REVOLVING DOORS

The True Account of the Full Spectrum of Fostering Abuses of a Boy Before Age Five

DAWN MAREE KETTERINGHAM, B.A., M.A.Ed.

Richard Ketteringham

Disclaimer
Identifying names have been changed
or omitted, wherever appropriate.

Dedications and Acknowledgements

From the Victim/Survivor

Thanks to my loving, supportive wife, son and daughter. Also, to "Susie" who guided me toward my life-long learning/healing process. I am also very grateful to my sister, "Dawn", who *"put pen to paper"*, to write my autobiographical novel, making sense of copious transcriptions and of my obscured memories and nightmares.

In addition, my deepest gratitude is to all who have been my support and my wings to freedom. Of course, with apologies, thanks to anyone I may have neglected to mention.
Richard Ketteringham

From the Author

I offer my deep gratitude and love to my birth mother Berneice Ketteringham, (undoubtedly in Heaven), for without her sacrifices, heartaches and unfaltering love and hope, this exceptional little family wound not even exist. Equally, I give my thanks also to my adoptive Daddy, William Alexander Stewart MacDonald, who loved me very deeply and whom I adored. He guided my path daily as he was an angel on this earth. Heaven needed him and called him home far too soon, in 1969. Thanks Daddy for making me the daughter, woman, mother, grandmother and author I am today!

My greatest thanks also to my son, Brandon, my daughter, Drew and their spouses, Lisa and Jeremy, for all of their loving support during my writing of this autobiographical novel for my brother, Richard. In addition, much thanks to my wonderful, amazing and very bright grandchildren, Troy (9), Kaylierain (7) and Daylan (5), for their love, endurance and encouragement, especially whenever "Gam Gam" was working on the book, while enforcing the rule of silence! (Of course, I must also give a wink and a nod to the father of my children, Michael Ray Simpson, of Hernando, Mississippi, for his 'vital' contribution to their existence.)

Thanks, also, to my other "sister", Renate, (Reni), McDonald, for life-long love, support and encouragement and to my good friends the Reverends Joan and Peter Gericke, for incessant, uplifting love and prayers.

*Certainly, my greatest appreciation is to my brother, who had to dig very deeply into his pain-riddled psyche to relate this story. Richard, I support your hope that **"Revolving Doors"** will encourage anyone living with such agony impeding their own self-fulfilment. Naturally, my sincerest apologies if I have overlooked acknowledging anyone.*

Dawn Maree Ketteringham, B.A., M.A.Ed.;
[Aka. Mary Lee MacDonald, (Simpson);
Nee: Dawn (Ketteringham) Faulconer]

Hope's Seed

The circumstances of a person's life may create around them, an invisible, protective outer shell to help each individual cope. However, it can never form too impervious a surface that a tiny seed of "hope" can't penetrate even a sliver of a crack and burst through with the exquisiteness of a life, well-deserved and worthy of living, blossoming, beautifying and regenerating.

Dawn Maree Ketteringham, 2013

Auguries of Innocence

"Every night and every morn
Some to misery are born.
Every morn and every night
Some are born to sweet delight.
Some are born to sweet delight,
Some are born to endless night."
*(Excerpt from poem by "William Blake",
Circa 1803, published 1863.)*

****

"Holding onto anger is like grasping a hot coal
with the intent of throwing it at someone else.
You are the one getting burned." *Buddha*

****

"The world is a dangerous place, not because of those who do
evil, but because of those who look on and do nothing."
Albert Einstein

Table of Contents

PREFACE

This memoir, which I am about to share with you, is my true representation of actual events which occurred in the first five years of my life as a foster child. This story is correct and factual to the best of my personal knowledge and recollection. I am describing my own life's struggles, the details about which are gleaned from my memories, dreams/nightmares, individual and group therapy sessions, hypnotherapy, diaries and journals, as well as from detailed information provided to me by the organizations named herein.

Many particulars and specific details were provided in from photocopies of microfiche notes from my personal adoption files. These were obtained through the Ontario Ministry of Children and Family Services, as well as from a few hundred pages of my originally documented records, transcribed from archives which were provided by the "Southwest York County Children's Aid Society" in Toronto, Ontario, Canada.

I have specifically chosen to present my story through the genre of Autobiographical Novel because this avenue allows me to tell the truth of my story, while incorporating enough literary license in order to round out the missing puzzle-pieces of my life. This way, I am able, humbly, to offer to you, my reader, a story, which flows somewhat better through the variegated scenery and undulating terrain of my memories. At the very least, I hope and strive for my story to move somewhat more fluidly than my young life ever could.

Because my own life's chronicle imprinted itself indelibly onto my brain, I am, of course, my own storyteller, and as such, I am the only person who can relate my own life's experiences. However, in order to best accomplish this task I required assistance in recording and presenting my tale in a format, which is readable, and interesting enough to make YOU keep turning the page. Therefore, I have enlisted the services of my sister, Dawn Maree Ketteringham, as "author", to actually write the manuscript of my story, since she has the necessary education, experience, professionalism and writing expertise. Therefore, she is the "author", I am the "generator", and together we have produced, "Revolving Doors".

[Sadly, my sister, Dawn Maree, is also a victim/survivor of childhood sexual molestation, abuse, battery and rape, which will certainly be detailed in her own future chronicles, the first of which is titled, RAPED!!! "PRESUMED INNOCENCE" My Fifty-Yearlong Painful Secret (Distributed by LULU.com).]

Over the past several years, even though we have been separated by the physical distance of several Canadian provinces, she and I have worked closely together on the manuscript for this novel. When I've been unable to visit her in person, I have "Skyped", emailed and, by phone dictated my daily thoughts and memories, in order for her to write my life's story of revolving doors. Additionally, I sent Dawn several hundred pages of hard-copy transcriptions of the details outlined in the photocopies of the original microfiche documents which I obtained directly from the "C.A.S.". It was my expectation that, in relating my childhood experiences, my sister would not only incorporate the information contained in the transcriptions, but also make sense of, and merge, my random, and often jumbled, memories, thoughts and their accompanying emotions.

I wanted Dawn to organize all the data I sent into a genre format which you, my reader, may deem worthy of you interest. I originally decided to relate, and record, my personal story for my own catharsis and healing. As my psychotherapy started and some memories began breaking through the chain-mail veil of my mind, I had difficulty believing I had indeed lived through all the once-masked memories. I was shocked and terrified to 'see', and 'feel', the sudden flashbacks of abuse in my life as a young child. However, the fact of the matter is, I did experience every one of the life situations, which, and as, I have detailed between the covers of this novel.

From 1947 through 1952, my two sisters and I were each taken from our young mother's loving arms and relinquished to the questionable services of Toronto's "Southwest York County Children's Aid Society". In my situation, I was temporarily housed by this "C.A.S." due to my mother's repeatedly failed attempts, and resulting inability, to financially provide a suitable home for me.

****

[In the situation of my sister, "Dawn", in order to rid our mother of the financial burden of a child, a conspiracy existed between her father, John Edward Richard Ketteringham II, and her husband, Donald Faulconer. Berneice was forced into the uncomfortable position of supposedly having to show off her new baby, only a few weeks old, to someone at the same "Children's Aid Society", (the hand-off location which the men had secretly prearranged). Quite oblivious to the real nature of the 'meeting', Berneice handed-over my baby sister to a nurse, but only for a "little look". The nurse, with my infant sister in her arms, then turned and quickly went back through one of the four, tall wooden doors in the great rotunda foyer.

To our mother's life-long grief and heartbreak, and as long as Berneice lived on this earth, she and "Dawn" would never get to see each other again.

In May of 1952, our youngest sister, Lynda, was born. Although we are not privy to the details of how she ended up as a ward of the "C.A.S.", we do know she was indeed, for approximately the first three years of life, placed in the general care of the same fostering organization as Dawn and myself. We also know she was 'rescued from neglect and abuse in a foster home. Lynda was returned to our mother, remarried at the time, due to her birth father, Donald Faulconer's, incarceration for bigamy. She remained with our mother, and her step-father, until she was an adult.

Unfortunately, each of us were unaware of the other's existence, as we became wards of the same system, (much to our helpless, hapless mother's chagrin and life-long deep sorrow). It was not until I was around the age of twenty-five when I actually found our mother. Of course, that was also the time when I met my youngest sister, Lynda. To the astonishment of both of us, our mother disclosed, the existence of our middle sister, Dawn, whom, sadly, she had never been able to find.

Around the same time when my original mental "breakthrough" occurred, in 2001, I literally found this lady, my sister Dawn, on April 26, living in Memphis, Tennessee. Incredibly it happened after approximately twenty-five years of personally searching and with the assistance and resources of the "Ontario Ministry of Children and Family Services". It was then, I discovered she had her own story of eerily similar abuses. I thought it might help her to know she was not alone in trying to suppress unbearable memories and excruciatingly painful thoughts. I wanted to help her understand, for certain, that the fault of the incidents was in no way hers, in the same way my abusive experiences were no fault of mine. This idea was contrary to the lies she had been repeatedly told, and led to believe, by her adoptive mother. (Thankfully, I was around six years of age, when sweet adoption plucked me from the cycle of abuse and torment while I was stuck in the 'virtual revolving foster doors. Of course, it's also when I became one of the "Thompsons".)]

Revolving Doors

****

Eventually, over the years of meeting others in formal group therapy sessions, or even over coffee at "Timmie's" [152], (in my "informal" group therapy sessions), I've found myself constantly responding promisingly to other's requests to "hear more of my own story". So now, in answer to people's suggestions to me, such as, "You should write a book!", or "Why aren't you writing your memoirs, or your autobiography?" I reply that indeed "I am!", and now, "Here it is."

Mine is the story of a search. It's the chronicle of my search for a mother's love, for acceptance, for a home and for a life without loneliness, pain, abuse, torture, anger, depression or despair. All of this self-exploration has become my life's journey which has resulted in my discovery of self. The result is my personal acceptance of unconditional love and love's sister, hope. It is this discovery of hope, deep within a worthless life, one which I had perceived to be most undeserving, nonetheless, I now believe, a life in as much need of hope as any other organism on this planet.

This hope is the miracle of my story. If I can dig deeply enough to uproot hope in my life, then I am convinced there is not one person with a similar history, who could not unearth his own tiny seed of hope. Hope is the catalyst to germinate a new life, as I can attest to have finally begun to do.

*What I never completely grasped, until I began dictating these scenes of my life into the chapters of my story, is that "hope" **is** my life's lesson. I am optimistic that, by sharing my story, my eventual introduction to 'hope' will clearly be my message. I truly believe that through this medium, (which you are holding), you will be able to re-live my story with me. If applicable, you too may find a long-repressed memory or two, which, once unleashed, will open your own floodgate of shaded memories allowing any of your own pent-up feelings and fears to flow*

5

Revolving Doors

freely. Due to the domino effect, they will lose their power to keep you in the fear and apprehension of "what might have been".

All I can add as a word of caution is to be prepared to face the darkness as it is exposed; however please embrace "Teddy's" unwavering hope of something better on the other side of the next virtual revolving door. Shedding a few tears for the little boy, "Teddy", might be an inevitability, but remember, I am "Richard" now and I am no longer crying.

INTRODUCTION

My Beautiful Mommy

My five-year nightmare in Toronto's post-war foster system began, of course, with my mother, Berneice Ketteringham. Without my mother, I would have no story. Certainly, I could not recount the chronicle of my own first years without imparting a little of my mother's personal struggles for 'answers', and of her hopes and prayers for some semblance of joy. Her futile quest for idyllic happiness and personal fulfilment was fuelled by her belief that it would inevitably follow, if only she could manifest the "perfect marriage" and, within the structure of such, would produce a couple of "wonderful and perfect children" of her own".

Berneice Ketteringham was a petite, slender, beautiful brunette. Her laughing hazel eyes barely betrayed her as little more than a youthful dreamer. She adored music and truly loved to sing, though her talent was somewhat debatable. Just like any other teenage girl, she was consumed with the hopes of one day marrying the man of her dreams and bearing him beautiful babies to round out their consummate little family. How could a naive and inexperienced girl be expected to discern that such unrealistic, and unattainable, ideals of love were only the puppet-portrayals by scripted actors, or flawless images contrived by prolific authors of weekly churned out, cookie-cutter paperback romance novels?

Berneice's energy and curiosity kept her continuously busy, although she was never as accomplished as she truly dreamed to be. Relentlessly she would try out her talents on one craft, or hobby, after another. If you asked her, she would rattle off a list of her interests such as painting watercolours, writing poetry, sketching or knitting, to name a few. She would be completely absorbed with one craft or hobby, then after one week of that activity she'd switch direction and totally immerse herself in another. In short, on the whims of her rapidly changing moods she would entirely over-indulge in each of the abilities she attempted to master, quickly relinquishing all previous interests in the process.

Naturally, being a highly intelligent young lady, Berneice continually sought to improve her life. After high school, she actually completed her first year of college, but her uncontrollable mood swings, depressive episodes and resulting confusion, forced her to drop out. She then opted for seven months of what was, for her, boring, repetitive, menial work in one factory after another. Although one of her various bosses reported that she had "many likeable qualities", she was often reprimanded for her inability to control her quick-tempered interactions with co-workers. In fact, she rarely made friends at work and on one occasion was purportedly described in her file as, "very moody and not well liked".

None of the people in Berneice's work situations could have known that she was incapable of either predicting, or controlling the devastating vacillations in her moods. In fact, her temper was simply the outward expression of the overwhelming depression, and ensuing anger, battling viciously in her brain. Whenever her taxed emotions and confusing thoughts subsided she would lapse into a day-dreaming state of mind. Of course even these calming breaks in her moods would sadly be misinterpreted by her supervisors as "laziness".

Ultimately, Berneice simply craved affection and longed for "some man" to take an interest in her. She was a hopeless romantic with elusive dreams and plans for the loving, stable home she, herself, never experienced. Lamentably, Berneice's immature, "little girl" hopes would never become her own reality. In fact, before closing her case, one of her social workers unjustly noted in her file that,

*"If she hadn't lost her mother at such a young, impressionable age, and if she didn't suffer from lack of a steady home life, she would be a **much nicer character."***

Had Berneice known of this terribly subjective and unfair judgement she would have been perplexed and devastated, since all she ever wanted was to be accepted and fit-in with her friends and co-workers. Of course, she could only be as "**nice**" as the unaddressed and unharnessed demons in her own head would allow.

Berneice's life started out uneventfully with an adoring father, a Canadian born in England, and a devoted mother who was a native of Canada. She was raised with two older sisters, and would have had two brothers, had they each not died at birth. Unfortunately the family unit, but most especially three-year-old Berneice, suffered a tragic blow with the untimely passing of their matriarch. Nevertheless, she still had her father, and their mutual devotion was palpable. In fact she jubilantly admitted that her "gentle-natured daddy spoiled [her], and certainly **never** corrected [her] forcibly".

However, soon after her mother's passing, Berneice's life took another unfortunate turn when her father remarried. Of course her father's inevitable decision undoubtedly followed his inability to properly care for his three daughters, while trying to earn an adequate living. But how could his little daughter possibly understand? The woman who was to become little Berneice's new "mother" was a plump, middle-aged woman, with dark hair and olive complexion.

But other than her appearance, which was so unlike her own precious mother's, the woman's personality was a polar opposite of her own. This step-mother was cold-natured, controlling, mean-spirited and completely overbearing, at least from Berneice's perspective. Little Berneice had to wonder how her father could possibly have chosen this abrasive woman to be her new "mother".

Tragically her father's decision to re-marry such a harsh and demanding woman would eventually trigger Berneice's mental and emotional downward spiral into a lifetime of disillusionment, disappointment and depression. Her perception of the re-marriage as a personal rejection by her beloved father, created unbearable heartache and shattered her expectations of having the simple, happy home life that any normal child would expect as a matter of course.

However, physical traits and personality aside, one predominant fact would make Berneice's life with this woman miserable at best, and that was this "mother's" stoic devotion to her religion as a stringently practising Roman Catholic. Despite the fact that little Berneice had been raised in the Protestant Anglican faith, as a strict Catholic, this woman forced the child to attend grade school in a Catholic convent. In there, Berneice tried her best to adhere to the rigid rules, practices, procedures and traditions imposed upon her by the convent regulations—and enforced by the nuns. However, everything about the religious grade school proved to be so completely foreign to her that she seemed to always be breaking one rule or another, and suffering the associated admonishments or physical punishments. Certainly she always felt like an outsider stuck in such an unhappy environment. This a situation which she could only hope and pray, would be temporary.

But after several years of failing to assuage her stepmother's strict rules and controls over every aspect of her life, Berneice was so overwhelmed with such resentment and anger that she could no longer contain her contempt for the woman. Sadly, as deeply as she loved her daddy, Berneice knew that continuing to live under the same roof with his wife would prove hopelessly detrimental, if not altogether impossible. Despite her young age, and lack of worldly experience, she felt forced into the decision to leave. Without money though, her only choice after moving out of her father's house was to head straight to her nearest relative's home. That action would mark the beginning of her life's rapid unravelling. Soon after settling in at one relation's home after another, she repeatedly felt that each of the adults quickly became controlling and unbearable. In no time it was as uncomfortable as living under the same roof as her father's wife.

Certainly Berneice's wildly swinging moods would have proven to be far too great a problem for her aunts and/or uncles to understand, manage, or even accept. Of course, no one could have known or understood that the driving force behind her overtly defiant attitude of independence, and frequently demonstrative, unbalanced behaviour, occupied its own region, in the innermost depths of her brain. Misunderstood, undiagnosed and untreated at that time, was her mental condition, aptly named, "Manic-Depression", [*currently labelled "Bipolar Affective Disorder", [117], although now discovered to be a genetically transmitted condition with basic symptoms of uncontrollable mood swings.*]

During an episode of either the mania or depression, Berneice's mood-swings, emotions and behaviours would be set off like an out-of-control pendulum. This undoubtedly created so much friction between Berneice and her relatives that the repeated house shuffling unfortunately resulted in exhaustion of all possible "family" boarding situations.

By the time she hit her teen years, Berneice found herself completely homeless and ironically turned to the further instability of boarding-house living. Finally, after staying in several different, increasingly degenerate and impossible boarding houses, she was permitted to "crash" on a small cot in a sort-of closet, in her eldest sister's home. This sister was the married mother of two young children and her impending pregnancy was causing a great strain on her health and her marriage. The physical and mental stress forced her to be in desperate need of assistance with the daily management of her home, and provision of her family's needs.

In exchange for room and board, Berneice agreed to help her exhausted sibling with the housework while providing live-in nanny services for her two, and soon-to-be three, young children. However, not long after her arrival, her sibling's family was served with eviction papers, making even this last-ditch living arrangement just another stopgap solution in her quest for a stable, loving home. Furthermore, daily existence with one foot out of the door, although seemingly innocuous, would eventually change her life, but decidedly not for the better.

It was soon after assuming her custodial position that one afternoon, on a break from her chores, Berneice and her girlfriend, Gloria, went to one of the local teenage restaurant hangouts. That's where Berneice's friend introduced her to the handsome boy in the next booth. He was kidding and joking around with the girls, but with Berneice he was most definitely flirting! Because Gloria knew "Robbie", as her brother's buddy, both girls considered this fellow fairly "safe" to get to know better. (Unaware the reason, my mother would always be drawn to the bad boys—like a hungry ant to a "picnic", and this fellow, proving no exception, had *picnic* written all over him.) Although he was only one year her senior, he had already acquired a serious reputation as a "bad boy".

Apparently this particular young fellow, whom my mommy would later name as my father, had been a constant source of friction to his own parents. In fact, both he and his brother had reputations of being "badly behaved kids" and "annoyances in school". Some teachers even reported that this youth was openly defiant of every school rule and continually created disruptions in the school yard. In fact he was labelled as "the worst behaviour problem the school had ever experienced". Therefore, at age fifteen, after yet another school suspension, his decision to permanently drop-out had come as no surprise to anyone who really knew him.

From her skewed perspective, Berneice seemed to be more impressed than dismayed, about the fact that her first beau had spent time in a reformatory, (and reportedly on more than one occasion).

She was amused by his bragging of the wild and crazy

misdeeds he and his brother allegedly committed while "incarcerated". She listened unquestioningly to his blow-by-blow description of the daily fights at his home, the worst ones being between his mother and father. Of course her undeniable physical attraction to this fellow had to be due, in part, to his being of Scottish-Irish heritage. Surely she was excited by that little touch of Irish-gypsy rascal in his nature. Admittedly, she was instantly infatuated by the smile from his ruggedly handsome face, and the curious drape of unruly cowlicks of thick, black, curly hair cascading over his forehead. But mostly, as she confessed to her diary, she loved when he held her. It made her feel so safe and protected when he, a muscular, stocky, five feet ten inches, enveloped her petite frame which was all of four feet, eleven inches.

Berneice was duly impressed as the boy proudly related stories of his "service" overseas in the Canadian Armed Forces. She listened with admiration as he, with equal pride, touted his firm plans in place to return for another tour of duty. He had been discharged earlier that year and, utilizing skills he'd learned in the Forces, had taken a job with a metal fabricating company in downtown Toronto. At that time, his thirty-nine dollar per week salary was fairly impressive for a young high-school drop-out, and reform school recidivist. At least it provided the funds for him to impress Berneice on their frequent dates. In no time, the two teenagers were spending the better part of every evening enjoying restaurant meals or attending movies. In fact, for the whole month, the couple went out daily, letting everyone know they were an "item" and that they were "going steady".

Of course, when this boy first smiled at the sight of such a sweet and beautiful young girl, he could never have imagined that their mutual attraction would soon interfere with **his** future career plans with the Services. He would never guess that his dreams would presently be disrupted and perhaps even abruptly terminated. Surely he was merely overwhelmed by Berneice's energetic and effervescent personality. At the very least, he would have been smitten by her natural beauty, inviting smile and most infectious giggle. After all, Berneice was a stunning, flirtatious and enthusiastic seventeen-year-old girl, who was already having considerable difficulty fighting off unwanted advances from more than a few boys her age.

About a month after their first meeting, the boy showed up one evening while she was babysitting at home. After shaking the rain off his clothing, he sat down beside Berneice on the living-room loveseat. This was not an unusual occurrence as they often liked to chat, play records or listen to the radio shows. The children were all asleep and Berneice knew her sister would not be home before midnight. Of course, as passionate as the two teens were, on this particular night, their talking or playing records would not last very long. They were soon overwhelmed by the natural stirrings of their fiery feelings of "first love".

Berneice's diary entry clearly described that it was on that very night, November 27, 1946, after the couple shared their first French kiss which sealed their mutual profession of love. Naturally their passion progressed quickly to their first experience of physical intimacy. Berneice was still a virgin at her tender age of seventeen, this boy was, of course, her first and **only** lover. Until then she had been able to preserve her precious virginity, fearing the **wrath of God,** or at least the wrath of the **nuns,** should she "give in" to any boy's pressure to have sex. [At least, such was the imbued belief system firmly imprinted onto her brain during her rigorous daily religious lessons at the convent.]

15

Berneice couldn't possibly comprehend the significance and consequence of their love-making. Certainly she would see herself as a *woman* now, and different from the girl she was until the moment of her deflowering. However, giving into this boy's pressuring would prove completely life-altering for Berneice. After only two more repetitions of intercourse between the young lovers, she became aware of the fact, which was then, and still is nowadays, most unwed teenage girls' worst nightmare—unexpected and unwanted pregnancy.

Yes, she was definitely pregnant, but because the boy was still living with his parents, she decided to keep her dark and forbidding secret hidden from him for as long as possible. She confessed to her diary that in her heart of hearts she neither trusted, nor respected him. She imagined he would probably spread their grim news all around town while insisting that Berneice was "falsely" naming him as the father-to-be. Berneice believed that telling him about her impending motherhood, and his imminent paternity, would end up back-firing and resulting in her acquisition of every young girl's much-dreaded reputation as a slut, or a whore.

Of course, as these things inevitably happen in the course of any pregnancy, before long her condition became too obvious to conceal. This panicked teenager was forced to concede to her frightening predicament and tell "Robbie". The evening of her admission to him, Berneice *screamed* to her diary that she could absolutely not believe how closely his immediate reaction matched her fears. In fact, he **did** deny any intimacy between them, and followed that with completely false accusations of her having repeated sexual encounters with many other boys. Feeling the ultimate rejection, although not completely surprised, she was deeply heartbroken, very much alone and terrified of the events and unknown possibilities to come.

Finally, after considerable time had passed, Berneice made a diary entry that the boy phoned her and sounded quite shaken while making his ultimate confession to her. Beyond admitting that he had indeed, and indisputably, been the first man to have sex with her, he could no longer deny that the timing of her conception was obviously singling him out as the only possible father-to-be. Then on the first of April, 1947, he went so far as to legally swear an oath attesting to this fact.

Later, during one of many disturbing phone conversations, the boy offered that he would be "willing to marry" her. However, she was keenly aware that it wasn't really the desire of his heart to be the husband she needed, or the loving father she instinctively knew her baby would require. The more she considered his condescending, back-handed "proposal", the more she knew it was not an acceptable solution. Although it hurt deeply, it simply wasn't her impression of the way she imagined her true love, marriage and family to be. She gave up on her belief that if she married him he would sweep her away to a life of matrimonial bliss.

Berneice confessed to her diary the hopelessness she felt because everything in her life was so terribly temporary: her mother's caring and warmth, her father's loving attention and adoration, her so-called "homes", family members, friends, jobs and even her boyfriend—all were present in her life, but sooner or later vanished. Ultimately, even Berneice's sister, upon discovery of her desperate, impending maternal predicament, unbelievably not only insisted she immediately move out, but also further betrayed her by alerting the "Children's Aid Society", ("C.A.S."), in her area of Toronto.

Her sibling attempted to justify her own actions by explaining that she believed Berneice would need to be accepted into a home for unwed mothers. Supposedly this was in order for her to be properly cared-for during her pregnancy. Ultimately Berneice feared what her sister knew—that it was a place which would be instrumental in **getting rid of her baby quickly** after delivery. Ironically, her stay at her sister's York

County, Toronto address, at the time of my conception, qualified her for that County's firm regulations for entrance to the Southwest Humewood House for Unwed Mothers. That was the residence which would become Berneice's home for the following months of her baby's gestation.

Once Berneice arrived at the Home she was given an intake interview which the nursing staff and workers could use in assessing her physical, mental and emotional health, attitudes, skills, personality traits and general needs and requirements. The results would help in determining where best she would fit-in with the other girls, all of whom were there, of course, for the same reason, albeit at different stages of fetal development.

[The initial "C.A.S." file entry read,

"Berneice is very friendly and related to worker quickly what had happened, but was quite undecided regarding her plans for the baby, and did not really know what to do. She gave the impression of being a very suggestible girl, who would simply follow the advice of the last person who talked to her. It seems important, therefore, that the decision regarding the future of her baby should be left entirely up to her."]

(Ironically, for some reason known only to Berneice, while awaiting my arrival my mother completely abandoned her most trustworthy and intimate confidante—her diary. Sadly, this left a void where her thoughts, feelings and personal struggles throughout the pregnancy would normally have been chronicled.)

Nevertheless...

PART I: "Hello World...I'm Ricky!

Chapter 1: Meeting My Mommy

I have decided that this day in 1947 would be a very good day to meet my mommy. The 75 degree heat and humidity, so common for Toronto in August, are making her *most* uncomfortable. We are sitting in a firm, wooden, Muskoka lawn chair, [59], and I am loving the warmth of the sun beaming down on her tummy—my bum! I am so anxious to see her face, of course, I already *know* her voice. One thing I am certain of, is that she is very, very beautiful. Whenever she talks, or sings, to me she is so sweet and whenever I get the *hiccups*, she gets the giggles!

Right now, I am being taken on a very bumpy ride and I am being quite jostled around while we are on our way to the Toronto Western Hospital. It's where the nurses are already preparing for my debut. When mommy was talking to me, she was crying and saying how much she was hurting. I promised I would not give her too difficult a time ushering me into the world.

At last, we have arrived at the Delivery Room! Ah, yes, it is time. It's finally the moment for my unveiling. I am moving into position now...here we go! Mommy, are you ready for my big *reveal*?

Revolving Doors

Chapter 2: I See the Light

Up until this very moment, I had been holding back with all the might my little body could muster. You see it's so very wonderful inside my mommy's perfect tummy! I am rethinking my decision to face the harsh environment awaiting me in the light at the end of the greatest, yet tinniest, tunnel through which I know I must eventually travel. As hard as I am trying *not* to be born, I feel bad because I've been forcing my mommy to labour for over eighteen hours now. I know she is so very tired. Actually, I too am exhausted and can no longer keep fighting the inevitable. I must give-in to the efforts of the sterile "handlers" guiding me into the blindingly bright delivery room.

Today is August 27 and I had kept myself coddled tightly inside mommy's tummy as long as I was able to stay there. However, now, "Here I am!" Although I am a full-term baby, my mommy still seemed surprised at all seven pounds of her little fellow. Oh yes, and mommy even calls me her "little man". I feel so very important when I think of the wonderfully significant name she has chosen for me, "**John Edward Richard Ketteringham III**"—me! However, because my name is so long and princely, mommy has simply nicknamed me "Ricky".

Oh my gosh! When I focus my gaze on her warm and adoring eyes, I know I had been sooooo right! Mommy is very, very beautiful, and she smells wonderful too! When she holds me tightly against her warm, soft breasts, without a word she communicates her deep love for me. When she does speak to me, she comforts me with the familiar voice I had been listening to for the nine months of my gestation. Mommy tells me I am handsome and very smart. However, she doesn't know how clever I *really* am! After only a few minutes in the world, I've already figured out how to nurse from her inviting and enfolding, white breasts.

I can't take my eyes off my mommy. I don't even want to fall asleep and miss looking at her for a minute. Holding me snugly and tenderly she starts humming softly as she rocks me. Ohhhh... I know how much she loves me, but how can I tell her how much I adore her! It's comforting to know we are deeply in love with each other and no matter what befalls us in life, we will belong to each other always and forever!

The soothing milk from my mommy's warm breast is putting me to sleep. I am loved. I am cared for. I am safe. I am happy, very happy. However, just as I drift into dreamland, I am wondering where my daddy could be?

Chapter 3: Going "HOME"

Only two days since my birth, the hospital discharges us both and sends us home, even though mommy has hardly recovered from bringing me into the world. *Home?* The only place we can go now is straight back to the rigidly ruled nursery at the Southwest Humewood House. [153] I know my mommy doesn't fare very well when expected to kowtow to the counsellors' demands, and adhere to their strict rules—she is simply too much of a free spirit. What is this now? Another meeting with the institution's Director has culminated with a letter from her to mommy's "C.A.S." Worker. The letter was "*a request for Wardship action with a view to adoption at a later date for the baby boy of birth mother, Berneice*". In any event, it has worked out very well that we only had to remain in the unwed teenage mothers' domicile, (my **first** residence), for a month before returning to my auntie's home, where my sweet mommy had been staying.

Wowee! It has been a few days now and I am already loving it here at *auntie's house*, (my **second** change of residence). She too is expecting a new baby—a boy like me, I hope—and soon! Moreover, her other two children are already my best friends because they play with me all the time. It's such great fun when they play with, and tickle me too. I really can't get enough giggle-time with my cousins. Mommy is too sad and busy to play with me very much right now. But I understand because she spends so much time cleaning this house, or washing the dishes and keeping up with everyone's laundry. Moreover, right now she has taken on the extra work of doing all the cooking for everyone in the household. I think the other reason she doesn't play with me anymore is that she is so tired. She looks so pale and worn-out from keeping up with all her responsibilities, not the least of which is caring for me. Moreover, despite her physical exhaustion mommy is unable to sleep very well at night.

It's very distressing to me when auntie, uncle and mommy all start yelling at each other. Whenever they send my big cousins outside to play, it's because they have to discuss some sobering issues which are very disturbing and, of course, affect all of us. Whenever they "discuss" these matters, it always comes down to the troubles about money. Debating money problems invariably culminates with my uncle banging his fists on the kitchen table and cussing at my auntie—my auntie bellowing at mommy—and my mommy crying her eyes out and running to our *room*, (which, incidentally, is really intended as a large storage closet, but now houses my bassinet and a child-sized, faded green canvas army cot in it, for mommy). Of course there is nothing *I* can do to comfort my sweet mother, nothing, so I cry right along with her.)

Of course, we children could not ever understand, but my uncle says he "can't possibly earn enough money to provide the basic necessities of life". He says, "Besides the rent, there are too many bills and expenses because there are six people living here!" (He had better get prepared because there are soon to be seven!) Although, mommy has been nursing me, and hand washing my diapers, my uncle insists that our presence in their home is "adding to his household financial burden". I guess he doesn't consider the rent mommy pays in the form of babysitting, laundry, house cleaning and cooking as our contribution to the family assets. (At least it's what mommy tells me, between her sobs.)

We've only been living here a week, but now the arguing has escalated so much, my mommy seems to be weeping all the time. She hugs me tightly and whispers about being uncertain of what will become of us. I can actually feel how scared she is, but I coo and try to reassure her that everything will be fine because we have each other. Then suddenly in the middle of our quiet little cuddle session, my uncle pokes his head in our *bedroom* door and screams at mommy, insisting we must, *"find another home immediately"*. This news is more disappointment than my frail mother can bear. She is so crushed, her volatile emotions cause her to suffer a complete emotional and physical collapse. Nevertheless, nobody understands her—nobody but me.

I am too young to comprehend the meaning, or implication, of the words "EVICTION NOTICE"; however, the predicament in which mommy and I find ourselves right now is directly affecting me in a negative way. Sadly, after uncle's final depressing words, I am able to sense my mommy's anxiety and tension immediately, whenever I try to nurse. *I* don't understand *why*, but suddenly, after this dysphoric event, it isn't long before mommy notices I am losing weight, and apparently no longer thriving from her breast milk.

My weight-loss is the reason why the "Children's Aid Case Worker" is stopping by here today. She wants to check my weight and help mommy figure out how to handle my newly developed breast-feeding difficulties. The Worker who comes through auntie's front door is quite scary-looking and more than a little off-putting. She has a ghostly, pale-white complexion, made-up to appear even more pallid against the frame of her platinum blonde hair. Her face has a shocking-bleed of cherry-red lipstick, her only make-up, and her perfume is a pungent scent reminiscent of bar soap. This woman is as petite as my mommy is, but her brusque manner is quite abrasive and completely the opposite of my own my sweet mother's.

I notice mommy is trying, unsuccessfully, to hide her nervousness. It's always her first reaction whenever she must speak with any of these type of authority figures or Social Workers, especially those from the "C.A.S.". On this occasion, however, she is especially uncomfortable watching as this woman undresses me, and turns me around and around to check out every inch of my little body for marks, or diaper rash, or who knows what. Her actions are ridiculous and unnecessary as, of course, she finds nothing amiss—not a mark on my little lily-white body, anywhere!

While this *sterile* woman is questioning the grown-ups about me, my cousin, (in auntie's tummy), is doing flips, and making her feel terribly sick. Auntie is so weak, she is unable to even sit-up throughout mommy's interview, so she answers all of "Cherry-Lips" myriad of questions while reclining on her chesterfield. Auntie tells the woman, *"Berneice is taking excellent care of her baby"*, and, *"She is very fond of Ricky."* However, I could not understand why auntie insists, *"Boarding home care is the only solution, because Berneice doesn't have any money and needs to go to work."* Then auntie explains to "Lips", *"**I** would take the baby, but I already have **more** than I can handle with what will soon be three children."*

It's then that she is unable to control her confession about the imminence of the family's "eviction" from the house. (I am now thinking one way or another, mommy and I are doomed to homelessness, unless something major changes in our lives, and quickly.)

Of course, one thing "Lips" did offer as an explanation for my weight-loss was, quite simply, I "can no longer be quenched by [my mother's] milk". (Certainly, mommy and I already knew this!) Therefore, in order to determine the best solution for this problem, right now mommy and I have once again returned to Humewood House. We are in conference with the dietician who seems very pleasant and kindly. This woman, who is at least a foot taller than mommy, is wearing a grey, box-pleated skirt, a plainly tailored white blouse and a stiff, white jacket, or sort of lab-coat. She speaks very softly, like my mommy does, and she explains her plans to "help us"--or, in other words, how to *fatten me up a little*. She leads us to a small white kitchen with huge, shiny, white-enamelled appliances, where she demonstrates how to supplement my nourishment with a formulation of "lactic acid milk" which is a mixture of regular cow's milk along with some nutrient-rich, but grainy-textured and vile tasting powdered ingredients.

Chapter 4: NOT My Mother's Milk

Naturally, mommy gets busy mixing my "formula" right away, and soon I find myself fighting a baby bottle in order to choke down the thick, lumpy, pasty white stuff. Oh, what a devastating disappointment *that* was, especially after having enjoyed my only sustenance, to date, from my mother's delightful breast! Nevertheless, in order to please my mommy, I am trying mightily to win the battle of the bottle. Because my mommy has such a special way of gently encouraging me, I can only comply when she tries to help me understand that the bottled formula is keeping my tummy from hurting as often, or as badly.

Quite soon after starting on the formula, it becomes obvious the nasty, pasty, liquid baby food is at least fulfilling my little body's current nutritional demands. In that respect, I guess it has been better for me, but I absolutely **hate it**. Nevertheless, my mommy says I am a *"pretty smart cookie"* and she is certain I will adjust quickly, and soon pick up the knack of bottle-feeding. Even so, as smart as I am, it takes me a little while to adapt, not only to the thick rubber nipple, but also to the icky smell, taste and texture of the bottled sand—oops, I mean, *formula*. Besides these non-redeeming qualities, the disgusting stuff is always either too hot, or too cold. Ahhh...lamentably, in every way it is most decidedly **not** *my mother's milk*!

After a short while, actually, as soon as mommy is satisfied with my feeding progress, we report back to "Cherry Lips" who meets us at Humewood in the First-Aid office. Once again, we are ushered into the freezing cold room to await the nurse who, no doubt, will use her cold, bony fingers to repeat her poking of every part of me. As usual, the nurse strips me naked, weighs, measures and inspects me closely—all over. I don't know what she is looking for, or whatever she thinks she'll find on, or in, me. Evidently, when nothing is discovered, mommy is ordered to put my clothes back on, (and just in the nick of time, because the room was so chilly my pee-pee almost disappeared). In any event, as mommy gently dresses me, the nurse is discussing my progress with "Lips" and making more notations about us, (adding to the copious volume of notes in her manila file folder, which already contains the *story of our lives*).

Once the nurse's examination is completed, "Lips" adds a few more questions of her own, specifically the *bombshell* question, "Oh, also, Berneice, we would like to know about your place of residence?" (Um, right, our *other* little problem.)

My mommy has not had much of a chance to explain herself; after all, whatever could my mother say? We have *no* real, permanent place to sleep, anywhere. Even though we currently have my nutrition problem under control, mommy and I are now officially homeless, and out of options. All mommy can do is agree with the counsellor. Since she has no job, no money and no living quarters for the *two* of us, the only place where mommy and *I* will be safe, and well looked after, is back in the Humewood nursery. (I did not know "Lips" could even be considering the possibility of some other similar fostering or group residence, which would make it even more difficult for mommy and me to live together.)

Shortly, after a few more comments and questions, mommy is pushed to her breaking point, and she starts sobbing. It is right before we could have made our escape, when I was devastated to hear my mother tell "Lips",

*"I guess I'll **have** to consider admitting Ricky to boarding house care."*

Revolving Doors

Whaaaaat? What can this mean? Where will we be next? I had absolutely no idea *I* would soon be facing a new type of existence, as a *ward* of the "Southwest York County Children's Aid Society", or "C.A.S.". It would certainly prove to be an existence which would forever alter my life in a most negative, and damaging way.

In any case, I breathed a sigh of relief when mommy adamantly insisted, "But, *I am NOT willing to give Ricky up yet—not yet!*" Mommy also told the woman, "*I still hope I will somehow be able to keep, and take care of, my little Ricky!*" She encouraged the counsellor by stating, "*I am planning to pay the 'C.A.S.' $20.00 a month toward my little Ricky's maintenance.*" (Mommy and I both knew she had *no idea* where she would come up with *that* kind of money—but it was her secret, and *I* was not telling.) I guess mommy was convincing, because the Worker made an immediate note in our file papers which stated,

"The baby has a stabilizing influence on [Berneice] who is eager to assume responsibility and should be encouraged to do so, (*but even if she has to give the baby up, the experience might have an invaluable effect on her future life).*"

PART II: Southwest York Co. Children's Aid Society

Chapter 5: The "C.A.S."

Right now, on this cold and snowy February day, mommy and I have been directed to an organization which is supposed to *help us* – both. We find ourselves shivering outside the main front door of the gloomy brown brick building with the name, "CHILDREN'S AID SOCIETY" chiselled in huge carved brick letters arching over the formidable entrance. To the right of the massive wooden front door is a small, brass-coloured panel with a lighted button in the centre. Once pressed, this button magically hails a homely, and rather forgettable, woman who arrives and silently opens the locked door. Brown hair and eyes, and matching brown suit and shoes, are the overwhelmingly understated manner in which she chooses to present herself.

This "Brown Lady" guides us into a large, and more than slightly intimidating, vestibule, which is actually a rotunda with a highly glazed, black marble floor. Four, floor-to-ceiling, heavy, wooden, monolithic doors are evenly spaced around the semi-circular wall, but curiously, the doors are not designated with numbers, or markings of any kind. Then, in a rather unremarkable voice, the emotionless "Brown Lady" greeter asks us to wait for a few minutes, before she disappears through the far right door.

Shortly, we hear quick footsteps, followed by the sudden squeak of the door, which is second from the left. Another woman steps through and greets us. This one is also rather plain, except she is quite overweight and has taken much effort to squeeze herself into a bulging navy blue shift-dress, with a wide, stiffly starched white, sailor collar. Her expansive white belt only emphasizes the bulk of her figure, and the large, flowery-looking, brown earrings in no way match her ensemble, (in fact, I'm curious if she borrowed them from the "Brown Lady" whom we met moments before). This woman's shapeless legs, which are cleverly disguised in thick, black stockings, seem unnaturally attached to her puffy feet. Her feet, (apparently five sizes too large), are pouching over her too tightly laced, black leather shoes. (This one will be, "Black Stockings".)

Stepping sluggishly, yet rhythmically, she leads us past two doors on our left, then opens then next one which is a glass-panelled door on our right. In an unnatural, mousey, screechy little voice, (which, shockingly, in no way matches her girth), she politely escorts us into an impressively large office. I can feel mommy's nervousness as she suddenly squeezes me tighter and whispers, *"Don't worry, little man, everything is going to be alright, I promise."* (The words were meant to be encouraging, but their delivery was anything but after all, who knows my mommy's true feelings better than I do?)

Upon glancing around the office, we notice two over-size wooden desks with a tailored woman sitting at each. One woman is sporting dark and heavy, horn-rimmed eyeglasses with very thick lenses, but the other's spectacles are tiny, and rimmed in gold wire. I notice neither of the women was a nurse, although they're both wearing a sort of uniform consisting of white blouses and navy blue skirts. (Their uniforms are merely everyday street clothing, and not the anticipated, and *unnerving*, rigidly starched, white nursing uniform.)

Under each woman's frantic fingers, the noisy typewriter keys are rapidly clacking loudly, with tiny, syncopated "dings" sounding regularly. It seems as if they're almost making percussive music together. I think they seem very strange, yet maybe a little bit funny. I try to attract their attention with my most impressive babble, but it's as if mommy and I are simply invisible because neither woman as much as raises an eyebrow in our direction.

Presently, "Black Stockings" shows us into a massive inner office, which is actually an interior room separated from the main office by its windowed walls. We are directed to seat ourselves in one of the two solid-wood, armchairs with black leather padding, fastened to the wood frame with hundreds of dull brass brads. Across the massive mahogany desk we are eye-to-eye with a matronly woman who, in a very curtly manner, and in a husky voice, introduces herself as "Mrs...", the "Director".

This woman, who is dressed in a crisp, navy blue A-line skirt and stiffly starched, high-collared white blouse, is positively horrid-looking! She is bone-thin and the skin on her arms and neck is wrinkled and pendulous. Moreover, she is sporting a big bump, or wart of some sort, protruding in a most distracting fashion from the very end of her pointy nose. The smoke trailing from the cigarette between her yellowed fingers is making me feel positively nauseated—well, at the very least, it's making me cough and choke! (My, how inconsiderate she is, especially for a person who is supposedly very important!)

I am feeling rather squirmy on mommy's lap as she positions herself, stiff-backed and motionless, in the great wooden chair. What this "Wart Lady" has to say to my mommy is terribly upsetting to her, and is making her clutch me more and more tightly in her arms. I start to whimper softly to get mommy's attention, but what she has to hear is making her cry more than I am. I see mommy's hand shaking as she is trying to write something on the papers handed to her while being demanded to "Sign your name!"

Of course, at only five weeks of age I can't understand the adult conversations. I could not know my mommy has signed some binding legal documents in order to arrange for my admission as a "temporary ward" of this organization. (Although this would be considered my *first fostering* situation, this asylum would not be considered a "Foster Home". That designation would come soon enough. However, this is, in fact, my *third* change of *residence,* since my birth.) In addition, I could not know what the signed papers would mean to mommy and me. The documents ensured, *for the next twelve months of my life, I would reside in this orphanage, and no longer live with my beautiful, sweet mother.* (If I could have understood, I would have been very sad and worried about where my mommy would be *staying—after all, if not with *me,* then where?)

All I do know is I need to comfort my mommy who can't stop crying as the "Wart" details what is to occur in our lives in the year to follow my admission to the orphan asylum. You see, my mommy *knows* what I could never understand. At this very moment, I've enjoyed the last nurturing nursing I would ever experience while nestled in the security of my mother's wonderful arms, with my cheek and lips against her soft, warm breast. I will never again know the sensation of being safe and protected by the permanence of my mother's embrace. How could I continue to live in the naive belief that, "*If I am in my mother's arms, all is right with the world and nobody can change that—ever!*"? Nevertheless, life goes on and mommy and I are out of options, and my mother is suffering under such a great burden of stress as she whispers to me,

"*Ricky, darling, we have come to the end of our time together, for now, and we have no more choices. Sweetheart, we must be very brave, and comply with whatever this nice lady tells us to do.*"

Certainly, I did not completely comprehend the significance of mommy's words. All the same, I babble my compliance, "*Yes, certainly, my sweet mommy dear, certainly."*

After my mother answers seemingly endless questions, the "Wart" gives some sort of hasty explanation of what she expects of mommy and me, and what the "C.A.S." has to *offer* us—specifically in the nature of a temporary "home" for me. She then escorts us through a door in the back of her office, and asks us to stand in the outer hallway, and *wait*. Wait for what? We wonder in unison.

Apparently, this outer hallway is one, which adjoins the main office building of the "C.A.S." to the first orphanage building. As we are waiting alone, I clearly see and feel how frightened she is, so I try to comfort her with my usual babbling. Strangely, my little voice starts echoing and bouncing off all the surfaces of the hall. I believe the echo is a result of the aseptic walls, which are tiled half-way-up from the floor with plain, ugly green ceramic squares, framed along the top and bottom by narrow, shiny black, rectangular ones.

Although mommy is as scared as I am, she is doing all she can to comfort and distract me. When she cradles me, I lean back in her arms and stare up at the ceiling. I can see it has many places where pieces of plaster have broken off, and through some attempt to disguise the disrepair, the resulting holes filled-in with thick, glossy-white paint. While we continue to *wait*, all I can think about is how the patchy, broken ceiling appears to be almost high enough for jumping giants! (Oh, my! Perhaps that is how it became so chipped!)

Nevertheless, right now my tummy is gassy and painful. Mommy changes my position and puts me over her shoulder to pat my back and burp me. Glancing around, I notice how the emptiness of the great hall seems to stretch on forever, broken up occasionally, on one side or the other, by ghostly, grey-white painted doors. Are there giants harboured behind the mysterious doors, I wonder? This can't possibly be any sort of real "home" for me, my mommy, or anybody else—I am convinced of that much! (At least, I desperately *hope* it's not!)

Chapter 6: The Orphanage

Suddenly, to my shock, the cries and screams of what sounds like many other babies, seemingly answer my babbling echoes. (They're probably crying because they *know* about the *giants*.) Anyway, inspired, and with the purpose of discovering what I might possibly be in for, I'm thinking it might be a good idea if I attempt to communicate with the babies who seem to already be hiding behind the doors. It's then I start wailing, only much louder this time, in order to get their attention. Strangely, the only responses I elicit are muted women's voices. (I can't help but wonder, if this is truly a foundling organization providing desperate single mothers with much needed help, or finding their children "loving" homes, why are there babies voices still echoing *here* in this ominous place?)

Ahhh, our waiting-time ceases! The "Wart-Lady" leads us from the hallway and puts us in a very small room which is virtually little more than just a broom closet, with only space enough for a metal cage-looking crib and a visitor's straight-backed wooden chair. Then, sensing how exhausted I've become, especially after all my extra crying and whining, mommy kisses my cheek and lays me down in the empty crib. She gently strokes my forehead in her very special, loving way and, of course, I can no longer fight back the slumber which has overpowered my current consciousness. I give into the sleepiness waves washing over my little brain. By now, I have already forgotten the events of the day as my eyelids meet in the middle. The very last words I do remember hearing are my mommy's soft voice and the promise she made to the "Wart", "Naturally, *I will be here to visit my little Ricky as often as **you** will **allow** me to.*"

"*Visit, visit?*"...What can it mean? However, because my mommy's lips uttered the words, I suppose whatever it implies

Revolving Doors
should be very encouraging news for me, so for now, I sleep.

Chapter 7: My Mommy is Taken Away from Me

Very shortly, some middle-aged woman approaches us in our closet. She is sporting scraggly grey hair sticking straight out sideways under her starched-white nurse's cap. She also has a matching sprig of grey sprouting bravely from a jagged, brown mole on her chin. Her funny little cap has a narrow black band along its edge, and is balanced—no actually perched awkwardly at the front of her head, right where her receded hairline meets her high forehead. At the top left corner of the cap is a tiny gold-coloured broach, which consists of two small, round pins curiously chained together. I'll later discover these imposing little pins indicate this woman is a "Duty Nurse". However, I am thinking that, for a woman who spends so much time caring for the foundlings in this nursery, she seems to be *awfully rough* about dressing *me*!

My mommy provided the adorable little yellow bunny suit in which to present me on this, a most inauspicious occasion. My talented mommy knitted the set for me while she awaited my arrival into this world. Oh, my, how happy it makes me feel when my mommy tells me how handsome I look in this outfit which she created! I am especially glad she thought of making a cap, which even has bunny ears to keep my head warm and snugly, because as it turned out, upon my entrance into this world, my head presented as bald as a cue ball, *tee, hee, hee*! How did she ever know? (I love her so much!)

Nevertheless, where is my beautiful mommy, right now? I am curious as to why this strange woman has so abruptly awoken me, and rushed me back from my dreamy lala-land'.

"Who are you? You smell awful! Ouch, stop twisting my arms! Your hands are so chafed, and scratchy, theyre hurting me!

Revolving Doors
What is going on? Where's my mommy?"

Oh, O.K., I hear her now—there she is, out in the hallway talking to the "Wart"! *"Mommy! Mommy!"* I am stuck in this small, barred prison, crying my very loudest now—screaming at the top of my tiny lungs. I don't understand the lamentable words she is uttering, or the tears raining down her soft, pale cheeks from her sad, hazel eyes. However, I *clearly* read the meaning of mommy's wonderful outstretched arms, as she struggles, unsuccessfully, to take me back from the nurse's rough grasp. I can only wonder why "Wart-Lady" has insisted my mommy return to her office immediately, but *without **me***.

Once mommy went through the door back into "Wart's" office, not a minute had passed when "Gold Pins" hands me over to a *man,* who also happens to be wearing a stiff white jacket. Can he also be a "man" nurse, I wonder? No, he is the porter—the one who carries the little ones to their assigned billets. I am uncomfortable and uncertain, partly because this strange man is holding me in a very uneasy manner, but mostly because I don't know why mommy is not *with me*. Unable to control my feelings, I begin fussing, squirming and even kicking in an attempt to reach out to my mommy. The stranger starts shaking me, and demanding, "Stop being such a cry-baby!" *"Hey, why aren't **you** talking sweetly to me? What's happening?"* I stare directly into his droopy brown eyes and screech back at him, *"Of course I'm a cry-baby! What do you expect? I don't even know you, and I am very frightened and I want my mommy! And, where has she gone without me?"*

Of course, I am certain he doesn't understand my utterances, so he pays me no attention. I really don't like this man with his grease-slicked, rat-like, grey-brown hair. Something about him scares me. He has the hugest ears I've ever seen! In fact, they're awkwardly stuck in an uneven arrangement onto each side of his skull, almost dwarfing his thick sideburns. I think I shall call him, "Big Ears"! I wonder why this unusual man is carrying me outside of the building and into the sunshine. Though the warm rays feel good on my face, their brilliance really stings my sensitive, tear-filled eyes. It's a good thing I am wearing my warm little bunny-suit with the feet and the long ears, because it feels quite cold out to me. In fact, I half expect to catch my every out-breath with my hands!

I try to lift my head and look around this fellow, but to no avail. Through the smoky cloud from his just-lit cigarette, I can't see my mommy at all now, in fact, I can no longer even hear her speaking. I don't understand these strange developments in my life, and I am terribly hungry and sleepy. I need mommy's kisses and cuddles. I need her loving looks. I need her caressing arms around me. I need her lullabies. I need to feel my cheek against her warm, soothing breast, and I desperately need to smell her wonderful, lingering fragrance. I am gone from mommy now, and she from me, and I am certain I will never, ever figure out why. I begin to wonder how I can exist for even a minute without my mother and if this tragedy will be my new "*forever-life*".

Chapter 8: The Asylum "CAGES"

Finishing his smoke, "Big Ears" then carries me over to a large brick building which is across the lawn, next door. We go through a heavy set of double doors into the comforting warmth inside. Immediately a middle-aged woman, wearing a white nursing uniform and cap, similar to "Pin's", confronts us. This new handler has jet-black hair rolled into tightly curled furrows. Her white roots loudly betray her store-bought hair dye colouring, which is long overdue for refreshing. She has a very ruddy complexion and rough, cracked hands, which stink of antiseptic.

This nurse carries me a little way through the building before abruptly depositing me into another barren crib, in a large room full of similarly occupied cribs. Then she promptly leaves without one single word of comfort for me. Surely, she must know what I am feeling. I tried to search her grey eyes for a glimmer of kindness, and when I found none, I wondered how she could be so cold-hearted to *me*, only a frightened little baby.

Of course, I am not only startled by this latest development in my life, but I am also petrified of what will happen to me next! However, no explanations, no answers and no words of consolation will ever be forthcoming to me. I am simply alone, without my mother, and apparently stuck in this unhappy predicament, which happens to be my *third change of address* even though it's only my *first fostering* situation, a lot of moving by anyone's standards.

This is NOT where mommy lays me down to sleep every night! It's NOT my cozy white wicker bassinet, with the blue gingham ruffle all around it. This strange, cage has nothing of comfort in it, whatsoever. There is no pillow or soft padding, and not even one teddy bear or toy rattle. This scratchy, white cotton crib sheet reeks of bleach and fits so tightly you really *could* bounce a coin off it. I will soon discover I am staying, temporarily I hope, with many others like me in a huge room full of very old cribs. A total of twelve of these infant cages take up the better part of this ward. They were originally a nickel-coloured metal, painted over with fresh white enamel, but are now aged, yellowed, chipped and even rusted in spots. The horizontal bars have suffered the greatest damage since it's there that many of the babies have, quite obviously, put their mouths, either to cut, or break, their teeth, or possibly out of boredom, to simply pass the time, I suppose.

Beside each crib is a change-table, the front of which lifts up to reveal a "Bathinette" [89], (for quickly sponge bathing us kiddies). Underneath are the few necessary supplies for each infant's most basic, daily toilet essentials. There is a conspicuous absence of any chairs for visitors, because after all, once there, we have been most likely been given up by our parents, and families. (Of course, I could not possibly know this right now.) Anyway, who else would ever be coming to the orphanage to *visit* any of the children, especially those of us who are unwanted, or worse--"hard to place"?

There is a special room, with a sort-of one-way window through which the "Prospective Adoptive Parents", or "PAPs", are able to view us babies and children, supposedly "interacting naturally" with each other. Ha! What a joke *that* is! There is absolutely nothing "natural" about any "interactions" in this Asylum! Nevertheless, the secret room is supposed to make it easier for them to choose the lucky child who will end up finally escaping this institution as an *adopted child. [I guess it's almost like picking out the best of us little "pups" from the rest of our mangy litter-mates.]*

I am just wondering where my mommy can be right now. I am

certain she is around somewhere arranging things so she can come right back and spring me from this antiseptic infant prison. However, I am starting to feel just a little confused because it seems as if I've been waiting a very long time for my mother's return, but she hasn't yet come back to get me. I can't understand it. Could I possibly have done something *so* terribly wrong that she would simply drop me off at this awful place, and walk out of my life, forever? No, no way! After all, I am *never* bad, I am *perfect*—mommy tells me so, all the time!

Where is the woman in the white uniform--"Grey Eyes,"--the one who initially stuck me in this nursery crib? Maybe she has some answers. At first, I felt certain she was just leaving to go fetch my mommy for me, but this is taking too long. I am beginning to wonder about the intense and disturbing conversation mommy had with the "Wart Lady" who is supposedly directing everything in this authoritarian institution. (...And what were all those important papers mommy had to write her name on?)

By now, a great deal more time has passed, I have not had any milk formula to relieve my aching tummy, and I have not seen my mother, or anyone else who could care for me. Moreover, the terrible mixture of smells in this nursery is aggravating my nausea. In fact, I'm certain if there was anything at all left in my tummy it surely would have come all the way up by now. Worse than anything else, I am experiencing a deep sadness which feels as if I have a large hole in my heart. Right now, I could really use a few of my beautiful mommy's "bunny hugs" and "butterfly kisses". I really hope she isn't lost in this big place, because it's so massive the giants could easily swallow someone up! Nevertheless, I'm physically very uncomfortable, and quite miserable. So right now, I am only able to think as far ahead as the hope of my next bottle-feeding, or diaper change—unless the invisible giants get me first.

Oh yes, I just remembered there *is* one thing which "Grey Eyes" took away from me, which I *know* would make my life in this cage much more bearable. I am referring to my soft, fuzzy, blue blankie with the doggies and kitty-cats and on which mommy used lovely cursive writing to embroider "***Ricky***". She also started making *this blankie* when I was growing in her tummy! Oh my gosh! It is soooo very stunning with beautifully finished edges. I would call it a masterpiece, even if she had never tried to make one before!

I like being "Ricky", but I truly miss my loving mommy calling me my other nickname, her "*Little Man*"! It's because *I am* the only man in her life, and *I am* the one who will love her forever, never betray her and always, always be there for her, no matter what! It makes me so happy to know how very important I am, at least in *my sweet mommy's eyes,* because, after all, who else really matters to *me*?

Even though I don't know how much time has passed, nevertheless I've decided I certainly don't like where I am right now. All of the children, and us babies, are staying in a very big, very old building. This place is cold, austere, and "unofficially" considered an orphan "Asylum". Outside of this nursery-room door, the hall walls, which are plastered and thickly-painted shiny white, stretch way up to meet the very highly arched ceilings. Every so often, down the hallway on one side or the other, is a large, dark-brown-stained wooden door, each of which has a noisy, tarnished brass latch and squeaky hinges. Every door has its own arched, smoked-glass transom window at the top. (*Presumably,* these open up for air circulation during the sweltering dog-days, which are so common of summers in Toronto.) Painted on each of these windows, in massive black numbers, is each ward designation. Hmmm? Lest anyone *forget* where he is, I guess.

Revolving Doors

All the many strange noises resound along the wide, battleship gray linoleum flooring in the halls. There are varying pitches and strange, noisy, haunting cries and screams emanating from the different rooms, regardless if they are other nursery wards, or those few which house the older children in our building. Of course, at times, when the dissonance becomes virtually unbearable, a hall buzzer will suddenly sound and the caregiver-aides, often seated right inside the doors, will put down their steamy, romance novels, close each door and latch its transom window, (probably to avoid a mass exodus lest we all try to escape). "Thud—click", "thud—click"! All the way down the length of the great hall we can hear the shutting-out noises reverberate!

I cry out for attention from any of the women who continually enter and leave this room, as if through some invisible revolving door. They all wear white skirts and blouses, and swish by in their white shoes with the thick, rubber soles. It's much easier to get the attention of the young girls wearing red-and-white-striped jumpers—the "Candy-Stripers". It is their generally known nickname, because their uniform resembles the red-and-white striped, Christmas candy sticks—or candy-canes. Of course, these girls are only the volunteers, not trained nurses, and are therefore, *not authorized* to actually *do* anything for us, (other than straighten up our change tables, or refill the bathinette supplies beneath). Nevertheless, some of them do speak in kindly voices, almost as if they even care one iota about us abandoned little charges. Maybe *one* of *them* will feed me. I squeal louder as they attend to one baby's area or another's, yet still give absolutely no attention to *me*. What the heck is going on? Am I simply invisible? I wonder.

I have noticed many others walking swiftly past our nursery door. Even when I am not watching, I still hear their parading footsteps, each with different rhythms and cadences. The steps vary depending on whether they're made by women or men, or if the sounds are a result of the nurses' rubber-soled swishers, doctor's pricey leather-soled Florsheim's, [163], or visitors' and office ladies' clacking stilettos.

Every now and then, someone peeks in our door and tells *me* to, "Hush! Hush, little one! Don't you know it isn't dinner time yet?" How would I know anything? Don't they understand I am not just terribly hungry, I am sleepy and aching with loneliness for my mommy? Regardless of my pathetic cries, I can't get anyone to come in and actually attend to *my* needs. I am sure I am crying just as loudly and despairingly as the other babies in here are, but regardless, all of the people's shoes just keep promenading past my doorway.

Sometimes I hear our so-called caregivers chatting, gossiping or mutually complaining about their working conditions. They natter on, and sound off about how very "over-worked, over-loaded and over-stressed" they are. They bemoan how they don't have time to pick us little babies up, or hold and cuddle us. Yet, not only do these "real" nurses continually berate and embarrass the high school candy-stripers, but they also scold the nursing "aides" who defensively excuse our needy screams by admitting they're only able to perform the most basic, necessary duties as assigned. For us kids, it means utterly no cuddle time! Of course, how could we little wards possibly understand what the adults are experiencing or thinking. We just feel empty, bothersome, ignored, unhappy, lonely and very, very needy.

I am certain that every single child in here, no matter their age, must ball their eyes out at one time or another. Many of us cry because we seem to be continually, incessantly sick. Unluckily, if any child succumbs to one malady or another, we *all* quickly develop the same disease. This is especially true when it comes to illnesses affecting our lungs such as bronchitis or pneumonia, or diseases which pass amongst us quickly, such as impetigo, influenza, or various intestinal afflictions. Often, we aren't yet well from one malady when we contract another.

[It seems as if the medical community, responsible for the day-to-day operation of this orphanage, has neither the time, nor the staff, to ensure the hands of all of us little ones are continually cleaned, and kept away from our faces, (which, of course, would reverse the high rate of repeat infections). However, I suppose it would surely be a nearly impossible task, requiring a great many more nurses and other aides, to provide such a level of care. The solution, therefore, is to keep us *semi-isolated* by having us spend the *better part of everyday* in our individual *cages*. We are only allowed actual physical playtime for a very short duration each day. Of course, the only other socially interactive time is when we are placed in the *mirrored viewing room*, being put on display for possible adoption.]

Therefore, due to illness, and all other sundry reasons, the noise level in this nursery can be quite unbearable at times. Yes, we all cry, and then we cry some more, but for me, personally, I usually cry because my tummy hurts so badly. Right now, I am screaming for some attention to get me out of this this rough and scratchy cloth diaper, which is soaking wet and hanging off my bum—again! I even screech sometimes because the diaper pin has somehow come undone and is sticking into my side—again! At times, I just need some soothing ointment for my pervasive diaper rash. Often I cry because I urgently need to be touched lovingly, picked-up, held and cuddled. I cry even more because I desperately need to hear my precious mommy sing me to sleep with her beautiful lullabies. Oh, how I miss inhaling the rich, sweet perfume which swirls lightly around her face, and settling, sleeps between her breasts. Mostly I cry because I now see I am gone from mommy now, and she from me, and I am certain I will never, ever figure out why. I begin to wonder how I can exist for even a minute without my mother and if this tragedy will be my new "*forever-life*".

From the very first moment when mommy and I arrived at the "C.A.S.", a domino-like series of events and changes in our circumstances has stood mommy, and me, on the brink of a hopeless and uncontrollable downward spiral. At every turn, such unhappy convolutions have brought nothing but misery to my mommy, and when *she* is unhappy—*I* am unhappy. Nevertheless we may only take each day as it comes right now, as we are unable to envision whatever may be in the future for us—if, in fact, there might even *be* a future for *us*.

I guess I should be glad I've been blissfully unaware of "Wart's" attempts to contact my mommy at the hospital where she last "stated" she was working. The only answer given to "Wart" was, "*Miss Ketteringham is no longer employed here.*" and, "*Unfortunately, this office has no forwarding information by means of which she may be contacted.*" The notations "Wart" wrote in my file after this disappointing discovery indicated I was, more likely than not, going to be one of the many pathetic children facing adoption, with the label, "*Hard to Place*", virtually stamped across our foreheads!

Chapter 9: *Where'd All These Homeless Orphans Come From?*

[There are far too many babies and children staying in this place. Of course, most of the youngsters here are awaiting adoption, at best—or at the very least a loving foster home. It's difficult to comprehend where so many of us orphans have come from, especially since we are not all blonde-haired and blue-eyed kids. In addition, we seem to babble in so many strange and different dialects. Obviously, there has been a variety of dissimilar situations causing every child in here to be "orphaned". When it comes to being chosen, (i.e. picked for adoption), no one particular child in here has any better opportunity than any other child does. Being chosen for adoption seems to be simply a matter of the "luck of the draw", (or so the "C.A.S." would have everyone believe).

Of course, the improved opportunities presented by the post-war economy are important factors contributing to the general over-abundance of children—in other words, the "Baby Boom", as it has been so aptly termed, was an explosion of new babies being born. [5] [5a] Although the employment/unemployment ratio has begun to improve, war-time life has created many single mothers attempting the impossible task of being both their child's/children's sole caretakers, while functioning as the exclusive providers of their family's income.

Mothers could be caregivers and not providers, but the income had to come from somewhere. Usually the "somewhere" would be the husbands, or partners, whose occupations brought some financial security into the home. However, the majority of these men, husbands or partners were physically "out of the picture" due in part to wartime, and post-war, postings in Europe and elsewhere. As well, the insidious nature of combat itself resulted in a great many men simply dying. Additionally, there were untold numbers of troops who suffered devastating injuries and, upon their return, were unable to handle the duties and responsibilities required to function in their former jobs, (though many of which had been held open, in anticipation of their return to work).

*Furthermore, many men who did return, were apparently physically able to work, but were actually silently suffering from extremely devastating, but **invisible**, mental health issues. These ravaging, and life-altering, problems directly resulted from either the stresses of battle itself, or the toll on relationships and marriages produced by post-war occupation at such great distances from the family homes. These desolating emotional results of trauma, which were once termed, "Shell Shock" or "Battle Fatigue", [12] [12a], are currently delineated, and only recently being treated, as a debilitating, complex medical syndrome, more accurately labelled, "Post-Traumatic Stress Disorder". [13] [13a]*

Quite often, many of the "single" mothers were simply not financially able to care for their children. Sadly, they were forced into what was, for the majority, the most crushing of life decisions. That was, having their children placed in large, over-crowded orphan asylums on a "temporary", or "semi-permanent", basis, or else, having their children moved out of the asylum and on to foster homes, (a decision, completely at the discretion of the asylum's Director).

*The Southwest York County "C.A.S." was one of many such organizations promising help to unwed mothers, and/or single pregnant women, during what would later be termed the, "Baby **Scoop** Era", (a somewhat shady time in the history of Canadian paid adoptions). [15] [161]*

{"Unwed mothers should be punished and they should be

punished by taking their children away."—Dr. Marion Hilliard of Women's College Hospital, November 1956} [161]

*Due to any desperate, pregnant woman's, or a single mother's, limited financial circumstances, this decision would have "seemed" to be the means to the end of witnessing their babies and children going hungry, or not receiving the proper quality of care. Even if the mother's original intentions were such that the placement was agreed upon as being, "only on a temporary basis", the reality created many more babies and children needing food, clothing, medication and general care for longer, rather than shorter periods of confinement in the asylums. However, the hardest reality for any desperate parent was losing any of their children "permanently", by having to give-in to completely **signing over** their care and maintenance to an adoptive family. Of course, this action would come with the understanding the parents would **never again** be able to contact, see or find out about the welfare of, these children. [14][160]*

{Am I talking about my own mommy right now? I guess I must be.}

*"The Home Children Movement", [2] [4] [4a] [9] [9a], the "Great Depression", [7] [7a], the "Children's Overseas Reception Board", [1], the Children of War Brides, [162], and the "Baby Boomers" were several of the major components contributing to overcrowded orphanages, children's homes, asylums and foster homes. They were all full to bursting, both during, and after World War II, in the history of Canada and the world, and, of course, to a no less significant extent in **my** little life. (See details in Appendix "A" below.)*

In any case, it's certain the flood of additional, destitute children only exacerbated the problems of the already over-crowded nurseries and children's wards. Of course, the prohibitive numbers of children, of all ages, surely added to the difficulties experienced when the youngsters were all competing for occasional adoptions by the few, and far between, Prospective Adoptive Parents, or "PAPs".

*However, with a limited number of actual adoptions, others had to be placed into outside fostering situations, in order to make room for those incoming children needing to be processed through the "C.A.S." system. Sadly, there was a disconsolate side to foster placements. More often than not, the prospect a child would be "happy" by simply moving on to a foster, or even a group foster home, was unrealistic. Happiness was not guaranteed to a child moving to live as potentially the second, third or perhaps even fifth youngster in the care of the harried foster "mother". As was frequently the case, many of children already placed in such homes were often well seasoned, worldly and, of course, controlling of their own little universes. This typically translated into cruel, vicious and resentful treatment of all newcomers—especially the easily bullied little children, like **me**! (However, that is a whole "nuther" part of my story.)]*

Chapter 10: What Kind of Folks "FOSTER" Kids?

I have to wonder why anyone would want to provide foster care to any of us needy little tykes. Sadly, the answer could only be that many fostering "parents" are only motivated to provide shelter for us children by the promise of remuneration, which amounts to a paltry few extra dollars per month of government-issued Baby Bonus payments, plus a little more income for foster parenting. These are our only dowries. Nevertheless, I am a smart little fellow and capable of quickly discerning I am just one more baby, occupying one more cage. I am in no way more or less special than are the other kiddies in this place. I soon figure out that, in here, I am, well actually we all are, unwanted, and unloved. How can I ever expect to be a *"chosen one"*, when there are so many of us competing for the same favoured placements, which, of course, are rare?

After staying here for only a few weeks, I am beginning to learn, by observation, the children usually picked first for the mirror room viewings, and potential adoption interviews, are the **quiet** ones, **not us screamers**. I *had* believed intuitively the, "squeaky wheel gets the grease". However, we are not squeaky wheels, are we? We are financial and emotional commitments, and daily burdens, in essence amounting to obligations lasting up to eighteen years, or more. Only the well-behaved, meaning the "quiet, mousey and non-aggressive puppets", are most often selected, for adoption. Too bad, because I'm sure, even if I try my very hardest, I certainly will *not ever* fit into *such a* category!

Nevertheless, I've learned to be much quieter, definitely not whiny, and to keep my discomfort, suffering and unhappiness to myself. Sadly, I am beginning to accept not only my physical hunger, but also the loneliness and emptiness in my soul, as part of my regular daily circumstances. I've discovered how to be secretive and to make myself small and invisible. "*Trouble-Maker*"—won't be *my* label— not *me*! If I am ever going to get out of here, I will *have* to be the quiet one, not the complainer. I'll make the cute faces which will induce the Prospective Adopting Parents to pick *me*. Secretly, though, I can't help but wonder if I am actually unlovable, after all where did my own adoring mommy go? Moreover, why, on earth, did she leave me here in this wretched place? At this minute, I am feeling very, very angry at this completely jumbled-up system of so-called "foster child care"--and, as it will eventually turn out for me, with *very good reason*!

Chapter 11: Is Mommy *Ever* Coming Back For Me?

Finally, my mommy contacted the "Wart" to inform the "Director" of her change of job. She apologized for having merely forgotten to call and notify their office. Mommy confessed, "*I really didn't like the work at the hospital, so I've taken a job at the '...Home for the Aged'.*" Mommy also assured the "Wart-Lady", she would be coming back into the office to make her promised twenty dollar monthly payments toward my maintenance—and, of course, *to visit* and *play with me*! The Director logged in her notes,

"*It was necessary to chastise Berneice for not understanding she must keep in constant touch with this office, regarding Ricky*".

She also noted my mommy "smiled sweetly" and said, "*I love my baby*" and, "I *definitely do NOT want to give my son up for adoption!*" Mommy insisted, "*I am sure, someday I'll be able to take care of Ricky, myself!*" However, when once again immediately challenged to pay the maintenance fees, my mommy apologized and said, "*It's just impossible at this time.*" (Obviously, mommy had not yet received her first pay cheque at her new, "Aged Home" job, or else I am certain she would have been happy to pay the "C.A.S." towards my maintenance.)

When asked about her "future plans" mommy's answer was quite firm, "*I want a real home for Ricky and me, more than anything else in the world!*" Why, of course she wants that for us! Mommy actually told the "Wart", "*I'm simply not interested in going out with boys anymore.*" (This would be good news since what I don't need right now is a baby brother or sister vying for mommy's attention!)

Revolving Doors

[The Director's immediate notation stated,
"*Berneice's plan was going to be quite impossible to adhere to, since she was <u>still a teenager</u>—and of course, <u>quite a pretty one at that.</u>*" (My gosh! *I* certainly know that *better* than anybody does!)

"Wart-Lady" added,
"*Berneice had a dreamy look in her eyes as she outlined her true hopes and desires for herself and her baby Ricky.*"

Mommy also told her, "*I only wish I could find a stable, reliable man who would marry me. That way I could raise my son at home. It's all I really want.*"

The Director continued,
"*It was natural for her to want a home as she, herself, had none.*" "Wart" tried to point out to my mommy the true reality of the situation. She tried to explain how mommy needed to be aware of the possibility she may not meet a man who would be willing to take-on Ricky and raise her little baby as his own son. However, "Wart" further noted,

"*Berneice rejected the suggestion and clung to her ideal of, 'having a little home, cheerful and bright, and of a daddy, {for Ricky}, who comes home at night, and who laughs and plays with **our** son'.*"

Then, according to the Director's notations,

"*Berneice appeared to have a mooning expression on her face, as she reminded me, 'What a wonderful baby my little Ricky is! Isn't he? Don't you think so?'*"

[From the "C.A.S." Director's additional notes,

Revolving Doors

"This Birth Mother's need for a 'home', in the physical sense, would drive her to seek only that, and not the emotional satisfaction which deep love could bring. She has been informed, at once, due to Ricky's transfer to a foster home, she would now only be able to visit her baby <u>biweekly</u>. This was done, of course, in order to consider the foster mother's feelings, and this directive came after the foster mother complained to this office that 'Miss Ketteringham's recent visitation was a great inconvenience'."]

PART III: The Foster Residences

Chapter 12: The "Cleaning Lady"

Well, it certainly is good to get out of *that vile place*! I am wondering if I am going home with my mommy today because she has not yet come to retrieve me. Therefore, now I suppose I'll wait and see how things pan out around here. Since I am less than two months old, I am certain I have lots of time to get situated, *somewhere* at least, until my mommy is able to "get on her feet". That is when mommy said she would be able to take me home with her—forever. It's all about the "money". I know her lack of money is the only thing keeping my mommy and me from going home together, forever. I heard mommy explain to the "Wart", when she has "improved financial circumstances, [she] will come right back here to pick me up and take me *home* with [her]".

However, each time the adults get me dressed-up and spring me from this awful cage, I have to wonder if I am being *"adopted"*. It's a term I've heard tossed around by these grown-ups in the asylum, and they tend to speak as if it's a good and desirable thing to happen to any orphan in here. Hmmm, "adoption". What possible meaning could it hold for my little life? If it's a bad thing, I don't want any part of it! However, even if "adoption" is a good thing, personally I will not find out for many years to come, what good it might be for insignificant little me. However, as I will soon discover, it's only temporary housing where I am currently being sent, and right now, I am not even sure why I am being moved out of this asylum. (After all, I thought this *orphanage* was only supposed to be *temporary housing, until my mommy could take me home with her.*)

In any event, this *second* foster situation was to be the *fourth* of my being moved *eighteen* times, in and out of *fourteen* different, (or in one case, repeated), fostering situations. These included "foster" homes, "boarding" homes, the "orphanage Asylum" and, failing to be chosen for adoption, one quickly aborted trial run at the first "Prospective Adoptive Parent's" residence. These moves would continue until I will finally be placed in the second "PAP's" residence, first, on a visitation, then later on a trial basis. Of course, nothing would be so perfect, or make me happier than my sweet mommy's return for me. However, in the unhappy event my mommy can never come and get me, thankfully this "PAP's" home would eventually become my *second* choice of a permanent home-- (through my "successful adoption").

All I know right now is the "C.A.S." ladies have had some sort of serious talk about my first placement being on a boarding home basis, which sounded to me an even more *temporary* arrangement than a foster home. They also discussed how they would be keeping this foster "mother" under "*close supervision*". I could not possibly know why they thought this necessary for my care. Nevertheless, I expect it will be an infinitely better arrangement than this asylum. Before long, I am being dressed in my baby-blue terry-cloth, one-piece jammie with the little blue doggie, yellow duckie and pink kitty-cat emblems all lovingly embroidered on it, by my mommy's talented hands, of course. I am certain I won't be coming back to the asylum too soon because they have already packed *all* of my belongings in a brown paper grocery bag with the words, "LOBLAWS, [17], Groceteria" emblazoned in bright red ink across the front.

A very pretty, blonde-haired "C.A.S." woman, who calls herself "Mary-Lynne", has been driving us around, in her whopping big old, blue-and-rusting vehicle. We have been travelling for such a long time, I've become sleepy, either from the jostling around, or more likely from the smell of gas fumes inside the car. Finally, she spots the small, narrow, faded-green clapboard house with the address numbers matching the one scribbled on the torn corner of an envelope providing her with the directions. We have arrived at the home of what is to be my first "foster mother". "Mary-Lynne" is very gentle about carrying me to the front door, all the while repeating, "*It's going to be alright Ricky, don't worry little guy, you'll like it here.*" Meanwhile, I am busy focusing on her mesmerizing sky-blue eyes.

Just then, a woman answers the door, and after a few short words with the woman, "Mary-Lynne" hands me over to the outstretched, welcoming arms of this 'foster mother'. Well, at least I am *feeling* welcome, and wanted, by this new "mother"-- at *first*, anyway. When the door closes after my "Worker's" departure, I decide to have a good look at the woman who was going to be acting as my mother for an indefinite amount of time, (at least until my *real* mommy could come and get me— or so I thought). The "mother" leans over and places me into a wooden playpen, which is in the living room.

As she raises back up, I am shocked by the realization she is an overwhelmingly tall person. When I see her walk into another room, I am more than a little unnerved by her overall size and her almost manly appearance and gait. Unlike anyone I have ever seen before, this woman is very heavy-set, or "big-boned", (as I would later hear her defend her own excess physical baggage). She is *so* unlike my beautiful mommy, or any other grown-up woman I have, yet encountered. In fact, I find her looks are more than a little off-putting. She wears her greasy-looking brown hair shortly cropped and, using the *kitchen vegetable shears*, (as I'll soon actually witness her doing), and she cuts her own bangs unnaturally short and *almost* straight across. She has probably done this in some effort to emphasize her dark brown eyes. Sadly, it has the opposite effect of accentuating the deep, dark, reddish-brown, semi-circular rings and bags, under her tired, blood-shot peepers. Between her hair, her reddened, bumpy face and the large, dark, blackheads constellating her nose, this "mother" altogether presents the appearance of a greasy-skinned woman, who is unkempt, very weary and far older than her actual age!

I also find it a tad strange, my foster mother also wears a "uniform" of sorts, just as the nurses and candy-stripers at the asylum did. Every day she dons one of her many stiffly starched, cotton print dresses, which are, without exception, white-based with blue prints. They are usually flowery, although some have, geometric-looking shapes or even *animal-skin* patterns. I like those ones best. Over the dresses, she puts on a full-length, blue-on-white similarly patterned apron. (Strangely, she never seems to be able to match the patterns on the apron with the patterns on her dresses, although by now it's obvious she, herself, is the creator and seamstress of these questionable adornments.) I watch as she, struggles to tie these aprons strings around at the back of her neck with quite a degree of difficulty. Then, she battles with the other strings, which she wraps around from the front of the apron, to the back, then back around to tie at the front of her waist, the precise location of which seems hard for her to determine.

From the moment I entered her house, I noticed my olfactory senses were insulted by her curious habit of disinfecting *everything* in her entire house, from top to bottom, with a potent, malodorous cleaning product containing chlorine as its bleaching agent. This woman always, and I seriously mean always, *reeks* of this disgusting bleach. When she picks me up to change my diaper, the overpowering nature of the disinfectant makes my little eyes sting and tear-up. Even the little rubber baby *spoon* she uses to feed me my yummy-mushy "Pablum Mixed Cereal", [18], smells *bleachy*. As incredible as it sounds, the formula from my baby bottle even tastes like the awful cleanser. (Could she possibly be attempting to poison me?)

During all my waking and sleeping hours, this woman restrains me in this horrid, old wooden playpen, which also stinks of this wretched cleaning agent! Try as I might, I have not yet developed the skills to be able to roll over in order to plan my escape from the deplorable wooden bars of this cage. In fact, the only occasions, under which I am *removed* from this confinement, are either for spoon-feeding in my highchair, (also well-worn from close familiarity with the bleach rag), or once a week on Saturday nights, for my bath. Ah, yes, my *bath*—I am bathed in her kitchen sink which was once a shiny white porcelain, but has long-since relinquished its gleam to intimacy with the surface-stripping chlorine. Of course, the tepid water, in which she I gingerly holds me, also contains such a level of the bleaching agent, it's a wonder I have any skin left! For these obvious reasons, I've decided to call this foster mother, *"The Cleaning-Lady"*. I can only hope my restriction at this this woman's house is, indeed, only, as it were, on a "boarding-home" basis, and as such, quite temporary!

Nevertheless, I must try to make my stay here as happy as I am able, considering I may, sooner or later, be permitted to go home with my mommy. That is what I am looking forward to, in order to, one day, make my chlorine confinement a long ago, almost-forgotten, bad memory! However keeping myself happy is going to be a difficult undertaking, considering the fact I am pathetically under-stimulated, quite bored and feeling more than a little lonely. You see, from this woman, I receive none of the attention any infant, like myself, would normally require for healthy mental and emotional development. In addition, there is nothing for me to *do* in this cage except look at my only toys. They consist of a matted, old, brown, one button-eyed teddy bear, badly in need of a *little* washing and a *lot* of stuffing, and a red ball missing chunks of rubber, (obviously chewed out by the last dog—I mean *child*, who occupied this loathsome cage).

I only wish I had even a fraction of the toys, or trucks, or blocks—or anything which the **other** boys in this house possess. These kids are the "Cleaning Lady's" **own** children. I mean they're not boarded, fostered or adopted. Sadly and shockingly, she has actually warned them **not** to share their toys with me at all! Nevertheless, you know, I would even give up having any nicer playthings and be satisfied if I could get my little hands on one of their cozy looking blankets which I could lay on and snuggle with! However, nothin' doin'! All of their, and my, belongings are kept separate, on purpose, as if I had some devastating and highly communicable disease—(which, at this moment, I do not have).

The only soft thing I've been given is somebody else's worn-out, moth-eaten, pale yellow baby blanket with a satin trim, which is loose and tearing away in several spots. The loops of trim keep catching on my arm or my foot and the itchy wool is bothering my skin, especially my sensitive face, as the "mother" always places me face down, to sleep on my tummy. Every time I move, the blanket moves away, so for the better part of every day, I am in no way comfy-cozy as my nose is stuck on the hard, wood bottom of this playpen.

As a matter of course, there are certain times when I am suffering one discomfort or another and it seems to be virtually impossible to get this woman's attention. I *must* cry to let her know I am poopy, wet or hungry. However, when I do wail, she gets a mean, angry look in her eyes, and then her face gets bright red, right before she explodes in a tirade of verbal diarrhoea, which, for a baby as sensitive as me, is tantamount to *mental abuse*!

Revolving Doors

I suppose I should be grateful, this woman, my first "pretend mother", is not *too* physically abusive to me. Certainly, she is **firm** with her discipline of me, but I would not exactly call her spankings actual "beatings". (After all, how often or how severely, would someone feel the need to spank an infant?) However, whenever she does beat me, it's with a long-handled, wooden stirring spoon, which she smacks against my bare thigh, or bottom. To me, it certainly feels like an unduly severe punishment for my only *vice* of "crying" to alert her of my need for her help. Nevertheless, any amount, or degree of my wailing, in her estimation, is "too much" and so virtually every needy sound I utter seems to require either the threat of, or else a real, "lickin'", (...*her* expression, not mine).

I am simply biding my time here, waiting for each wonderful visit from my mommy. Constantly, I am reminded I am *neither* part of this family, nor may I expect to be staying with them for very long. It's fine with me because, frankly, I would not want to become any permanent part of this "Cleaning Lady's" household. I feel like an outsider and a disturbance to them. In fact, I am aware I will never fit into her little brood which is comprised of her *own* two boys, four-year-old Davey and Freddy, who is about six. Unlike me, both of these rotund brothers have eerie looking dark-brown, almost *black* eyes, like their mother. When I first arrived here, the brothers had straight, dark-brown, mop-like hair, (obviously trimmed with those infamous kitchen shears). Of course, that was until Freddy came home from school one day with a teachers note, which indicated the school nurse had observed some of those nasty little critters, head lice, in his hair. Once their mother had stopped screeching at **both** of them, she shaved off *all their hair* and then **all of mine too**—although I hardly had enough to shave off. Nevertheless, she scalped me, all the while rationalizing she was doing it, "*Just for good measure*"!

Through the wooden slats of my cage, these brothers

relentlessly poke at me, pinch me and tease me something awful, but only when their mother isn't watching. They know quite well, once they get me crying, *I* will be the one to catch hell with another lickin'! Apparently, they find this quite amusing! Of course, *they* never get into trouble, ever! However, as for me, it doesn't matter what I fuss or cry about, the mother's response is always the same—first, she screams at me, and then she goes looking for the long-handled wooden spoon! Sometimes she just glares at me and screams for Davey to "Run and git me the *damn* spoon!" I desperately wish I could squeeze myself into the corner of my cage and become invisible. Of course, that can't happen because she can always reach my arm or leg, grab me by my jammie collar, or occasionally, even pull me by my hair, (when I still had some).

Unlike the sounds of bedtime routines I hear coming from her sons' room, there are no cuddle sessions, or kisses "Nite-Nite", not for me anyway—not ever. The only times I am picked up and actually cuddled are on the occasions when my own beautiful mother comes to see me. Sadly, I am feeling very lonely and empty right now, and I am missing my mommy terribly. I am positive she would bring me some other play-toys or cuddly bears if only she knew of my desolate plight. As my mind drifts and my thoughts wander, I am curious if mommy can even get me away from such a wretched, so-called "foster-care home", which is, of course, in no sense of the word "caring" nor is it in any way, shape or form a "*home*"--at least not for me. Maybe mommy has given up on me entirely. Regardless, it hurts my little heart so much, but I really don't dare let my thoughts wander in that direction right now, lest I receive further punishment, for my sobbing.

At first, I thought mommy did not even care I had so few playthings in my cage at this house. However, on one of her visits to me, I heard her demand of this foster "mother", "*Where are the toys for my little Ricky?*" Unintentionally revealing her level of education and grasp of the English language, the "foster" woman abruptly responded, "There ain't no extra toys what *me* own kids ain't already playin' with."

Apparently it was all mommy needed to know, and luckily the very next day, she arrived with my *favourite* teddy bear, "Teddy Boy" dressed in his crisp little sailor suit. She also brought my little black stuffed Poodle doggie we named, "Scamp". Mommy did not even forget my two little yellow rubber duckies who chase each other around in my bath, (of course they're named, "Lucky" and "Ducky" and, though they're identical, *mommy and I* can always tell which one is which).

Mommy also brought me the big fat book with all the nursery rhymes told by M*other Goose*, [157], which she always used to read aloud to me. I really love the fairy tales, nursery rhymes and poems in the tattered old book, but the best ones are *any* ones she **sings** to me! However, *this foster mother* is not inclined to read anything to me, at any time and she certainly would *never* sing to me! Sadly, the book stays way up on the high bookshelf in the front foyer, where the foster mother stashed it, (obviously with the knowledge that, "out of sight, out of mind"--it will be soon forgotten).

Of course, mommy's spontaneous return with my playthings today was a problem for the "Cleaning Lady". The unscheduled and unannounced visit was visibly disturbing to her—and it would be the catalyst for new, even more stringent, visitation regulations to be imposed upon my mommy. Notwithstanding the foster mother's attitude, mommy has come to see me again, and it's only one week later, of course, *this time*, she contacted our old friend the "Wart Lady" first, for permission. (Just imagine a grown woman needing permission to see her own son.) Right before she answered the door to mommy, I watched curiously, as the "Cleaning Lady" reached down my fairy storybook and put it beside my playpen on the end table. This was obviously intended to give the impression that she most lovingly attends to my every need, even so much as regularly reading to me from my book!

Immediately after removing her overcoat, mommy starts her usual smothering of me with butterfly kisses everywhere, even on my nose, which is very ticklish and makes me giggle! However, the *second* thing mommy does is read me one of my favourite fairy stories. This feels quite wonderful! Not only do I get to *see* my mommy, but also I am able to *hear* as she reads my favourite fairy tales, or even sings me a song! (Mommy really has a beautiful singing voice, too.)

It's quite soon apparent that, most regrettably, mommy is not able to stay very long this time. This is because the "Cleaning Lady", who has impatiently been interrupting our giggle-cuddle-story session, is sternly suggesting to my mommy "You should git outta my house, *right now—immediately!*" Oh, this is not good. It seems to me as if it has only been a few moments since she had only just arrived. Oh, how I cherish whatever little time I do have with my real mommy. There are simply no words to express how much we adore each other. I treasure her hugs and kisses, and the secrets we share. No one knows mommy whispers her intentions to spring me from this, my latest infant jail, in which I am currently incarcerated. I think she truly sees I am getting very little positive attention from the foster mother, and I am exceedingly lonely. Mommy senses the sadness in my heart; however, what can she do? She cries when she leaves me, because she is so helpless to change our circumstances. I cry too, but only very softly. (My crying sounds like the whimper of a frightened puppy that has fallen into a deep, dark hole and can no longer see, or hear, its own mummy).

Naturally, my mommy has to *obey* the foster mother and leave me immediately. However, after she steps off into the abyss, on the other side of the heavy, wooden, front door, the foster "mother" quite rudely *slams* it behind her. Then she watches out of the front window until she is satisfied my mommy is far out of sight, and can no longer hear my puppy sobs. It's then that I am *whacked* with the wooden spoon—again! This is my punishment for crying-out for my mommy—or for crying-out at all, I suppose.

I could not know it, but this foster mother's attitude was greatly upsetting to my mommy, and, so much so, that on December 1, 1947, my mommy's United Church Minister contacted the "C.A.S." Director's office about the issue. Right after her last visit, mommy had spoken with him about how very distressed and frustrated she was with the new limits of her "biweekly visitations" with me. Explaining to the "Wart-Lady", the Minister said, "Berneice couldn't believe she was being kept from seeing her baby simply because [the child's] foster mother complained about the birth mother's visits somehow "*upsetting the daily routine of the children*". Moreover, the shocking response from the "Wart" was even more disturbing to him— and to mommy. She told him, "Miss Ketteringham is already getting more visits than the normally allotted **one day per month**". To mommy's dismay, the *following day* she received a phone call from the "C.A.S." Director, who firmly insisted visitation with me, would now be *restricted* to only ***a few hours***, on *one day per month*!

Of course, nobody is telling *me* anything! Sadly, after a while, when I come to the realization my mommy's visits with me are now being further limited, it makes me feel terrible. I am unhappier than ever, now that I will be seeing my mommy less and less. The worse I feel, the less I am able to eat, and now I am much sicker with a nagging cough. In fact, lately my health seems to have quickly gotten so much worse, the doctor is now calling it a "serious bout" of "Brown Kites", (at least it's what the word, "Bronchitis" sounded like to me). Or else, he said it's possibly, "New Onions", (which is what "Pneumonia" sounded like). Of course, these are such scary sounding and confusing names, that whichever he decided to treat me for, I really can't remember.

(Personally, I think it's the _bleach,_ which irritates my lungs and makes me gag and cough something awful. But no one would ever guess such a germ-fighting substance would be the culprit triggering the "New Onions"!)

It has not been long, since I first began coughing so badly, I now seem to end each coughing spell by vomiting, from _my toes_! That was when, as my luck would have it, the "Cleaning Lady" made a frantic call to the "C.A.S.", reporting on the debilitating state of my illness. It has quickly become apparent to those _powers that be_, I am not faring terribly well in the presumed "care" I am receiving at _this_ "foster/boarding house".

[In fact, the "C.A.S." Director's own file notations would later indicate, "_Ricky is only receiving an average level of care at this foster home, which is quite inadequate for this baby's needs._"]

These latest developments quickly followed the two unannounced, surprise visits from different "C.A.S." workers. A very short time later, I witnessed their very stern reprimands to the "Cleaning Lady" after which the Workers vehemently discussed their plans for "moving me" to a different foster home. Oh nooooo! I am scared where I might end up next! Right now, my life is spinning far out of my own control, and I feel like I am caught up in the twirl of a great, huge centrifuge—a great spinning—revolving door!

Revolving Doors

Chapter 13: Mommy Loves Me Enough to Let Me Go

Two days after my mom was informed of the completely devastating news of the "once-a-month" limits to her visitations with me, she went again to talk to the "C.A.S." Director, only to discover the "Wart" had reassigned us to a new Case Worker. This new woman was one of the Workers assessing my requirements, and determining my need to be reappointed quickly to another "foster care" facility. Apparently, the only focus of this woman was clearly delineated as, primarily, "the child, John Edward Richard Ketteringham III", after which her secondary concerns are for, "the Birth Mother, Berneice Ketteringham". However, her duties with me would quickly become a great deal more *complicated*, and in her dealings with my mommy, considerably more *delicate*.

Apparently, to the shock of everyone in the "C.A.S." office, but especially to the surprise of this newest Worker, at her next appointment, my mother strode right up to the Case Worker's desk, then after a curt, introductory, "*Hello*" mommy simply announced, "*I've been thinking the whole thing over and I've decided to place Ricky up for adoption.*" When this new Case Worker questioned what prompted my mother's changed decision, mommy explained in an almost rehearsed response,

"*I have spent the past weeks at my church, [participating] in the activities of our 'Youth for Christ' group. While enjoying the little children and their games, I completely broke down and told my Minister **everything** which had happened regarding my premarital intercourse, my unplanned pregnancy, and the resulting, [illegitimate], baby—my little boy, Ricky.*"

The response from mommy's Minister had been the main factor in redirecting her purpose from her previously intense desire to,

"...work, marry 'anyone' and raise baby Ricky in the home which [my husband and I] would be able to more than adequately provide for him."

It seems her Minister had reacted to the confession of her plight as a single mother, by admonishing her, stating, *"Berneice, in all thoughts and actions regarding the baby, you have considered only yourself, and you are being quite selfish."* He also reproved my mommy, stating,

"You should start thinking about the welfare of your little baby, and what will be in store for his future if he is forced to remain in the 'Children's Aid Society's' foster care system."

Unrelenting, he continued,
*"For you, Berneice, I believe that allowing **adoption** of your baby is the only unselfish solution to your problem."*

When his words settled into the depths of her brain, mommy clearly recognized the sad fact, if an adoptive family did not soon choose me, I would probably bounce around from one fostering facility to another. Of course, it only added to the weight of such a decision on mommy's heart when the Case Worker further explained, *"We are already searching for another foster home which would be more sensitive to Ricky's needs, but if none is available, he will be returned to the "C.A.S." residence, [the orphan asylum]."* The prospect of having no real home, nor roots anywhere, and moving from place to place to place, was a loathsome scenario, the negative implications of which my mommy, personally, understood only too well.

The Case Worker tried to explain to my mother,

"True adoption is the best known solution as far as your baby

is concerned; however, giving up all the rights to your child is a very important decision." The woman also explained to mommy, *"Once you have signed the 'Adoption Consents' forms, you can't change your mind, and therefore it is extremely important you are completely, (both mentally and emotionally), ready to give up your child. You must understand, in other words, by relinquishing your little baby Ricky to an adoptive family, it means you will never be able to see, or contact, Ricky again."*

[At this time in the history of adoption in Ontario, the Ministry's documents and files were kept private, sealed and locked away from any possible public disclosure. This remained in effect until the year 2000.]

Continuing, the Case Worker asked my mommy once more, *"Berneice, do you really think you are ready for such a huge decision?"*

[Logging mommy's response to this question, the Case Worker made the following file notation,

"Again, Miss Ketteringham repeated,

'I want to sign the Consents for Adoption.' However, as the interview with Berneice progressed I noticed she sat rigidly on the chair and seemed to be very remote. She did not share any of her true feelings, instead, she kept repeating the phrase, *'I want to place Ricky for adoption.'* However, as a professional I do not feel she is ready to give up her child, (especially when she presents with such a defeatist attitude). In order to give her a little more time to contemplate her decision, I suggested to Berneice, we would prefer to see her wait on *signing* until our office is able to find out more about the birth father, in order to ascertain if the child is indeed adoptable. Berneice then reminded me of her previous

statement,

'I signed the Declaration of Paternity while still at the Southwest Humewood House, naming the one and only boy with whom I've ever had relations, (intercourse).

As a result, I promised to inform Berneice immediately of any developments after obtaining whatever further information might be relevant to the paternity investigation in this case. Berneice was visibly relieved upon leaving this office."]

Four days later, after the Case Worker inquired at Humewood House as to what Berneice had declared, in writing, was the *name* of Ricky's father, the boy was finally contacted. Sadly, "Robbie" vehemently denied his responsibility for paternity, then immediately offered a slander to this young mother's reputation, falsely declaring she was indiscriminately sexually active, or as he actually stated, "*I know she sleeps around with lots of other boys in town!*" Once this information was passed along to Berneice, her Case Worker asked her, "Could you come up with any proof of relations having indeed taken place with *this* young man?" According to the Worker, "Berneice then became confused and did not even know how to prove her claim." She said,

*"It happened at my sister's while her kids, that I was minding, were asleep. I distinctly remember telling my sister as soon as she got home from the movie that night. Moreover, when I talked to 'Robbie', he never tried to deny it. In fact, he even offered to marry me—**over the phone**!"*

The Worker noted her "emotionally depressed demeanour", and then delicately suggested, "Berneice, you must think it over very carefully and *try* to somehow find some proof of the incident, before we are able to again approach the man you're naming as Ricky's father."

However, irrespective of mommy's inability to provide proof the boy she named is actually my daddy, by January 7, 1948, she called her Worker to say, "*I have changed my mind and have decided to keep my baby.*" The Worker noted, "*Berneice sounded much, much happier and said she was so glad she didn't 'sign', (the Consents for Adoption forms).*" However, the Worker then spoke very softly, suggesting to my mommy, "*You should not visit with the baby quite so often.*" In fact, this woman insisted, "*From this moment on, you must always notify my office, or the Director's, ahead of time, of your intention to visit with Ricky at any foster home in which he is being cared for. You should try to understand this change of visitation is being made so as not to disturb any of the foster parents in their ability to interact with, and relate to, **your son**.*"

This latest regulation was very distressing to my mommy's free spirit. She had never been good at adhering to stringent rules or schedules and she hated alarm clocks! Mommy wondered how she would cope with being unable to visit me whenever she wished, or, as was often the case, whenever she had the *bus fare*. Nevertheless, mommy stated, "I will endeavour to do my best because I know you are only following the rules in order to, first and foremost, consider my little baby Ricky's basic needs and his specialized health requirements."

Revolving Doors

Chapter 14: But My Name is "RICKY"!

[From the Case Worker's notes,

"The issue of a twelve-month temporary Wardship was discussed with Berneice, since it has now become obvious there is little possibility of her taking Ricky home at any time within the following calendar year. When the birth mother understood what the Wardship entailed, she was also informed of what she might expect at the court proceedings.

The court case for John Edward Richard Ketteringham III to be established as a twelve-month 'Temporary Ward of the Southwest York County Children's Aid Society' was held on February 3, 1948. Outside the courtroom that day, Berneice arrived with a large parcel for Ricky and was utterly delighted when she saw her little boy. Since she had been adhering to the greatly limited visitation schedule, she seemed surprised and really could not get over how cute and clever her little five-and-a-half-month old youngster had become, since her visit the previous month. While awaiting the proceedings in the courthouse foyer, mother and son hugged, kissed, cuddled, played and revelled in their love for each other. Additionally, we have determined it to be in the child's best interest, as a ward of this Children's Aid Society, he shall henceforth be known by the name, '__TEDDY__'"]

****

The Worker has brought me to the courthouse where we wait in front of the courtroom inside which my following year's fate is about to be determined. Regardless, I have now, finally, seen my mommy and can't stop hugging and kissing her, I've missed her so much. Oh, wow, mommy brought me a large package today! When she helped me to tear the wrapping off it, she held up a *beautiful* new baby blanket she had saved up her money and bought only for me. It was light blue and had little navy-blue sail boats, with red decks and white and yellow striped sails all over it. It was also quite soft, and absolutely perfect to keep me warm and cozy, and wherever my mommy touched it, her wonderful fragrance lingers. I vowed never to let it out of my sight, never, ever!

Then, as soon as mommy and I were enjoying our intimate, albeit fleeting, moments together, this new Case Worker suddenly became visibly upset. Naturally, I was quite bothered by the nervous manner of this petite woman. She was middle-aged, and rather *mousey* from head-to-toe. She sported a sterile, almost nurse-like appearance in her gray, two-piece linen suit, with a starched white blouse underneath, and a yellowing, white lace handkerchief timidly blossoming in the breast pocket. Her hair was a plain, average brown, although I could see, secretly it was quite long, and divided into two braids which twisted at the back, pinned in a circular manner, and married at the crown of her skull. I decide I shall have to call this Worker "Mrs. Mousey".

Although "Mrs. Mousey's" words had not yet vocalized beyond a whisper, suddenly, she sounded unrelenting while reprimanding my mother for purchasing the blanket, instead of paying toward my care. "Mousey" told mommy, "I can quite understand your desire to bring [the baby] a gift, but you should be paying on his maintenance instead!" The woman insisted, "You should pay whenever you have even the smallest amounts of money, instead of buying the baby any *gifts*!" Quite suddenly I witnessed my mommy's complexion change from its usual pallor into a rush of ruddiness! Mommy, biting her bottom lip, then became uncharacteristically hostile and sternly, albeit *politely*, suggested to "Mrs. Mousey",

"**<u>You</u>** *should know what it means for me to buy my own baby* *boy a treasured gift!"*

Of course, to the next question mommy posed to the "Mouse Lady", there would be no forthcoming reply....
*"Tell me, 'Miss...' (So-and-so)...do **you** have any children **of your own**?"*

Of course, my mommy knows what I could not, that this short visit at the courthouse would have to last us a very long time. I am so confused and trying hard to stay awake, but I just can't help falling asleep in the security of my own mother's embrace. She is so warm and soft, and of course, she always smells sooo wonderful. Oh no! Not the "Mouse-Lady"--not yet...mommy can't be handing me back over to *that* woman before we even leave the courthouse! However, unhappily, it's done now; and down the divided double steps, and out through the polished, brass-fitted, double set of revolving glass front doors, there goes my beautiful mommy. She can't be leaving me again. Why did the "Mouse Lady" insist mommy leave first? In my loudest babble, I call to her, "Mommy, Mommy, please don't go, not now, not this time, not ever again! Please!" Oh, not the waterfall of tears again—I can't see her clearly through my tears. Nevertheless, as always, there have to be the mandatory "Good-Byes", and always more tears and more sobs, always an ache in my heart, (and in mommy's heart too, I am sure of it!).

Where will I go, and who will be my "pretend mother" now, I really wonder? You know, if it's not my really, for really, real mommy to love me and take me home, I feel as if I just don't care anymore!

Revolving Doors

Chapter 15: Back to the Asylum for this Miserable Kid!

The next two months of my life are wasted, and miserably endured back at the institution, which I had desperately hoped I would never set my eyes upon again. This will be my *fifth* residential move into my *third* boarding situation. By now, of course, the decor and the routines have remained unchanged, feeling all too familiar and stirring up bad memories of my first stay in here. I am back in a paint-chipped metal cage—and I mean "*cage*", since there are high bars on all four sides, allowing absolutely no possibility of escape!

Early the next morning, I am awakened by a change in my routine. After my bum is cleaned up and I am fitted into a clean, albeit scratchy, cloth diaper, the warm, one-piece, footed jammie I am wearing is replaced by a clean, quite cold one, which is identical. Shortly, I am carried to a room, adjacent to a kitchen of sorts, or at least the emanating sounds and smells certainly seem to indicate some sort of meal preparation is going on in there. The striking arrangement of sixteen baby highchairs seems a little strange to me. They are lined up in two equal rows, and are back-to-back, for ease of feeding us little ones, I suppose. I am strapped into one of the wooden seats alongside, and in back of, the many other babies and toddlers who are also being fastened in place.

After the required bibs are choking our throats, the nursing aides begin spoon-feeding us some yummy-mushy "Pablum" baby food, [18]. On the box is a picture of a cute baby who looks exactly like me. I love this stuff, and I am starved, so I rush to get the spoon into my little mouth bite after bite, even trying to grasp the implement from my server. After we have mostly finished this first course, we are fed warm, soft fruit, sometimes applesauce, or minute pieces of cold, syrupy canned fruit such as peaches or pears. In the event any of us are constipated and not pooping as well as *they* think we should be, mushy stewed prunes are on the menu. (Some kids whine and complain, but I don't care—I even like the prunes.)

When we are all done, the bibs are removed to complete a quick swipe to wipe-off our little faces and hands. We are all unstrapped and carried, not to a playroom, but back to our cages. (Personally, I think it's this lack of any real movement or exercise, which makes it so hard for us to poop.) We are given warm bottles of milk, or lactic acid formula, depending up on our individual requirements. Then, whether we try to fight it, or not, we can't help but doze off to dreamland. A few babies are given pacifiers but it's definitely something which is discouraged by the nurses. When my mommy arrives for a visit, she brings me my brown rubber "pacie", but is firmly told to take it with her when she leaves, and so as not to make any trouble, she always complies. (I am thinking maybe the cross-rails on our cribs might not be so chewed up if more of us were permitted pacifiers—Ah, but what do I know?) "Dreamland"-- the place where we babies all head to for a little visit, and some playtime with, our *real* mommies.

After a couple of hours of quiet nap-time, the noise level in this nursery room starts to slowly increase as we each awaken and, in varying stages of diapering requirements, one-by-one notify our caretakers, with individualized vocalizations. Although I hate those awful dry, rough diapers, I guess I hate it worse when they're soaking wet and heavily drooping low off my bottom. That is when I start squirming and fussing, but only a little, to alert someone of my need for a clean-up. Depending on who is here to change me at the time, I am often stuck in my side from the "safety-capped" baby-pins. (Oddly enough, these pins are only safe *after* they have been *snapped closed*.) I hate when it's one of the *nurses* coming to change me because they are usually in quite a rush and may be depended upon for giving hard pin-sticks. However, most of the nursing-aides, and especially the nice little "candy-stripers", are much slower at the repetitive task, and these ladies can be pretty much relied-upon to keep their two fingers under the diaper, and against our little bodies, while they push the sharp-ended pins through the cloth, missing our sensitive flesh altogether.

Soon it's lunchtime and I am having another feeding in the high-chair room. Shortly, I sense the rubber nipple of another bottle of formula, warmed just right this time, inserted into my mouth in the aim of rapidly putting me back to sleep for my afternoon nap. Even if some of us are alert enough to desire some "playtime", there are no toys permitted in our cribs, because, of course, it would require some effort at keeping them individually cleaned and sanitized. Sadly, we are not given any "mat" time either, or any other such activities, which are designed to help us develop our arm and leg muscles. There is very little of our day devoted to our much-needed "playtime" with the other infants or toddlers, or any other such activities which are actually the beginnings of our developing important "socialization" skills.

The exception occurs when we have been *chosen* to go into the one-way-mirrored, "Viewing Room" to be spied upon by Prospective Adoptive Parents. There, we understand we are expected to act "naturally" alongside a few others who are also, awkwardly acting "naturally", (whatever *that* means). We can only look at each other quizzically without a clue as to what we are supposed to be doing in there. So, I suppose, if you can sit up, you do. Otherwise, you are either flat on your back staring at the ceiling, which incidentally still needs re-painting, or you're on your tummy staring into the carpet, which incidentally, still reeks of filth and vomit.

Oh my, such excitement can only be followed by, what else, a nap, which, in turn is followed by another diaper change, then another "meal". We are all trapped, barely existing in a constantly cycling survival mode. It seems we only know what time of day it is by the type of food on the spoon. I feel uncomfortably hungry between feedings but we are never offered snacks because it would require removing us, and once-again, fastening us in our high chairs, and so on. The rule is very strict, "No food, whatsoever, is permitted in the cribs." This is rigorously enforced by all, except the young "candy-stripers". It's important because, in the event any crumbs might be left behind, we might meet a late-night scavenging visitor, in the form of a rodent, (whose only measure of detection are the little "raisins" which pop out of their behinds)! Ooooh! Yuck—yes, I **have** eaten *rat-raisins*!

Day after tedious day brings the eventual passing of a couple of months, as I wait for something—anything, of interest to occur which will break the boredom and bring a little stimulation into my brain. Unless something creates a great racket when dropped, there is nothing of much interest happening around here. I do pay attention to the vocalization uttered by the other children, and I've gotten quite good at being able to tell who is making the rounds at diapering time. If there are screaming utterances, one after another, it's definitely a *nurse*. It's then, I stiffen my little body in readiness of being stuck next. It is soooo painful when the nurse sticks the pin into a hole in my skin left by the previous pinning accident. However, if any footsteps, especially a visitor's, are detected approaching the nursery door, it is quickly closed and, pin-sticks or not, we are ordered to, "Hush-up now, little ones. Be quiet, or be punished!"

However, one day it all seems so unimportant to me and that is the day mommy arrives for a visit. I am so excited I can't contain myself. I am so *happy* to see her, though I am giggling on the inside, so overwhelming are my emotions, all I can do is cry on the outside! My beautiful mommy is allowed to pull up a chair and sit down right next to my crib; however, she *isn't* even permitted to let down the side and lift me out. *I* can only *wonder* why she isn't picking me up and holding me, or why she only reaches through, or over, the crib rails to tickle my cheek, hold my little hand or play, "This little piggy went to market..." with my toes. I guess it really doesn't matter, I can still feel her love, even from the infinitesimal brush of her finger across my forehead.

I try to talk to her and let her know how unhappy I am in this asylum. I implore her, "Mommy, please, please take me home with you! Please don't go away and leave me here any longer, not this time." Just then, however, as I am almost certain she understands and is sure to comply, it seems as if no time has passed when an aide returns to the nursery and reminds mommy her time with me is up and she must leave. Mommy kisses the tip of her finger and touches it to my lips. It's the best we can manage, considering the nurses won't allow her to hold me in her arms or caress me, as she would normally do. Then after a very quick lullaby, the impatient aide escorts her across the nursery floor. Glancing back over her left shoulder, she starts crying ever-so softly and calls back to me promising, "Ricky, sweetheart, I'll come back again very soon, you'll see, very soon."

"*His name is '**Teddy**', miss!*" the irritated aid gruffly reminds my mommy.

You would think I might be used to mommy always having to leave me in someone else's care, but I am an eternal optimist. I just can't allow myself to believe the day will never come when she might sweep me up in her arms, walk boldly out of the asylum door and take me home with her, (whatever a "home" with mommy might mean, or wherever her home might be).

Revolving Doors

Chapter 16: The "Fearless Foursome" and Lil' Ol' Me...

I guess I am just not meant to go home with my mommy, not yet anyway, because it appears to be, "*getting ready time*" again—and she isn't here yet. The sweet little candy striper called "Queenie", is chatting softly with me as she collects my meagre belongings and bags them in the same brown-paper "LOBLAWS", [17], bag which accompanied me to this institution two months ago. I guess I'll miss seeing *my half* of the other kids at meal times, but there is nothing else, whatsoever, about the ugly old, orphanage which I'll be sad to leave behind. I am seven-and-a-half months old now, and I am beyond excited, albeit a bit apprehensive, about my being "placed" into another, promised to be "much better" foster home. This placement will be my *fourth fostering* situation, but it's actually my *sixth place of residence*—a lot of moving around for this little guy.

I am starting to feel just a little excited because I've been told this time it's someone's *real home* which will replace the institution as my new abode. Well, surely it won't be any worse than the "Cleaning Lady's" house. Right? This time I am taken by bus in the company of the same man who first carried me from the "C.A.S." Director's office over to the residential building where the nursery was located. I easily recognized "Big Ears" by, well, the prominence of the protuberances still managing to dwarf his, now, ridiculously bushy sideburns. After a little riding around in the huge human transporting machine, I am sort-of enjoying the ride, and the views. Curiously, I notice as one passenger after another pulls on an overhead wire which rings a bell, next to the bus driver's head, alerting him of someone's desire to get out at the next stopping-off place. Repeatedly I hear the little bell ding until "Big Ears" jumps up, with me in-tow, and rings for our stop.

I thought we had arrived at our destination, but I soon discover we have not come to the end of our bus travels. "Ears" carries me across the road to await another bus, which will come along to take us in a different direction. However, this transporter only conveys us a short distance, when "Ears" jumps up, and once again rings the wired-bell so we may hop off. Hey, I am thinking this is sort of starting to be fun. This time, "Ears" carries me as he walks a short way down a narrow side street. Then he turns into the front walkway of a small, rather nondescript, brown brick house. When the front door is opened, he speaks to the rail-thin woman who is introduced as my new "foster mother". After each adult nervously exchanges a few pleasantries, I am once again handed over into the arms of this woman, who is, of course, just another *stranger* in my eyes.

Although I can't really understand the words and explanations by the "mother", nevertheless, I'm quickly made aware, I'm expected to *exactly* follow her demands, and adhere to the routines in this household. As well, I soon discover I am not the only fostered child in this home. I am not sure if it's a good, or bad, thing, but apparently, I am the youngest of the *four other boys* already living in this place. I wonder if maybe this will be a lot of fun being one of *five little kids*!

However, when I meet the boys I see they're definitely *not* little! These other foster children are five, six, nine and ten-years-old, and in no time at all, these kids let me know of their resentment of *me,* and of the extra "care and attention" which will have to be given to me by the "lady". (Well, of course, I require more attention; I am only a little feller-- a toddler, *right*? They certainly can't expect me to change my *own* diapers!) Nonetheless, they quickly inform me of my lowly place at the bottom of their pecking order, and, as such, am the last in line for the *food*. What the heck do they mean? Won't we all get the same food, at the same time, in the amounts tailored to each of our specific requirements? (I am also wondering why they refer to the "foster mother" as, "our Mother".)

However, it isn't long before I have my answer. I've watched as this woman repeatedly insists, and constantly reminds us, we must refer to her, and always *address* her, as our, "Mother". "Mother, MOTHER!" Boy oh boy, that will soon prove to be quite an overstatement! In very short order, I will observe this finger-shaking witch does not have a mothering bone in her skinny body and little less a nurturing or caring heart. In addition, as I'll soon discover, this woman is the *only* foster parent in this house, although the "C.A.S." folks seem to believe otherwise. The Workers and Director discussed, amongst themselves, the fact this foster mother is not only married, but also has the daily help of her husband to assist her. After all, handling the repeatedly revolving requirements of the now, *five* of us fostered kids is a daunting task for any fostering mother on her own.

I figure the "C.A.S." is mistaken because she *no longer* **has** a husband. It's a little sad to see from the dusty wall with the faded wedding photos, this woman was, at one time married to the groom who appears to be the epitome of a "tall, dark and handsome" young man. The wedding photo shows this fellow, probably in his early twenties, wearing a white, serge suit and standing beside this lady who was an *almost pretty* bride in a navy blue A-line skirt-suit and dandelion-yellow blouse.

However, this foster mother is now a homely woman whom I would guess to be in her mid-to-late-thirties. I am not surprised in the least she no longer has a husband, simply judging by her quickly revealed, mean-spirited nature! This woman is forever crabbing and yelling at us innocent young kids. It seems we simply can't do anything right in her estimation, and I am guessing her husband must have felt much the same way. It is my understanding, like many other young men, her husband left to volunteer in the war efforts, (or at least it's how I've heard this woman tell the story). Yet, she gives no reasonable explanation why she is now alone. Either her husband died, or he was still stationed overseas, (or maybe he simply refused to return to this hag! Who would blame him if he purposely never came back to her?)

Nevertheless, I don't know how this woman thinks of herself as our "Mother", because she does little or no "mothering" from the vantage point of her kitchen table. This woman virtually *lives* at the table, sucking back her beers, and from morning until night, stinking up the house with the smoke from her cheap cigarettes—the ones with no filter tips on them. (Hmmm, I am thinking her second-hand smoke can't be very good for my very sensitive lungs, either. Oh, well, who cares about *me*, right?) Anyway, the only time we see her without a beer bottle in her hand is when she is drinking the disgustingly harsh, and malodorous black coffee—and smoking more cigarettes.

The smokes have left a sickeningly orange tinge to skin the first and second fingertips of her right hand, and caused most of her thickened, striated fingernails to turn yellow. However, it would seem her voice has suffered the greatest insult from her ciggy habit. She sounds like a weathered, old sailor-man when she speaks. Then, every time she gets terribly angry with any of us boys, she actually trembles and shakes. (All the others may have to call her "Mother" but now I've got a much better name for her—I'm calling her, "*Nervous Nellie*")

You would think with the monthly income she receives for fostering five boys, that instead of mishandling, wasting and spending it on the beer and fags, the woman would be happily motivated to spend at least some of her time preparing and cooking nutritious and tasty meals or snacks. However, she says she has no time for feeding us properly, or for cleaning the house. She certainly would have no time at all for keeping up with the mountain of weekly laundry we *would be creating,* that is, of course, if she ever gave us clean clothes, bedding or towels! Nevertheless, this self-centred woman is interested in *none* of these maternal chores. Instead, our "Mother", "Nervous Nellie", is always on the telephone jabbering and gossiping about the real, or imagined, disgraces of *this* person, or *the other one*. It is astounding to me, how much time this woman can waste gabbing on the phone.

This woman, although short in stature, seems like she towers over us boys, especially when she is wielding the long wooden yardstick, which she uses to "discipline" us. Believe me, she uses her wooden weapon for her own personal enjoyment and entertainment, more than discipline—or measuring. Naturally, it means she uses us boys as whipping posts, on which to take out some deep-seated personal angers or frustrations, (probably aimed at her "ex"-husband)! Yes, we are all beaten, and a lot-for seemingly no reasons at all. Strangely enough, she really seems to get the angriest when we don't eat the food she "cooks". However, sometimes we just can't get it down our throats, because it's sooo bland and tasteless—and either too creamy when it should be thick, or too lumpy when it should be smooth.

You would not think that our leaving food on the plates would matter in the least! After all, what *we* don't consume, why wouldn't she herself eat, or at least she could set it down for her fat little brown wiener dog, "Schnowzie" to gobble up? (Oh, yes, did I fail to mention the other "baby" in the house?) Actually, it would soon become apparent there is a very good reason she takes issue with us foster children refusing to eat. Quite simply, her anger is financially motivated. The problem is simple. Our refusal to eat may cause our weight to plummet. Of course, it would not reflect well on her as a foster mother. If such a problem could not be expediently remedied, hers would be disqualified as an "acceptable fostering home"--and she would lose her regular, and repetitive, source of income which continually fuels her distasteful habits.

This "mother" also becomes especially concerned when *I* am the one getting thinner, since the "C.A.S." makes surprise drop-in visits to *actually check my weight*, (something which had been a previous problem, and a serious concern to "Mrs. Mousey" and the "Wart" at the "C.A.S."). The main problem is, we growing boys have to eat more the than the disagreeably tasteless potatoes and noodles she pushes at us to force us to eat and fatten up. We deserve and crave meat, fresh veggies and fruit! Every now and then, would it kill her to bake a few cookies? Still, it doesn't happen. In fact, I have yet to discover what it's like to eat even a "baby cookie" in this house. But we don't dare complain or ask for her to bake us anything, because it would certainly lead to more discipline with the wooden cooking implement—and certainly no cookie—or anything else, would be worth such punishment!

More often than not, her swats with the yardstick are in carefully chosen places on our bodies—actually usually on our heads, or the *bottoms of our feet*, where bruises don't show, but where it's nonetheless, excruciatingly painful! Sometimes she swats us on our legs, where even the most horrendous looking marks could easily be excused as the rambunctiousness of "boys being boys". To whom could we go for help? To whom could we speak of our quandary? No adult would consider believing a word coming out of any of the mouths of us little orphan kids! Grown-ups NEVER take seriously the whining or complaining of us fostered children, versus the calm explanations of the so-called adults who supposedly have complete charge over us!

The plight we boys share, living under this woman's tyrannical rule over our lives, prompted the pact into which all the other four kids, purposely, (and I, inadvertently), have entered. They formed an internal brotherhood of a sort, though in fact, only two of the boys are actual brothers. Nevertheless, while chanting, "We are all-for-one, and one-for-all!" we permanently seal our promises via the temporary discomfort of the blood-brother *pin-sticks* on our right index fingers!

Of all of us newly indoctrinated blood brothers, Joey, who is five, is the next youngest after me. This little boy is awkwardly shy and usually quiet, that is, of course, when he isn't *whining* like a three-year-old girl! This boy is short, thin and very pale, with watery, baby blue eyes and bright yellow, bowl-cut hair, one piece of which, at the back, is always sticking straight out sideways, like a bent flagpole! Like his unruly hair, this little fellow has a mind of his own, which is convenient considering how he seems to exist in a *world* of his own. All Joey does is play by himself, sleep and whine, on a continuously replicating cycle. I've never actually seen this kid eat—anything! Correction—I do often see him eating *candy* and he doesn't seem to care where he finds it! He will ingest anything, which even remotely resembles candy or "ABC" gum, (Already Been Chewed!), no matter whether it's on the floor, in the dirt or even stuck on Felix's tail! (Oh, sorry, I omitted mentioning Nellie's doggie has a kitty-cat "brother", who in fact *had* an exceptionally long and fluffy tail—at least until Joey started prying the candy out of his fur.) Anyway, if you place any kind of real food in front of Joey, he goes into this amazing act of fussing, gagging, violently shaking his head back and forth, and complaining, saying, "*Noooooooooooooooooo! Gimme candy! CANDY!*"

There isn't much for any of us boys to do around here. The foster "mother" only allots us kids a handful of mostly broken toys. Somehow Joey always manages to hoard the very best one—the smooth little wooden doggie on wheels, which you pull-along by the knotted string around its neck. By the way, I don't want either the toy car or the truck, nor do I want the pretend garden tools! That dog is the *only* toy *I want* and Joey refuses to relinquish it! Little Brat! Blood Brother', or not, I *hate* him, and *I want his dog.* Ive tried to ask the other boys for help but they just can't understand my baby-babble—but I know *Joey* does and he chooses to ignore me! (I am thinking it's just too bad I can't get my hands on any candy, or else I would bribe the little bugger—and get me **that damn dog**!)

Anyway, the next oldest is six-year-old, David, and he's not the least bit interested in the wooden doggie, so in that respect he is no threat to me. "David" is actually his nickname because his real name is unpronounceable, especially when he stutters. It sounds something like, "Davadovitsky". (No wonder he stutters!). He talks funny too. I guess he speaks with an accent; all I know is he is hard to understand sometimes, especially when he mumbles. This mumbling stutterer has thick, brown, curly, matted hair, dark eyes and dark olive skin. He is quite tall next to me, but then again, who isn't? Anyway, whenever the mother is not looking, David is the one scooping up all of Joey's "leavings" from the meals he never eats! Of course it's the reason he is a whole lot fatter than anybody else is. However, David is a bossy know-it-all and makes me sick the way he pushes me around and bullies me. Because I am such a little shrimp, he often knocks me down, or pounds the back of my head with his fists. He only does this when no one else is looking, because he says he knows that fists don't leave a mark there. (You know, he could boss me all he wants to if he would only snatch the little wooden doggie from Joey and hand it over to me!)

The two older boys, John and James, are brothers from the same family, of course, not this woman's natural children. "Johnny", (his nickname), is quite tall for a nine-year-old and skinny too, with light brown, bowl-cut, hair and brown eyes. He has a lot of sores on his arms and legs which he picks at most of the time, but tries to cover up if there are any *strange grown-ups*, (translate: *"C.A.S." Workers*), around.

"Jamie", which is what James calls himself, is ten, and is a little taller with greenish-blue eyes and white-blonde, bowl-cut hair, (and by now, I've figured out who's doing all the "bowl-cutting" around here!) "Jamie" brags on how he stays darkly tanned all summer, unlike the rest of us, "pale skins". Oddly enough, he is also the one who stays sick—regularly coughing his guts up, too. I've also noticed how his coughing fits seem much worse when he is playing with "Felix" because the kitty is a long-haired, grey Persian, and being so long-in-the-tooth, he leaves his fur behind every time he lays down somewhere.

These boys call themselves the, "Double J's", and segregate themselves away from David and me. Of course, they hoard the best corner of the one big room we all live in, camping-out right next to the small, noisy radiator. Whenever they're outside in the yard, they spend an inordinate amount of time up where the "Y" forms from the great branches of the backyard's oldest maple tree, which happens to be the only good-climbin' tree out there. Either the "J's" are whispering to each other, or else, talking in a made-up slang lingo, they call "Pig-Latin", [33]. (Which, incidentally, they *think* nobody else can understand.) They're constantly plotting stuff and getting in trouble for making their escape and running away from "Mother". I don't blame them, if I could run, I would be out of this room, and gone far from this house, with a *quickness*! In fact, "I ould-wa, et-gay, ar-fay, away-ay, om-fray, ere-hay, oo-tay ay-day"! (Hahahahahah! They're not so smart!)

It sounds like a broken record, but it's true! Once again, I am lonely, bored and very, very despondent. None of the boys will play with, or entertain, me—not ever. They complain that I am too little, or too slow. Of course, the woman never cuddles or rocks me because she *says, "I'm always too busy taking care of the rest of the boys to be picking you up all the time!"* Ha! What a laugh! Anyway, right now, I am sick again, and I have caught another cold, or "Brown Kites", or maybe, "New Onions", from "Jamie", I guess. I am so sick and feverish, I've stopped eating. Our "Mother" yells at me and swats my head with the back of her hand to force me to eat. She doesn't understand, even when I am in the best of health I can hardly swallow the revolting mush she calls food; but, now, I am so sick I can't eat *anything.*

Late last night I overheard this foster mother, and her newly acquired boyfriend, argue over whether or not to "**get rid of the baby**". Wait a minute, <u>*I'm*</u> the baby! Holy cow! I am not a goldfish she can flush down the toilet the way she did last week after she noticed "Mr. Jingles" had spent two days bobbing upside down at the top of his fish bowl! However, then, I overheard this fellow, who is now her "live-in man", insist they need the "monthly income" which the woman receives from the "C.A.S.". (It's paid to foster parents for providing us orphan kids with "loving, caring and healthful foster home environments". Ha! That's another laugh!)

Anyway, while still discussing and trying to decide if I should stay or go, quite suddenly, the woman became really upset and started weeping on the man's shoulder. During her crying jag, she let slip out, something quite disturbing. While expressing her fears about "losing the 'C.A.S.' income" if I were "moved out of her foster home", she blubbered out, *"Teddy might die! What if he dies?"* Whaaaat?

Of course, the man tried to console her repeating, "Die? What do you mean? Of course he's not gonna die! Stop crying, dammit!" However, then the bombshell dropped. Our "mother" went on to explain to her lover, how, quite unbelievably, another child "actually died" while in her care and custody!

Then she started pounding on his chest and screaming, "Oh my God, Fred! What are *we* going to do? What in the hell should I do now?" I had been listening intently to their words, up until I heard the words, "Die?"..."*Died?*"!...Did she actually say some other poor little boy, whom she'd been supposedly taking care of--"***died***?"! Boy oh boy...holy cow, am I ever in a terrible predicament!

At the sound of these words, my mind begins reeling, and all I know is I *have to* get out of here, and I mean yesterday would not be too soon for me! The question, however, is, "*How*?"

Thankfully and miraculously, the answer to my frightening dilemma arrives unexpectedly two days later. It's a fact, the foster mother must report to the "C.A.S." weekly on my progress, my health and any changes or special needs, which may have arisen during my stay at her house. Certainly, there are many reasons why I've not eaten properly, or at least only in very small amounts; but the ensuing result has been a considerable weight loss, especially for a little feller my size. When this bad news is reported to "Mrs. Mousey" she takes no time before making an unannounced visit to see me, along with, none other than, the "Wart Lady" herself, gracing us all with her presence.

At least this is what I *thought* was happening. However, this fostering situation was in a far more precarious position than I, (or any of us kids), could have known. Naturally, I can't fully understand the meaning of their words, but I can certainly feel the desperate sincerity as the "C.A.S." women discussed the improprieties of the foster mother *and* her new man. Her "boarder" as she refers to him, is how "Nervous Nellie" tries to excuse their intimate and improper living arrangement.

[Of course, since it's *1948*, a man and woman living in an intimate relationship, outside of a legally recognized marriage, is *very much* against the norms and mores of "proper living in society". At the very least, it would certainly disqualify her as a model "foster mother".]

The "C.A.S." women were expressing the seriousness of my losing weight, and resulting health issues, such as the upper respiratory infections to which I seem to be continually succumbing. Now, after only nine weeks at this house, the "C.A.S." is moving very rapidly, stepping-in to find me another, *more appropriate* home.

Seemingly, something else is happening here which I could not really understand. Apparently, this foster mother is very ill. She isn't coughing like me, but she is kind of sick "in her head". Lately, she sleeps a lot more than usual—which is *more than a lot*; but when she is awake, she screams at us for the least little thing, and her crying spells drag on, day after day. Her *man* is gone now, more than he is here, and the older boys are talking about the "Mother" saying she is "going totally, around the bend, crazy"! Although she still collects the money for our care, she has not had any food for us for three days now. In fact, *she* won't even heat up one of three cans of "Campbell's Soup" in her pantry—and we aren't permitted to use her kitchen tools for any reason. [19] Sadly, the most the big boys are able to find for us to eat is plain bread, or a few stale crackers.

Miserably, I stay in my dirty cloth diapers often for a whole day at a time. The only thing stopping me from leaking-out everywhere is the rubber pantie covering my diaper – but its tight elastics leave sore, red rings around my legs and waist. Of course, beyond my lack of care and cleanliness, which are obvious, how could I communicate an even bigger problem to the Workers? I only wish I could inform them how this so-called "mother" has been so terribly mean and physically abusive to me, since day one of my stay here.

We are all in a very bad situation at this foster home, and her man, "Freeloader Fred" seems to have already figured this out. In fact, right as he packed up the last of his belongings and was moving out of the house, while pulling the door shut behind himself, he shouted, "*I'm gonna get as far away as possible from YOU!!!*" Nevertheless, it was what he **did** next which ended up **saving** all of us kids. As I would later overhear it re-told, "Her fella telephoned 'Mrs...', (the Director), and insisted, 'You people need to get right out to the house and find *all* of those kids new homes—immediately!'" So now, the two "C.A.S." representatives are also discussing the overwhelming logistics of, "having to find additional appropriate housing and care for me, Joey, David, John and Jamie, while 'hopefully keeping the latter two together'!"

[Certainly, it's common knowledge how hard it is to place *older* children, especially boys, into any well-run foster home, (never mind, attempting to meet the ultimate goal of finding and placing all five of these children with *adoptive* families)!]

Nonetheless, the bureaucratic machine was moving far too slowly and before we all had our newly assigned "homes", the unthinkable happened! The woman began acting *really* crazy and seemed to lose her mind, screaming, crying, throwing and breaking things and punching her fists, in several places right through the walls, until her hands, and her walls, were a bloody mess! Luckily, it was not long after this series of incidents when the "C.A.S." workers knew they had to take swift and immediate action for all five of us boys, and to our utter amazement, they *did*.

One Wednesday, a whole bunch of strangers arrived in a couple different vehicles to "rescue us". Then right after they had gotten to the house, some doctors, (or whatever they were), dressed in white suits, put "Nervous Nellie in an ambulance and took her off somewhere! Then the woman, living in the house next door, came over and put Felix in a little box to take him back to her house. He didn't seem to care, and was too weak from near starvation, to fight her off. However, we kids were all getting really worried about Schnowzie, so the big boys asked another man what to do about the doggie. The man said he knew a person who really needed a little dog; so off with him, Schnowzie went! I don't think he really minded because the foster mother had not fed **him** in three days either!

Personally, I am wondering with what new foster "mother" *I* might end up next. Though, I don't really care, because, if she is not my *real* mommy, it just doesn't even matter to me anymore. Besides, I was never allowed to play with the wooden doggie anyway, so moving on to some other foster home—well, truthfully, it's all the same to me. Anyway, a better "foster mother" maybe one who even bakes cookies, or one where there are oodles of toys, is surely awaiting me, right now! On the other hand, at least, all I can really do is hope for it to be so. As far as the other boys are concerned, frankly I don't care where they go, as long it's in a *different* place from wherever *I'll* be ending up.

In any case, who could miss the evidence I am in dire need of medical attention. I am still severely undernourished and always seeming to be coughing my guts up while in the throes of one-after-another upper respiratory infection. This time I heard the doctor say it's definitely, "New Onions". In fact, one doctor told my Case Worker, "This child is in very poor condition; in fact, he's not only critically undernourished, but he's also in an advanced stage of Pneumonia." Did he not know they were already well aware of this?

Chapter 17: "Revolving Doors" to "SICK KIDS"

Off *I* go in an ambulance with the siren blaring, while we are absolutely tearing through the streets of Toronto. We are heading straight for the one and only hospital devoted entirely to the treatment of children. Of course, that is exactly where I end up—at the *"SICK KIDS"*, the nickname for The Sick Children's Hospital. [26] [26a] I sure hope they can fix me quickly and don't force me to spend very much time staying here. I hate the smells, and the sounds and the antiseptic caregivers; but I especially loathe the needle-sticks!

How is a sick little fellow supposed to get any much-needed rest around here? It's the same thing day-after-day, until my confinement here has already passed ten miserable days. Worse than being here this long, is the fact I am not simply lying in a normal bed and able to enjoy a little interaction with other children. I am in scary solitary seclusion, confined to an *oxygen tent*! [154] It just isn't fair because I can watch the other children laughing and playing in this room, from the restriction of my see-through plastic cage. However, I am stuck in here and *never* allowed out!

****

Anyway, finally it's time for me to get sprung from here, but now I am once again in need of a safe, secure place where I might lay my head at night. I am certain I would *not* be welcomed back at "Nellie's", so for me, I'll be off to the next *"frolicking fun foster family"*. {*Y*es, I am being *facetious*}. After another quickie two-week stop-over in the asylum, (which I am not actually "counting" as a residential "move"), this next move places me in my *fifth foster residence*, but I'd have to count this as my *seventh residential move*. I'm already getting weary

102

Revolving Doors
of *living out of my paper bag.*

Chapter 18: Out of the Frying Pan...

This really can't be happening! What can these folks at the "C.A.S." be thinking? I AM right back at "Nervous Nellie's"! However, this time it's only me...no "Fearless Foursome"...no Schnowzie...no Felix...only me, and the "Mother"! I thought she went crazy. She DID go bananas, I know it! So what could I possibly be doing back here? Some strange, smelly, grey-haired, old man from the "C.A.S." brought me here in his car and I slept all the way to the front door, otherwise I would have recognized where I was going and fought and kicked the whole way here! Oh well, I guess it doesn't matter now because my really, crinkly "LOBLAWS", [17], bag and I are already here, so I will simply have to deal with it in my own way.

I wonder what could be in the bulky little rectangular package the man carried up to the front door. It was wrapped in brown butcher paper then tied securely with a string around this way and that. Anyway, I am back in the big room we five boys called home for a while; however, it certainly isn't the same around here without them. It's quiet and lonely and there is nothing to do by myself. The good thing is I've now taken up residence next to the radiator—no "Double Js" to fight with for *that* coveted corner of the room. I wonder if all the boys went "home", or went to other foster houses—or even to the asylum. I guess it doesn't matter where they went—it's only *me* here, right now.

I am sitting on the bed looking around the room, which is unchanged from the day we were all so suddenly whisked away from this house. What is this? I "see" the little wooden doggie laying on his side completely under another bed in the room! If I did not know about it, I would never have noticed the knotted string sticking out. Ah, yes...he's all mine now...no Joey to fight with, this time. Yet, even having the doggie all to myself is not very satisfying. I thought it was all I wanted—but it seems I would rather begrudge Joey having him, than my having to play alone all the time.

"Mother" doesn't say much to me. She walks around in a sort-of daze as if she is sleeping and walking at the same time—if that is even possible. She feeds me from her plate at her kitchen table—because, it seems she just can't break herself away from her favourite spot. She is still drinking the coffee and puffing away on the cigarettes. (Oooh...the last bite of applesauce had nasty cigarette ashes in it, yuck!) Of course, she still swills her beer; but this time she is all alone—no "Freeloader Fred" living here and mooching off her.

Boy, I just realized, am I ever soaked! Even the plastic diaper-covering panties are not working well-enough to hold back a day's worth of pee. "Mother" changes my diaper when she thinks of it, (which obviously is not nearly the same thing as *when I need it*). I guess I am alright here, simply bored, wet, sore from new diaper rashes—and ever so lonely.

Every day is the same. Morning turns into day. Day turns into night. Night turns into morning. After three or four boring days of this repetition, the woman brings me the paper-wrapped package the man had brought with me to this house. She says, "It's to stay in this room, but you can have it for now." Oh boy! What secrets could this stiff brown paper be disguising? Quickly I rip the string off and tear the package open. What is this? Only a bunch of stupid books? Books! What am I supposed to do with these? I am not able to read, and there is nobody to read *to me*.

Oh, I know! I get the brainwave to stack them up and climb on them in order to look out the window, which has always been too high for me to see out. Well, nothing much to see out *that* window, only the back fence and gate which open out to an alley, where everybody else's fences and back gates open in the same manner. Of course, now I am bored again. So, I decide to have a look at these books. Naturally, I can't read and I can't count, but if I could, I would be more than extremely excited because what I have in front of me is a brand new series of children's books with twelve colourful little titles in all! These books, which are just my size, all have pretty pictures on the covers and throughout every one of their myriad of pages.

Oh, if only somebody would read to me or tell me the stories...I could memorize them and go over them many, many times from looking at the pictures. However, without a reader, the best I can do is to have a glance through the pages and make-up my own stories to go along with the pictures. Let me see, this one has three little kittens on the front, and the next one is a picture of an adult reading to a child who he has tucked into bed, all warm and safe. What could this big lady goose wearing a flowered hat be a tale about? I wonder what's the story in this other book with a red chicken on the front.

I take another one from my pile and see there are little children singing, and then there is another one with big letters on the front. Oh, here is a story I know all about...it's a little puppy dog. It's so cute, this will be my favourite. Another has a baby surrounded by lots of things. I recognize the barn animals on the front of another one about a man in a straw hat. There is also one with a little pig and some numbers. Ah, yes! Here is one I do recognize. It's a book about *fairy tales*. Some of these I know from my mommy reading and singing them to me! [27] Both this story and the puppy dog one will be my two very favourites! I decide it would be best if I stow these way far away under my bed, in case the "Mother" gets a notion to get rid of them, (because you just never know with her).

Almost two weeks have passed and all I do is stay in my room with no other stimulation than my new found treasury of books. I look through them repeatedly until I've dog-eared many of the pages by accident. Just then, all of a sudden I hear this huge loud noise outside of my high window. Using my book collection for its non-intended purpose, I climb up and look out. There is the "Mother" out in broad daylight in her **underwear**! Now, she is at the end of the backyard throwing things *over* the fence...not through the gate! There goes a lawn chair, and the trash can, which was full...a lamp from the living room, a bunch of laundry and the basket it was in and what were those last two things—the toaster, and her coffee percolator? Her coffee-making machine! Oooh, I am thinking this can't be a good thing at all. Wow! I am curious as to what, the heck, is going on? (Could it be *fall* cleaning day? Nope, she would **never** get rid of the coffee perk...Hmmmm!)

The moment I climb back down off my book stool, I hear her back out there screaming *something*. Up I go again, and peek-out so she doesn't notice, in case she is screaming for *me*. I see her turning around and around and absolutely screeching into the air like a big old peacock! "Ayyyyeeeeeahhheeee!" What a nut case! Suddenly, the woman from next door, who took poor old Felix the last time I was here, has come out of her house and is trying to speak to the "Mother" over the side fence. "Mrs...Are you alright...do you need any help...should I come over there?"

By then the man, who lives across the back alley, is standing in the middle of the lane-way, with his hands on his hips. I can see him scratch the single hair on his bald head and stare blankly at the huge mess she has created. Of course, some of the laundry never made it to the ground because it was hanging off both sides of the fence! However, never mind all that! She is standing in middle of the yard wearing nothing but her "*Living Bra*" and yellowed, baggy old granny panties, drooping down under her rubber "*Living Girdle*"! [28] [28a]

Holy cow! Here we go again! She is acting absolutely nuts and I am not the only one who thinks so. I understand this for a fact a little later on when the lady from next door has come over here and dressed the "Mother", changed my diaper twice, dressed me and has already fed me lunch, and a snack! Oh yes, this could be a very good thing for me! The woman is very nice and speaks softly to me, spending more time in my room after she put the foster mother into her *bed*. When she asks me what I would like to do, I don't really know of anything. Nonetheless, deciding she can be trusted a little bit, I reach under my bed and gingerly slide out my storybook, but only one, in case she is only tricking me and is going to take it away, or destroy it. The book? Why, it's the one with the doggy on the front. "Do you want me to read this story to you sweetie?" ("Sweetie"--that was nice to hear.) "Yes!" I nod my head wildly up and down in agreement.

Then she starts, "The Pokey Little Puppy" [27]. I listen in rapt amazement as the little pictures take on a life of their own, but not the one *I* had assigned to them. Oh, no...it's over. "Do you want another story?" Do I? Do I ever! I reach under my bed again, without even breaking my glance from her eyes, lest she change her mind. I know exactly where it's at...there, got it! "Oh, you must love doggies and kitties. Do you?" Again, I nodded my delight until my head was almost falling off. "The Three Little Kittens" [27], she begins, and then turning her attention back to the pages she relates this story, exactly as it was written. (I can do this; I can remember these stories after she leaves.)

Now the words and the pictures all came together and made sense. I wonder if she has time to read *all* my books. Just then, a loud banging at the front door interrupted my answer to her question. It was more people wearing stiff, white uniforms and this time a policeman was with them. I heard them say repeatedly, "It's a 'nervous breakdown'...'nervous breakdown'...", and I am thinking, see, I didn't call her "Nervous Nellie" for no reason at all! I knew she was certainly not right, in her head—in her mind! She was, and is, a nervous nut case!

I went back into my room as instructed by the neighbour woman. There I repeatedly read, front to back and back to front, in my two, now familiar, storybooks. I motionlessly waited to hear, or see, what will next unfold in this household's drama. I did take a quick little peek-out through my door, which I had cracked open only the width of my nose. It was a scene reminiscent of the last time I saw this "Mother". Again, she was escorted away, right before everyone's attention turned to me. "...Yes, certainly...I'll get him over there by bus—this afternoon." Who? Over where? Not me...I am O.K. right where I am...this nice neighbour can care for me. Right? You could care for me, couldn't you? Why not?

As usual, my moments of joy or contentment were to be only fleeting. Either this woman, or her house, or both, were "unacceptable" under the "C.A.S." terms of standard requirements for fostering a child. She seemed great to me. What are they expecting to find for me? I know what they *will* find for me...another *abusive, mean, selfish, greedy, crazy person with long wooden punishing implements, and certainly no food, no books, no toys—or, something even worse...no doubt!!*

Nevertheless, within the hour, "Mrs. Kind Next Door Neighbour Lady" takes me on a bus ride back to the "C.A.S." office where "Mrs. Mousey" greets us. "*Is he going to be alright?*" she asks the Case Worker. "Mouse" reassures her. Then she leans down to me, and kissing me on my forehead, says, "*Bye Bye, Teddy dear. You be a good little boy, now.*" "Bye-Bye" I wave, but with a very heavy heart.

Oh, nooo! I suddenly remembered nobody knew about the book collection under my bed, because I had hidden it very well. Sadly, for me, it was a day to wave good-bye to my "Little Golden Books" series, [27], not to mention the little wooden doggie, forever. "Did anybody remember my grocery bag?" I babble.

Chapter 19: "Hi Everybody, I'm BAAAAAAK!"

Well, at least during this next transition I only had to spend three days back at the asylum, and it wasn't so bad because I was there on the same weekend when my old friend, "Queenie", my favourite candy striper, was on duty. (Again, this is too short a stay for me to count as another residential placement, but you get the idea, I was in and out of the virtual "revolving door", countless times.)

PART IV: The Beginning of the Beginning of the End

Chapter 20: The "Boys" and the Lady Upstairs!

For what seemed like ages, now, "Mrs. Mousey" has been driving us around in her husband's really humongous, sort-of navy-blue-black, 1934 Buick, four-door convertible. [20] [21] Because it's a very hot spring day in Toronto, her husband secured the stiff canvas car roof *down* in its compartment before she drove to work this morning. However...considering the car's interior upholstery is entirely *black leather*, this might not have been the best of ideas. The problem became evident by the little squeal she let out when she sat down and her sleek tight-skirt rose up, barely enough to expose her nylon-stockinged-thigh to the blazing-hot seat.

However, the steaming-hot leather doesn't bother me. *My* problem is how to avoid being just about blown completely out of the front seat, by the tornadic rush of wind circling around inside the vehicle, as this lead-footed *lady driver* speeds around one corner after the next! I am just trying my best to squeeze tightly up against her side and just hang on!

[*Of course, this car-ride, with me unrestrained in the front seat, occurred decades before Ontario regulated the mandatory use of children's car seats. It was also long before the strictly enforced driving regulations, which require children to ride, securely harnessed into specialized age/size-appropriate car seats, and fastened into the **back** seats of all vehicles.*]

Finally! "Mousey" has pulled over and is stopping in front of what purportedly will be my next foster home. It's a humble, grey stucco bungalow in a lower-income part of the city. From the lack of toys, ride-on kiddie-cars or children's trikes/bikes out front, you would never guess there are, or will be, *any* children staying at this house. The cement path from the front sidewalk to the house has cracked badly, with chunks missing in many places, causing my Worker to trip, not once but twice—*with **me** in her arms*! Then, after regaining her vertical stability, she actually has to squeeze us between an unkempt wall of shrubs on our right side, and the virtually impenetrable wilderness of Weeping Willow, *raining* its very curious looking "leaves", down, on our left.

As we ascend the front steps, I look down to see they're shabbily displaying their dark green, painted wood which is in bad need of a touch-up. For a few minutes we are waiting in a small, outside foyer, which is a sort of veranda, arched on two sides, forming window shapes, (minus the glass of course). I am distracted for a moment while my gaze shifts upward as I follow the sound of a couple of quite exquisite robins, (the "daddy" sporting the telltale red breast). They're tweeting frantically as we pass too closely, and threaten the little eggs in their nest, which the birdies have tucked securely under the corner of the eaves.

A few seconds pass, while the "Mouse-Lady" repeatedly pushes the button to ring the door buzzer. Suddenly, a shockingly short woman, who is as big around as she is tall, opens the door. After a minute, or so, of polite adult niceties being exchanged between the two women, we are invited inside of the house. Immediately, the rotund little woman needlessly starts apologizing for the "state" of her home. Actually, it *looks* fine to me, except it has an overwhelming odour of "garlic" permeating the air; and this unpleasant stench was *more* than just noticeable as soon as the woman opened the door.

Immediately, the obese woman lovingly introduces the child, hiding behind her backside, as her daughter, "Isabel", or as she pronounces it, "Eee-zabel". The girl clutching the back of the woman's yellow-and-grey-vertically-striped, shift style house-dress is about seven or eight years old. The little girl, who has below-the-waist length, dark brown hair and piercing, deep brown eyes, utters not a sound, until "Mouse", wondering where they could possibly be, inquires about the *three boys* already being fostered in the tiny house. (What!? I saw no evidence of any children.) Before the plump "mother" could answer, "Eee-zabel" starts giggling and won't stop, even when her mother gently reprimands her about it.

Nonetheless, in response to the question about the "others" the corpulent little woman hems, haws and stammers, then walks over to a door next to the kitchen. She cracks it open, a little, and screams down into the darkness, with the remnants of an Italian accent, "Boys, c'mon up here, there's someone who wants to speak to you!" After no immediate response, she again screams into the abyss, "I said, git up here, now! Freddy, Freddy, Fre..." She is in mid-scream when, thump, bang, thump, bump, up come stumbling three young-looking boys!

"Mrs. Mousey" and I are sitting quietly on the long, orange-brocade chesterfield, which the lady has covered entirely in fitted plastic. The first thing I notice is, the kids are all wearing nothing but ragged, dirty shorts made from cut-off, frayed and faded old denim jeans. We are waiting to see what might happen next, when, by a wave of her hand, the youngsters understand they're to sit down beside *us*. After a second look at them, it's obvious the boys are so shockingly dirty, they appear as if they had been playing in a coal bin! (Ahh...the reason for the plastic furniture coverings, I suppose.) The foster mother, realizing what "Mouse" and I are looking at, quickly dismisses her boys' appearance by explaining they were playing downstairs in the rec room. Yet, even more appalling than the boys' lack of hygiene is the appearance of their scrawny little bodies. They all look like a child's drawing of *stick figures* popping out above and below their loose-fitting, cut-off jean shorts!

The "mother" tells us that the boy she calls "Freddy", though skinny and small, is eleven-going-on-twelve-years-old, and he is the biggest of the three, standing only as tall as this pear-shaped foster "mother" does. He has curly black hair and naturally olive skin, feigning a dark tan. Yet, his eyes are the feature, which have really caught my attention—they're black—not dark brown—actually **black**, and severely sunken-in. The middle-sized fellow, introduced as "Frank", at age eight is a head shorter than the "Big Boy". This kid has an easily maintained brush-cut of flaming-red hair—which, as I'll soon discover, is the reason for his nickname, "Red". All of "Red's" visible white skin is so freckled it appears as if the spots seem to join up in several places! He has bluish-green eyes and tries to keep them turned down, and away, from us strangers. The youngest of the three ragamuffins is six-year-old "Sonny"-- which is his name, and his nickname. He is almost as tall as "Red" but is so painfully shy, he appears diminutive as he slides tightly up against the sofa's wide arm at the other end of the couch—as far away from us strangers as he could get.

The fat little woman keeps trying, unsuccessfully, to hush "Sonny" as he keeps *coughing*—quite uncontrollably. Finally, she tells him to, "Get back downstairs to the *playroom*, right now!" Then turning to "Mousey", she says, "You know...he's putting it on! Trust me...he's not really sick, he is just pretending, faking—you know what I mean, just for attention!" I am thinking the fat woman sounds very harsh towards the boys, and I wonder if "Mousey" notices it also. Huh! Apparently not! All *she* has to say is, "Does the little boy need to come in and see the doctor for a check-up?" Then, convinced of the foster parent's explanation', in no time at all she hands me over to this stranger, along with my "LOBLAWS", [17], grocery

Revolving Doors
bag of belongings.

All during the time of our visit, the remaining two boys have been whispering to each other, and staring at me, giggling. However, the scene quickly changes when the front door closes behind my Case Worker. First, "Rolly Polly", (*my* nickname for her), eases back the sheer curtain on the long, rectangular slit of a window beside the front door. Then, when she is convinced, the Worker is out of ear-shot, suddenly, this "mother" screams at "Big Boy" and "Red" to, "Get the hell downstairs with Sonny, and I mean—right now!"--and, of course, they do. Wow, I am a little scared now, and wondering, hopefully, if this foster woman will be any kinder to *me*. However, for the moment, everything seems alright with me as this brusque woman has placed me on the living-room floor while she looks through my brown paper shopping bag of necessities, extras and my few paltry toys.

I have arrived well prepared. There are two empty baby bottles and four cloth diapers folded neatly at the bottom with two special "safety" pins attached. As well, there are two pair of rubber diaper-covering "panties", three changes of fuzzy blue, footed jammies, a little box of baby biscuits, a small rattle, (which I had long forgotten about, and no longer need), "Teddy Boy" "Ducky" and "Lucky". Great, all my stuff came along with me, but now I am inquisitive as to where my crib is set-up. Then, after only a few moments have passed, I've been stripped down to my rubber pantie-covered-diaper, and am also being shuffled off down to the basement of the house. At the same time, I am watching this foster mother *eating my baby cookies,* right in front of me—and not even sharing one of them!

I really don't understand what is happening to me, or why? I have arrived at the bottom of the basement stairs, having absolutely no idea as to why I am here. I wonder for what length of time we four boys must actually live in this basement, (and I do mean *basement*—not recreation or playroom!). After this "mother" silently deposits me at the bottom step, she returns up the stairs, quickly slipping through the door into the comfort of her house. All I can hear is, "Eeezabel...do you want a baby biscuit, dear? There's a whole box here in this kid's bag!"

The first thing I am quite overwhelmed by is the reeking stench of human waste! Its insult is so overpowering that it actually makes my eyes begin to water. Although a little daylight comes in through the solitary window, it's quite small and caked with years of collected filth on the inside and out, so it takes a few minutes for my eyes to adjust to my dim new living arrangement. I am only around ten-months-old and still quite frail and sickly, after the so-called "care" I received in the previous "home". However, even though I am young, I immediately understand this is *not* a good situation for me, or any of the other boys who are quite solemnly staring at me right now. For whatever unknown reason, the woman has exiled us to her small concrete *basement,* which, I will soon discover, stays dark, dank and smelly. In addition, being underground, regardless of the outside temperature, it's painfully cold on the boys' bare chests, and on *my* whole body.

The first thing my adjusting eyes recognize are the two, green army cots forming a ninety-degree angle against two of the walls. Where are four boys supposed to sleep? Yet, that is it— only two skinny cots for three skinny boys and a sickly toddler. Rumpled on the beds are two very old, dirty, nasty, ragged, faded pink, twin-sized, chenille, [22], bedspreads! The next thing I see are three chipped and cracked china plates, dirty with old bits of some unrecognizable food stuck all over them There are no utensils, as we are all expected to eat like animals, with our dirty paws, um, I mean, *hands*. In addition, I notice the lack of chairs so, obviously, we may only sit on the cots, the steps or the cold, hard floor.

Under the window, there is a deep laundry tub with only "cold" running tap water. We are supposed to drink from, wash in, or (the big boys), pee down into the washbasin! They must stand on cinder blocks in order to pee right into our water fountain/bathtub. (Nevertheless, sometimes they pee into the drain in the centre of the room—and when they miss the drain cover, their pee goes all over the floor. It's slick too...you slide and fall if you step in it.) Tap water, poured into the jam or jelly jars for drinking glasses, is all we are allotted to quench our thirst. What are we supposed to do about food, I wonder? There isn't even an icebox—so where do we keep the food for us *four* boys? I am even more concerned wondering how we are supposed to keep my milk-formula from spoiling.

Nonetheless, of all the lack of amenities the worse one, at least for the others having to use it, (but for us *all* having to smell it), is the lack of a toilet! The only place for three boys to poop in the basement is into a tube, which sticks up out of the dirt, underneath the stairs. I suppose it's there for the purpose of drainage as well, in the event of basement flooding, but for these unlucky three, it's the "shitter"! Of course, that is *their* **outhouse**! Fortunately, however, it's not mine—I wear diapers—(which is how I will be kept clean all the time).

Nevertheless, of course, that did not turn out to be the case as I soon found out, I would be living in wet/and/or poopy diapers for hours, or even a whole day, at a time—again! I had to wait until the foster mother opened her door to the cellar, tossed a clean diaper-cloth down the steps, and removed the dirty one in a little bucket we had to leave on the top step. "Big Boy" had to get the nasty diaper off me and put the clean one on. However, he was always so very careful not to stick me with the pin—not like the nurses back at the prison...oops, I mean orphanage.

Anyway, after the boys poop down the tube they have to pour some sink water in after it and somehow it seems to wash the excrement further down into the dirt. Most times, the poo stays all over the top and sides of the pipe, or on the loose soil around it. Then, what do you think they have to use to wipe their bums after they do "number two"? There is no bathroom tissue, there is only the "Sears Wishbook" [32] [32a]. (A "Sears, Roebuck and Company" [32] [32a], catalogue is always a good resource for wiping when nothing else is available—and, for us, nothing else was *ever* available.). Then the boys have to throw the poopy catalogue pages into the furnace. However, the furnace won't be turned on until the fall cold weather so until then, it becomes a humongous reeking receptacle of poopy pages!

(How undignified, how inhumane are these terrible living conditions! This is such an overwhelmingly sad home, and we are all so very desolate, there simply aren't any adjectives appropriate enough to describe the extent of our individual, or collective, devastation.)

There are no books, because we don't get enough sunlight by which to read them, or even to only look at their pictures. At first, I don't notice any toys at all which makes me wonder what we kids are supposed to *do* down here. I also wonder when we get to go back upstairs. The answers respectively are "nothing" and "never"! Later on, after the boys see I am no real threat to their individual caches, they bring out some of the so-called toys with which to pass the time and amuse themselves. "Big Boy" has a cigar-box collection of colourful, little die-cast, lead-based toy cars he says are called, "Dinky Toys". [23] He plays with them repeatedly all day long, making car-sounds, and even making them "crash" into each other! He says, one day when he gets away from this house he's gonna steal a car and drive and drive—forever! That is it! It's all he has with which to amuse his mind—little toy cars, and a *dream of a great freedom ride.*

"Red" has a very small, pretend, farm with tiny animals, none of which are bigger than my little finger, and upon all of which he has lovingly bestowed names. There is "Bessie" the cow, "Porky" the pig, "Jake" the horse, "Mrs. Cluck Cluck" the chicken, "Mew Mew" the kitty-cat and "Spot" the doggie. Like "Big Boy", "Red" plays pretend farmer all day making the tiny, painted, animals, (also wrought from *lead*), do this or that, or he sounds their noises, acting exactly as he imagines they would on any real farm. (His *dream* is "to live in a big barn with all [his] favourite animals".) Sonny has a dirty, old, boy-doll called, "Raggedy Andy". [24] He doesn't actually play with the doll. Instead, he clutches it *all* the time, while watching the other boys play with their own personal toys. He asks them repeatedly to let him share in their imaginary games and their answers are always, "No—get your own toys!", or "No—why don't you get rid of your stupid doll!" (Either of which, of course, he can *never* do.)

Since none of the others will share their toys with me, I've decided I must also keep mine to myself. (Oh yes, after a few days, "Rolly Polly" has now allotted me a couple of my own toys, from my bag.) Therefore, whenever we are all playing, we sort-of go to our corners, like boxers do in the ring. We can't really make much noise because she'll yell at us, so we quietly pretend in our imaginary worlds. Actually, we don't really even fight, except when the food comes down, then it's every man for himself. The "Lady Upstairs", (as I realize she is called by the boys), once a day sets a small tray of food on the top basement stair-step. We never know what time of day the food will come, so whenever the door opens and we see her slide the tray onto the step, we all scramble to get to it first. The hungry, bigger, faster kids knock it down the stairs virtually every time she sets it there. It's terrible though, when sometimes the tumbling food lands in the dirt under the stairs, and not on the not-quite-so-dirty cement floor. (There is no food for us to pick up at all whenever it, unluckily, happens to fall down onto or into the poo-tube.)

Depending on the nature of the meal, such as soup or stew, usually we can't wash it off. However, now and then, if it's just bread and luncheon meat, such as bologna, wieners, or even if it's boiled potatoes, we *are* able to clean it off well enough to be edible. Personally, *I am* hungry enough to eat white bread with little black specks, of dirt—I don't even care! However, no matter when or what food we are provided, the "Lady Upstairs" has never yet sent down any fresh vegetables or fruit, never. Nor, by the way, has she ever given me a bottle of formula, or milk.

Even if it's sunny and warm outside we hardly know it because of the dirt film on the window. Also, no matter what the outside temperature, the cellar's dampness makes us feel quite chilled, and we can't seem to get warm. Adding to our misery, the air, which is so heavy with dirty, black coal dust, makes breathing very difficult. Even when I don't seem to have "Brown Kites" or "New Onions", I am coughing so much more down in this dirty, damp environment, I seem to be imitating "Sonny". At night, which seems to start in the afternoon, when we boys try to rest, we must huddle together with two kids sharing each of the two flimsy cots. Since I am the youngest, I always get to curl up beside "Big Boy" who has assumed the self-appointed task of watching over me. However, even "Big Boy" can't stop the annoying, crawling, itching and biting bed-bug attacks on our bare skin, in the darkness *every night*!

Actually, "Big Boy" does try to take care of all of us boys, but especially me. It's the only time I can actually feel any warmth, when I cuddle with my foster "big brother". Moreover—it's the only time I am not frightened of the huge coal-burning furnace monster. Normally, I never get too near it, because I can see how such a great monster, (whose over-sized arms actually support the basement ceiling), would have no trouble reaching down and grabbing me. I am certain, in the cold weather, when we feed the furnace monster the chunks of coal from the great black-stained, wooden bin, it will roar its intention to *eat me!* Of course, I'll be so petrified, I'll be frozen in my tracks, providing an easy meal for the monster's cavernous, devouring, flaming cavity!

I am not long in this challenging new environment when I am informed about, and shocked to discover, the real reason why we kids are never allowed upstairs where the foster mother lives. This woman may expect the same moniker of, "Mother", as have the others I've previously encountered, but she too is entirely undeserving of such a special name. (I reserve the name for my own sweet mommy.) Just like the "Cleaning Lady" and "Nervous Nellie", this one is greedy and cruel and she thinks nothing of abusing and starving us. I understand why the boys only ever speak of her as, "The Lady Upstairs".

I could not realize this yet, but my young life is about to take a turn for the worse as I try to maintain my own existence in these harsh, and difficult, living conditions. Unlike the others, I am unable to do much to take care of myself, or even reach down a snack for myself from the bag they hang from the ceiling behind the furnace. By the way, I wonder what all is in the bag and why "Big Boy" controls it and hangs it so high.

In any event, my captive siblings leave me out of everything. I am never included in any of the games with the other boys. Yes, they do sometimes play games like Jacks, Tiddly-Winks, [25], Marbles or Dominoes, if they're lucky enough to get their hands on any such treasures which might be quickly concealed, should the "Lady Upstairs" suddenly come down, unannounced. Sometimes we make shadow puppets when the light permits. Otherwise the games are, "Simon-Says" "Red-light/Green-light" and others. However, it's pretty much impossible to play "Hide-and-Go-Seek", considering the small size of our basement *play* area. Heck, the only place to hide is behind the furnace and every kid, except me, has already been found there! I guess it's probably a good thing we are unable to move around much, because it would require energy, which would necessitate the ingestion of many more calories than we are allotted by "Rolly Polly".

Not long after I've been relegated to stay down in this dungeon, "Big Boy" lays down the law of our societal microcosm—in other words, the rules of my new "home". Whether self-appointed or not, he is the biggest and oldest and he's very kind to the rest of us; therefore, he is unquestionably the leader of us three other boys. What I couldn't know yet, is, he has also been living in the cellar of this house long enough to figure out a way to bring food, and other such basic necessities of life, down into our meagre underground "home". I have no choice but to believe him and do whatever he says I must. We are like a pack of dogs, united in our collective dependence on "Big Boy". He is our pack leader—our alpha dog and he makes the rules we live by— and he somehow, provides for much of our unmet needs. How does he do it? I wonder.

Eventually I get my answer. Sometimes, as timing and weather permit, "Big Boy" must lead "Red" and "Sonny" outside of this house on their secret nightly ventures to scavenge for food. They all silently squeeze out of the small basement window to salvage *anything* edible. They grab garbage-food from the trash cans and dumpsters, which are out in the dangerous Toronto streets and back alleyways. Of course, I am too young and too small to be of any help yet, so I must remain behind and stay quietly hidden, and safely tucked into my *hidey-hole* until they return. (I have omitted mentioning about my "hidey-hole", as I call it, because it is, of course, a very secret and safe place for me to go when I am confused and trying to understand things—and up until now, I have not felt the need to share this secret.) My own personal little hiding space happens to be under the curtained pee-tub, where I am able to be very quiet and safe while the boys are gone. This is the first, of what will be many such, "hidey-holes". When I am in there, I don't really mind sharing the space with the spiders, rolly-polly bugs, ants or black beetles, because I curl myself up into a tiny foetal position. Then, I *know* I am able to achieve the impossible -- "*invisibility*"!

Because I am too young and too little to accompany the boys on the midnight food-runs, it's only fair I come-in last when it's time to enjoy the spoils of the kids' surreptitious ventures. But it's tough for a little guy like me, always being last to be fed, because I always have to wait while they all finish eating, before I get to sop-up their *leavings*. My tummy always hurts and I never seem to have enough to eat. Despite my fatigue and weakness, I need to fight for my own tiny bits of food either left over or discarded by the others. Often I only get to eat whatever they drop onto the filthy floor. The excruciating pain of hunger permeates my body, and makes my head hurt almost as much. I am weak and tremble from the dampness and from the fear of never having enough to eat. My unreal world feels like a dream—no, more like a series of unending terrifying toddler nightmares! Nevertheless, I *know* it's real. I know from my hunger pains, and my coughing, I am not asleep.

Every now and then, the group of scavengers brings back a can of food with a picture of a doggie on it, (and nobody loves doggies more than me!). "Big Boy" says, at least we are eating *some* kind of meat. Although this stuff is awfully mushy and stinky, when I glance up from gorging on it, they're all chuckling because they know something I don't know.

Whatever! I don't care if it's kangaroo meat, as long as I am not eating the dog in the picture, I'm happy enough, (or at least, I *hope* I'm not eating *that* doggie!).

We kids all think it's very strange our highly respected leader continues to insist the boys steal enough extra food to "pay" the "Lady Upstairs" first, and only then do we get to eat what's left over. I wonder why he takes so much of the stolen food up to her. How could she not *know* the boys are sneaking out at night to find the food? I know the woman certainly does not *need* the food—she is virtually as big as her own house already. However, we boys certainly *do* need it—and desperately! Does our leader think she'll be just a wee bit kinder to us? Well, it never works—never! Perhaps he believes it will keep her *away* from us boys. If she stays away and leaves us all alone—at least she won't be physically punishing us, (which, apparently is what happened *a lot more* before "Big Boy" got the idea to start "paying" her off with pilfered food!)

I have learned quickly from the others, the summertime is the best time for gathering food and other supplies. Now and then, when my roommates sneak out during the evenings as hunter/gatherers, they use moonlight to work under, while stealthily collecting fruit from yard trees, or even digging raw veggies from gardens. When they're exceptionally lucky, they can sometimes grab an item of clothing from some unsuspecting woman's clothesline, thus providing us with the odd necessity, other than our basic food requirements. However, as summer moves unrelentingly forward, the promise of autumn's approach is right around the corner. "Big Boy" knows we must not all eat everything they bring back to our basement. He says, "We have to start hoarding cabbages, potatoes and apples for the oncoming fall days which will quickly turn cold, giving us no more summer gardens to raid."

I am young, malnourished and so small. I don't understand

why I am here, in an even worse place than I've been in the previous foster homes. Most of the time I feel worthless, powerless, insignificant to my "pack", and lost to the world. There is no love or any sort of affection for me in this house, or maybe not even in this great big world. (I have come to this realization, after listening under the cellar door to the upstairs, and hearing the *loving* exchanges between the woman and her real daughter.) Sadly, we kids may be staying in a person's house, but "foster" or not, as far as we boys are concerned, it's certainly far from our idea of what a *home* should be.

Chapter 21: Just Toddler "Night-Terrors" ... or *Are* They?

We four boys have all quickly become so very unhealthy as the onset of the brisk fall air has brought illness to us all in the form of "New Onions". Because the woman forces us four boys to sleep on only two small canvas cots, "Big Boy", though sick as well, protects me, allowing me to snuggle with him. My own coughing and gagging keeps waking me up as soon as I doze off, but I know from their relentless coughing, none of the others is getting any sleep either.

After a couple weeks of all of us being so terribly sick and continually coughing our guts out, one night I lay awake just listening to the others who seem to be sleeping. Gosh, I'm figuring "Big Boy's" "Onions" must be completely all better now, because he hasn't coughed at all tonight, or come to think of it all day yesterday either. By the next morning, I feel good that our leader has been getting some much-needed rest while he has been asleep for the last two days. Heck, he has not woke up once! But even though I am not really trying to wake him up, I'm miserable because my bed-mate's been hogging our pink blanket, and has somehow gotten himself all wrapped up in it, (I'm softly giggling a little, thinking he is like a pink piggy-in-a-blanket). Anyway, at a moment when I am pretty sure he won't notice, I yank the bed covering hard and try to grab it back to wrap around myself. Nothing happening! Then I decide I need to wake him up and ask him to share half the blanket. It's very strange, but when I tried to shake him awake and then poke his bare back, I notice he feels sort-of slick, clammy and unusually cold and stiff.

But right now, I'm more concerned it must be somebody's poop that is really stinking around here, and so much so, it's taking my breath away and making my eyes tear-up. [It's probably good that it's so very dark in this basement, otherwise I would have been terrified by the sight of his body which had turned completely black after *decomposing for three days*! But I had no experience of death so how could I know he was dead?...I have only known about *illness, sleep deprivation, starvation, beatings, pain and abuse*...but not *death*, at least not until now.]

Right after "Big Boy" *got well* and stopped coughing, the other two boys also stop their relentless hacking, and lay very still, no longer moaning or tossing and turning, (which always caused the other cot springs to squeak half the night). Well, isn't that just *great*! They all get better and stop coughing completely and *I am* the one who is still sick – as always, the *last* one!

[At least, those are my thoughts. I never want to be left out again. I neither want to be the only one sick, nor the only one well. However, I could not possibly fathom how my being left out this time meant I was the only one *still alive*, and they were all **dead**. I have no experience with the concept, and finality, of death—except for the time when a very still, upside-down, floating "Mr. Jingles" was flushed through a swirling abyss toward fishy heaven somewhere! Whatever is going on with the other boys, I KNOW nobody is going to flush any of us down the commode! Ha—we don't even have a toilet down here! Actually, now I am wondering if maybe they all have "Brown Kites", and I certainly don't want to catch the "*Kites*".]

On the third day of "Big "Boy's" great long nap, the "Lady Upstairs" comes to set the tray of food on the top step. Of course, she never speaks to us, except when she is screaming for one imagined reason or another. She certainly never asks how *we* are. However, this time she growls, "Why aren't you kids eating my good food?" Then she starts down the stairs and stops short at the bottom step. "What the hell stinks down here?" she screams. Then with one foot still on the bottom step and the other one on the basement floor, something makes her come down the last step to repeat her question. Just then she suddenly starts gagging as if she were about to puke. Then she reels around and *runs,* blubber bouncing, back up the steps, slamming the door behind her. Upstairs she is running around the house, frantically blabbering in Italian. I really can't comprehend what's going on above our ceiling boards, but something is definitely changing about our situation below her floorboards.

Regardless, on about the fourth morning of my friend's stinkin' nap, the third day of the others *getting well* and sleeping deeply, it's quite early and I am very tired, having awakened myself off and on all night with my own coughing.

"Now what! What's this...and who are you?"

I vaguely recognize a very big, strong man, in a bulky, grey-wool winter coat, having run down our cellar steps, is swooping me up in his arms, and is now cocooning me in a thick, dark-wool blanket. I have no idea where we are going, nevertheless, I am not leaving without my bag of toys and belongings. I reach and grab it while asking him, *"My friends, my friends!"* however, I can't seem to make him comprehend my babbling! Then, almost understanding me, he speaks softly in my ear and says,

"Hey little feller—don't you fret—everythin' is gonna be alright now—and don't worry 'bout your friends...they's all gone 'home'."

"Home! Home? When can I go home?"

I wonder this, babbling, even louder. What about "Rolly Polly" upstairs? She is carrying-on, and fussing, and balling her eyes out as she is being questioned by *three* very large policemen! As we squeeze by them in the hallway, on our way to the front door, the big man who is carrying me doesn't utter one word to her. Nevertheless, this "foster mother" has plenty to say to him—screeching and screaming her *obscenities* at *him—and me. She is actually complaining about us "stinking up her house".* (As if it is somehow **my fault,** the three boys died and their undiscovered rotting corpses were reeking to high Heaven!)

After this kind gentleman carries me outside he starts to head down the front walk, and with every step takes me farther and farther away from *her* house! Maybe I should be scared, but I am not. I am actually comforted as this hero holds me snugly, with my face turned in such a manner as to prevent me from looking back. As I study *his* face, neither does he look back. No matter, I am so very, very ill, I can no longer think about my friends or even about what it will be like at my next "home". I can only hope the "C.A.S." ladies do a better job of investigating the residence and the "foster parent" before I am placed anywhere else.

However, right now, I keep falling asleep while we are riding in the back of yet another very, very big car. This man has bundled me up so snugly in a warm woollen blanket, I am only able to see his eyes every now and then, when I force my own to open. I notice the man's clear blue eyes are all wet and dripping on my face, as if his eyes are raining. However, as he wipes his tears away, he assures,

"Sorry I'm crying, little boy. I'll be fine. I hate to see what you kids had to live like in that terrible woman's basement."

I am more puzzled as to why he would be *crying* over wild children like us—crying over unwanted, homeless little guttersnipes—crying over *me*. At that instant I start thinking about my own mommy and wonder what she would have done if she knew the way I've been forced to live in the basement of the horribly neglectful and abusive foster home run by "Rolly Polly"--the "Lady Upstairs". Now, I too am feeling like I want to cry; so I try to cry. I try very hard because crying usually makes me better, (like *hugging* myself in the dark basement, when I'm alone and scared). However, I am so dehydrated and weak from my illness, no tears will even come!

Maybe it's wrong, but I feel absolutely nothing about losing my friends, or about my being removed from the house while the other three were able to go "home". Well, maybe I am a little jealous, because, well, I am *not* going home, am I. Besides, I've been so terribly ill myself, the loss of my so-called brothers hardly matters to me. Maybe I'll be able to sleep with jammies and a cover on me, instead of freezing and being kept awake with the other boys coughing fits. Nevertheless, once more, I've become so desperately sick with my own unrelenting cough, it's fated somebody would send me back to "SICK KIDS Hospital". [26] [26a], I'm sure it's either, "New Onions" again, or maybe it's "Brown Kites" I am sick with this time around! (Although, I still don't even know what *these diseases are*, other than the "Kites" make your cough a lot, almost as much as the "Onions" do.)

****

["*Teddy sits alone, fair hair, blue eyes, well-tanned, good-natured...Cold the last few days.*"

For the several months of my endurance at this foster home, these are the last couple comments entered into my file on the "Director's" desk. There seems to be a conspicuous absence of any further notations regarding the unspeakable incidents at this horrible foster home, and/or whatever reprimands or punishments "Rolly Polly" received as a result of her neglect.]

131

Revolving Doors

Chapter 22: At "WELL KIDS": Near Death/After Death....

The man who rescued me has brought me back to the big, familiar building in Toronto with the words, "SICK CHILDREN'S HOSPITAL", [26] [26a], in huge, yellow, neon-sign letters across the main entrance. He is taking me around the corner of the hospital to a different way in, and this doorway is clearly marked in huge *red* neon letters as the, **"EMERGENCY DEPARTMENT"**.

After he hands me over to a nurse, suddenly everybody is rushing around me. They lay me down in one of those over-sized, shiny, chrome-looking crib-cages, (scaring me, a little, as they remind of me of another frightening place where I lived in a metal baby "cage"). Right now, people in white, women and men, are rushing around and all seem to be getting me ready for something. I wonder what it could be.

Now they have stripped me down to my diaper and are affixing something into a vein in my lower right leg. [34] Suddenly, my body is shaking and jumping wildly on the white sheet and so much so, they have to get two of the folks in white to restrain me. Hmmm... It *is* odd, but I don't actually *feel* anything, although I think I should. *Shouldn't I?*

Wowee! The absolutely strangest thing is happening to me right now. I seem to be able to see and hear what everyone is doing and saying, from my vantage point way up in the corner of the **ceiling**! I can see everyone as they come and go from this room and I can even peek into the hall and see the doctor and nurse discussing my condition out there. That is correct— **outside** of the room in which the nurses have completely constrained me. Wow! This is sooooo neat and the sensation is virtually indefinable! I've floated up into the ceiling somehow, but it would be impossible—wouldn't it. Perhaps I am coming in and out of feverish dreams...dreaming again? Of course, that explains it. I can clearly see my eyes are closed now, and there are tubes and wires going in and out of me and being taped to my body everywhere, [34] [36], not to mention the huge thing they have stuck down my throat to keep my breathing airway open!

****

[*This procedure is called an orotracheal intubation, [35], and is performed using a Magill Laryngoscope blade which, at the time of this procedure, may or may not have utilized the improved Macintosh Blade which was invented in 1941, and is* **still** *in use today. [34]*]

****

If I am awake, why do I not feel anything, or open my eyes and look around? However, you know, somehow this strange dream feels so very real. Now, I am actually looking at myself sprawled out on a table or a bed, or some such thing and the "white" people are all zipping around me and doing things to me, or at least to my limp and lifeless little *body*. Now, I find this very odd, since I *know* I am *actually* up in the ceiling! But, strange as it sounds, I can clearly make-out all of the goings-on around me, including the flashing lights and beeping noises on the machines which have, through the various tubes and wires, been hooked up to me. [34] [36] Somehow, I have an understanding that my body, which they're all fussing over, is actually unconscious—which explains why my eyes are shut! I am not asleep. Oh-oh—I think *I might just be dead.*

Yes, quite definitely, I am dying, right this minute! (Gosh, I sure hope they don't flush me down some great, huge, people-sized whirlpool of a toilet, giving me a final "Good-Bye!" just

134

like poor little, pale orange "Mr. Jingles" got when he could not swim around anymore.) Anyway, all of a sudden the pace of the frantic activity picks up when someone says, *"We're losing him!"* Then someone else yells, *"He's gone! He's gone!"* I notice one of the machines, which were constantly beeping has stopped completely and is now producing only one very high pitched, continual tone. And the matching zigzag light pattern on the machine's illuminated screen has changed to one continuous, flat line running straight across.

At that moment, I decide to jump on this bandwagon and let them all know what *I* want. *I* start screaming at all of *them*, **"Let him go! Let him go! Let him die!"** I wonder how they could ignore me. Maybe they're unable to hear me. However, *I* can hear me! So I try once again to get their attention and stop them from restarting my heart and bringing me back to life. However, it just isn't my day to die, I guess, because they don't understand my pleas, and *I do not* die. Of course, reviving me in the emergency room allows them to tack yet another lengthy hospital visit onto my "itinerary of places to go, people to see" and more "frolicking, fun, little-fella activities to enjoy". (*Not really!*)

Well, naturally, I had to come down off the ceiling eventually, but I did not get in trouble for being up there because actually, I just never tried to tell any of the grown-ups what I had experienced. (Who would believe me anyway?) However...I never expected to come down quite so fast! One second I'm floating around in the air and feeling not a single tinge of pain, then in the shortest nano-instant, I am suddenly sucked right back into my suffering body. In that moment, comes the rush of all the pain in my chest, my leg and various other places where I've been stuck with needles and other life-saving equipment!

Even though an oxygen mask is completely covering my

mouth and nose, making it a little easier for me to breathe, I still want to cough my guts out. Oh, why did they have to do this to me? I was happy floating on the ceiling. I certainly was not in pain or misery as I am right now. Nevertheless, these folks at "SICK KIDS" [26] [26a], are determined to ensure my swift return to health and wellness. If only anybody had stopped to ask *me* what I really want for my life—if only...

I have just completed another miserable stay in the confinement of a high-sided metal crib cage, in another oxygen tent, and definitely not having any fun at all! Now, the time has come around for me to go *home*. Wait a minute, I don't even *have* a home. Shortly after trying to face this harsh reality and speculate about what might await me in my next fostering situation, I overhear a conversation concerning the fact I *"should have been discharged three days earlier"*. *Whaaaaat?* I listen intently as the women, (who are changing my bed sheets and cleaning up my area of the room), are discussing a fact about which I had absolutely *no knowledge*. I know they aren't medical staff because both women are dressed in regular, frumpy, street clothes. The first lady, who has bright orange hair and a thick Irish accent, tells the other, *"This wretched little fellow is only still in here because there is no place for him to go—poor wee tyke."* *"Yes, yes...sad state of affairs when even the 'Children's Aid' can't find him a place to lay his wee head."* This was the empathetic reply from the other lady, who is an older, matronly type, with thick, curly, steel-grey hair, but no accent.

The major problem is they have no foster family ready to take me yet. Apparently, the powers that be in the hospital, or else at the "C.A.S.", are reluctant for me to spend another hiatus at the orphan asylum. Well, in any event, I never unpacked, so I suppose in that respect, I am ready to go through the next revolving door of my life to meet my next foster family, (whenever they're able to find me a *suitable* one). In all truth, however, I am very ready to leave this hospital, regardless of how kindly the staff here treat me.)

Of course, I only have one regret about living and not dying at this time, and it is the fact that *I am alive*! After all, of the four of us boys existing in those horrible circumstances, I alone survived. Why? It just isn't fair. I want to go home where the other boys went, and if it is to some ethereal place in the sky, then it's where I want to go! Why should they all die, and I, the most unwanted of all of us, be forced to live-on? Oh, yes, by the way, I've now acquired a new label ... I am termed a "Sickly Child". Those are the latest words, which the "Director" entered into my file at the "C.A.S.". It will really put me in the front-running in the race for a loving "foster", or "adoptive", home, now won't it? {Of course, I am being facetious.}

[I have had to face countless more battles with Pneumonia and Bronchitis, off and on over my lifetime. However, I've had to fight the "survivor guilt" every single day! Of course, I know which battle is worse.]

Revolving Doors

Chapter 23: The *"Perfect* Little Family"...Without Me!

Although I am too young to understand the frightful feelings and distress, I am experiencing, I am only a little boy and I am *very* scared now, every time I see "Mrs. Mousey" coming my way. It's simply because her presence means there is going to be yet another move for me, and who on earth knows what horrors await me at my next place of residence. The only good thing about the "Mouse Lady" showing up this time is that she has picked me up *immediately* upon my discharge from the "SICK KIDS". [26] [26a] At least this time I won't have another reservation at the "C.A.S." "Hotel for Unwanted Orphans", (the *asylum*, of course.)!

Oh, yes, she is once again, driving me in her husband's big old Buick, although this time, we do *not* have the top down. However, it's still lots of fun because she has not gotten any better at driving, and I am still sliding back and forth every time she turns a corner. However, this time I don't slide all the way over, because she has a passenger along for the ride—and to be a personal baby-bumper-pad, for me. The female passenger is a quiet, very plain, sort-of librarian stereotype, complete with brown hair fastened in a tight bun at the back. I listen intently to their conversations because I am trying to figure out what sort of home I'll end-up in *this* time. Unfortunately, the "Workers" seem to be talking in some sort of code which I can't seem to crack, (unlike the "Double Js" *pig-latin* which I deciphered easily).

"Wheeeeeeeee!" This is fun anyway. "Mouse" tells my human buffer she is going to try to *slot* me into another "normal" family's home. I have absolutely no idea what it means to be slotted-in, and now I am more scared than before. I wonder if it will hurt. My natural reaction to this latest adversity is to start a little *puppy-sobbing*, but ever-so softly. When "Mousey" notices how upset I am, she tries to reassure me,

"Everything's going to be alright, Teddy—don't you worry one little bit—you're really going to love your new home. We have checked it out very carefully to make good and sure this family will be an excellent match for you."

I may hate to see her coming, nevertheless, she has always been very caring in nature and so, ever the optimist, I smile acceptingly, first up at her, then back at "Miss Librarian" who is nodding her head in reassurance.

[However, no matter how much I am addressed by it, I KNOW I am "RICKY" and I just can't get used to being called by my so-called *new name*, "*Teddy*". Anyway, isn't, "*Teddy*" a name reserved for stuffed, toy bears, like **my** "*Teddy Boy*"?] [151]

Finally, after another very long car-ride, we arrive at my new home. I could tell from looking at the homes and cars up and down the block, this neighbourhood is a little ritzy. When we pull into a driveway, I am quite stricken by the perfect little house straight in front of me. It appears to be a cute redbrick, five-room bungalow, which, from the outside, seems to be very clean and well kept-up. My escorts each take a hand and walk me, between them, to the front door. We are just waiting for an answer to the musical door chime, which sounds when the doorbell is pressed. "Dee Dee da Ding...Dee Dee da Ding..." A little girl, about four or five-years-old slowly opens the door and asks what we want. However, before the women can respond, the mother arrives and with a wide, bright smile, invites us in.

As we stand in the foyer, the adults exchange pleasantries. I can't help but notice how clean and shiny everything looks. The area of the home I am able to see, is as neat as a pin, and is very modern and smartly, though sparsely, furnished. The house smells like the fragrance emanating from the rather impressive arrangement of multi-coloured roses on the narrow little, polished mahogany table beside the door.

The "mother", "Jennie-Marie", is quite young, slender, strikingly pretty and, truthfully, she reminds me a little of my own beautiful mommy, (though my mental pictures of mommy have recently begun to get a little faded and blurry). This woman has a baby boy on her hip, maybe about five-months-old, whom she tells us is named Samuel, or "Sammy", for short. I thought to myself, how funny this baby is with one bare foot stuck in the side pocket of his mommy's apron, and the other foot caught in the loop of the bow tying the apron at her back! Just then, my attention is drawn back to the little girl, whom her mother introduces as, "Anna-Marie" or "Annie for short. These are her *own, real* children. (At this point, I am wondering what would possess her to take on a stranger, a foster kid—*me*.)

While I am ruminating over this question, a man enters the house from the door to the back garden. He is dressed in work clothing and immediately washes the mud on his over-sized hands before introducing himself as, "John". At this point, I am thinking this could certainly work for me this time, even though it's my *ninth* home address, and my *seventh fostering* situation. Maybe this latest home would be the lucky one. What I could not know is, this foster home placement is considered as a "*supervision transfer*" for me, because of the abuse I suffered in the previous foster homes. Apparently, I am to be very closely monitored to ensure I'll "thrive well and begin to heal my emotional and mental wounds from previous mistreatment".

[The "C.A.S." terminology for my resulting state of mind is that I am, "*suffering from anxiety and depression which would be one-hundred percent remedied by a proper placement of (me) in the environment most suited to (my) needs*". Does nobody understand? Does no one get it? The "environment most suited to (my) needs" is at "home" with my "real mommy" even if "home" is in a cardboard box, in the gutter of a filthy back alley!]

My Case Worker's companion, the "Library Lady" is schooled and trained as a "Social Worker", with special emphasis in working with children from abusive situations. The "Wart Lady" has especially chosen, and added her, to the others on my "C.A.S." team who are working on my case. I pay close attention as the two women stay and visit with the Perfect Little Family for a short time. After a few minutes of chitchat with the "C.A.S." women, the new foster parents take us on a tour around the house, and yard, to ensure it all complies with my needs. After all, I am now considered a "sickly child" with "special care" requirements. However, when they point out the homemade swing set with a slide attached, in the backyard, I decide it complies with me—just fine!

They also show the "C.A.S." representatives where my bed is going to be, right in my own corner of the *baby's* room. (It suits me just fine, considering my Worker has neatly folded my "entire world" inside of a *new* "LOBLAWS" paper bag! [17]) This place is going to be great for me! I'll really "belong" with someone and, for once, I will even have a semi-permanent address.

The parents make an encouraging comment to "Mrs. Mousey" and "Miss Librarian", "Teddy's fair hair and blue eyes will let him fit right in with the features of our *own* children." They're right too, because, from where I am sitting on the sofa between "Mousey" and "Library Lady", I am staring straight at the children on the carpet in front of me; and I am amazed to see two kids who are absolute carbon copies of their mother. The only difference is, the mother's platinum hair is really long, hanging straight down almost to her waist, and both of the kids have very straight, white-blonde, shortly-cropped hair-styles. Certainly you can't miss the fact they too, like me, have very pale complexions, only they have sky-blue eyes and, of course, mine are bluish-green—I think. They're all quite right though...I *will* "slot" right in with this foster family, (and I bet it won't even hurt).

Just then, the foster father, "John", redirects the conversation, explaining the importance of the fact he attends the University of Toronto and is working towards his D.V.A. Degree, [Department of Veterans' Affairs]. He points to his "office"--a modest little desk, right beside which, is a shelf, overstuffed with books and papers shoved-in, and hanging off everywhere. The entire office only takes up a small corner of the dining room, just off to the side of the kitchen, (convenient for this foster father's late-night raids of the pantry, or the icebox). However, getting back to our tour, the man is trying to explain something about, "needing *silence* in the household", due to his "heavy course load". Actually, his exact words are,

"Due to the gruelling demands of my courses, I must insist on complete silence in the household every evening, so I can study."

Hmmm, I am wondering exactly what he means, and what will be expected of *me*? I'm a pretty quiet little guy though, so I'm sure I won't be a problem for John, (as long as I don't get the "New Onions", or "Brown Kites", and start my uncontrollable coughing again. Maybe I had better not unpack my little grocery bag of stuff yet. Guess I'll wait and see, just in case I need to leave in a couple days. Who knows—aw nuts, who cares?)

I have not been in my new house but a few days when things here have already started to go sort-of sideways. I guess this pretty, young, "foster mother", "Blondie", seems to treat me alright; however, I find it peculiar that she always feeds *me* in a high chair, only *after* both of her children have finished their meals and have left the table. I presume I am receiving the same nourishment as her kids but, I have no way of really telling. They continue to grow bigger and fatter every day. I, on the other hand, seem to be hovering around the same pathetic weight I was at when removed from "Rolly Polly's" house. If I am not mistaken, I believe the scale tipped at a meagre nineteen, or twenty pounds on the day the medical team treated me in the emergency room. I also think my stomach must have shrunk during my time of confinement in the horrid basement. It *must* be the case because when I was presented with each meal in the hospital, my eyes said, "*Yes, yes!*" but my tummy stopped after only a few bites with a noisy, cramping, gurgling, "*No! No!*"

I remember when they first brought me to this house, the "C.A.S." ladies were quite insistent with this new foster mother. They instructed her to give me my formula "according to a strictly enforced schedule". They also firmly suggested "Blondie" should:

"Feed Teddy your regular food at the table with the rest of the family, in order to help him assimilate as part of the family dynamic."

However, this mother knows I can't possibly divulge to my Workers any details of my stay under this roof; therefore, she can pretty much do as she pleases, and feed me whenever it crosses her mind.

Nevertheless, management of my nutritional needs is not the only area of parenting in which she comes up somewhat short of skills. Regrettably, she either never remembers to change my "diapee" or else she chooses to ignore my cries, and *decides* not to clean me up. Either way, it renders the same result—a smelly, flaming-red, oozing, opened-sored diaper rash! This terribly blistered diaper rash is all over my buttocks and both my thighs too. (I wonder if this mother knows the ammonia in my urine is causing it. Such a harsh chemical as the ammonia in my urine, is pressed up against my skin for too long a period, literally **burning** my sensitive baby flesh.) These blisters occur simply because of her neglect in not changing my diapers as soon as my cries indicate I am *miserably* wet. In addition, this woman has never applied any of the soothing white ointment the nurses at the asylum are forever slathering on our bums. I know, from experience, the "Penaten Cream" [30], in the flat little blue tin, would quickly heal the excruciating wounds on my buttocks, thighs and my pee pee.

It is very early on a Saturday morning and we three children are sitting on the floor watching television cartoons. Suddenly I hear the familiar, "Dee Dee da Ding! Dee Dee da Ding...!" "Hmmm, who can it be?", "Blondie" wonders aloud. Oh, glory! What a great and marvellous day! My beautiful mommy has just come to see me! What a surprise! Equally as surprising was the man whom she has brought along on the visit, "*Ricky, this is my special friend, Don.*" "Hi, Don", I acknowledge, however within seconds, he is already busy on the floor playing with the foster woman's own two children. "*Don...this is* **my** *baby boy, Ricky!*" Mommy repeats while gushing over me. "**His name is 'Teddy'!**" the foster mother interjects with an attitude. "*Right, that's right...of course. Don the court changed his name to Teddy, but I just can't seem to get used to it, you know.*" However, Don, who is quite young, seems to be purposely acting very callously toward me. In fact, he doesn't even look up from playing with the kids on the floor, and is embarrassing my mommy by really making an overly great fuss over **them**. It seems he could not care less if my name was Teddy, Freddy or Betty! He obviously has absolutely no interest in me! His is very strange behaviour, indeed.

Nevertheless, I certainly don't care one little whit! Right now, I am playing with *my mommy,* which makes everything right with the world. Oh, and she has brought me a really cute little monkey she fashioned out of brown socks, stuffed and tied off in the proper places to make arms and legs, cute little ear bumps and a long tail. She has sewn-on big yellow buttons for eyes, a pink button for a nose and has embroidered with red yarn to make a big, wide, smiley mouth.

[Of course, this occurred decades prior to the stern warnings to parents of, "the choking hazards of small parts on toys for children under three years of age".]

Mommy even cut red felt material to make a jacket and blue felt for shorts. We are both giggling over the monkey as she walks him around and makes monkey noises for him. Then mommy asks me, "*Darling, what shall we call him?*" I wonder too. "Good question!" I babble. "*How about 'Mikey the Monkey'?*" she asks me. Oh, what a perfect name! Thank you so very much mommy. Now I've got a "Ducky", a "Lucky", a "Teddy-Boy" and even a "Mikey the Monkey"! I am very, very lucky and I am never, ever letting anybody even touch the newest addition to my little "toy family"!

When mommy notices I am wet, she asks the foster mother for a diaper. "He's alright, don't worry about it. I'll change him when you leave." is the foster woman's snippy reply. But, mommy insists and removes my soaking wet diapee, awaiting a clean one. However, when she sees my horrendous, pervasive diaper rash, she is absolutely aghast!

"What on earth is this, 'Mrs...'?
Oh! My good God!
How did this ever get to be so bad?
Has he seen a doctor?

Revolving Doors

Don't you have some rash ointment, or any Penaten? [30]"

Mommy rattled off her string of questions, one after the next, in such quick succession, she never took a breath between them. However, the foster lady had no answers, none satisfactory at any rate.

Therefore, her response was,

"I believe it's time for you to leave here *Miss* Ketteringham! In fact, you really had no right to just drop-in unannounced, as you did today! I think you should know this will **not** be happening again, and I will personally see to it!"

Nevertheless, all mommy could keep repeating is,

"*But my baby is miserable, and suffering! He really needs some medical attention! Why are you being so obstinate and ignoring my little boy's needs? You know, I will be reporting this to the 'C.A.S.'!*"

Right now, "Don" is already at the door and pulling my mommy's sleeve insisting, "C'mon, now Bernie—c'mon, we should leave."

Apparently, my mommy *did* report this foster "mother", because today, the foster mother and I have been required to stop-in at the Medical Clinic for my examination by a very nice old man named "Dr. Samuels". "Blondie" is bringing me in for a check-up, which my Social Worker ordered, (apparently right after my mommy called her.) Once we are at the clinic, the nurse instructs my "foster mother" to undress me completely before the doctor comes into the room.

At first, when he enters the small room, the doctor's back is turned away from the examination table, on which I've been laid down on my back. I watch as he is seated at his huge old brown wooden desk with lots of books and papers strewn all over it, and I wonder what he is doing. He swivels around in his huge old wooden pedestal chair, with inlaid black leather on the seat and back, matching his desk. I can also make out he's writing something on a piece of paper while he asks a few simple questions of the foster mother.

Then he stands up, and walking towards me, in a gentle, honeyed voice, he asks "Blondie", "Now, let's see here, 'Mrs...', what seems to be the problem with this little fellow?" However, before she answers him, the Doctor is already close beside me, gently rolling me from side to side. He is visibly upset, at what he discovers to be my problem. (Oh boy, this room is so cold and I really need to pee...all I can think of is, *"Don't pee, Ricky, please, please don't pee on the nice Doctor."*) Suddenly his tone of voice changes dramatically and "Dr. Samuels", rather emphatically, demands of the "foster mother", *"How long has—Teddy, did you say, had this 'Episode of Dermatitis'?"* (asking this while writing down exactly *what he hears*). (Yikes, now I have, "Exploding Darn Didees!" At least that is what it I *think* the doctor said. How the heck did *that* happen?)

Nonetheless, it's what the mother tells him *next* which makes him write something, at length, on the paper fastened to his clipboard. [I could not know this, but the remarks he is jotting down will, once again, change my life.] "Blondie's" glib answer is, "I have just not been able to check that. Really, I didn't notice it." At that moment, he asks his nurse to come into the room, as he wants to discuss his finding with her. What these health professionals are concurring on is the blatantly obvious fact that, ***"This foster parent has been appallingly neglectful of the child's needs, personal hygiene and general care."*** [These are the exact words in the follow-up letter he sends to the "C.A.S." Director, after this office visit.]

As the nurse is tending to my wounds, the doctor repeats the question to my foster mother, "*How can you be changing this child's diaper, repeatedly every day, and not see these infected, oozing, open sores all over his little body?*" (Actually, the mother, and **I,** both know the answer to these questions hangs on the clothesline at home. There are many of family members' items, but no little cloth diapers for me because she leaves me in my wet, nasty nappy for hours and hours at a time.)

"Dr. Samuels" then asks the mother, "*Why doesn't Teddy seem to be crying or fussing about the painful lesions all over his little body? If I did not know better, I would say he has endured a beating evidenced by these wheals and bruises shaped like...well...a belt-strap! Please tell me I am wrong about this, Mrs...!*" Yet once again, she chooses to ignore his prying and simply reiterates, "He doesn't seem to mind, I guess it's why I never noticed the sores." (*I am* remembering the butt whipping which the foster father gave me the other night. Surely, it must have burst many of the blisters on my bum.)

From the back-and-forth glances I notice between the doctor and his nurse, it's easy to tell they're both well aware how this foster mother is blatantly, straight-faced lying to them. Then he asks **_the_** question, "These red striations absolutely look like belt-marks to me. Has this little child been harshly disciplined?" She lies, "NO, of course not." The doctor then gives "Blondie" a small, blue, sample tin of Penaten Cream, [30], so she can get started on the business of slathering me up and getting my wounds to heal, finally. He also tells her she must keep applying this soothing ointment as long as there are open lesions anywhere on my body. His final instruction is the foster mother must also,

Revolving Doors

"Rinse the diapers in the chemical, Anorizine, in order to dispel the bacteria which is so deeply embedded in the material of the diapers; because normal detergent washing can no longer be effective against the stubborn bacteria."

I am lying naked and freezing in the doctor's office, and I really just want to get out of here and go home. However, "Dr. Samuels" has not yet finished his questions to this foster mother. After determining my weight, he tenderly laid me back down again, and used a measuring tape to see how big I am. He comments to "Blondie", "For his age and length, I find the child's weight quite below the normal scale. How is his appetite—is he taking in enough calories for proper growth and development?" She back-peddles her reply, stammering, "Actually, he was brought to me in a sort of emergency situation, and he was just as skinny as this back then! It isn't anything I've done, I can assure you of that!" Before we leave, he asks his nurse to,

"Prepare the pertinent information sheets for 'Mrs...' to take home so she'll be more properly attentive to this child's cleanliness requirements and nutritional needs as well."

Oh, I am thinking, and trusting, this bodes well for me...no more diaper rash, and no more hungry tummy aches! Yaaaaay! Back at the house in the evening, "Blondie" tries to explain to "John" what went on in the doctor's office today. He insists, "Just you keep on doing things your own way because, after all, you have *our two children* to care for, and their needs must be attended to first!" Then he asks her about the pamphlets on the kitchen counter. "Oh, those—the nurse gave them to me today to help me do a better job." The father collects them, and stepping on the white enamelled trash can pedal to flip-up the lid, he tosses them in, with a flicked wrist and an *attitude*.

The foster mother is quite satisfied by the father's reaction so she turns back to the stove and starts making *their* supper. I'll just *have* to wait for mine. Don't anybody worry about me. I'll be quiet as a little mouse and just sit here on the living room floor to wait for my supper. No use complaining or trying to notify her of my soaking wet, pee-pee diaper, because she'll just change it when she "darn well gets around to it". Or so I've overheard her tell her husband.

While I'm sitting on the carpet, I'm just quietly playing with a short stack of wooden blocks with letters and numbers in different colours engraved on each side of the cubes. "Sammy" is in his high-chair awaiting food and "Annie" is sitting on the chesterfield watching me. "C'mon over here and eat your supper sweetheart." are the father's caring words to his daughter. "Come to the table, right now!" the mother demands. Anna-Marie stands up and just as she passes me, she goes out of her way to kick me in the side of my right knee, as hard as she possibly could. The parents don't see what actually happened. All they see is the result of her kick, which was the tumbling-over of my fabulous block-stack castle, and my crying, (not over the knee kick—or over the castle either).

Of, course I can't explain to the parents, but I also can't stop my crying. It isn't as if I am unable to build another castle. The castle reconstruction is certainly not a problem with *my* talented little hands. It's not because "Annie" is laughing at me so hard. Even when the mother comes over and yanks me up onto my feet by my left ear, yes it hurt, but I am not crying about that either. I am easily able to endure such abuse. For a short moment on my feet, suddenly I had the realization, I think I am finally crying over *my losses*: my mother, my foster siblings, my companions in anguish, my foster pets—but especially "Big Boy", my protector and friend. Everyone and everything I have ever had in this world, I've lost. E.V.E.R.Y.T.H.I.N.G!

As much as the foster "parents" yell at me, nevertheless, I can't stop crying. Finally, I am leaned over the father's knee and given a bare-bottom spanking. He thinks nothing of removing his leather belt and folding it in half to make the loop, which he uses to strap my bare skin. Whack! Whack! Whack! With every hit, I feel the few remaining unopened blisters and sores on my buttocks and legs popping and my skin splitting open. The belt is slipping and getting wet from the watery substance oozing from my sores. Three more now, *whack, whack, whack!* Now, I am silent—silent as the graves in which my three skinny little stick-friends must now be laid to rest. I am silent as the clouds on which I concentrate my mind—the beautiful, fluffy, faraway clouds where I wish I could be at this very minute. I am as silent as *my own grave*—soon, I *hope*— maybe this beating will do the trick. I can only *hope so.*

As further punishment for my crying, the "parents" send me to bed without any supper. Too bad, too because the smell of her Shepherds' Pie was making my mouth water and my empty tummy rumble. The whole house is quiet now, but I don't dare cry to draw attention to my wet bottom. The mother is cleaning up after the meal and the father is studying at his desk next to the kitchen. Baby "Sammy" and "Annie" are in the living room playing with the ruins of my block castle. I don't care. Tomorrow will be another day. I'll do better, somehow. I certainly won't be doing any crying over all the spilled milk in my life. No, no more tears, no matter what. My gosh, I can scarcely bear the pain of the sores and blisters on my body, and the pee-soaked diaper is burning and stinging these newly-opened wounds.

Is this it? Is this my life? How can I ever get out of this situation? I don't really understand why I am not able to do things to please this woman. I think I am trying hard to behave well—and to make friends with her children. What else could these parents possibly expect of me?

A few days after my severe butt-whipping incident, I find myself, once again, in the presence of "Mrs. Mousey", and I am quite surprised to find out *she* is the one who has arranged today's meeting. Apparently, upon receipt of the doctor's report, she decided to call us into her office, where she, "Librarian Lady" and the "Wart Lady" are ready to question "Blondie" regarding my care, or lack thereof. Oh, if only I could tell her of the newest abuses within this latest foster home. Sadly, all I can do is listen to their conversation, and cry, but, of course, only on the inside. Then, "Mouse" suggests they undress me and "have a look at the healing progress of [my] diaper rash".

The moment my diaper was peeled away from my raw, red, blistered bottom, a little of my skin and blood came off sticking to the cloth. There was a collective gasp from the three "C.A.S." employees. "How on earth did it progress to such a state?" the Director demands of my "foster mother". "What have you been doing to help Teddy with this dreadful problem?" my Case Worker asks. Then they tell the mother to dress me and they all leave the room together, whispering softly as they obviously discuss my newest health issues.

[Exactly what they were discussing was immediately entered into my file, and read as follows,

"Originally, this foster mother spoke affectionately of Teddy, and this office was hopeful it would be a good placement, and a very good match. However, we have currently witnessed how the foster mother obviously feels no warmth for the child, and the decision regarding this placement is now in question."]

Revolving Doors

They never even got around to weighing me; but I think from just looking at my emaciated little orphan body, they could easily tell I'm not receiving proper nutrition.

While they're out of the room, the mother dresses me and whispers very sternly in my sore left ear, (the one she pulls and stretches regularly), "If you are trying to get me into trouble here, it's not going to work! So you better not start crying or else you will get double the whipping with John's belt when we get you home." I babble loudly in agreement because I absolutely can't imagine taking another butt whipping like the one I endured the other night. Therefore, as we sit in the little room, we wait for who knows what is next. When the women return to the room I could never have anticipated what was about to happen.

"Wart-Lady" speaks first, saying,

"We have been discussing the situation regarding this child, and we think he is not being cared for in the manner in which we, and his physician "Dr. Samuels", expect. We gave you clear instructions as to how to manage the dermatitis and additional instructions about Teddy's feeding schedule and eating habits. However, it appears as if you and your husband are unable to manage these special requirements for Teddy."

Then, my Case Worker adds, *"Is there anything you are not clear about? Or, do you wish to ask us anything about the boy's care?"*

My foster mother stands right up and, pulling her shoulders back, shocks everyone with her answer, which was recorded, and entered, word-for-word,

"I think there is something you should know about this little boy. First of all, he is lazy, and is completely disinclined to

154

make any effort to develop."

The "C.A.S." women each looked sideways at the others, as the foster mother continues,

"As a matter of fact, I must insist you test him for mental retardation because I believe it's the main problem holding him back in his development."

Again, sideways glances, halted abruptly when the mother offers to demonstrate what she means.

(Uhh...I am once again wondering where my LOBLAWS, [17], diaper bag is at, because it's starting to sound like a good time to start packing again.)

"Blondie" lays me down on the floor to demonstrate, "Look at that, will you...he is quite *unable to pull himself up!"*

Then she sits me up and awaits their response. However, just then, as I am sitting on the floor, her little girl runs at me with full force and knocks me back down, causing me to bang the back of my head, quite hard on the marble floor. Ah Ha! I saw this as the perfect opportunity to show the "C.A.S." women, I am *such a good little boy* and I never make trouble or fuss at all! So...I lay there quietly, not allowing myself to cry or show any emotion at all.

Oh nooooo! My perfect plan backfires when "Mrs. Mousey" says, *"He certainly does appear to be abnormal because he doesn't react in any expected way, whatsoever."* The Director then adds, *"I am not sure of a diagnosis of retardation because neither you, nor we in this office, are trained properly in order to offer such an identification of Teddy's stage of development. Therefore, I will arrange for this child to be seen at the Paediatric Neurological Clinic at 'SICK KIDS'."* [26] [26a]

Revolving Doors

Great—and I don't mean that in a good way! Now the "C.A.S." is arranging to send me to the "Peanut Clinic", (or at least it's how it sounds to me!).

(Oh well, it's alright, I already have one foot out the door anyway! After all what is one more "revolving door" to the next, foster home in my life?)

It has only been a couple days since we were in "Wart's" office and now "Blondie" is having a heated phone conversation with "Miss Librarian". This is the part of the conversation I hear,

"But there's something wrong with him. He is always off in a daydream and doesn't always obey my husband or me, no matter how much we discipline him. We think he must be mental, or something strange like that."

(Again, *she and I knew* the truth was, they simply wanted me out of their house.)

Nonetheless, the formal resolution regarding my purported retardation came two weeks after this phone call. In another correspondence from "Dr. Samuels", there is no doubt as to my diagnosis. The letter clearly stated,

"Neither I, nor his Speciality Clinic physician team, can find any physical or mental reason for, or evidence of, any retardation."

After she reads it aloud to her husband, he snatches it from her, steps on the trash can peddle and, again, pitches it straight in; nevertheless, I *know* they're talking about *me*, again. Regardless, I guess I am still here and probably staying, even if they don't believe the results from the "Peanut Clinic" and just think I am stupid, or backwards.

Revolving Doors

After a few more weeks have passed, it's now approaching the end of November. The "Perfect Little Family's" perfect little Christmas tree has already been erected, and, I must say, quite beautifully decorated by "Blondie". In fact, her homemade Christmas crafts litter the house, but...*I* happen to know she has a secret behind the beautiful items. She has had quite a bit of *professional* help with her decorating ideas from the magazines she regularly receives in the mail. They're called: "House Beautiful" [36], "Better Homes and Gardens" [37], "Redbook" [38], and the "Ladies Home Journal" [39]. Every one of these magazines approaches the Christmas season with zealously designed covers of red, green, gold and silver; and all the covers have tantalizing hints of the inviting articles and recipes filling their pages! These cleverly contrived periodicals are designed to show even the least crafty woman how to fashion everything from the season's best cookies to the homemade Christmas tree ornaments and stunning dining table centrepieces!

This house is all abuzz about the events the family is planning for the holidays. With each day now drawing closer and closer to Christmas, Anna-Marie is maniacally dancing and singing "off tune" carols all around the house! Even though I can't understand it, I too am a little excited to see what the mysterious, great and benevolent Santa Claus would bring *me* to open on Christmas morning. I really hope he knows I exist! After all, Santa could finally *find* me because I live in a house, with a mantle and a tree where he can stash my wonderful and amazing present. Wowee! I just can't wait until the most exciting and fateful children's event—ever!

Nevertheless, then it happens. "Blondie" makes another phone call to the "C.A.S.". My "foster mother" is complaining and insisting, "We need the little boy to be *moved out of our house by the first week of December!*" Oh, my gosh--"the little boy"-- that would be me. Oh noooo! This can't be happening! It's only a few days away! What am I going to do? I'll be good! I'll be better! Let me stay until after Christmas morning—please.

Then she deals the killing blow saying, "He simply **has** to be out of here by then because we are going to our relatives for the Christmas holidays and we **don't want the child along**!" "*The boy?*", "*The child?*" Whatever happened to, "Teddy"? I was slotted-in, wasn't I? I thought I fit-in to this "Perfect Little Family". Didn't I? Don't I?

It's obvious from the conversation, the mother is being met with some sort of argument. So then, she spills the *real reason* for wanting me to move out, demanding, "The child is just too much to handle, along with our own two children. We want him gone, right now!" According to the notes in my file at the "C.A.S.", the Worker insisted, "It would be devastating to Teddy to move him once more." Luckily, this guilt trip actually seems to work, making the "mother" give me a reprieve of a couple more days in her house. However, just two more days go by before she calls my Workers urgently demanding, "*the immediate removal of this foster child*". This time her excuse is, "Our whole family has head colds and we don't want Teddy to catch our colds". Sadly, that ship had sailed, and I am *already very sick—again.*

A couple of hours later my paper bag is packed and placed, along with me, by the front door. When the "Librarian-Lady" arrives, I am soaked with fever from waiting so long inside the front door, all bundled tightly in my coat, hat, scarf, mitts and boots. On my way to the next foster home, the Worker notices how sick I am and decides to make a point of telling the new "foster lady" at the next house to "give Teddy some aspirin, [57], and he'll be just fine".

Revolving Doors

Chapter 24: *HAPPINESS* is the Cruellest Invention

"Librarian Lady" has picked me up in a taxi from the latest foster home where I am **no longer wanted**. I think she must be rich because I've never known anybody who rides in taxis. It isn't bad, but far too tame for my new love of car riding, or should I say, car-sliding. Nevertheless, while we are seated in the back, a burly looking man with thick, wildly curly grey hair and an agreeably thick, Greek accent is chauffeuring us around! "Yady, where to go? Where you go, yady?" he asks my chaperone in his best attempt at English, albeit broken. She hands him a small slip of paper on which "Wart" has written my next living assignment.

Actually, between the words on the little piece of yellow, lined legal paper, my future has been written out. "Where *are* we going?" I babble, though she doesn't understand me. We aren't in the cab for very long when he suddenly pulls to the curb and stops in front of a rather unimpressive white, stucco, four-plex apartment building. My Social Worker pays the cabbie with a little extra and receives a, "Zank-you, yady!", and then we head up the paved walk.

There are only four, extra-wide steps up to the main entrance of the building. We are standing on a grey cement veranda and my escort is inspecting a small panel of lighted buzzers on the left exterior wall. She decides on one and pushes the illuminated button for apartment "C". "Hey, '*Wadee*'!"--tee, hee, hee, I try to babble using the cabbie's vernacular. I would like to push some buttons too—but, of course, it just doesn't happen. After a few minutes of no response, she buzzes the suite once more.

Shortly there is a voice coming out of the small, circular, slatted intercom, and the person inside the tiny box is telling us to, "Wait a minute, I'll be right there—just a minute, please." In no time, a tall woman with medium-length brown hair, not particularly styled in any way, opens the door for us. We walk a few steps to her apartment marked with the letter "C". (This will be my *tenth residential* move into my *eighth foster home.* You would think I might be getting good at this moving around business. Nope! I still hate to hear the almost imperceptible *sweep, sweep, sweep* of just one more revolving door in my short little life.)

This new foster mother introduces herself as "Gerda". She is wearing what appear to me to be a *man's* pair of tailored grey trousers with a black-on-white pinstriped blouse, neatly tucked-in at her waist. "I've been waiting for you", she says in a voice, which seems unusually deep, for a woman. "Sit-down, please", she suggests, pointing to the big, long sofa.

Smiling, she offers an oatmeal cookie with what she admits are big "raisins" sticking out everywhere. (Those black lumpy, wrinkled things remind me of the "rat raisins" I ate in my crib at the asylum, so I am not planning to try one of *her* rat's raisins, which incidentally look like they came from a decidedly massive *rat!*) It's a very highly piled plateful of the cookies and I am wondering whether *the* mouth-watering scent might be what I've smelled since we came down the hallway. Such a lovely fragrance, so warm and inviting, but I had better not take one of those cookies it *could be* a trick.

Then "Gerda" asks my Worker, "Coffee or tea, 'Miss...'?", but "Library Lady" explains she can't stay, and that she is expected right back at the office. "Oh yes, before I forget, Teddy has been ill again with another nasty chest cold. It doesn't seem to have turned into Bronchitis or Pneumonia, however, the nurse at the "C.A.S." instructed me to mention you need to give the baby "half an aspirin"*. [57] Actually, I've brought a few for you; they're right here in my purse, somewhere." (She searches frantically until she finds the small paper envelope in which the nurse safely tucked away the aspirins, [57]. Because they each contain adult dosage tablets, she already cut them in half, to avoid any possibility of an overdose.) "Also, please observe him carefully and if necessary, call "Dr. Samuels". Here's his number."

*[Half an Aspirin? [57] Because this was prior to the 1952 introduction of "Bayer's Children's Chewable Aspirin",[57], which were small, easily administered, pleasant-tasting, orange tablets, this adult pill had to be crushed and the powder added to a bottle, or food. This was also long before the research uncovered the link between the administration of "Acetylsalicylic Acid", (the ingredient commonly known as its pharmaceutical brand name, "Aspirin"), [57]), to children with fevers, or Chicken Pox, and the often deadly result which was the condition known as, "Reye's Syndrome". [31]]

"Oh yes, and before I go, could you give us a quick tour, please?" "Gerda" complies, mainly showing the small spare bedroom which she has prepared for me. It has light-blue walls and a bare, hardwood floor. Against the wall, under the window, is child-sized bed with a white headboard, which serves double duty as a book-or-what-not-shelf. The bed, which has a blue quilt with brightly striped balls, red wagons and yellow trucks all over it, sits very low on the floor, (easy for this little guy to get in and out of, but I notice it provides very little stashing space underneath).

The other furnishings include a wooden, child's rocking chair, on the seat of which is a picture of a little boy and girl, each holding the handle of a pail between them. (They would presumably be the storybook characters, "Jack and Jill" [60]). Also in the room is a sturdy, handcrafted, wooden rocking horse with a stringy, mop-like mane and a short, little white dresser for my clothes and diapers. At the foot of the bed is a massive, shiny blue chest, or steamer trunk, [40], which "Gerda" indicated is for toy storage—but certainly far too ample for my simple little collection. What is going to be especially nice about my new room is the very large window reaching down low enough so I can easily see out of it, (without the aid of my previous ladder invented from my clever use of my "Little Golden Books", [27]).

"Library Lady" then excuses herself and bids me good-bye. I am sitting politely on the living room floor when I notice the Christmas tree. I am quite pleased to see that even though it's still November, "Gerda" also has put up her little tree—and I do mean "little", because it's no taller than me. It's sitting on top of a round, darkly stained wooden table with four legs sprawling out from underneath it, each of which is tipped with shiny, polished brass *bird's* feet. There is also fake snow, (really just cotton batting), arranged in an attempt at disguising the table under the tree. On the tree are small, multi-coloured lights, beautiful shiny balls, fluorescent *icicles*, some assorted little ornaments, a strand of tiny, shiny gold-coloured beads, a fuzzy twist of red garland, and everything is draped over with oodles of shiny silver slivers of tin foil. In total it presents a quite magical-looking little tree, itself is no bigger than any of the numerous, imposing, green houseplants which are strategically placed on every flat surface in this woman's apartment.

Of course, you know what I am wondering right now. Right! That's right! Will **Santa** know I've moved to this place? However, almost as if she were reading my mind, "Gerda" asks me, "What did you *ask* Santa for this Christmas?" Me? How was I supposed to *ask* Santa for anything? Maybe I still have time. I know I want Santa to take me back to my mommy. I wonder if he could possibly have enough magic dust inside his red velvet sack to accomplish such a grand magic feat. In any event, if I am going to ask the "Big Guy" for anything, I'd better get on it, and I mean, yesterday. (I really, really hope this new foster mother, "Gerda", can help me with such an overwhelming task.

"*HOPE*"... hmmm...it's not a word I've used much in my short life, so far.) We'll just see how my new pretend mother handles this monumental task for me.

Anyway, as I glance around, I notice the rest of my newest "foster mother's" home is very nicely furnished with all dark-wood furniture and a long, bright, couch with matching chair in an over-size floral print. There are lots of pictures and oil paintings on every wall, conveniently concealing the grandiose and hideous grey, red and yellow, floral wallpaper! "Gerda" explains how *she* actually painted all of the pastoral-scene oil paintings, which are mounted on every wall around her apartment. Hmmm, I am impressed.

Down the long hall going to the two bedrooms and the bathroom, "Gerda" has lined the walls with framed photographs of many people. Old, young—all kinds of people, two of which are photos of women who look remarkably like my newest "foster mother". "Gerda" explains the photos are the faces of all the people in her family. She has a long story to tell about every one of them, which is quite nice for me, because I enjoy *lengthy* stories.

Before long, we are eating supper, which consists of mashed potatoes, little green peas and a bit of pork chop, cut up into teeny-tiny, me-sized pieces. After supper, this latest "foster mother" puts me into a nice warm bath, which makes me think I just might enjoy my stay here at "Gerda's" house. It's quite comforting to me how she seems so prepared to take care of a little boy. After she cleans me up, she gently applies the salve to my dermatitis, and then she dresses me in a pair of flannel jammies, which are also me-sized. They're so warm and soft, and are decorated with little choo-choo trains all over them. Because this foster mother is being so nice and kind to me, I almost believe things could work out for me here—*almost*.

However, before I can climb into bed, this foster mother makes me perform a strange ritual she calls, "*saying my prayers*". I must kneel down on the floor beside my bed, with my elbows on the bed and my hands clasped together, with fingers pointing upward, in front of my face. Then I close my eyes and repeat the words after her,

"Now I lay me down to sleep,
I pray the Lord my soul to keep.
If I should die before I wake,
I pray the Lord my soul to take." [42]

I try hard to say the words but what comes out of my mouth is only,

"*Babble, babble,*
Blah, blah, blah...,
(Of course, her version sounded better).

Goodness, the words in the little prayer are quite profound and I can really relate to the rhyme in a way, which she can't possibly imagine. "*I pray the Lord my soul to take.*" Fine—but what in the world is "my soul", and where would he/she take it, and, incidentally, who is this "*Lord*" anyway? Would it be *so* easy to "shuffle off this mortal coil"? [43] [43a] Maybe it's a trick and something very bad will happen to me after I fall asleep.

Although, this woman is being very sweet to me, even to the extent of smearing on my bum cream, I can't really trust her. I am just a little afraid she might sneak in and hurt me, *after I go to sleep.* No matter, I am too drowsy now because I've already had my nighttime warm milk and crackers to make me sleepy. Yes, this woman is very, very nice, indeed; however, I really hope I'll dream of my sweet, beautiful mommy tonight.

Morning comes streaming through my window, prying my reluctant eyelids open and waking me to this nice new room— *my* room. For a moment I had forgotten where I was, because last night I was so sleepy, I never noticed the walls with all the neat pictures of toy trains, hobbyhorses and brightly costumed circus clowns. I would say my favourite is the brilliantly emblazoned carousel with a striped canopy and darling little painted horses, each one chasing, but never quite catching up to, the others.

After gently changing me into day clothes, "Gerda" props me high up on cushions she has arranged on a dining room chair. I am definitely up high enough for her to feed me easily, without my nose hitting the table's edge. Right in front of me are two boxes of cold cereals called, "Kellogg's Corn Flakes" [41], and "Kellogg's Rice Krispies" [42], and "Gerda" holds them both up asking which one I would like to eat. (Do I have a *choice*? Wow.) The pieces of Corn Flakes, [41], look a little big for me to manage, but the Krispies are tiny and look like more fun anyway, so I point to the one with the three elves on the front. "They're named, 'Snap', 'Crackle' and 'Pop'!" she informs me. Well, what a yummy, delicious decision *that* turned out to be!

Many days repeating this cycle of "brekkies, lunch, dinner, bath, prayers and bedtime", came and went in this latest "foster mother's" apartment. Of course, each day moved me closer and closer to the *big event*! Besides the regular food rituals, this "foster mother" makes a point of taking me for an outing almost every day. One especially enjoyable day, we went to a huge building, which was packed full of books! This "mother" told me, "It's a 'Library', and all the books are there for us to *borrow*. In fact, we even chose some books to *take home*." "Gerda" then helped me pick out, "*Curious George*", [164], which she told me is about a funny little monkey, like my "Mikey", who is always getting into trouble. We also borrowed,

"*Alice's Adventures in Wonderland*", [165], and the pictures in it show it's about a little girl who falls through a rabbit hole and ends up having the strangest adventure of her life!

On another day, "Gerda" took me to a big park with swings and a slide, a great huge sandbox—and dozens of children, all running around, playing, laughing and squealing with delight! That day was heaps of fun. Another time, we rode on a very big "streetcar" [47], which looked a little bit like the "bus", people-transporter, which I had ridden in with "Big Ears". But instead of rolling on big black tires, this vehicle moved with noisy, squealing steel wheels, on steel rails, just like those on trains. (The "Pull-the-wire-to-get-off" rule was the same, though.)

Today, however, "Gerda" has prepared me for a very special surprise! Today she is taking me to an imposing downtown department store called, "SIMPSON'S" [44] [44a] [48] We are standing on the street corner out front of it, and are facing a choice of either of two sets of entrance doors, one on each street incorporating the corner, on which the building's *own* corner sits. Choosing one, we step toward the entrance itself, which has regular doors on the right and left and very special one in the middle. It is an actual "*revolving door*", [49], and when you step inside it turns around and around. I've noticed this kind of door on another large building—the bank, where my new foster "mother" regularly visits.

After a few minutes of watching patrons enter and leave

through this peculiar, highly arched portal, I follow in amazement as its mechanism rotates in almost, non-stop circles within a humongous, tall, glass cylinder. Suddenly my "foster mother" decides it's our turn to jump *into* the ride. She pushes me in ahead of herself and we become squeezed together into one of the four pie-shaped spaces created by the centre crossed-wall. This people-powered, divided cylinder continues to turn, moving us, or rather slowly *s-l-l-i-i-d-i-n-g* us right into the store. Once "Gerda" pulls me out of the revolving part and into the shop, I am quite happy to be on solid ground again, although it *was* kind of fun.

Wowee! This is a place of wonderment, just chock-full of brightly lit and amazingly beautiful displays, and items, all screaming, "Buy me!" "No, buy me!" As we wander around in the store, I am mesmerized gazing at one thing or another, when whom should we come upon face-to-face, live and in-person, but *Santa Claus* himself! Yes, there he is, all dressed in his red velvet suit, trimmed with white fur cuffs and collar! On his feet are large, shiny black boots, which match the belt around his voluminous waist, all of which sport golden buckles. With his huge, white, fluffy beard, he looks exactly like the pictures I've seen, which is how I recognized him on sight. Santa Claus is seated in an over-sized wooden chair which is quite obviously sturdy enough to hold himself and each the children sitting on his ample knees, one, or even two-at-a-time.

The line of children waiting to see him is worming and snaking all around the store display cabinets and shelves. They all eagerly queue up to get up on his lap and rattle off their lists of must-haves from him for Christmas. "Gerda" is holding my hand as we take our place at the very back of the line. In her manly voice, she assures me all I need to do is, "Wait, patiently, and [my] turn will surely come, then [I] can ask Santa for [*my*] very special requests this year."

Revolving Doors

"I want my mommy! I want to live with my mommy! Please bring my mommy to get me." I repeatedly rehearse these thoughts so I know exactly what to babble when I get up to Santa Claus. However, while waiting, I get distracted listening to the Christmas carols playing continuously over the store's loudspeaker system. Then, every so often, I also catch the store's famous jingle,

"You'll enjoy shopping at Simpson's,
With their money-back guarantee,
Satisfaction in ev'ry way,
And your money refunded cheerfully.
You'll pay no more at these great stores,
With so much more for you:
Service! Selection! Value! Satisfaction!
And Free Delivery too!
You'll enjoy shopping at Simpson's..." [44] [44a] [48] [50]

I am busy listening to the music, but my attention is on the kids in this line who are jumping around, whining and complaining to their parents. Then, before I know it, my turn finally arrives. Now, I am the kid being lifted up onto Santa's lap by a nice elf-lady wearing a green velvet dress, which is also trimmed in white fur. She is also wearing a matching, pointy elf-hat and sparkly gold shoes with toes, which come to a pointy upward/inward hook, and have a jingling bell dangling from the tips. The bell tinkles a little when she steps over to whisper something into the "Big Guy's" ear, which I notice is immediately before each child climbs up.

Now, Santa is *speaking* to me, in a softly rumbling voice, saying, "Ho, ho, ho...*Teddy*, and what would *you* like for Christmas this year?" Oh my gosh—HE KNOWS MY NAME! I am so dumbstruck, I can't get even a little babble out of my mouth. Actually, I am almost a little afraid, but only *a little*. However, then he asks me, "Would you like a nice red fire-truck, or 'Tinkertoys', [45], or how about a little choo-choo or a farm set?" I still can't get one syllable out. "Lemmie see...I bet you'd like a cute little pull-along doggie, now wouldn't you?" [46] "Yes, oh, yes! That's it—exactly what I *do* want, Santa!" How do I let this over-sized elf really know for sure I certainly *do* want the doggie? I nod my wild agreement with his last suggestion. I am so beyond excited to think he might bring me my own wooden puppy, I plum forgot to ask him to bring me my *mommy*! Before I know it, my time with Santa is over, and the diminutive, green, elfette lady is lifting me down off Santa's expansive knees.

"Gerda" picks me up at the "SANTA'S WORKSHOP" exit, asking, "What did you ask Santa for, Teddy?" I am trying to figure out how to respond to her when I *see* what I want on the toy shelf right in front of us! There it is, along with a *red fire truck, Tinkertoys*, [45], a *little choo-choo* and a *farm set*! I point to the *doggie on wheels* and she smiles, reassuringly, saying, "Well if you have been a very good boy this year I am certain Santa will bring you exactly what you want!" Oh, now *I am* not so certain about getting the wooden doggie.

Then, "Gerda" says we need to go *upstairs* and have some lunch. As we leave the "TOY and GENERAL MERCHANDISE" floor, we step into a big metal cage—one of three in a row all along one wall. Next to each of these cages, there are three sets of lighted plastic, white "UP", and red "DOWN", arrow-shaped buttons. On the wall, above each of the cage's solid brass doors, (which incidentally are engraved with huge sun-ray patterns), there are very weird brass arrows pointing to, and swinging past, a semi-circle of numbers, apparently corresponding to each floor of the tall building. The arrow over each "elevator" moves around from one number to the next as the moving-cage people-transporters reach the corresponding floors. Once inside, I can see these metal cages have vertical metal bars around the three sides, with mirrors comprising the spaces in-between each. The cage's floor is a stunning black marble and is so highly polished you can actually see your face reflected in it.

There is a pretty woman permanently stationed inside the elevator doors, and "Gerda" explains, she is the "Elevator Operator". (I am thinking it's a lofty position to which I can certainly see myself aspiring, one day—just in case, "Circus Clown", is already taken.) I notice that this attractive "Operator" lady is wearing a smart navy blue skirt-suit which is the exact same uniform which all of the sales ladies behind each of the store counters are wearing, but this one is also sporting clean, stark-white *gloves*.

I notice the young woman alternates standing, or sitting on a little stool, while operating the tools of her trade. Her gloved right hand pulls the long brass lever which makes this great machine move, while her left hand safely holds back the folding metal, inside doors as the numerous patrons get on and off, (lest a door should try to close on, either their many packages, or their *behinds*). Then this woman in charge of getting everybody where they need to shop next peeks out of the doors, looking from right to left, to make certain no customers are running to catch *her* elevator. When the "coast is clear" she slides the fourth wall of metal bars back across the elevator doorway opening. Then, pressing a large white button, she makes the solid door close with a hydraulic *hisssss* sound. Then the cage moves up to the next floor and the Operator repeats the ritual.

As our cage starts to rise up into the air, I am having the sensation that the motion of the elevator cage is making my tummy go up in the air too. I swallow and steady myself by staring at the "Operator's" dazzlingly shiny brass badges. The one on the left side of her chest has the "*SIMPSON'S*" name engraved in cursive writing, with the woman's job "title" printed below, "ELEVATOR OPERATOR". The corresponding badge on the other side of her dress has her name, also engraved in large block letters, "ELSIE". "*Hello Elsie!*" I whisper-babble.

Then, as we reach, or pass each floor, the corresponding number button on the panel of buttons lights up and the people get off and on according to what merchandise they're interest in looking at. The "Operator", without actually making eye contact with anybody, speaks continuously in an unnatural, sing-songy, nasally sort of voice. She is actually talking about what is for sale on each floor.

"Second floor: *ladies' wear, shoes and lingerie.*
Third floor: *men's wear, shoes and accessories.*
Fourth floor: *bedding, linens and household items.*
Fifth floor: *home and patio furnishings and tools.*
Sixth floor: *home furniture...*"

On and on she prattles. I am completely amazed at how in the world she remembers what is where, as she tells everyone about "Simpson's'" many and varied offerings!

Up, up we go, all the way to our stop, which is on the eighth floor, at the very zenith of the overwhelming building.

"Top floor: *Arcadian Court, [48], Ladies and Gentlemen,* please *enjoy your dining experience!*"

We step out and, with another *hissss*, the doors close behind us, startling me a little. "*Beautiful!*" What I am now staring at is so lovely I really have to wonder where exactly we have ended up. Might this be "Heaven", where "Gerda" told me "God" lives? I soon discover it isn't "Heaven", but mighty close to it! We are actually facing the entrance to a stunning and extremely classy restaurant, (yes, certainly, *almost* "Heaven", I am thinking). Apparently, everyone, but me, knows what my foster mother is explaining to me, "Teddy, this is one of Toronto's most exclusive and ritzy dining places!" I am not sure about everybody else, but I, for one, certainly plan to do as Elsie suggested, "*enjoy my dining experience!*"

Another woman in a navy skirt-suit, and white gloves, escorts us to a nicely detailed table in a room full of straight rows hosting a multitude of the same. The beauty of this dining room, with its seemingly unending mirrored walls, which reach from the floor, all the way up to the ceiling, and capped in arches, completely overwhelms me. [48] My latest foster mother continues to explain, "This is one of the most famous department store restaurants in the entire world." [48] My goodness, I certainly can believe it!

Gosh, "Gerda" knows about some very nice places to go to in this big city and I am a lucky little boy to share these experiences with her. Before long, approaching our table, is a woman in a starched white, belted dress, with a funny little white cap perched precariously at the very front of her head. I am a little apprehensive, in case she is a nurse, but then I notice she is bringing "Gerda" the small plate of lunch she ordered. It consists of four club-sandwich triangles, each standing upright and daintily held together by a toothpick with colourful, blue plastic fringe on one end. I am having chicken noodle soup, which "Gerda" is to spoon-feed me with an over-size round spoon—minus the fringe. Yummy! The soup is delicious, although quite messy and drippy. It's then I figure out the intended purpose of the accompanying little square crackers—they're for sopping-up the soup.

Soon, we have finished our meal and are taking another tummy-floating ride down in the gilded cage. However, just as we stop, right before we exit, "Elsie" gives me a little candy-cane and wishes me an especially "Merry Christmas". Wow, this is wonderful—what a super great time I am having!

"Gerda" smiles at me. On our way walking to the front door, she stops and quickly purchases some navy-blue cotton gloves to match her coat, mentioning to the Clerk, "No—no bag, thank you, I'll just wear them out.", (and she does).

When we step back outside, away from the warmth and lights of the massive store, we are once again standing in the freezing cold. Although it's only four o'clock, it has already turned dark outside.

Fresh snow is blowing wildly, yet refreshingly over the dirty, brown-grey slush covering the streets, which have already begun to ice-over. Despite the freezing temperature, I really don't want to go home yet. I just don't want this day to end. Then, as if to read my thoughts, I realize we aren't leave the storefront quite yet. My new foster mother has something else to show me now. We join a crowd of children and adults standing around and watching something in the lighted window-display insets on each wall, either side of the stores main corner doors.

Then my newest "foster mother" lifts me up high so I am able to see some of the best and most amazing things I've ever witnessed! Everyone is looking at a *living* picture of "SANTA'S WORKSHOP", complete with the old Elf trying to read the evening paper, but he can't find his gold-framed spectacles. Hee, hee, hee! It's so funny because he has forgotten his reading glasses are stuck up on top of his head! There are many elves with little hammers making toys, and a miniature train rattling down a track, carrying the toys through a big tunnel which somebody blasted out of the mountain.

Mrs. Claus is bending down and handing Santa some hot cocoa as he rocks forward with outstretched arm, in order to grasp it. Outside Santa's house, the reindeer, including "Rudolph", [61], are intermittently lowering their heads to eat some straw, or lifting them up and looking around from side-to-side! Everything in each of the large windows is animated and seems full of life. And the colourful little scenarios are accompanied by the Christmas music being loudly blasted out into the streets!

I can't believe my own eyes, and I am very grateful "Gerda" likes me enough to show me all of these wondrous things today. However, right now, I Am quite tired and a little overwhelmed from meeting the Big Guy! I *really* hate how I forgot to ask *him*, of all people, for my mommy to take me home forever, or, well, at least for Christmas. Nevertheless, I did forget, and I think it might have been my last, best hope for my dream to come true. Anyway, "Gerda" isn't so bad—at least she doesn't scream at me or hit me, and my bum sores are definitely getting better!

As she is tucking me into bed, after my prayers of course, I smile at her, thankfully, for taking me to "Simpson's" today. I am indeed a very lucky child. Now all we have to do is wait and see if Santa stays true to his word and pops down the fireplace chimney with a wooden doggie on wheels—for me! (Wait a minute... "Gerda" doesn't have a *fireplace*...oh well, I'll let Santa figure it out...after all he *is* the Elf with the magic fairy dust, right!?)

More cold, snowy, blustery winter days and nights come and go outside of my apartment window. "Jack Frost" [51], has made the most incredibly stunning, fern-like ice-patterns on all of the glass panes. Oddly enough, the frost is on the inside...you can even scrape it off with your fingernail. I am amazed and am suspended in wonderment as to how this newest fairy gets inside this apartment and paints my window with ice! Oh well, it doesn't matter so much now because I actually have something else to think about today. Correct! It's *Christmas Eve*, which means tomorrow morning I will discover if Santa is all he's cracked-up to be! Will *it* be there? Will my little doggie be there under the tree?

I don't know *how* I am going to sleep tonight! But my "foster mother" just takes me through all our usual nighttime rituals, and after my prayers are said, then it's under the covers for this little guy. I tell "Gerda", "Nite, nite.", and she responds with,

"Nite, nite, sleep tight; *don't let the bed-bugs bite!*" [62]

"Aaaayyyeee!" I scream under my breath. Oh my gosh, I absolutely HATE that nasty rhyme! (Because I happen to *know* for a fact, bedbugs *do* bite—and bite hard!) If only she knew, I'm sure she would never say it to me again, but, of course, I can't tell her about my personal experience with bedbugs. I guess I'll just have to put up with the rhyme, at least until I'm moved out of this apartment and taken on to the next "foster" place.

I am awake so early on Christmas morning, I almost believe I did not even go to sleep! I tiptoe to the living room with my eyes tightly shut! Then I peek...a little...then a lot! There is a bright-red, gift-wrapped package under the tree and it has Santa's face all over the paper. There is also a wide red ribbon around it and the elves have tied off neatly at the top with a big red bow. "Is it for me? Is it for me?" I babble and stammer! "Look here, Teddy, this is from Santa Claus for you—it says so right here on the little tag!" "Gerda" fairly erupts with excitement *for me*.

"Here, dear, open it, go ahead and tear it open!" So I do! Oh my—it really is the wooden doggie I asked of Santa! I am so excited and overwhelmed. I don't know whether to laugh or cry...so I cry. "Teddy, what's wrong, isn't it what you wanted?"

"Gerda" asks with a look of disappointment. Yes, of course it is—it *is* the toy I've wanted ever since that brat Joey had one, and wouldn't share it with me. I am happy, and satisfied knowing Santa is *real*, and, I don't know *how*, but he *found me* at "Gerda's" apartment.** There's nothing more I could ask of life right now, except of course, the usual—*my own mommy*. I am, however, just a little regretful I forgot to ask Santa for **my mommy**, because, well, what if he could *really* have brought her to take me home? Nevertheless, I can't dwell on that right now—it's time to play with my new pet! I think I'll name him, "Pom Pom"--and why not?

**(What I will figure-out in years to come is that it was "Gerda's"
decision to hang the Christmas lights around the living room window, which clearly directed Santa's reindeer to our apartment, where prior to my stay, no other child had ever lived at Christmastime.)

"Gerda" explained to me, since today is Christmas Day, it's important for us to "share our blessings" with the lonely old neighbour lady named "Ruth", in apartment "B", and also with the one who is much younger but, I think, equally as lonely, called, "Linda", in suite "A". By "sharing", I mean, "Gerda" says she has invited them over so we may all enjoy a "togetherness" celebration buffet of turkey, stuffing, mashed potatoes and carrots. I must say incidentally, this "mother" is quite a good cook because she prepares everything with a "pinch of love", (which must be the special, secret ingredient she is always talking about).

Ruth brings along a big, deep-dish, Dutch-apple pie with steam escaping from the fork marks in the top pastry crust, and one of my favourites, white ice cream. Linda brings rolls, pickles, tomato juice, Brussels sprouts and sweet potatoes! A "buffet"--indeed, it's a feast, and with all the chatting, it takes two hours for us all to eat through it!

"Linda" brought *me* a gift also. It's a little red fire-truck, with a real-sounding horn! "Honk! Honk! Honk!" I am off to fight fires and walk doggies. However, before I do, "Ruth" says, "Teddy, dear, I also brought you a little gift. It's just a little boo though." Then she adds, "But sometimes very good things can come in tiny packages!" Well, let's just have a look-see inside the green tinfoil gift-wrap. I rip and tear it off to reveal a little book; but when you open it up, it's full of rolls of different flavoured "Lifesavers" candies. "Ruth" blurts out, "Teddy, dear, it's a 'Lifesavers Christmas Sweet Story Book'!" [58] I open it up with great delight to see not only a cute little story book about Santa eating Lifesavers, but also several rolls of the delicious little hard candies with the centres missing. Then "Gerda" passes them around and everyone tries one of their favourite flavours—after which, the remainder are all mine! (I'm just wondering where all the *centres* went.)

Several more days have been waxing and waning until today's arrival. I can't believe Santa came an entire week ago and now I will have to wait another *whole year* before I am able to ask him to bring "my mommy". Nevertheless, here it is already "New Year's Eve". Although there will be no skyward visitors bearing gifts, it seems equally as special a day for the adults, as "Christmas Eve" is for us kids. It *must be* a pretty big deal because the apartment neighbours are all out chatting in the hallway about it being, "*New Year's*" and, "*What are **you** doing?*" and "*Where are **you** going?*" I don't get it, but because it seems to be so important to her, "Gerda" has arranged to have the widow-lady, "Mrs. Smith", in apartment "D", to come in here and baby-sit me tonight.

"Gerda" is going to a big party called a *dance* and I can tell it's some big "to-do" because she's dressing in her finery. She bought a brand new, knee-length dress with a little peplum waist-flair over a full-skirt. It has such dramatically padded shoulders, it makes *her own* waist seem almost miniscule! The dress designer created the entire ensemble from a shimmery golden material which swishes and moves from side to side with Gerda's every step. [52] My "mother" is also wearing jewellery consisting of earrings, with a matching necklace and bracelet. Though modestly designed, I've never seen her adorn herself in anything like these, before today.

Oh, my! "Gerda" is also wearing makeup, including bright, Elizabeth Arden Red lipstick, [53], which she purchased at the salon this morning. I hardly knew her when she returned from the stylist's with her formerly ordinary-looking hair, fashioned in the latest, unmistakable, "Joan Crawford" style, [54], (sort-of a severely backswept up-do, with curls in the back). Frankly, as long as I've known "Gerda", which is all of thirty-one days, I've never seen her looking so beautiful, and so much like the "Movie Stars" in the magazines on her coffee table, (the ones I am *never* supposed to touch—but I do anyway).

"Mrs. Smith", (I think that happens to be her *only* name), and I have a nice, quiet evening. She spends her time knitting what appears to be a winter scarf for a very big man, and I am just playing quietly with "Pom Pom". Before long, my bedtime rolls around and, she too, knows about the nighttime prayer. She tucks me in warmly and hums a little lullaby I've heard my own mommy sing a very long time ago. After she turns out the light, she leans down to kiss my forehead and says—no, no, please don't say it, Mrs. Smith, please don't—"*Nite, nite, sleep tight, don't let the...*" I close my eyes and cover my ears so as not to hear what I know comes next! "...*ugs bite!*" [62] Oh, why do all adults, except my "real" mommy, say that horrible, awful rhyme? How is it reassuring to a child in any way, shape or form? It makes me dream of my own remembered nightmares of real bed-bugs snacking on me at night!

Revolving Doors

Well, it's the morning of "New Year's Day" in 1949, and I'm up early as usual, but "Gerda" is sleeping-in, which is most *unusual*. I play quietly until later on when she has had her morning coffee. However, instead of playing with me, she is stuck on the telephone rattling incessantly to her girlfriend, "Nancy", about what a wonderful time she had the night before, at the dance. After "Nancy" makes her excuses for an exit, "Gerda" gets on the phone nattering to her other sister, "Vera" who lives a very, very long-distance away, in another country called, "The States". "Gerda" is telling "Vera" about some man—some "old high-school boyfriend" she had not seen in years, but with whom she "*danced the whole night away*". My, how she is chattering on and on about him, and "how well they got along, blah, blah, blah"!

I am just wondering what today will have in store for "Gerda" and me, when, the buzzer announces someone's arrival. "Mother" looks out the window and, recognizing the visitor, she quickly primps before the mirror before pressing the buzzer to allow him entry to the building. A man is coming down the hall and when she looks out her door, he says, "Mornin' *Greta*! (He is silly. Her name's not "Greta"--it's "Gerda"!) "Tee, hee, hee", she is giggling like a little school girl, then turns to me and says, "Teddy, this is my very special friend, Robert. He thinks I look like Greta Garbo, the movie star!" [55] Then the adults loudly laugh in unison.

"Hello there, Teddy-boy, nice to meet you!" He says the words, not looking at me, but as he is leaning-in to kiss "Greta" on the lips! Yikes! That is nasty! "Teddy-boy" is my *teddy bear's* name! I creep across the floor in the completely opposite direction to, "Mr-Thinks-He's-Robert-Taylor-but-he's-NOT"! [56] "Garbo" [55] and "Taylor" spend the whole day together, flirting, reminiscing, and eating and did I mention *flirting*?

Several more days of the same activities by the adults in this apartment and, frankly, I am a little nauseated by it all. "Gerda" seems to be paying less and less attention to me and it has gotten to the point, she is even been *forgetting to change my diaper.* In fact, I am starting to get more painful diaper rash sores and those nasty, excruciating, liquid-filled pustules again. Everything seems to be changing since this man has been coming around. This "mother" used to read to me, but she has no time for those types of family activities with me now. Her every waking moment is spent either preparing to see her new/old man...seeing him...or talking about seeing him, the *morning after the night before.*

Last night, "Gerda" called her sister, "Frieda", who is also a very long distance away in another country called "Germany". She just *had* to tell her, "Frieda, I'm absolutely *in love*! We are in love with each other, and he has asked me to marry him! Frieda—do you believe this is happening?" Apparently, "Frieda" is just as surprised as I am to hear "Gerda" is getting married, *at her age*, (which is probably at least forty—ancient—ooh, yuck!). Anyway, now "Gerda" is busy every waking moment making the hurried plans for their soon-to-be nuptials. I guess I am happy for her; however, I can't really say how this will affect her ability to care for me. We will see.

Today is January 6, 1949, and I am about sixteen-and-a-half months old now. I can move around the apartment quickly because I've been getting stronger and healthier with each passing day in "Gerda's" care. I've decided I am glad she has someone to love her. I know how it feels. After all, she has been that someone in my life who has given me, well, kindness, and a sort-of love, even though I am only fostered and not her child by birth. We haven't had much time with each other since she met "*Robert*" the other night at the dance party, which was only six days ago. Nevertheless, I'm sure we'll soon get back to our routine of going to the library, the park and, of course, to "Simpson's".

Revolving Doors

Just now, "Robert" has dropped in, unexpectedly, and he and "Greta" are having some sort of angry discussion about—well—about *me*. "Robert" says, "The boy has to go!" "Go"--go where, I wonder. To his repeated demands, "Gerda" is saying, "No, Robert, I can't." But after their arguing becomes quite heated, "Gerda" gives in to him. "Alright, honey, I'll call the Director next week." "Go", where would I be going? However, "Robert" is not satisfied with this suggestion, "Gerda, dear, I want you to call them right now! We need to take care of this immediately!" Although she tries to reason with him, he'll accept none of her suggestions.

"O.K. honey, hand me the phone, there, will you?" she says.

"Go!" What the heck is going on? I have but a minute to question what is happening when "Gerda" dials the phone and is calling the "C.A.S.". "Hello... Miss...?" (She is talking to "Library Lady"...Oh, no...nooooo, not again!) Then I hear her say something, which I know for a fact to be an out-and-out lie. "He has to go because I just can't *take* to him!" (Whaaaat? She "takes" to me just fine! Really, we are friends.) Then I hear, "I understand what you are saying, but I absolutely can't give the boy what he needs because, as I said, I can't *take* to him!"

There it is—she said it again. What does "take to [me]" mean, exactly? She never mentioned "Robert", or the wedding plans; she just blamed it all on me. Well, I don't want to be with her, either! So—where is my "LOBLAWS", [17], sack? I am ready to get out of this place. In all honesty, though, I am very sad, because I really hoped and believed this time was going to be my *last move*, before my mommy could finally take me home with her.

Revolving Doors

"*Sweep, sweep, sweep...*"--here comes the invisible revolving door again!

A few hours later, I am dressed neatly and sitting on the Chesterfield by the front door, where my paper sack of belongings is already waiting. When the buzzer sounds, she looks out, buzzes back and in comes "Mrs. Mousey" whom I am almost glad to see. My eyes implore, "Take me away from here—take me somewhere I'll be loved, or at least, sort-of *wanted*. Please, please..." My Case Worker picks me up, along with my bag, and smiling, says, "Teddy—my goodness, you have put on some weight, dear! How wonderful, son."

"Greta Garbo", [55], and "Robert Taylor", [56], are standing, arm-in-arm, just smiling and waving good-bye to me, as if it were the contrived happy ending of some great flick they'd just finish acting in. Well, I hope they're happy—no, I don't! {I am being facetious again}. Nonetheless, I refuse to let "Gerda" see me cry, so I must cry on the inside, (a skill which I am beginning to perfect.). Anyway, I don't wave back. In fact, I can't even *look* back because I don't want to see the face of another foster mother who *no longer wants me* around. I find it very depressing not only being unloved, but also—unwanted.

Chapter 25: I BOUNCE... (Right Back)!

Today the "Mouse Lady" has come to pick me up in her husband's big Buick, only this time *he* is doing the driving. (I am guessing from the big dent on the front passenger-side panel, that her husband will be handling the vehicle from now on.) Anyway, without a word, my Case Worker deposits me between them on the front car seat and we drive off. (I find it very weird how my "Worker" and her husband look so much alike. He seems very mouse-like himself and he never utters a sound all the time I am in the car.)

"Mousey" is trying to soothe me right now, because she thinks my fussing is just my nervousness about her *husband* driving us around. That's not it—I am fussing because I am feeling scared about what might await me around the next corner of my life. I decide I don't really care anymore where I live or who looks after me. It only matters to me whether or not the next foster parent is mean, or belts me, or leaves me in diapers so long I get bum sores all over again! That's what is really concerning me right now.

Once we are back at the "C.A.S." building, we enter the "Wart's" office and await the next directions for my life's journey. "Mouse" comments to the "Director", "I think you'll find Teddy seems very much improved by the environment at this last foster placement." Then, watching me, "Mousey" exclaims, "Oh, now look at him!" (I betcha I'm impressing them both right now, because they see I'm able to sit up without falling over! Ha! Watch this! Now I'm showing off my creeping/crawling skills and I'm really speeding around on my hands and knees in "Wart's" office!)

Then comes the bad news. The "C.A.S." Director tells my Worker, "There won't be another place available for the child for at least three weeks." Three weeks—that's *forever* if I have to spend it at the orphan asylum! But then the Director makes a couple phone calls and now tells my Case Worker to take me over to the residence building. (Oh nooo! Not the orphanage again!) Nevertheless, I have *no* say whatsoever in expressing my own feelings about bouncing right back into the asylum! However, considering the fact it would be less than a month, once again, I am not counting this as another actual "residential move".

PART V: All Hope is Gone

Chapter 26: Permanent Wardship

Today is February 1, 1949 and the Court held another hearing for consideration of establishing my status as a "Permanent Ward of the Southwest York County Children's Aid Society". This occurred as a result of my mommy not being able to keep up with her promised commitment of twenty-dollar per month payments for my maintenance. (They just don't understand my mommy, or know her as I do.) The judge determined my maintenance is *now*, and for the duration of my imprisonment, I mean *care*, the *responsibility* of the *"C.A.S." system*. Anyway, all of this was accomplished in an hour in the courtroom and my mommy was just not there, because either she had something else to do, or else, they never notified her about the court meeting. (Maybe she didn't have enough money for the bus.) Well it's a done deal now, so no use fretting over the consequences of the judge's decision, because no matter how much my mommy might beg him, his decision won't be changed.

[This move to Permanent Wardship removed all responsibility for Teddy's care from his birth mother, "Berneice". The "C.A.S'" main goal now was now to keep Teddy's time in "Foster Care" as short as possible, and find him a permanent home, through a*doption*. The motive is unclear, however, this would soon ensure Teddy's never being able to return home with his mother and in effect, ending their relationship—forever. This was a result Berneice never foresaw, as she clearly, repeatedly insisted she eventually planned to remove her son from the "C.A.S." and take him ***home***.] [160]

Certainly, no matter to whom they all say I belong now, day and night I do still dream my real mother might sweep me up in her loving arms, and carry me away to a perfect life full of love and happiness. I pray she still wants me and needs me as much as I desperately need her.

However, day after day she doesn't come. (Of course what I could not know right now is, on this very day, the responsibility for my care is now permanently assigned to, and I have been made a "Permanent Ward" of, this Children's Aid Society. This means my hopes of mommy and me going off hand-in-hand to our own home are now scattered to the wind. I wonder if she feels the way I do. I wonder if she even knows what has happened here today. I very much doubt she knows.)

Chapter 27: "NIRVANA" [63]

"I'm certain I can make it work, this time around—I just know it!"

After a couple more miserable weeks stuck in the toddler ward with a bunch of screaming brats, I am ready for my next placement to be just about *anywhere*! I had only been here at the asylum for three days and I already caught the "Brown Kites" from one of the other children sharing the same stale, disease-filled air as me! I hope this doesn't mean I will miss-out on being moved as soon as an opening becomes available! (Gosh, I am so sick of the rigid routines, and the hurried, harried nurses' diaper-pin sticks.)

Well, here we go again. Today it's "Big Ears" who is picking me up, along with my little brown paper sack, which contains the few belongings which follow me from one foster residence to the next. "Well, hello again little guy! Are you doin' alright? We are going to take a nice big bus ride today, all the way across town to your new home. It'll be great fun, you'll see, there, Teddy." "Ears" picks up his instruction note from "Wart", and we are off on a big new adventure. (I don't care where this latest escapade takes me, at least I am out of the whiny little baby-brat's ward!)

We soon jump onto the steps of the second bus, which arrives at this place called a bus stop. As soon as we are seated, (with me right next to the window, of course), "Ears" reaches into his hugely over-sized coat pocket and retrieves a miniature red and white striped candy cane in a plastic wrapper. Wow! It's exactly like the one which, "Elsie" the "SIMPSON'S Elevator Operator", had given me at the end of our ride down from the Arcadian Court, [48]. Where does everybody get these delectable little peppermint sticks? I would certainly like to know! "Here Teddy" he whispers into my ear, "I brought this for you from my home." (I think it's pretty darn nice of him—so I babble my best, "Thank-you, Mr. 'Big Ears', thank-you!") Yummy, it's delicious and I think it's actually soothing my coughing too.

We move to the front of the bus and my escort inquires as to where to get off to find, "Such-and-Such-a-Street", and the driver assures "Ears" he'll alert us when we arrive at our destination. After riding around on this great people-carrier for the longest time, I've been in the same position for so long, my bum has gone to sleep! Ooooh, I don't like this strange tingly sensation. Then, thankfully, "Here you go, sir—here's your stop coming up.", "Mister-the-Bus-Driver" announces. Then "Ears" thanks him politely and we disembark.

We are standing in front of some sort of low-income housing complex, which consists of a long, low building with one residence directly attached to the side of the next, and no grassy spaces in-between them like real houses have. I am just surveying the area when I notice a handful of children playing in a large communal play-yard. Four of the kids are having lots of fun with toy cars, shovels and pails in a very large sandbox, but another one is crying and rubbing his eyes, (adding more to the sand already in them). I wish I could play in there. I tug on this man's coat and point, to inform him of my desire to go with the others and jump in the expansive wooden sandbox.

However, he is ignoring me and just walking along the sidewalk in front of the apartment-house entrances, while he re-checks the correct address from his instruction note. Finally, he turns in and takes us up the few steps to a door. Before anyone answers the door, I can hear some music playing, and it's coming through the adjacent window, which is open about an inch or two. I recognize the tune and recall it as one which is actually a nursery rhyme my sweet mommy used to read and sing to me all the time. As well, coming through the window is the smell of something I think must taste quite yummy.

"Big Ears'" second knock is quickly answered by the woman who is about to become my next "foster mother". This woman is petite, like my mommy, and has brown hair and hazel eyes, also just like my precious mommy. "Hello!" she bubbles, "C'mon in here you two before you freeze out there!" While they make their introductions, I notice this young woman is very pleasant to look at, and is wearing a bright and happy, white-and-pink flowered dress with a puffy, full skirt. She also has a plain apron in a matching pink tone, tied in a big bow in the back. "Excuse the kitchen—I'm doing a little baking for Teddy." the lady says. How nice—baking for me! Is she serious or is she just saying that only to impress "Mr. Big Ears" because she thinks he is a Case Worker?

Shortly, my escort *passes the torch*, handing my grocery bag of stuff and me, over to my newest "foster mother". "Won't you stay for some tea, and fresh-baked butter tarts, 'Mr'...?" However, he makes his excuses and a hasty exit, and here I am once again facing my prospective "foster mother" and "foster home". "Butter tarts" –I am not exactly sure what they *are*, but they sound, and smell, yummy! I suppose it can't hurt if I try just one.

"Sit down here at the table Teddy and we'll get you unpacked and organized. Here's a glass of milk and a tart, but be careful because they're kind of hot right now." I observe as this young woman fusses over me and flits around me like a big bug. While I await her cutting my tart in half, I can't help but wonder if she'll abuse me, hurt me or beat me. Is it possible she'll be kind to me and even put bum cream on my diaper sores? On the other hand, will she, dare I even think it, *love me*? I am pondering these issues while facing this latest term of fostering incarceration which will be my *eleventh* residential move and my *ninth* fostering placement.

"Let's have a look here, Teddy, and see what you might need right now." She hangs my coat on a high-up hook along with several others. Then she takes my bag, and me, into the room where I'll be staying, (for who knows how long this time). "This is your little bed over here, Teddy." she indicates pointing to my newest accommodation. Although it's of a poorer standard than a mattress/box spring bed, it's of much better quality than the canvas cot I shared with "Big Boy". "O.K., that'll be fine." I babble and smile. "Oh, I'm glad you like it" she responds. What is this? Could it be she understands what I am saying? No way! I think maybe I'll just test her out. "Say, lady–(I haven't got a good nickname for her yet)--how about a nice snack, maybe some ice cream?" Then, reaching something down from the kitchen cupboard she turns and asks, "Teddy, do you want a bite to eat?" (Wow! That was easy.) "Yes, yes, yes." She "gets it"--I think she "gets me"!

I wonder what other little kids might live in this house? From the hung-up jackets by the door, I would guess they're boys. In the bedroom there is a larger bed with drawers all around the bottom and a straight-back wooden chair with larger boy's clothes flung all over it-but no sign of a kid. There is also a baby crib with the side rail in the down position—but no sign of a baby. The woman sets my paper bag of belongings beside my bed on a very small nightstand with a lamp on it shaped like a ship's wheel.

The fun music is still playing on a little radio in the kitchen and this new "mother" is humming along. I like it—I really like this happy, singing woman. I've decided to name her, "Songbird". Yes, that's a perfect name for her. After my milk and butter tart snack, just a little time has passed for us to begin to know each other. Quite suddenly, her door flies open and in walks a *very big* man who is carrying a small baby, about three months old. I guess from his head-to-toe blue garments, this little kid is a boy, and not a pinkie, girly-girl. Following quietly and sombrely behind this man and baby is a big kid, around eleven, or twelve-years-old.

"Teddy, this is my *husband, and...*", but the man cuts her off mid-sentence, rudely insisting, *"I'm your EX-HUSBAND!" "I'm her 'EX-EX-HUSBAND'! I'm her EX!"* (As if I really give a hoot who he is!) What do I care? So I just tell him, "Good-bye Mr. EX-whoever you are!" Despite my babble, he got my message and without another word, turned-tail and rushed out of the squeaky kitchen door allowing it to slam, with an attitude, behind him.

"Teddy, this is my son, Daniel and my baby boy, Evan. You will be sharing their bedroom. "Daniel" steps forward and gives me a nuggie, messing my hair with his knuckles. "Hey, there, kid...you're gonna like it here." (That's encouraging, I think.) Of course, "Evan" doesn't *do* anything. He just stays asleep, which is something I'll soon discover he is good at and enjoys doing very, very much. "Teddy, why don't we all go out on the swings?" Is she talking to me? "Swings, Teddy?" she suggests again. "Yes, yes!" I kick my legs as if I were running to the door like the good little puppy I am. "Danny, are you coming outside?" A grumbling, "Naaaaww..." is heard emanating from our bedroom.

The way things have been going with my foster placements, I was certain this was going to be a *terrible* foster home for me, but this nice lady isn't showing any sign of being mean or neglectful—yet. (Maybe I just haven't been here long enough. We'll see.) So far, so good. I can't believe this "foster mother" is pushing me on the swings! This is fun, and it doesn't end there. Next stop on our rounds of the playground equipment is what she says Danny calls the "Get-Sick-Quick". It is a round wooden platform with four metal railing handles, which the bigger kids hang onto while they make the platform spin around and around, trying to make each other take-off flying. "Yikes, stop-it, stop-it, I want to get off!" As soon as "Songbird" notices my discomfort, she grabs one of the railings to stop the ride for me. Goodness is she ever strong.

Anyway, overall, I've enjoyed a sweet day of swinging, sliding, (on the baby slide), and sand-box-castle-building. Now my day is wrapping up rather nicely with a warm bath shared with both of my old friends, "Lucky" and "Ducky" and I can assure you a great time is being enjoyed by all three of us. Then, some warm milk and three or four banana coins, and I am off to bed, with the foster "mother" tucking me in tightly. What! No "Bed-bugs" rhyme and, no "prayers" at this house? I suppose I will just have to wait and see if either the bed bugs bite me, or if God "takes my soul" tonight—or not.

The warm morning sunrays wash my face. Once awake, I'm happily aware that I did not go to "Heaven" in the night. Instead, I spent my sleep-time in another dream of mommy and me, only this time we were romping around on my newest playground equipment. I love being with my mommy in my dreams, and oh, what a wonderful night we had. We were drinking hot chocolate with big, fat, floating marshmallows and we are going higher and higher on the swings, all at the same time! Mommy is always so beautiful and, in my dreams, she tells me repeatedly she loves me, *"very, very much"*. I only wish I never had to wake up, ever again. Back and forth, back and forth... "Higher, mommy—way, way higher, pweeeeese!"

Oh, but I am awake now, and am surveying my newest bedroom. Daniel is still dead asleep and looks so funny with one leg hanging all the way off his bed. Anyway, I try to be very quiet while I glance around. Hmmm...I don't see the baby anywhere. Immediately I sense that I am thirsty, hungry and very wet. "Mrs...!" "Lady...!" "Songbird...!" I babble. She rushes in to get me and is going on about, "Did [I] have a nice sleep?", and "Poor little guy...all wet...", and all these words of concern while she cleans up my bum and puts me in a clean, yellow, one-piece, terrycloth sleeper, with the trap-door bum fasteners and the feet attached.

Once all of my immediate needs have been satisfied, I am *ready to play*. "Where's 'Pom Pom'?" comes out sounding like, "Eeewahz, ppp ppp ppp?" The "mother" leans down to me on the floor and asks, "Are you looking for your little wooden puppy?" Wow, she's good! Besides understanding my babble, she amazes me because she always knows where everything is located. I've decided she'll be quite handy to have around. I must strive to obey and not make any trouble! Therefore, I creep around the house, check out all the nooks and crannies and eat things lying around on the floor. Mmmmm...it's a good day, I found some not too yucky, ABC candy!

"Doo dee, diddly dumm, dee dee, doo dee, diddly dumm dee dee..." I know this song! Our "mother" is always playing music, which is familiar to me. It's not so bad here, really. The only bad part is happening within me! I've been growing new teeth, and they're painfully erupting right through my gums. My goodness they hurt so much too. The "mother" helps me a little by massaging my sore gums with something smelly, stinky and burning hot liquid, which comes from a big brown bottle with a tall neck. [I can't read, but if I could I would be reading, "CANADIAN CLUB WHISKEY" [64], on the bottle's shiny label.] Oh, yes, when the burning sensation stops my gums feel much better. Now I can go back to playing with my toy doggie. "Let's go for a walk, 'Pom Pom'...c'mon now..." I pull him all around the house by his string leash.

Daniel is nice to me and appears to enjoy taking me outside to the playground. Although he seems to spend a lot of time with me out there, his real reason for getting out of the house is to meet up with some of his friends, both boys and girls. These kids all talk amongst themselves in a funny lingo. It isn't Pig-Latin, nevertheless it *is* some sort of made-up, secret language and, for the life of me, I can't decipher it. No matter, I am having fun in the sandbox right now and I could care less what they're talking about in secret. In fact, I could care even less about the fact the kids all sneak around back of the apartment garbage cans and stealthily puff away on their smokes. Heck, who cares! You will never see me doing anything to make this new "mother" unhappy, or mad, because I know how it feels to live in a worse place, under the tyrannical domination of a much worse "mother"! "*Dumm, dee dumm dumm....wawawa...I'm a-singin' my little dittie...dee dee, and a-stayin' outta twouble...dee dumm dumm...*"

Today "Songbird" has been very busy cutting-out and hanging-up a whole bunch of red and pink hearts all over the house— many of them in the windows. She informs me she is doing this because it's a very special day. She calls it, "Saint Valentine's Day and explains it's a day for people to show how much love they have for the other people in their lives. While the kitchen music plays joyfully, it's my job to hand the "mother" each of the hearts so she can stick them up. This is great fun and we are certainly making the house look even more inviting and appealing than usual.

Daniel, who has been busy hogging the bathroom, has made himself very handsome, indeed. In fact, just now, as he is heading out the door, I tell him in my clearest babble, "You are looking more dapper than I've ever seen you.", but he seems to be ignoring me. "What's up?" I'm wondering. Then, as if he read my mind, he leans down and confesses in my ear, "There is this really pretty girl named Cindy who I like very much and I'm taking her to a dance tonight." Then he shows me his school-dance invitation ticket, which is also red and heart-shaped. (Frankly, I don't get it. I know I love my real mommy and will gladly give her every heart in this whole house, including mine. However, I certainly won't give my precious heart to anyone else, especially some icky girl!) Wait a minute—did he say, "dance"   --I hope he is not getting married too!

Ooooh...my gums hurt so much today. I guess another tooth is poking through, or at least that's how the "mother" explains it to me. She knows I need some comfort, but she is so busy getting the house straightened up, she becomes sidetracked and forgets my tooth-cutting pain *medicine*. Apparently, someone special is supposedly coming over here today. "Here, Teddy, let me fix your sore gums, dear." Oh, *finally* she remembers me and rubs some whiskey into my sore, raw gums. Before I know it, I am quite sleepy though it's not even bedtime. However, then, I am alerted to a, "tap, tap, tap" sound, at the front door. Oh, that's interesting, it's "Library Lady". It's alright, because she doesn't bother me anymore.

"Hello Mrs..." "Yes, hello, 'Mrs.'...won't you come on in, please." "L.L." steps inside this modest row house and, quickly glancing around in order to assess the environment, says, "What a nice home you have here." I would have to agree. "How's *our* little Teddy doing?" "Well, see for yourself!" she replies, then shouts, "Te—d-dy, dea-r, come in here and see 'Mrs...'" I creep down the hall and into the living room and see her familiar face. "He's about seventeen months, now, am I right?" "L.L." asks. "My, but he seems to be coming along very nicely now."

I climb up on the "mother's lap and snuggle up under her chin like a kitty-cat. Then, much to the surprise of the grown-ups, I decide to show off some newly acquired, and secretly practised, skills. I slide down and grab onto the side of the coffee table. Then I move along grasping one safe and sturdy piece of furniture after another. Of course, I am not yet ready to let go and walk unaided—but it will all come, in good time, which is something I am certain I will have a lot of here in this house--"good time". I am confident this foster "mother" is quite satisfactorily meeting my personal needs; however, I could care less that the Worker is writing a note, which reads, "*Teddy is* not *kept as clean as he might be, but he receives good care.*" (Who cares how clean she keeps me? At least I don't have any more bum sores.)

My Social Worker actually looks into my mouth and counts how many teeth have been bursting through my gums. "One, two...five! How wonderful—keep up the good work, Teddy!" Then she turns to my foster mother and remarks about the, "distinct smell of alcoholic spirits coming from the child's mouth". The "mother" explains the fact I require the assistance of distilled spirits to get me over the teething pains. (Frankly, I could not agree more!) "Oh yes, it's the 'CC'..." she explains, smiling as much as I am, "Well, *that* wou...wou...would be strictly forbidden and we wou...wou...would frown on the usage of distilled spirits on any baby for any re...re...reason." The "Librarian Lady", visibly disturbed, explains *with a stutter,* which I've never heard from her before today. (I guess she's pretty upset about the booze, nonetheless, much to my delight, the "mother" ignores the Social Worker's sage advice. So, booze it is, to numb every newly erupting tooth!)

[Back at the "C.A.S.", the Worker prepares her report to the Director and, glossing over the "booze" problem, remarks,

"There is a great deal of love in this home, and Teddy seems /to thrive on it. He is doing very well scooting around holding onto furniture, but not yet letting go and taking a step on his

own. He does have five teeth and seems happy and contented. The only hint of a problem was when the foster mother explained to me that the little boy doesn't put anything into his mouth'."

(Ha! That's what *they* think.)

Then the report continues, explaining,
"Even when given a cookie, Teddy does not know what to do with it."] (They just don't understand me—I know pl-en-ty, p-l-e-n-t-y! I am just too afraid to try eating things with lots of other little black things sticking out of them. It is my bad past experiences with the rat raisins, you know.) Nevertheless, now they're talking as if it's some sort of a problem for me not to grab *five cookies* whenever someone offers me one! I can play the game, in fact, I can play any game you choose! Just you hide and watch me.

Whew! The interrogation is over and I must have passed the test because the Worker did not take me with her. So, now what? I am determined to be a very good little boy and I won't do anything to get myself into any trouble at this house, ever! So, day-in and day-out, I'm playing, eating, getting cleaned up, picking up toys, then repeat, repeat, repeat. Right now, it's the end of April 1949, and I now have eight teeth! I can stand alone and I can walk all around holding onto the furniture. In fact, I can even take three or four steps all by myself, although I am not yet able to walk without holding on. Often, when the "mother" leaves me alone outside in my playpen, she encourages me to walk around holding onto the slatted sides. I am just not very steady yet.

During another follow-up visit, "Librarian Lady" seems to ask many more questions than during her last inspection. I'm a little concerned because she is make long, wordy notations in her little book, and I *know* all of her notes are entered into my file.

[In fact, this Social Worker's notations include the following comments,

"This foster mother has done a lot in helping Teddy to develop. He gets an abundance of love in this home. Teddy has improved much in this environment, in fact, he doesn't even look like the same child."]

More time passes, one day melding into the next, for me. I am getting bigger and stronger and have not succumbed to any lung attacks lately. Today the "mother" is taking me to see a new doctor in the Newmarket subdivision. "Doctor Urquhart" says I'm "looking great"! I am twenty-one months old now and I weigh twenty-one pounds! Yippee! My bum sores have all healed up and the doctor says I am in "good physical condition". The only bad thing about today's doctor visit is my having to get my second toxoid shots.*** Hey, this calls for some ice cream, "mom"! She reads my mind and agrees with me. So on our way home, we stop off at the little family-operated, corner grocery store and pick up some of the three-flavour kind. This way, everybody in our whole house can pick a favourite flavour! Naturally, I call dibs on the CHOCOLATE!

***[The toxoid shots would be somewhat equivalent to the immunizations for several of the most devastating of childhood illnesses which most Canadian children receive, from infancy until around age five years, or whenever starting kindergarten. At later ages, they're administered as "booster shots".]

It is a very hot day today, even for July, and we have come back from another visit with "Doctor Urquhart". He is quite pleased with my progress because, at twenty-three months, I am running all over the place and he comments, "Teddy is a very handsome little boy!" "Mother" agrees! Then she starts discussing her concerns, "You know, doctor, Teddy is *not* toilet-trained at all." She explains, although she has been "trying to work with [me] on this issue, [she is] only meeting with occasional success". Aw, big deal! I have better things to do than run and squat on the potty all the time.

On my second birthday in August, the foster mom baked a little cake for my brothers and me to enjoy. There was a huge white number "2" on the chocolate-iced, chocolate cake, which had two candles for me to blow out to get my birthday wish granted. For my gift, she gave me a beach ball and a sand-pail-and-shovel set. "Danny" didn't stay very long after he ate his piece of cake, but "Evan" and I didn't care, we just spent the rest of the day out playing in the big sandbox. It was a *great* birthday party, complete with a bunch of balloons, which we were able to pop, laughing our heads off every time!

****

{I could not know this, but approximately around September or October of 1949, when I am about twenty-five to twenty-six months old, my real mother, (at this point married to "Don", Donald Faulconer), became pregnant with my sister, "Dawn". Of course, this pretty much sealed the deal making it impossible for my mommy to come back into my life, rescue me and take me home with her—ever. This unending dream of mine was never going to happen—certainly not now.}

****

Today is October 27, 1949, and I am twenty-six months old now. The "mother" has brought me to the "H. S. C.", (the "Health Sciences Centre"), [65], back at Sunnybrook Hospital. Once again, I am back in the office of old "Dr. Samuels", whom I haven't seen for some time. "Hello there, young man! My goodness, it's been awhile since you have stopped by, and I can see how much you've grown, Teddy!" Yes, of course, because I am more than two years old now. "Dr. Samuels'" nurse, "Cathy", weighed me and announced I am "twenty-six-and-a-half pounds" now!

"How would you rate his development, 'Mrs.'...? Are you having any problems or difficulties with little Teddy?" the doctor asks her. "He's certainly running all over the house. Oh yes, and he's saying words, sometimes putting two words together. He *is* bowel trained but still wets day and night. Oh yes, and he's has very few colds since we last saw you." the foster "mother" offers. "Dr. Samuels" then comments, "Well he certainly has lovely rosy cheeks. Let's have a little look at the boil, you mentioned—on his buttocks, correct?" Then the doctor ordered sulpha ointment to treat the one huge sore on my bum—after he lanced it first—which really hurt, a lot!

I only wish we had left his office right then, because it's what the "mother" said next which started getting me into a completely new mess of trouble. "I wanted to ask you about this new habit Teddy has developed. Whenever things don't please him, he's been banging his head in bed, on the headboard, or on the wall." "Songbird" said. The old gentleman commented, "Well, he's in good physical condition, and I can see no obvious reason for his actions—I mean, no ear infections, or such. Why don't we keep an eye on this new behaviour and come back if it becomes a larger problem?"

Darn her, anyway! Neither you, my so-called "mother", nor the good doctor could possibly understand what I am *trying to shake loose out of my brain*! How could you even guess? You have not lived the horrors I've endured in my short life span. So back off, and leave my head-banging issues for me to deal with by myself!

Today's weather is very, very cold and snowy, and quite

typical of Toronto winters right now. There is an icy, chilled wind rushing off the lake and it slaps your face and grabs your every breath. Unfortunately, the weather is keeping us from playing outside, nonetheless, I am a happy little boy because I know, regardless of the climate, it's almost time for Santa to come again! As far as I am concerned, I've been a very well behaved boy and did not "pout" even once this past year! So yippee, and wowee—Santa's gonna bring me a very nice present, or maybe even two!

Christmastime in "Songbird's" house is a very happy time, indeed. We have all participated in decorating a huge, beautiful, *real* Pine tree which "Songbird", Danny and I dragged home from the "Santa's Village Christmas Tree Lot" where the Boy Scouts are selling them. My big brother then found the ladder and climbed up through the large, square hole, in the hall closet ceiling. The hole opens up into the expansive, dark attic, where "Danny", using a dim flashlight, bravely crawled around in order to search for the previous year's decorations. As he dragged out numerous boxes all labelled, "Xmas", he called down for our mother's help with the biggest ones.

These boxes hold every imaginable sort of tree-and-house, decoration and we are all having great fun sorting through everything! Other than in the department store, I've never seen so many beautiful and colourful things. We have the usual shiny, glass ornaments of every possible colour, and many beautiful tree lights also. I must say, most definitely, Christmas is my favourite time of the whole year! It is even better than my birthday!

Of course, no tree-decorating party would be complete without popcorn, and, we certainly have plenty of that! However, I am curious as to why there is so much more of the delectable, fluffy white snack, until the "mother" brought out her darning needle and some thread. It's then, we all get down to the business of making the "popcorn garland". Nevertheless, I wonder how will we leave it on the tree, and not have it all eaten by the time Santa magically appears in our living room. Perhaps that's the whole idea, maybe we are supposed to enjoy the garland in more ways than *looking at it!* Anyway, right before we are ready to drape the garland, we stretch it out, all the way from the front of the house to the back! My gosh, but this is so much fun—we even have to make a third batch of popcorn in order to finish the tree, tee hee hee.

Then "Danny" shows us all how to use different coloured sheets of construction paper to cut strips and make loops, alternating the colours to fashion the perfect paper garland. My "brother" does the cutting and the fastening, but *I* hand him the paper strips! Then, we string the beautiful garland not just all over the tree, but all around the entire house too. We even loop some around the windows and the doorframes. We are all ready with our Christmas lights around the front windows, *and even the back* ones, just in case. It is starting to look like "Santa's Village" around here, and *I*, for one, thoroughly love it.

Today, we are once again visiting with "Dr. Samuels", who asks, "*Teddy, do you know there are only ten days left until Christmas Eve? Have you given your wish list to Santa yet?*" I nod violently with excitement—I most certainly have! (I was not taking any chances *this* year.) Then he writes something on his clipboard paper which he will later forward to the "C.A.S." Director who will enter it in my file as follows,

"*Teddy is developing nicely now at 28 months. He is a lovely little boy with fair hair and **blue** eyes, quite nice looking. He has completed toxoids, feeds himself. Just recently, his foster mother reports, he has been telling her when he needs to use the toilet in the daytime. He still bed-wets.*"

Then the foster "mother" asks the doctor, "What on earth should I do about his head-banging? He is doing it more and more often now, and with greater force. It gets so bad that sometimes he even gets a knot on the back of his head. Other times he wakes the baby up from his nap. I am feeling very frustrated. Can you suggest anything I should be doing for him?"

My physician responds with, "Well, first of all, if he has a lump come up, just put a cold compress on it. Otherwise, have you noticed what seems to set off one of these episodes? I can't see anything physically responsible for such behaviour. Would you say he's trying to express anger about something, or perhaps—is he frightened—or even bored?"

"Songbird" tells him, "He acts like that when he doesn't get his way about something or sometimes right after he's been disciplined." Then the Doctor asked her how she disciplines me and she explains how spanking me is not permitted, because of the "discipline" abuse in my past. She confesses how she usually ends up "yelling and screaming a lot", or "taking [my] toys away", but beyond that, she said she "can't do anything else to reprimand [me]". This doctor agrees and gives her a little pamphlet suggesting alternative means of discipline, such as the latest idea of, "putting a child in time out". (I think it's what happens when you are sent to bed without your supper...but I can't say for sure.)

After seeing the doctor yesterday, the "mother" is being a lot nicer to me when I am being a little bit bad. Now she puts me in my room and leaves me alone. I can't see how this is very much of a punishment because I really don't mind it. I play with my toys until she says I can come back out into the living room. I am not bad very often, but I do get really angry when baby "Evan" takes, and/or breaks, my toys! It is at those times, when I just can't help myself, I start the bang, bang, banging my head against the floor or the wall. She can't stop me from trying to bang the bad thoughts out of my head! Oh-oh, here she comes. "TEDDY—STOP YOUR DARN BANGING RIGHT NOW!" When she calms down, she thinks of a *better* threat, "You'd better quit it, or else *Santa Claus* will know you are being a bad little boy and all he'll bring you is a lump of coal!"

Since I have no use for the proverbial lump of coal, I am trying to be a much better-behaved boy for the next few days or at least until the "Big Elf" comes on Christmas Eve. I am even trying to share my toys with baby "Evan". Although, I'm keeping my eye on him so I can quickly retrieve my toy from him if he seems as if he is going to break it. The "mother" just poked her head in the bedroom to remind Evan and me, it's only "two sleeps", until Christmas morning. No problem! I have this under control. I am not going to "pout", "cry", or fuss, or bang my head! Then we'll see if Santa rewards me with something special, and by *special* I mean, toy DOGGIES or HORSEYS or even some MOO-COWS!

O.K., so tonight is the big night! It's "Christmas Eve", and the "mother" has bathed us and tucked us into our beds. I am determined NOT to WET my bed tonight, of all nights. (I *know* I can do this.) "Songbird" sang all the Christmas songs to us while we were getting ready for bed. I am *so* excited, I can barely contain myself. However, everyone knows, if you aren't asleep when Santa Claus comes, he won't leave you any gifts. I just need to *pretend* to be asleep, and maybe I'll be able to drift into dreamland for real.

It's just that I can't stop thinking about the long list of toys that I asked Santa to bring me. I want one of those little sets of either a toy "Ranch" with horses and cows, or a toy "Farm" with horses, cows, pigs and sheep, or a toy "Circus" with doggies, horses, lions, tigers, clowns and a funny megaphone-wielding Ringmaster--in a fancy top hat! That's it—my whole list—no wait a minute, I almost forgot I also asked Santa for toy cars, trucks and a pretend Filling Station to drive them up to. I wonder what he'll bring me. I wonder how he gets into the houses. I also wonder how he carries all the toys for all the children in the world. I wonder...I wonder...I... (I am asleep).

Oh my gosh! Finally it's Christmas morning and we kids are tearing the pretty paper wrappings off of all the gifts under our great tree. Santa really *did* come and he actually brought me *three* presents. I got the "Circus" with all the animals and three little 'rings for the performers, and the Ringmaster. Then I opened another package and it was two toy plastic cows and two tiny horses. The third gift was my "Ranch" with pretend grass and trees, fences you can fasten together, a big gate and the ranch house. WOWEE! What a Christmas morning I am having! Danny and Evan got some nice things too, but my stuff was the greatest—and I am off and playing in my little pretend worlds.

The foster mother has been cooking for hours—about the same length of time I've been playing *circus*. The house smells wonderful, mostly because of what appears to be an oversize chicken' in the big oven and beside it, her famous, yummy, delicious cinnamon-apple crisp is hiding in the warming oven. Ooooh! I have such a tummy ache because Ive been eating too many of those truly delectable "Laura Secord Chocolates" [70], which the "Songbird" received from her very good friend, "Mrs...", who lives right next door. They sit and chat on the phone with each other sometimes, but at other times, the woman comes over to our house and has her morning "wake-up" coffee with my foster "mother".

Oddly enough, this woman next door is also a "foster mother", only she is not taking care of any foster children at the moment. Actually, she has a son of her own, "Sid", who is around fifteen and it is about this kid she always seems to be complaining. "Sid did this...", and, "Sid did that...", and, "Sid...blah, blah, blah." I guess he is hard enough to care for—after all, he is so doggone rude to her! You should hear him mouth-off to his mom all the time. Last weekend he dragged his dad's old motorcycle out of the garage. (It was not drivable, so it remained when his father left them a year ago.) Sid "played hooky" from school all week, so he could stay home and work on the cycle. Nonetheless, I often hear his mother yelling at him, "You're NOT gonna ride on that damned thing!" However, you would not believe what he "yells back" at her.

Today, I am having another visit with "Dr. Samuels" but I can hardly believe seven weeks have zipped by since I last saw him. In his office, the nice doctor just takes a quick glance at me, and makes his usual diagnostic notes on his clipboard paper.

[As always, the "C.A.S." later received a transcription of those notes, which reads as follows,

"*Teddy looks well and very lively. He talks well. He is day-trained but still bed-wets. He has fair hair and brown eyes.*" (What? Now, they say my eyes have changed colour from blue to brown. Really—is that even possible?) *The foster mother reports the child is still demonstrating head-banging behaviour, therefore I have ordered some follow-up "Psychometric, [66], testing"**** to determine if there has been any change in his IQ, [67, 68, 69], level.*"]

Today is May 22, 1950, and I'm headed back to the "H.S.C" [65], again; however, this time it's for a "Psychometric Test," [66]. My IQ has been previously measured at *seventy-one*.**** I am not sure if it's good or bad, all I know is, Dr. Samuels is now recommending I be "retested in six-months, to a year". Fine with me, the tests are quite fun to do—almost like games.

Revolving Doors

****

****{*These tests were performed specifically to measure a child's developmental levels of knowledge, abilities, attitudes and education as well as to determine personality traits. The resulting grading is more commonly known as the "IQ", or "Intelligence Quotient". [67] "IQ Reference Charts", [68], were developed associating the number grading of the "IQ" with actual developmental levels, abilities and future potentialities. Over the decades since the first introduction of these numbering systems, it has been argued the most they achieve is the ability to pigeon-hole students and too often limit their own personal development and abilities by labelling some as* **developmentally limited.** [69]}

****

{*On July 2, 1950, my sister, Dawn, is born to my mother Berneice Ketteringham Faulconer and her husband, Don Faulconer. Of course, of this event, I'll have no knowledge for several years to come, and I will not be able to locate, or make contact with this sister, for almost five decades later, (and, unfortunately, four years after our sweet mother's passing).*}

****

The summer zips along ever so quickly for me at this foster home. I get along pretty well with Danny, whenever he can find some time to play with me, or talk to me. Actually, I don't really mind the baby too much. Evan is an ordinary kid and nothing about him is especially bothersome or annoying, except he demands an inordinate amount of our "mother's" time and patience. Of course, the foster "mother" is still very nice to me and I don't have any problems being fed, or having my diaper changed. As well, she doesn't beat me or hit me very much— maybe a well-deserved spanking now and then, though.

208

Nevertheless, she sure can *scream*, and I mean a lot, and very, very loudly!

However, the play-yard is the best thing about being here because there are many kids around here to play with—and all ages too. I can always find someone to join me in the sandbox, or push me on the swings. In fact, I've made friends with a little girl named Betty, and a little boy named Bobby. These two kids are brother and sister and both look exactly alike, (except, obviously, one is a boy and the other is, well, a girl). "Songbird" says they're called, "Twins". I don't really care about what they're called. What matters to me is who builds the biggest and the bestest sand castles! Personally, I am certain, *I* do!

Sometimes we play with our little trucks and cars, driving and racing them up and down on the sidewalk. But I suppose *my* most favourite thing in the playground would have to be the big kid's slide. I love going wheeee all the way down the shiny metal surface which is actually made with a hump in the middle which sends me flying up, then down, down, down again. Yep, it's the best!

"Songbird" says today is very special because we are going to Betty's and Bobby's birthday party! I've never been to another little kid's birthday party, let alone, two little kids! The foster "mother" has wrapped two gifts for me to give the twins. (I call these kids the "Double Bs" for obvious reasons.) Betty's little dolly is wrapped in pink tissue paper, and Bobby's big red fire engine is wrapped in blue. "Songbird" says she is certain they will like their gifts, and I am sure they will too! We take off on a short little walk down the sidewalk, to the third house down from ours. Hey, even if you were not certain where the party was being held, you could certainly find it from the colourful balloons tied to the front porch railings! (I love balloons and I really hope there are more inside for all of us to play with and maybe even take home!)

This is amazing! There must be a million balloons inside—and there are bowls of candies, popcorn, peanuts and pretzels! For lunch, we are served dainty little sandwiches with all the crusts cut off. They're made with bread which has somehow been dyed in pastels colours of pink, green and blue! When everybody has finished their lunch, it's time for the white ice cream and chocolate birthday cake. Yummie!

In no time the effects of all the sugar overwhelms our little brains and bing, bang, boing—we are all running around and just about bouncing off the walls like crazed maniacs! We are jumping, skipping, dancing and just plain screaming! I really don't know who is having more fun, the "Birthday Boy and Girl"--with all their new toys, or me! I would say it's "Teddy"! Just then, "Songbird" says, "C'mon Teddy, dear, time to go home." However, I don't want to go home, so I protest! Of, course, she, being the grown-up, wins every time, hands-down, so *home* we go.

Yesterday may have been the big birthday party for the "Double Bs"; however, last night was no party for me! I spent a long time throwing-up and feeling generally yucky before and after the heaving! The "mother" said I got so sick because I ate too much ice cream, cake and candy. [Man-oh-man! Damned if you don't, (eat sugar), and damned if you do!] Oh well, finally I stopped barfing and fell asleep, and I'm feeling much better today—just don't show me anything sweet, (you know what I mean?).

"Songbird" is walking around singing and humming, much more than usual today. Apparently, her mood is connected with the phone conversation she just had. I don't know who she was talking to but there were an awful lot of, "*I love you's*" and "*I love you too's*" and "*Oh you're so sweet!*" and, "*Mwah!*

Mwah! Mwah!" (kissing sounds), and, "*Yes, baby, yes of course!*" (Apparently, she was talking to somebody's "BABY".) Anyway, I am just glad to see her in a happy mood—difficult for her to yell at us kids when she is in a great mood, right?

She has been cleaning like crazy for the past two hours, and the knock at the front door is probably the reason. Oh, no! It is her "EX-" "EX-EX-...SOMETHING-OR-OTHER"! Oh, now I remember, he's her "EX-husband"! What in the heck, is **he** doing here? I hope they don't fight!

I hate it when grown-ups argue and fight. "C'mon in sweetheart!" "Songbird" gushes. Whaaaat? Then the "EX-EX" leans in and whispers something in her ear. "Yes, oh, me too sweetheart." and she gushes again. "I...I've really missed you." was the "sweetheart's" reply. This whole scenario should probably be a good thing, but somehow I don't think it will be good for me. We'll just wait and see.

Their visit is over and now he is gone. Well, I am glad because it was just a whole lot of gushy, mushy, fluffy, stuff and a bunch of smooching too. Oh, yuck! When I grow up, I am NEVER, EVER going to kiss a girl, NEVER! Oh great, now she's **really** singing around this house. "*La...lee...la...la...dee, dee, da, da...*" "*Brrrring, Brrrring...*" "Hello, oh, hello sweetheart!" What is this? I thought he left, and now here we go with the mushy, kissie-face stuff again!

However, this visit and phone call were just about to be the beginning of my newest nightmare. In the days to follow, the "EX" came by every day with flowers, or chocolates and even the new Frank Sinatra record album, "*The Voice of Frank Sinatra*"! [71]. This last gift really won her over! She *loves* that crooning fellow, Frank Sinatra! What a sneaky move! "Teddy, dear, I'm going to make a quick run to the store, but Mister Martin will take care of you for a few minutes. O.K.?" (He's her

"EX-EX".) Anyway, off she went, and I never thought anything about it. I'm just playing with my toy circus on my bed, while Evan does his favourite thing—he is sleeping.

It is taking a lot longer than a couple minutes. In fact, it seems more like a couple hours. The "EX-EX" has been sitting in the kitchen, listening to some truly awful music on the radio and drinking his beer. Bang, bang, bang...I can't help myself! I just can't stop bashing my head on the wall while I am nervously waiting for the "mother" to return. Good, now "Songbird" is back and it's about time. I suppose the annoying man will be leaving, but not before another knot has raised up on the back of my head.

Aw, nuts...more mushy, gushy kisses, yuck! "Blah, blah, blah, blah...and more..." They're seriously talking about something right now...something about, "no longer need the income from the Children's Aid...moving...your house...remarrying...Kew Gardens", [72], and so on, with some other strange sounding puzzle pieces of *plans*.

After two more weekends have gone by, I notice the "mother" is very busy sewing a big, fluffy white dress. Today she has finally finished it and she is modelling it while twirling around and around in front of the mirror. I would have to say, she looks very pretty. Now, she is styling her hair, and is applying her make-up extra nicely today. When she says it's *time*, we three boys are all dressed in our best duds and squished between the adults in the torn-up seat of her "EX-EX's", big, old, ugly, rusty green pick-em-up truck. After too long awhile of bumping noisily along and almost gagging on the exhaust fumes, we arrive at the Kew Gardens, [72], which is part of "The Beaches" area of Toronto. It looks like either some little elf, or somebody else, has already beat us here. They have been quite busy decorating the tree trunks, picnic tables and benches with pink and white balloons, fluffy pom-poms, ribbons and streamers. So far, it looks like a very pretty start to somebody's party, and I, for one, am *always* ready for a party!

Of course, it's unfortunate for me, but this isn't the kind of party *I am* thinking of. The area is distinctly decorated for a wedding, and the post-ceremony reception party. "Songbird" and "EX-EX" are being *remarried*. Now I understand the pieces of conversation. She is planning to move into his house, along with Daniel and Evan, who are, of course, his children too. However, *I* pose the biggest problem because I don't fit into any sort of "Norman Rockwell", [76] [76a], depiction of their perfect lives. This means, once they are *wed*, I will no longer be welcome as a part of their family. This unhappy fact is quickly about to become my personal reality.

"Hello, 'Mrs...', this is 'Mrs. Martin'". My foster mother continues on the phone, "I wanted to let you know I have remarried my ex-husband and, well, I'm sorry, but we find it necessary to move into his house. Unfortunately, it isn't located in York County, and I understand this makes our family no longer eligible for fostering Teddy under this County's jurisdiction."

Oh, no, this just can't possibly be happening again, not again. I am feeling so sad right now, all I can do is just curl up, make myself invisible and wait to see what will happen to me next. I don't understand it. I thought everything was going so well at this house. I thought she liked me. Did she really have to go and get herself *married* to this man, AGAIN—*REALLY*?

"Teddy, I want to explain something to you, dear." O.K., so I'm listening. "Teddy, it isn't anything you have done, or not done, which is forcing us to have to <u>*give you up*</u>. (There are those *three magic words* I hate so much.) You know I think you are a very sweet little boy and I love you very much, and so do Danny and Evan. Danny is certainly upset about this change in our lives because, of course, he enjoys your company, and always says how much he likes to play with you, and teach you about things. However, for us, it's a matter of finances and geography. We won't be living in the right area here in Toronto, in order for you to continue living with us. I know you can't possibly understand what I'm trying to explain, but, well...I'm sorry."

Well, now I am more confused than I was before she started to explain things to me. If she is sorry and doesn't really want to leave me behind, then why is she doing this? I can't possibly understand how the grown-ups think, or what their motivation is for doing this or that. I suppose I have no choice but to accept my sudden expulsion from this foster family as simply, "the way things have to be".

Right now, I am thinking my time would be best spent in my special "hidey-hole". So it's there I'm headed—to the little space in the back corner of my closet, behind some cardboard storage boxes which contain Danny's old ice skates and other stuff. *No one* would think to look for me in this place. As well, in this hidey hole, I can't *see* what is happening and often am unable to even *hear* what is going on. I am insulated, and safe, but I won't be spending much more time in here, as I suppose I'll soon be moved to my next so-called foster "home".

Oh no, I *knew* it! It is my Case Worker at the door. I am already scrambling for the security of my little closet hidey-hole. (No matter what sort of fostering situation I find myself in lately, or from now on, it's going to be the first thing on my to-do list. I need to hunt for the most impossible hiding place—and make it my own safe space.) What could *she* want? I thought I was doing quite well here. I like the woman and her boys, and I thought they liked me too. In fact, I've even sprouted more teeth now, too. (Who is going to give me the booze for my sore gums now?) In addition, I can get around quickly now, although I am still too afraid to let go and walk without hanging on. However, I don't think "Songbird" would want to get rid of me for that. Would she?

"Hello, 'Mrs...', come in." "Thank-you, '*Miss...*'" the "Mouse Lady" replies. "Actually, I'm 'Mrs. Martin', *now.*" the foster mother corrects. "Oh, of course, I'm sorry...", "Mouse-Lady" stammers while stepping around the edge of the over-sized, "FOR RENT" sign, which the landlord attached, crookedly, to the porch railing. "Excuse the mess. We're all boxed-up and awaiting the moving van in the next hour or so." (I have noticed "Songbird" has not been singing anything today, and right now, she is talking quietly and solemnly to my Case Worker. Maybe she feels bad about "giving me up". Maybe she'll change her mind.)

"Yes, well, this is a rather unusual circumstance." my Worker says. "Where do you think he could go next?" the foster "mother" asks. "Well, actually we don't usually divulge such information, but in this case I think it will be beneficial for Teddy, and you, to know what's next for him. We are planning on moving him to the house next door." "Do you mean 'Mrs...'?" the "mother" inquires. "Yes, exactly. She only has one son who, as you know, is a teenager, so she would be willing to take Teddy, at least on a temporary basis. Of course, it's my understanding, as your neighbour, she already knows the child. Am I right?" "Mousey" asks. "Yes, certainly she does." the "mother" replies. She is a good friend and quite a nice person too.

Am I hearing these women correctly? Are they talking about moving me next door into 'Mrs...'s' house with her awful teenage son, Sid? I certainly hope not! He is a terrible kid, and very rude to his own mother. I can't imagine him being any nicer to *me* if I am stuck in their house for any length of time. However, as I listen a little longer, I am sickened to discover, indeed, that's *exactly* what they're planning to do with me. Why can't I stay in *this* house? Bang, bang, bang...my head is bashing itself against the wall in the back of my closet hideout, again. Bang, bang.... "Teddy, dear, please come out here, 'Mrs...' wants to talk to you." Bang, bang, bang, bang.... "Teddy, come *here!*" ***BANG!!!***

"There!--There he goes again! Do you hear him banging?" "Songbird" asks "Mousey". "It's Teddy banging his head again! It's what I've been talking about!" the foster lady exclaims. "What does 'Dr. Samuels' say about it?" the Case Worker asks. "He's referring him for another round of Psychometric, [66], testing." "Hello, Teddy dear!" the Worker addresses me cheerfully, while tousling my hair as I step past her. "Oh, my goodness, 'Mrs. Martin'," she says, examining the dampness in her hand, "*Oh!...his head is bleeding!*" In minutes, my foster "mother" has cleaned-up my head, completely unaffected by what I've done to myself—again.

The two women chit-chat a little longer, before we all walk over to the house next door for an official visit to my next "foster mother". After a few minutes of chitchat, "Mousey" announces, "Teddy, you will be staying here now, with 'Mrs...', and her son, Sid." I know who she is, and I know who *he* is! This feels like the worst possible solution. I wonder if this can really be the only answer. Is there nowhere else where I could move? I would almost agree to return to the asylum right now—well, *almost.* Nevertheless, I am over here now, and I am supposed to stay here. (I'm thinking, as soon as my Worker leaves I'm going to run right back home to "Songbird".) Of course, that doesn't happen, because later the same day, a moving truck arrives and my foster family's belongings are packed up and driven away, with them all following closely behind in her husband's ugly excuse for a vehicle.

Today is September 18, 1950, and I am over three years of

age. I am so sad and weary of always trying to "make nice" and fit into each new family where I am stuck, I mean, *placed*. I so very desperately want a real home and I need a real, loving "mother". (I have not seen my own, sweet mommy in such a long time that I've pretty much given up on moving back "home" with her.) I don't understand all the changes and I hate the resentment shown toward me from the kids already "belonging" in each new "foster family". Of course, Sid will prove to be no exception.

Nobody *wants* me and certainly, from what I've witnessed, nobody *loves* me. It is just one more day in my life, and one more prayer to some invisible God, or Santa Claus, both of whom seem to have forgotten me, or at the very least, they don't recognize me as a normal little boy needing, and worthy of, love. No matter—I just don't care anymore, really—I don't care! ***Bang, bang, bang, bang, bang***...!

Chapter 28: *What the Hell?!*

Because I've been so rushed into this new foster living arrangement, I have hardly had enough time to think about this latest home and family. Nevertheless, I am counting this as my twelfth residence and tenth fostering situation. I already know I don't like the woman's son, because he is such a meanie and he is a *brat*, even though he *is* fifteen. The "mother", a woman of thirty-something, is a very anxious type of person. In fact, she actually shakes and trembles a lot of the time. She excuses her tremors as the result of her habit of drinking a whole percolator full of coffee every morning, but I know differently. I know her son's behaviour puts her on edge and keeps her as nervous as a long-tailed cat in a room full of rocking chairs.

She's rail thin, and ever-so pale, with brown hair, highlighted with prematurely silver threads. As well, she smokes an awful lot of cigarettes every day. It is a bad habit, which she says, "calms her nerves", but I don't buy it. I think she smokes so much because of her son's awful behaviour! He cusses her out and disobeys her at every opportunity. Sometimes she jokes about him saying stuff like, *"Sid's the cause of my grey hair and all these wrinkles too!"* With this, I *do* agree, although I would have to say the *smokes* certainly aren't making her look any younger. (Nevertheless, *I* happen to know what her son is *really the cause of* it's the big, fat plaster cast on her broken ankle! She blows it off as having happened, *"due to a fall down the front steps"*. However, behind closed doors I've heard her going on and on to Sid, repeating her frustration, saying, "You and I both know, I wouldn't have this broken ankle if you hadn't *tripped* me on purpose!")

Sid is a belligerent youth with an attitude, which out-matches his short, stubby stature. He has jet-black hair, which he greases back with so much "Brylcreem", [74], I swear, it drips all the way down the back of his neck! Yuck! Maybe it's the reason why his neck is starting to match his zit-covered *pizza-face*. Oooh, more yuck! Anyway, he has taken to wearing an old, faded-brown, cracking leather "flight jacket", which is thickly lined with sheepskin. [75] (This was something else his father left behind in his rush to escape, I mean, *leave* them.) Sid really thinks he is pretty slick and spends an excessive amount of time in front of mirrors. I have no idea why he acts so angrily toward his mother, or why he is so terribly mean to her too. He certainly makes no bones about blaming her for his father's decision to fly their coop. However, I don't really know this for certain, I'm only guessing.

Sid is not particularly nice to me either. He doesn't hit me, but, under his breath, he says threatening things when he knows, only he and I can hear. I have determined the best way to handle living with him is by staying out of his way. It isn't as if we have to share a bedroom, because I sleep on the pull-out sofa/bed in the living room. As well, I am very careful to keep my own toys in my paper "LOBLAWS", [17], shopping bag which still follows me from house to house. This way Sid can't get them and break them, *accidentally on purpose*.

I have decided to call this newest foster mother, "Shaky Sheila", because Sheila is her real name and, well, the rest is self-explanatory. I do not think this woman was the best choice for my latest foster mother because she focusses so much on her son's latest antics, she actually forgets to change my diapers. Sometimes she doesn't even remember to feed me unless my aching tummy makes me cry and "bother" her about it.

Yesterday, Sid stole her package of smokes right out of her purse, along with some paper money. *She* never noticed the money was gone, but *I* saw him do it. She only found out when we walked to the corner store and she tried to pay for some more ciggys, but discovered she had no money in her wallet. She actually started crying in the store. "Mister Sam", the proprietor, took pity on her need for her nicotine fix, and fronted her the smoke pack, telling her to, "Just send Sid back with the money tomorrow." Fat chance *that* will happen! In a low grumble, she vows she's "gonna keep a tight rein on [her] purse from now on".

Later in the day, when Sid got home from school she tried to discipline him and make him stay in his bedroom. However, he just laughed at her and told her to, "Go jump in the lake!" (See what I mean—he is *so* awful to her.) Now she is crying again. There is nothing I can do to help, except make myself scarce. So, I head for my latest hidey-hole. (This time I've found a small crawl space, which I get to from inside this new "foster mother's" broom closet. There is a little trap-door at the back. I saw her slide it sideways to open it one time when the landlord came by to fix the kitchen plumbing. Nevertheless, in the absence of emergency plumbing issues, this has the makings of a perfect hiding space for little ol' me.)

Right now, she thinks I am outside playing in the sandbox and she is phoning somebody. It is *her* ex-husband. "Ralph, I don't know what to do about Sid. You know, he's being so impossible! I've totally lost control of him." Ralph must have said something not particularly nice, because she defensively replied with, "Why would you say such a thing to me? Why would you call me that? Sometimes I absolutely *hate* you! No wonder Sid is so difficult, he is turning out exactly like you, and I'm starting to *hate him* too!" Then she hung up the phone with an attitude, a slam and a cuss word I won't repeat.

I don't like this tension around here. Frankly, it's scaring me because I am not sure what is going to happen to me next. "Teddy! Teddy!...Come in here!" she's shouting out the door.

Revolving Doors

When I do appear from the broom closet, I startle her a little because she thought I was outside playing. She demands, "What on earth were you doing in *there*?" I try to explain, *"I'n hiding, I'n hiding."*

"Never mind. You sit down here, right now, and eat some lunch!" Nevertheless, she is still sobbing and it's hard to work-up an appetite when your "mother" is so unhappy. (Now, *I* hate Sid too.) However, "Shakey Sheila" insists I eat, and since she's serving me canned spaghetti with little meatballs in it, (my new, all-time favourite), I gulp it down quickly. Then I run and play with "Pom Pom", because *always* makes *me* feel better whenever I'm sad. (I wonder if I should share him with the "mother". Nawww...she's a grown-up woman, she'll be O.K., she'll probably just eat some chocolate ice cream again.)

Since today's chilly weather is making it impossible to play outside, I decide to play with my wooden doggie in Sid's room. (Sid won't be around because he has been staying at some friend's house, and has not been back, since he was busted for stealing the smokes and the money from his mother.) Nevertheless, it seems as if so much happens in a very short time in my life. I have only been here a week and "Shaky Sheila" is already having the curiously familiar telephone conversation with someone at the other end of the wire,

"If you could just stop by, I think I could explain my position a little better...yes, but my ankle is in a cast and I'm not getting around very well these days...it would better if you could come here...thank you, tomorrow will be fine."

Dare I attempt a guess? Could it possibly be "Mrs. Mousey"? The answer comes the very next morning when, who do you suppose walks through the door? It's "Librarian Lady". She has not spotted me yet, so in two seconds I slip into my hidey-hole. "Where's the boy?" she asks. "Oh, he's alright. He's playing back in my son's room. He won't be able to hear us." my "foster mother" responds. "Well, good, because I must try to impress upon you the seriousness of your request for us to move him *again*, especially since he has only been living here for *one week*! Do you *really* think you've given him a fair chance?", "L. L." impresses in a very stern tone. "In fact," she continues, "what I am confused about is y-you-your phone call to his other Case W-w-worker only two d-d-days ago. You said, and I quote, "Ted-d-ddy is settling-in m-m-much better than I expected he wou-wou-would, and he f-f-feeds himself very well." ("Librarian Lady" is really stuttering badly. I guess she is pretty upset.)

"Well, it may well have been true a couple days ago, but I have now discovered that *two* children are too much for me to handle, especially with my broken ankle.", my so-called, "mother" says. "Is Teddy having any p-p-p-problems with your son?" "L. L." inquires. "My son, Sid, is *not* the issue here. The problem is simply, little Teddy requires too much care and I am not prepared to handle such demanding needs of a child." the foster woman retorts. The Social Worker then wraps up the discussion with, "Alright, then, if you are certain it's how you feel, we'll work on f-f-finding him another home as soon as p-p-possible. Naturally, we simply don't know how long it will t-t-take, so, for now, p-p-please don't let on anything to him about this conversation, p-p-please."

When I hear the familiar, slap-pap, slap-pap, I figure the outer storm door has shut and now I feel like I am about to explode. All I can do is bang, bang, bang my head until the bad thoughts escape with the blood trailing down into my ear. I feel nothing. I am totally numb. I can't believe my ears, or my bad luck. Maybe it's not luck at all. Maybe I'm just a terrible little kid and nobody wants to take care of me. Oh, these are such horrible thoughts, I want to bang and shake them out of my skull. I am so defeated. The most I can do to alleviate my frustration is to lie on my tummy, and bang and kick my fists and feet, screaming until I have no voice left! Of course, that is exactly what I do.

"Stop it, Teddy! Stop that tantrum right now!" the "mother" screeches. "God Dammit! I said stop it!" Then she hits my head with her shoe! (That's right! She actually removed her shoe and used the heel end to hit my head, with a few hard whacks.) Nevertheless, I am unable to simply stop. I am totally out of my mind, and out of control. Where and when will this nightmare ever end for me?

However, even as I am pondering my plight, and right in the middle of our confrontation, you would never guess who should walk in the house. It's Sid. "What the hell are you *doing* to that little kid?" he demands of his mother. In response, she just swings around and screams, "What the hell are you *doing here*? You can get out **right now**!" I start to run out but she catches me, "Get the hell back in here, *right this minute!* I'm not finished with you, Teddy-boy!" Then she starts hitting *Sid* with the same shoe—and when he runs out the door, she throws it at him. Ooooh—the shoe hits the door frame at the very instant the door is doing its "slap-pap", causing the pointy heel to snap right off—making her *even madder*! In this instant, she is so out of control, she is screaming hysterically and hobbling around looking for her smokes. Oooooh, I am outta here, and into hiding, before she "tans my hide", (whatever *that threat* means)!

After Sid high-tailed it out of the house, we immediately hear a very loud, "*VRRRMMM, VRRRMMM*" sound. "Shakey Sheila" limps to the kitchen window to see Sid way off down the sidewalk on the motorcycle he has been "restoring". "Oh, no!" She heads out onto the porch screaming her fool head off, but he is already a blur in the distance. Then she turns around, lights a smoke and makes herself a cocktail. She is looking right at me with her all-familiar evil eye, as if to say, "Don't you even make a peep!" A little while later, she is still crying with her face in her hands, and is shaking her head back and forth, when we hear the strangely unfamiliar sound of a siren. Police, fire engine, ambulance? I wonder which. They all sound the same, so I just ignore it and go find my doggie. There she goes phoning her "Ex" again. "Hey, Ralph...is Sid over there with you?... Well, I thought he might have rode over there...on the damn motorbike you *left* here! Well, he has been fixing it and it's working now!... O.K., but you call *me* right away if he comes there. I have a bone to pick with him!"

I am actually hungry right now, but I figure it isn't the best time to whine for food. As any good doggie knows, sometimes you have to wait until your caregiver is ready to take care of your needs and so I wait, while she takes a nap. Almost as soon as she laid down, the "*Brrrinnng*" of the phone breaks the house's silence. "Yes, this 'Mrs...', Whaaat?...Oh, God! Oh no!!...Where is he?... I'll be right down!" Then, without explanation, she quickly deposits me with the twins' mom and excuses herself, telling the woman something about "Sid [being] in the hospital emergency room." (Apparently, he had raced off so fast, he had wrecked the motorcycle—and his own body, in the process.)

The next morning she came over and retrieved me from the "Bobbsey Twins" house, [91], (at least this is what I started calling them after I heard the story). She explained how Sid was in a bad wreck and is going to need a great deal of extra care and help when he gets home from the hospital. (I am already beginning to get the picture here.) Then she tells me, indeed, I must be moved out of her home, immediately.

This is not good, for me. I feel like a puffy, fat teddy bear who just lost all his stuffing! I am feeling very sad and the only thing to do now is head to my hidey-hole where she will *never* find me. I can stay there for a long time. In fact, I have even put a little towel and a few crackers and cookies in there. I'm just crawling in when I hear another, "*Brrring...*" of the phone. "Hello". She steadies her voice so as not to let on to the caller how badly she has been crying. "Oh, yes, that'll be fine. I guess I'll have to wait it out, won't I?" (Wait *what* out, I wonder?) She gets off the phone and pours herself another cocktail, even though it's only ten o'clock in the morning! (What's that noise? "*Sssweeep, sssweeep, sssweeep...*")

Chapter 29: Two "*STORY*" House

Several awkward "sleeps" later, after staying only twenty-one days at "Shakey Sheila's" residence, "Librarian Lady" once again picks me up. I wonder where she got this brand new 1949 Plymouth Suburban Station Wagon. [81] Right now, she has plunked me down in the very back of this humongous shiny black, gangster-looking automobile. When I try to "speak" to my "Worker", driving this hunk of steel, I have to use my outdoor voice to make myself understood all the way up to the driver's seat. (This is a little like riding in the back of the great bus with "Ears", only there is no wire to alert the driver.)

I really have many questions about my new home and family, since this will be my *thirteenth* residential move into my *eleventh* foster home. Predictably, however, my Social Worker doesn't explain anything. She just offers the usual,

"Oh, Teddy dear, you're gonna like it at your new home. This family consists of a mother and her two very nice daughters. They are all anxiously awaiting your arrival. I understand they also have a nice big cat! You like kitty-cats, don't you?... Blah, Blah, and a swing set, Blah, Blah..."

Her voice goes up and down with the stream of comments and questions, but I am not really listening. I wish she would just turn the radio on and shut up. I will judge whether it will be a *"nice new home"*, after I've been there for a little while. Nevertheless, she just asked me a question about "kitties"-- requiring an answer from me. I responded with, "Uh-huh." (Translation: "Yes, I suppose cats are O.K., but I'm more of a dog person.")

Then I asked, "Is there a little boy for me to play with at this house?" (But it just came out sounding like, "...wittle bo?") I am trying very hard, but I am not exactly certain I am making myself clearly understood. "Doddie?" I ask, as I keep trying to elicit the answer I *want* to hear, but get nothing in reply except, "Oh, here—we're here now—here it is, Teddy." I look out the car's side window and see a two-storey, whitewashed, clapboard home. It's so big I am immediately encouraged it will be spacious enough to be inviting to this pathetic, unwanted little orphan. Maybe I'll have my own room. Maybe they have monkey bars or a slide in the backyard. Maybe the girls "L. Lady" mentioned will be my new best friends. I wonder, and hope.

"L. L." parks the massive vehicle and gets out. She reaches in and plucks me from the rear seat, taking my hand to walk me up to the front door. I *am* digging my heels in and pulling back on her hand, because I'm scared and I don't think I'm gonna like this place very much. However, just then...what's that I hear? "Do you hear the doggie, Teddy?" she asks me. Yes, I do, and she heard it too! Oh, this IS going to be a good foster home. I am, convinced of it now, because we *do* hear the welcoming barks of what must be a very large doggie!

As we approach the front door, I am positive I'll quickly make friends with him, so now I'm no longer resisting my Worker. In fact, I count eagerly as we go up the seven front steps to their big black door. Oooh! Now I am starting to get butterflies in my tummy with each step closer to the doggie! Will he be black or brown? Will he like me? (Of course, he will!) However, when we ring the door buzzer I notice the barking has stopped completely. In fact, sadly, I now recognize it had been coming from the backyard of the house *next-door*. Oh dear, a little gloominess drizzles over my disappointment. No doggie here—too bad for me. However, when I think that maybe I should still be able to pet him through the fence slats, it makes me feel a little bit better.

Revolving Doors

While we wait on the covered porch, I notice the two girls' bikes leaning on their kickstands. Both are quite new looking, and both are painted red and white with lots of shiny chrome. (You can tell they belong to girls, because there are no cross-bars, which I have seen on big boys' bikes.) On the wooden-slatted floor of the front veranda, beside the two-wheelers, is a small cache of miscellaneous toys. There's a red-white-and-blue striped rubber ball, a doll the size of a small girl seated in a little white wicker baby carriage, (which is tipped over a little, due to the missing front wheel), and a very large brown teddy bear with one of his button eyes missing. The sad looking teddy is sporting a stringy, threadbare, pale blue ribbon-bow around his neck. I clutch my bag of belongings tighter. For darn certain, they're not getting *my* stuff or ruining *my* toys!

As soon as the new foster lady answers the door, "Librarian Lady" starts to introduce me, "Hello, 'Mrs...', this is little 'Teddy'." Nevertheless, I know the game now and I know the routines. I squeeze right past both women and head into the living room where I can already see my two new "foster sisters" playing some game on the floor. "Hi-Ya!" I shout. Then I spot their great, huge, fat kitty coiled sleepily in the corner! I try to make kissing sounds to get the kitty to come over to me when the smaller girl interjects saying, "His name is Midnight". I try to make conversation and tell them how impressed I am with their humongous, record-shattering feline! However, the girl is already back concentrating on her strategy for the next game move, because her older sister keeps nagging, "C'mon, 'Rosie'! It's your move—never mind him—make your move—or d'ya want me to make it for you!" (It sounded more like a threat than a question. Very soon I'll discover why "Rosie" decided to ignore me.)

I hesitate to interrupt, but I can't help myself. "What's dat?" I ask the girls. "We're playing a *board game* called, 'Monopoly', [78], and you are *too little and dumb*—so you *can't* play any *board games* with us!" This is the friendly, welcoming response of the younger girl, "Rosie".

{Oh yes, that *was* a facetious remark.} Who cares about their stupid old "bored" games anyway? Not me! I have my own, much better stuff to play with!

I sit myself down on the living room floor to play alone, but I'm just far enough away that they can't see what is in *my* secret sack of stuff. All my junk and my secret stuff are in my well-travelled paper bag. I still have "Pom Pom", and "Ducky" and "Lucky" as well as a few little metal "Dinky Toy", [23], cars and my farm with the tiny animals. I decide to remove the cars and start to play with them because, as everyone knows, girls don't like playing with cars! Therefore, no chance of them trying to steal my little vehicles. "Vrrrrm, vrrrrm, vroooom, vroooom, **CRASH**!" (I make the best car sounds!) "Shut-up, kid! We are trying to concentrate on our game! Go somewhere else! We don't want your stupid noises in here!" the older girl scowls. (Hmmm, so *this* is how it's going to be at my new home!)

All the time I've been trying to get to know these sisters a little better, the "Librarian Lady" has been discussing my latest fate with the "foster mother". I pretend to be playing, but really, I am watching the two women chatting while still standing in the foyer. I notice how much these daughters resemble their mother. Both girls have jet-black hair which is thick, coarse and wildly curly, resembling wriggling snakes! Like their mom's, it's styled in a shortish bob, obviously some attempt at management, I suppose. I see also, they're wearing dresses made in the exact same, hand-sewn print styles as the one currently worn by their mom.

Oh well, since I can't play the board game with the girls, I decide to put my car-cars away and make friends with their big cat. "Hi-ya diddy-dat!" However, the very second I start to pet the cat, the older girl, "Rita" says, "You shouldn't touch him! He will slice your eyes out! He doesn't like *anybody*!" "Especially boys!--he *really hates* boys!"

"Rosie" chimes in. Nevertheless, *they* can't stop me, and I pet him anyway. I rub his head, and then run my hand down his back all the way to his tail, then I gently pull the fluffy tail up into the air. "Brrrrrrr, Brrrrrrr, Brrrrrrr..." he purrs, in obvious delight at being rubbed. Ha! To their shock, Midnight *does* like the petting and he *does* like me too! At least I've made *one* friend in this, thus far, cold and unfriendly new household.

After a few minutes of chitchat, the "mother" takes my Social Worker and me upstairs where there are three bedrooms and the bathroom. One is the mother's and the other two are where the girls sleep. I'm in mid-thought of wondering where the lady will be putting me when, out of the hall closet, she rolls my obviously "temporary" accommodation—a fold-up canvas guest cot on wheels, explaining, "Because 'Rita's' room is a little bigger, this cot is going to be in there for Teddy. Then she suggests, "If there are any issues which arise with either girl, we can always move Teddy around into one of our other bedrooms." "Uh-uh! Not—not mine!" "Rosie" stammers negatively. (Hmmmm... the first half hour at this new house is not exactly proving very pleasant or welcoming for me, now is it?)

After the tour, we all go back downstairs and my Worker sits down at the kitchen table to go over an important list she had prepared. She explains it's all the things my new "foster mother" needs to *know* about me:

> 1. *Teddy completed his toxoids some time ago.* (Oh, yes!   Thank God and Santa Clause *those* are all finished!)

> 2. *He does not express his toilet needs but he dances when he needs to go.* (Do I? O.K., so maybe I do.)

3. *He needs a firm hand for discipline. (Spanking? Nuh-uh, no way, no I do not!)*

4. *Occasionally, he bangs his head when he is cross. So don't worry if his head bleeds—just clean it up and he'll be fine. (O.K., so maybe I do this, but only a little, and only out of desperation.)*

5. *Other than this, he is very obedient. He certainly is friendly. ("Yes! Yes!--I certainly am!")*

6. *Lastly, Teddy is used to an afternoon sleep, and goes to bed right after supper. (Doesn't everyone?)*

"I believe that's all." "L. L." finishes. The mother then calls the sisters into the kitchen, but they don't respond. Then she goes to them and instructs, "Now, girls, I want you to get along with your new little *brother*. Show him some of your toys or books. Please, girls." She is talking to them but they're not even looking up from their boring game. "Also...", the "mother" then directs our attention out of the kitchen window to the backyard, "...there's a swing set with a slide and a sandbox in the corner of the yard." "*You* can use them." "Rosie" gripes. "We're too big for baby games now." (O.K., fine by me.) "Don't you still have your little tricycle "Rosie"? Where would it be now?" Then, answering her own questions the mother says, "Oh, I believe it's in the crawl-space under the front porch, isn't it Rosie?" "I don't know! Who cares, anyway?" is "Rosie's" rude reply. "Well, Teddy, we'll look under there later because it would be just your size, I believe." It is commendable the way the foster "mother" is trying so hard to accommodate me. (However, I certainly can't say the same about the girls.)

By the time the Social Worker leaves, we are all quietly playing in the living room. Then the "mother" suggests, "Teddy, why don't you and I go upstairs and get you unpacked and settled-in?" O.K..., sounds fine to me. It only takes a few minutes to unpack my few jammies and other clothes onto the temporary, tin TV-tray-table, [114], next to the cot. When she and I go back downstairs, I sit on the bottom, green broadloom-carpeted step and run my finger around and around in the little indented swirls of pattern woven into it. I just want to be a little fly on the green-and-white on grey, flowery, papered hall wall. From a distance, I want to listen to the sisters and get a sense of what they really think about me, when they think I am out of earshot. However, now they're whispering and I can't hear them anyway.

I decide to remain on the stair-step and just sort of oversee everybody's activities. I'm wondering if I'll be able to find a decent hidey-hole at this house. In fact, I could use one right this minute. Nevertheless, the step is a good enough place for me at the moment. I sit back and observe as the girls' mother runs around the house picking-up this item, and dusting-off that one. I am a little amused as she sweeps and cleans because with every movement, her big, fat bum moves back and forth sort-of dancing. I notice she is another very short, bottom-heavy, "pear-shaped" woman. Her inky-blue-black hair has recently been coloured with a drug-store box of dye. (It's obvious from the drippy spillage of the runny black dye along the top of her forehead and on the tops of her ears). As I will soon discover, this foster woman wears only apron-covered dresses, nylon stockings and flat shoes. And, oddly enough, she wears the same tiny gold-coloured hoop earrings, all the time, even to bed. (Hmmm...I have never met any women who wore earrings to bed before—curious, very curious.)

This woman speaks very calmly and nicely to me, and as I will eventually come to realize, does not raise her voice to any of us. Speaking of voices though, she does have an unusual accent—obviously European—perhaps Ukrainian, maybe even Polish, I would guess. (Her hairy black moustache is a dead giveaway and should have been my first clue.) Anyway, I believe I decide to nickname this foster "mother" for her annoying habit of always smiling and grinning! Naturally, she'll be "Mrs. Smiley". She actually chuckles a lot too, as if it were a sort of nervous habit. She will say a sentence or two then giggle, say another and chuckle again. Personally, I don't see the humour in what she says; but, then again, I don't see much humour in anything these days.

Later on, after our supper of sausages and potato slices fried in oil, "Mrs. Smiley" gives me a bath, after which, I am snug and warm dressed in my familiar flannel jammies. I sure hope I can sleep tonight; however, just in case the bogeyman starts tapping on the window, I grab "Pom Pom" and slide him under the covers with me. Oh, noooo! Just as the "mother" is about to turn off the lights she starts in with a sing-songy, accent-laden, version of, *"Night, night, sleep tight! Don't let the..."* [62] I hold my ears and hum...I just don't want to hear the doggone rhyme tonight—or ever again! *"Blah, blah, blah, blah..."*

The morning sun rouses me and I guess I did eventually fall asleep last night—in spite of the icky, nightmare-producing, "bed-bug" rhyme. My roommate "Rita" is still sleeping right now, so I tiptoe out into the hall and peek in to see if "Rosie" is up, but she is dead to the world as well. I sit on the top step and bum my way all down the stairs, then run into the kitchen. "Good Morning, Teddy." "Mrs. Smiley" says with a big grin, adding, "Would you like some cereal and milk?" I nod in agreement then go into the living room to pet Midnight again. Believe it or not, "Midnight" can actually talk to me. He says he is very lonely and he's glad I've come here to be his friend. I guess I'm glad too, but I can't really say for sure yet.

Suddenly, "thump, thump, ka—thump ka—thump" down the stairs the two girls bound, elbowing each other out of the way in a close race to the kitchen. "Hey, I want toast and jam." "Rosie" demands. "Gimme me some cereal, mum." "Rita" orders rudely. "Deeed you girls forgeeet your manners theees morneeenn?" their mum asks, almost a little nervously.

"Ah, who cares?" "Rita" shouts back from the hall. Then, addressing me, she says, "Oh, hey kid." Then she adds, "You'd better stop petting Midnight!" "Yah! We told you he's gonna scratch you! He'll tear your eyes out! I've even seen him do it!" "Rosie" adds her threat. "Stop saying those things!" the "mother" orders from the kitchen. "Weave me awone!" I protest their interference. However, the girls get more and more unreasonable. Why won't they let me pet the kitty-cat? Oh, no! My little brain just popped a gear and slipped into overload! Now I find myself down on the kitchen floor, kicking and screaming, in the middle of a temper tantrum. Oh heck! I certainly did not want to expose this darker side of myself, not yet anyway, at least not until I am sure I can trust all of these new people.

"Oh, no! Theees won't do. Stop-it, right now Teddeee!" the "mother" interjects, adding, "We don't *allow* tantrums in theees house." Oh, darn it! Right now, the girls are *laughing at me* and I am most definitely out of control. I can't stop myself, and I know it. Bang! Bang! Bang! My head is bashing itself against the floor. The woman tries to pick me up to get me to stop thrashing about, but my arms and legs won't stop flailing around. I probably look like a Tasmanian Devil, [93], at the peak moment of crazed excitement. When this round, little woman is unable to control me physically, she grabs a wet rag and begins wiping the back of my head. I didn't even know it but it appears I've bloodied myself *again*. If this is not humiliating enough, it seems as if I've peed in my pants too! Oh, gosh—I am *so* embarrassed! This is *not* how I wanted to start things out at this new foster home. I HAVE to find myself a hidey-hole, and fast! I'll be alright then.

Later, the same day, "Mrs. Smiley" stops grinning for a minute while she calls the "C.A.S." to get some insight as to how to stop, or at least manage, my tantrums. She tells whoever answers the phone, "The little boy is quite obstinate and disobedient". (How can she judge me or say such a thing? After all, I've only been here since yesterday. Nevertheless, this is only the beginning of what will eventually be *many* such phone calls.)

Happily, this foster "mother" has a very quiet manner and seems exceptionally understanding. She handles my, now daily, outbursts of emotion, by either ignoring me, or being firm and insistent, saying, "Get a hold of yourself!" I can certainly see she is not easily rattled by my tantrums. I don't do it to upset anyone on purpose. I do it because I can't help it. She says I am "probably upset over this additional move", and, "He only needs a little more time to settle down and make the adjustment". She is probably right. We'll see how I feel after two, maybe three more weeks, are behind me.

The routines in this house aren't unlike the other places I've lived. Of course, here, the "girls" always come first, and the "girls" are always "right", (whether they are, or are not—and they usually are *not*). One good thing is, I've inherited "Rosie's" tricycle after the "mother" dragged it out from storage and gave it a good once-over with a cleaning rag. As far as foster "mothers" go, this one isn't too hard to take. She's not a bad cook, and I especially like the way she leaves me *by myself* a lot, without interrupting my coveted playtime. She also walks away and leaves me alone when I start to lose my temper, which is apparently, what the "C.A.S." women told her to do.

Not surprisingly, I have not experienced quite so many tantrums lately, because, after all, when you don't have an audience, there isn't much incentive for a performance. However, I have not yet gained mastery over, and control of, my other little temper-related habit of head-banging. I can't seem to help it. However, with Santa's impending visit so very close at hand, I am constantly reminded by "Mrs..." who repeatedly sings the Christmas song about, "*not crying*" and "*not pouting*". (Although, I notice there is nothing in the little Santa Claus jingle, [92], about not "banging your head".)

I have been living with this family for a few weeks, and it's already *my favourite* time of year again. That's right, it's the Christmas season! Of course, today we are going to be decorating *our* tree. (The "mother" bought it for two dollars from a man selling them in the parking lot of the big Catholic Church, and he was kind enough to *deliver,* I mean, *drag,* it to our house.) The tree selling man nailed a wooden "X" on the bottom of the trunk to make the tree stand upright on its own. After he and "Rita" wrestled it into our house, I think they must have forgotten to shake it off because bunches of pine needles made a trail from the front walkway into our living room. The man excused the mess with, "Lady, don't worry, they all lose a few needles. Just give it a little water 'n' it'll perk right up. O.K., Lady?" (Hmmm...How does a chopped-down, dead Christmas tree drink water?) Regardless, in only a couple minutes the whole room is starting to smell very familiar, and comforting, from the pine's emanating scent.

I wonder what we'll be using to decorate it. Maybe we'll be making some popcorn garland. I no sooner ponder this thought when, holy smokes—I'm in shock as the girls start bringing the "Xmas" boxes down from the attic. This can't all be Christmas stuff, I'm thinking. Wow! This family has just produced such a huge cache of fabulous ornaments, which I am certain they must have been saving up since the "*first* war", the woman's always talking about! [94] They have boxes and boxes, all varying in size and each marked on every side with big letters, which spell, "XMAS". I think it will take forever to sort through all *nine* of these cartons of decorations in order to determine what is useable, and what the moths or the mice ate while the ornamentations were stored up there.

Obviously, we must arrange everything, which needs to go on the tree, in the correct order so we may begin our cooperative tree artistry. "We start with the glass balls..." "Rosie" says. "No, stupid! We start with the lights...", "Rita" interrupts. "Correct. The lights go on first" the "mother" affirms. I decide the best job for me is unravelling the tin-foil garland strands, so I take one end of the red one, and start walking through the house with it. In no time, I have stretched-out red, blue and silver garlands so each reaches all the way up to the top of the stairs. They were a little flattened-down from being in storage, so I've been delegated the job of running my fingers all along each of them to fluff them back up. Easy-peasy!

It takes quite some time, but eventually, with a little cooperation, we get it right. Then we all sit on the couch while the mother does the honours of plugging the light strands into the wall socket. My, but the tree has shaped up quite beautifully. (Of course, I know, no matter what you do, it's hard to make a Christmas tree ugly.) "I'm making the popcorn!", "Rita" yells from the kitchen. (Do we even need a popcorn garland?) A few minutes later she walks in with a humongous bowl of popcorn which has oodles of butter drizzled all throughout. She and "Rosie" start to chow down and I realize *this popcorn* is for eating—not for decorating. So—I dig in too! Then we all sit back and enjoy our snack, which is the perfect reward for our hard work and collective creativity! (By the way, I seem to be having a little *fun* right now—sure hope it lasts.)

Now, with the tree all finished, the "mother" tells us to give her our Christmas "wish" lists so she can send in our letters to Santa. Gosh, I have *no idea* what to ask Santa for this year. The girls, on the other hand, know *exactly* what they want. "Rita" writes, Board Games, [82], such as "Sorry" [86], and some items of make-up like rouge or lipstick and "Chantilly

Revolving Doors

Perfume" [90]. "Rosie" wants the Board Game called "Candy Land", [87], and a great big bottle of pink bubble-stuff for the bathtub. Then the "mother" makes some suggestions to me and helps me write my own letter to Santa. (Well, actually, she writes the letter.)

"Dear Santa Claus,

I have been a very good boy this year and I would like a new 'Slinky', [83], a 'Tinkertoy Set', [45], or some 'Silly Putty', [84]. Santa, I love you a lot and I am going to put out some cookies and milk for you—and a carrot for Rudolph. [61] Thank you very much. Love, your friend, Teddy."

It is a perfect letter! O.K., now I am ready! "But, I thought you wanted to ask Santa for the electric train set you saw in the Wishbook? [32] [32a] Or, did you want to ask for a ride-around-on toy 'Hobby-Horse', [88]?" the foster "mother" sort of urges. "No", I insist. (Actually, I really, really *do*, but I tell her I don't because I'm not sure Santa has enough money for those things, and I really wouldn't want to be a bother to him, or cost him too much, because he might get mad, and punish me, and just bring me some of his dirty old *coal* instead.)

Now we've emptied all of these boxes, I am a little concerned because there weren't any "outdoor" lights to put up around the windows. Just then, the mother brings up a large bundle of outdoor lights, from her basement. Apparently, it was not packed away very carefully at the end of last Christmas season and as a result, it has a knot in it. However, the "knot" is the size of a basketball and the girls are *not* volunteering to untangle it. So, by herself, poor "Mrs. Smiley" has to get down on the floor to start working on untangling the big mess of lights and wires. Eventually, it begins looking more like a snake than a ball, and when she finds the end with the plug on it, she pokes it into the wall socket to check it out. However, nothing happens—nothing! Oh no! The lights are not working. So then, she explains,

"You know kids, if even one bulb is loose or burnt out, the whole strand won't come on. And you can't find the bad bulb unless you replace every one with a new one, and keep moving down the wire until the lights turn on." "I already knew that, mum.", "Rita" complains. (Oh no! Is this woman serious?)

[*My gosh, you'd think somebody would invent a new way for strands of lights to stay on, no matter how many tiny twinkling light bulbs happen to mysteriously burn themselves out while in winter storage. Oh, well, this is, after all, only December 1950.*]

Nevertheless, now my biggest concern is how Santa will ever find us without being directed to our house by twinkling coloured lights around our windows. But "Mrs. Smiley" has a solution. She says she is going to leave the Christmas tree lights on all night, with the drapes left open. This way, Santa, and Rudolph, [61], will be certain to find our house. "You're just being stupid, mom!", "Rita" complains. However, *I*, am completely satisfied with the "mother's" plan.

Oh yes, speaking of "Rudolph", [61], the "mother" says, besides the carrot, we have to leave out some other "reindeer food", so all the reindeer are able to keep up their energy too. What a novel idea, and a good one too! I have never actually considered the toll on all of the reindeer flying around to every child's house in the world in one night. O.K. by me! So, we prepare a dish of carrots and prickly, pointy holly leaves, with the red berries, which are poisonous if we eat them, but alright for flying reindeer. We set it out next to Santa's plate of homemade cookies. By the way, you would not believe how great the Christmas cookies ended up. We *cookie-cuttered* them into shapes like Christmas trees, bells, candles and even some like Rudolph, [61], with red candy noses! We put candy sprinkles on all of them too. Of course, lastly, we couldn't forget Santa's glass of *milk*! Just now, the foster "mother" announces it's bedtime. I am the first one upstairs and under my covers while tightly clutching "Pom Pom".

My eyes are squeezed shut and, though I may not be asleep yet, I know how to pretend I am until the "Big Fellow" stuffs himself down the chimney into our fireplace. I sure hope he drops-off a bunch of presents for us! Hopefully, he'll bring everything from the lists we all mailed to him earlier in the month—especially mine.)

The morning's sun slices yellow ribbons through the bedroom curtain openings, announcing *today's* wakey-wakey time as "Christmas morning". Oh boy, I am outta my fold-up cot so fast and bumming my way down the green stairs into the living room. It worked! "Mrs. Smiley's" idea to leave the curtains open and the tree-lights on all night, worked great! Santa Claus had indeed found us! There are oodles of beautiful brightly coloured and ribboned packages! However, I am going crazy because I can't read, so I don't know which are for me. Even more agonizing, now the mother says we have to wait for the girls to wake up before we can open anything.

Hmmmm...I'll handle it! On all fours, I scurry back upstairs and jump on "Rosie's" bed, "Ded-up Wosie!" She stirs a little, almost forgetting what surprises *this* morning has in store for us. Then I run into "Rita's" room, "Ded-up Wida, ded-up!", and she glowers at me until I remind her, "Danta dumd, Danta dumd!" Then she too jumps out of her bed and all three of us tear back down the stairs. Immediately, "Ooohs" and "Ahhhs" collectively come from all of us as we start to demolish the exciting coloured papers, ribbons and bows disguising the gifts inside the *first few* packages. However, the "mother" stops us, insisting on *slowly* reading the little labels and distributing the parcels to each of us.

After a very little while, we have opened all of the gifts, even losing some under the mess of paper and ribbons strewn across the floor. This Christmas morning is truly delightful for all of us, but especially for me. Santa brought many wonderful presents from everyone's list, and even some unexpected ones. The girls got their board games, [82], "Life Savers Christmas Candy Storybooks", big huge candy canes and stockings full of oranges, apples and tiny packages of "Sun-Maid Raisins." [80] I got my "Slinky", [83], some "Silly Putty", [84], and Santa even included a nice "Life Savers Christmas Candy Story Book" in *my* stocking! Oh, wow! The "mother" gave each of us a big solid chocolate reindeer! My reindeer has a red candy stuck on its nose, which is how I knew right away it was "Rudolph". [61] The only problem is I don't really want to eat him. I don't know where to start and I think it might hurt him if I were to eat his tail or his foot. Nevertheless, knowing the chocolate is going to be so delicious, I give in to temptation and start with his candy nose! Yummmm!

Christmas has already been over for a couple weeks now, because today is January 11, 1951. I overheard "Mrs. S." on the phone mentioning "Someone from the 'C.A.S.' is coming by to check on [me] this afternoon." I'm not worried because I know I am doing **a lot** better now. I am even seeing a little success at my attempts to communicate and make myself understood. Oh, it's the door buzzer. Hey, it's my old friend "Mrs. Mousey". "Hi, ya!" I announce. "Hello, Teddy, how are *we* doing today?" But before I could answer, the foster "mother" butts-in and offers, "The boy is doing quite a lot better—I mean, he's had no tantrums at all lately." "How is his head-banging problem?" the Worker asks. "Almost stopped.", "Mrs. Smiley" says with a typical grin. "Very good" my Case Worker replies, while jotting some notes for my file. Then the foster "mother" interrupts "Mousey's" notations with, "He can hum very nicely, too. You should hear him do the Christmas songs."

"Teddy, was Santa Claus good to you this year?" I respond to "Mousey's" question with a wild nod of excitement, and immediately start to drag out some of the things Santa brought me for being such a *good* little boy. (Wow, how nice. I think she actually seems impressed.) I try to tell her what each item is about, but I think she only understands every third word. Then the "Mouse Lady" stands up to leave and says, "I'll be back in a couple months, Teddy, until then you be a good boy for Mrs…" "Uh-huh, Odee Dodee" I reply with every intention of complying.

More days come and go in this house, and as each passes I am getting along better and learning so much I am even talking a little better, (at least *I* think so, anyway). Christmas 1950, and New Year's Day 1951 are only distant memories now, because it's now February already. I am getting much bigger because I am now all of three-and-a-half years old. I am even big enough to recognize, and remember the reason for, the box of pink and red hearts and streamers on the kitchen table. "Valentine's Day" is quickly approaching and I remember from experience, those are the *decorations*. So, I eagerly help the "mother" with her embellishment of our home by sticking the paper hearts all over the windows and on the walls too.

"Mrs. Smiley" has been humming something vaguely familiar all day, but I just can't put my finger on where I've heard it before. The girls are busily writing their friends' names on little Valentine's cards so they can pass them out at their school parties tomorrow. Me, I'm helping the "mother" bake, because, of course, what Valentine's celebrations would be complete without home-made, cookie-cutter heart-shaped cookies decorated with pink and red icing and little heart-shaped cinnamon candies? I put the little hearts on. However, for every two heart-candies I place on the iced-cookies, I sneak one and eat it myself. (They are yummy, but oh, how they burn my little mouth and tongue.)

The next day the girls bring a bunch of candy home from their little class parties. There are red hearts, chocolates and a lot of suckers too. I think it's very nice of them to share their stashes of goodies with me.

As well, their mother bought each one of us humongous hollow chocolate hearts. This time I am saving some of my goodies and hiding them in my hidey-hole. This way I won't get a bad tummy ache from eating too much sugar all at once. Ah, yes! After it was over, I must say, "*A wonderful Valentine's Day was had by all!*"

Oh, yes, my "hidey-hole"--I neglected to mention the special place in *this* house which I've discovered is perfect for hiding little ol' me! This one is a sort-of wooden frame, or box, built along the length of the front hall disguising the radiator inside. The box provides a mantle-type shelf on top, with hooks all along the front latticed *window* area which are intended for drying-off wet mittens and snowy woollen toques. I discovered, on one side of the frame-box, the wood panel pops off. One time I noticed the "mother" draining some water from the radiator, which is obviously the reason for the small release-valve at the bottom of the green-painted metal heater. The removable side wood panel is my entryway into the box, but it's amazing how I can actually *fit inside*. Then I easily pull the wood panel in after myself. I am serious! I really like my small, safe hiding places, and this one is really warm too. Nobody can find me, or get me, in there, but I can quietly watch and listen to all the goings-on through the screen. Whenever I need to escape, I slide inside the box, stay outta trouble, listen and wait until the coast is clear for me to exit.

Revolving Doors

More weeks come and go, and today it's time to start getting out the decorations for a different holiday called, "Saint Patrick's Day". I am not even surprised the "mother" actually has a storage box with that moniker written on it in large green letters. On each side of the box, it even has drawings of green clovers with four-leaf petals. While she sorts through all the stuff, I am playing with my Slinky, [83], making it go down, down the stairs.

Just then, I hear a knock at the door. Oh, it's the "Library Lady". She comes right in and, immediately spotting me on the stairs, asks me, "Hello Teddy! So—how're *we* doing these days" (Why do they always say that? Why do they call me, "we"? Oh, never mind.) I start to tell her, "See my Swinky on da dairs? An' Danta bwinged me Silwy Puddy! (Wow, I think I'm doing a pretty good job of telling her all about my "Slinky", [83], and my "Silly Putty" I got from Santa.)

When she sits down on the sofa, I lift-up Midnight and drag him over to her to show her the kitty. However, when she recoils in fear, letting out a little yelp, "Mrs. Smiley" scolds me and tells me to, "Get him away from 'Mrs...'!" I comply, dragging the poor, heavy, hapless cat by his front legs all the way to the front door. On the way, though, I try to fit him and me into the hidey-hole, but Midnight is having none of it! Then, outside he goes.

"Teddy is really fond of music, you know, and he can keep a tune very nicely too." the "foster mother" touts. "Yes, I believe you've mentioned it. I seem to remember such a notation in his file. Well, I must say, he certainly is an attractive little fellow with his hazel eyes and brown hair." (Sounds like my eyes have gone and changed their colour again? Brown hair, I thought I was a Nordic-looking blonde-haired, blue-eyed child.) "I can see he has improved a great deal from being in your home, 'Mrs...'" "L. L." remarks. (Yes, I am doing very well and getting along nicely with the daughters as well. A-n-d...I haven't had a tantrum in a long time and very soon now, I'm certain I'll be able to stop my head-banging—in fact, I *know* it.)

Chapter 30: Appearances Are *Always* Deceiving

Whenever I think things are going pretty well in my life, or whenever I feel a little happiness, or joy, something comes along and kicks me in the bum—really, *really* hard! Recently, during the Easter break from school, "Rita" and "Rosie" went to stay at their Uncle Franklin's house in the country. I understand he has a great big farm with a barn, and lots of cows, a big, fat, pink pig and even horses you can ride on. The girls' daddy moved there with his brother when he split-up with his wife, my "foster mother". I guess by the way they all talk about the arrangement, it seems everyone is reasonably satisfied.

The girls' plan is to stay from the sixteenth of March until Easter on the twenty-fifth. I don't care about the girls not inviting me to go along with them, although I would like to go if only to see a *real* farm. However, this break from the girls will be good for me because, with them gone, it leaves more one-on-one time for "Mrs. Smiley" and me—and maybe even a few more cookies for me too. (You would not believe how many icing-sugar-covered Bunny cookies I have already stashed in my little hidey-hole! Oh yes, I believe I am prepared for *any* possible emergency. However, it's a real mystery, because two of the cookies now have a bunch of little scratches, bite-marks and pieces missing, and I know *I* didn't cause the damage.)

However, something unexpected and unforeseen happened while the sisters were over at their uncle's farm. Today is "Good Friday" and they have returned after only a week over there. This is much sooner than the "mother" expected, and *their* return is now interrupting *her* plans. Naturally, she wants to know why they have come back so soon. However, only minutes after they arrived home, she is talking to them in muted whispers and, of course, I am unable to hear their actual words.

All I *do* know is, "Rosie" has returned with a bad attitude, which is following her around like a stinky fart. "Rita", on the other hand, will not stop crying, and stomping her feet, and even screaming! In fact, she has been absolutely wailing and *cursing* at the top of her lungs! Her strange behaviour doesn't stop there. Now, she has also started *biting* herself—not her fingernails, but *her arms*! Over the phone, her mum told her daddy, "'Sharon', (her girlfriend, who's a nurse), thinks, *'Rita' is trying to relieve some anger or frustration by pushing it inward towards herself.*"

(Anyway, I want to know what the heck kind of anger or problems would cause her to make bloody bite marks all over both of her own arms?!)

"Mrs. Smiley" has not been smiling at all lately and, in fact, is spending more and more time on the phone, yelling at the girls' *daddy*. She is complaining about *something* "Rita" said her "Uncle Franklin" apparently **did** to her while she was staying at his farmhouse. I wonder what it could be. Maybe he spanked her. Whatever her problem is, now this foster "mother" is screeching on the phone into her ex-husband's ear and after she bangs down the receiver, is balling her eyes out as well. (What the heck could've happened when the sisters were away?)

Something is going on around here which is changing our everyday lives, completely. Although we had started to prepare for Easter Sunday, and the Easter Bunny's much anticipated arrival, everything came to a screeching halt and Easter preparations were not only stopped, but also all decorations came back down and were boxed up immediately. In fact, I would not even know it, but Easter Sunday came and went—and the Bunny missed our house completely! It's pretty sad how whatever happened at the farm could change our world. How could it stop all the fun we should have been having, hunting for the Easter eggs and such? (Right now, I am thinking it's a good thing I've been hoarding my candy and chocolate since Valentine's Day. I never, ever know what might be around the next corner, or through the next *revolving door*...sweep ...sweep... sweep... sweeeeeep.)

The girls' mother is lecturing them in the kitchen right now. She's saying, "You'll both have to forget about *it* and get ready to go back to school tomorrow. And, by the way, "Rita", take "Rosie's" sweater off—it's too tight on you!!" However, "Rita" is acting more and more frustrated and angry right now and shouts, even cusses, at her mother saying, "No, mummie, I'm not going to *fucking* school and you can't make me!" "Rita's" hissy fit continues with the words, "And I'll wear whatever the hell I want, and go out with whichever friends I want to! And—you just try and stop me! And, by the way, everybody can just stay out of my damn room too!" (She is actually raising her balled-up fist and making a threatening motion to her mother! Where did all *this* come from?) "'Rita', stop saying those things!" her mom pleads, while backing away from her. (Ooooh, I've already snuck into my hidey-hole. I'm only too glad I'm hidden and out of everybody's way before I get socked in the eye by any of the things "Rita" has now started *throwing* at her mum.)

Nevertheless, school's back in session and "Rosie" seems to have put behind her whatever "happened" at her Uncle's house, but some things about "Rita" have definitely changed now—and decidedly for the worse. She has become quiet, ultra moody, withdrawn and soooo angry she fairly bursts with her own form of tantrum whenever she is asked to do, or *not do*, the smallest thing, or even if she's spoken to at all. Everybody irritates her, and everything bothers her to no end.

Revolving Doors

Her mother and sister are virtually walking on eggshells so as not to "set her off" on another rant or tirade of screaming obscenities.

I would surely like to know what happened at her Uncle's house during her visit. No, forget it. I don't want to know, considering how negatively it affected everyone in this household the way it has. "Rita" is so disturbed now, she has started to lock herself in our room and bellows at any of us, ***"Don't anybody dare knock on my bloody damn door!"*** Then she plays her record player so loudly you can't even hear yourself think. I don't have any idea what is wrong with her, but I decide to keep, myself *invisible*, just in case it has *anything* to do with me. (Unfortunately, in the evening, the "mother" is still putting me to bed on the little cot in "Rita's"/my bedroom.)

Chapter 31: When the *REAL HELL* Begins!

Before long, the school year ends, with "Rita" having missed so many days she was unable to squeeze through to the next grade. Fortunately for her, summer school provides her only opportunity of making up all of the missed lessons so she may matriculate into grade nine as a high school freshman. Otherwise, she would have to repeat her whole grade eight school year.

Of course, with the advent of summer, the girls' get their, *previously*, eagerly-anticipated, invitation from their father for them to return for a summer stay with him at his brother's farmhouse. With only a little hesitation, "Rosie" agrees, but "Rita" is adamant and screams at her mother,

"I'm never going back over to my "uncle's" stinkin' rat hole—never, ever again! Mum, I hate you for even suggesting it! What do you think I am?"

"Of course, you're right "Rita". I wasn't thinking. You have your summer school to attend." her mother condescends. Then "Rita" screeches at her mum, ***"You know damn well this is NOT about my fucking summer school!"*** Then, controlling her voice, her mother replies, "'Rita', dear, let's not discuss this in front of "Rosie"--or 'you-know-who'." she adds, glancing sideways at me. (I wonder why I am always, "You-Know-Who".)

"I don't care if "Rita" can't come, I'm going anyway! Daddy promised to teach me to swim in the pond this year. And, guess what, "Rita", I'll get *lots* more attention, and ice cream, from daddy without *you* along!" "You stupid brat! I don't care about fucking ice cream! Go idiot! Go! And have fu-uh-unnn!" A few days later, with "Rita's" apparent blessings, "Rosie" does go off to stay with her father, (and uncle), with the planned visit arranged to last for, "*a month or so*".

[Shortly I will understand that the "ice-cream" days of my own life have now ended and the real "*fiery burning hell*" of my bare subsistence is about to begin! (Oh, shit! There I go again. Bang, bang, bang! I am in the back of "Rita's" closet and am trying to hide myself from the bad thoughts, feelings and associated cuss words flying around this house, but my head-banging has just given away *this* secret location. Dammit, I *hate* myself and I hate my world!)]

"Mrs. Smiley" just announced her decision to take on a night-time job, at least for the summer. She explains that "It's necessary to "supplement [her] income." "Rosie" needs braces on her teeth, which is going to be a great deal of expense, and her father completely refuses to help with that cost. Then, right before school ended, "Rita" came home with a note indicating she was going to definitely need eyeglasses before the start of the fall school year. The eye doctor and the special prescription glasses "Rita" needs are going to cost around seventy or eighty dollars, and of course, her *no-account* father is refusing to help with the purchase of those as well. Of course, both of the girls are going to need new clothing and shoes before school starts and, as the "mother" repeatedly complains, "It seems the expenses just never end with these girls!"

Their mother sounds off about the girls, "always needing or wanting some damn thing" and about the fact her, "money always gets spent even before [she] gets it", which is a little confusing to me. However, I sure don't know what she means whenever she complains, "All these kids are gonna put me in the *poorhouse*!" (I sure hope *I* don't have to go to the "poorhouse" whatever *it* is, because it certainly does not sound like a very welcoming place—and I am fed up with *un-*

welcoming places!) Anyway, these are some of the reasons this "mother" has taken a job in a garment factory, sewing clothing for other people. I overheard her on the phone saying, "*You know, Sonja*", (her sister), "*I considered taking-in another foster child, but thought better of the idea, because this one extra **boy** is really more than I can handle right now*." (Maybe I should be thinking about packing my bag again. We'll see.)

Unfortunately, the many hours the "mother" now has to spend away at her new job are loading a lot of responsibility onto "Rita's" shoulders, (much of which is due to the extra job of caring for *my* needs). Basically, "Rita" has had to become the "mother" to me, handling my morning and evening routines of feeding, bathing and dressing me. She even washes the laundry, hangs it out on the line then irons it later. She certainly is not very happy about this new system and she is not hesitating to let anyone, (especially me), know what she thinks. Nevertheless, what can we three kids do but accept and adapt to these new living, and caring, arrangements.

The "mother's" new job in the factory takes her of the house every evening, and she doesn't return until very early the following morning. I am left in "Rita's" so-called "care" to ensure I am given supper, bathed and put to bed. Then in the morning, she has to give me breakfast and get me dressed. We all must be very quiet so we never wake our mum who has only just returned from her night shift, and always needs to sleep in the daytime. Of course, there is nothing I can do to help the situation. I am unable to care for my own needs and it is *not* my fault how "Rita", simply by virtue of her birth order, has been forced into the role of my caregiver. Despite this disturbed teen's protests, it's just the way things must be, for a little while anyway, until the real mother can "get on [her] feet."

However, after less than a week of this change in our routine, "Rita" has acquired a new attitude. She has become *very mean* toward *me* lately, as if any of these changes are my fault. She is quite short-tempered and quick to severely punish me over my least little mistake or petty misdeed. Nevertheless, something else has started happening between us. It's something which feels creepy and *bad* to me, and I DON'T LIKE IT ONE LITTLE BIT! (***BANG BANG BANG!!)***

Of course, I know "Rita" is in charge of my "*care*"; however, her newest form of *taking care* of me is nothing like I have ever before experienced—in my whole life. This girl has begun to *use* me as her own personal, private **toy**! She *uses* me in a way, which is neither playful nor fun, but is in a mean, demanding, deviant, sick, abusive and, yes, *sexual* way! She has started to touch me, and bother me in a manner which somehow gives her pleasure. What she does to me, and forces me to do to myself, and to her, makes her giggle and laugh, but it makes me feel dirty and yucky, and makes me want to cry—and puke.

It all started around the fifth morning we had to get up and get ready for the day. While the "foster mother" was dead asleep, this girl decides to *play* with me. I don't mean she wanted to play games, or ball-toss or toy cars'. What I mean is, she wanted to *play* with me—to use me as her own personal little "*toy*". It began when I first woke up in the morning. Of course, like any other little boy, (or, also for any grown-up man, I suppose), I wake up with a stiff little pee pee—a "woody". I just need to go pee and relieve myself, in order for it to shrink back down to normal size. Well, on, this, my first incident of *molestation*, "Rita" stopped me from using the bathroom. In fact, she stood in front of our bedroom door, blocking it so I couldn't get out! She was laughing and making fun of me, but I was frustrated and scared. I thought if I end up peeing in my bed, or even on the floor, I'll definitely be in really big trouble and certainly catch heck from "Rita", and even more likely get the "firm hand", (a spanking), from the "mother". Instead of letting me go to the bathroom and pee in the potty, she sat down, facing me, and leaning back against the bedroom-side of the closed door, absolutely refusing to let me get past her.

At that point, as I am standing in front of her, she yanks-down my jammie bottoms and starts to touch my woody. (Oh, gosh! I wonder what the heck she is trying to do to me.) It's then she starts to fondle and stroke my pee pee! Then, leaning forward, she actually puts it into her mouth and sucks, and sucks on it. What a *terrible* feeling! It's really awful, having to go pee so badly, and trying to hold it in so as not to let go of any pee into her mouth.

Suddenly, she actually pulls her nightie up and doesn't have a thing on underneath it! Oh God and Santa! What was I supposed to think—or do now? Moreover, what is the tangled jungle of ugly, writhing black hairs doing, reforesting the very spot where her pee-pee had obviously fallen off? (In the event her pee pee has not dropped off, then where is it, and how does she use it? I wonder if she is deformed, or a freak of some sort.) However, I have barely time enough to form these questions in my mind when she pushes me down onto the floor on my back and, straddling my diminutive body, she tries to sort of sit on my little "hard-on" and stick it into her "sex"! [vagina]

I have no idea what "Rita" is trying to do to me, or why, but once she gets my pee-pee into the hole between her legs, I feel a warm, slickness and I almost can't control myself, or hold back peeing. I don't know what is happening, but she is a very stocky teenager and her weight alone has pinned me in place. She is simply not allowing me to squirm away and get my little pee-pee out of her hole. The pain I am experiencing is beyond description. My little wee-wee hurts because I still have to go pee, and I've been holding it back so long now, that I have an ache *deep* in my belly. However, it also hurts because it's stiff and the delicate skin is stretching—and staying unnaturally stretched.

Nevertheless, after a few moments of her twisting and wriggling the strangest feeling has just washed over me. The more this girl squirms and writhes around with my pee-pee into her gaping sex-hole, the more she moans and it sort of tickles and hurts me, all at the same time. I mean it makes me feel terrible as if I am being a bad little kid, but I am completely confused by the co-mingled rush of physical feelings which are strangely enjoyable at the same time.

[This girl may be completely self-serving in her urge for sexual pleasure; however, her molestation, and *rape* of me, like it or not, has just introduced me to my first, (albeit immature), sexual climax to *orgasm, (the delights of which, I was unable to fight or ignore).*]

In my gut I *know* what she's doing to me is not right. In fact, I sense it is very, very wrong. Otherwise, if this activity were a completely normal part of any little boy's development, why wouldn't I have experienced it a multitude of times over my short lifetime? As well, I know it's a *bad* thing because she is being really quiet and secretive so as not to let her mother know what is going on behind this closed door. When I try to complain and wrestle out from under her, she puts her hand over my mouth and tells me to,

"Shut the hell up, brat—and you stay fucking put, until I'm done with you!"

("...*done with me!*"...My brain floods with questions:
"When will it be?
What is she doing to my body?
Why on earth is she forcing me to partake in this ritual?"
I wonder if this could possibly have anything whatsoever to do

with the strange activities, which occurred up at her uncle's farm.)

I'm crying at this point and I try to tell her to, "DOP-IT!" But she pinches my cheeks *really hard* between her thumb and forefinger, then she leans down and *whisper-yells*, quite firmly, into my ear,

"Shut the hell up you little fucking brat—or I'll really give you something to cry about!"

(**Bang, bang, bang!** I really wish a revolving door would sweep around and scoop me up and out of the situation which I am in right now! However, all I can do is *hope* I'm just dreaming the worst nightmare of my life.)

I am so confused. I can't understand what in the world is happening to me, or what I've done to deserve such terrible treatment from this girl. However, just then, when I thought it was all over because my woody had subsided, she grabs my pee-pee and starts pulling hard, really hard on it. In fact, she squeezes it so terribly tightly, and starts pulling it up and down, up and down. It is so very painful, once again, I open my mouth to scream a marriage of *agony* and *fear*. It's then she slaps her hand over my mouth, again, so I can't make a sound, but this time she is choking me and not allowing me to breathe! She won't let go of her grasp on my woody, though I am moaning and crying, until finally I can't hold it any longer and have to release my pee all over her bare body, on her nightie and, as she squeezes and purposely aims it all right *into* her *sex*.

It doesn't matter if she stifles my crying, or squeezes my face, because right now, my belly is even more painful. However, after such abuse, I am whimpering like a puppy who's been kicked across the room and doesn't understand why. Then, still not letting me get up, she takes my little hand and shoves my fingers into her sex, moving them around and around until some stuff, along with my pee, has all dribbled out of her. It feels so strange, like nothing my hand has ever felt before. It is hot and wet and the slimy excretion feels just like the snot that dribbles out of my runny nose.

But then "Rita" starts making moaning sounds and funny squeaky noises while she moves my fingers around inside her sex faster and faster until she makes some more gooey slime come out of her, run all over my fingers and down my little hand. Now my wrist hurts too from her pulling and forcing my hand into her hairy hole.

Still not done with me, she forces my slimy fingers into *my* mouth and tells me to suck them while she puts fingers from both of her hands into her own "sex-hole" and does something to herself, which makes her sway and moan and groan even *more*! Then she crawls up my body and sits on my little face with her sex-hole covering my mouth and my nose. It's impossible to catch my breath. I am absolutely in shock and I can't believe what is happening when she says, "*Suck it, lick it, more, faster, suck, suck, move your tongue faster you little brat-fucker!*" Finally, she falls over and lays down beside me, gasping and breathing hard.

Her slime tastes awful and smells disgusting, exactly like a dead fish which has been sitting-out too long in the summer heat of the farmer's market! However, unfortunately, my torture is not over yet. Although I am gagging, she is still forcing my fingers down my own throat. Then she says, "*You goddamned fucking little brat—if you say anything to 'Rosie', or to mom, I promise you, first I will torture you way worse than this, then __I will kill you__!*" (Of course, I believe her.)

All I can think of is, "Well just go ahead and kill me now,

because I'd rather be dead and feeding worms, than go through *this* experience again and have to eat any more of *your fishy slime!*" Once she seemed to be done with me, I roll sideways and start to puke and once again, she squeezes my cheeks, this time causing me so much pain, it actually halts my vomiting reflex.

Finally, gratefully, *it*, whatever *it* was, is all over. She gets up and tells me to stand up and clean up the pee-and-vomit-mess I've made all over the floor. She strips her nightie all the way off, because it's all wet with her slime and my pee. That's when I first see her small, pointy titties and her dark brown, erect nipples. I am at once terrified and curious, because, of course, this is my first sighting of a girl's boobies. (Such a strange mix of feelings and emotions are coursing through me right now and I am confused to find myself fighting some *very strange feelings* of my own.) At least I know "Rita" will leave me alone now because I no longer have to pee, and my pee-pee is flopped over and my woody is gone to sleep.

She is just about to leave the bedroom, when once more she bends down and starts to suck on my pee-pee. Oh noooo! Oh my gosh...! "Wida dop! Dop, Wida, dop, dop! Pwease, pwease Wida..." However, it's too late, she has made my pee-pee big and hard as a little stick again, and her sucking is both frightening, and the cause of unspeakable pain. I hate it, yet I want more of her stroking and sucking, all at the same time! Then she plays with my little hard-on and swirls it around in her mouth with her tongue. She licks her lips and says I taste delicious and tries to suck every last drop of pee out of my little wee-wee—but to no avail because there is nothing left in me.

Finally, this girl stands up, saying,

"Get ready for more, kiddo, this is just the beginning of the fun we are going to have together! I promise you, there will not be

*a day or night going by without me playing really hard with your pee-pee! Guess what, brat—I have more than one surprise for you! You don't know it yet, but even if it hurts, I can make your wee-wee feed my tongue with pee, again and again! Nevertheless, we'll save some surprises for tonight and tomorrow morning, little guy. I'm warning you—you'd better remember this—when you see me coming for you, you might as well go ahead and take off your pyjama bottoms, because you will already know what I want, and why I coming for you. Don't you dare try to fight me, or struggle and wake mum up! Just get your little dicky-wicky ready for "Rita's" nice warm, slick cunty-wunty—because if your little hard-on isn't good enough, I will suck and bite your little baby-dick until it gives me everything I want, and then some more! So, get ready because you can never, ever get away from the fun little tortures I am going to force on your body! And the next time I'm gonna bring something very special to use **on** you, and **in** you—to really, **painfully** torture you if you are a bad little brat and cry, or try to scream!"*

Oh! *Bang! Bang! Bang!* What the hell is she talking about? I am sore, sad and stupefied. I don't know why she wants to use me this way. I don't understand the confusing simultaneous good and bad feelings I'm experiencing. Nobody has ever forced me to hold-in my pee until my belly aches. No one has ever touched my pee-pee the way she did. I mean, of course, my different foster "mothers" have had to clean me up from a dirty diaper, or bathe me and wash my pee-pee; however, nobody has touched it, pulled it or *sucked on it*! I am terribly sore and my tummy aches too. Nevertheless, it's my pee-pee, which is hurting an awful lot right now, and no wonder, because all her abuse has caused a painful lesion on its thin skin. Shit, now my pee-pee is broken and bleeding! Oh hell, how I *hate* her damn guts! ***BANGGGGGGG!!!***

However, now, to add to these loathsome feelings I have

toward "Rita", I am terrified of her! I fear her and hate her all at the same time! What else could she be planning to do to my pee-pee to make it hard and spit pee all over her again? I don't know what to do, so I *do* nothing. I don't know what she'll do if I tell her mother, so I *say* nothing. Thank goodness, at least she has to go to school for most of the day, so I will have a short reprieve from her molestation. How will I ever go through this day as if nothing has happened? Even if I could make myself understood, I don't dare tell the "mother" because of the unspeakable torture which "Rita" has threatened.

Although I have time to breathe a little, the whole days passes with me not feeling like playing at all. When school is out and "Rita" returns home, the minute she comes through the front door, she pushes me into the corner of the hallway and scream-whispers into my ear,

"You little fucker—you'd better not have told mum about our little secret fun time! Did you say anything to her? Did you, brat-fucker?"

I shake my head with an emphatic, "No—no!" Thankfully, she's momentarily satisfied. She *knows* she now has total control over my body and my mind, so she releases me from the hall corner and storms up to our room.

Everything seemed to be alright throughout supper, which made me think maybe "Rita" had forgotten her promised threat to me about "tonight". However, I was wrong, because later in the evening, when it was time for her to bathe me and get me ready for bed, she says, "Teddeee, get your play-clothes off and come get in the tub!" Of course, I *need* to, and I'm *supposed* to, *go pee in the potty* before I get into the tub. However, she won't let me go potty at all and forces me to get into the bathtub. Then she climbs right into there with me! Then she plays with my pee-pee, stroking it until it's really painful for me, all over again. I beg her to leave me alone. I tell her repeatedly I can't hold my pee any longer. Then she forces me go pee *on* her! (I think she's gone totally nuts! Why would she want me to pee *on* her and not *in* the potty?)

However, "Rita" is still not finished playing this horrible game with me. She takes my hands and forces me to rub the pee all over her little breasts and her belly. (I am getting really scared because I'm certain she has gone totally loopy.) I try to whimper quietly, but she slaps my face with her wet hand which makes it hurt more than ever. *"Shut-up, stupid brat! I warned you not to cry—and I meant it!"*

However, it's not over yet, because right now she's sitting-down on the side of the tub with her legs spread wide apart. Then separating her "pussy" lips with her fingers she forces me to look right inside of her sex-hole. *"Look at it, little brat-fucker! Look inside of me! It's where* **you** *are going, right now."* Then she pulls me towards it and makes my lips touch the hairy lips on the outside of her hole. (I'm wondering what happened to her pee-pee which must have been like mine. What could have made it fall off and disappear? Actually now I'm seriously getting nervous thinking, *if "Rita's" abuse doesn't stop, my wee-wee might suffer the same fate!*)

Nevertheless, this abusive, molesting teenager has her own agenda and is hell-bent on having me pleasure her. So she grabs my head with both her hands and says,

"Stick your tongue out, stupid! Stick it way far out. Lemmie see you do this." So, having no other recourse, I oblige. *"There's a good little fucker. Now we're gonna playing a new game. You're gonna fuck 'Rita's' little pussy-cunt with your tongue!"*

I try to fight her but she starts pushing my head back and forth hard, making my tongue and my nose, heck my whole face, go in and out, in and out, of her disgusting hole until her sex-hole squirts sticky, smelly slime into my mouth. (Oh, *nuts!* All I can think of is, "*How am I ever going to get out of this bathtub and run way far away from "Rita" and her new craziness?!!*")

Though I think, and wish, this torturous treatment must truly be over now, I quickly discover, for "Rita", it's still not the end of my bathtub *play* time. She makes me lay down in the shallow water, face-up, and then she strokes and strokes my sore, raw pee-pee until we both see it grow bigger and harder. Nevertheless, by now, probably from the cool bathwater, I have to pee again. I can't hold it this time and I dribble some pee into the tub. Now she starts hitting my head and whisper-screaming at me, "*What the hell are you doing, brat? You are supposed to let me lick and swallow your pee! Now you've wasted it and we'll have to do this all over again!*" (I am exhausted and I just want to go to bed and sleep, or *die*—I really don't care which.)

Eventually I do get to go to bed, but not alone, because "Rita" crawls right in beside, and facing, me in order to execute her promised threat. Then, with our pee pees touching, she wraps her legs around me, she tries to make my pee-pee hard again so it will stick out straight and go inside of her sex-hole. I know it isn't getting hard but what she is doing to me, apparently *works for her*, because in only a few minutes she is writhing and squirming with delight and I have to admit, as creepy as it feels in my head, my body feels something quite different. My wee-wee is cut and sore and aching, but after my dead little pee-pee falls limply out of her sex-hole, I experience a sensation of floating on a cloud. In fact, I feel like I too, in a strange sort of way, simultaneously want more—and NO MORE—of what she has started doing to me today. (Maybe I *am* dead.) In any event, I really hope she forgets about all of this by the morning-time when she is supposed to get me dressed again for the day.

After she is done using my body this one last time, I pass-out, asleep from exhaustion. Nevertheless, at some point in the middle of the night, I wake up crying and screaming from a nightmare, or perhaps it was a memory. "Rita" quickly jumps over to my cot and leans down to my ear to whisper-threaten me with, "*Shut-up brat, and go back to sleep – or I'll knock you asleep! And you know—I will!*" I am shutting up and pretending to be asleep now. If I can fool Santa, I can certainly fool "Rita".

The morning's sun ribbons beam across my face and wake me up first, as usual. Immediately I think I must have had some horrifying nightmares. When I sit up, I become acutely aware my pee-pee is super sore, and my morning pee-woody is hurting me today. When I notice "Rita" is still asleep, remembering yesterday's horrendous abuse, I grab "Pom Pom", sneak out of the room and quietly bum my way down the stairs. As soon as I spot Midnight in the kitchen, I run over to pet him and have a little telepathic chat with my safe furry friend. "Oh my gosh, Midnight! It was so terrible yesterday. Did you know how badly 'Rita' was treating me? She was so mean and did such awful things to my pee-pee. I hope she's back to normal today—and leaves me alone!"

"Shhushh...Sheees". Oh, oh...it's the toilet flushing! Is it "Rosie" or "Rita"? Doesn't matter...I am already slipping into my hidey-hole so my tormentor doesn't find me today. My body is terribly sore and my spirit is very broken. I did not know another person could be so devastatingly evil to me. I have suffered much mistreatment in my short little life, but absolutely nothing could have prepared me for "Rita's" torturous abuse. I still don't really know what went on at her uncle's farm at Easter, but I think I am starting to get an idea. It's too bad if some of the things she did to me yesterday happened to her on the farm. But that's no reason, or excuse, for her to turn and repeat the perversions she learned at the farm on my innocent little body! Since the "mother" has taken the night job, "Rita" is supposed to be taking care of my needs—not abusing, molesting and *raping* me! This is soooo wrong. It makes me a much sadder little boy than I would ever have thought possible.

Thump, ka-thump, thump, ka-thump...! It's "Rita" coming down the stairs, "Teddy—where are you—Teddeeee?" "'Rosie'--is Teddy up in your room?" I hold my breath in with one hand and clasp my pee-pee with the other. I listen while she searches for me. Then, when I am certain she is out in the backyard, I slide out from my hiding place. When she comes in, she yells at me for not showing up when she was calling. Nevertheless, it's almost time for school and I hear the "mother" stirring now, so I'm sure it's safe, for a little while anyway.

After the girls catch the school bus and I am sitting eating my "Krispies", I breathe a little easier knowing, for a few hours anyway, I won't be treated like "Rita's" personal sex toy. Boy, do I ever need a nap. However, the day passes all too quickly and it seems as if no time has passed when school's out and the girls come running in. Immediately they both head to the kitchen for a snack before starting on their homework. Except "Rita" refuses to do any homework since she's just repeating grade eight anyway. I'm really not certain where I stand with "Rita" today, but I'm sure that nothing will be happening, at least until bath time. Strange, though, "Rita" keeps slipping me glaring sideways glances. I think she's mad at me, although it's hard to read her. Later on, after "Rosie" has had her bath, she leaves her dirty water in and it's my time. (Most nights we have to share bath water to save money on the hydro-electric bill, which the "mother" complains about having to pay.)

Suddenly, "Rita" comes in close behind me and pushes me further into the bathroom. Then she locks the door and turns-on the little radio which is up on the high plant shelf. (I'm curious because she has never done that before.) "*Get your clothes off, brat!*" she demands, adding, "*And get in the tub!*" I comply. "*What's this? Is your tiny little dick sore, little brat? It looks very red and sore—maybe I can make it feel better, okee dokee?*" She reaches into the tepid water and grabs my sore, red, cut and dying pee-pee. Then she pulls it and strokes it up and down. "Dop-it Wida, Dop-it! I dot boo-boo!" I try to beg her. "*Oh—too bad—let me kiss the boo-boo on your pee-pee and make it all better kid!*"

Oh gosh noooo! Not this shit again. "Please God and Santa get me out of this terrible situation. Please." I pray, but to no avail. I am alone in my misery and torture. I am a little kid and don't have the strength, or the wherewithal, to fight her. She has planned to molest me and I may as well sit back and take it until she is done with me. Her next move is to take her own jeans and panties off and sit on the side of the bathtub with her legs spread wide, again. (I guess I know what happens next.) Then she takes both my little hands and pokes as many of my fingers as will fit into her wide-open, ugly, red, fleshy sex hole. When she decides she's 'hot' enough, "Rita" starts to squirt her slime down my fingers and hands. Then she pulls me over to her "pussy hole" which is alive with its curly, snaking, black forest entrance-way. Then she pushes my face into it. "*Lick me, brat! Move your face all around in my cunt and lick me until I pour my sticky stuff into your eyes!*"

What the hell is happening to me? (What the hell has my little life become—just morning and night of sexing her hole? Is this it? I do as she says, but I am crying about it.) "*Stop it you little fucker! Stop your fucking whining!*" She ceases her writhing for a second and stands up only to turn the little radio up louder, in order to muffle my cries and mask her moaning and heavy-breathing. Then she sits back down on the side of the tub facing me with her legs spread even wider apart now. I have gotten back into the water, which is quite cool against my skin and actually feels better on my sore, red pee-pee. However, then she stands me up and pulls me to her. *"You're going to fuck me, little brat, or else I'll* **torture you***. I will stick some very hard things up your bum—like mom's wooden spoon!* (As she says this, she glances over her shoulder to the counter where sits the "wooden spoon"--quite *out of place* in the bathroom. Oh, no! This is the implement of torture she has been promising.) *So bring your little pee-pee over here and stick it into momma 'Rita's' nice, big, warm, wet, slimy cunty-wunty, baby-boy!"* Again, thinking of the alternative, which has seriously been threatened, I comply. What the hell else can I do?

At the point when she seems to act *satisfied*, I am sure the torture is over, at least for another night. Then, she gets me dressed in my jammie *top,* but not the bottoms—those she is holding as she directs me to get into bed. She, too, re-dresses before exiting the bathroom, (a good sign, I take it). I crawl into my bed and grab "Pom Pom" for a little extra security. *"Not your bed, you stupid little shit—my bed! Get up there into* **my** *bed!"* She locks our bedroom door and off come her clothes again, as she mumbles something about her *"plan to try something a little different tonight"*. No...Oh noooo! ***Bang! Bang!!***

This time she sits with her pussy-hole on my face—*completely covering my mouth and nose*! I wiggle around and squirm like crazy but she won't move off me! In fact, she seems to get greater pleasure the more I struggle and writhe underneath her. I gurgle and choke, trying to push her off me, imploring her to stop. However, she keeps doing this to me until finally, I can't breathe, and I actually pass out, completely unconscious! When I do regain consciousness, my face is completely wet and slimy, and I can still smell the fishy stench of her dirty, rotten sex! My gosh! Her stink makes me so nauseated I start gagging, retching and then throwing-up all over her.

Every night now, when "Rita" is supposed to be putting me to bed, I know I will have nothing to look forward to but this horrendous ritual. (**Bang, bang, bang...**)

In the morning, I find myself on my own cot although I have no idea how I got here. Apparently, I passed into unconsciousness again and "Rita" must have moved me. I can't believe I actually lived through her sexual torture yet again. I will soon wish, more than anything, that I had never awoken today, because, of course, this abominable girl is also in charge of getting me dressed for the day. It is then, another nightmarish cycle of molestation, torture and rape starts all over again!

After a couple agonizing weeks of the same morning and evening sex rituals, "Rita" decides to ratchet my abuse up a notch. Now, she is making me **wear her panties**, and even her *girdle*, under my clothes. She doesn't allow me to go to the bathroom first, even though she is well aware how much torment I am suffering. Anyway, once she gets me trussed-up in her lingerie stuff, she viciously teases me and belittles me. Now, she is pretending I'm her baby and she makes me suck on her titties. (Oh, dear God and Santa, my pee-pee hurts and my belly is aching for relief and release of my saved-up nighttime urine.) However, "Rita" keeps on tickling me and playing with my pee-pee, until I can't hold it for another second. I squirm and struggle to get myself out of her tight rubber girdle and panties. However, on those occasions when I can't escape the binding I'm in, I end up peeing, in her panties! Then she punishes me for doing it! *"Brat! You little fucking weakling, brat! You shouldn't have done thaaat."* She slaps my face really hard, actually knocking me clear over sideways.

Revolving Doors

[Suddenly I've become acutely aware *I* am lost in "Rita". I mean, I have no idea where my self ends and this girl's self begins. I've somehow lost my being, my spirit, my "ME-ness" somewhere in this vile teenage, molesting rapist's sex-hole. Oh hell! BANG! BANG! I just want to bang, bash, and push all these newly formed, horrendous thoughts out of my little head. *I want to die*. I want to be dead and never, ever wake up again. But first, I want to kill "Rita"!!]

This vile and evil girl's controlling sexual abuse of me never seems to end. Her daily behaviour becomes increasingly deviant and wicked toward me. Her favourite thing is to control *when* I am permitted to urinate. Being a boy, I'm unable to control the "woody" I get because I have to pee, first thing in the morning. Now she even uses this to her perverted advantage. She has started to force me do *things* to her while *she* is only wearing her panties and a bra. For instance, she makes me go pee down her into panties, or down her bra, on her little pointy boobies. She even makes me kiss and lick her squirmy, slimy pussy-hole while she squirts her reeking gooey ooze all over my face and *in my mouth*! Sometimes she jams my little hand right down her panties and makes it as icky, soppy, and smelly as her slimy cream makes my face. I hate it! I really hate it! And I *hate her*! I hate "Rita"! ***BANG! BANG! BANG! "I WEALLY, WEALLY, WEALLY, WEALLY HATE YOU!!! I HATE YOU Wida!!!"***

Life goes on, week-in and week-out, with the same repeated ritual sex games she forces me to "play" with her. I know deep down in my guts her abusive behaviour is really, really wrong and I absolutely KNOW she is a *very bad person*. Although, right now, I wonder if I am a really bad person too. I feel embarrassed, ashamed and dirty—but can *I* squeal to anyone about her? Of course not! I am unable to tell on her, out of fear—and she knows it!

However, even though this girl is so much bigger and stronger than I am, I've now decided something has to change in my life. So, when she came at me yesterday morning I decided to rebel against her. However, in the very moment I actually tried to fight back, I discovered how much more powerful she is than I am. She got so mad at me, she pushed me right down, hard onto the bedroom floor! Then she began kicking me in the ribs! The pointy toes of those hard, black, patent-leather shoes, [121], which she's so fond of wearing, actually *broke* one of my ribs! She broke my damn rib, on the lower right side, shoving the, (now excruciatingly moveable), piece of broken rib right up under the next rib above it. The pain was of such a degree, I actually passed into blessed unconsciousness for a few moments.

When I regained consciousness, I was curled up, not only in *pain*, but I was also having a great deal of difficulty breathing. It was this moment when she threatened,

"Alright, little brat-fucker, if you try to fight me again, or tell on me, I'll do even worse to you! I could easily kill you and make it sooo look like an accident, and nobody would ever guess I did it. And—little baby pig-sticker, if you even let on, or hint, to mom about the pain in your ribs, first I'll push the wooden spoon handle right up your bum-hole, then I'll kick you in your other side and when I'm finished, I'll fucking kill you anyway!"

(Oh God and Santa, not the wooden spoon handle—not the patent leathers—please not again!)

*"Either way, little brat, you're **my** toy and you will do everything and anything I say, whenever I tell you to! So, roll over on your back, "Rita's" cunty-wunty wuvs Teddy-boy's little red pee-pee. Get it hard, stupid—get it harder! Here comes my sex-hole, now eat my slime, brat-fucker—eat it and tell me you love it!"*

Revolving Doors

Again, she sits on my face covering both my breathing orifices until I spit and choke, and slump back into unconsciousness. *"Wake up! Wake up, stupid!"* She's whisper-screaming into my ear *and* slapping my face. However, it is when she twists my pee-pee around like a piece of liquorice, I am definitely awake.

Now it's Saturday and the girls have gone out for a little while. I am still lying on my little canvas cot trying to breathe, with every breath causing agony where my rib is broken. "In-out, in-out—keep going Teddy", I tell myself, "In-out, in-out". I need to just try and keep going. I know if I let on anything to the "mother", I'll be tortured and killed by this horrid girl. So, I am quiet. When the "mother" asks me why I'm not getting up, I point to my chest and say, "Dot a boo-boo", and, of course, she thinks I simply have a tummy ache so she leaves me alone to rest.

If only she knew. If only I could let on even a fraction of the truth of the torture and rape. If only I could tell her of the misery I'm being forced to endure every day and night. Nevertheless, I can't tell. So I must resign myself to accepting my fate, at least for as long as I have to live in the same house with "Rita". However, all the while I am praying to God and Santa to make the "mother" quit her night-job!

I am so sad because I now have been forced to live with these excruciating and deplorable sensations in my chest. It is very hard to stand up straight now and even putting on my T-shirt elicits unspeakable pain. Agony in every form is what I've been forced to accept as the norm of my everyday life in this hell-house. I suppose the physical pain in my chest is not much worse than the rest of the painful abuse "Rita" inflicts on me daily. Right now, I am depressed, tired and very sick once again with the "Brown Kites". However, I could not know it yet, but my life is about to turn a hundred-and-eighty degrees from where it's at right now. Finally, today, Sunday, is the day on which, either God or Santa Claus has decided to rescue me from "Rita's" stinking, slimy clutches.

This morning started with the usual sex-game ritual, nothing different, *except for my broken rib!* "Rita" likes to begin our day with "Miss Cunty-Wunty" squirming and writhing on my face, alternating with her "mouthy-wouthy" sucking on my pee-pee. Now she's turned my wee-wee into a hard little woody again and, in fact, is trying to suck the pee right out of me—as she's repeatedly done before. We are both entirely naked and now, once again, I am pinned completely under this heavy-set teenage girl who is sitting on my face and choking the life out of me.

Suddenly the bedroom door opens and my "foster mother" is standing there watching us. "***That fucking door was locked mother! I locked that goddamned door!***" "Rita" screeches. Her mother looks almost as shocked as "Rita" does. For a brief second, as she tries to assess what it is she is actually witnessing, she seems to be unable even to speak. But then she starts screaming at "Rita", using a tone of voice I'd never before witnessed from this rotund little woman:

"What in the hell are you doing to that little boy?
You get off him, right now!
I can't even believe my own eyes.
Oh my dear God!
Oh, my God! Teddy, are you alright?
Come here Teddy."

I try to crawl over to her but I am somewhat embarrassed because my whole face is covered with "Rita's" slimy, reeking cum, (which smells no less fishy today than any other day). But when I stand in front of the "mother", I am leaning a little forward and to the right side, because I have to clutch my chest tightly, where the rib is not only broken into two pieces, but also shoved, and lodged, up under the one above it. As well, there is a great, huge, ugly bruise right over the spot. However, even the bruise can't mask the awful looking lump in my chest, (resulting from this unusual and unnatural new arrangement of my ribs).

The foster "mother" is crying now and shaking while she cradles me like an infant and asks me, *"How on earth did you get such a terrible bruise, Teddy?"* She goes to touch it and I wince in pain because she couldn't know there is a badly broken rib underneath the grotesquely swollen lump. *"What happened?"* she again insists on a reply. I glance backward at "Rita", and then I cut my gaze over at her terrifying, pointy, black patent-leather pumps gleaming in the corner of the bedroom. *"Did "Rita" hurt you?"* I start to sob ever so softly. Then the foster "mother" demands, *"Rita"! What did you do to this little boy? How did you bruise his chest? Tell me, right now!"* *"No, mummie, I never touched him at all, honesssst. HE's making this up."* ("Rita" lies, feigning her innocence, in a very unnatural little girl sort of voice.) *"I don't believe you for one minute! Just you wait until I figure out the best punishment for what you've done here, today!"* ("...here, today"...this foster mother has no earthly idea how long this abuse has been going on, nor to what degree it has escalated.)

"Rita" is standing a few feet away and will know for sure if I squeal to the "mother" right now. Anyway, I can't even get the words out. They are stuck down in my throat with the remainder of the vomit which has not yet come out, *today.* As for me, I am certain of my fate if I tell-on "Rita". Of course, I really don't want to be tortured to death, so I couldn't bear to answer her question, truthfully. Nonetheless, the "mother" already knew the answer, even before she questioned me.

Was it over? Could all this hell possibly be at an end for me? I am not sure, but I do have the tiniest seed of hope right now as I am being held in the "mother's" arms. Dare I allow myself to feel safe again, if even for a moment? The "mother" is no longer "Mrs. Smiley". She is furious at "Rita" and, quite obviously, beside herself with the whole situation. *What to do? What can I do? What should I do now?*" She is talking to herself, while pacing in circles around the room.

Her solution? Within the hour, the foster "mother" is calling the "C.A.S." for an *emergency placement* of me somewhere, (*anywhere*), else. (O.K.--I know the routine, but this time I am *happy* to be packing my paper grocery sack of belongings, and putting my shoes on.)

I am a little confused though, because I hear the foster "mother" explain over the phone to the authority at the "C.A.S.",

"*It's not working out with Teddy at our home.*" Then I hear, "*No, nothing he actually did. He is just not a **good fit** with us. Yes, I know he has been doing better, but I insist you send someone immediately to pick him up! Of course, that's too bad, but I honestly believe a short stopover at the children's asylum is preferable to him staying under my roof for one more night! Yes...but not over the phone...I will explain more details when I come in person to your office.*"

The reasons I am being sent away are always the same. Apparently, *I* have to leave because of something "*I did, or didn't do*". How could I ever tell on "Rita"? I could not squeal after I am moved out because everyone would think either I am lying, or it must have been entirely my fault. Besides, who would ever believe me? Who would ever imagine a girl *raping* a little boy? Therefore, *I* did not ever tell anyone about "Rita", or about the abuse, or the molestation, or the sex, or even about the torture—never! Once again, I am so perplexed. I can't imagine *how* I lost my home because of the torture this girl *inflicted upon me*! Everything had been going so well, or so I thought.

Later the very same day, I could not believe it, but my old friend, "Big Ears" is banging on the front door. (Oh my – he shaved his bushy side-burns off, now giving the illusion his ears have grown even more immense! In fact, they are usurping both sides of his head.) "Mrs. Smiley" is all smiles and grins as she invites him inside. As he stands in the foyer looking around, his soft eyes meet mine. I am sitting quietly, making myself invisible in the oversized, overstuffed chair nearest the door. My bag is packed and on the floor next to my feet. ("Rita" and "Rosie" are upstairs and are under threat to "*not*" come down whenever the "C.A.S." Worker arrived. Incidentally, "Rosie" still doesn't have a clue as to what has happened between "Rita" and me. She thinks I've been a bad boy, somehow and her mom is getting rid of me.)

Anyway, "Ears" says, "Hi there, little guy! Are you ready to take a ride on the big bus with me?" He has *no idea* just how ready I am! He reaches his great, big, rough hand towards me and folds my diminutive little-boy hand inside. But right before we are to go out the door, the "foster mother" says, "Oh, 'Mr...', I just wanted to say we're sorry Teddy didn't work out for this family, but you see *he*..." My escort stops her mid-sentence,

"You know, Missus..., I'm not supposed to say anything about the little boy. If you have something to talk about, you really need to call the Director's office."

Then with an unexpected yank, he quickly pulls me up into his strong arms. I bury my head, heavy with *bad* thoughts and *horrendous* memories, deeply into the security of his warm, strong chest. He smells clean, like soap and safety.

"Wait, wait a minute, 'Mr...'", the "mother" adds, "Don't forget to take Teddy's tricycle with you; it's around at the side of the house." She directs him with a wave of her hand. "O.K., thank-you, missus..." he says. As the door closes behind us, and I count the seven steps down to the lawn, I know in my heart, and my spirit, I have been plucked from "Rita's" vile reach and taken right out of her hell-house, forever. I let out a little sigh because I know now, nothing I would ever have to face in my life could be as bad as the torture "Rita" has been inflicting upon me. ("Ears" did not forget the tricycle, either.) Oh, wow! I feel as if I am floating amidst the clouds. I'm as light and soft as a downy little feather. My mind is in a slow-motion, drifting free-fall! I'm freeeeeeeeeeeee!!!!!

****

[*Over. It is over. Is it over? Will it ever be over...ever? The answer to this is, of course, a resounding, "NO"! The bad memories and self-loathing triggered by what "Rita" both did to me, and introduced me to, (from the tender, innocent age of three-and-a-half years), will **never, ever, ever** stop haunting me. At the time of writing this, I've lived more than sixty years, and if I close my eyes and allow myself to meditate, I am still unable to **clear** my mind. The mental dissonance in my head keeps battering my thoughts with the details of each session of "Rita's" molestation, as if it all happened yesterday. In my brain, and my heart, I can never turn-off the memories or their associated feelings and emotions. From the start of "Rita's" sexual abuse, my spirit began to wither outwardly from the centre of its spiralling double helix. Emotionally speaking, pieces of whom I am, or was ever meant to be, festered and rotted right off.*

From the first moment "Rita" started abusing me, it made me feel as if I was a wicked, dirty little animal with a stained and soiled spirit. I mean, not an animal like a cute, friendly little

275

dog, more like some sort of filthy, depraved, debased and demoralized monster, unworthy of existence. I was not even four-years-old and I was experiencing several daily bouts of molestation, torture and rape, via manipulation, fellatio, cunnilingus and intercourse. These are intimate activities, which should only be experienced between consenting ADULTS! This sort of worldly carnal knowledge should NEVER be introduced to a child, let alone a TODDLER! A toddler should never know such consequential feelings of "filthiness" and "self-loathing". A toddler, or any child, should innocently experience what life has in store, and remain as unacquainted with such carnal debasement as he was on the day he was born. However, it was too late for me. It was far too late for me to reclaim my innocent heart and soul. These have been lost to the self-serving actions of the vile, disturbed and evil teenager which "Rita" had become.

While it was happening, I continually asked myself, "How can (she) be doing these things to me? Who can I ever tell about my pain? Who would believe a little kid like me?" Now I am an adult and sometimes I, myself, don't believe it actually happened to me, although I know for certain it did. I believe when the foster "mother" discovered "Rita's" depravity, the plump, little "Mrs. Smiley" could never confess to anyone what she witnessed her daughter doing to me. When she contacted the "C.A.S.", she led them to believe I was somehow responsible for her needing to have me quickly removed from the household. Again—it always appears as if I've done something very wrong, or I was a very bad little boy. The "C.A.S." Workers will never know what went on behind "Rita's" hellish locked doors. So how would she ever be punished for the torturous abuses she forced and inflicted upon me? (Even worse, what if this woman opens her door to take in another foster child! What if "Rita" abuses the next foster child?)

These secrets have had to remain so for all these decades, until I am now both, able to face the memories, and work through the nightmares, which have haunted my slumber for decades. This chapter is my recording, and final confession, of what went on behind "Rita's" closed doors. In order to arrive at this place, psychologically, I've had first to acknowledge the disgusting and depraved details to myself, before even considering confessing them to the rest of the reading public, (or whomever may be remotely interested in my story).

I have not related this part of my story for any sort of salacious value, but for a true and honest representation of the torture I suffered at "Rita's" hands. I feel the need to apologize for the raw, lewd nature and very graphic language used in presenting this chapter; however, there is no other way to bring forth the honest feelings and emotions I experienced. I was just a tiny, terrified, hopeless little kid, with nowhere to run, and certainly nowhere to hide, from "Rita".

I understand now that memories of my horrific experiences in the hell-house while my live was controlled by "Rita's" tormenting behaviour, had been somehow safely isolated from the other areas of my brain. In order for me to function in life and in society, these horrendous memories had to be shut down and locked away by some invisible, mental gatekeeper. They were never intended to be brought out into the light of day. I am convinced I would never have purposely, and consciously, reached so deeply into my psyche to retrieve and rediscover such loathsome memories. However, my decades of recurring nightmares, unimaginable anxiety, mood-swings and dark, prolonged depressive episodes needed to be assessed, addressed and treated.

I experienced years of intensive individual and group psychotherapy, as well as a strict medication regime, which somehow unlocked the **gate***. Of course, I can never change the fact that all of the abusive memories are comprised of* *actual incidents in my life. These memories are driven by the repeated, ritualistic, terrifying, perverse physical, and depraved sexual, assaults, which I experienced before the age of **four years**. These corrupt events **really did happen** to me—just an innocent little boy—only a small, unprotected child.*

Now that I've gone to the darkest place in my head, I am facing my demons and am daily working to move past what effect the abuse had on my heart, and my spirit, six decades later. Certainly, even to this very day, for me there is no such thing as "forgiveness". I still think of "Rita" with the most intense hatred, and probably always will.

Even as a grown-up, I still have a "hidey-hole" to which I retreat for many hours, or days at a time. Currently this small, safe place for me is in my kennels with my own dogs, (and those for which I provide board for clients). It's very strange, but even now, the lump remains in my chest and my head often hurts, as if I were still bang-bang-banging it. I guess some things will never change...Sweep, sweep, sweep...]

PART VI: Changes, Always Changes

Chapter 32: The "Big House" Revisited

Mr. "Big Ears" hurries down the street clutching me in his arms and sort-of slung over his shoulder like a sack of flour, with my wrinkled old paper bag of stuff I'm grasping, flapping up and down against his back. He waves wildly to flag down a bus coming along in our direction and on we get. It's quite crowded and I see a sea of many strange and unfamiliar faces. We move down the bus aisle looking for a seat which will not only fit us, but also have room for my trike. There is only one remaining, so we squeeze-in next to a very fat man with three stomachs, a huge ugly nose with black hairs sticking out of it and a four-day growth of unkempt beard hair. A few seconds beside this ape and we look at each other having recognized the pungent marriage of garlic and whiskey odour is emanating from this fella's every pore. (I hope this ride is a quick one because I am getting nauseous from the insult of his stench.)

As the bus bumps further along down the road, I happen to glance down at this offensive stranger's mammoth feet. He has somehow stuffed them into big, old, black-leather workman's boots—size sixteen if they're an inch, I'd say. (Wow, I'm thinking I would *not* want to be kicked in the ribs by *those* gunboats!) I look away and wince from a painful memory.

As our ride continues, with every passing telephone pole I know I am getting farther and farther away from "Rita" and all of the abuse I suffered at her hands. I start to daydream a little and I sense my body, previously tense and tight, let go a little—just a little. I feel as if I am finally able to *exhale*. My ribs are still so painful but I'm sure they will get better, eventually.

At least with "Rita" away from me, they shouldn't get any worse, but I can only *hope*. Shortly, "Ears" stretches his long arm up to pull the cord and alert the driver that this is *our* stop. Then, just as we get up to leave, the fat man *grunts* something unintelligible and simultaneously *farts* the same message. (I stifle a giggle and "Ears" gives me a big, wide, toothy grin, and a wink.)

Back at the "C.A.S.", we go straight into the "Director's" office where she, "Mrs. Mousey" and "Librarian Lady" are all seated looking rather sombre. There is one empty chair left, and I am instructed to sit in it. "Teddy, dear...", the "Wart" starts out to say, "we are sorry about things not working out very well at 'Mrs'...' house. Is there anything you would like to talk about now you are back in here with us?"

(Am I back here—with them? I certainly hope not. I want no more stays in the orphan asylum. Certainly, they can place me again, or better still, find me a *permanent* home. What was it called? Oh yeah, right, *adoption*.)

A few minutes into my debriefing, the nurse enters the office. "How are *we* feeling today, Teddy?" (There's that damn *we* again.) I tell them I'm a good boy. Then the nurse whispers something to "Wart" who nods in agreement. "Come along with me, Teddy. *We* are going to play some games and have lots of fun." (Is she serious? I'm tired of fun and games! I want rest and medical attention for my ribs. Nevertheless, I have no choice other than to tag along with her.)

When she ushers me into a sterile little examination room, she says, "Teddy I want you to take your shirt off so we can have a little look at you." I groan at the thought of raising my arms. "Here, let me help you. Have you gotten taller? I'm sure you have put on some weight too. Haven't you? Why don't we listen to your lungs and your heart? I just want to make sure all of you is in tip-top shape!" (Is she gonna touch me? I am tired of touching games, and I don't think my little cut pee-pee will ever recover from "Rita's" unbearable and persistent sexual violations.) "No-no!" I try to tell this nurse-lady to get away from me and leave my damn clothes on! I protest, "Stop touching me—*anywhere*!" (But, of course, she doesn't understand me, or *get it*.)

Of course, as always, I lose, and the grown-up wins. In no time, she has removed my shirt and is closely examining my sore chest with the hugely sensitive, purply-black bruise-over-lump where a normal rib-shape *should be*. "Oh, my goodness, little fella...does it hurt you right there?" she's asking while poking my chest lump. As the immediate pain from her touch takes my breath away, all I can do is *groan* and *moan* my answer. She makes some notations on her notepad then, excusing herself, hurries back to "Wart", presumably to *blab* of her findings.

Minutes later, all four women march into this little exam room. "Oh, my gaaaaaaaaaaad!", they all gasp in unison. (Please God and Santa, don't let them all hurt my pee-pee too!) "Nursey" then insists, "This little boy is in dire need of medical attention, immediately!" I thought they were all mad at me and going to hit me, or something. That was until she had shown them my chest and they collectively gasped with matching expressions of sheer horror on their faces. After their shock, they whisper a few things to each other, then leave. The nurse binds my chest up with a very long, stretchy, skin-coloured material. Though the binding action is very painful, the tightness actually begins to make my ribs feel a little better. The best I can do is inhale softly and shallowly.

When "Nursey" and I re-join the women back in the main office, "Mousey" then takes my hand and my bag of stuff. I try to elicit a little information from her, so I ask, "Where are we going? I sure hope we're not going to the asylum." Sadly, it just comes out my mouth as, *"Bere doin? Huh...bere doin?"* Without answering, she walks me straight over to the orphan asylum in the building next door. (I've been here before—a few times—didn't like it then—am gonna hate it now!) However, this time she doesn't leave me in the nursery, but gets me settled into my crib-cage in the three-to-five-year-old ward. It's right through the next door down, along the great hall. This place is so packed with cribs, they had to squeeze an extra cage for me, very tightly in between two others. (Hmmmm, this time I'll have some very *close* neighbours.) Then she asks if I am hungry and, satisfied with my negative nod, she walks out, leaving me to wait upon the arrival of all the other kids who normally occupy this ward. (Right now, they're all out enjoying their suppers.)

All I want to do is curl up and sleep. Nevertheless, when I start to, as I am drifting into the nether world between wakefulness and sleep, I welcome the intrusion of a beautiful memory. It is my real mommy sitting beside a crib such as this one, and gently rubbing my arm, stroking my forehead and singing me a lullaby. (Oh, God and Santa Claus, how I still miss her at times like this.) Nevertheless, if I can't be with my mommy, at least being alone in this steel cage is better than living at "Rita's" hell-house! So I release my dark thoughts and drift, float and dream my way to a safe, sparkling, emerald-green harbour in a beautiful, lavender sailing ship with wispy pink sails and my mommy's warm arms embracing me! Oh, I inhale her unmistakable scent; it's the softly, soothing, swirling kiss of my beautiful mommy's wonderful *"Shalimar"* perfume. [153]

[Of course, my mommy could never afford to buy this costly fragrance; however, it was so special to her, it was the first item on her Christmas and Birthday lists every year. Later in life, my youngest sister, Lynda, (who, of course, at the age of three, was rescued from her own foster home nightmare and reunited with our mother), explained how our mum would even water-down her tiny Shalimar perfume bottle in order to make it last the whole year!]

I don't know how I slept through the stampede of all the kids returning, climbing and clamouring into their allotted cages in this big room. However, it's morning once again and I am *soaking wet*! My hair, forehead and neck are all sweaty from a feverish night, and, oh—not again – I have peed my jammies. (Although I am old enough not to wear a diaper, now, because of "Rita's" abuse, I become confused sometimes and pee when, and where, I'm not supposed to.)

"Now—will you just look at this mess?" Oh-Oh...it's one of the crabby nurses and she is hopping mad at me for making a mistake in my crib. They don't understand. They will never know how confused my little wee-wee gets now. Actually, after "Rita's" unending episodes of molestation and control, sometimes I hold it so long I can't even pee at all and I end up with the miserably familiar ache in my belly.

"Sandra, will you get in her a minute, please." This angry nurse is hailing an aide who is just walking down the hall. She tells the girl to come and clean-up my crib, and *me* too. Then she starts in on me, *"Young man, you are far too old to be wetting your bed at night! This better not ever happen again! Do you understand me?"* I nod my compliance.

Shortly, we kids in this ward are told to climb out of the dropped-down sides of our cribs. I soon see I must join in their marching line so we can all walk in an orderly fashion to get our breakfast. There are fifteen of us little kids and everybody, but me, is chattering, humming or singing. (I'm just "paying attention".) A few of the children are bumping or pushing the others and when they do, they are yanked to the back of the line. In the lunchroom there are fifteen highchairs aligned in an oval arrangement. This is done to make it easier for the women, wearing the ugly hairnets and stiff white dresses, to pass the food trays around. (Oh yeah, I remember this routine, and this *food*.) Nevertheless, I am happy and thanking my lucky stars, I am absolutely ANYWHERE but hell-house! I decide to adhere to the rules and accept the routines at this asylum, for however long I am forced to stay here:

Dress,
Eat brekkies,
Play in the playroom,
Nap-time,
Eat lunch,
Play again,
Quiet/nap time,
Eat supper,
(Baths on Saturday nights),
Jammies on,
Get into bed,
Lights out and
Shut-up!

The days and nights come and go without one single molestation incident. Nobody ever touches me in the bad and creepy way "Rita" did, certainly not in this toddler orphan ward. The worse problem in this place is the boredom. However, one lucky day my routine changes. After I wake up and am dressed for the day, I am removed from the crib-cage and taken to a playroom alone. However, this is not the usual playroom. I happen to know it's the viewing room, with the half-silvered, (one-way), mirror. I wonder who is going to be having a look at me. I decide it doesn't really matter who takes me next, as long as they don't abuse me. Yet, I wonder if it's just too much for me to hope.

Shortly a new lady comes for me. "C'mon here, Teddy", she

encourages softly while down on one knee. "I'm 'Miss...' and I will be taking you to your new foster home this morning." (O.K., I guess.)

During this short abatement of my "Brown Kites", I am being taken to yet another group home. This one will be my *twelfth foster home,* but my *fourteenth residential placement.* Maybe this will be the home I've always dreamed of. Ever the optimist, I am hoping, perhaps this time will be different from all the others. Maybe this time my *revolving door* will sweep me around to a beautiful and wonderful new forever home.

My newest "Worker" already has my bag of stuff in one hand and takes my hand gently with her other. "My twike? Where's my twike?" I'm trying to elicit where my tricycle could be but she obviously doesn't understand me. Oh, well, I guess it doesn't really matter. Right now, I'm having a good look at "Miss...". She is quite slender, and is dressed in a sheer, light grey blouse under a darker grey peplum jacket, which rides gently over its matching tight-skirt. My latest "Worker" even has grey flats on her feet, which I can attest was a good decision this morning, since she is already so very tall, especially up against me.

This young woman's feline eyes are sea green and her facial features are quite soft and delicate. She is certainly beautiful in an understated way. However, what offsets all of the grey in her ensemble is her long, thick, curly, flaming red hair—*a la* "Rita Hayworth"! [96] (Hmmm...What shall I call this woman? I once lived with a little boy with red hair, called "Red" but *he* is dead, so I can't name her "Red". *I know!* She will be, "Cat's Eyes"--Yes, it's the perfect name.)

We leave together with my old "Workers" waving, "Bye-bye", to me. This time we are *walking* to my new foster home. She insists that it's such a beautiful day outside, we should enjoy it on our way to the new house, (which she promises isn't too far to walk). Because it had rained overnight, the sidewalks are still damp, with a few little puddles, remaining here and there. Of course, I decide it's a good idea to jump into the first couple of puddles, but I am quickly discouraged from doing so, (because I might "splash" her pristine skirt). Anyway, I soon notice how the very smooth leather on the bottoms of my shoes is perfect for skating across the grass as it dances with glistening water droplets. I can't help but notice how everything smells so fresh and clean. I simply inhale the purity until I am satiated.

About twenty minutes later, we stop in front of an inviting little yellow bungalow with a grey, wrap-around porch. The stones of the six fieldstone pillars, which support the roof over the veranda, are all fashioned in a pyramid-style of arrangement. "Cat's Eyes" leans down to me, straightens my shirt, flattens-down my cowlick and buttons my sweater. Then she says, encouragingly, "I want you to be a very good boy, now, Teddy. I am sure you are going to enjoy living in this house. And, guess what? There are already *four* foster boys living here so you'll have lots of kids to play with." I don't say anything. I don't care about "lots of boys to play with". I just want to find a safe hidey-hole and climb on in. "Scared?" Of course, I'm scared…and I can clearly hear the *sweep-sweep-sweep* of this next revolving door pushing me around, either to a wonderful new adventure—or, God forbid, to another nightmare.

Revolving Doors

Chapter 33: The "Bowery Boys" [95]

"Cat's Eyes" and I walk, albeit a little timidly, up to the front door of my new foster home. She rings the doorbell a couple of times, but no one responds. While we keep on waiting, I notice rain drops from the broken eaves are dripping down onto my arm. As we continue to wait for the foster "mother" to answer the doorbell's chiming, we can hear several boys' voices playfully nattering from the backyard. Taking my hand, she leads me down the side path and she unlatches the gate. The four foster boys she had mentioned are apparently the ones playing and climbing the trees in the yard. "Uh, excuse me boys. Do you kids know where 'Mrs...' is at?" she inquires politely.

The biggest boy yells down, "She's inside the house havin' a nap. D'ya want I should go get her?" (The other boys start to giggle.) "Um, well, yes please, young man.", "Eyes" stammers while blushing a little. "You can tell her, 'Miss...' is here with the new little boy." my pretty escort adds, albeit with a little hesitation in her voice. "Hee, hee, hee—*young man*--ha, ha, ha!" chortles the large kid up in the other tree.

In a few minutes, my new foster "mother" appears at the back screened-in door. "Oh, uh, won't you come in.", she says, while trying to flatten-down her unruly hair, and straighten her crinkled dress. By the looks of this new "mother" I think I can probably guess she's gonna be a good cook and is probably a baker too, (because, of course, she's twice as wide as her own back door).

Once we are inside, she ushers us through the kitchen where I notice some burnt biscuits on a tray next to a large glass pitcher of yellow lemonade. (I would pass, on the biscuits, but I could certainly use some of the lemonade right about now. In fact, I haven't had anything to eat or drink yet, and it's already ten in the morning. However, nothin' doin', no lemonade, or even water, comin' my way.)

Anyway, the foster lady takes us through the dining room, which has some very handsome dark mahogany dining furniture pushed tightly into the corner and up against the window, leaving available seating for only two normal-sized people. (That's strange, because there are currently five people living here, or six if you count her as double and, of course, *I* would then make seven.) However, from her girth I am guessing the new "mother" needs the extra wide space in order to waddle through into the living room.

She then shows us into the front room, which has what should be a *bright* bay window, but instead, it is heavily curtained with dark green velvet drapes. In the living room are two pretty, flowery, over-stuffed couches, both of which are fitted with made-to-order stiff, protective plastic covering. The woman sits in her own chair, which incidentally has no plastic and we squeak down onto her plasticized couch. (I am wearing shorts so the skin on the backs of my bare thighs immediately bonds to the clear plastic--"Ow, Owie, Ouch!")

"Well", the new foster mother crosses her arms over her expansive belly and sighs, "You've obviously met my boys out in the yard. Do you have any questions for me?" "Cat's Eyes" says, "Yes, well, of course this is little 'Teddy'. We would like to see him settled-in as soon as possible. Here's a list of what you will need to know about him." "I'll read it when I get my glasses on." the obese woman responds. "Eyes" continues, "And he has his own little bag of clothes and a few toys here." Then she asks, "Exactly where will he be sleeping?" "Upstairs, of course, with the other boys. There are two bedrooms with three bunk beds for them—plenty of room for Teddy too. I would take you up but my asthma is bothering me right now, and I don't climb those darn stairs until I *have* to. But, don't worry, he'll settle-in just fine.", "Wide Load" (the perfect name for her), offers reassuringly. "Oh, alright then", "Eyes" acquiesces, adding, "…and thank you, 'Mrs…'"

"Oh yes, I've got something for the little boy." this new "mother" adds, while retrieving a small outfit of a sort, from beside her chair. "Here, Teddy, it's a little cowboy suit which the youngest was too big for, last Halloween. I think you might like to wear it to play in.", she suggests while handing it to me. "Oh, yes, yes, dank you!" I emphatically tell her *how* much I would like it. Then "Cat's Eyes" says, "Well now, isn't the lady nice, Teddy? Thank you 'Mrs…'" Then my beautiful Worker leans down and whispers, "Bye-bye now Teddy, dear." (Oh gosh, she smells so nice too—not like mommy, but nice just the same.) "Please be a very well-behaved little boy and mind your manners too. Alright?" I assure her with a promise, "O.K.". Then my beautiful escort leaves.

I am still sticking quietly to the plastic sofa, literally quite planted in place. As I survey the living room, I get the distinct feeling that *nobody* actually ever does any "living" in here. Papering the walls, are eerie old photos, which are barely visible under layers of years' worth of collected dust. Most are sort-of sepia-coloured—very old pictures, I would say. All the strangers on each wall are also *stuck in place* like me, and they seem to be whispering *something* to me. But what? "Tick-tock, tick-tock…" are the actual words spoken by the very ornate grandfather clock in the corner. However, to my nervous ears it sounds more like, "Get out! Get out!" (I can feel the panic welling up inside my throat and I want to bang my head and make the voices stop—but I can't.) I am holding onto myself. I can't run and there is nowhere to hide, not yet anyway. I start to hum so I no longer have to listen to the clock, or the photos or whatever is trying to scare the bejesus outta me.

Unable to move, I can only look on, as "Wide Load" waddles slowly back toward the kitchen where she screams out the window at the boys, "Git the hell in here, right now—all of *yous* brats!" ("Brats"--oh I really don't like the sound of that at all. It's what "Rita" kept calling *me*.) Anyway, into the house they all run, but stop short—each kid bumping into the next while trying to get their shoes off at the back door. "Teddy come in the kitchen and meet your new brothers." "O.K., I'n doming." "Sprrrlllt", off I pull one leg, then "Sprrrlllt", I unstick the other, (in the process, losing a little surface layer of flesh from the back of both thighs). Ignoring the pain in my legs, I run into the kitchen to meet my four new, ragamuffin, so-called, *brat-brothers*.

I am summarily introduced to the boys by age or height, I am not sure which. The first boy is "Arthur", ("Art" for short). He's thirteen-going-on-forty. He's loud, boisterous and, even upon first meeting I sense he is a little obnoxious. This kid is over five feet tall and has very greasy, slicked-back, brown hair and dark brown eyes. He has a real air about him, which fairly screams, "I don't belong here and I'm making my break at next light!"

Then there is the boy, who's a stair-step down in height, "Walter", ("Wally" for short). He is ten-and-a-half and pretty much acts six. He is a silly-heart and is always joking around and pulling April Fools tricks, when it's not April Fools' Day. This boy has white-blonde hair, which is sort of shaved around the sides, but is long on top. His light blue eyes seem very sorrowful, even as his mouth is trying to make funny jokes. Wally had some kind of accident when he was little and somehow lost the thumb on his left hand, (but we aren't supposed to notice it and I dare not ask about it.) Although it looks awful, all the same, it doesn't seem to slow him down any, because he's always up for the next tree-climbing race.

The next kid in descending age is "Ronald", ("Ronnie" for short). He is almost eight, and for some strange reason, he insists on being called, "Charlie". O.K., so, "Ronald", "Ronnie" and/or "Charlie" is a real beanpole. He is the same height as "Wally" but he's so skinny he's almost inside out. He has bright orange hair, which he keeps slicked-back like "Art's" only this kid never stops combing it—and I mean never! He has strange, squinty sort-of eyes, which, certain ways you look at him in the sunlight, appear more orange than brown. This kid is always complaining about being hungry. In fact, if you don't hold onto your plate, he'll have eaten its contents before you look down. I don't get it. How can he always be hungry and eating, but be rail-thin? *He says* he has a pet tapeworm in his stomach. Oooooh, yuck, bad thought, bad thought!

The last boy is "Henry", ("Hank" for short). He isn't much older, nor much taller than I am, but he is pudgy, nevertheless. His face is terribly disfigured by a cleft palate. Otherwise, he is an average looking kid with an average build, ordinary brown eyes and a shaved head. He is always scratching his scalp, armpits *and* his groin. His head and underarms even have sores and scabs all over them—I'm not certain if his groin does, though. I sure don't know what he's got, but in case it's a bad case of cooties, I make a point of keeping my distance from *him*. (I have heard those lousy little buggers can jump!)

Learning all these names, and the "for short" names too, is just too much for me to remember. I think I'll just make my life a little easier by assigning them names of *my own* choosing. After all, it's what I'm especially good at. I've decided the biggest boy, "Art" with the slicked-back hair, will be called, "*Slick*". Next in line is "Wally" who has one unruly piece of hair which stays sticking straight-up at the crown of his head, very much resembling a spike. So, *his* name will be "*Spike*". The third kid, "Ronnie" has so many freckles, he could almost pass for a little coloured boy, though he isn't. It's a perfect new name for him, "*Freckles*". The last kid's facial deformity gives him the appearance of having a face like a fish. So, he will hereafter be known by me as, "*Fish*". (Of course, this doesn't necessarily mean I am going to *tell* these boys their new names. I'll just have to wait and see.)

Right after introductions, we all go out back to play. Before you can sneeze, "Slick" and "Spike" are, one, two, three, racing *straight up* the trunks into the two big Oak trees! "Freckles" is over beside the rattletrap old shed, "working on" his upside-down bike, and "Fish" is walking around bashing the bushes with a broken tennis racquet. Me—I am headed for the dirt pile with the dump truck and cement-truck parked on top. Now this is my kind of fun, unless, of course there is a doggie! This isnt too bad of a set-up. Maybe I could like it here. However, I find it weird that everyone is playing and jabbering away, but the moment *I* come around them, everybody stops talking.

I am hungry and thirsty and I'm wondering when the new "mother" will be coming out with the pitcher of icy lemonade. However, it never happens—she never comes out. In fact, I soon learn how to quench my own thirst by watching the boys, one-by-one, stick their heads under the faucet which protrudes from the back wall of the house. (Oh, so that's how it's done.) I decide to try it too, but I don't seem to be doing it right because when I put my head under the tap, the water runs up my nose! They're all having a really good laugh at my expense, right now. (Though the tap water is wet, it's too warm and yucky-tasting to quench *my* thirst.)

The sun's tired rays signal our time to finally go in the house and get ready for bed. I am so hungry and the pain in my tummy is almost doubling me over. How did we kids play all day and miss lunch and supper? I ask myself, "Why aren't these boys hungry too?" Once inside, the foster "mother" demands, "Alright now, *yous* kids show Teddy where yous *live*." I grab my war-weary little brown paper sack from the floor inside the back door, and head towards the front hall where the steps lead to the upstairs. "Not up there, dummy!", "Slick" says, stopping me in my tracks. "This way...", he corrects, pointing to the door and stairs going *down* into the basement. NO WAY! Not another basement existence! In-out, in-out. The revolving door of my life keeps sweeping me right back around to where I *really* never want to return. "No! No! No!" I protest vehemently. (Now, how in the hell am I gonna get out of this damn mess of a situation? I wonder.)

Regardless of my attempt at disagreeing with "Slick", I follow as the others shuffle down into the abysmal, dusty and very damp cellar which, thankfully I suppose, is somewhat bigger and has one more window than the last one to which I was previously exiled. When I wipe the airborne cellar-dust clouding my eyes, I can see on this floor are two double-bed sized mattresses. This can't be where all five of us boys are supposed to sleep! Or, can it? What about the three "bunkies" that the lady told my "Worker" were upstairs? Aw nuts! Nothing surprises me anymore. (Though it's my fifteenth residence, and my thirteenth foster situation, my newest home is not holding very much promise for me right now. And, frankly, I'm getting sick of moving around.)

With the understanding that "Slick" is the obvious Leader of our pathetic little pack, it is to him I plead for something to eat. "Um, I'n hundwy, I'n hundwy, pwease." "All I can give you is an apple and some dry crackers." he answers, grudgingly "O.K., oh...dat's dood, dat's weawy dood." I am very grateful for him sharing *anything* with me at this moment. Then he says, "You know what kid? You are gonna hafta learn ta pull your own weight 'round here. We all work. Every day we hafta make the effort or else we don't eat nuthin' at all. D'ya understand what I'm saying?" (Well, yes, I understand the words, but I have no idea what he's talking about when he says I need to "pull my weight". After all, I am the smallest and arguably the weakest of all these kids. Besides, why wouldn't all the food be coming to us from the foster lady's kitchen?)

Whatever! I have a little food in my tummy now and I am going to sleep no matter how puny my sliver of the mattress. (My head thought about banging itself against the wall, but then it thought better of it.) I grab "Pom Pom" and pull the corner of the ratty, old, faded-blue, chenille bedspread up over my eyes. [22] (Oh, it smells terrible—like stinky feet.) Then, to be sure, I feel around for my wee-wee, to make certain it didn't fall off, like I'm positive "Rita's" must have. Oh, good, though it still hurts to be touched, at least it's still intact. Ahhh, maybe this is all just a dream. I'll know for sure if I wake up in the morning and none of this happened. Maybe when this nightmare ends I'll actually wake up in my sweet mother's soft arms and my head against her lovely white breast. But, no matter what...I'll be happy if I wake up and "Rita" isn't sitting on my face!

Morning barely announces herself through the grimy, clouded windowpanes. My eyes open, half expecting me to be in "Rita's" room. However, I am, in fact, in another horrid cellar with four older boys. Sadly, I must face the fact that this newest existence, is my new reality. Surely, the "C.A.S." women would not approve of such accommodations and, once discovered, they would quickly usher me out of here. However, fat chance of that happening! Life seems like an ugly, rusty old merry-go-round, with all the pretty horses gone. As always, I am the smallest and weakest of all the kids. Looks like another permanent basement existence. The only difference is, there are four boys already here ahead of me this time. (Oh yes, and I have a broken rib poking and pushing the rib above it almost all the way through the skin of my chest now.)

When the oldest boy is awake, I am soon apprised of the strict rule of law down here. We do everything according to age, height and abilities, (which, of course, amounts to "physical strength" and, as might be expected places me last every time). We must *all* always obey "Slick" no matter what—oh yes, and never question his judgement. I don't understand how these young kids are taking care of themselves in this shabby cellar. If "Wide Load" isn't providing for our needs, what then is she doing for us? And, how are we supposed to find food while stuck down in this filthy room?

Actually, I *am*, yet I'm really *not*, surprised at the answer. It seems these four boys are all quite savvy at making their own nightly escapades into the Toronto streets to scavenge food and sometimes they even find good stuff to drink. These boys are all quite adept at this craft. In fact, I'll soon observe how "Slick" and "Spike" are both tall, and gutsy, enough, to snatch items, right off the neighbourhood clotheslines. Sometimes they grab clothes or even a sheet now and then. This "teamwork" philosophy is what I discover helps keep these boys, (and me too), warm, dry and reasonably well nourished.

This basement lifestyle reminds me of my previous experience, with one important exception. When we need to go number two, (poo-poo), we have to climb out the side window and do it, like dogs, in the one corner of the backyard where we never play. The worst thing about it is, day or night, rain, snow or shine, we must climb outside the window. Believe me—I soon learn the art of pooping quickly—and before bedtime! Thankfully, for going number one, there's a drain hole in the lowest part of the basement floor and whenever we need to pee, we do it in there. (Sounds familiar, doesn't it?)

This new leader is much tougher, bossier, and meaner to me than "Big Boy" ever was. I rapidly discover, if we don't all contribute to the group's efforts by stealing for the pack, we will get a crack on the head, or a backhand across the face—and no share of the spoils! In fact, each kid in this whole gang of boys is entirely much rougher on me, and each other, than I had experienced in the first basement group-home. There is no room for slackers—or sickies. We are all being taught by the best sneak thief amongst us and, no doubt, the best in the city of Toronto! He not only knows how, and where, to get the choice food or supplies, but he's keenly aware of all the tricks to pull in order to avoid, or escape from, "*Johnny Law*".

There is also an unwritten, unspoken pact among all of us, which dictates we must first *steal* the food, and various sundry goods, and secondly we *divide* it up. All of these boys really resent "Wide Load" because—again—half of everything pillaged goes to her **first**, then one quarter of the remainder to each boy. The problem is, you can't give five boys very much from the other half. That means, since I am the last foster kid coming into this house, I am in essence, the last man to be dealt a fair portion of the food.

I was just wondering out loud why the kids think they have to "pay" the "foster lady" with their plundered swag, but when "Slick" removed his shirt, the answer was clearly written in the markings on his back. Forging a trail right down his back are the weirdest arrangement of a series of scars which are more like gouges than bruises. When I try to touch one of the eight markings, he pulls away, saying, "Stop-it kid!" Then I ask, "Boo-boos?" He explains they were a result of the "foster lady" repeatedly hitting him with the buckle end of a long, thick, man's leather belt. He says he discovered, as long as he keeps furnishing her with free food and other goods, the belt stays hung on the hook next to the basement door. However, if he misses a couple days of tapping on the basement door with a cornucopia offering for her, she'll open the door and scream down, "Are yous brats looking for this leather strap? I can certainly GIVE IT to yous boys, unless yous have something good for meeee!" (That usually means she wants something special, not veggies, probably treats such as doughnuts!) Whether he wants to, or feels like it, or not, "Slick" will make the extra trip out into the back alleys to find something to allay her cravings and keep the leather belt-strap hanging in place.

For the first couple of weeks at my latest residence my assigned job has been to tidy up the cellar and keep our food-storage container wiped clean. The container, our *pantry*, is a decent sized, wax-lined, cardboard grocery box with pre-cut-out handles. I need to ensure there are no pieces of bad fruit or anything else, which could spoil the fresh food they bring in. This minimizes the amount of wasted fresh fruit and veggies. Right now, there are two apples, a potato and a handful of carrots with their long green stems attached, and a little soil still on them, (and it's my job to clean everything off before it goes into the box.)

There are also a few cans of "who-knows-what", which have no labels, (one of which is bulging badly). As well, there are one each of tuna and salmon, and four cans of "SPAM". [97] (I have seen "SPAM" cans before, but I've never tasted it myself, so this will be an interesting experience.) Oh, yes, and I also have to *do the dishes* which means I must wash of all five of our little tin army plates, as well as the mismatched forks or spoons allotted to each of us. Of course, the only *knife* in our possession belongs to "Slick". It is a "Swiss Army Knife", which quite mysteriously, opens up to provide many different tools. Other than the knife blade, it has a tiny screwdriver, a bottle opener, teeny scissors and a small pick. [98] This, a much coveted, tool hangs securely from the belt loops on any of our Leader's shorts or jeans. Nobody touches it, but "Slick"--ever.

Up until today, when the boys went out the basement window toting their pillowcases for a *shopping* trip, I've had to wait behind. However, today our Leader says I will be 'working' too.

"Slick" digs through the little steamer trunk, [40], under the steps and pulls out a man-sized white shirt. He dresses me in some jeans which are too small for "Fish", but have to be rolled up for my short little legs. Then he tucks the shirttails into the tops of my jeans and *ties* me up, belting me with a piece of cord from the junk box. Then he sort of fluffs-out the shirt so it billows all the way around my waist. I look like a pirate and I am completely in the dark as to why he is dressing me so strangely; however, when we hit the market I will soon understand.

Chapter 34: "BOX, SWEET BOX"

One day our Leader decides it's high time for a change in our situation. (Of course, it might have something to do with the fact, the foster woman strapped him hard last night when he didn't have anything to give her. The buckle cut stripes down his arm and the only thing he has to clean up the blood and wrap the wound is a dirty, old piece of rag.) Therefore, not unexpectedly, "Slick" announces, *"We're outta here! I'm sick of the fat bitch running our lives and I'll be damned if she hits me with the damn belt, ever again!"* Then, "Freckles" who never says anything, chimes in with, "And I'm sick of her always screaming at us, or scolding and threatening us!" Then, *I* try to ask what "outta here" actually means. "Slick" tells us we're moving down into the "***Don***".

[This refers to the "Don River valley" which at the time was a very large, heavily wooded and brushy area of Toronto with a few tributaries and creeks branching off the Don River. Reputedly, it made the perfect hideout for bums, hobos and other derelicts of society.]

It will make a superb area for our outdoor camp, or so he is leading us to believe. So we just wait-it-out for a good night to embark on our new adventure. It must be warm and not raining, with enough light from the moon to help us find our way. On the chosen night, instead of trying to carry our stuff *and* our clothes, we dress in everything we each own, including multiple pairs of underwear and socks if we have them. We are using the pillowcases the boys have stolen from clotheslines, and we are throwing in all the stuff that's important to each of us. (I am wearing my cowboy suit and I have packed my LOBLAWS bag, [17], with all my little toys. I am not leaving anything behind.) Then out the basement window we all scamper, always in the same order: biggest to smallest, *always.* However, "Fish" is so fat with all his clothes on top of his own blubber, his bum gets wedged in the window and *I* have to push him out! We all want to laugh our heads off, but we have to be silent and get far away—and quickly!

Where are we goin'?", "Fish" asks "Freckles". "*Search me! **He** knows.*" "Freckles" replies nodding in "Slick's" direction. We can't let anyone see us running away, so we scuttle as quickly as we are all able, considering we are each toting a bulky pillowcase full of bunches of junk crucial to each of us. The big boys have to carry extra. "Slick" has the waxed food box and "Spike" has a bulging pillowcase full of the remaining saved-up hoard of eats. Then reassuringly, "Slick" says, "I've been out here before. It was a long time ago when I ran away once. It will be a perfect hideout for us all. So everybody can just shut-up and stop whining—I've got this problem covered!"

Anyway, on we trek, hiding behind a tree or cowering next to a bush. It takes at least twenty minutes until we reach the Valley—and it is, in fact, the much disreputed "Don Valley" where we're gonna make camp. (I sure hope he knows what he's goin', 'cause I don't have a lot of confidence in our plan right now.)

Finally, we stop hiking down the steep ravine wall from the highway. We are standing in the midst of a thick overgrowth of small trees, shrubs, weeds, poison ivy and poison sumac bushes and this is where we are instructed to make camp. Obviously, "Slick" has indeed been here before because there is already a bunch of flattened cardboard boxes awaiting our arrival. Also, we can hear the sound of trickling water coming from a creek nearby, and we're told we'll be getting our drinking water from there. "Slick" orders, "*Drop all the stuff over here—we'll fix the card-board good enough to crash on tonight and sort everything out at first light.*" Of course, we do exactly as he says.

Revolving Doors

As soon as the sun's warmth rouses us all to life again, the big boys start getting our "house" organized. To construct our makeshift shelter, the two oldest boys collect some large pieces of discarded wood, more cardboard and even metal, including a huge slab of galvanized tin, abandoned from some construction site. It is especially perfect for fashioning our shelter's roof because our leader assures it won't rust. "Freckles" and "Fish" have already dragged over some large wooden crates for us to sleep in, and they're fastening them together with wires. Everybody is working to set up our camp, except me. I don't know what to do so I just start collecting the little sticks for starting a nighttime bonfire.

After a few days and nights, we are really settling-in rather nicely. (Hey, who needs grown-ups? or houses!) Last night I was running around trying to catch some lightning bugs in a glass jar I found near the stream. But I nearly broke my ankle when my foot went down a gopher's, or rabbit's, or some animal's burrow entrance. *I* was concerned about the pain and swelling, but the boys were happy I accidentally discovered a poo-hole for us! (Although we sometimes pee in the stream, we didn't really want to poop where we drank, nor did we want to get poison-something-or-other on our bums! This way we could fill the deep hole with poop, cover it up with a rock and use it until we need to hunt for another one. Also, nobody is accidentally stepping in, or smelling, anybody else's poop. Perfect!) Anyway, "Slick" fixed my ankle up by tightly tying the old piece of rag from his belt-whipped arm, around the swollen area, making it feel a lot better. (I often wonder *how* he knows all the stuff he knows.)

Typical of Toronto summers, this one is stiflingly hot. There isn't a lick of breeze on this side of this ravine. In fact, virtually all of the greenery has turned brown and dry from the abundance of heat and lack of rain. It is so doggone hot that we actually take a couple of daily swims/baths in the stream. The only green plants growing under our feet are the weeds— these unwanted intruders are the *survivors* out here, like us kids—I guess we are the unwanted *weeds* of this society.

Livin' out in nature is great and all, but yikes, I could do without the deer flies we are constantly having to battle. I discovered the hard way, those buggers can take a very nasty chunk out of your flesh. "Freckles" is scared as hell of the bees! In fact, he says he was stung once and ended up almost dying. (I think he is exaggerating.) I'm not scared of bees, or spiders or even the garter snakes. Not much out in nature frightens me except the earwigs and the mosquitoes out here, which are the size of small cars. These awful parasites are especially bothersome during their nightly devouring attacks on our unprotected little white bodies. (Huh! Feasting on us is probably the reason they grew to be so darn massive!) Of course, to add to *my* personal misery, I am blistering everywhere from a sunburn on a sunburn, while at the same time, I'm miserably itching all over from poison ivy, or poison oak, or that horrid poison something-or-other!

Right now, because it's summer, thankfully there is no shortage of food. "Slick" and "Spike" have been in the business of stealing fresh fruit and veggies since last summer, so they know where the best gardens and fruit trees are located. Naturally, "Fish's" tennis racquet comes in handy when we need to harvest apples or pears from the trees in people's yards. (However, I learned the hard way not to eat the ones already laying around on the ground. Unfortunately, I once bit into one and was eating away when I looked down at my apple to discover **half** a worm still wriggling like mad! Yuck, and double yuck! Even worse than rat raisins!) The big guys also know which fresh garden foodstuffs will **keep** the best and don't turn rotten too fast. Other than the apples, the potatoes, rutabagas, carrots and even cabbages tend to keep better for a long time in the basement, but not so very long out in this heat. We rarely get tomatoes because once you pick 'em, they don't last but a couple days. Still, a fresh tomato now and then is an especially nice change.

When we go into town and all around the areas with grocery stores and delicatessen shops, we are occasionally lucky enough to find sources for meat, like hot dogs and salami. These meats are thrown away in the big trash cans out back of the stores because they're not fresh enough to sell to normal people—the *paying customers*. (We don't care how fresh stuff is, we are only happy to get some source of meat to satisfy our growing little bodies' cravings for protein.) Occasionally we get food from a restaurant's trash can. It's the stuff they scrape off people's plates before they wash them. Nevertheless, if it's still recognizable we snatch it up. Some of the tastiest cured meats come from the Italian butcher shop, but if there are any green parts on the meats, we just scrape those off—simple and effective!

There are even two bakeries in our shopping area, so finding old loaves of bread isn't too difficult. However, if they're green with mould, we have to tear any of it off before we indulge. Luckily, every now and then we can also find some three-day-olds—doughnuts which were being sold as day-olds, two days before. They're hard and often dried-out, but still a sweet treat if you pick-out the ants first. (Actually, on a dare, I *did* eat a great big black ant once, but I didn't die.)

We have to plan our food-runs carefully. Obviously if we're hitting a fruit market, or grocery store, we have to go when they're open for business. However, for the searches in the trash cans and industrial garbage receptacles, it works best if we go right after the stores or restaurants close, (before the discarded food has a chance to rot, or be gnawed on by the rats who homestead there). As for digging in people's gardens, it's best to go in the middle of the night because no one is awake to catch us and people's dogs have usually been taken into their houses.

Any other scavenging trips are only crimes of opportunity, such as running past the fruit-store's big wooden display boxes full of fresh loot for us to snatch up along the way. A few times, though, "Fish" and I have been accessories in the big crimes. Our job is to crawl under the bleacher-type shelves, which house the fruits and veggies for outdoor display. Then, "Freckles" runs around inside the shop purposely knocking into the people and food displays, and generally making a big distraction, and an even bigger mess. Outside, while we are hiding underneath, the two big boys sort of make stuff fall down from the outdoor trays and then they kick it all under to us so we can both stuff it in our over-sized, tucked-in shirts! I've always thought it was just a whole lot of fun. I've *never* been scared—and I *never, ever* was caught.

I have been taught well to generally stay away from, and never trust, any adult humans, NEVER, (nor trust any outside kids, either)! Occasionally, though, there are circumstances which bring us right into the middle of many people, mostly adults. Those are the times when the various sports games are going-on over at any of the local parks. Baseball, football, whatever—because it doesn't really matter what the game is, our interest is in positioning ourselves under the stair-step bleacher-seats. Under there, we can always pick up a little spare change as it drops from men's cluttered pockets, or kids' slippery, ice-cream-covered hands. A bit of money always comes in handy for buying, what else, **candy,** of course! (We don't usually *steal* candy, unless it's only a penny's worth from the corner store. "Slick" always says we should only *take* what we really need' and not steal for the thrill, or for junk.) Of course, there is another benefit for going to the games. No, it's not what you would think. It's not for the sport, it's for the ciggy butts! We can pick up hundreds of cigarette butts, (for "Slick"), which have been tossed down. Even though most have been stepped-on and flattened, we don't care 'cause we can always scoop the tobacco outta them.

At our "Box", "Slick" has created order out of our chaos by determining *where we sleep, who's in charge of the food storage and preparation, who's on clean-up duty, who collects sticks and fire-wood,* and even *who eats first,* (that's all of them), and *who eats last,* (that would be *yours truly*). Content that we kids have everything we need to keep us alive, we experience such a sense of fearlessness and freedom that we are able to have a little fun as well. Sometimes we smaller guys play "Hide-and-go-Seek", sometimes "Red Rover", or "Simon Says", or often "Leap Frog" or "Monkey in the Middle", (But guess who is always the "monkey"?). "Fish" has decided to share his prized, peeling-leather softball so we can play catch and we've even found a way to play baseball with it, using some small slabs of base-board-finishing wood.

For fishing, we use a stick with a string tied on the end of it and an open safety pin for a hook. (These items are never hard to find—you just have to be looking down wherever you go through town.) Then we try to catch fish in the stream, but there really aren't any decent-sized ones, only minnows and tadpoles which are only worth the effort for the sport, certainly not for the eating. Other times we chase the newts and gophers, dig for crayfish in the mud or catch grasshoppers until they spit "tobacco" in our hands. (Actually I think they're scared of us and are pooping in our palms, but "Freckles" says it's "tobacco".) The big guys still climb the trees but us two littlest ones still can't get up them very well.

"Slick" and "Spike" are teaching us little kids about the sounds of nature which we need to pay attention to—and the ones which are insignificant. This way we will all recognize if something is actually a threat to us. If ever we hear heavy-step, walking sounds in the underbrush or leaves, we can be assured its most likely a deer. Scooting sounds are probably rabbits. "Swish, swish" noises are most often something small and fast, like gophers or squirrels racing through the fallen grasses and leaves. Often we hear a very busy

Woodpecker working constantly to find the bugs inside a tree trunk. ("Tap, tap, ratta, tap, tap…" It's a wonder their eyeballs don't pop out.) At other times, if we are very quiet and pay attention, we can spot teensy, weensy, quick, and amazingly colourful, little Hummingbirds harvesting nectar. I have noticed them mostly drawn to the red, orange and bell-shaped wildflowers. However, if you're trying to observe one, you'd better not blink because they move *so quickly* you would miss them.

All of the birds have different and distinct songs, and even the songs and calls are different within each type of bird. For example, the big boys have shown us how one sound, or song, is a bird's call for his mate, another alerts of danger and so on. We have also learned how most bird-calls are unique to their own species. The Robin's call sounds nothing like the little Sparrow's. However, there is one bird which can actually feign the calls of most of the other birds. It is called a Mockingbird, but as knowledgeable as our leader is, even "Slick" doesn't know why these birds do this, and he says he "really couldn't care less". Still, I wish I had a few more answers about my fascinating surroundings.

The first time I heard an owl I was petrified because I thought it was *talking to **me*** and saying, "You! You! You!" I called back, "Who's there?" but then it said, "Who! Who! You!" At that point, I hid under a shirt until the big boys returned from a scavenging hunt, and by then I was crying out of fear, but they just laughed and told me what it was. Whew! Anyway, eventually I've come to recognize all the rest of the busy nighttime animal and insect noises, and they're no longer alarming to me. I'm not even afraid of the bats flying around in the evenings, because they fly through the swarms of insects, swallowing mouthfuls of millions of the annoying little bugs with each swoop. (They're doing us kids a big favour, especially if they eat the army-tank-sized mosquitoes—or the horse-, or deer flies.)

Very few animals are interested in our food hoard, except for the one that came around yesterday. The biggest, ugliest rat you ever saw visited us! This massive rodent thought he could out-smart us and scavenge from *our* cache. We all sat still and quiet and the minute he got really close, "Spike" sent "Mr. Rat" an unmistakable message when he chunked a rock at him, nicking his hind-quarters. We think he took the message back home to his friends because he was unable to steal anything from us. Of course, to the best of our knowledge, neither he, nor any of his big, fat ratty friends ever came back around our "Box".

"Slick" has also educated us so we are aware of the sounds specific to any of the real predators such as wolves, foxes and even raccoons. I had always been under the impression that those cute little bandit-looking animals were friendly, and cuddly. However, "Spike" set us all straight on that point, making sure we little guys didn't think we could make them our pets. However, all his talking about the raccoons being mean and hateful was one thing, but maybe we were not a hundred percent convinced. That is until one night two of them wandered near us right after we had eaten the last bits and pieces of somebody's discarded pizza. It was quite the feast for us and I guess the smell was also so enticing it drew the raccoons out of their hiding places. When "Slick" got up to scare them away, one of them reared-up on his hind legs and clawed and hissed into the air at our Leader before turning to run off. It was so vicious-looking, that I, for one, got the point right then and there—*not pets—no problem*.

"Slick" also told us, as long as any noises seem far away we don't need to be too concerned. I was scared of bears but he said they might be much more of a threat if the foliage in our chosen settlement area was not just small trees, shrubs and grasses. "Slick" says bears prefer densely treed areas like forests, of which there are certainly plenty in this vast Don River valley, just not really near our encampment.

"We're close to the sloping sides of the ravine, so we really don't have to worry about bears.", or so he says. Nevertheless, just to be extra sure we immediately consume any meat we scavenge. We store everything else in the waxed-lined, produce shipment box, which we set into a hole "Spike" dug into the ground. We keep it tightly covered with a mammoth flat rock.

Naturally, just to be certain of our personal safety, in case any real threats get curious or do happen to wander too close, (including those on two feet), the big boys take turns "sleeping with one eye open" right by our "door". They keep two thick lead pipes and couple of huge, stripped branches right beside them for the protection of all us kids and our camp. (As for me, with the big boys taking all these precautions, I have no problem sleeping with *both eyes closed*.)

However, it isn't the wild animals we need to be the most wary of, it's the humans, the derelicts, who are on the lam for one reason or another. These bums usually reside, and remain, mostly under the large, nearby bridge spanning the Don River. However, on three separate occasions we have been harassed by one of these hobos, or other shady type of characters. In fact, on two of those instances, we felt threatened enough that we picked-up stakes and moved our *house*, and all our belongings, to a different *secret place* in the vast Don Valley.

After the last incident, the two big boys worked-out an escape plan, in case of a repeat visitation, or even an attack. From our "door", we are supposed to run either straight *up* the ravine wall behind our box, or straight *down* towards the creek, depending on where the threat is coming from. Then whenever we are chased, we stick to our well-rehearsed plan, running along the little goat trails the boys already plotted-out and cleared of underbrush. Each trail goes along for about an eighth mile through the valley's unending maze of trees and bushes, and both meet-up at a safe-enough distance to observe and wait-it-out until the threat is gone.

It's important for us to keep our camp off any sort of actual trail and far away from the accidental view of any person who might be simply taking a hike in the valley. This way we can ensure the security of our cache even when we are all gone on a hunt ourselves. Our Leader says this is now of utmost importance because, our well-hidden camp won't accidentally be stumbled-upon and raided by any of the derelicts hanging out in the valley. In fact, the importance of hiding and disguising our Box house was driven home on one occasion when we all came back from a shopping run. Immediately we discovered every single bit of our food stores gone! At first, we thought it was animals like raccoons or possibly a bear drawn by the smell of our apples. However, when we noticed the can opener missing, (it was the one "Slick" had kept when we first escaped from "Wide Load's" house), and then we noticed the little box of vitally important wooden, stick-matches was also gone, the wild animal theory went straight out the window. That meant, until we could steal more food, another can-opener and/or some more matches from somewhere, we couldn't eat anything, either canned or cooked, and we had to go back out on a hunt in order for us to have any fresh fruit or veggies.

Chapter 35: My New BEST Friend: "DOG"

Our chosen outdoor lifestyle seems to be working quite well for all of us boys. I can't see that there is anything else we really need. We each have our designated role to fulfil which ensures the smooth and efficient operation of our little family-style wolf-pack. Luckily, for us, people often drive by this expansive ravine and toss useless items out of their vehicles. We absolutely can't believe what some people must think is junk. For us, every now and then, it's almost like Christmas. In fact, this past weekend somebody chunked a big, old, pee-stained mattress down the hill. Of course, we snatched it up right away, but now we have to draw straw grasses to determine the sleeping order, since only one person at a time will fit on it. (Why the heck do I always come in last? Oh well, every fifth night, the mattress is all mine! Let's hope I can count right.)

Tonight, however, it's a piece of cardboard for my mattress, and I'm sitting here on it, watching the moon and the stars perform their nightly ballet across the skies while dancing to nature's nightly orchestra of chirping crickets and bellowing bullfrogs. Every few minutes the crickets' music is overshadowed by the bullfrogs, sounding so very strange, while performing their mating calls. The lightning bugs have gone to bed now, and so have the other boys, but I can't seem to sleep tonight.

Uhhhh, what's that noise? Oh-oh, I think somebody is coming down the hill behind our shanty shack. "Skriiiitch, skriiiitch, huh, huh, huh, huh, skriiiitch...." I hear the dry grass and underbrush rustling and some very heavy breathing getting *closer*. "Wake-up, wake-up!" I am whisper-screaming in the big kids' ears! I'm *really* scared and can't seem to get anybody to awaken. (What happened to "sleeping with one eye open"?)

Just then, as I lean over to reach for the lead pipe weapon, my scary, noise-making intruder walks right by me as if I am invisible. I *am* invisible! And I am frozen to the spot! And...I just peed in my pants. My gaaaaawd—it is a deer, big enough to be a moose! (I sure hope he doesn't have any relatives following him—but it's my experience they aren't often alone.)

Now, I am *never* going to get to sleep. Oh, gosh, now what's that sound? Oh-oh, he must have a friend tagging along behind because I am now hearing the underbrush rustling again, only with lighter, quicker steps. I sure hope it's not a wolf hunting his dinner that just ran past me. What on earth? It's a doggie. It's a cute little doggie that was chasing the deer, but when he sees our *house* and me sitting there in my peed-in shorts, he comes right up to me for a little petting. (I hope he doesn't have rabies—"Spike" said his brother once caught rabies from a squirrel and had to get a whole lot of needles poked straight into his stomach! I sure would not want that to happen to me!)

"Hello, little guy. Are you lost?" I notice he isn't wearing a collar but, where a collar *would* be, all the black fur is gone, leaving a white collar-pattern and scabs around his scrawny neck. My gosh, he looks half-starved. (Maybe he was planning to *eat* the big deer.) I can feel his ribs sticking out when I pet him and I can also feel he's absolutely matted everywhere with those nasty little brown burrs that stick their hooks into, and hitch-hike on, *everything* brushing past. The poor doggie's tongue is hanging way out and he's panting like crazy so I decide to get my drinking can and take him down to show him the stream and get both of us a drink. (After all, I've already peed my pants, so what does it matter now if I take a little drink of fresh water before sleeping?)

While the pathetic little canine is slurping away and enjoying the cold running water, I start pulling some of the burrs off him, starting with the poor little feller's face. "Stay still! I know it hurts, but I'm trying to help you! You know, little feller, if you don't belong to anybody and don't have a home, let's ask 'Slick' in the morning if you can stay with us. O.K. by you?" He replies, "Yes." by pushing his face up under my chin. I understand him and he understands me. The doggie and I curl up on my cardboard bed and I have no trouble sleeping now.

It seems as if no time at all has passed when the morning arrives, announced by the jackhammer sound of pounding rain. The raindrops insult us morning sleepy-headed kids, sounding as if a freight train were driving through our little camp. Then, as each boy shakes the dreamy fog out of his brain, of course, they all stare at me. Then "Slick" demands to know, "Where'd the mutt come from, kid?" While I am resuming my de-burring of the pitiful little stray, I explain how he came along in the night, needing my help. Then I fairly *beg* "Slick" to allow me to keep him. "You know we can't keep the damn dog. We can barely scrounge enough food to take care of our own selves, never mind feeding your ugly mutt! In fact, we should just drown him right now and put him outta his misery."

I start to cry because, other than my sweet mommy, I've *never* wanted anything more in my whole life! "Pwease, pwease...I wiww tate care ub da doddie!" My pleading must be working because our Leader takes pity on ME and reluctantly agrees I can care for the stray for a few days, 'till *he* "can decide what to do with it—maybe we'll eat it.", he suggests, laughing right out loud at my reaction which is hysterical screaming of, "Noooo, don' eat da doddie, noooo!" Then, laughing his butt off, he says, "Not the dog, maybe we'll eat *you*!", and the rest join the chortling choir. "Noooooooooo!" is my only reply.

The next couple of days go by with my doggie settling more and more into our routines. I happily share all my food with him, though it doesn't seem to be helping him get any fatter. Nevertheless, before long, I understand "Dog" has decided to adopt *me*! ("Dog" is what I named him, because, after all, *we boys* only know each other by our *own* first names, or nick-names.) Then, before we are to go on our next run, the big boys decide on a plan to make the dog more useful to our team, and somehow help us when we go "shopping". My job, as their "mule", has always been to run, with my tucked-shirt full of loot, all the way back to the "Box", (which is our equally unimaginative secret name for our shelter). "Dog" stays by my side and barks at any people, or other dogs that attempt to approach me while me and my stuffed-shirt try to make it safely back to our woodland shelter.

Of course, most of the time, my doggie and I always do as we are told. Because, as I quickly discovered about living with this pack, compliance in our criminal activities is the only way to earn the privilege to eat at all. Howeverrrr...I may only be a dumb old *pack- mule* for the rest of them, but I'm smart enough, and brave enough, to take a couple items from my shirt and stash them in *my own secret place*, **before** I get back to the "Box"! This is because, as I have discovered in my life, *you really never know what is around the next corner,* or *when the scary revolving door will sweep around and get you again.*

Revolving Doors

Chapter 36: Me and "DOG" Go "House-Hunting"

Things are changing for me again. Just when I felt like I had a sort-of safe little home, these boys have now made the decision to disallow me to stay *inside* their shelter at nights anymore. They say it's because I am always peeing in my pants. (I guess I stink—they say I do, anyway.) Even though I am four, after all, I've never had a chance to be properly potty-trained. The kids tease me and call me a "baby" because of this. I've even tried to hide my problem by stealing extra clothes for myself so I can put them on whenever I've wet my pants. Nevertheless, the boys make me feel so embarrassed and ashamed of myself. Well, who gives a crap what they say! I'll be fine sleeping on my cardboard right outside their shelter. Anyway, my new, true-blue, little friend, "Dog", likes me just the way I am! He doesn't mind if I wet my pants! In fact, he *loves* me and he even *told* me it makes him very sad the way the boys tease and beleaguer me.

I have been two nights now, exiled to the "outside" of our *house*. I pushed my cardboard under an evergreen's low branches and put a blanket over the branches for protection—making a sort of fort. I was managing alright until this morning when the gang approached me. Apparently, my being in exile is now no longer good enough for these fellows. They got together and announced to me, I wet my pants too much, so now I'm not allowed to live with them anymore, not even on the *outside* of their shelter. They say, "You'd better go and find your own crate, or a cardboard box, in some alley and go live there!" (Wow, they sure are mean—after all, I am only four.) Anyway, I am not staying where I'm not wanted. So, now that I'm kicked-out of their entire shelter area, my companion, "Dog", and I take off on our *own* adventures, exploring all around in the valley for a new home. I'm positive we'll find an even better place to live in than their stupid ol' "box".

I grab my pillowcase and stuff it with my clothes and other junk and we two little unwanted strays take off hiking. In no time, I come across a large area of berry patches which none of us kids had ever found before. I know they're all good to eat because we've previously swiped these kinds of berries at the markets. That's when I stuff my pockets and myself too, with fresh raspberries, blueberries and blackberries. Yummie! There is a chokecherry tree here too, although "Slick" has said we shouldn't eat its tiny black berries. Ha! He's not the boss of me, now, so I eat some anyway. Oh, oh...ooooh, very bitter, not for me, yuck! Next, I'll try some of the wild rhubarb. Woooo, woooo....is it ever sour! It makes my mouth pucker up just like "Fish's" face. I'll certainly remember where my newly discovered stash of nature's bounty is at, all except for those darn choke-cherries and the rhubarb—oooooh! The only thing rhubarb will be good for is using the large, soft leaves to stuff my pillowcase for my tired little head to rest on.

Say, this newfangled independence isn't so bad! Who needs those bratty kids? Not me! Anyway, we two little friends keep wandering until we find ourselves hiking up in a place where the ravine wall is gently sloping. We are in a different area than we kids had ever explored before. When we reach the top of the hill though, I notice we're really not too far from our...I mean *their* shelter. However, I'm looking straight ahead at a new discovery. It's a very ancient cemetery, which is more than a little scary-looking. "Com'ere 'Dog'!" I immediately discover that our 'getting inside' the fenced area is simply a matter of crawling over any of the bent-down or broken parts of the rusted wire which once delineated the perimeter.

Granted, it *is* a little eerie, but, no matter, my brave little partner and I start down one of the numerous carriageways and walking paths. In every direction, I see a panorama of uneven rows, each housing scads of curiously shaped grave markers. I turn down one of many smaller trails and end up in a peculiar-looking part of this cemetery. Here many of the residents' headstones are leaning way over, as if some great tsunami of energy rippled through the graveyard. "Spooky"? Yes, I would call it very "spooky", but not bad enough to scare me off. However, the deeper I get in this old boneyard, the more the little hairs on the back of my neck are standing at attention. I do actually start to feel a wee bit frightened now, remembering some of the ghost stories the big boys were constantly relating to us gullible little fellows. However, when I look down at "Dog" and see he isn't scared in the least, I am reassured.

As we wander through the paths, which wind around the gravestones, I am amazed at all the beautiful sculptures. (I never, before now, thought of anything in a cemetery as beautiful.) Many of the shiny marble markers are shaped like someone's head, or carved like the dead person's face. I can also see a whole lot of sculptures shaped like crosses in one form or another. Some of the tombstones look like little children playing or flying angel-babies with wings. There are also many other angel sculptures, some of which are women and a few are men, but they all are *very* lovely.

"Dog" and I keep going deeper-in until we make our way to a tucked-away, sort-of corner area. Then, what do I see right in front of me, up against the fence? It is a little house—*a house just my size!* [*Unbeknownst to me, of course, it's a small mausoleum housing one individual corpse.*] Cemetery or not, I am just too curious not to investigate my newest discovery! First, I try to open the front door, which is an ornately carved slab of wood, but as might be expected, it's locked. (I wonder if it's locked to keep somebody from getting in or to keep *someone* from getting out). Anyway, next I examine the house on every side. I soon notice some pieces are worn away and broken off from the bottom back corner of the strange little building. I wonder what, or who, the heck could be in there. I find a sharp-edged rock and start chipping away at the hole which, right now, is only about the size of my head. Before long, however, I've scraped-out a hole the right size for "Dog" and little ol' me to squeeze in and out of. It's perfect!

Once inside, my eyes adjust to the sliver of light coming in through a very long, narrow, glass window, which is stained dark yellow. I can make out one small, white box. I don't think there is a dead body in it because it isn't big enough. In fact, it isn't any longer than I am tall. Oh, maybe it's a kid's corpse— after all, kids die too, as I well know. Either way, it doesn't frighten me, because, being as I am in the middle of a cemetery, I more than half expected to see a couple of dancing *skeletons* rattling around inside! Lacking that sort of spectacle, I am just fine with this arrangement.

While I am sitting on the cold, stone slab floor, I begin thinking—holy cow—this is a real eureka moment for me! "You know what, "Dog"? I can move right in here and there is even enough room for you too. At least *this* time I'll have my own house--and *this* little boxed-up "roommate" won't be kicking me out! It isn't too far from the other kids either, so I can easily still be their "mule" and *earn* food for you and me. It will be absolutely perfect for us, my little friend!"

What a super duper discovery this little house is for me. Nevertheless, I know I absolutely *have* to keep my special find a secret! No problem! After a little time of sitting on the floor of my new house, I realize my bum is freezing cold, so I decide to grab some cardboard to lay down on the fieldstone floor. I know right where to get some already-flattened, and dry, cardboard, but I must wait 'till all the kids are *gone* from their "Box". Then all I have to do is grab a dry slab of it from one of the many layers of cardboard lining their shelter. They won't even notice it gone.

That is exactly what I do, and I drag the big pieces up to my new house in the cemetery. I bend and poke them through my entrance door and spread them all around on the floor inside. Now, what's next? I decide I'm gonna need some food supplies for me and my best pal, and I know where to get them too. Since I'll be using it mostly for sleeping, I think these two necessities will be sufficient for my home.

Later on, I go back down to the shelter on the pretence of "just wanting to hang out with the kids". (Actually, I am here to find out *what's new* and *when* the kids might be *leaving* long enough for me to sneak back and take some other miscellaneous items I'll *need*.) I never respond to the kids' repeated questions regarding the whereabouts of my own shelter, instead I stay quiet and listen to *their tales* of plunder, and *plans* for the next excursion. Then, after an hour or so, I announce I'm returning to my own "Box" and they all act as if they couldn't care less. So I take off, but I only go a little distance away because I want to eavesdrop and find out when they might all be leaving. When I hear them talk about their next planned scavenging trip which is to occur, "tonight as soon as it's dark", I know exactly when to come back down, and bring my empty pillow-case along.

Once darkness washes over our little part of the city, I use the light from the moon and stars to guide my trek back down the ravine slope. I sneak into their hideout and grab a few old clothes and a blanket from their cache, then I high tail it right back up to my own little house. I also snatched an apple, potato and a few of their grapes, but not so much they'd really notice anything missing. Oh yes, and I got my best friend a chunk of salami, because, of course, he is not as much of a vegetarian as I am forced to be these days.

Revolving Doors

Back up at our new digs, I make a little bed for "Dog" and me, and then I stuff my pillowcase with some of the rhubarb leaves, rags and my cowboy suit. I wedge some cardboard, and the rest of the pillaged clothes, snugly back into the door-hole to keep some of the colder night air out, and to ensure no curious animals could entrap us in there during the night. I tuck us both in snugly, by wrapping the blanket right around the two of us. (My best buddy doesn't seem to mind being wrapped up at all.) Then, as we huddle and snuggle safely in the blanket, I'm thinking it's really a nice, yet strange, sensation. Because, sadly, it is actually the **first *loving*** physical contact I've ever had with *any living thing* up to this point in my life.

The morning's warmly whispered breath is my reminder I have a job to do. *I* have to be the scavenger now, for both of us. So I empty my pillowcase before taking off to town on my own salvaging, shopping trip. I know where a crab-apple tree is at, so I head there first. (The fruit is a little bitter but still edible.) I've learned from the big boys how to run and bash myself against the trunk to shake the branches free of their ripest fruit. Then it's easy pickins as the apples land on the grass. In the front yard of the very next house I find some lawn onions, (I don't know what they're really called but they look, and taste, like tiny, skinny green onions and, it's weird but they grow right in the middle of some people's lawns.)

As I continue down the street, I decide to check out somebody's side-yard, vegetable patch. It has been picked clear of most of its plants, however in the corner I notice a little bunch of mint leaves growing wildly. (When you chew on them, they almost taste like spearmint gum, except a lot more bitter and, of course, lacking in the sweetness sugar adds to actual gum.)

One more stop, a few houses down, and I get carrots fresh outta the ground. I cross the lane onto the next street and I pick up a large, dented metal beach pail, which some kid left lying in a yard. (Too bad for him, but after all, EVERYBODY knows the rule, "Finders—Keepers—Losers—*Weepers!*") The pail proves not only good for carrying foodstuffs, but it will also be perfect for bringing water from the creek up to my safe little stone house. On the way back along my own goat trail to my house, I grab some of the last of the raspberries on one bush and toss them in my new pail for *my* own secret cache.

Although the boys did try to pry it out of me, I never told where I am staying at night now—never. I'm positive, if they knew, they would first kick me out and then fight over who would get to stay inside. Heck, they would probably even kick out my silent, uncomplaining roommate—the one in the white box, not "Dog" of course. You know, I sure do love this ugly little doggie. In fact, this funny little feller has helped me understand that, I truly no longer have to rely on any of the human species for my security or my spirit's basic need for love. Ahhhhh, I am finally *adopted*. I am needed. I am loved. I am the new Alpha dog in my pack of two—*I* am Leader, (even if I am only master over my four-legged friend)! My life is good now and I think I can finally say this foreign feeling in my head and my chest must mean I am happy at last. At least I know for sure, *I* am smiling.

It is starting to get colder now and the leaves are bursting with brilliant colours of yellow, orange and vibrant red. When I stand at the hill's edge and look out over the vast ravine below, the spectacle is so stunning it takes my breath away. I feel like a king, as if I am ruler over all I survey below, and my red carpet is actually a multi-coloured patchwork of the regal yellow/orange/red/purple canopy disguising the ordinary valley beneath it. I may be young and little, but I certainly recognize pure, unadulterated beauty when I behold it. Sometimes I just sit here watching and wondering about everything from the bears to the ants. Many times, I lay back and read the

Revolving Doors
Heavenly messages which the ever-changing clouds present
to me.

Most times, I just enjoy being all by myself and not having to
answer to anybody, or do stuff for anyone else or always come
last. Just "Dog" and me—we are all the family that we will ever
need, ever!

Revolving Doors

Chapter 37: "Cemetery Angel": Death and More Death

With the approach of the colder weather, and the chilly fall rains, all of us kids have started to get sick with chest colds. Unable to obtain the proper daily balance of nutrients to nurture our ever-growing bodies, we have all succumbed to illness and all of our coughing is quickly getting much worse. A couple of the boys have started really coughing their guts out. We all are plagued with fever also and although we are burning up to the touch, inside we feel like we're freezing cold. In fact, all of us are shaking and shivering uncontrollably. (Now, I remember this kind of coughing and fever.) I tell the boys I've been sick like this before, and it's sometimes called, "Brown Kites" and sometimes called, "New Onions". They don't have the faintest clue what I'm talking about. No matter because any way you look at it, we aren't able to get medical attention or any medicine which might help our fevers. So, day-in and day-out, we suffer.

Regardless, I am too sick to stick around in their "Box" because the autumn wind has changed direction and is blowing hard and cold right through the two open sides of their shelter. Something is different tonight, however. I notice "Spike" has taken ill with terrible coughing spasms and he seems much worse than the rest of us. He is coughing and hacking all over the place. In fact, he sounds like the next thing to come up will be his lungs, or his toes! I stick around and try to help by fixing him some hot potato and carrot soup with some rocks added to the boiling pot, (for "more minerals"--or so "Spike's" grandma told him). I bring him some icy-cold trickling creek water for him to drink. However, I am also getting sicker and need to get back up to my secret little house before I get too weak to climb.

Revolving Doors

The morning sun's warmth has barely kissed the air and already "Dog" has pushed his way out of our doorway to go pee a few yards away. I don't really want to move out from under what little warmth our coverings offer, but I force myself to crawl out when I hear the sounds of shouting and screaming! "Dog" and I race each other through the graveyard and slide-climb down to the "Box" where I see the boys shouting, jumping around and just going completely nuts. "He didn't wake up. He went to sleep and never woke up!", "Freckles" is shouting while pointing at Spike's grayish-blue body. "We weren't sure if he was gonna be O.K. or not, but when his body turned stiff as a board this morning, we figured for sure he's dead, now.", "Slick" stammers. ("Fish" is crying and crying.) "What's stinkin'?" "Freckles" asks "Slick". "He's shit his pants, that's what." he grumbles. "How the hell can a dead guy shit his pants?" again, curiosity from "Freckles". "Slick" scowls, "It just happens sometimes stupid, so shut-up and help me." (I'm wondering if "Spike's" pet tapeworm will try to get out.)

Anyway, they're all just about pulling their hair out trying to figure out how to handle our newest problem,

"How to dispose of a dead boy's body without involving adults, or taking a risk of being caught and sent back to the asylum and/or horrid foster homes."

I had not ever told the boys about my cemetery because I didn't want them to know about my new, perfect, secret hidey-hole. After all, it's so much better than their cardboard, crate and tin shelter that they would definitely steal my shelter from me. Nevertheless, now it's time, at least to mention my discovery of the place where dead bodies are supposed to go.

I tell them I'm staying in the nearby cemetery; however, I neglect to mention my house. "Slick" and "Freckles", while coughing and gagging like crazy, are both asking, "You're living in a boneyard? You're making this up!" "No, I'n not!" I protest. "Why didn't you tell us?", "Slick" asks. However, before I can answer he adds, "Well I suppose it'll be handy to solve the little problem we seem to have here, right now. C'mon, kids, let's go see this supposed boneyard, and what the little baby is talking about, then we'll decide what to do." (They *never* believe me, and certainly never trust me.)

Shortly, after I indicate the direction, we all hike over to the old graveyard. Then the two older boys climb on up the sloping ravine wall to determine if they can possibly find a newly dug grave to bury "Spike" in, or maybe slide him in with somebody else's body. (I never told them about the protective stone structure housing me, so I was praying to God and Santa they wouldn't notice it.) My gosh—we all sound like a bunch of old sailors, choking and coughing so loudly! It is a wonder our clandestine little venture isn't discovered by anybody else who might be alive around the old cemetery

The two kids hurry right back to where we are perched and order us to, "Stay-put! Just stay right there!" Down at their "Box" our Leader and "Freckles" roll "Spike" onto a big piece of cardboard that had lined their shelter's floor. Pulling very hard on it, they eventually drag, and/or push, the body's dead weight all the way to the top of the hill, which, although not terribly steep, is problem enough when two kids are dragging another kid's *dead weight*. We two littlest fellers are left about halfway up, so we poke along behind as they pass.

At the top, we peek out and see the big fellas. "Fish" is still crying softly and shakily admits he's "scared to death" of the ghostly old boneyard. He whispers to me that he knows for an absolute fact, "There's zombies roaming all around, waiting to kill us little kids and eat our brains." (What a helluva thought— and according to my own first-hand experience, quite wrong, but who am I to argue. So, I say nothing.) "Fish" shadows me as we witness the others drag the dead boy's body over to a very big grave-marker, which is shaped like a *huge stone Angel*. The whole structure is a good twenty feet or more, from its base to the tip of the Angel's upraised fingers as they point to Heaven.

How did I never before notice this ANGEL, whose name "Shekhinah", [149], is inscribed on the base on which she is mounted? I can't believe how beautiful and welcoming she is. This Cemetery Guardian Angel looks like a very beautiful young woman with a flowing, belted gown fashioned with softly draping material. Her shoulder-length, hair has a centre part and the sides are blowing back as if being styled by the fingers of an invisible breeze. She is perched on top of a very tall stone structure which is kind of an archway held up by two massive pillars. (I bet you could stand inside of it and not even be rained, or snowed, on.) This gorgeous Angel is standing with huge, inviting wings spread wide open. Her right arm is pointing to Heaven and her left arm is lowered, with out-stretched hand, as if she is clearly saying, *"Bring him to me; I will see he gets to Heaven."* Of course, the boys are thinking the same thing I'm thinking, so they lay his skinny body inside the arch, and under the promising Angel's feet. After all, what else can they do?

By dawn's first winking light through our window strip, we are awakened by some commotion outside of my little cemetery house. As usual, "Dog" is out before me. When we follow the hysterics, we see the kids over at the Angel, yelling and jumping around. "He's gone! He's gone!" They are screaming in unison, between duelling coughing spells. Then we all run around, searching the area as if somehow he had tried to get up and walk away. Nevertheless, "Spike" is absolutely nowhere to be found! His skinny, blue, poopy, dead body is gone without a trace. Holy cow! We are all completely stumped. The kid's body is gone—clothes and all! Obviously, those of us remaining can do nothing but agree, "God must have noticed him at the Angel's feet and took him on to Heaven"! Then "Slick" exclaims, "See! It just *proves* God is *real*!"

[*This was an instantaneous follow-up conclusion to a long-standing philosophical argument regarding the "existence of God".*]

"Slick" insists, "God took 'Wally' to Heaven!" We all agree; however, I get goosebumps when he adds, "And, *I've decided*, this Angel is who we'll all come to when we die." (I may be coughing as if I'm dying but I'm not planning on dying—at least not yet.

The three other boys remaining continue to share their "Box" shelter, staying down there in it, even though the colder fall/winter weather has already overtaken the valley. After all, what other choice do they have? At least, they've given up on discovering where I'm staying. They figure I'm "boxed-in" under some big evergreen, or else I've made a fort between some tombstones. However, I still have our safe, warmish little place for "Dog" and me—and it's still our secret—and I know *he's* not telling anyone. Because we are staying in this safe little house, it's a darn good thing too. After the first huge snow blizzard, kazillions of the sparkling crystals covered everything in the cemetery, even many of the larger tombstones. Nevertheless, it doesn't bother us and, of course, no snowfall could completely enshroud our lovely Guardian Angel. "Shekhinah". She always rises above—well, above almost everything in the whole Necropolis.

The fact is, although I am getting sicker with the lung gunk, I can still eat and get around, and I credit this to being protected by my stone house and by "Her"--by "Shekhinah". However, though it has only been a couple weeks since "Spike" went to Heaven, here we are staring at another dead boy. It seems some combination of illness and starvation has just claimed "Freckles", and now *I* have to help drag *him* to the Angel. I am afraid to look at him because he died with a horrible, freakish look on his face and his eyes are open and kind of rolled back! (I didn't even know you could die with your eyes open, but then I didn't know you could sleep with one eye open either.)

It has taken a heck of a long time to get him up the embankment. Although it's not terribly steep, it's still enough of a slope to cause him to keep sliding off our makeshift cardboard stretcher. The other problem is, he died with his right arm sticking out sideways and he is so stiff we can't push it in without breaking it right off, which is such a gross thought nobody volunteers to perform the operation. So as we pull him through trees and bushes his doggone arm keeps grabbing them and swinging him around sideways off his cardboard stretcher. (I am the smarter feller of our bunch, staying upwind of this boy's body; because, of course, *he's* shit in his jeans too.)

Eventually, of course, we do get him over to our Angel. She has not changed. She is still so beautiful, still welcoming, and, eerily still *waiting for the rest of us*. As we slide him off onto her large, solid marble platform, we hear someone coming toward us. "***Shittt-hitt-hit-hit***!" "Slick" cough-scream-cusses. We've been spohh—ohh-ohh-tted! Let's get the hell outta here! Go, go you kids, go, go! Without hesitation, we run in our predetermined and well-practised directions.

Indeed, it seems as if somebody *has* been hanging out in the cemetery very near our "Guardian Angel" statue, and upon spotting us boys, gives chase. He is a very big, heavy-set man in a long overcoat and he's awkwardly trying to run in great, flapping, galoshes which make their own pounding sounds between his huffing and puffing. We scatter and lose the stranger while scooting in two different directions. We hightail it under and over the broken fence and through the deep snow into the thick underbrush surrounding the outside perimeter of the cemetery. "Slick" runs one way while "Fish" and I run the other way. Later, when we meet back up at the "Box" we agree to wait-it-out a good couple of days before we all sneak back over to the Angel. They're sick and I'm sick, nonetheless, I need to get back to my little house, huddle with "Dog", and rest.

Three days later, when we return to our Angel, sure enough, as expected...the *second boy's* body is gone up to Heaven! It is amazing, yet anticipated, at the same time. Although now, it only leaves three of us remaining alive. It hasn't been very long since "Freckles" died, and now the oldest, "Slick", I mean, "*Art*"--our Leader, has gotten much sicker. His, sounds like the same kind of coughing I was plagued with when I ended up floating in the corner of the hospital emergency room ceiling. The doctors said it was the "New Onions" and concurred with each other, "It's often a death sentence to a lot of adults, and even more so for many children." I know this, from my own experience with the three roommates I lived with in a previous basement group home, all of whom I witnessed die from this very same, devastating disease.

"Fish", the second youngest, and I are sick as anything with this same creepy, crawly lung crud which is killing our friends. Even so, we now have the job of "feeding and watering" "Art", to try like crazy to nurse him back to health. After all, we can't let him die on us because he's our Leader, and we wouldn't know what to do if he wasn't here to lead us. Anyway, whatever we are doing must be working because yesterday he said he felt "good". So, we little guys decided to make a run to the grocery store area of town. Then later, we checked-out the garbage cans behind the Italian restaurant, where we actually found some semi-hot food and a container to carry it in. It was spaghetti and was even still a little warm by the time we got it back to our patient. After he ate it, he felt even better. (We divided-up and shared the remainder, and we too felt a little healthier.)

Though it has only been a week since our spaghetti feast, (which, incidentally, was actually my first experience with sketties), we two youngest returned this evening from an all-day shopping trip. To our complete shock, we find "Art" had joined the other two boys, but not before he coughed up a big pile of red blood, which was splatted all over the cardboard bed. We figure he must have tried to get outside the shelter because more blood was all over in the snow outside the doorway. "Slick" was dead, stiff and bluish all over, which has now made ours a very desperate situation. What are we supposed to do? We discuss it and we know "Art" *has* to go to the Cemetery Angel in order to get into "Heaven"--and *he* believed in "God's Heaven" long before any of the rest of us did. Nevertheless, he's an awfully big boy compared to us.

So the next night, the two of us little guys remaining, get his body on a huge piece of cardboard, which had obviously housed somebody's new refrigerator during delivery and which was subsequently discarded by tossing it into the "Don". Anyway, "Fish" pulled, I pushed, and we tried for hours, only getting him halfway up the hill. (Poor "Dog" doesn't have a clue about what we are trying to do.) Utterly exhausted, we had to stop for the night, so we just covered his body over with snow and branches and went back down to their "Box" to sleep.

Then, the next night we go back at it again. Though coughing and sputtering all the way, we finally get *his* body to the Angel. Again, we are spotted by *two other* very large, stocky men, also in long, dark, heavy, woollen-type overcoats. (It certainly is weird how all these big men *happen* to be hanging-out up here.) Nevertheless, somehow we scoot away without being nabbed, once again. (It is very strange, but these men don't seem the least bit interested in our little *dead* friends—it's *us* they seem to want to snag.)

Right now, we are talking things over and I'm drinking my can of warm water, which I heated on the car grill, over our little fire. "Who should get the knife?" I ask. "Fish" says he is oldest, so he should keep it. However, right now, I am looking at my last little companion and I'm thinking he doesn't look so good. (I think the Swiss Army Knife, [98], will be mine, *sooner* than later.) Though we are both deathly ill, he is even sicker than I am. Right now, I'm not so much feeling sorry for him, but I'm thinking about when he dies, how I'm gonna drag his pudgy body all the way up the hill to the Angel, by myself. ("Dog" would definitely help, but after all, he is just a dog, and lacking the proper digits would need to pull with his teeth, which simply would not work in this situation.)

I wonder how I will be able to take care of my little doggie and myself. (Thank God and Santa, "Dog's" not coughing!) It is probably a good thing "Fish" doesn't know what I'm thinking. I **know** we are both seriously ill, and both coughing our guts up—all the same, I figure he is much worse than I am. I'm certain, pretty soon it will be *me* dragging *him* up to the Angel by myself—and it won't be easy because we are about the same height, only he's a lot heavier than I am.

So, I suggest we move the basics of the "Box", (the cardboard floor, metal car grill, blankets, extra clothing and some food), up top, closer to the cemetery fence. He wants to know what has prompted my suggestion, so I convince him we'll be nearer to the stores and restaurants for stealing food, especially *hot* food. Of course, we no longer need to be so near to the stream, because we can melt the *snow* in our drinking cans. Either "Fish" believes me, or he's too sick to argue. Anyway here we are at the top of the vale, setting-up housekeeping, and ensuring we are well-hidden in-between some barren, but thick, bramble bushes.

When we have moved just about everything up, he lies down. I tell him, "I'll go put out the fire and bring the food and the last blanket up here. O.K. with you?" (No answer from my sickly friend. I guess he is just weak and exhausted, and talking makes him start coughing again.) So, down I go, grab the last things, some extra jeans for me, and I snuff out the fire with some snow, then head back to scramble up the hill, which due to my exhaustion seems steeper every time I climb it. I am coughing so often and so loudly after all this exertion, I don't even notice my last little roommate is *not*.

When I get up to the brambles, I start talking to him. I tell him I brought the stuff to get us settled into our new digs. Then I ask him for the matchbox so I can get another fire going for us. When he doesn't answer, I figure he's asleep. However, when I roll him over to get the matchbox out of his pocket, I see how *he too* has turned phantom-white. I figure only moments before he must have given up the ghost. He actually peed his trousers, but I don't smell any poop. (Maybe it's not very nice what I'm thinking, but I can't help thanking God, and Santa, I don't have too far to drag *this kid's* body all by myself.)

Of course, he is already lying on the cardboard, so I throw the blankets aside and start dragging him towards our Angel. I guess I *should* be feeling sad or lonely, or even scared of what is to come. But I'm actually not feeling anything at all except the shivery cold nipping small bites out of my flesh wherever it's exposed. Anyway, I drag him to the fence and raise it up with a big stick, then slide him under, into the graveyard. Lucky for me, the top layer of the snow had frozen solid the previous night and dragging his body on the cardboard sled was much easier than I anticipated. Nevertheless, it's a good thing we were already at the top of the slope because I would never have been able to get him up out of the valley by myself.

When I had "Fish" almost all the way over to our Heavenly marble Guardian, I see that I am once again, not alone, in this desolate cemetery. I can hear three different men's deep voices speaking in hushed tones. Because it's the sort of crisp, clear winter night which carries sounds over greater distances, I'm hoping the men are much farther away than they actually seem to be from their whispers. It boggles my brain to comprehend what in the heck three more grown men are doing out here in the freezing night just standing around and smoking!

[Our Leader used to talk about the "cemetery-men" who were always hanging out in graveyards, "boozing it up". Of course, that explains the presence of large, glass, long-neck bottles with funny labels and really stinky "pop" residue left inside. However, why would they have to go to a freezing cemetery in the middle of the night to smoke and booze it up? Don't they have homes either? If not, where are the "Boxes" they live in?...And, I would certainly like to know where they're getting such warm, heavy overcoats and boots!]

I quickly understand how wrong I am in assuming the men are probably not very near our winged statue. Because I had not slid my last little dead friend, (who is right now, also starting to look a little bluish), all the way to *her* cold, marble feet, when I *see* them. As soon as it's clear they have spotted me, I have no choice but to drop "Fish" right where I'm standing. I take off running like the scared little rabbit I am right now, and bro—ther, they're sure coming after me in a big hurry, and bellowing curse words at me all the way!

Of course, I always know exactly where the best spots are to run and squeeze under the fences. "Don't look back! Don't look back!" I have to keep telling myself. Nevertheless, I am very curious to know why *they* are chasing *me*. Do they think *I* am killing the boys at the Angel's feet? Do they think I've *witnessed* something I shouldn't know about? Who are these men? Obviously, they're not vagrants—I can tell as much from their warm, winter attire. Nevertheless, all I can do is run like the wind right now and cough later.

[We kids would not have heard the whispers and rumours about the gangsters and their prospective "hits" hanging out in this very cemetery. Nor would we have kept up with local current events reported in the newspapers. We only knew our little cemetery usually appeared to be abandoned. Ironically, it was originally intended as a "Potter's Field", then later designated as a "Stranger's Burying Ground, for the burial of indigent or unknown people." (How ironic?)

Gossip on the streets apparently had mobsters dropping bodies into the already occupied coffins—squeezed-in on top of the newest Necropolis residents. Personally, I had no knowledge of mobsters' activities, such as "murder for hire". I was still quite young and never taught to read. My limited knowledge of evil deeds like "bumping people off" entirely consisted of stories the bigger boys related to us, or read us from the comic books they "borrowed". In reality, I was in no way savvy in the ways of the real world at the time and in the massive metropolis of Toronto.

Looking back from an adult's perspective, I understand, even if the men were indeed, gangsters, we boys would never have been in actual danger in the cemetery—at least not from them or mob guys. We were innocents, and even mobsters purportedly had their own code of conduct, which did not permit the vengeful killing of innocents, especially children. In fact, they could murder someone right in front of a little kid, and they would not be concerned whether the child would "talk" or could testify in court. Because in those days, children *would not even be <u>believed</u>, never mind be expect to swear an oath and bear witness in a trial of murder.]*

Chapter 38: *BUSTED!*

Now I've been spotted, I bolt like the bejesus is scared right outta me, again! Then I head for one of the many familiar openings in the bent and twisted, old wire fence. Almost there—Ahhhh—Freedom is inches away! I scoot under the fence and between some thick evergreens. *Suddenly* I am face-to-face with, and right in the waiting arms of—a *copper! A cop*—who happens to be out there, (looking for *me*, I guess). (At least it's what I thought)! If he is *not* looking for me, it's an incredible coincidence he's waiting in the exact spot where I am trying to escape from the cemetery men. I suppose it really doesn't matter because whatever the reason, *I'm* caught—apprehended, and "arrested".

"Hey! Hey, hey, little fellow! What the heck are *you* doing out here in the freezing cold? And, where do you think you're you going? Don't you worry son, I'll get you into a warm, safe place. You'll be fine. Trust me." Why would I trust a copper? "Wemmie do! Wemmie do!" I'm screaming at the flatfoot! "My dod, 'Dod'! I hab a doddie!" I try to tell him he can't take me away because I have a little doggie which needs me very much. "My doddie, my doddie!" I protest with every breath left in me, which, considering how far my own health has deteriorated, isn't much. "That's right little guy, we'll find your daddy." he condescends. "Noooo...doddie, doddie!" I try hard to make myself understood, but to no avail. I am screaming so much I can hear "Dog" barking from inside our house, where I had barricaded him in while I got us two boys moved up from the bottom of the hill.

However, the cop doesn't understand what I am clearly telling him. Despite my squirming around, he has a tight grip on me and just keeps trying repeatedly to reassure me, "Everything is alright now." No, it's not! Really? Can he be serious? All my buddies are dead, and I *am not*. Of course, the only true blue friend I've ever had in my life is now locked away in the little cemetery house! I suppose, when he chews his way outta the cardboard door, he'll be out there somewhere running all around in the boneyard, or even in the vast Don Valley, looking for food, for love, for rest—and for me. "Good-bye, 'Doddie', good-bye, I will always, always love you. I'm sorry, but this mean old copper is forcing me to leave you behind. I love you."

I am arrested now and sitting in the front seat of the cop car while my rescuer is talking to a fellow officer outside my window. He has wrapped me in a thick, grey, woollen blanket from his trunk. It's both comforting, and itchy, at the same time. The parked car is still running and the heater is forcing warm air up past my feet and around my legs. I would have to admit the warmth is actually very soothing. In fact, as frightened, and sad, as I am, I am getting so sleepy now, it's not mattering quite so much.

"Blah...blah...blah...buzz...crackle...crackle", the cop-car radio is blabbing away. A few minutes later, the copper gets into the car and asks me if I'm alright. "We're gonna take a little drive over to the station and see if we can find out where you belong." he announces. "What's your name, little fellow?" he asks, but I'm not telling. Then, as soon as another police car arrives alongside us, we take off.

At the police station, I am escorted through a large office, windowed on three sides. Then I'm placed in a smaller, interior room, also windowed, instead of walled. Filling this little office is a huge, brown wooden desk. I am instructed to sit in one of three, large brown, armchairs with black leather seats and matching padded backs and armrests, [apparently a very popular style of office furniture]. There are life-size pictures of men in police uniforms on one wall, and a smaller picture of a lady who is dressed in a beautiful, pale blue evening gown. She is wearing a jewelled crown on her head and jewels around her neck, which make her appear quite stately and regal. I'm feeling very small in here and scared of what will happen to me next, but I'm also a tiny bit glad I'm caught, because at least I'm warming up a little now.

"Little fellow, would you like some hot cocoa?" my captor inquires. (Would I? Is he crazy? Of course, I would!) I give a small nod of agreement, without giving away my true feelings that I am starting to be glad I'm caught. However, I'm not sure if it's caused by my coming in from the cold to the heat of the office, but I have now started coughing uncontrollably. The uniformed officers, including a sort-of lady policeman, [99], are scrambling around trying to find some warm, dry clothes for me. One brings a big sweater, another offers a man's work-shirt and they start peeling my damp stuff off, right down to my cowboy suit which is next to my shivering body. When they try to take *it*, I protest vehemently, so they leave it on me and just layer me up with the other items.

They are all bustling around in the office like a swarm of bees, or a colony of hard-working ants. I guess they're trying to get someone to adopt me. It doesn't matter where they take me now because I plan to run away, and I now know I'm able to do so. I also know how to find my way back from this area of town to the valley, to my cemetery house—and to my pal "Dog", of course. So all I have to do is wait it out and see what they have planned for me next.

For now though, I sip on the most delectable treat I have ever had in my entire four years of life...and I wait.

Revolving Doors

Chapter 39: Back to, Where Else?... The *ASYLUM!*

After an hour or so, who do you suppose should appear in the outer office? It's "Big Ears"! When he spots me, he almost shouts, "Hey there kiddo! It's *you*, Teddy! What are you doing in *here*?" Then he turns to the constables and assures, "*I know* this boy!" "Teddy, you know everybody's been looking for you, for a very long time now. I'm sure glad you're found. (*I* was not *lost!*) Do you have any idea where the other four boys are at— you know, the kids you lived with at "Mrs'..." house?" he inquires. "Dey went to da Ainzul, 'n' she dot 'em to Heben.", is my best attempt at an explanation. However, he has absolutely no idea what I'm trying to tell him. So then, I just shut up.

Suddenly Mr. "Big Ears" remembers something to tell me, "Oh, guess what, son, we have your little tricycle over in 'Mrs'...' office." (Hmmm, really? It's in "Wart's" office? How the heck did it end up there? Anyway, it's nice to hear, because I figured it was thrown out long ago.) After a few more minutes of "Ears" and "Flat-foot" speaking softly in the outer office, we are leaving and heading out the door for my second cop-car ride of the night—of my life. Where are we going? Where else! We're off to the "C.A.S." once again.

Once there, I am *so* sick and *so* exhausted, I fall fast asleep on the hard wooden bench outside the "Wart Lady's" inner office. Oh, no! I am awake now and I am in a crib-cage back in the same asylum ward from which I escaped when my previous confinement ended. How in the hell did I end up back here? I don't really want to be here, but it's better than the cemetery, I suppose. "We lost track of them after they all ran away from 'Mrs'...' group home. You know, the others still haven't shown up anywhere." This is what I overheard one nurse telling another nurse.

(Actually, I happen to know, for a fact, they won't be finding them anywhere either. Because I know they all floated straight on up into Heaven with a little lift from our Guardian Cemetery Angel's up-stretched arm. All, of the kids, except for "Fish". Poor little, deformed, fish-faced kid never made it to the Angel's safe little marble platform. Too bad because he might have gotten a new mouth in Heaven. Anyway, his body probably won't even be discovered until the snows melt away. Unless the bad guys who hang around in the cemetery find him first, and throw him into a coffin with somebody else, {lest *they* be found with his body and suspected of murdering *him*}.)

I wonder how long I'll have to stay here this time. How can these people keep pushing me into one foster home after another without ever checking on my actual progress, or without finding out what is really going on in these so-called *homes*? I don't even care where they send me next, because I am determined, I will run away again! However, I am having another problem right now. I am stuck in the itty-bitty baby ward, and bro—ther, can these little kids ever scream! Actually, I don't even think I'll wait 'till I'm placed into another foster home. I will simply escape from this horrid place and run away where none of these nutty people will find me. I can do it too. I know how to stay alive out there now, and all I have to do is find my old cemetery and I'm sure "Dog" will be waiting right there for me. But I think I'll wait 'till tomorrow to make my big break. I'm gonna take-in a few meals around here, just enough to get my strength back.

Oh gosh, I can't believe I've already been back here in the baby nursery for a couple weeks now. I haven't found a good way to escape yet. However, right now I have a bigger problem. It's my lungs—they're still full of the "creepy, crawly lung crud", and I don't seem to be getting any better. The nurse called in a visiting doctor to have a listen to my chest and, no surprise to me, it's "New Onions" again! Geeeze, I can't catch a break, or a breath. Oh great, here comes the doctor with a two-foot-long hypodermic needle to shoot some "Penicillin", [156], antibiotic into my bum cheek! "Owwwiee! Dat hurt me! Dop-it, dop-it!" O.K., so that is absolutely it! I am outta here, somehow—tomorrow...

The tomorrow, which became yesterday, sleeted until another week has passed by again, and I am still stuck here. I got even sicker before I started to feel the effects of the antibiotic shot a couple days later. "Librarian Lady" decided to check up on my mental health too. She took me for *another IQ test.*, [67], [68], [69]. This time I did a little better, scoring a **ninety-two, which** is much higher than my first score of **seventy-one**. Although I am chronologically *fifty-one* months old, this score slots me in at a mental age of *thirty-six* months.

(My problem with those damn psychometric tests, [66], is, I know a whole lot more about whole lotta stuff, but the person testing me didn't ask me the *right questions*.)

[The ONLY comments in the "C.A.S." file regarding this test situation stated the following, *"Teddy was quite friendly with everyone in the office and was quite at home in the test situation."*]

(These people are all a bunch of clueless dodo-brains!)

Anyway, I think I must be getting really sick again, because more weeks have passed since I got the bum-shot and now I have completely lost my appetite. Nobody knows why I've stopped eating and now I can't sleep either. This time I have to go to "Doctor Malcovitch's" office to find out what is wrong with me. Once there, he is shocked to see my weight charted at only ***thirty pounds***. He prescribes a nutrition supplement to help me catch up on my weight and get even stronger. Oh, noooo! Here he comes with another bum-shot of "Penicillin" to "really knock-out" this lung infection, or so he says. (How in the hell does a shot of medicine in my bum "knock-out" infection *in my lungs*?)

[The following is an excerpt from the Doctor's letter commenting on Teddy's health status and is exactly as recorded in his file at the Director's office,

"Teddy was very cooperative and is an attractive, lovable little boy. He is prepared to go to a new home, and talks of things he is going to take with him. He seems well adjusted, and when he is well prepared, will probably go on to an adoption home with the minimum of adjustment. The *results* of his psychological *testing* for mental *retardation* are *negative.*"]

When they're testing my brain, I've learned how to go along with these adults. If they ask,
"Don't you want to go to a nice new home with very nice parents?"
I reply, "**Yes**."
Then, in answer to leading questions like,
"Do you have a favourite toy you would like to take with you to your new home?"
I reply, "**Yes**" etc. etc.

Then they turn it all around and write garbage in my file. They say what they would like to think I am thinking...and nowhere near what I am *really* thinking and planning! See what I mean—dodo brains!

I am getting another taxicab ride today as "L.L." and I return to the orphan asylum after additional prodding doctor visits. However, I must say, I am really getting tired of all these comings and goings through the psychological revolving doors of my life. I really wish I had died right along with the other four boys. Then I would not have to keep going through all this stuff, including the bum-shots of antibiotics. I would be right up in Heaven with my little friends. I would get to see "Spike's" new thumb and, hopefully, see "Fish's" new face! Then I would be playing all the time, and certainly not seeing doctors or taking ridiculous "IQ" tests, [67], [68], [69], which tell everyone how damn *stupid* I am. (I may not actually be called "stupid"; however, I'm pretty sure the labels, now noted in my "C.A.S." file, which are: "**Recidivistic**" and "**Feral**", are just as bad, if not worse! Does this mean I am an incorrigible child with no hope of ever having a real, loving adoptive home? Through how many more revolving doors will I still have to spin and pass? Awww, who cares about me anyway?

PART VII: The Baby "Garden"

Chapter 40: "*NO* News"...is GOOD NEWS!

How long am I going to be forcibly detained, being fed and watered in this baby garden? I sure miss my dog, "Dog". I have nobody to talk to around here. Well, of course, there are other kids I see at feeding-time and so-called, "playtime", but I mean I have nobody I can *trust* to talk to about my current big secret'. I have formulated a new, perfect plan now, and I know *how* I'll be able to escape from my confinement. I'm just not exactly sure *when.*

I have observed a pattern, of a sort, in the way strangers are permitted to visit here in the, *all-whiny-brat-babies-except-for-me* ward. One day is pretty much exactly the same as the next around here. Although, I have noticed on the same day the sounds of the bells hail the churchgoers, strangers, usually in the form of young married couples, come here to do a little "baby window-shopping". What I mean is, they come and browse around the ward looking wistfully and lovingly into every single crib, *excluding mine.* Without exception, when they get to me, invariably the comments are:

"*Oh, my, and how old is this baby?*" or,
"*Is this little fellow just visiting here?*" or,
"*Where does this little guy belong?*" or,
"*Looks like this little boy crawled into the wrong crib!*"
...then always the hurtful laughter, "Hahahaha."

When they laugh at their own jokes, I decide I am very glad they are *not* picking me to go home with them.

Nevertheless, the response from the nurses or the Workers is always the same, *"Of course this young man belongs in our 'Three-to-Five-Year-Olds' ward. Unfortunately, the appropriate ward is simply too full at the moment, but, he's certainly still available for adoption."*

Nobody ever asks the begging question, "Could we adopt him?" (Incidentally, neither does anybody ask *me* what *I* think about being stuck in here with these damn screeching baby-brats!) Neither do any "nice young couples" ever ask if *I* would like to go for a Sunday drive in the country—*none, not even one, ever!*) In fact, on one of these Sunday visitation days, I was actually removed and taken to the high-chair room where I was given a *snack,* when it was not even snack time. This was done so the handsome young couples could parade around in the nursery, during an open-house pre-viewing shopping trip. Who cares anyway? Dammit, not me! I never get any hopes up anymore. Why would I? It just always ends in heartache. After all, if I expect nothing, I am never disappointed.

However, I've decided, this is how my perfect escape plan will come into play. When everybody's attention is on the babies, and nobody's attention is on me, in the feeding place, I'll climb out of the highchair, run out the back door and never look back! See, my plan is simple, but perfect! I *have to* escape because there is absolutely no hope for me if I stay in here. That's because, on the only occasions I am ever *removed* from this orphan asylum, it's only to shove me into one horrific foster home, after another. "I am taken *out of the frying pan—* have one swirl around in the revolving door, then I'm shoved back out—*into the fire.*"

Huh? Now what's *she* doing here? It's "Mrs. Mousey" and she is chatting with the floor nurse, and nodding and glancing in my direction. (You can just forget taking me somewhere else to stay...that ain't happenin'!) That's odd—I just heard my

Revolving Doors

"Case Worker" introduce the man next to her as her husband. I wonder what *he is* doing here today and I am curious to know what he is carrying.

However, I sure don't have to wonder very long, because a few minutes later, they're both standing beside my crib-cage and they're talking to me in their best *nicey-nice-nice* voices. (However, *my focus* is on the blue box the man is carrying by its handle. It appears to be the perfect size for *me* to fit-and/or-escape-in.)

"Here's his bag of things, oh yes, and don't forget his tricycle over next door, just inside the main office doors." explains the crabbiest nurse of all, (I call her, "Snake Lady", because her hair looks like wriggling, crawling, slimy snakes). "We brought him a little suit-case to pack instead of his old paper bag. Alright?", "Mrs. Mousey" asks in her best, extra nicey-nicely voice. "Snake Lady" wriggles her hair while nodding in agreement. My Case Worker instructs her husband to start putting my clothes and small toys, including "Pom Pom", into the box, which is, upon closer inspection, a cute little, light-blue, hard-sided, over-night-sized travel case. He complies and then, with a "clack-clack" he snaps it shut.

Well, that's nice. Nobody has ever given me a brand-new, little suitcase before—only a paper bag. I am feeling very important right now, albeit a little apprehensive about what is to come next. "I guess you have figured out we are here to take you on to a very *special* home today, Teddy." "*Pecial*?" I ask. Today you will be having a visit at a house with a family who are very interested in keeping you forever. "Pfor eber", I sputter, wondering what "forever" can possibly mean in the life of a recidivistic, feral, stupid, bad, skinny, pee-stained, little guttersnipe. "Yes, forever!" my Worker adds with a touch of glee in her voice. "We'll go see them today, and if you're a *very* good boy and they like you—maybe you can soon move right in with them. Isn't that *niiiiiice* Teddy?" she prods, looking only for a "yes" from me.

I don't know how "*niiiiiice*" it is until I get there. Nevertheless, I respond with the reply she is trying to elicit, "Yes." Say, this is likely the opportunity I've been waiting for. Maybe my means to an escape from this baby-cage dungeon. "Oh, nurse, *I'll* get him dressed and ready." my Case Worker offers. "Let's see what you have in here to wear, Teddy." she says while riffling through my meagre belongings. "My cowboy doot!"--I clearly explain my choice. "O.K. Teddy, dear, here's your cowboy suit, so let's get this on you, then we can leave right away." So, she does, and so we do.

"Do you have all your favourite things packed Teddy?" she inquires of me as we are already speeding down the road. I am thinking, "How the heck would *I* know? *You* folks packed my little suit-case, not me." "Do you hab my twike...where's my twike?" I ask them. "Yes, we've got your tricycle, dear." she replies. "Aren't you looking forward to playing with your new big brother?" she asks me, encouragingly. "Uh-huh." I answer without a shred of enthusiasm. "Won't it be fun to play at your new house?" she leads. "Uh-huh.", again, without any positivity in my voice. "Won't it be nice to be in a house with a new mommy and daddy", she continues. "Dess so." I grunt. "Teddy..." she starts... (Oh, give it up, lady, enough with the positive-response-eliciting questions!) "Oh, this is it, Fred. Pull over right here." she instructs her husband, thankfully giving up on prying answers out of me.

"How long are you gonna be in there? Don't be too long, I have things to do at home, you know. I'm not sitting around out here all day!", "Mr. Mousey" presses, in a less than polite tone. "Never mind, Fred, just keep your shirt on, I won't be long.", is her pat reply. Then, after getting me, and my stuff, out of the car, she leans down and tells me, "Now, Teddy, this is "Mr...'

and 'Mrs'..." house. They've been waiting and wanting a little boy like you to come and live with them for a very long time." Then she says, while brushing the wrinkles out of my cowboy suit and sticking my hair down with lick-dampened fingers, "So remember, now, you must be on your very best, and most polite, behaviour." "O.K.", is all I feel like saying, but it certainly is *not* what I'm actually thinking.

"Fred" stays in the car, keeping it running while he waits impatiently, as she marches me up to the front door of another *two-storey* house. This one is a gray brick, semi-detached in what is obviously another of the nicer areas of the city. We squeeze past a big, beautiful, gleaming, blue vehicle in the driveway. (It is a brand-new, 1951 Ford Country Squire Station Wagon, with the wood-panelled sides and back hatch. [107]) I guess these folks must be rich! I wonder why they are taking-in a homeless little gutter rat like me.

Just as we start up the steps to the front door, she notices a note on the door. Following the instructions, we head around to the entrance on the right side of the house. Then she presses the buzzer on the brick wall, right next to the door. I hope the buzzer will alert someone inside of our presence, and we won't have to make my Case Worker's husband wait out front too long. However, when it's apparent the buzzer likely isn't working, "Mousey" opens the storm door and taps lightly on the inner door.

Shortly, a nice-looking, plain-Jane sort-of woman comes to the door. "Oh, yes, hello, do come on in, please.", "Jane" encourages. "Mousey" introduces herself then says, "This is Teddy, the little boy you've been informed about, 'Mrs...'." "Stevie, c'mon down, 'Stevie', 'Stevie', c'mon downstairs and meet your new little *brother*." my new "mother" says, (jumping the gun a little here, I would say). Shortly a young boy around the age of six or seven comes bounding down from upstairs and comes to the side door. "Hi-ya kiddo!" he blurts. "What's new?" (Well, *this* is new, for one thing ...at least it's what I'm thinking; however I don't say anything aloud.) "Hey, d'ya wanna come upstairs and see my toys?" he asks. "Hold your horses a minute, 'Stevie'. Let's get these folks inside first."

So waving us through the kitchen, this newest "mother" invites us all into the dining room to meet her husband. He's sitting at the table, doing some kind of paperwork requiring the use of a very large, heavy, grey adding-machine which is making regular and repetitive, 'click-click-click-clacking' noises. "This is 'Mr...', Teddy, and he's your *daddy* now." she affirms. "Say 'hello' to 'Mr...', Teddy." "Mousey" urges. So, I say, "Hi ya!", but he never even looks up. "Oh, I forgot something!", "Mousey" says. Then she runs back outside and shouts, "Fre-ed, Fre-ed...Bring the trike up here! Will you please, dear?"

"Why don't you boys go upstairs now, and play?" the "mother" suggests. "C'mon up and see my room kiddo. I've got lots of toys I'll let you play with!", "Stevie" boasts, adding, "Say, what's that you've got on? Halloween's over you know!" Then he starts laughing at me. I don't understand. This is my most important outfit in the whole world—my cowboy suit! A few minutes later, while I'm still holding onto the "Mouse's" hand, "Stevie" runs up and down the stairs *twice*, bringing armfuls of toys down with each trip. "Here, let's play soldiers, or auto shop, or farmers, or Tinkertoys, [45], or..." and on and on and on he blabbers. I look up at my escort who indicates, "It's alright for [me] to go ahead and play with [my] new big brother's toys".

"Take all your toys right back on up to your room this very minute!" "Stevie's" mother insists, sternly. "We're just gonna have a little adult talk down here." she finishes. So up we go while the three, well really only two, grown-ups have a little chat about *me*. ("Be good! Be good!" I keep telling myself repeatedly. No head banging, nor crying or fussing! I can do this.) From my new brother's room at the top of the stairs, I am able to hear the women talking and laughing every so often. I also catch bits and pieces of conversations, such as, "...his list of...you should know...toxoids...IQ test results, [67], [68], [69],...feral...chest colds...'New Onions'...call us...Dr. Malcovitch..."

(Yet, I did not hear one word about "TORTURE" or "ABUSE" or "RAPE" or even "MOLESTATION"...not a single syllable.)

I wonder why "Mousey" was acting as if this house would be any different than any other foster home I've been placed in? [If I could hear the entire conversation downstairs, I would already know the answer to this question. This is not a foster home. It's a "Prospective Adoptive" home, whatever *that* means.] I will try to be good but as soon as nobody is looking, I know where the doors are. I'm just temporarily turned-around, so I'm not exactly sure what area of town I'm in right now. However, despite what my "IQ" test, [67], [68], [69], results tell the so-called professionals, I am a very *smart* little person and I'll figure it out. "Teddy, come down and say good-bye to 'Mrs...'", the "mother" insists. I go right down and stand at the front door beside the woman who is supposed to be my new "mommy", and I wave "Bye-bye" to, *Nancy,* *was* it? (Who knew she had a first name?) Well, *I am* here now and I guess that's that. So I run right back upstairs to resume playing with my newest, temporary "brother".

In a short while, we are summoned, "Boys, boys...come back down here and get some fresh-baked peanut-butter cookies and milk!" the "mother" insists. I'm up for that. These days I am always up for cookies and milk, I guess. From the kitchen, I wave a little 'hello' at the "daddy", while wondering if he is really going to be *my* "daddy". It will be different to have a daddy around, not necessarily better, just different.

"'Stevie', did you show Teddy where he'll be sleeping?" the mother asks. "Well, uh, no, 'cause I didn't know if he's staying." he replies. "Of course he's staying; he's your *new kid brother, forever!*" she retorts.

(Really? I am? I thought I had to be very, very nice and good to earn the right to *be* the brother and *stay* forever at this house. Oh well, if I'm staying for sure, maybe I am already *good enough.)*

"After snacks, let's go back upstairs and get your stuff unpacked, and then we can keep playing with *my* toys. O.K?", "Stevie" insists. Sounds fine to me, so I nod my agreement and follow him back upstairs again.

A little while later, the "mother" announces, "Boys, I'm going to the grocery store to pick up a little something for supper", adding, "Did you boys want to stay here with your dad, or come along with me?" "We're comin'!", "Stevie" answers for both of us. Then, back out we go and scramble into the rear seat of her fancy-schmancy Station Wagon. In minutes, we are in the parking lot of a very large grocery store. (Good thing for me though, it isn't one of the stores I had been stealing from for the past few months of my home address being, "*The Mount Pleasant Necropolis*". [149])

Inside the "super" market, I get to ride in the buggy while "mother" shops for the supper stuff. "Can we buy this?", "Stevie" whines, "...or this?...or this?...or that?...or these?" On and on, he prattles, as we go up one aisle and down the next. He is always begging his mother to buy him something. I am quiet, and ask for nothing, absolutely n-o-t-h-i-n-g. Hmmmm, I'm thinking she sure needs a lot of stuff for supper because this shopping cart certainly is filling right up.

Revolving Doors

Suddenly three young boys go running past us at top speed! One of them knocks the cart I'm sitting in, almost all the way over. "Would you just look at those little *brats*? Where's their mother? A bunch of ragamuffins is what they are!" she complains quite loudly. (Whaaaaaaaaaaat? Is she serious? Doesn't she know they are just hungry little kids without a home, or a mommy and daddy?)

In no time, after we have filled the basket with most of her needs, and *all* of "Stevie's" wants, we head to the women who ring-through everybody's cartloads at the checkout counters. "I would like to speak to your manager." she insists of our checker. "Certainly, ma'am—I'll just call for him." our young little, blonde check-out girl replies politely. "*MR. FLEMMING...ING...ING...*" the store's loudspeaker screeches and reverberates. Shortly, "Mr. Flemming-ing-ing" descends, god-like, from the upstairs office, and speaks to my new "mommy", "Yes, ma'am, what can I do for you today?" Mother details her complaint about the little boys who are wildly running around in the store, "bothering the paying customers". "Yes, ma'am, I'll see what I can do about the problem, but I'm sure you know they're probably gone already."

Two minutes later, I see him running through the store on the heels of the three kids, swatting at them with a broom as if they are pestilent rodents! "Get out! Get out you little gutter rats, and don't show your dirty little faces in my store, ever again!" He yells at them, loudly enough to be heard by actual gutter rats two blocks away. Then, satisfied with his own efforts, he glances back over his shoulder at my new "mother" and nods and smiles, pleased with his own job well done—the job, that is, of keeping a paying customer happy. (Nevertheless, I am wondering, "What about the poor kids?") Anyway, pay she does! Her order actually totals a staggering twelve dollars and ninety-two cents! Are they kidding? Is that really what this junk adds up to? Is she serious? Is she actually going to pay these highway robbers? Whatever! Now I am positive *she is* the stupid one.

Once we are back at the house she starts telling her husband about, "...those darn little guttersnipes running around in the store, again..." ("Guttersnipes"? There is that darn bad name again. Doesn't anybody get it? I'm in shock and don't know what to do, so I play quietly and keep *my secret* to myself...the secret that *I* am really a little guttersnipe **myself**.)

Before long, we kids are seated at the L-shaped breakfast nook in the kitchen, eating... sketties. Oh, wow, this is interesting. I am discovering sketties are especially good served really *hot*, dripping with tomato sauce, and with fat little round meatballs rolling around in the sauce! Hmmm, so far— so good at this new house. Then suddenly "Stevie" starts singing some little dittie, to the tune of "On Top of Old Smokey" [167],

"On top of spaghetti,
All covered with cheese,
I lost my poor meatball,
When somebody sneezed.

It rolled off the table,
And onto the floor,
And then my poor meatball
Rolled out of the door...." [109] [167]

I decide it's a funny song, so, enjoying music as much as I do, I absolutely *have* to join in!

Soon it's bath and bedtime. Bathing here is fun, and I share the bath with my new brother. He has oodles of toys for playing with in the tub! (And, *he doesn't* "play with", or "touch"

me!) The mother washes my face and behind my ears where she says, "some potatoes could grow". I have no idea what she's talking about. All the same, I would like her to leave a *little* skin on my neck, potatoes or not. "Bedtime boys." she announces. This should be fun because it's bunkies. "You get the bottom—I *never* sleep on the bottom." "Stevie" declares. "Yes, of course you know very well you do!" his mom corrects. "No, I don't, not anymore, anyway!" (Fine with me, either way—I am just grateful to have a bed.)

I notice the teensy weensy little chair beside his nightstand and wonder why the "mother" is sitting in such a midget-sized chair. "O.K. What will it be tonight? What would *you* like to hear tonight, Teddy?" she asks. Hear? What is she talking about? Then, recognizing the confusion on my face, she clarifies, "What's your favourite story?" Oh, my story? "Uh, I dunno." So "Stevie" points to the one they started the previous night and she begins reading it.

I certainly don't remember falling asleep. In fact, I don't remember whether or not she said the, "Night, night, sleep tight...blah...blah... bed-bugs bite." rhyme. I hope not. "Deebie, what you doin'?" I ask "Stevie" why he is getting dressed-up to go somewhere right now, since it is quite early in the morning. "I go to school, Teddy. I get to ride on the school bus every day. Have you ever been on a school bus? Don't you go to school yet? How old are you?" he asks. So many questions are annoying, besides, how am I supposed to know how old I *really* am? "Never mind" he says, and runs downstairs for brekkies.

There are three boxes of cereal on the breakfast nook table. The only one I recognize is the "Rice Krispies" with the elves on it. So it's the one I point to, when asked by the "mother" for my preference. "Stevie" starts singing another little ditty, "Row, row, row your boat...", and I try to join in, "Woah, woah, woah your boat..." I am doing my best to get along and fit-in with this family. Soon, "Stevie" leaves for the day, and takes his silly little songs and verses with him.

With my new big brother gone for the school day, there isn't too much for me to do except play with *his* toys, and he sure has enough of them. While I'm playing in his, I mean *our* room, the "mother" gets busy washing dishes, then washing the clothes, then washing the floors and for fun, she vacuums—everywhere! Her day is jam-packed full, and I am bored as anything because it isn't very much fun playing with toys all by yourself. So, what is a good thing for me to do when I am all by myself? Well, it's find a hidey-hole, of course. So, I go hidey-hole-hunting. However, this place seems to be locked-up drum-tight. I check out all the usual possibilities but no luck until I'm watching the "mother" who is now folding the laundry in the master bedroom. When she leaves the room and goes downstairs to answer the door, I go snooping.

Hmmm...There is one place in here but I'll have to be very, very sneaky. I discover a funny little trap door in the wall, at the very back of the "parents" big, walk-in closet. It's a cinch to open with its little knob, and, guess what—it's just my size. Inside the "me-sized" area is a crawlspace, which goes back the length of the house. It's probably intended for storing stuff too large to haul up through the trapdoor to the attic. There are taped-up boxes with printing on them, bags of summer-wear clothes and numerous old picture frames, minus their pictures. The thing is, I could sneak up here and go into my little hole any time I feel like it, and nobody could ever find me. I decide it's a great plan. Once I get accustomed to the numerous spidery webs, and their inhabitants, I decide—it is definitely the *perfect* plan!

"Teddy? Teddy where have you gone?" It's the "mother" calling for me. "I'n wight here." I tell her while quickly scooting out of the closet and on down beside the bed. When she reaches the top stair and sees me, she waves, "Let's go to the school and pick up your big brother." (Doesn't he ride a school bus back home?) Oh well, off we go again in the luxurious Station Wagon. But when we get to "Stevie's" school there aren't any kids running around, and "Stevie" is standing all by himself outside the main doors. (I have to wonder what's going on.) Then his mom yells, "Come on, hurry up, Stevie! We'll be late!" He jumps in the back with me and off we go to...well to...uh, well...I have no idea where we are going.

The mother then takes us to the top floor of a three-storey office building in downtown Toronto. Up there, we go into a funny office with some sad people sitting in the waiting room— a few of them clutching their faces or holding one cheek in their hand. I must have a completely confused look on my face because the "mother" notices and says, "We had to bring "Stevie" here to the dentist to get his tooth filled today." Dentist? I wonder what a Dentist could be? What is *it* going to fill his tooth with—and why? My gosh, this place stinks! (It smells like the hospital I already died in.) What on earth is the strange *squealing* sound, which I keep hearing every few minutes?

In no time it's "Stevie's" turn and his mom accompanies him, while I wait alone in the outer office, rather glad it's not me going into such a strange place. In a few minutes, every time I hear the squealing machine, I also hear "Stevie" screaming! "Ah! Ow! Ouch! Ahhhowee!" Then, no more screaming, not a sound, and I'm thinking maybe *he's* dead. Suddenly he leaps all the way from the back hallway into the waiting room, where he throws his arms out and with a wide, toothy grin, announces, "All done!" "And, here's a sucker for being such a good boy today, 'Stevie'!" says a big man in a white suit. "Oh, tucker, can I hab a tucker, pwease?" I beg, politely. "Here's one for the little boy, 'Mrs...'" "Tank-la." I say, remembering what my Case Worker said about being a polite little boy for this new "mother".

Back at the house, the "mother" starts dinner and I begin thinking about what I will be naming her, and this new "family". Right now, we kids are sitting on the living room carpet. "Stevie" is doing his reading homework and just I'm looking at the family photos on the cluttered fireplace mantle. I decide this family is rather ordinary looking. I mean, they're not really fat or too skinny, nor very tall or short—just average and ordinary. The father and son look identical; both have medium brown hair, parted right down the middle. The mother also has ordinary brown hair which is straight, cut in a "page-boy" style, with a centre part. She very closely resembles "Buster Brown"! [100] There is nothing left but to label this plain-looking family, "The Browns", which is not only the colour of their hair, but also I think it's a plain, ordinary sort-of colour. So—"The Browns", it is. (I haven't really looked anybody in the eyes yet, but I'd be willing to place a bet they're all brown too.)

This morning my Worker phoned here, and the fragment of the conversation I was able to hear went something like this,

*"Oh, hello, 'Mrs...', fine, thank you...yes we are quite pleased...he does seem like a **nice little boy**."...*
"No, no tears at all, just a story and right to sleep..."
"Ha, ha, ha, ha—they've actually been singing all morning."...
"No, in fact, I think he's taken quite well to my husband" ...
"Yes, we both think he's going to be a good fit in this family"...
"Well, thank you...yes...of course I will call you...goodbye now."

It almost sounds like good news. Dare I guess my staying here is already "working-out" for this family?

[After meeting this family, and having the above follow-up

conversation, the Case Worker noted in the Director's file,

"The Prospective Adoptive Mother seems quite pleased with Teddy. The Father seems to be a very kind man who would have a good manner with children." (I have no earthly idea how "Mrs. Mousey" could possibly judge this about the "father" in this house because he barely even gave her, or me, the time of day.)]

Sooner than later, at this house, the hours become days without much departure from the usual routines. "Stevie" and I get along great and he has no problem sharing his toys with me. I am kind of bored when he's off at school, but at least I'm being looked after, and have a warm place to sleep with plenty of food, if I want it. However, my appetite has lately become my problem. I don't feel too much like eating these days. Instead of getting bigger and stronger, I am getting thinner, weaker and definitely losing weight again. (I can tell this by the loose fit of my cowboy suit.) One issue I have with the food is the fact it is *cooked*, especially the vegetables! I've gotten so used to having crunchy, hard, raw ones and not mushy, cooked vegetables. Sometimes I just can't get the slimy-feeling veggies past my tongue and down my throat. This is probably why I've been experiencing a lot of tummy aches lately.

"Teddy, eat your lunch." the "mother" urges. It is something weird called a 'grilled cheese sandwich', which is fried bread with mushy, stretchy, gooey cheese inside. "I don' wanna!" I protest, and thankfully the lady doesn't force me to eat it; however, neither does she offer me any alternative. Then, later the same day, it's the "father" insisting, "Teddy, eat your supper! If you don't eat this delicious supper which my wife has worked hard to prepare, you will be going to bed immediately—and no bedtime snack, either!" "O.K.", I agree, and grabbing "Pom Pom" from below my chair at the dining table, I run upstairs and slide under my covers. I am not trying to be difficult. I just can't eat the reeking fish the "mother" cooked for supper because it smells like "***Rita***"! How can I be expected to eat when I am slapped in the face with such an awful memory? So, it is off to bed I go, hungry but nauseated, (if that is even possible).

I am insulted by the sun's rays, blanching my face and reminding me, on this fresh new morning, I am even hungrier than when I went to bed the previous night. When I sit down in the breakfast nook to wait on my cereal, what do you suppose I am looking at? It's the stinky-fish supper I couldn't eat yesterday evening. "Teddy, your father said you must eat this before you get anything else today." this "mother" insists. (If I couldn't eat it last night, how am I supposed to gag it down today?) "Noooo!" I protest. "Then, no breakfast either." she retorts, firmly.

Come lunch time, there it is, the dead fish adjacent to the mashed potatoes, (which *touched* the fish), and the dehydrating little green peas which have long since turned brown, and their life's goodness withered right out of them. When pressured to eat the meal, "Noooo!" is all I can say. Why can't they trust me? They couldn't possibly know what I'm thinking or experiencing, so why can't they throw the dead fish away and give me whatever the rest of them are having?

By the time supper rolls around, the "father" is furious with me. "You eat that damn meal or you'll feel the strap on your bare bottom!" he demands, and threatens with the same breath. The menacing strap is one of his black leather belts and it hangs in the kitchen, right beside the wall-mounted, black telephone. By now, my tummy has been hurting for twenty-four hours, so I poke my fork into the potatoes and pretend to be licking them off the tines. Tonight, they're all eating pork chops, green beans and a baked potato topped with grated cheddar cheese and dollops of sour cream. Every ounce of their meal looks infinitely fresher and more appetizing than my long-since deceased, fishy dinner. All I can do is chase my withered little peas around with my butter knife. Every now and then, I flick one off my plate, and it lands where it's camouflaged by the pea-green broadloom carpet. Unfortunately these folks don't have a dog who could help me get rid of the evidence!

"Alright, enough! You can march right back up there to bed without your supper again!" my "father" demands, angrily. I can see he is absolutely fuming mad, because there is a big vein which fills with blood and protrudes from his forehead whenever he is this angry. If it were possible, I am positive steam would be wooshing out both his ears, and blood would be shooting out of his eyeballs! He is so mad his whole face and neck has turned beet red! However, I am not scared of him or his notorious leather strap, and he knows it. Now it has become a matter of *his* will against *my* will. However, I know it is **fear** which can break a person's will, and **I am not fearful** of his threats. "Oh, dear, let's just throw it out and give the boy some supper." the "mother" gently urges. "Absolutely not! He'll eat this damn food sooner or later!" is his stern reply. That's what HE thinks.

I get into bed, pull the covers over my head and listen to my tummy growling, while I wait-it-out until the parents also turn-in for the night. You see, I have a plan. When I am certain everyone is fast asleep, I sneak downstairs and get a carrot and an apple out of the deep, filled-to-bursting, pull-down fridge drawer. Then I grab the can opener, a flashlight, a little box of stick matches and another of the many cans of green beans from the amply packed pantry storage closet. With my collection tucked into my pillowcase, I creep across the master bedroom floor and slide into their closet, unnoticed. Then I ease the trap-door open, get inside my hidey-hole and quietly pull the small door shut. I certainly don't want to make any noise eating so I creep a few feet down the crawl space. After I consume the carrot and the apple I open the can of long green beans and carefully pick them out, munching them down one at a time. Ahhhh...relief from the tummy pains. I am *so smart*!

Chapter 41: PARADISE *IS* Lost

The "father" is fuming mad at me right now. He insists on continually presenting me with the, now shrivelled-up and much stinkier, fish dinner. The "mother" says there is no use trying to heat it back up because it has gone *bad* anyway. I do not appreciate being *forced* to eat *anything*—not one little bit. Nobody knows better than I do that food is costly and precious, so if *I* can't eat something, there is a damn good reason. Of course, I can't explain myself, so the "father" interprets my refusal to consume the nasty plate of long-dead garbage, as my being "rebellious". However, he is very wrong, because this stand-off is not about rebellion.

Nevertheless, once again, he is threatening to use the strap to discipline me. He actually took it off the wall this time, doubled it and slapped it a couple times against his palm, saying, "Never you mind the misery of going to bed hungry, because if you don't eat this meal, you will get to know the *business end* of this belt, little mister!" Actually, this is a consequence I truly didn't anticipate at *this* house; nevertheless, I certainly can't eat the fish. So, over his knee I am bent, and *whack, whack, whack, whack, whack, whack*—I become intimately introduced six times to the "business end"...Oh, this is definitely not good. However even this beating can't break my will. So, I *do not* cry, not even a whimper. This way, you see, I win.

"Was it really necessary to strap him?" his wife asks, hesitantly. Then almost with the same breath, and obviously changing the subject, she says, "Stevie—see if you can find the can opener in the junk drawer—I don't see it anywhere." (Oh—oh! *I* know where it is, but I am not telling.) My bum is red and killing me and my mind is racing a-mile a-minute. I need a plan. What is my plan? Lemmie see... matches, check... blanket, check... canned foods, check... can opener, check... flashlight, check... that'll about do it, I believe.

When it's night-time, I grab my pillow and a soft blanket from the folded laundry pile, then I sneak back into the closet crawl space to do some serious thinking, with my bum well-padded underneath. While hidden and protected, I begin formulating a plan of escape. Nobody is going to strap my bum and expect me to wait around for them to do it another day—nobody! I have to get outta here, and somehow get really far away. Bang, bang, bang! Oh, shit! Bang, bang! Oh shit! Shit no! Not now! Now my head is bashing itself against the wall in my crawl-hidey-hole-space. My head is doing this because I don't know how to get myself out of this really bad situation.

Oh-oh, I woke-up the "mother". "Did you hear that noise?" she asks, rousing the "father". "Someone's banging or trying to break-in downstairs!" They both get up and check downstairs, but of course it's only me, banging my head in my hiding place in the back of their closet. "Where's Teddy?" she asks next. While they're looking everywhere for me I sneak back into my room and pull the covers over my head. "What are you doing, Teddy? Where were you just now?" she demands upon finding me. I just pretend to be asleep and don't answer. They go back to bed, satisfied it was only me running around in the middle of the night.

O.K., now I need to get moving on my plot to escape, if I am ever going to be able to leave here. Tonight, yes, why not? Tonight I'll put all of my clothes on and grab some of "Stevie's" clothes, which are big enough to fit over layers of mine. Lemmie see, a warm sweater, extra socks..., oh, and I'll grab another warm woollen blanket from the hall closet. All my 'supplies' can easily be stuffed into my spacious hole in their closet wall. However, in light of tonight's developments, it turns out tonight is not the best night for my escape. It's alright though, tomorrow night will be soon enough.

Revolving Doors

These last several mornings I am extra sleepy because I am spending a lot of what should be bedtime sneaking around collecting important survival necessities, and hiding-out. However, lately, a new hitch has started occurring in my developmental difficulties. When I finally do get into a deep sleep, a few times every night now, the "mother" comes running to my room and shakes me awake. She says, I "must be having a bad dream". She tells me I am screaming and crying in my sleep, and when I check, in fact, I do have wet tears on my cheeks. "What's the matter, dear?" she asks. "I dunno" is all I can answer. I suppose I thought I was safe here in this house. At least, until the father and I had our "Mexican stand-off" over the fishy meal and also, until his discipline strap and I became intimately acquainted. I no longer *feel* safe here. In fact I am *not* safe here—and—I am not *staying* here!

Revolving Doors

Chapter 42: "Return to Sender"

I knew things were about to change around here because last night I had a particularly bad session of night terrors. Everyone was standing in my bedroom when the "mother" woke me up. I guess I am the cause of the family losing *their* sleep. Of course, in the morning, she makes another phone call to the "C.A.S.",

"Hello, Mrs...I am having a few problems with the little boy, and I would like your advice.
...No, nothing like that. He's just not sleeping very well and has gone off his food again.
...Oh, and he's banging his head on the head-board.
...Remove the head-board?
...Well we were just wondering if we should bring him into your office or perhaps take him to our family doctor.
...Alright, yes, I'll do that, thanks."

This was the "mother's" conversation with "Mrs. Mousey" and before the day is out, we are already at the office of this family's physician. This doctor, who has never before met me, prescribes a *sedative*—for the family. Well, actually it's really for me, to make me sleep, because I am the cause of the family members waking up at night. However, it tastes disgusting and I sputter it out of my mouth when she tries to force it into me! I'll be damned if I am gonna swallow such nasty stuff! (I have had to swallow some foul things in my life, but this vile-tasting concoction takes the prize.)

The following day I overhear another phone call to one of my "C.A.S." Workers,

"Hello, 'Mrs...', it's 'Mrs...' again...We are still having the same problems with Teddy. In fact none of us are getting any sleep

with his crying-out and head-banging on the wall now!
...Well, he just wouldn't take it—he wouldn't swallow it.
...We are at our wits end and don't think we can go on very much longer like this.
*... Yes, in fact we **are** all on edge!"*

She is complaining about these problems to my Worker. They think *they* can't sleep, they should see the night from the inside of *my* head! Between the night terrors, anxiety and constantly being awakened, I am not getting any rest either. Then she continues, "*Steven is starting to exhibit resentment towards the little boy, probably because of all the extra attention I must give to this child...I am worried their relationship is at risk now.*" ("Steven"? Doesn't she even know her own kid's name?)

Another day has passed and the "mother" is back on the phone with my Social Worker, "Librarian Lady". "Well, you see, we discussed it, and "Mack", (her nickname for her husband), and I think we are not the best parents for this child. We have looked at the problem from every angle and we have concluded it's our age. We are a little too old to have the kind of patience, that caring for this little boy requires, so we've decided we need to **give him up**." (I HATE those three little words!)

[The following are the Worker's notations in Teddy's "C.A.S." file following the above conversation with the *Prospective Adoptive Mother*,

"*I discussed this thoroughly with her, reiterating what I had previously said on the telephone about the problems which arise when a child is moved. I suggested, if she could keep trying and could reassure Teddy, eventually he would settle down. I emphasized how sometimes it takes several months for a child as old as Teddy to adjust to a new home. I* *reassured her about her ability to handle the present problem and tried to help her understand why Teddy is reacting in this manner. Although she was quite discouraged about it all, she said she would try for **another week** and see if she could not work out Teddy's problems. I asked her to keep in close contact with me and not to hesitate about calling me for help, or merely to discuss how she is getting along. I plan to make an unannounced visit to the home next Monday."]*

I am feeling poorly today, probably because I was awake half the night, hiding out and trying to think how to escape. The "father" got really mad at me again last night. I was playing cowboys and Indians near his feet as he was sitting on the sofa, reading the newspaper. "*Teddy!*" "Stevie" suddenly screamed at me, "*Teddy...stop it! Stop it!*" I am not exactly sure what I was doing but his shout startled me and I dropped the shiny, metal, six-shooter, which is a little heavy I suppose. It fell, barrel-point down, right on the "father's" slippered-foot. Boy, oh, boy! Did he ever shout at me! "I'n sorry, I'n sorry!" I try to explain it was an accident. I certainly never *intended* to hurt him—it just slipped out of my hands. Anyway, he jumped up and headed toward the kitchen to grab the belt and strap me again, but the "mother" butted in this time, and, standing directly between us, also insisted it was an *accident*.

Nevertheless, now I'm certain I can be disciplined any time at all, without warning or without having done something terribly bad. It's crystal clear to me now, I absolutely have to get away from this house—and soon.

"Buzz, buzz, buzz!" It's the side-door buzzer announcing someone's arrival. "Oh, c'mon in, please. I wish I'd known you were coming I would have certainly straightened up a little." the "mother" nervously stammers, realizing what this visitor *almost witnessed*. Whaaat? It's "Mrs. Mousey". I wonder what *she is* doing here today—although I *am* glad to see her right now. "It's O.K., 'Mrs...' we wanted to observe Teddy's attitude without him trying to be on his *best behaviour.* I'm sure you understand.", "Mousey" explains. Then turning to me she says, cheerfully, "Hi there Teddy! Don't *we* look well today?" "Hi, ya!" I reply, (thinking, *we* don't really feel so good).

"Tell me how you are getting along with your big brother, Steven." she pries. "Deebie has wots ub doys!" I explain. She takes a little notebook and pencil out of her purse and starts writing a few words. Then she and the "mother" chat a little, oddly enough, spelling some of their words. Me? Well, I go ahead and do what I do usually and naturally, which is play by myself on the floor.

I don't know why I am feeling nervous and shy right now. In fact I am feeling so insecure, I find myself climbed-up onto the "mother's" lap, while the adults continue talking. (Incidentally, I've started coughing these last few nights and I don't feel too good today. It might be all the dust I'm breathing in my hidey-hole, but I sure hope I am not getting the "Brown Kites" again.)

[Later, this Case Worker would make the following notations in the "C.A.S." file,

"Teddy does give the physical appearance of having a big struggle to adjust. He has obviously lost weight and there are big dark circles under his eyes. During my visit, he seemed to show a great deal of affection for the Prospective Adoptive Mother. He sat on her knee, hugged her and seemed to want to be near her. He seemed to be making a great effort to be accepted by her. I discussed with her the effect upon Teddy if she decides he must be removed from their home.

She seemed to understand how Teddy would feel **he** *had failed. She said she would also feel very guilty, if she did not succeed with Teddy."]*

Revolving Doors

These two carried on talking as if I was not even in the same room. It's clear now, these "parents" want me out of their home. Another invisible *revolving door* has just now opened up and is preparing to sw—swee—sweep me out of their house. Who knows where I will end up next? I hope to Heaven I don't have to go back to the baby ward! It is high time I start fighting-back against all these moves. Right now, I am headed to my *hidey crawl space* for a little thinking time. I'm very sad and surprised at this new development. I really thought I was being good and doing everything right at this house—well, almost everything, except for the 'fishy dinner' issue and, of course, today's 'six-shooter to the toe' incident. How come every time I do the tiniest thing wrong, I am shuffled back out one revolving door, circle through a couple rotations and slide back in through another.

Chapter 43: "Forever" Always Means:
"JUST VISITING…"

It's December 1951, and from the appearance of the shops and stores, I am guessing the Christmas season is certainly upon us. However, you would never be able to tell this from my "forever family's" house. Apparently, they don't celebrate the holidays with the rest of the world. Nevertheless, I figured I could even give up Christmas and Santa if I could stay in a permanent home with a loving family and not in need of life's basic necessities. At least, I believed from all appearances I had been fitting-in nicely and getting along with everyone. Wasn't that exactly what everyone hoped would be the case?

However, as has been the reality so many times in my young life, "appearances" can be deceiving. In fact, this very morning my "mother" phoned the "C.A.S." office and, to my absolute shock and astonishment, these are her exact words,

*"We can keep on with Teddy **no longer! He must go!** My husband and I have talked it over and we both feel this just will not work! Of course we are all upset but we don't feel matters will improve at all."*

[The Worker receiving this call noted in Teddy's file,

"I talked to her for some time but she seems to have definitely made up her mind. In fact, I feel if Teddy remains there, she will only reject him and he would be very unhappy. I discussed the situation with the other Case Workers, and it was decided it would be best for Teddy if he moved back into the home of 'Mrs…' and her family, as he is a very upset little boy, and she had previously been so successful in settling him. It was felt the sooner he returned to her care, the better it would be for him."]

After only two weeks at "The Browns", my so-called, "forever home and family", they now want me gone from their house. Therefore, after one additional week following this phone conversation, I am packed-up and waiting on the decorative, little, black, wrought-iron chair in the front foyer. I really thought these were my "forever adoptive parents and brother". I thought I could never be "taken" away from here. I suppose I assumed it meant I would never be "*sent*" away from this home. Nevertheless, it's clear now—I have done something so terrible, I am being returned to the horrid baby asylum. So, I can do nothing but wait in front of my latest invisible revolving door, which is about to, once again, sweep me around to...what? As usual, I don't have a clue.

Soon a chime announces there is a visitor at the *front* door. "Yes, can I help you?" the mother inquires. It's "Librarian Lady" introducing herself to my so-called "mother". "Oh yes, do come in, please." "Hello there, Teddy! How are *we* today?" the familiar woman asks me, (again with that *we*. "We" are depressed and angry and once again without a home! "We" are scared as hell, confused and very lonely. How the hell do you *think* "we" are?) "Oh, yes, uh, well, we're very sorry this isn't working out, but the child has such serious problems, we can't act like a normal family anymore." My so-called, "mother" just about trips over her own tongue while trying to spit these words out—words which I had witnessed her previously rehearse in front of the bathroom mirror.

"Well, sometimes these things d-d-don't work out.", "L.L." accedes with a noticeable stutter. "Do you have somewhere else to place him?" the "mother" inquires. "Yes, in f-f-fact we do, but of c-c-course I can't discuss this with you—y—you understand." (My Social Worker's stuttering is something I've noticed her doing every now and then when she appears extremely frazzled.) Then she asks, "Well, is he all p-p-packed?" My "mother" hands her the suitcase and tells her my tricycle is at the side of the porch.

Then "L.L." says, "Teddy, you won't b-b-believe it but you are going home today. You're going to 'Mrs'...' home!" Who? Does she mean, "Songbird's" house—or apartment—or wherever? (I thought they moved far away.) "Wis Danny 'n' Eban?" I question. "Yes, they have m-m-moved back to this area and she has been inquiring about y-y-you, d-d-d-dear."

Chapter 44: Going to My *NEXT*: "FOREVER Home"

This "foster mother's" house, to which she is referring, had previously been my eleventh residence and I was terribly happy there. That was until her "X-X" showed up, and had to go and re-marry her. Why did they all have to move to *his* house, so far away? While I am wondering why they have moved *back* to this area, we wait in the foyer until my Social Worker's ride shows up. Oh, O.K., good—it's another taxi. The taxi driver has hung a little plastic, lit-up Santa Claus from his rear-view mirror. I have to wonder how close it might be until Santa comes, but then a horrible thought washes over me. I wonder if *I* don't know where I'll *be*, how will Santa know where I have *moved*?

"Verr tu, laydeee?" our driver asks with a very thick accent. She gives him the address then my escort turns to me and condescendingly begins explaining how I am "going home to 'Mrs...' house" and how I've "just been visiting at this latest residence". I wish they would make up their damn minds. Was it my "forever home" and "forever family", or is this going to be my "forever home and family", or what? Regardless, it will be nice to see Danny again, and I guess Evan is a little older and might be more fun to play with too. We'll see.

While still riding, we pass right by the "C.A.S." buildings and keep going until we reach a funny-looking house. It resembles a very long, white, tin box, which is sitting in a row of many similar very long boxes. I am thinking this is a very unusual-looking street, as my Social Worker tells the driver to pull in front of number eighteen. At the front end of the box is a big picture window with a little brown wooden flower planter in which several plastic flowers are sorta planted. Oddly enough, these are forever in bloom. I notice how strange and out-of-place this seems, considering it's a freezing-cold, snowy

Revolving Doors
December day.

Chapter 45: The "HOMECOMING"

From the road, I can see a woman who is wearing a popular thick, tweedy-type of winter jacket and is sitting outside on her porch steps, smoking a cigarette. "L.L." points her out and explains she's waiting for us. Suddenly, delighted, I recognize "Songbird"! (That's weird though—I don't remember seeing her smoke cigarettes before.) Then I recognize the small child playing beside her is Evan. He too is warmly bundled in a red snow-suit. As soon as the car is barely stopped I start banging on the window, "Hi-ya, hi-ya!" Then "Songbird" jumps up and runs to the taxi, letting me leap right out the door into her waiting arms. What a good surprise! Oh, yes, this is very, very good! (Fortunately, I didn't even have to exist for any length of time at the stinkin' baby jail.)

"Songbird" greets us with, "Hello, 'Mrs...'!" and, for me, "And, hi to you Teddy, dear! Do you remember Evan?" (I almost do, but not looking like this kid. He was much littler and didn't have any hair, the last time I saw him. I wonder if he still sleeps all the time now.) "Please come in..." (She tries to turn and go behind the Worker, but she can hardly move because I've tackled her so hard with a big bear hug around both her knees.) Once we are inside the white tin box, the conversation between the women is of little interest to me, except for the part about her, "husband". Is she still with the rude man? He was already her "X" then he became her husband again, and now—who knows? I guess it's fine by me either way.

"Where's Danny?" I ask her. "Daniel's gone with his daddy to stay with his grandma and grandpa, Teddy, but you'll see him when he comes home after the holidays." Oh, this makes me sad because I had loads of fun with Danny and will miss him lots, especially the way he played outside with me all the time.

Revolving Doors
She did say "holidays", didn't she?

Certainly, that would be Christmas holidays—of course. I easily guessed from the decorations around the house, but I had no idea we were close to Christmas, or if it had even come and gone, especially judging by my most recent "forever family" or their residence. They never discussed "Santa", or spoke of "Jesus Christ", or "Christmas".

[I couldn't know the significance but my previous family worshipped in a faith termed, "Jehovah's Witnesses" [101], and they were not Christians who celebrated Jesus Christ's birthday, on "Christmas Day" which is, December twenty-fifth each year. They also did not believe in Santa Claus, or in exchanging gifts annually on that special day.]

"Come in here and see your new room, dear." "Songbird" warmly urges. "How do you like your bed?" I am not sure which bed is mine because they look the same, since both are draped in blankets of navy blue with red, white and yellow decals. "Yours has the comforter with the trucks on it, and Evan's has the balloons." she says, adding, "Come in here, there's someone I want you to meet." In Danny's bedroom, she points to a big cardboard box in the corner and inside of it is a tiny, black, fuzz-ball of a puppy! (Oh, yes, indeed, this is very, very, **VERY** GOOD!) "His name is 'Blackie', Teddy. Would you like to help me take care of him while Danny's away?" my now ***favourite*** "mother" urges. "Yes!" I virtually shout with delight. A wonderful, favourite, singing, foster "mom" and a puppy too! This is certainly *my* day—and I am *positive it's my* forever home!

While I play with the little guy in the box, the adults have a conversation in the kitchen. I pretend not to be paying any attention, but really, I am. I catch the "mom" saying how "thrilled" she is at having me here. My Worker, having heard this at least once before, reminds the foster "mother" I am here only on a "boarding home basis", but whatever this means, I am not sure. However, I think I must be imagining things when I hear the "mom" say she and her husband *would like to adopt [me] if possible*".

My worker responds with,

"When I told Teddy he was coming to live with your family again, it was the happiest I've seen him in a very long time. I explained to him how he'd been on a 'visit' and now he was going **home***. He was so happy about going 'home', he didn't seem to need any reason for the move. In fact, Teddy was so happy all the way here in the car, he couldn't wait to get to his new 'home'."*

It is nice to know you are wanted and loved by someone who is so wonderful and kind. I am such a lucky little boy now that I have this old/new mommy and brothers, and maybe a new daddy too; however, we'll have to wait and see about him. I am sure this is destined to be my *last* exit from a revolving door. I am certain this is it! I'll belong and get along with the boys, and be loved by "Songbird"…and…and…and…I am beyond excited about this move.

[According to the "C.A.S." file notations, the following is what the Worker remarked regarding meeting with 'Mrs…', and Teddy's move back to the family,

"'Mrs…' insisted she and her husband could never see (Teddy) moved again and they would like to keep him permanently, either on a 'free home' basis or an 'adoption', as we at the "C.A.S." saw fit. I asked this mother to 'give Teddy time to settle down again, and then at a later date, to have a discussion with his new Worker about the basis on which they will be keeping him'. Therefore, on this date, December 18,

Revolving Doors
*1951, Teddy was transferred from adoption probating with
'Mr...' and 'Mrs...', the Prospective Adoptive Parents, back to
boarding home care with 'Mrs...'.]*

Apparently, I am four-and-a-quarter years old, and now that I
am in my seventeenth residence, (my fourteenth fostering
placement), I finally have a place to call "home".

The next day, "Librarian Lady" stops by this tin-can house,
unannounced. "How's he doing, 'Mrs...'?" "He, he—Teddy—go
put 'Blackie' in the backyard, dear. Oh and open the new can
of doggie food on the counter, and set some out there for him."
"My" doggie was so excited to see the visitor, he was jumping
up on her legs and threatening the pristine condition of the
new, sheer hose, which she valiantly tried to protect from his
little claws. When I let him out-side, he really makes me laugh
because he's rolling around on his back in the snow pile *I*
created for the ants and rolly-polly bugs to live in, (just in case
they were not already asleep for winter). What a cutie-wootie! I
sure love this little black mutt!

Once back inside, I hear the "mom" reply to "L.L.", "Teddy ate
good yesterday and, although he was a little restless last night,
he did finally settle down and sleep." I am in the kitchen
wrestling with the new can opener she bought. I hate it
because it's an *electric* one and too hard to use; nevertheless,
they're not getting *mine!* I took it when I left the "Browns" and
hid it in my jacket pocket, so nobody ever knew I had it!

(However, right now something is bothering me about this new
brand of canned doggie food. I remember the exact same can,
with the doggie pictures on it, which "Big Boy" and the others
brought back to our cellar-residence, after their scavenging
escapades. I remember them all roaring with laughter as they
watched *me* eagerly consume the contents. When I do finally
get this can open, the additional bad memory of the smell of

this stinky dog food floods my mind. Oh, yes, I remember eating the same kind of reeking, mushy, disgusting meat. In fact, I hesitate to feed it to my doggie right now, but he is jumping all over and wagging his tail, so I guess it tastes good to him. I'm just really glad I don't have to eat that stuff anymore.)

Then the "mother" mentions how I've started coughing a lot and she wonders if I am allergic to the little dog, because, she confesses, "It sleeps in the bed with the little boy." "L.L." tells her I was starting to get a "little head cold" before I left the last house. Then, "mom" says, "But it's such a harsh cough and I'm worried about those dark circles under his eyes—and he's so awfully pale-looking. He doesn't appear very healthy." Nonetheless, they both agree that moving me back in here with this family is a very good idea. Apart from the fact my damn lungs are getting cruddy again, I suppose I generally feel alright.

It is five days until Christmas and high time we go pick-out a Christmas tree! Off we go then, to the Boy Scout's "Santa's Village Tree Lot", where we pick the biggest and fluffiest one we can find—although reduced in price. We wrestle it all the way, while walking home, and then we fight with its slapping branches while manoeuvring it into the living room. My "mom" has already dragged the boxes, labelled, "XMAS", in from the tin storage shed out back of her tin house. Then we all get right down to the business of decorating, and this time, I KNOW what I'm doing! Although baby Evan is getting into everything, I am being a good boy, helping to unwind the blob of tree lights, while little "Blackie" thinking this is all a great game, tries to bite the wires and pull them across the room. "Dop-it Bwackie. Dop-it!" Next is the garland, then the balls and other ornaments. Oh, my goodness, this is absolutely my favourite time of the whole year! I can't believe I almost missed it while living with the "Browns".

I have not seen Santa at a store, or written a list, nor do I have any earthly idea what to ask for this Christmas. "Mom" gets out the "Sears Wishbook", [32] [32a], and helps me sort through the toy sections. I point out a *"View Master"* with the *"Disney" reels*, [102], or a *"Muffin the Mule"*, [103], with moveable parts. Or, maybe... "Oh, Oh, wook, wook at dat!" It's a *"Hopalong Cassidy Cowboy Watch"*! [104] Then "mother" asks if I would like a board game, like "Monopoly"[78]. "Nooooo" I scream with the memory of "Rita" and "Rosie" and their damn "bored" games! (Besides, I can't even read, so how could I play a game like which requires reading skills?) Anyway, the "mother" writes Santa a letter and puts my requests in it, then mails it off to him. (I sure hope we're not too late—I *really* want one of those "Hoppy" watches!--who cares if I can't tell time yet—it's a "Hopalong Cassidy" for Pete's sake! (However, what I *really* need to ask Santa for is a new set of lungs! "Cough, cough, cough, hack, hack, hack...")

How can Evan be sleeping? I'm not tired in the least. I'm as wide-awake as if it's already morning-time tomorrow—*Christmas* morning, to be specific! "Teddy, what are you doing? You need to close your eyes and get to sleep so Santa can come! You know he WON'T come in the house unless **all** the children are asleep. So close your eyes now, dear." my foster "mom" urges. "I'n not sweepy!" I protest. Then she says, "Well, 'Blackie's' tired, so why don't you roll over on your tummy and put your arm around the little doggie, and I'll rub your back so you can pretend you're asleep and then Santa Claus will bring you presents." "O.K" I reluctantly agree—but a back rub—what fool would ever refuse a back rub? Then she starts to sing, "Si-I-lent ni-ght, ho-o-ly ni-ght...", and I don't remember much after that. ("Songbird" is a very nice mommy—In fact, I think I'll *keep* her.)

"Ahhhhh—eeekkkk—eeyeeee!!" It's Evan, screaming his

damn lungs out. What the hell does the whiny little bugger want now? Lemmie sleep, dammit. "Oh, look at you, will you. What's wrong sweet-heart? Oh, my goodness, Evan, you've been sick all in your bed again. Teddy, Teddy dear, wake up!" (*Shut up and shut the kid up too! I am asleep.*) "Yes, I'n up, I'n up.", I answer with no enthusiasm. "Teddy, don't you know what day it is?" (*No, and I don't care!*) "Uh-uh.", I reply in the negative. "Teddy, it's Christmas morning and guess what? Santa came last night when he knew you had fallen asleep." she says with exuberance in her voice. "***OH! I'N UP—UP, I'N UP!***" I jump out of bed and trip on my pyjama bottoms, pulling my jammies, with the brown horseys on them, halfway down my bare bum. Then I pull them back up, scramble across the hall and race into the living room! "Blackie" is close on my heels—in fact, he is never, ever very far from me.

I absolutely can't believe my own eyes! Santa *did* come and there are approximately one million beautifully decorated packages of every imaginable size and shape. How I love Christmas—and Santa Claus! I really wish it was Christmas EVERY DAY of the year. Which ones are mine, I wonder. She's in the bathroom where she's cleaning Evan up from another night of puking in his bed. I don't know what's wrong with him but he gets sick at night, a lot. Then she says, "I'll be right there sweetie." reassuring me. When she finally comes into the living room she starts to separate the packages into little piles. One for Evan, one for Danny and one little pile for me. "Now? Can I open dem, now, pwease?" I ask, barely able to contain my excitement. "Yes, dear, yes, go ahead."

Oh, my gosh! I got EVERYTHING I asked Santa for, except the "Hopalong Cassidy Watch". [104] But Santa also put a "Lifesavers Candy Book", [58], in my stocking for an extra surprise. I love them! However, I was definitely disappointed when I realized there was no Hopalong Watch for me. I hug "Blackie" because he cheers me up when I am a little sad. Oh well, thank you for everything else Santa Claus. "Teddy— what's the little package way inside the tree branch—back there—yes, there in back of the tree?", "Songbird" asks leadingly while she points directly at the gift she seems pretty certain is there. I crawl under the tree, with "Blackie" helping me, and I see, right there stuck in between the branches is a little package. (I sort of remember once hearing the saying, "Good things come in small packages.") I hand it to her and she reads the tag, saying it's for me.

"Oh, oh! Uh, O.K." I say, while trying to rip the Santa Claus paper off the small box inside. Wow, I can't believe my eyes! It is the "Hoppy" Watch! It's my "Hopalong Cassidy Wrist Watch"! [104] What a Christmas! I got my Watch, the "View Master", [102], "Muffin the Mule" [103], (with all the moveable parts), two colouring books, new crayons, a Lifesavers Candy Book, [58], and a chocolate Santa! Wowee! This is the best Christmas of my whole life. Now, if I can only get well and finally heal my lungs, life will be perfect.

"Let's clean up this mess of papers, and here's a little bag to save the ribbons and bows in for next year's gift-wrapping." my "mom" says. (Wait a minute, I thought *Santa's Elves* did all the gift-wrapping at the North Pole. Don't they? Oh well, I suppose it doesn't *really* matter.) Anyway, we do as we are told. Evan got a whole bunch of baby junk, but I'm curious what Santa brought for Danny in a box as big as *me*. (Of course, when Danny returns he opens the huge gift to reveal a brand-new wooden guitar—and was he ever pleased!)

Christmas day was only four days ago, but I haven't really been able to enjoy my new toys very much, because I've been sick—again. I haven't caught the "stomach flu" from Evan, but I've been coughing and hacking so badly the "mom" thinks I might have the "Whooping Crane" cough, (at least I think it's what she called it). Whatever *that* is I don't know, but I do know I'm very sick and lately when I experience a coughing spell, I hack uncontrollably until *I puke*. In fact, it's so much worse at night, I actually keep Evan, the "mother" and myself awake. (The "daddy" in this family is almost never here, because he has a job driving a big transport-truck on very long, long-distance runs across the country.)

I don't seem to be getting any better, so today we're heading out to go see this family's regular physician, "Dr. MacInnis". I sure hope this guy can fix my lungs. When we get to his office, I find it strange because it's located in the basement of his house, which is in "Leaside", a very nice area on the outskirts of Toronto. Inside the office is a small room with the usual desk, chair, examination table and numerous filled-to-capacity bookshelves lining the walls from floor-to-ceiling. The doctor who enters is an older man with no hair on his shiny head and a face so deeply etched with worry-lines, they look as if they were actually drawn on with a brown pencil-crayon.

"What's the prroblem herrre, 'Mrrrs…'?" "This is my foster child, Teddy. He seems to have a very bad cold, or something. Actually, it sounds to me like Whooping Cough." she responds. "Come herrre, son, and we'll have a little listen to yourrr chest." I look at the "mother" and she gives me an encouraging nod. "Let's get yourrr shirrrt off. O.K. son?" he continues in a barely understandable, thick, Scottish accent.

Anyway, I comply, but then, with a very shocked expression on his face, he asks the "mother", while feeling the lump in my chest, "What's happened herrre?" I wince—it still hurts me— and she says she doesn't know, adding, it must have happened before I came to her house *this time*. "*This time*?" he questions. "Oh, yes, well I've taken care of him on a previous placement but it was necessary for him to go elsewhere when we moved out of the area.", "You'rrrre a skinny little fellow, arrren't you, now?", he asks, rolllllling every "rrrrr" off his tongue. "How old arrre you, son?" "I'n fowww 'n' a half!" I boast.

"Now, take a deep brrreath, therrre, young man." "Ahhhh, cllchllcll, hhoohhoo, cllchllcll, hhoohhoo." I just about choke to death trying to comply. Anyway, he tries to listen to my front and back but is interrupted by Evan's holler-whining. "Ahhhhhhhh! Mamaaaaa!" (I look at him with my eyes screaming, *"Shut the hell up Evan! You are being a whiny brat and keeping us all in here longer than necessary!"*) Finally, when his mommy sticks his binkey in his mouth, and Evan shuts up for two damn minutes, (after all, you can't suck and scream at the same time.) The doctor then resumes his listening to, and gently touching, me until he is satisfied.

"You'rrre quite rrright, Mrs..., it does sound quite crrroupy but I'd say, for certain, it's Brrronchitis. What arrre you doing forrr his feverrr?" (There are too many rolled "Rs" for me to clearly understand anything this old codger has to say!) Again, I don't catch her answer. Aw...crap! I'm too busy thinking about having "Whooping C*rrr*ane/B*rrr*own Kites" *again*. The doctor writes something on a little piece of paper and gives the "mother" some verbal instructions to follow. However, after she whispers something to him he retrieves the note he had given her and adds more writing to it. What do you suppose this new doc gives me? It is another *sedative*! (I am not even five years old, for Pete's sake!) He also prescribes some wretched-tasting cough syrup containing a stinky ingredient called, "Sulpha", which is supposed to make my lungs stop these awful spasms. However, the problem he seems to be much more concerned about is my "weight". Apparently, I am far too skinny for a kid my age. But, it's because I'm always so sick with "Brown Kites", "Whooping Crane" or whatever, and I really don't have any appetite. I can only *hope* I can keep some of this new cough medicine down long enough for it to make me well, once and for all.

Revolving Doors

Yesterday was the start of the New Year 1952. I tried so hard to stay up 'till midnight and actually see the new year come in. But I am consuming these sedatives now and whether I want to or not—I pass out, dead asleep by six o'clock every night. I'm still sick with lung crud and now Evan has it too, and he's whooping away just like me! We sound like the Canada Geese, when they fly overhead in their big "V" formation, on their way south for the winter. "Whoop—Whoop—Whoop!" We both sound as sick as we feel, and we are "running the mom right off her feet", or so she complains.

Danny and his dad got back today from Christmas at his grand-parents place. (I don't have much to say about the "dad" in this house. He is gone most of the time and when he's around, he pays me very little attention—which is perfectly fine with me. I don't exactly have a good track record with *fathers* anyway.) After being home just a couple days, Danny has also taken sick with his own version of cruddy lung junk. We are all as sick as dogs! Speaking of dogs, "Blackie" has chosen to sleep with *me* in bed every night and now that he's housebroken, the "mom" doesn't mind. However, Danny *does* mind, as "Blackie" was *his* doggie, until I arrived. Nevertheless, I'm sick as anything too and have no energy to fight or argue, so for tonight, if "Blackie" wants to, he can go sleep in Danny's bed.

The next day, Evan, Danny and I are right back in our beds by two o'clock in the afternoon. "Ching—chong—ching— chong...." is the front door's musical announcement of somebody's arrival. The "mom" answers the door with, "Oh, hello 'Doctor Lambert'. Come in, come on in." So, he does. "Where are the children?" he inquires, a little irascibly. (I know what comes next. I've been down this road before. He is carrying his little black leather doctor's bag, with who knows what horrors inside of it.) [By the way, this was back in the day when doctors actually *did* make house calls.] "Mom" brings him into the bedroom and he checks on Evan commenting, *"It's only a cold, or perhaps a slight touch of Bronchitis."* (So, I'm not the only one who gets the "Brown Kites".)

He had already had a look at Danny and told the "mother", *"He just has a cold and it'll resolve itself."* However, when he listens to my chest, both sides, and my back, he says, with deep concern in his eyes, *"This child has a very bad case of Pneumonia."* (Oh, that's just *gr—eat! They* both get off easy and now *I* have the "New Onions"! I am furious, because this isn't fair at all.) Oh, hell, what's he holding in his right hand? Not the bum shot of Penicillin! "Oh-oh-oh, ow, owieeeee! Dat hurt me!" So then, he says, "Sorry about the little pinch-stick, but we've got to get you well so you can start eating again, and gain some weight, little fella." Then he finishes the visit with the obligatory tousling of my hair.

I suppose "Doctor Lambert" knew what he was doing because it's barely a couple days later and I am starting to improve. In fact, today I've even stopped those coughing-'till-I-puke spasms. Also, I've started eating some soup, especially chicken noodle. It's my favourite whenever I'm sick with a cough. A few more days pass by with everyone getting better and better, including me. Now, it's the end of January and the "mom" says I am doing great. She's pleased with how I am trying to eat and catch up with other kids my age. Of course, I still sleep like a log because I am drugged with sedatives every night—in fact, it now seems I can't sleep *without* taking this new medicine.

This morning, the "mom" has taken me to the "C.A.S." to meet with "Wart Lady", "Mrs. Mousey" and my newest Case Worker, the lovely, "Cat's Eyes", (who today is wearing a soft, sheer, sea-foam green ensemble). "Mom" washed and pressed my cowboy suit and helped me get the "Hopalong Watch", [104], on properly. All of the women are quite impressed with *my* coordinated outfit and smart looking, "Hopalong Cassidy Watch", [104]. "Can you tell time with your new watch, Teddy?" the Director asks. Of course, I can't tell time—I don't even know what day it is. What a dumb question. Rather than tell her I think she is dumber than a bag of hammers, I just don't bother answering.

"How are *we* feeling today, Teddy?", "Wart-Lady" asks in such a way as to seem to want me to answer with, "Well, I'm perfectly fine, thank-you!" (Oh, p-u-l-eeeese, you old wart hog! It's that damn collective "we" for which I have no use!) So what do I *actually* say? "I'n awl bedder." (Chicken!)

Then comes the *real* question she directs at my foster "mom". "So how do *you* think he's coming along, 'Mrs...'?" The "mom" responds honestly to the Director with, "I'm concerned his behaviour has caused him to regress, I'd say, to around the age of three or three-and-a-half. Of course, I'm not a professional, but it's what I witness of his behaviour." Yikes! I am busted. "Exactly what do you mean? Can you give us an example?" "Mousey" asks. "Well," she starts, "he's been demanding his own way a lot and always wants to be first among the children." (Well, du-uh! I am a much bigger kid than Evan!) She continues, "He also needs constant reassuring and seems to now be resentful of *my own* children. Also, if things upset him he runs and hides somewhere until he hears me calling with a *promise* not to punish him." she answers, albeit a little too thoroughly.

"Of course, I'm sure you know this, but in several of his placements he has been through a lot more trying experiences than we are at liberty to discuss.", the "Wart" protectively explains. "Yes, I understand he's been through *an* upsetting experience, but all I am able to do in the way of helping him, is to try and handle his sensibility." the "mom" responds, unable to hide her defensive attitude.

Right now, I am bombarded from all sides and I feel like I could use a good hidey-hole! The four women continue to discuss me as if I am invisible. I *am* invisible, and I wish I were deaf too, because, hearing this conversation is making me very nervous. It's upsetting me so much to hear the way they're talking about me! As soon as I get home, I am gonna hide in the only place left for me—underneath *Danny's* bed. The "mother" looks everywhere for me, but has never yet discovered me there, probably because it's so low to the floor it would seem impossible for somebody to get under there. However, it doesn't stop me! I quickly disappear into the midst of the cluttered assemblage of more meaningless junk than I would ever hope of collecting, all of which seemingly supports the weight of Danny and his bed. Under there I really don't always hear her calling me somehow. I think it's the clutter, which buffers the sounds, but because I don't always respond to her calls, now she thinks I don't actually *hear* properly.

It is already February 1952 and Danny has been talking and carrying on about some girl he likes at school. He showed me her picture, which he keeps in the coveted, clear plastic photo-slot, in his wallet. "Her name is Sally-Ann." he gushes—and blushes! She is quite petite and pretty, and like "Cat's Eyes" has flaming red hair. Danny tells me he's "in love" and wants to marry her someday. "Kiss, kiss?" I motion my lips to ask him. "Uh-huh" he replies in the affirmative, nodding his head and grinning like a Cheshire cat! [111] "Oh! Yuck, yuck, ble-ah!" I let him know exactly what I think by the faces I'm making and my tongue sticking out. Personally, I am never going to kiss a girl or get married either. But being as it's February, Saint Valentine's day *is* right around the corner, again—and I, for one, am eagerly awaiting a whole bunch of *candy kisses* on that day.

However, today is definitely not a fun, "candy" day. Today we had to come to "SICK KIDS' E. N. T.", (the Ear Nose and Throat Clinic at Toronto's Sick Children's Hospital). [26] [26a] It is where the specialist says my "Tom Sells", [tonsils], are diseased, and my "Add-a-Noise", [adenoids], are very large also. In fact, he says, "They seem to be affecting [my] speech." That's why they put my name on a list for "Tom and Add Outside", (or it's what I think they said). [The procedure was actually going to be a Tonsillectomy and Adenoidectomy in the Out-door, (i.e. *the Outpatient facility*).] Geeze, they sure have some funny names for stuff in a kid's body.

We have a quick conference with a couple doctors. However, before we could get away from the Clinic, my "mother" *had* to throw her two cents in and ask one of the specialists, "Due to the fact that Teddy has so many repeat bouts with colds and other upper respiratory issues, I wondered if his hearing may have been adversely affected?" (I hear her just fine—silly woman, doesn't she know I am choosing to ignore her?) Nonetheless, the response they sent the promised response in a report to the "C.A.S." Case Worker, stating, "As soon as possible we suggest the child should be hearing-tested." (Oh, g-r-e-a-t, {of course, it's a facetious comment}, more poking and prodding into my tiniest places.)

Wasting little time, in fact within the week, my Case Worker took me to a Hearing Clinic where a therapist and I played a bunch of games, while I wore some strange-looking headgear. All I had to do was raise a finger or press a button when I heard different sounds. However, the testing session was cut short because the doctor, who is supposed to interpret the test results, indicated he would not do any more extensive testing until after my "T-and-A" surgery, if hearing-testing was still deemed necessary at that time. Waiting until I am healthy is probably a good idea. Anyway, I've been settling down slowly, and becoming more like myself at this new home with my old family. Everyone says I look better and I am really trying to eat better, and of course, I'm still sleeping well—with the drugs, at least.

I can't believe it's "Saint Patrick's Day" already. Valentine's Day zipped right by so fast, and it was extra great because I got lots and lots of candy kisses and chocolate! Danny got his "kisses" too, but they were not the candy kind. In fact, Danny brought "Sally-Ann" home to meet us all and announced they were "goin' steady" pointing to the ring, which was a barely visible piece of wire on her finger. I have no idea what "goin' steady" means, other than you get to do lots of smooching! Oh, well, it may not be my cup of tea, but Danny's happy.

Anyway, as of today, Valentines is ancient history, and as of last Friday afternoon, so is "Sally-Ann". Today is March 17, 1952, and Danny is in love with another girl. This one is named, "Marilyn", and she is a pretty girl, as tall as Danny is, with black hair, styled in a sort-of "Tinker Bell" pixie cut [158]. "Songbird" has gleefully decorated our entire house in green clovers and little leprechaun cut-outs and I helped. Other than the usual exciting events of this *everything needs to be green day*, the other thing I have scheduled is my visit to the Sick Kid's Medical Clinic for my overallcheck-up prior to tomorrow's scheduled medical procedures called, "Tom Sells 'n' Tony" and the "Add-a-Noise 'n' Tony" ["Tonsillectomy" and "Adenoidectomy"].

After waiting three months for this appointment, I was finally examined and, of course, weighed on the scale. At four-years-and-seven-months of age, the highest number I can make the scale jump to is *thirty-five-and-a-half* pounds, which is *underweight* by approximately *twenty-five pounds*. The doctors determine that indeed I am well recovered from a recent "cold-chest" (or, is it "chest-cold"). Anyway, they say I am "alright for both of the surgical procedures to be carried out tomorrow."

Revolving Doors

[In the follow-up report to the "C.A.S." regarding today's check-up, the doctors' only comments were, *"Teddy was very good and didn't make a bit of fuss."*]

Is that *all* everybody can think about—how good I am, or how much fuss I do, or do not, make?

I think probably the reason I let those doctors poke and prod and look in my throat without me *making a fuss*, was because I was already getting pretty sick—again, and didn't have the energy to fight back. It is now two days later, after both the surgeries, and "Songbird" is on the phone to "Doctor 'Bum-Shot' Lambert", saying, "Teddy has a temperature of 102 and is very, very miserable. Also, I can't make him drink enough fluids." (Didn't she ever think Popsicles, and even ice cream are fluids too? Guess not. Although, it *is* what they gave me in the hospital after the surgery.) What strange names these docs have for all their even stranger, and excruciatingly painful, procedures! (By the way, who the heck is "... 'n' Tony"?)

Anyway, the doctor tells "mom", "Such a high degree of fever is unusual and worrisome for a post-op, so I'll drive right on over and have a little look-see." Indeed, Doctor 'Bum-Shot' did come by, with the needle of Penicillin already in his hand, even before he entered my room. "Owwww! Owieeeeee! Dop it! Dop! Dop!" (Damn those 'bum-shot' needles have to be ten feet long and boy, oh boy, they hurt like hell!)

[After this visit, according to the "C.A.S." file, *"The doctor's written report stated,* 'The child has had a *cold* on top of the operation'."] (Really, a little "cold"?)

Again, it's only two days after the new damn bum-stick, and I am able to take-in fluids and soft food. In fact, I want to get up and play, and, of course, so does "Blackie" who, by the way, has remained loyal to *me*. In fact, he stays *only* in my bed all the time now, never in Danny's bed. (I seem to be a fur magnet...or at least a furry-friend, magnet. Tee, hee, hee.)

"Songbird" has been in an unusually great mood these last couple of days. Now I see why. She has retrieved a large box from the tin shed and is struggling to get it into this tin house. "What's dat?" I ask. "It's Easter decorations, Teddy. You've been pretty sick lately and I bet you forgot all about Easter and the Bunny coming didn't you?" she asks. "Dess so." "Well he's coming on the thirteenth so we only have three days to get the house ready. You need to help me with this, O.K.?" I nod in agreement and we start getting out all the junk to decorate for the Bunny's arrival.

When Danny suddenly comes bounding through the door she tries to commission his help also, but he says he is too busy and is taking "Jennifer" skating. "Did you say 'Jennifer'? What happened to 'Marilyn'?" the mother asks her eldest son. As usual lately, he just grunts something unintelligible and runs right back out. We could have used Danny's assistance because of course, Evan is no help at all. Nevertheless, it's left to mum and me to decorate the windows, doors and walls with paper Easter stuff. "Just three sleeps until HE gets here, Teddy! Aren't you excited?" She has no idea just how excited I really am! I can almost taste the chocolate already—I am *not* kidding.

"Wake up, Teddy, dear—wake up!" I open my eyes just a little because it's very hard to sleep-off, and wake-up out of, the heavy sedation I am under every night, lately. "What's goin' on?" I ask, in case, (hopefully), it's unimportant and I can go back to sleep. "The Easter Bunny—Teddy, the Easter Bunny came last night!" she bursts with all the enthusiasm of a child. "You too Evan, dear, up! Get up boys!" We both jump out of our matching beds and bump into each other hurrying to be first into the living room and see what the Bunny left for us. Oh, wow! There are three great, big, huge chocolate eggs with beautiful coloured icing patterns dribbled all over them. "We have to go have our Easter Egg Hunt now, boys.", "mom," bubbles. So we put sweaters on and go traipsing out into the backyard, still in our jammies, and, of course toting our matching Easter baskets filled with the pastel, multi-coloured excelsior into which we are supposed to softly set all of the collected eggs. She follows along behind and takes pictures of us with her new "Brownie Hawkeye Flash Model" camera. [112] (It was a Christmas present from her husband.)

We run here and there and look up in the trees and under the bushes, while our "mom" pops in flash bulb, after bulb. We search under the lawn chairs and in every nook and cranny, we can see. We both hunt with great success, finding so many colourful and yummy eggs. Some have patterns on them, some are plain, but the few I find, wrapped in foil, well they're the best ones as far as I'm concerned. They're the "c-h-o-c-o-l-a-t-e" ones! Then our "mom" says it's time to come inside and count all the eggs we each have found.

Oh yes, and now it's time to start painting the real eggs she hard-boiled and refrigerated for us last night. I think it's really the best fun of all, because you can paint any shapes or colours you want on the eggs! When we are right in the middle of our Easter artwork, she starts taking more pictures, and giggling because we look as if we've been painting each other instead of the eggs. Oh well, it's all in good fun, and it has been a super-d-duper *great* Easter Sunday. We eat so much candy we don't even want lunch, but supper is a baked-ham roast and I definitely have my appetite back now.

It has been ten days since Easter and it's less than one month after the infamous house call by "Doctor Bum-Stick". If I thought Doctor Lambert's bum-shot hurt, I had not yet felt today's insult of the HUGE syringe I was poked with, almost all the way through my left arm. Well, at least it *felt* as if it was ten inches long! It's my booster-shot of "triple toxoids" which I have to get before I can start school in the fall. Boy, oh boy, that bugger hurt like hell! Good thing "Songbird" brought me some candy suckers to soothe me after the painful stick, (because as everyone knows, candy has magic powers and, as always, will ease a little of the sting).

[Today, also, an age verification letter was sent from the "C.A.S." to the school administration office for September 1952 Kindergarten pre-registration.]

****

{It's May 5, 1952, and I couldn't know this, but my youngest "half-sister", Lynda, is born in Toronto to my mother Berneice (Ketteringham) Faulconer and her husband, Donald Faulconer. Of course, of this event I'll have no knowledge for many years to come. It seems as if my real mommy finally achieved her ultimate goal—marriage and now two children born to the perfect little married couple. It's just too bad it happened this way. Now, I would never be able to share in their idyllic home and hearth scene. Although I'm certain Lynda's birth would make my mommy very happy—truthfully it makes me very, very sad as it completely locks me out of mommy's life, for-ev-er.}

400

Chapter 46: My *Very Special "Fifth"* Birthday

The rest of spring and the summer of zoomed quickly by without incident, including no lung crud, and no more 'bum shots'. I am doing better in every way and, considering today is August 27, I think it's a darn good day for a birthday party and it will be a pretty big deal for me! "Songbird" has been busy all morning cleaning the house and baking cookies and a cake for my celebration. The cake is a big, fat, triple-decker, dark chocolate one with chocolate fudge icing! Drawn on it is a truck, made out of blue icing! In green icing are the words, "HAPPY BIRTHDAY TEDDY". It is such a wonderful cake. I can tell it has been made with a lot of *love*—just for *me*.

At my party, I am having Danny, of course, and Evan, naturally, and three other kids I've met around the neighbourhood—Alice, Davey and Joey. Alice is a funny-looking little girl, with yellow hair wildly sticking-out all over, making her look as if she stuck her finger in a light socket! The boys are *twin* brothers, but it's weird because they look nothing alike. One kid looks like his mom and the other looks like his dad. We are all good friends, get along, and play together all the time, (even though Alice *is* a girl.)

"Awwre we habing ice cweam, Teddy?" Alice asks politely. "I dunno." is what I answer on the way to the kitchen to ask "mom". On my way back through the grey, plastic, accordion-style, folding door, I am giving the answer they all wanted to hear, "Yes, ders chawkwate 'n' white ice cweam!" Danny takes off to go on his date with his newest girlfriend, but we little kids will have much more fun, spending the afternoon singing songs and playing party games. My favourite is, "Pin the Tail on the Donkey", because I somehow always get his tail on his nose, and it looks really silly! Hee, hee, hee. We are also playing "Hot Potato" and "Musical Chairs".

Now it's time for me to open my presents. I rip open the first of the colourful birthday papers to reveal, from Alice, a toy truck, nearly big enough to sit on and ride around the yard. What a great gift! Then, from Davey and Joey I pull a brand new cowboy suit out of a big, flat box. Oh, goodness! I can't believe it! It's my favourite thing in the world—a new, dark blue cowboy suit! "Gee-whiz, tanks a wot, guys!" I'm wondering why Danny has given me one of our mom's big, round, flowery hatboxes, but when I pry it open, I see it's full to the brim with a million of his old Tinkertoys. [45] (I don't care if they're not new. It's an especially nice gift, because Danny knows the few pieces of Tinkertoys, [45], I have remaining in my own collection, aren't enough to actually build even an outhouse.) "Tanks, Danny!" Now I can build a castle to the sky!

"Mom" and Evan have given me a stuffed "Hopalong Cassidy", ("Hoppy"), cowboy doll, [104] and a new View Master, [102], reel of "Hoppy and his horse, 'Topper'!" [105] What a great birthday—it's almost better than Christmas! After the papers are all cleaned up "mom" comes in with my birthday cake which has five lit candles on it and tells me to "blow them out", but not 'till after I, "secretly make a special wish". I think it's is a strange thing to do, but she insists everybody does it whenever they have birthday candles. Then everybody sings, "Happy Birthday" to **_me_**. This is really wonderful. Wow, I guess I'm getting to be a *big* boy because, now I am five! Hmmmm? I don't really *feel* any different. Maybe I'll feel *five* tomorrow.

Chapter 47: Send That Little "Stray" Back to the Pound!

It's the twenty-fifth of September and I was supposed to begin school before no, but for some unknown reason I've been held back and not permitted to start with the other kids my same age. I wonder if it has anything to do with those damn "Psychometric Examinations" [66], like the one I had to participate in again, yesterday. This time I received a score of **one-hundred and eleven**, which the test person informed the "C.A.S.", now gives me a mental age of "*five years*", (which is just about right on the money, because my chronological age is actually five years and one month.) So, if I am where I'm supposed to be, why "hold me back"?

Oh, *gr—eat!* {And, yes, that was facetious.} Right now, this entire family, including the "father", is headed to some meeting at the "Wart's" office. (Of course, I still think of the "C.A.S." Director as the "Wart Lady" because she *still* has the nasty, ugly, protruding, hairy, distracting wart, on the tip of her nose. Somebody should tell her about it. It is so hard to look her in the eyes as she speaks to you because her annoying wart moves up and down with every word she utters). When we get to "Wart's" office, not only are all five of us supposed to squeeze into the small glass room, but all three of my Workers are also there. Obviously, the topic of discussion will be "me".

Evan is allowed to sit on his daddy's knee in the room. However, as for *me*—I am the only person who is told to take a seat on the hard wooden bench *outside* the glass-walled office. Curious, I assume there just isn't enough room for me. "Mousey" instructs, with a pointing finger for emphasis, "Sit down right there, Teddy, and be a good boy. We are going to have a little chat with the family. We won't be very long." (Hmmm...I'm asking myself if *I'm* no longer a part of this family?)

They all think I'm not able to hear what they're saying, but I can hear every word. I am "playing" with my View Master, [102], pretending to be engrossed in what I am doing. While, in fact, I am listening intently to the future of my life being played-out right beside me in the little see-through room. The adults are all having an agonizingly serious discussion, and it's definitely something about, "adoption". The "C.A.S." Director is asking these "foster parents",

"We would like to know what you have decided regarding the adoption of Teddy. I understand you have expressed to each of his Workers, you are considering making Teddy a permanent member of your family. If this is correct we would like to get started immediately on the necessary paperwork to enact this adoption process."

My two-time "foster mother" answers this question by stating the following,

"In order to best explain our position on this matter, we have prepared a letter which I would like to read aloud so I am able to best express our wishes."

[The following words are **exactly** as the mother *reads* them aloud from her letter. These words are also recorded by a secretary who is seated in the corner, transcribing every person's exact words in her shorthand notes. They letter states, as follows,

"While everyone in this foster family is very fond of Teddy, we do not wish to adopt him *at the present time. He has been boarding with us during two separate placements totalling many months. For the first while, (the first time around), we had a great deal of trouble with him. He had temper tantrums,*

banged his head and rocked. He gradually got over this, but unfortunately, after the failure of the attempted, (Adoptive), placement last fall, Teddy regressed and was suffering all those symptoms again, (this second time around). We now realize there is some emotional instability, and have to wonder how this is going to affect him in later years. Of course, we are willing to give Teddy a home for the rest of his life, if necessary, but simply do not want adoption now."]

The parents, having cemented their decision regarding keeping me permanently, stand up, shake hands with "Wart" and exit the office. "C'mon, Teddy, we're going home now." the "foster mother" says, while reaching for my hand. What can this conversation mean? My head is spinning. I can't think straight. Oh noooo! Oh noooo! This can't be happening! I love them and they loved me, so why wouldn't they want me "forever", like they said they would? I've been so happy, and settled in this house. I get along with the whole family and rarely have to revert to my hidey-hole, security-seeking behaviour.

"Songbird" has no idea I overheard the conversation behind the windowed Director's room. She is putting on an act and being the same as she was before today's office visit. I am so confused and I just don't know what to do or say. When this happens, as usual, I do and say *nothing*. (I have not yet tried to run away from this family; however, if I ever felt like it, *now* would certainly be the appropriate time.)

The depth of my sadness is unfathomable. They aren't aware I now know exactly what they truly think and feel about me. Nobody is saying anything in the car. We have been on our way driving home for a little while and I am feeling sick to my stomach thinking my "foster parents" are certainly not the people whom they appear to be. On the outside, they both seem so *nicey-nice* and very loving, but apparently, below the surface facade is a totally different story. Why is it always blamed on *me*—or *my* fault?

We're at the tin house now and they haven't said a single word to me about what went on at the "C.A.S.". They don't know I *know everything*. "Take those muddy shoes off outside, Teddy." the "foster father" insists sternly. Am I in some sort of trouble? Evan's shoes are as muddy, but nothing is said to the perfect little baby who lives, and *belongs*, in this household. Right now, I can see how things have started to shift sideways, just a tad.

From here on, things will become more and more skewed for me. I'll receive greater amounts and severity of discipline, whether warranted or not. I will seem to be the problem child and the shit-disturber, every time, whether I am guilty or not! However, right at this minute I'm hungry so I ask the "mother", "Can I pwease hab a cookie, pwease?" She tells me "No!", and after pouring the sedative down my throat, insists I "go right upstairs and get into bed". So, I do. They just don't want me around to overhear about my having to move, once again, to some other home. I am beginning to see the imaginary revolving door sweep-sweep-sweeping around, and about to catch me up, once again in its slow spin.

Once in bed, I roll over to face the wall. She could have given me a little cookie. What have I done? When she pokes her head in my door and asks, I tell her, "No.", (because I don't even want a phoney story or a pretend-happy song). "Why are you moaning, Teddy?" my so-called "mother" asks me. I tell her my tummy is hurting. (However, I'm actually moaning more from fear and self-pity than from an actual stomach pain). However after a few minutes alone, I jump up and run to the bathroom to throw-up. I keep puking until the "mother" hears me and comes to help. "Teddy, what's the matter with you?" she asks, with what I swear I recognize is, genuine "concern" in her eyes. "Dunno." is all I can get out between the retching spasms. "Well, look you've thrown-up all your medicine. I suppose there's no use giving you any more right now."

"Well, let's get you tucked back-in and you can try to get some sleep, *sweetheart.*" Why does she call me names of affection when she really doesn't want me in her life? I roll over and try to sleep. Then suddenly, I really don't know what is happening to me, but just as I lie back in my bed, my whole body becomes as stiff as a board and I can neither relax, nor *move* in any natural sense. Then I start shaking violently and my head is bashing itself against my headboard. Bang, bang, bang! (I'm thinking I haven't experienced this for quite a while. In fact, as far as I know, *this time around, the* family hasn't *seen* my head bashing itself at all. Well, at least I don't *think* they have.)

"Oh, Teddy...Teddy!" The foster "mother" is *acting* all worried. "Teddy, you've cut your head open! Stop, stop thrashing about, dear! Let me get you cleaned up." "Honey, come here! Please come in here and help me with Teddy! He's having some sort of seizure!" She implores her husband to help, but he ignores her. When I finally settle down, she cleans my head, the sheets and the wall, washing off all my blood, while at the same time murmuring something about, "get off his lazy ass and help"...and something else about... "how badly head wounds bleed!" Then she tucks me back in and sits beside me while I try to sleep. She is behaving as if she has no idea why I would be acting-out like this. I can't possibly control my brain having a meltdown, or, as it would indeed, later in my "C.A.S." file, be recorded as a "*seizure*". I certainly couldn't, wouldn't and didn't, do it on purpose.

After the rough time I suffered through last night, as might be expected, we are now in the waiting room, about to see "Dr.

Lowder". I hope he'll be able to shed some light on what can possibly be happening inside my little head lately. At least we might gain some measure of understanding or insight to help us avoid future seizures. The nurse takes us into a small examination room where we sit and wait some more. "Dr. Lowder" is a middle-aged gentleman with thick, curly, salt-and-pepper, hair. He is very short and looks as if he's only *pretending* to be a doctor, because his white lab coat is far too long. In fact, it looks so ridiculous he seems as if he just walked off the set of a "Three Stooges" film. [110] Oh-oh! I guess he hasn't yet noticed his breast pocket is housing a pen, which seems to have leaked all its blue ink.

Anyway, the doctor directs his nurse to weigh me and she complies. "Let's look at your weight first, young man, and then we can all talk about your progress." (Is he loony? I am not here about my weight or my progress! It is the *fit* I experienced last night—the *seizure*!) I couldn't believe this, but the first thing he does is *congratulate* me on my small amount of gained weight-- over a pound! (Really... is he kidding me? Is my weight all you're interested in?) Then after a few redundant questions, a tap of each knee with a little metal stick with a rubber thingy on the end, a little shining light aimed right into each eyeball and a pokey thing in each ear, the doctor reports to my "mother", "There is nothing *physically* wrong with Teddy." Then, he writes something on a small slip of paper and instructs her to take it to the pharmacist who will prepare the required daytime medication—another *sedative*, of course.

He follows our visit with a written report to inform the "C.A.S." of the exact details of my examination,

"There is nothing physically wrong with this child. He worked himself into a state of emotional tension. I have ordered another sedative for the boy to take in the daytime. Of course, he will continue on his regular dosage of the sedative

prescribed for sleep."

Therefore, now I am not only drugged at night to sleep, but I am also drugged in the daytime so I "will stop getting so *emotional*". Doesn't anybody wonder why, at such a tender age, I am experiencing problems requiring day and night sedation?

Later in the day, on the phone to one of my Workers, I overhear the foster "mother" say,

"I feel perhaps Teddy has connected our family's visit to your office, along with the psychometric test, [66], to somehow give him the negative connotation of *having to move, yet again*".

That may well be part of it, but the other, worse part, is living with this two-faced family. They all act in front of me as if they love and want me forever, but when they think I am not aware, or not within earshot, then the truth obviously prevails. The truth is, they all want me gone from their lives! My natural reaction is to withdraw from this family and from life in general. So, where I am headed right now is off to rekindle my friendship with the dust-bunnies under Danny's bed. In this hideout, I am so quiet I barely breathe. Good thing for me that Danny is sleeping-over at his friend's house again. At least *he* won't be the one to discover my hidey-hole.

"Teddy—Teddy, wake up—where are you? Come now, I don't have all day to wait on you. Are you getting dressed?" the "mother" calls down the hall. I don't want to get up. I am hiding-out under my covers because I've heard bits and snippets about more changes coming soon in my life. In fact, I'm so concerned about what will be around the next corner for me, now I have virtually stopped eating completely, except for my fingernails. The "mother" thinks I'm sleeping, but really I've got my head all the way under and I'm petting "Blackie", my sweet little friend who never lets me down, never, ever!

Anyway, now she's on the phone to "Wart Lady" at the "C.A.S.". (I always know when the "mother" is talking to the *Director* because she puts-on this phoney voice. It's sort of sing-songy and ever so proper.) This is the side of the conversation, which I am able to discern,

"I just don't know what to do with him.

*All of you know I've—I mean **we've**, tried and tried, but he is a very unhappy and confused child.*

Well, you tell me what you think is best.

No, of course we don't want to see him go to the orphanage again...nor another foster home. He's been in what, three or four?

***Seventeen** residential moves? ... Oh, dear!*

But you see, we're also concerned that his emotional instability will have quite a negative effect on him in later years.

*Well, we're very sorry but **another month** is all we can realistically handle.*

No, really, another month and that's it. I'm afraid we must be firm about this decision."

So, this is it, one more month and I'm outta *here*. (Sweep-sweep-sweep. Here comes the revolving door and I have nowhere to hide.)

Certainly, I couldn't understand the changes about to occur around this house, though I *am* aware of the fact, the family wants me moved out. I heard the words, "another month", but I am unable to tell time or understand days, weeks or months. I can't possibly grasp the significance of what "another month" might actually mean. As well, there is a great deal of tension around here, and, of course, tension is something I *do* understand, or at least I can feel. I am just bumping along in a routine, which is the same, day-in, and day-out. The only thing which has changed is how the grown-ups in this house literally cross the days off the calendar with a big black "X" while they await *their* day of emancipation, which is the day I leave this house and this family gets rid of me—*forever.*

I too am eagerly awaiting that day, because "Songbird", and the rest of the foster family members, have all changed their attitudes towards me. These days, I am not being treated the same as their real kids. I am yelled at, and strapped with the belt almost *daily* now. It is usually the "mother" screaming at me repeatedly with, "Why did you wear your shoes in the house? Look at the mess of milk you spilled! Stop teasing the dog! Are you going to finish your meal, or not! Stop chewing your fingernails! You will eat what is set in front of you! Stop fighting with Evan!"

Even when it's Evan who is misbehaving, I am still the one who is punished. The other day Evan stole "Pom Pom" from my bed, and refused to give him back to me, even when I said, "Pwease." So, I grabbed my wooden doggie from his grubby little baby fingers. Then, the "mother" ordered *me* to, "Give the damn dog back to Evan!" I answered with, "But, dat's my doddie, 'Pom Pom'—he's mine—dat's 'Pom Pom', 'n' he's mine!" However, she ignores my pleading and gives my little second-best friend back to Evan.

It seems, these days my transgressions never end. The foster parents are obviously not happy with me, and I am no longer happy with being here. It has turned out to not be the home I thought, hoped, it was. I almost wish I could go back to the asylum for a short stay—at least until they find me a real, permanent adoptive home. No more "foster" living arrangements, dammit! I want to run away but I still haven't figured out where this *tin box* house is at in relation to the old boneyard—where I *know* I can survive. However, for now, we all must wait it out until the day of the last "X". Then I'll, once again, be removed from a "foster home", just to take another spin in the revolving door. I'll go around and around, then I'll be swept out to *wherever,* (but it'll be better than *here*! At least I certainly hope so).

You know, life around here is just not good for me at all, right now. I really think these grown-ups are very unkind and selfish. On Saturday, they all went to the park to play and left me at the tin box next door in the care of the elderly neighbour lady, "Mrs. McDiarmid". I don't like it here because she smells funny, wears her nylon stockings rolled over a garter below her knees and hasn't got any teeth! So, all I can do here is just sit on the floor and play with my View Master, [102], while being a "very quiet, good little boy". When I look up, I am curious to see the withered, two-hundred-year-old, woman taking something very strange-looking out of a glass of water on the flowery, tin "TV Tray Table" in front of her. [114] I am really shocked to see her put this strange-looking item into her gaping, toothless mouth. Whaaaat?! Now she has teeth!? She cough-laughs when she sees I've been intently watching her.

I must have a heck of a queer look on my face because she starts explaining a shocking story about her teeth. She says these are called, "false teeth" which she is able to remove, or reinstall, whenever she wants to, "for cleaning and such". I guess I still look very puzzled so she just says they're "pretend" teeth. Oooooh, I get it, but it's still gross! "Watch this!" the next-door, toothless-wonder exclaims. She then commences to flipping the dentures around and upside-down in her oral cavity. Oooooh, that is disgusting and really, really gross!

Anyway, for the finale of this boring circus act, the ancient woman makes me sit through a stupid bowling show on her "colourised" television. (It really isn't a colourised television set, it's a "colourising", [113], plastic film taped over the black and white screen to make it appear as if the picture is in colour! It looks ridiculous because it consists of a band of purplish-blue across the top third, a red band across the middle third and a green band across the bottom of the stuck-on plastic sheet.) [113] Anyway, the moronic, boring bowling show, colourised or not, was so tedious for me to sit through, it almost made all *my* teeth fall out too!

What seems like many hours later, the *perfect* little family gets home and I notice Evan is proudly toting a huge red balloon, which he had received from some new store's "Grand Opening" promotion. In his other hand is a candy-apple, which his parents obtained free from a street vendor at the same event. I guess nobody thought to bring home any balloons or candied apples for me. It really makes me sad to be excluded from having a little fun, like all the rest of my so-called "family" obviously have been enjoying today. (Of course, this is not the first time, either.) I feel as if I am being punished for something I haven't done.

Something else is changing in this family also. I've begun to notice "Songbird" isn't going around the house constantly singing these days. Even worse, she displays a short temper, snapping at me, but in the same breath is extra nicey-nice to Evan. I wonder what's up with Danny, because these days, he's spending more and more time having sleep-overs at his friends' homes. I don't guess he misses playing with me at all, although I *really do* miss playing with him.

Revolving Doors

PART VIII: Nightmares End...Sweet Dreams Begin

Chapter 48: Here's Your Hat! Where's Your Hurry?

I guess it's time for me to go again. This morning there are fourteen "**Xs**" on the fridge calendar ever since the family's meeting at the "C.A.S.", when I overheard their plans to have me removed. Though it's early, I've already been dressed-up in my brown, *almost good enough for Sunday*, corduroy jacket and white shirt. (It's the one which *still* has the two middle buttons missing because the "mother" here is just *too busy* to sew them on for me.) My suitcase is packed and *most* of "me" is ready for something, except for my hair, which sure could use a good combing. All my toys are in a plain brown paper grocery bag on the floor beside the little blue suitcase and my trike is in the yard, on the edge of the grass, right where it meets the driveway. Everything is ready and waiting—but for what? Although, whatever I am waiting for is not immediately apparent, I know I'm supposed to be leaving, but I still really don't know "why".

As I await whatever fate has in-store for me through the next revolving door of my life, I find myself in a daydream about my beautiful, loving mommy. We are at the beach, walking hand-in-hand, but only our toes are getting wet. Mommy's feet are very pretty, and I notice the water is beading on the shiny pink polish on her toenails. As always, she is petite, slender and ever so lovely. When I look up at her and our gazes meet, her eyes are happy and with a gentle little smile on her lips she says,

"I love you Ricky, dear—I love you so very, very much. Don't you worry about anything because everything is going to work

out alright. You'll see, my darling little man. We'll be together very soon."

I don't seem to drift back to those warm memories too often lately, because *life* keeps getting in the way of my *joy*. As always, suddenly my daydream is jolted back to reality when little "Blackie" starts bouncing around my feet and licking my hand. "I'n gonna miss you, wittle 'Bwackie', I wub you bery much." (I may not say it right, but he *gets* it—he *gets* me.)

Suddenly, the familiar sound of the front door chimes fills the foyer. When "Songbird" opens the door I see the woman who is coming in this time is "Cat's Eyes", and oooh, she looks stunning today! She's wearing a navy-blue tight-skirt with matching jacket and coordinated overcoat. The navy is brightened by the sunny warmth of her pretty yellow blouse ruffled daintily to fashion a high collar around her neck. Completing her lovely ensemble are matching yellow pumps. Today, she has her hair pulled back from her face and it's held in place with a wide yellow ribbon, which looks lovely against the warm, rich, red hues of her hair. (Other than the red hair, her loveliness reminds me of my real mommy.)

"Hi, Teddy dear...I've come to pick you up today. I'll tell you all about the *good news* when we are on our way. Alright with you, sweetie?" (I like when she calls me "sweetie". It sounds so genuinely affectionate coming from her.) "O.K." I say while barely nodding in agreement. I decide just to check one last thing with the "mother", so I ask when I'll be coming back here. She replies with a most unexpected, "Teddy, I thought you understood, this is going to be your new, wonderful forever home you've been waiting for your whole life."

Then before I could ask anything else, "Cat's Eyes" inquires of the foster "mother", "Do we have everything of his ready, 'Mrs...'?" "Yes—yes!" I butt-in and answer for the "mother", then I try to inquire as to where we're going this time. "Well, first we need to stop by and say 'hello' to 'Mrs...' and 'Mrs...' over at the office." she explains." (That's "Mouse Lady" and "Librarian Lady". Hmmm, I was thinking it's probably a good thing they don't all know what I call them because it might make them angry with me—and they wouldn't like me anymore. Anyway, it's so much easier for me to remember them, in the way I actually see them.)

Then, "Cat's Eyes" continues, "Later on, I'll be taking you to a very, very special place, you'll see." (I have been to some *very*, and some *very, very*, special places before, and I, *very, very, very* much, didn't like any of them. However, how could I distrust this beautiful woman? Of course, I can't. So I decide to go along with her and wait and see what happens next in my recidivistic little life. It seems as if I'm pathetically, forever caught up in those damn spinning doors.)

Quickly, my escort and I depart from "Songbird's" tin box house, sadly, without as much as one little kiss, or even a "Good-Bye" hug, from the "mother". Then we summarily exit the halfway broken-off, little wooden, access gate, leaving the "trailer park" at our backs. In doing so, we are also leaving behind my second "forever mother", "Songbird" and her husband, my second "forever father", and also my "forever big and little brothers". However, it isn't even so much this second "forever family" I'll be sad about leaving. I am terribly heartbroken over having to leave behind *my*, I mean *their*, doggie, "Blackie". I will really, really miss the faithful little fur ball the most.

As my escort and I are apparently trying to catch a streetcar, [47], to ride back to the "C.A.S.", I suddenly remember my tricycle. "My twike...my twike...where's my twike?" I ask her with urgency since, minute-by-minute, we are getting farther and farther away from the tin-box row houses. "Oh, right. I forgot your tricycle, Teddy. I'll tell you what, tomorrow, I promise, I'll stop by there and pick it up, then I'll bring it by the office so we can be sure it gets to you. O.K.?", "Eyes" vows. "O.K." I reluctantly agree, having no other recourse but to trust her implicitly.

As we are choosing a seat, I'm thinking the streetcar, [47], sure is a strange way to travel. It can only go where it attaches to the wires running way up high over-head, and only in a *few* of the bustling downtown Toronto streets. Also, it can ride only where its tracks go, just like a choo-choo train—very strange if you ask me. As we ride along, I am especially enjoying the abundance of windows, which, as always, permit me to busy myself by "people-watching". On this cold, blustery day, the city streets, despite the weather, are nonetheless hustling and bustling with strange and sometimes, *amusing* people. For instance, we just passed an old man who was trying to read a newspaper while standing at the streetcar stop. [47] Naturally, the wild north wind had a different idea! As it raced and swirled around him, it swept his paper high up into the air. Then, as he tried to jump up and grab it, his *hair fell off*! Tee, hee, hee, hee, hee! It was really funny. I didn't know somebody's hair could fall off. (However, then again, remembering "Rita's" *strange* anatomy, I didn't know somebody's wee-wee could fall off either. Ooooh, bad thought, bad thought. I need to shake my head violently to get rid of it. Bang!)

Anyway, as our mode of transportation rattles, squeals and bumps along, I continue my people-watching. Oh-oh! I just saw some little kid, who was screaming and stamping his feet because he let go of the string attached to the large, red balloon he had been holding, (the same kind Evan had recently brought home). With aspirations of its own, the balloon went on a windward journey, in seconds sailing all the way up to the farthest reaches of the sky. I think it must be going to investigate the fluffy, cloud-animal parade up there.

Revolving Doors

Oh-oh! Just now, a very well dressed lady just sat down directly in front of us. My gosh! Around her neck, she is actually wearing a REAL, (once *alive*), fancy furry red fox which is held together by it "biting" his own tail! I just couldn't help myself—I leaned forward and started to pet it! However, my Worker just about had a conniption, stammering and stumbling over her words of apology! It really wasn't necessary—I only wanted to pet the furry thing. Anyhow, the lady was very nice and said, "I understand the child's natural curiosity." (Does she really "understand" *me*?)

Regardless, my attention is already out my window and focused on another woman in a big, huge, fluffy white fur coat, which is unbuttoned and sort-of floating over a shiny green dress. I observe as she accidentally walks over a grate in the sidewalk causing the stiletto heel of one of her bright green satin shoes to catch and break completely off! I can tell by the way she's waving her arms around and yelling something, she is definitely not happy about her broken heel. I guess now she'll have to walk home with a limp.

Oh, now—look over there...it...it is...

"Here we go, Teddy, this is our stop.", "Cat's Eyes" announces while pulling the cord to alert the driver. Then, we disembark the strange, noisy, squealing bus/train at the intersection where we find ourselves kitty-corner to the "C.A.S." buildings. Then we break the law by j-walking, corner to corner, diagonally across the intersection, heading over to my *second* most "UN-favourite" place in the world.

"Hello there, Teddy!" As we enter the inner office where they're waiting, the three women officially greet me in unison. Then "Wart Lady" asks me, "And how are..." (Don't say it! Don't *say it*!)...*we* today?" (Oh my God—she just *had* to say it!)

Well, let's see:
"*We*" are all alone!
"*We*" are unwanted!
"*We*" are homeless!
"*We*" are skinny, sickly, lonely and pathetic!
"*We*" are alive! ... But, of course ...
"*We*" are terrible!

How the hell do you think "we" are? Why the hell don't you ladies just go ahead and sing the "...bedbugs bite" song, and completely top-off this awful day?) However, regardless of what I am really, secretly thinking, *"I'n pfine."* is what comes out of my damn mouth, instead of the truth, which is that I am the absolute polar opposite of fine! (Chicken!)

["C.A.S." file notations, *October twenty-fifth,*

*"In yesterday's Adoption Conference, a decision was finalized to **immediately** place Teddy in a permanent, adoptive home. Teddy's Case Workers are in agreement with the Director that a permanent home is the best option to offer Teddy what he needs most—**security**. After two interviews with 'Mr. and Mrs. Thompson', of Weston Ontario, we are in unanimous agreement that it will be in Teddy's best interest to be placed in such a **stable** environment."*]

"Were you able to carry all of his belongings and toys on the streetcar, [47], 'Miss...'?", "Mrs. Warty Nose" inquires of the lovely Miss "Cat's Eyes". "Oh, 'Mrs...', I'm sorry, I forgot his trike—I, I promise I'll get it back here by tomorrow." my beautiful escort assures. "It's alright, we'll just get 'Mr...' to run by there and pick it up for Teddy, on his way-in to work tomorrow. He says he's bringing something special to the office for Teddy. I think Teddy is going to be especially thrilled because it's a little red, "W-A-G-O-N". ("Mr...", he's the fellow I call, "Big Ears"—I feel better now because I've found him to be a very kind and trustworthy gentleman, who often has little candy cane surprises for me. I wonder what surprise he could have in his big pocket today. (Of course, if I had been old enough to spell, I would know already.)

"Well, Teddy, we have some things to talk about and then you'll be going to some place *very special* later-on today.", "Wart" says with obviously feigned enthusiasm. (What's this *very special place*? I'm getting a little nervous at the way everyone is acting so overly optimistic about my next placement. I'm starting to wonder if it's just another dungeon they plan to stash me in somewhere. Sweep...sweep?)

"'Miss...', why don't you take little Teddy over to the barber shop in the plaza, and get him a nice hair cut?" "Oh, what a great idea! You like haircuts, don't you, Teddy?" she asks. "Dunno." is my response. "Well, when we go in there, you be a big boy and say to 'Mr. Mac', 'I would like a haircut, please.' O.K.?" Therefore, without even removing my coat, we are right back out the door and headed to the little strip-plaza at the corner. "This'll be great fun, you'll see!" she bubbles.

Then, that's exactly where we go, into the place called "Mac's Barber Shop". It has an eye-catching revolving pole out front which is painted with red, white and blue diagonal stripes. It's neat because, as it turns around and around, it looks as if the stripes are moving all the way down then starting at the top, and going down again. It's a pretty neat little barber sign. Anyway, in we go and "Eyes" says, "Mac, I've got a new little customer for you today." Mac replies, "What'll it be there sir? How about a nice, close shave today?" (Is he nuts? I don't shave.) "A haircut, pwease?" I ask, using my very best manners. "What, no shave?" he says, chuckling away. "Mister Mac Daniels", ("Mister Mac" for short), is the old, wrinkly, white-on-bald-headed barber who is about to somehow remove all my hair. It's interesting that this skilled artisan is wearing the exact same kind of white suit which was worn by a certain dentist, with whom I recently became acquainted, (or more specifically, befriended, especially considering the nice sized lollipop he gave me for doing *absolutely nothing*!).

[However, when I think back about the lollipop-wielding dentist, I believe, more than being generous and kind, he was simply setting me up to be his next new patient.]

Anyway, before *this* white-suited gentleman gets me to climb into the over-sized black leather-and-chrome barber chair, "Mister Mac" reaches down into the cabinet under the stand on which sit his "barbarous" instruments. These already lined-up implements are placed neatly across a small, white towel. They consist of two different-sized combs, one brush, several razors, two styles of scissors and a *styptic pencil*. Next to the towelled instruments is a tall glass cylinder with a metal lid. It's full of a pretty turquoise-blue liquid and inside of it several more combs are soaking, (or actually disinfecting).

I wait anxiously, my mouth watering as I half expect to be presented with another lollipop. What colour? What flavour? How big will it be? However, what he retrieves is definitely not a lollipop. It's a homemade contraption, which is a sort-of board with a padded brown-leather seat. He sets it snugly across the arms of his barber chair, then has me climb up the chair and onto the board-seat. Quite efficiently it raises me up high enough so he doesn't have to bend down to see what he's doing as he *scalps* me, (I mean *styles* me). Neat. Next, he puts a great big, red-and-white-checkered picnic table cloth around my neck, fastening its two corners with a clothespin at the back if my neck. "Brush cut, sir?" he asks, still cracking himself up with his own jokes. "Dunno." I reply, not having the remotest idea what the hell a cut with brushes could possibly mean.

Meanwhile throughout all of his banter, the lit cigarette he's *not smoking*, is trailing its noxious cloud of fumes all the way up from the ashtray, directly into my face. It's really bothering my lungs making them want to spasm into a tirade of coughing. Though I am trying to sit perfectly still, the second-hand cigarette smoke is really too strong and irritating! I try to hold my breath in, but the smoke makes me suddenly cough. The moment I do, he pokes the pointy chrome scissors deep-down into my left ear, nearly cutting my ear off, or possibly stabbing my brain, I think. Seriously—he hurt me! "Owwwe! Owwwwieee! Dop it! Dop it!" I wail. "Oh, my goodness, it's a good thing *that* doesn't happen very often or I'd be out of business, now wouldn't I, young mister! Well at least you match the drape cloth now." he remarks, in another feeble attempt at a joke. (This old fool is nuts! Somebody had better get me the hell outta this contraption, right now!)

Then, if it isn't bad enough I was just stabbed almost to death, "Mr. Mac" rubs the end of the ever-waiting, white styptic pencil against the wound, in order to stop the profuse bleeding from my ear! "There, that'll do the trick." he comments with a smug look of satisfaction on his face. It may be "doing the trick" and might even be stopping the bleeding, but it stings like hell! In fact, it's so painful, it's making my eyes water! "Don't cry, Teddy", "Cat's Eyes" says, reassuringly. "I'n not cwying!" I protest, adding, "I'n *not* a baby—he just hurt me *wealwy* bad!"

Watching as I become increasingly distressed, "Cat's Eyes" interjects, "Just cut it the way it is, only a lot shorter please. Do you know what I mean? Just neaten it up please, Mac." She is evidently becoming impatient with his juvenile joking around, and she is visibly upset because his lack of attention resulted in my ear being stabbed. I keep trying hard now not to cough because I'm quite terrified of those shiny, pointy, sharp, barbarous, sword-like, scissor-weapons—and the maniacal, *unfunny*, "Mr. Mac the Stabber" who is wielding them!

Well, well, in under fifteen minutes I am all *neatened up* and looking dapper enough to never again be called a guttersnipe or a ragamuffin! So, other than the big wad of bloody cotton batting sticking out of my sliced ear, and after nearly bleeding to death, it's turned out an O.K. day, I guess. Anyway, back we go the "Children's Aid" office where everyone says stuff like, "Who are you, little boy?" "We hardly recognize you!", and, "Where's Teddy gone?", and, "Don't you look smart!", and, "What a nice hair-cut you got!"... and "blah, blah, blah"... and on, and on they blabber.

O.K., never mind all this bull crap, will somebody please tell me where I'm going today that's so special? "Wart Lady" just read my mind. "'Miss...', you can go ahead and put Teddy into 'Mrs'...' office because she'll be taking him over to the 'Thompsons' today. I need *you* to do a 'preliminary' on our next Prospective Adoptive couple in an hour.", "Wart" explains to "Eyes". "Certainly, 'Mrs...', of course." "Eyes" replies. It means "Librarian Lady" will be taking me to "*the Thompsons*". O.K., I give! What the hell is, "The *Thompsons*"?

"'Mrs...', do you have your vehicle at the office today?", "Wart" inquires of "L.L.". "I have my sister's station-wagon; but it's a little full with her laundry and bedding needing to get cleaned at the Laundromat. However, there's no *problem* using it." she replies. I am listening to this conversation, which may as well be in Greek because I don't know what a "Laundromat" is, or why a car would be full of laundry and bedding. (I thought laundry and bedding had to be washed, dried and put-away at somebody's house, not in their car.) Oh well, as with everything else, I suppose I'll see what it's about sooner or later.

Revolving Doors

"Come on, Teddy", "Librarian Lady" urges as she reaches for my hand. Momentarily, I am being packed-in as tightly as a sardine while squeezed into the only space left inside the once-spacious interior of this automobile. I'm in the far back seat, squished between the loads of laundry, which are piled up to the roof of the car. I know "L.L." referred to the vehicle as a "station-wagon". However it looks absolutely nothing like the other "station-wagon" the family had at the **almost forever, not quite adoptive**, home I just left. Theirs was a brand-spanking-new 1951 Country Squire model and this is a 1940 Ford de Luxe Station Wagon. [110] Both cars happen to be "woodies", designed with wood-panelling on the side and back doors, but the resemblance ends there.

I guess it doesn't matter; at least this is a *ride*. Without it, I suppose we'd either be walking quite a long distance, or else catching buses or streetcars, [47], and sitting next to nasty old, smelly fellow riders. So, I just sit back and enjoy the bumps which, every now and then, send me sailing right up into the roof! [*Of course, this is still decades before the mandatory imposition of child restraints or seat-belts.*] "Say—huh—hay", (whoops a bump). "This is great fun—hu—hun", (whoops another bump). I have the best viewing place out of the back window, so I turn around and kneel, watching as the telephone poles run their races past us.

Just then, a car comes up quite close behind ours and the woman in the front seat starts waving at me. Do I know her? She sure seems to know me. O.K....so I wave back...then the man driving starts waving too. This is weird—two total strangers waving wildly at little me, sandwiched by piled-up laundry. Then, quite abruptly, their car turns right at the light, as ours continues driving straight ahead. "Hello." Here comes another car, so I start waving wildly at the people inside! Nonetheless, these elderly folks are not amused and don't even wave one wrinkled up, bony finger back at me.

Revolving Doors
Hmmmm? Curious.

"We're going to be at the 'Thompsons'' house in a little while, Teddy. Now, do you remember what you've been told about this placement?" (I haven't been told *anything*.) "I'm not positive if we've mentioned this or not, but it will be a home where there's a mommy and a *daddy*. They're a nice young couple who very much want *you* in their lives. If you are a very good little boy, they will want to *adopt you* and *keep you forever*!" she encourages. "Pfor eber, 'n' eber?" I ask with a hint of pessimistic apprehension, after all, I've been down the "forever" road a couple times already. "*Right, forever, and ever.*" she calmly reassures. "Am I goin' back to Danny 'n' Eban's house?" I pry. "No, you won't ever again be going back to live with Danny and Evan. Their parents wanted to make sure you would be able to go to a forever home, and they knew they would not be able to provide it for you, Teddy." (In fact, now I'm being reminded of it, "Songbird" did tell me I could not come back to their family anymore, as I did this last time.)

"In this new family, you will be their one and only child—their *only* little boy—forever! O.K.? Doesn't it sound like a nice place, Teddy?" my escort encourages. "Dess so, uh, der only widdle boy?" I question, with less than a shred of hope or enthusiasm. (After all, this may only be my *second Prospective Adoptive home—but it's my **eighteenth residential placement**.*) "I believe you will find this new mommy and daddy very kind and understanding. They are well aware of *all* the difficulties you've been through in your numerous foster homes, Teddy, and they seem well-prepared to work with you and help you get settled."

They're "aware of all the difficulties I've experienced". Are you serious? That's what *you* think! **No one** is aware! Nobody is talking about the first "basement" residence, and the three boys dead in there! Moreover, *me dead too* and floating up into the corner of the ceiling in the hospital emergency room! How about the horrors of my torture and repeated raping by "Rita"? What could you have told them about those things? Nor are any of you Workers aware of, or *willing to discuss*, my last bunch of roommates. Nobody's talking about the fact that all of us were forced to escape the foster home and eke out a basic existence on the run, unbeknownst to all you Workers, although almost right under your noses—right down in the Don Valley.

Ab-so-lute-ly nobody's talking about how all those boys' spirits sadly ebbed away with each out-breath of their lungs, which were diseased by the relentless infections, and with no relief from having to live, unprotected out in the winter weather. Nobody even knows how those of us boys who were still alive, dragged each dead kid's pale and lifeless corpse to the Mount Pleasant Necropolis, and how they, (all but one), were placed gently below the feet of the beautiful statue of the Angel, "Shekhinah". Nor do any of you know about this saving, Guardian Angel. Nobody knows how each of those pathetic little guttersnipes, (all but ugly little "Fish", of course), were gently lifted to Heaven, leaving behind them not as much as a grave, or a marker-stone—hell, not even a shoe!

Nobody knows it *all,* except me—nobody else has even a clue to what went on when we were all living our **feral** existence! Therefore, it's a mystery to me exactly *how* you people think *you've told* these new Prospective Adoptive Parents everything they need to know about me. Because *I* know you couldn't have, or wouldn't have, and certainly didn't!

"Teddy, these folks really want to give you the wonderful home you need very badly, and certainly deserve." We'll see, yes, we shall see what we shall see. Today is the eleventh of October, 1952 and I am five years and seven weeks old. "We" will just wait and see if this placement will be the lucky one, or not. (Sweep—sweep—sweep! It's the damn revolving door coming around to sweep me inside only to push me back out to the "Thompsons'" residence. Will *this* one be marvellous and joy-filled, or another abominable hell?)

["C.A.S." File Notation,

Oct. 11, 1952. *On this date, Teddy was placed on Adoption Probation and supervision will be carried on by the Adoption Department. This case is now closed in Boarding Home Care.*]

"Teddy, dear, I really think you are going to like *visiting* the 'Thompsons'' home. You know they live on a farm.", "L.L." says, with a reassuring broad smile. "Weally? Dey hab a pfarm?" "Yes", she adds, "with pigs and cows and chickens and even a horse, I think." "A doddie? Do dey hab a doddie?" I plead, hopefully. "I am not positive, but you know, I think, in fact they might have a doggie, a big one, Teddy. Let's just get there and see. O.K.?" "O.K." You don't have to ask me twice!

"Oh," she adds, "I almost forgot to mention, today is just a *visit* at their house—for *afternoon tea*." What's "afternoon T"? I wonder. (I know what an afternoon nap is.) Then she continues after seeing the puzzlement on my face. "Well, you aren't staying overnight, just visiting for today to see if you *like* Mr. and Mrs. Thompson, and if they like you also. So, again, sweetie, you need to be on your best behaviour." (Aren't I always? As far as I'm concerned, it's the family members who are not on *their* best behaviour!)

Chapter 49: And...We're Off to the "PFARM"

We seem to be driving for a very long time. In fact we have gone quite a ways out into a rural area called "Weston". But, before too many more telephone poles have scooted past, we turn into a country lane marked only by a black, lacquered mail-box with "THOMPSON" printed on it in large white block letters. As we travel down the very long country lane, I notice it's bordered, on both sides, with lined-up rows of lots and lots of big, craggy old trees—the ones which I happen to know are the best for climbing. I also notice the country lane is running directly parallel to a good-sized creek, (and, from experience, I know *exactly* what creeks are good for). As we approach the house, I can see, just down the hill a short distance behind it, is a large, quite sturdy-looking, pen, but I don't see any animals in it. Also, not far off, huddled together, are two massive Black Angus beef, (not dairy), cows.

Before "L.L." can even get the car stopped, a large doggie comes running up to us, wagging his tail and barking, but not in a mean way. Oh GREAT! There IS a doggie at this house! He is a very beautiful, long-haired, brown and white Scotch Collie with a long, slender, pointy snout. I can see how he's guarding the house and the people living in it. The house is a modest single-storey, red brick bungalow with a large picture window in the front. Looking at me, looking at her, is a pretty "Siamese" kitty-cat, sitting motionless in the window, as if she were a statue. Also, in the front window, (beside what I will soon discover to *be* a *statue* of a kitty), is a lady. It must be the new "mother", one of the "Thompsons", I suppose.

Then, before we can exit the car, the lady is already running out the front door—very excitedly. "Skipper!" "Skipper!" "Get over here!" "Skipper", come here!" "Oh, I'm so sorry, he too is really excited to see you." the lady excuses, as she fastens the frantic doggie to the veranda rail by his blue leather leash. "Skipper" What a cute name for an adorable doggie. I think "Skipper" and I are definitely going to be very good friends. "Can I pat him, pwease?" I inquire politely. "Of course, go ahead—he's very friendly." is her response. "I weawy wub doddies!" "Oh, wonderful!" the lady says with a pretty, red-lipstick, grin.

"I'm 'Mrs...,'", "L.L." says, offering her hand. "Of course, we've spoken on the phone, haven't we?" the new "mother" replies. "Well, let's not stand out here all day, come on in the house and we can get to know each other." So, in we go right behind Mrs. "Thompson" and "Skipper" who is very eager to show us the way. Inside I have a better look at this "Mrs. Thompson", whom I notice is a very pretty, young woman, around thirty-something. She has a pale complexion like mine, and very beautiful, perfectly coiffed, brown hair. She offers to show us around the house which turns out to have three bedrooms. I know this because I've been permitted to run around and look into all of them. Hmmm? I wonder why they need so many bedrooms. "This little room would be perfect for you to sleep in, Teddy, if you ever come for a sleep-over.", the nice woman offers. What I can't get over is how this house, which looks rather small from the outside, is quite ample enough on the inside. I am thinking I could *probably* live here quite comfortably—especially if I am to be the only boy here, forever.

As "Mrs. Thompson" shows us around, I can't help myself but ask some of the many questions popping into my head. "Who's sleeping in there? Who is in here? Who is in this picture? Do you have any other children? Do you want me to stay here? Whose doggie is Skipper? Where can I go potty? Is "'r. Thompson' your daddy? Do you have a horsey? Can I have one of those muffins, please?"...and on, and on I prattle.

Revolving Doors

Of course, she has to sort-of guess at what I'm trying to ask, since my spoken words are not easily understood yet.

However, she does a fairly good job of interpreting my babble. The most important thing she said was, if I want to stay here some night, "Skipper", (who usually stays outside in his doghouse), **can sleep in my room, or even on my bed** if I really want him to.

Really! *I don't think I heard a single thing after those inviting words.*

"Where you doin'?" I ask when she seats us back in the living room and walks around the corner. "Oh, I'm just in the kitchen putting the kettle on to make some tea, dear." (Oh, good—she understands me.) Then, I go right in there after her to observe this curious activity called, "making T". Shortly, a man of medium build, also with a pale complexion and dark brown hair, comes through a back door and up the four steps to the kitchen. "Hi-Ya!" I blurt. "Hello there, you must be Teddy!" the man says, seeming genuinely pleased to make my acquaintance. I nod in agreement. "I'm 'Mr. Thompson', Teddy—and it's very nice to meet you." this gentleman adds. Then he kneels down to shake my small hand, which disappears inside his big, strong, rough, manly hand. I shake his hand too, but right now, I am fighting the doggie for his master's attention.

I can tell how excited "Skipper" is to see "Mr. Thompson", because the doggie's tail is *wagging him*! I can't stop laughing at the silly doggie, silly "Tipper"! "Tipper's pfunny, wteally pfunny! Hee, hee, hee, hee..." "Would you like to give the doggie a bone, Teddy?" the man asks. "Dess so." As if previously arranged, "Mrs. Thompson" hands him a soup-bone, long past its usual usefulness, and "Mr. Thompson" gives it to me, demonstrating how to hold it and what to say to the doggie. "Tell him to sit. Say, 'Sit, Skipper, sit!'" "Tsit, Tipper, tsit!" It wasn't perfect, but "Skipper" gets the message—and complies by sitting utterly motionless. "And..." the man continues, "when he does what you ask, say, 'Atta-boy! Atta-boy!' O.K.?" Carefully, I reached the bone toward the doggie and he eased it very gently from my hand.

Now, we are friends—dare I say, *forever*? "Atta-boy! Atta-boy!" (Though I am unaware of it at this time, this is actually my *first* of a multitude of "life's lessons" which will be taught to me by the "adoptive" father, "Mr. Ralph Thompson".)

"Is the tea on yet, Lillian?" he asks his wife, but before she can answer, she is summoned by a soft tapping at the front door. "Oh, it's our nearest neighbours, 'Mrs...' and her little boy, John. I told them you were coming for tea today and she promised to stop by so you boys could meet each other." Then she opens the door and ushers them inside. It's a woman, younger in appearance than "Mrs. Thompson" is and she is holding the hand of a little feller who is about three-years-old. In the living room, the boy is very quiet and sits on his mother's knee, keeping a stranglehold around her neck. While the adults drink their tea, everyone enjoys something from the large plate of homemade cookies our hostess is passing around. I wonder if this woman might be my next "mother".

"Teddy, John lives on the next farm over. I'll bet you two could become very good friends.", "Mrs. Thompson" eagerly suggests, waving her arm in the direction of their place. I don't really care about the boy, after all, I am here to see if I like the "Thompsons", and if they like me. (I'm not interested in the suckie, little *baby* on his mommy's knee.)

"Would you like a soda, Teddy?" the woman, I mean, "Mrs. Thompson", asks. "Dunno. Dess so.", is my answer, because I don't think I've ever tasted a *soda* from any bottle which looked like the one she's holding. She pops the metal top off the glass bottle of root beer and hands it to me. A thin, ghostly plume, like a genie, is winding its way out of the bottle. I figure-out pretty darn quickly how to drink from the soda-pop bottle without spilling a drop, (except for the first fizzy spritz, which went straight up my nose. Ooooh, *it* tickled!) In between bites of several of "Mrs. Thompson's" delicious homemade *peanut butter* cookies, she asks me if I don't like the oatmeal-raisin, or the chocolate chip, ones. (Oh, I wasn't gonna try anything with little black things in it, just on the off chance they might be rat-raisins—ooh, yucky, bad thought, bad *memory*.) "I dess so." Bravely, I try them both, and boy have I been missing-out on some deee-licious treats. "Say thank-you, Teddy.", "L.L." whispers in my ear. "Tsank-you pfor da cookies and da Woot Beer pop." (Good enough.)

Then, "Mr. Thompson" asks me, "Teddy, would you like to come out back and see the farm animals? We have pigs, cows, chickens, ducks, geese and turkeys out there." "Yes!" I reply followed by a wild nod of agreement. "John, you come along too." he suggests. However, John declines, while clinging tighter to his mother's neck. When the man and I go down the steps to the back door, I notice a few steps to the side going further down into a basement, which is visible from the daylight streaming in through its windows. I shudder a little, as some bad "basement" memories wash over me for an instant. These thoughts are followed by my hope this will not be another horrid basement existence.

"Whe-wee, whe-wee!" The man whistles for "Skipper" to join us as we head out back of the house. The doggie knows the routine and races on ahead of us, his tail still wagging him! Just as I am pondering the awful possibility of another cellar existence, we arrive at the pigs' pen. It's where I noticed the fenced area when we drove up here. It's adjacent to a tractor shed with a very large lean-to attached behind it, on the leeward side. It certainly looks a great deal bigger when you are standing this close—and, of course, so do the piggies.

As we get nearer, I hear some grunting and snorting and see the two grown pigs lying down in a dip at the corner of their pen. They are quite terrifying, because they're so humongous! Of course, they're really, really, really stinky too! One pig is the "sow"--the girl, and the other is the "boar"-- the boy. (This would be my second lesson from the man, I mean, "Mr. Thompson".) They're absolutely massive and the ugly old boar looks at me as if he could *eat me,* if I came over on his side of the rail fence. "Teddy, be careful to always stay away from 'Bobby-Boy'. That boar's even meaner than he looks." (O.K., I got it! You don't have to tell me twice.) "Sally-Girl", the sow, is lying on her side and seems to be ignoring me completely— except I can see her one tiny little eye follow my movement past her. I believe I won't be trying to pet either of those pigs too much—probably not at all.)

As we drove in, I noticed the two cows as well, but they certainly look a whole lot bigger when you're standing right beside them. Then we go under the lean-to, which is around on the other side, sheltering the poultry and keeping them warm enough to all stay there right through the winter. "We get our fresh eggs from our chickens, Teddy." the man says, (lesson three). Inside the coop, the chickens are pecking away at stuff on the ground. There is also a big white rooster running towards us with his wings spread wide. He's squawking like mad because we are getting too near his brood. Then, a little nervously repeating himself, "Mr. Thompson" says, "We get eggs every single day from our chickens, Teddy. If you come back another time, I can show you how we collect the eggs, if you'd like to come back and see." this nice man gently suggests, without putting any pressure on me. However, I *do* want to come back and I *also* want to see how they get the eggs. So I nod wildly in accord. Sounds like a very good plan to me.

Back up the little hill we go, with the doggie joyfully running ahead. Every few steps he turns around as if to say, *"Come-on, you slow-poke people! Come-on! There's bones and cookies a-waitin' up at the house! Hurry up!"* He is actually running and turning around in excited circles at the same time. He's such a happy doggie and I am happy too because I know I'll be spending a lot more time with him, if they'll *let* me come back. I've already decided I'd like to come back here to gather eggs and help him with the farm animals. However, most of all, I'd like to come back here and play with "Skipper". I am halfway convinced that any parents who care for such a nice doggie, might possibly care for me the same kind and gentle way. Yes, I am hopeful for a return visit here.

Back at the house, the neighbour-lady excused herself and left just before my visit was to end also. I waved "Bye-bye!" to John, thinking maybe we can play with each other another time. "Thank you for coming to tea today, Teddy!", "Mrs. Thompson" says warmly, as we are getting ready to leave. Then she adds, "Won't you please come back to visit us another day? Maybe you could come for a sleepover, too, if you'd like. Remember, there's a spare room here with a bed just for you." "Mr. Thompson" nods in agreement adding, "Don't forget—you can help me get eggs from the chicken nests and feed all the animals too, when you come back. O.K.?" I wonder if these folks really *mean* what they say. Actually, it all sounds almost too good to be true.

While "Librarian Lady" squeezes me back into the rear seat where I am *re-wedged* snugly between the laundry piles, the "Thompsons" are waving their "Good-Byes" from the front door. Then "L.L." goes back to speak to them once more, but I can't hear their conversation. She returns, and we are off to, well...where to now? "Did you have fun today?" she asks me.

"Yes!" "Would you like to come back for another visit sometime soon?" "Yes!" "Can I take my twike?" I ask. "Certainly." is her answer. "Is diss my new house?" "We'll see, Teddy." "When can I come back?" I ask, and she responds, "Very, very soon." "Where we doin'?" "I'm sorry Teddy, but we do have to get you settled in the 'Children's Residence', but only temporarily, I think. (She means the *orphan asylum*, and I hope "temporarily" means "a few days". I can handle that, knowing I have a place as nice as the "Thompsons'" farm to go back and visit.)

[When the Social Worker stepped back inside to question the "Thompsons" about the visit, they both said they, *"are **thrilled** with Teddy and truly want him back soon for another visit, so (they) can all get to know one another a lot better".*]

Chapter 50: My Very Own "WADIO FWYER" Wagon!

I have only been back in the "baby" ward for two days when Mr. "Big Ears" comes to see me. He says he picked up my tricycle from "Songbird's" tin house, but he had to try to straighten out the big front wheel because "Mr...", "Songbird's" husband, had accidentally backed his car over it. "Oh—O.K., I dess." Nevertheless, he said he had a big *red* surprise for me. What could it be? Then he took me outside and showed me a red "Radio Flyer" wagon, just my size. [115] Wow! For me? It is absolutely great! I just can't even believe he brought me a wagon! He said it was too small for his son to play with anymore and it was all mine now. Wowee! I can already think of *many* uses for a red wagon on a farm. Maybe I can help "Mr. Thompson" collect the eggs and put them in my wagon. On the other hand, I could put some ducks, or even a turkey, in it and ride them all over the place. Or else, John could pull me in it. (No, that would have to be the other way around.) Of course, I could collect some neat rocks and keep them in my room, or maybe I might find some huge boulders and build a fort. The possibilities are endless when you have a little red "Radio Flyer", [115], wagon just your size! "Dank you!" I use my best manners!

"Teddy, you only need to just stick it out here for a little longer, because, before you know it, you will be going back to the farm." Does he know something I don't know? He must have inside knowledge because he is very encouraging to me. In fact, he actually winked as he said this, as if he is privy to some great secret. So I decide to do exactly as he says and stick it out here, for now.

Revolving Doors

Chapter 51: "High Tea" and *Horseys*

I woke up to sunshine's bright grin today and immediately I was happily informed about my return visit to the "Thompsons", which will be this *very* afternoon! One of the nursing aides is getting me dressed and organized to go for another nice visit. "Can I take my wagon?" I ask. "I'll find out for you, Teddy." she assures. "Mousey" pokes her head in the baby ward and asks if I am ready yet, because her husband is waiting in the car. In no time at all, I am in "Mousey's" husband's big Buick, (with the panel now repaired), and we are headed back out to the country to visit my new, possible forever parents. I remember some of the twists and turns of the long drive and, thankfully, it seems to go a little faster this time.

Before I know it, I am sitting in the living room and "Mrs. Thompson" is offering tea to "Mousey", and soda pop to me. Of course, a *huge* plate of cookies always accompanies the drinks in this house. ("Mrs. Thompson" explained to me, that "having tea", or "high tea time", are expressions which simply mean having an afternoon snack around three or four o'clock—you know, a drink with some cookies, muffins, or a slice of cake, or sometimes even pie. I believe I could really get used to this "high tea" time.)

"How would you like to go see some horseys, Teddy?" the lady, I mean "Mrs. Thompson" asks me. "Dere's no horseys in da backyard." I tell her. "No, dear, let's go for a little walk to the neighbours place—to John's daddy's farm, because they have the horseys over there. O.K.?" "O.K.!" So we walk over to John's house to see the horses in the field beside his big red barn, (naturally, being accompanied the whole way by "Skipper"). These beasts are massive when you get up close to them. When they breathe, they're so loud and hot air comes out of their drippy nostrils. When they "speak", they say, "Neigh...Neigh...Neigh...")! *But*—when "Mrs. Thompson" scratches under their chins, it makes their top lip lift up as if they're laughing. But it also exposes their huge chompers, making me just a little bit worried, wondering if horseys eat little boys.

"It's alright, Teddy, they won't hurt you. When you get to know them a little better, we can get you up on one for a ride!" "Mrs. Thompson" promises. She is visibly pleased to see my interest in the animals. "Here Nellie-girl, here Nellie, Nellie!" "Mrs. Thompson" is making kissing sounds and is calling one particular horse over to the fence by us. Then, responding to her *kisses*, a beautiful, tan female "Quarter-horse", with a pure white blaze between her eyes, walks right up to us. "Mrs. Thompson" lets me pet "Nellie" on her nose, and give her two little cubes of sugar to eat. Her face is so soft and almost silky feeling. "It's good to see you making friends with Nellie because she actually belongs to us. We just board her over here so she isn't lonely, and has a warm place to sleep with the other horses in their big barn." "Mrs. Thompson" explains.

Oh boy, that's great! They even have a horsey! I love "Nellie" already. Right now, "Mrs. Thompson" has helped me climb up onto the top fence rail to get a better look at the horsey, sort of eye-to-eye. I look deep into her shiny, black eyes. The light makes them dance a little, but there is something else—it is something her solemn eyes are saying to me. I listen for her thoughts and I think I hear in harmony with her every out-breath, *"It's alright little boy. It's alright. It's alright. It's right..."* For a little while, as I sit on the fence, I totally forget who I am, what I've been through and what is on the other side of the next revolving door, *after I'm forced to leave this house.* I believe I can safely say, "It's almost good." Right now, at this very minute, it is *alright,* indeed.

We head back over to the house and see "Mr. Thompson" who has arrived home from work. His *other* job, the one he does when isn't being a farmer, is working in a big office building in downtown Toronto. He's a "Cost Accountant for the T.T.C.", (the Toronto Transit Commission) [166]. I don't know what exactly he does but he says it draws the wrinkly lines on his forehead and is going to make more gray hairs pop right outta his head! [Of course, I will understand, as time goes by, he simply meant the job makes him *worry* a great deal.]

While I play with "Skipper" "Mr. Thompson" asks if I would like to brush the big doggie. While I do, his wife starts to make her husband's supper of pork chops, green beans and macaroni and cheese. For a snack before I have to leave, she offers me some of the steaming hot little macaroni noodles dripping with melted cheddar cheese. I've discovered it is the one thing I *do* like, which is served hot, slimy and cheesy! So, I chow down on a big bowl as if I've never seen food before, but every so often, I'm secretly slipping my new *bestest* friend a cheesy noodle. Hmmm...I think this woman may possibly do just fine as a "mother" for me and she's not a bad cook, either.

"We have to get going now, Teddy.", "Mousey" urges. "I'm sorry we didn't have much time to play today, but I promise next visit we'll do lots and lots of fun stuff!" the man called, "Ralph" says, encouragingly. "My wadon? Where's my wadon?" "Oh, right. He brought his newly acquired little "Radio Flyer", [115], wagon with him on this visit, but it's still out in the car." "Mousey" explains. "Can you pwease put my widdle, wed, 'Wadio Fwyer' wagon in da daradse?" "Of course." the man agrees, without hesitation, then he remembers to tell me, "Next time you come, bring your PJs". "What's dat?" I ask. (I just forgot for a minute). Then he explains, so, of course, I agree. I have to wonder though, if he really means what he says. (I am just the tiniest bit nervous about putting on my jammies in front of these folks, but I quickly push the *bad* thought, {and creepy memory of "Rita"}, right out of my mind.)

Even though we have to return to the orphanage, every day is looking a little brighter now I'm getting to know the "Thompsons" and what nice folks they appear to be. Of course, I can also play with "Skipper" and now the beautiful "Nellie" too. It's already dark as we head back down the long driveway to the main road. I notice my escort has turned the lights on in front of the car. "Do you put da wights on because you're afwaid?" I question her. However, she explains why the car lights have to be on when it's dark outside. "Oh, uh, if I'm afwaid, can I hab a wight on at da 'Thompsons'' house? Will dey wet me?" "You know what, Teddy, I'm sure the "Thompsons" won't have any problem with you keeping a little light on in your room, especially if you are a bit uneasy there at night. In fact, if you like, I will mention it to them." It was the perfect answer. "What do you think of all the farm animals you met today, Teddy?" she asks. I tell her I like the horseys, but I don't like the big old pigs—they're scary! I'm gonna shoot them with my six-shooter gun! Oh, and I added the chickens and duckies are nice, but I don't like the big *boy* turkey called "Tom".

Back at the asylum, I settle into bed without any fuss. I don't need to worry about missing supper because I ate so many cheddary noodles I'm full enough to go right to sleep now. Besides, I know it's only a matter of a few more days or weeks, before I can go back to the farm and play with my new-possible-maybe-adoptive-forever-parents. It is much easier to bear the routines and the stuck feeling in here when I notice the imaginary revolving door is slowing down and—almost— yes, almost...stopping to let me in for, hopefully, my final ride.

It has been four sleeps since I saw the horseys and played with "Skipper" and, guess who just showed up in here. It's "Librarian Lady" and she is telling me to get up because we are going to see the "Thompsons" again, in a very short while. "My cowboy suit...can I wear it?" I plead. "What a wonderful idea, Teddy. I guess "Mr. and Mrs. Thompson" haven't seen your new cowboy suit yet, have they?" she asks. Then, we get me dressed, including my "Hopalong Cassidy Watch", [104], and she brushes my hair in place.

I explain I want to bring along my "Hoppy" doll with his horse "Topper", my "View Master", [102], my "Muffin the Mule", [103],...and..." "I think you've got enough toys to bring with you today, Teddy. Oh, and I've already got your trike in my sister's car, so let's get going—O.K.?" (Oh—her sister's station wagon again. I hope she finished doing her laundry by now.) Out at the car I ask her to double-check the tricycle is truly in the car. She reveals it, explaining it had been a little crushed by her husband's car, (my last "forever father"). However, "Mr..." (that's "Ears"), straightened it out for me. (Isn't he a nice man?)

Off we go, stopping only momentarily for some gas at the "Texaco" filling station. [116] (I know this from the big sign with the red and white star and the letter "T" for "Texaco", not for *tea*.) When "L.L." went inside to pay the man, she came out with a black liquorice stick surprise for me! This day is certainly starting out very, very well! It is so strange but the drive out there seems to be getting shorter and shorter. I spend a lot of time turned-around in the back seat waving at all the approaching vehicles' occupants. Some won't wave back, but it really doesn't matter because I am going somewhere very, very special, and this time I really like it, very, very much.

As we pull up to the front of the house, "Skipper" is already jumping up and down wildly as he recognizes us in the car. "Hi—hi there!" "Mrs. Thompson" comes running out to greet us right behind the doggie. (The statue-cat is still sitting in the front window. She looks so real, as if she could jump right down and start playing.) I rub "Skipper's" head and pat his side. We are very glad to see each other again. "Wanna bwush Tipper? Wanna bwush?" A rush of wonderful-smelling baking envelopes us, as we step inside. "I'm just about to remove the cookies from the oven, Teddy, are you ready to eat some nice warm ones?" she asks. "Yes!" I most certainly am—no matter *what is* sticking outta them!

"My goodness, what a handsome cowboy suit you have on! And, are you wearing a 'Hopalong Cassidy Wrist Watch'?", [104], she asks with genuine interest. So, I demonstrate my special watch and my "Hoppy, and horsey "Topper", dolls. "What is this? Do you have a 'Muffin the Mule'? [103] I've never known anybody who had a *real* 'Muffin the Mule' before." "Yes, an' his arms an' wegs move too—see!" (I demonstrate to this nice woman how my "Muffin" moves all around.) "My goodness, but aren't you are a lucky little boy, Teddy!" she exclaims. Right now, I am feeling pretty big and important with all my neat stuff, a-n-d I'm quite surprised she knows about all my neat toys. Next time I might bring "Pom Pom" too. (He isn't a famous toy; nevertheless, he's very *important* to me! I'm just hoping maybe she can help me replace his broken pull-along string.)

"I have something to show you too!" she whispers. I wonder what it could be as she slides it out from under the end table in the living room. Oh, it's a record player. (I have seen an identical one in the playroom at the orphanage.) I didn't know the "Thompsons" had a record player—I really love to hear music. "Teddy, we have some records but they're mostly music for grown-ups—you know, for "Mr. Thompson" and me to dance to. I'll make you a *promise*. If you come back to us for another visit, I'll buy you some records of your very own." the lady gushes. Let's look in this book and you can tell me your favourite songs so I can pick the right records. (I can't believe she is really going to spend her good money on music records—for me!)

I'll hum some of the popular tunes and you tell me which ones you know, O.K.? So we do, and she writes a list then puts it right into her pocket-book so she doesn't forget her promise to me. The list of all the ones I'd really like to have contains all these songs:

1. "Old MacDonald Had a Farm"
2. "I'm Popeye the Sailor Man"
3. "The Good Ship Lollipop"
4. "Grandfather's Clock"
5. "Puffin Billy"
6. "Tubby the Tuba"
7. "All I Want for Christmas (is my two front teeth)"
8. "Looby Lou"
9. "The Teddy Bears' Picnic"
10. "Flick, the Fire Engine"
11. "Sparky, the Talking Train"
12. "The Pied Piper"
[167]

Twelve songs! She is going to try to get me twelve songs! It's a whole lot, and she promises she'll teach me how to use this record player too! (But I'm so smart I could probably figure that out by myself).

"Would you like a soda, dear, or would you rather have some ice cold *milk*?" she asks while reaching into the fridge. "Milk, pwease." "O.K., dear, milk it is. Say, I thought you could help me gather some eggs from the chicken coop today. What do you think of that?" she asks—already knowing what my answer will be. "My wadon? Can we take my wadon pfor da eggs?" "Oh, yes, it will do very nicely, dear." she agrees. She grabs a soft cloth, lines the wagon and out we go to the barn. ("L.L." had to leave for a while but said she'll be back to pick

446

me up at suppertime.) Out at the shed "Mrs. Thompson" gives me a pan of grain and shows me how to feed the chickens. This is great fun! Then we open the gate to the pen where the cows usually stay, and let them out to the fields to graze. "Skipper" helps with all the chores, (or at least he *thinks* he's helping). "Atta boy, Tipper, atta boy!" Then, right back up to the house we hurry with a wagon full of eggs.

The next thing I help "Mrs. Thompson" with is carrying a little basket of dirty laundry down to the basement, to wash in the strange looking machine she uses down there. It is a large, cylindrical, white metal tub on legs with wheels. Across the front it's emblazoned with the manufacturer's name, "*Maytag*". [155] It also has a ringing-out attachment on top, which consists of two parallel rollers, which are pressed tightly together. She feeds the wet laundry through the rollers and they squeeze most of the water out of the items, before she hangs them out on the clothesline. This woman says although it's "old", it still does the job "just fine".

There is nothing noteworthy about the basement, except of course, the monstrosity of an octopus furnace whose great arms reach and stretch all around, attaching to the basement ceiling in several places. As with many basements, part of the floor is cemented, but part is still dirt-floor. You would think I would be a little scared or at least bothered being down in this cellar, but this lady is so kind to me I'm not thinking of anything except asking her a million more questions while she makes the white tub wash their laundry. My favourite part is when she puts stuff through the ringer and it squeezes it as flat as a pancake. It looks funny. "Teddy, dear, don't you *ever* touch those rollers. It would be very dangerous and you could get injured, dear." (I was *just* thinking about doing exactly that! Does she read my mind, too?)

She brings the wrung-out laundry upstairs to the kitchen and puts some of it onto the bottom shelf of the *fridge*. When she sees my astonishment, she explains those few items are made from a fabric called linen and need to be kept damp until she is able to do the ironing. [*Obviously, before irons provided their own steam and spritzing features.*] The rest, of course, she says we'll hang out to dry on the line. Then she asks me, "Do you like wieners, Teddy?" "Yes!" No problem here, I happen to *love* wieners. By the way, what food goes well with wieners? Why, it's macaroni and cheese noodles, of course. I get busy making quick work of eating lunch, but as always, sharing a little with my new best friend.

My gosh...I'm having so much fun here, at least for now, anyway. (Every now and then I think I hear the whispered *"sweep, sweep, sweep"* of another revolving door slowly coming around for me, and I'm afraid it will suck me in. It is just that, right now, I am having a great time here, and I don't want to leave the "Thompsons'" house! After all, what house, {or parents}, could possibly be any better than this one, {or these}?)

"After lunch, I thought you and I could play 'Candy Land'." the woman suggests. "What's dat?" I query. "Oh, it's a children's *board game,* and it's a whole lotta fun, dear." "Noooo! Oh, noooo! Pwease, noooo!" is my reply, of course. (She doesn't *know*—she can't understand why I don't ever want to play a *bored* game—never!) She seems a little startled but doesn't press the issue. "No problem, sweetie. What would *you* like to do?" I don't know what I want to do. I only know what I *don't* want to do. Then I remember and ask her, "Can we do see da horseys?" "Excellent idea!" She says she couldn't agree more.

Off we go, with the doggie, of course, to go see "Blinkey", "Chesnut" and "Dapple". Those aren't their real names but what I'm gonna call them. "Blinkey" is a very big black stallion who does a lot of blinking with his long eyelashes. "Chestnut" is a large girl horsey, the colour of, well, chestnuts and "Dapple" is a much smaller little girl and I chose to name after her dapple-grey colouring. "Did I tell you there is a new little pony on "Mr.'s..." farm?" "Mrs. Thompson" asks. "No." (Did she say, "Mr.'...s" farm? Wasn't that John's mommy's and daddy's name? That piece of information somehow didn't sink in before now.)

"Let's knock on the door and ask if we can go into the barn to see the new pony." Then, after a few polite taps on John's door, his dad not only gives us permission, but also escorts us into their very large red barn, with the huge, grey, grain silo attached. Inside, lying on a pile of clean, dry straw, is a beautiful, sleek and shiny, black "Friesian" pony. We are told his name is "Midnight Blue Star". What a perfect name for this deepest, blue-black little colt, with a perfect white star on his "forehead"! He *is* the most beautiful thing I've ever seen. I love doggies and kitties too, but my newest love is going to be horseys and ponies, especially this perfect little colt.

"Can I pat him, pwease?" I ask of the farmer, (John's *daddy)*, who nods affirmatively. I don't know why but as I pet this amazing animal's warm, soft nose, I find myself crying, and the more I pat the pony, the more I am crying, uncontrollably. "Teddy, dear, what's the matter Teddy? Are you alright?" the "mother" asks gently, while kneeling and hugging me firmly. "I dunno." *"He won't bite you—I promise you!"* the farmer says, a little defensively. (However, that's not the problem.) Anyway, I keep petting the stunning "Midnight Blue Star", and "Skipper" keeps wagging his tail and pushing his long, slender snout up under my chin. *"Skipper" knows.* Shortly, with the nice doggie's cuddles and encouraging face licks, I stop making my *own* face wet. "Let's go back home now, alright, dear?" "Mrs. Thompson" suggests. "Say 'thank-you' to 'Mr...' for letting us see the pony." she urges. "Tsanks pfor wetting me pet da pony." I choke-out my best manners, considering the

Revolving Doors
circumstances.

It's very late in the afternoon and "Mr. Thompson" is already home from work when we arrive back at the house. "Where'd you two get to?" he asks us. "We were over next door seeing their horses, and the new little Friesian they got." "I bet you had lots of fun, Teddy, wasn't it?" he adds, encouragingly. "Mrs. Thompson" explains, "Something upset him and made him start to cry when he was looking at the pony." "Were you scared, Teddy?" "No...I dunno what made me cwy." is all I can say. "Oh well, let's get the dinner started so you can eat before 'Mrs...' comes back to pick you up.", she suggests.

I sort of *did* know why I was crying. It had something to do with how wonderful my life *seems* to be today, especially compared to the way it always *has* been for me. When I saw the beautiful pony, I thought this might be a good place to hide, (whenever the "Thompsons" change, and become mean to me). I know they're being very nice now, but from my experience, I am certain it's only a matter of time before they change. I don't know when that day will be, but I do know it will most certainly come—it always does, sooner or later. If they ever start whipping me with one of "Mr. Thompson's" black leather belts, or if I ever have to stay down in their basement instead of in the bedroom they pretend is just for me, I'll climb out one of the cellar windows and run right over here. "Midnight Blue Star" and his straw bed will keep me warm for sure, and he'll keep me company so I am not frightened or lonely. This is my plan, and it's a good one too.

"Is 'Mrs...' running late today?" the man asks his wife about my Social Worker. Then, reading his mind, she says, "Right, dear, I think we'll just go ahead and give Teddy supper here, anyway." Then, while awaiting supper, "Mr. Thompson" and I go down to the basement to clean-up my "Radio Flyer", [115], wagon after the egg collecting dirtied it up so badly. (I never knew the eggs didn't come out of chickens' bums all nice and clean. They're all mucky with chicken poop and need to be washed off in the basin and wiped dry, one at a time—and you can't hurry the job or you'll end up breaking them. Today's lesson is the fourth which "Mr. Thompson" has taught me so far.)

After he washes-out my "Radio Flyer" wagon, he dries it with a rag and gets some kind of oil from a small can with a long, pointy spout. "What's dat?" I ask, genuinely curious as to what he is doing to my prized wagon. "Pay attention, son, and I'll tell you exactly what we're doing." As he pushes the bottom of the can in and out to get the oil onto the metal wagon, it makes a funny noise, sort of, "Click-clack, click-clack." Then he shows me how to wipe it all over, first spreading the oil, then following-up with a dry rag to polish it. "This will keep it from rusting, and ruining, Teddy." he instructs. Then he oils the wheels also, explaining the oil makes them turn better. (Lesson five—well, don't you just learn something new every day—especially around here!)

While we are still down in the cellar, we hear "Skipper" announcing "Mrs'..." arrival, so we hurry back up the steps to the kitchen. She is making a breathy apology, "I'm sorry for being so late. Something came up, last minute, at the office. Are you ready, Teddy?" "L.L." says. "I'm sorry you won't have time to eat supper, dear. Oh, well, here's your jacket...here, Teddy." "Mrs. Thompson" says this as she helps me on with my coat. Then both the "Thompsons" walk me out to the car.

"Did you have a lot of fun today, Teddy?" my escort asks me. "Yes, an' we got eggs an' cweaned da poop outta my wagon!" (I was hoping the lady wouldn't tell her how I cried like a little baby while visiting the pony—and, thankfully, she never said a word. She did not spill the beans! I'm not certain, but I am beginning to think maybe, just *may—be*...she can be trusted. However, the man knew also, and he did not tell on me— maybe he can be trus... Oh, never mind.) I'll just take it as a good omen that both of the "Thompsons" were asking repeatedly for me to, "Please come back again!" I nodded my agreement. (I'll be alright the next time. I won't cry again. Moreover, when they **do** start to be mean to me, as all foster parents end up doing eventually, I've already started formulating my escape plan. Until that day comes, I'll just have to start collecting a few necessities and find a good hidey-hole somewhere in the house to stash them in.)

Before we leave, "Mr. Thompson" comes up to me, shakes my hand like a gentleman and says, "Teddy, we really want you to come back to see us, won't you promise?" Again, I nod my answer. Then I give "Skipper" a great big teddy-bear hug around his neck, and "Skipper" stands up, puts each of his front legs on my shoulders, and hugs me right back. He sure makes me giggle! Not one to be left out of a tender moment, "Mrs. Thompson" kneels down and hugs me too; in fact, I think it was more like a squeeze! Then she said this funny little rhyme,

"Apple pie without the cheese is like a hug without a squeeze!"

It feels nice, very nice indeed. I could definitely do with a few more of her huggy-squeezes in my life, (and maybe a little of the apple pie with cheese, too.)

Chapter 52: My Big "Sweep-Ober" Weekend

Today, when the sun whispered, "Good Morning Teddy", I was already wide-awake and jumping up and down in my crib-cage. "Get me outta dis cwib!" I want to get dressed, and hurry up and leave this ward today. I can't wait to get to see "Mrs. Thompson" especially because she promised to get me some recordings of my favourite music, and I believed her. It seems like *forever* before "L.L." comes to get me—I mean *for-ev-er!*

There she is, now. "Hi Teddy, it's time to go to see the 'Thompsons' again, O.K.? Do you want to wear a cowboy suit again?" I nod my 'yes' reply. "Which one, blue or brown?" she asks. I point to my new dark blue, besides I'm actually getting too big for the old brown one I got from "Wide Load". While I am dressing myself, she is packing my little blue suitcase with my other clothes and some toys. "Don't pfordet 'Pom Pom', pwease, an' my pfarm aminals." "Do you want to bring along this box of candy our Aide, 'Jenny' brought in for you?" Of course I do, because after all, *"A day without candy is like a day without sunshine!"* ("Mrs. Thompson" invented that little rhyme, as well. I think she is very clever, and funny.)

We are ready for anything now, so off "we", I mean "*I*" go—for the whole weekend. When we get to the farmhouse, "Mrs. Thompson" opens the door and has a big, wide grin on her face. "Did you wemember my wecords?" I ask her. "Oh, no, I forgot, Teddy." "Weally? Oh." "No, not really! Of course I remembered, but you'll have to hunt for them because I hid them very well." Oh, I see. I guess she reads my disappointed expression, because she quickly says, "It's a game, Teddy...a fun little game for you to hunt and find them. O.K.?" "Oh!" I get it now. So I run around the house and look here, there and everywhere and I am almost about to give up when she tells me, "You're getting warmer—even warmer—now you're hot!"

Revolving Doors

Oh, there they *are*, in the end table drawer.

Oh my goodness...there are *so* many records. "I had to get a lot to find all your favourite songs, dear.", "I'n a wucky wittle boy!" I tell her while skipping in circles around the living room. "Let me help you work the record player, Teddy." "No—I'n doin' it, I'n doin' it." However, it's a little more complicated than I expected so she does have to help me, (this one time anyway). This is such great fun! I can sing along to all the songs I've heard and I can quickly memorize the words. It was very nice of her to buy me these records. She is very kind to me. "Oh, I brought my candy box. Can I put it in da pfwidse?" She says it's fine, so I do, taking one at a time. Then I run and play, take another candy, and on and on, back and forth 'till all my candies in the fridge are gone.

Just when I'm in the middle of playing my music, John and his mum come over again. They just walk right in this time since we didn't hear their knocking. How could we? I'm dancing around to the music and "Mrs. Thompson" is singing along and clapping her hands, and we are both laughing our heads off! Soon after he gets here, I discover John likes music as much as I do, and he *is* impressed with my new record collection. In fact, there is not one selection he doesn't like. Also, I can't believe it but his very favourite is also "Old MacDonald's Farm"! So we sing and sort-of dance and jump around, being fire engines, or trains. Then we dance to "Looby Lou" and sing "Old MacDonald Had a Farm" *five-hundred* times.

We are having so much fun, in fact, we don't even want to stop for lunch, but we force ourselves. I really like chicken noodle soup and "Mrs. Thompson's" is homemade, and not out of a can. She even taught me how to scrunch-up little crackers all over the top of my soup too. So far, there isn't one single thing I don't like about this nice woman. Of course, I will reserve my final judgement until I've been here on a more long-term basis than just one little weekend sleep-over.

"Are you staying to supper, Florence?" "Mrs. Thompson" asks. "Well, I guess we could, Lillian, because Fred will be late coming home tonight." Then "Mrs. Thompson" excuses, "We're just having an upside-down-supper tonight. I hope you don't mind." "What's dat?" I ask, because it sounds as if we are supposed to eat while standing on our heads. "Wike dis?" I ask, while trying to stand on my head. "Mrs. Thompson" and "Florence" start laughing so much. "No, dear, it only means breakfast for supper, but I suppose we *could* try eating while standing on our heads. Why not?" Now everybody is laughing! Anyway, I get it—like bacon and eggs and fresh biscuits, (breakfast, only served at suppertime), and it sounds just fine to me. "Teddy, will you and little John please run out to the barn and gather a few more eggs for our supper? Here's a basket—be careful and try not to break any of them. Oh, and steer clear of the darned, mean old rooster, 'Russell'. He seems to be on the warpath these days."

John and I take my "Radio Flyer", [115], wagon and go to collect some eggs. We steer a wide path past "Bobby-Boy". Then our only obstacle to a fresh, eggy supper is the rooster, because he doesn't seem to want us to get near his chickens, or his eggs. He keeps running up to us and squawking and waving his wings out and acting as if he's gonna bite us! (Do roosters have teeth?) So, John, who has the same breeds of birds on his farm, jumps around waving *his* arms and scaring the daylights out of all these birds, while "Skipper" barks his head off, and I grab the eggs! The three of us make a perfect team. We carry them back to the lady, I mean "Mrs. Thompson", and she is very pleased to see how many we got and exclaims, "You boys didn't break a-one! I'm very proud of you both!"

Revolving Doors

While we wait on the grub, I ask John if he likes Tinkertoys, [45], because I have a million of them that Danny gave me for my fifth birthday. John does like 'em, so we play 'building with the Tinkertoys', [45], until "Mr. Thompson" gets home which is the signal it's time for *eats*. (However, this time I am not leaving.) It certainly is lots of fun having a little kid like me to eat with, so I try to eat a big upside-down supper to please the "Thompsons". Right after supper, "Mr. Thompson" lies down on the chesterfield in the living room because he's not feeling very well tonight. (I betcha it's all those grey hairs poking through his head are what's causing his headache.)

By the time John and his mum are barely out the door, I am already in the tub—with bubbles! Say, I'm thinkin' a feller could really get used to such treatment! The bubble bath, I must admit, was quite enjoyable, and "Mrs. Thompson" even washed my face, ears and neck very gently. *She* never said a word about *potatoes* growing behind my ears, but she looked extremely concerned when she washed my chest and felt the lump However, when she questioned me, I just turned away in silence. After all—what *could* I tell her?

Anyway, moments later, I'm outta the tub, have my jammies on and "Mr. Thompson" has joined us for my bedtime story. He says his head feels a lot better now and asks what story I would like to hear. They show me the two books on the nightstand which they *bought* just for *me*. One is titled, "*Fairy Tales*" and the other is "*Fairy Tales Told for Children*". [118] The author of both is a man from Denmark named, "Hans Christian Andersen". "Mrs. Thompson" told me this, and how each book is a collection of several stories which this man wrote for *all* children to read, or to have read *to* them. I choose, "The Emperor's New Clothes", because "Mrs. Thompson" says it gonna be a funny one. (Naturally, she's right, as usual.)

Revolving Doors

Then it's lights out time, except for the small little lamp sitting on the brown wooden dresser. It is shaped like an old balloon-selling man. He's sort-of bent-over, wearing shabby clothes and holding colourful red, yellow and blue balloons. They're the part of the lamp which stays lit for me all night, or at least these folks, the "Thompsons", have promised me this. Shortly, they both say, "Nite, nite...", and I am horrified—but mistaken, because they continue with, "...sleep tight, Teddy dear." That's it! No bed bugs tonight! I'm alright now. I can hardly believe my good fortune today. I can rest now.

Though the sun is working hard, it's forcing very little light through my bedroom curtains in its pronouncement of today's fresh start. I am not sure for a moment where I'm at, but then I look down at the foot of my bed and there is "Skipper" snoring, as only big doggies are able to. When I see that I am not still dreaming, and remember where I am now, I jump out of the bed and run to see who else is up. It's Saturday and "Mr. Thompson" is drinking coffee at the kitchen table because, thankfully, today he doesn't have to go to his job which makes his gray hairs stick through his scalp. Today we can play and work in the barn, and he can teach me things and we can have lots and lots of fun together. I certainly *hope so* anyway.

"Mrs. Thompson" is making fresh biscuits in the oven and I'm working-up an appetite. "Mr. Thompson" tells me that always on the weekends, the eggs are scrambling in the pan, and sausages, bacon or kidneys are sizzling in the heavy, black, cast-iron skillet. "Teddy, sometimes my wife makes her speciality, Home-Made Chilli, and it has actually won awards!" her husband proudly boasts. [By the way, *I am still making my mother's chilli recipe to this very day.*] "Do you like farmer's potatoes, dear?" "Mrs. Thompson" asks me. "Dunno." (I'll at least hold off my judgement until I've tasted the so-called, "farmer's potatoes".)

There is a little jar of "Mrs. Thompson's" great-great-grand-mother's recipe, home-made strawberry preserves on the table next to the silver rack of toasted white bread awaiting generous dollops from the pot of hand-churned butter. "Here's your milk, Teddy." the woman says. Then she hands me a very big glass of fresh, cow-made milk, from *John's* daddy's cows! (My lesson about *exactly* where our milk comes from will come later on.) "Why don't we all go for a little walk around the property after breakfast, Teddy?" "Mrs. Thompson" suggests. "We'll just tend to everybody first, Lillian, alright?" "Of course, dear." (I can't help but notice how *polite* these parents are to each other, and to me also. However, knowing grown-ups the way I do, I'm fairly certain it's really just an *act* for my benefit.)

"Mr. Thompson" and I hike out to the coop and feed all the birds. It amazes me how these dumb birds are smart enough to know when it's feeding time. As soon as we start spreading the bird-feed around, the chickens and "Russell" rooster, all the ducks and both the turkeys come hurrying and squawking over to us. "The pigs need feeding too, Teddy." "Mr. Thompson" reminds me. I don't like the pigs because they're awfully stinky! They're pretty darn big too, at least compared to me, so I'm afraid to get too near them, especially "Bobby-Boy". I tell the man I forgot the name of the girl piggy. "You mean the *sow—*she's *Susie-Girl*" he replies, with lesson six, of course. "Skipper" is having lots of fun chasing the chickens and especially the squawky rooster! My goodness it certainly is loud around here with the pigs snorting, the ducks quacking, and the chickens clucking, but I think "Russell" is the loudest of everybody!

Later on, after we are all tuckered-out from the big walk around the whole farm, we end up back in the kitchen, where I help "Mrs. Thompson" prepare the snap beans for supper. She shows me what to do and I'm really enjoying helping her. I am not big enough to peel the potatoes, because I could accidentally cut myself, but I am very good at washing them. The woman, I mean "Mrs. Thompson", seasons the steaks and we pretty much have supper almost ready.

"Let's play some music, Teddy! You choose, alright?" she suggests. I drag out the record player and "my records", and start with, "Old MacDonald Had a Farm", because, even after I've played all the other songs it's still my very favourite. She and I play around in the living room and she turns me into a human wheelbarrow! Then I fall down on purpose and we both laugh so much. She also bought me a new colouring book and my very own, brand-new large box of many, many crayons. (Yes, I am a lucky little kid.) Before too long it's the end of another day and bath and bedtime are just a repeat of last night. For my story tonight, I've picked, "The Wild Swans". Lights out, well almost all of them, anyway. Then after huggy-squeezes and butterfly kisses, they say, "Nite, nite...." Yes indeed, nite, nite to you folks also, (and no bedbugs!)

Chapter 53: "Jesus, GOD, the Holy Spirit and Heaven"

Sunday morning has its own set of surprises in store for me. First, of course, is brekkies which consists of a sizzling skillet of farmer's potatoes, which, incidentally, I decided immediately upon my *previous* first bite, I really like, especially with a little of "Mrs. Thompson's" homemade ketchup. However, today we are having her "walk-a-mile for", award-winning Chilli. I quickly discover it to be unquestionably worthy of its title and awards, as it most certainly is the absolute yummiest condiment I could ever imagine tasting.

Then, as soon as we're finished brekkies, I need to get washed-up right away, hair combed, teeth brushed and then dressed-up in—in—what's this? "Mrs. Thompson" bought me a new suit of clothes! It is a navy-blue sport jacket with gray wool slacks and a white, dress-shirt with a little blue bow tie, just like the outfit in the Sears' catalogue. [119] She even bought me shiny new black, "patent-leather" shoes to wear. [121] (While regarding my reflection in their lustre, for a minute I feel myself rubbing my chest where "Rita's" black patent-leather shoe-weapons kicked me and broke my rib. But, it's all healed now, so I quickly push the awful memory out of my mind.) I can see how very handsome my new shoes are, so I simply thank these nice folks for their generosity.

It is not only *me* getting cleaned and spiffed-up. The "Thompsons" are also getting quite spruced-up today. "Mr. Thompson" is wearing a navy-blue, three-piece suit and "Mrs. Thompson" is in a lovely tailored dress, also navy-blue, with a small, round, silver-coloured lapel pin. As ALWAYS, her hair is meticulously coiffed and today she's even wearing a little rouge and lipstick. "Help me with this tie, will you sweetheart?" the man asks his wife. "Double Windsor, today, dear?" she asks. Then with his response she quickly twists the knot around for him until it's just right.

The question is, "*Where are we going that requires all of us to get so gussied up?*"

The answer is, *It's Sunday, and on Sunday, many nice folks, like the "Thompsons", dress up and meet at local places, such as Saint S...'s Anglican Church, to join in Christian worship services.*

Whenever he decides it's time to leave, "Mr. Thompson" backs the car out of the garage and we are off and riding in the family automobile! This stunning car is a brand, spanking-new 1952 Chevrolet, which is massive, with *four* big doors. [120] Wow, it's a beautiful, shiny green on the outside and has a spotless, beige cloth interior and coordinated, beige leather dashboard. I really like this car a lot! (Are these folks rich?) Wow, what a ride-- like I imagine "floating on a cloud" would feel like! No bumpity-bump-bumps here. (I believe I might be just getting luckier by the moment)

At the church, we follow as most of the folks walk straight in through the double front doors to a large room where "Mrs. Thompson" explains the "main services" are to take place. I am getting a little frightened because I don't know what this very large, unusual building is, who all these strangers are or even what the loud music has to do with me. I am quite intimidated by all the folks who are walking in and chatting as they enter in the big church hall, because many of them keep approaching the "Thompsons", shaking their hands and offering sincerest "congratulations".

All I can do is cling even more tightly to "Mr. Thompson's" large, strong hand on my left side and "Mrs. Thompson's" soft hand on my right. She senses my uneasiness and leans down to quietly whisper in my ear, "Don't worry, Teddy, there's no need to be frightened. This is a very nice place and nice folks too. Stick by me, dear, and you'll be just fine." I feel better immediately upon hearing these soothing words.

As we enter this place, I can see many rows of wooden benches lined up on either side of a main, centre aisle. The arriving families are quickly filling-up these pews. (I think it's a funny name because it's what "Slick" said whenever he smelled a skunk and pinched his nostrils with his fingers, "*P— U!*") "Ralph, let's sit here." "Mrs. Thompson" suggests with a wave of her hand indicating the perfect spot. We take our position on the end of a pew adjacent to the main centre aisle, and about halfway up the rows. I am seated between the "Thompsons" who are speaking quietly and grinning with affirmative smiles to those folks nearest themselves. In the benches, everyone has suddenly quieted down and we are all sitting in respectful anticipation, but of what, I certainly don't know. That's curious—I know I saw many children coming in at the same time we did; however, looking around this large church, I can no longer see any of the already-seated children. I can only see the tops of a *few* of their heads.

As it is explained to me in lesson seven by "Mr. Thompson", the nice music we have been hearing is being played on a very large musical instrument called a pipe-organ, or organ'. The change of music is the indication to these churchgoers, and me, that we should now stand up. O.K., so what's next? The sounds also announce the entrance of about twenty men and women, all identically dressed in very long, royal-blue dresses with over-sized, stiffly-starched white collars. The music changes again and these oddly garbed folks begin very slowly walking in, from the main foyer at the church's front entrance doors. Then they start singing in unison as they walk, stepping in time to the music. The "Thompsons", (and everybody else), have opened identical small, blue, leather-bound books which apparently contain words to accompany the songs the "Blue People" [the choir], are singing.

All of these "Blue" folks are intently watching their leader, the "Choir Master", who is standing at the front of the big room. This man is also in a blue dress and looks quite funny to me as he waves his arms all over the place, sort of in time to the organ's tunes. The choir's unified voices and the organ's purely, perfectly unadulterated sounds, and even the attendees', not quite so pure vocalizations, are all so overwhelmingly beautiful, I can hardly believe my ears. (I soon discover "Mrs. Thompson" has an even lovelier singing voice than I had noticed, and she knows all the words to each hymn without even looking at her little blue hymnal. "Mr. Thompson" has a nice, deep, quite pleasing singing voice also.)

When the singing is finished, and we are again seated, "Mr. Thompson", (never missing an opportunity to *teach* me something new), points to the very tall, shiny, golden tubes attached to, and spread across, the entire front wall of the church. He whispers to me about those numerous, gold-coloured, hollow cylinders. He says "They're actually metal pipes of varying sizes through which the pipe-organ is pushing air and making the sounds which our ears receive as purely beauteous music." That is utterly amazing! I am sitting, quite stunned while pondering the question of how could air, being forced through hollow, metal tubes, of varying length and circumference, possibly create such lovely music. But then he tells me the metal pipes work on the same principle as a whistle...only they're huge and have loud, booming sounds which *fill* the church. Oh, O.K., now I understand, sorta.

When I look around, I notice how quietly all the folks are acting, while they appear to be in obvious anticipation of something which is going to happen next. Then, seconds later, two men enter the front of the church where the "Blue People" have taken their seats on either side, (obviously divided by gender). One of the men is in a black suit, with a white shirt and dark-blue/black tie, but the other man is quite differently dressed. Strangely, this gentleman is wearing a black *dress*, reaching all the way to the floor. Over top of this first under-dress, is a not-quite-as-long white *dress*, trimmed in frilly, girly-looking lace. (Hee-hee-hee...he looks like a big girl to me. I wonder if somebody is making him wear girl's panties under those two dresses, just as "Rita" forced me to do, so many, many times.)

The "suited" man sits in one of three, ornately carved, high-backed, wooden chairs, all of which have red-velvet seats and are arranged together in front of the choir. This is the absolutely most unusual place I've ever been in. (Certainly, if it were not for my folks' calm and reassuring manner, I would be quite frightened to death of all this foreign "pomp and circumstance".)

Shortly the organ is silenced and the man in two dresses steps behind a wooden podium. Then, speaking into a microphone, he offers greetings to the regulars after his words of welcome to the visitors. Then he starts talking *a lot*, while reading aloud from a book. It's not any kind book that I am familiar with and I have no idea what he's trying to explain to the congregation. I want to ask some pressing questions, but I decide it's best to just keep my mouth shut instead.

After he reads us one story, the choir stands up and sings a beautifully, moving song about "....The Light...blah, blah...and the Heavens open up...blah, blah, blah". Then the gentleman talks a bit and reads aloud again. At that point in the services, we, the congregation, stand and this time we sing along with the choir, as we follow the words in our little blue hymnals, (assuming, of course, we are able to read). This happens a couple more times before the organist plays a long piece and all the *children* get up and walk in quite an orderly fashion, out of the church, (the same way everyone came in).

"Mrs. Thompson" takes my hand and escorts me to the place where all the kids are supposed to go at this time in the services. We head down some stairs and into one of several small classrooms, all of which are collectively referred to as the, "Sunday School". "Mrs. Thompson" then explains she has to return upstairs to the adult's services. By the nature of the music, she knows the service has already resumed after the children's mass exodus. Before leaving me with the teacher, "Mrs. Thompson" whispers to me, "Don't be afraid dear and remember to mind your manners. Then, in a little while, when you hear the church bells ring, I'll be waiting at the top of the stairs for you." Then she kisses me on top of my head.

I am standing against the wall, waiting for the other "three-to-six-year-olds" to assemble in the small room. I guess, then, we'll be able to get started, but on what, I don't have a clue. I am somewhat uncomfortable as "Mrs. Thompson" leaves me, because this is a little intimidating and I don't know anybody at all. As I glance around the classroom I've been left in, I notice the cheery classroom, though small, is painted bright yellow, with stuck-on decals of children, animals, babies and little lambs, all over on the walls.

There are six teeny-tiny wooden chairs pushed neatly under a long, wooden table also painted bright yellow and sporting similar decals. In one corner of the room are books and art supplies and in the other is a pile of mats, which I assume are for us kids to take a nap on. (These nap mats are making me wonder just how long I'm gonna be staying down here.) Anyway, on the third wall are three wooden toy bins with numerous, assorted, colourful toys overflowing from each. Next to the door is a cart with juice cups and a pink, cardboard bakery box. Along the same wall are hooks for the kids' coats, and when it's wet outside, there's a place for your rubbers, or galoshes, underneath the hanging coats.

I am still leaning against the coat-wall, quite bewildered as I watch all the kiddies' faces as they enter the classroom and take their predetermined seats. Then *John* walks in! It's my friend *John*! "Hi-ya John!" I call to him. Now I know whom to sit beside, and I am not feeling so out-of-place and apprehensive. Ohhhh, now *this* is nice. We are immediately being served apple juice. Hmmm? Now, what's this in the pink box, which is tied crossways with thin, shiny, white string? Wow! It is from a local bakery and contains a million, different kinds of cookies with colourful icing patterns on them!

(I've certainly noticed one thing while visiting with these nice folks, the "Thompsons", and that is, around these parts, people are certainly serious about their cookies!)

Of course, being the newcomer to this Sunday School class, I am told if I need to go *"potty"* to *stick my hand up in the air and wave it around and around.* (Seriously? Will that really help? Oh, I bet *that* was the Choir Master's problem. He just needed to go potty.)

In our little room, after the snack, we sing some songs I've never heard before, but I pick-up quickly. Then our young teacher, Miss Marilyn Banks, sits at the top end of the table and starts telling us stories about some man, named "Jesus" who wasn't really a man. Apparently, this feller was, and wasn't, "God". In fact, he was born in a barn hay-stall, to a humble, impoverished couple. Then he grew up learning the skills of a carpenter. However, in his early thirties he rode around to different towns on a donkey. That's when he became a "fisher-of-men", (which we are informed is *not* the same thing as a "fisherman"). She tells us Jesus really lived in a very far-away place and besides being a man, and "God's" son, he was also "God", and another feller called, "The Holy Spirit" or "The Holy Ghost". (However, she *lost* me at "God".) Anyway, all of these guys live in a place in the sky called "Heaven". She says it's where we all want to go and meet "Jesus" and "God" too, when we die. (I have heard about Heaven before; but I don't quite understand how we *go* anywhere when we are dead, unless we're placed at the Necropolis' Guardian Angel's base, under the feet of "Shekhinah". That part, I *do* understand.) Nevertheless, I'll just listen, keep quiet and go along with whatever they are preaching at us little kids. I suppose it sure can't hurt me, right?

Suddenly some loud organ music and even louder churchy bells, both announce the grown-ups' services upstairs are finished and we can all go home. John and I race each other up the steps and find his *parents* waiting for him and *my paren..*, uh, I mean, the "Thompsons" beside them waiting for me. I didn't notice that John had a handsome daddy until today. (He certainly looks different on the farm, with his face and hands all grimy and his faded, denim overalls equally as grungy.) He seems like a nice man though—a lot like "Mr. Thompson" or maybe a bit younger, I guess.

The "Thompsons" then take me by the hand and walk me around to meet some of the people who are standing and talking in small groups, here and there, in the back of the church, near the doors. They gleefully introduce me to many nice folks who seem genuinely glad to meet me, and all express being "*happy*" for the "Thompsons" too—for their "*good fortune at finally getting [their] little boy*". This is all very nice, however, I'm not sure what all this happiness means for me—or how long it could possibly last.

Finally, they introduce me to the "Minister" (the man wearing two dresses). Oh! He is, as I now understand it, the boss of the church. This seemingly kind man is exceptionally tall and bone-thin, with deep black hair and absolutely no colour in his face, except for the watery, ocean-blue of his eyes. "This is *our* Teddy!" "Mrs. Thompson" says, while absolutely effusive with delight. This girly-man leans down and shakes my hand with his haggard-looking hand. However, I notice, unlike "Mr. Thompson's" hand, the skin on the Minister's palm is strangely soft, indicating to me *his* real job could not possibly be as a *farmer*.

"Very, very pleased to make your acquaintance, Teddy." says the man in the two dresses, and speaking in an unexpectedly deep tone, as if he were still talking through the microphone at his church podium. "Welcome to our church. How nice it is to see you at our services this morning. I suppose you met 'Miss Banks'. How did you enjoy Sunday School, young man?"

Too many questions for me to answer even one As this minister bends down to greet me, I notice he is wearing a silver chain around his neck, and suspended from it is a black wooden cross, about three inches long. While the man in the two dresses bends forward, this cross sort-of swings and hits me in the nose. At that point, I am certainly able to have a very close look at what is on it. Somehow, a tiny carving of a man is attached to the crossbar with little nails through each of his outstretched hands. However, on the up-and-down bar, one of the man's feet is on top of the other one, and both are held in place, having been driven-through with another tiny silver nail. This manly wooden figure is so skinny, his ribs are sticking out, and he has very long hair, down to his shoulders. His face looks very sad, or perhaps he is grimacing because he is in a lot of pain, or something. All the tiny man is wearing is a loosely draped cloth around his bum, which looks very much like the diapers I used to wear in the asylum', (only *his* diaper would certainly be much bigger). I can't seem to take my eyes off the man on the cross, and I wonder what this little figurine might represent.

When the two-dress gentleman notices me staring at his cross, he asks me quite directly, while grasping the sort of talisman, *"Do you know Jesus, son?"* "Uh-uh", I reply negatively. "Jesus is the man who loved *you* so much he died on the cross for you." he tries to explain. (I believe he is obviously jumping at an opportunity to minister to such a sinful, ungodly, pathetic little guttersnipe.) Wow, first, I certainly can't comprehend why this feller, "Jesus" would die on some cross for me, when I don't even know him. (Secondly, exactly *how* do you *die* on a cross, anyway?) I don't even know this man, "Jesus", who wears a diaper. All I have heard is he is a *"man"* like any other man, except He's *sinless, (whatever **that** means)*; He's the *"Lamb of God"*; He's the *"Son of God"*; He's *"God Himself"*; He's everybody's *"Heavenly Father"*; and He is the *"Holy Spirit"*, and so-on and so-on. *Clear as mud!*

I don't understand why he *is, or* how *he could be,* so many people, nor do I see why they all took up residence in some town called "Heaven" way up in the sky. (Where is this "Heaven" in the sky? Is it on the moon? Is Jesus a "Martian" from Mars?) This morning's Sunday School teacher, "Miss Banks", said Jesus' Father, who is supposed to be "God", well, he has a "house" which must be more like a city because inside it's supposed to be really, really big—large enough to contain "many mansions". She also told us there are so many of these places to live in, and how there's a place for everyone to move into when they die, (but then, she clarified, "everyone who says they love Jesus, that is..."). I am totally bewildered and baffled. I certainly don't know why I even *need* to know about the diapered sufferer who got himself nailed up on some big, wooden cross and died—for me. Why didn't he just kick somebody, climb down and run away? (Oh, this is all so darn

Revolving Doors
confusing.)

When the Minister sees that I am completely befuddled, he decides this mini-lesson in one of Christianity's most basic premises can wait for another day. Then, standing back up, he turns to the "Thompsons" and says,

"I am so happy for you folks. Isn't it wonderful when our prayers are answered in a way which is even better than we could have hoped? Congratulations to *all* three of you—and I will continue to pray for things to proceed quickly and smoothly." [*I couldn't know what he's talking about, but he is actually referring to having the "Thompsons'" dream of "adopting" me, finalized.*]

"Go in peace, friends.", he says, smiling a long-toothy smile and waving his arm toward the open main double church doors, as if we might not be able to find our way out.

Anyway, I'm hungry—after all, juice and icing-sugar cookies only last in a little feller's tummy, for just so long. "Ralph, dear, stop at the little corner store and we can pick up a small brick of ice cream for Teddy", "Mrs. Thompson" suggests, obviously reading my mind—again. "Chocolate O.K., Teddy?" she asks, already knowing the answer. "It's Sunday, dear, they won't be open—remember the 'Blue Law'." Ralph replies. [122] "Oh, yes, Ralph, but *I* heard it from a 'little bird', they only have to pay a small fine to get around the law." (Later on, I'll discover, this "mother" is in the regular habit of communicating with "little birds".) Down the road a little way, we *do* stop at the small convenience store and get the ice cream. Yeah! (Lucky for me, I guess the store owner must have paid his "*Blue*" fine.)

Then, it's on home we go, and right in time before a sudden rainstorm hits, with a vengeance. "We wanted to take you back to see the horseys again, Teddy, but now it's raining so heavily, what do you say we play some games instead?" So, we decide to sing, and play games such as, "Red Light-Green Light", "Simon Says", "What Time is it Mr. Wolf?", "Ring Around o' Roses", "Here We Go 'Round the Mulberry Bush" and a bunch of others too. Lunchtime comes and goes and before I know it, it's bedtime. The weather has gotten steadily worse all day and now it has turned into a frightening thunder and lightning storm. [*You have never witnessed a real thunderstorm until you've experienced a southern Ontario thunderstorm—one which is raging off the Great Lakes!*] Anyway, I am tucked into bed and "Mr. Thompson" reads me, "The Steadfast Tin Soldier", which I also like very much because it makes *me* feel a lot braver.

The "Thompsons" tell me goodnight, tuck me in, then each gives me a kiss on top of my head. I must admit, I am just a little bit scared of the storm but I would be a whole lot more frightened if "Skipper" was not up here in the bed snuggled right up tightly beside me. (However, even he's whimpering and whining a little because *he* doesn't like the storm either.) "Mrs. Thompson" knows I am a little nervous so she pulls down the shade and closes the darkening curtains in "my" room. She's trying to hide the lightning flashes from "Skipper" and me. (Just for me she sewed the nice curtains and matching bedspread, with pictures of different doggies all over them.) She thinks of a great idea to keep the thunderclaps from frightening the dog and me. She brings a small radio into the room and turns it on to very nice music playing softly. It is quiet enough to let me sleep, but just loud enough to mask the thunderbolts.

The final storm-coping strategy comes from "Mr. Thompson" who tells me—yes, another lesson—the secret of how you know the storm is passing over—and *getting farther away*. It's a system of counting between the "flash" of lightning and the "crash" of thunder. The more numbers you can count between these occurrences means the storm is getting farther and farther away. It's a good lesson for tonight. Now I *can* sleep.

!!Flash!!...one-thousand-and-one...one-thousand-and-two...one-thousand-and-three...!! Crash!!
!!Flash!!...one-thousand-and-one...one-thousand-and...

I did sleep well last night, especially after all the things the nice parents did to comfort me. Of course, the security of having "Skipper" snuggled up next to me really can't be beat. It reminds me of having little "Blackie", or even "Dog" cuddled up beside me. However, I notice "Skipper" isn't in the bed this morning, so I jump up and run to the kitchen to see where he could be. Oh! I am stopped dead in my tracks. It's "Librarian Lady" having tea at the table with "Mrs. Thompson" (What is she doing here so early?) "Oh hello, Teddy" she greets me with a big smile, and, "How are *we* today?" (Boy if I never hear *that* again it will be too soon!) "O.K., I guess." I reply, a little hesitantly, because I am not sure what I've done wrong and where she'll be moving me to next. (I start imagining the revolving door, turning slowly, with its opening just *swe-swee-sweeping* around to pull me in.)

Was it the storm? Do the parents want to get *rid* of me because I was scared of the storm? Was it because I cried when I saw the beautiful pony? These are the thoughts filling my head as "Mrs. Thompson" sets my place at the table. "Here's your milk, dear." she says, adding, "Would you like some cereal this morning?" "Yes, Wice Kwispies, pwease." "Oh, I really love those nice manners, Teddy." "Mrs. Thompson" reassures. (Why then, is she *getting rid* of me?)

"Teddy", "L.L" starts to address me...(Oh-oh, here it comes—no more horseys, no more "Skipper" no more bubbly baths, no more cookies, no more records, no more lessons)...Then she

says, "Teddy, I've got some very good news for you today."
(Nevertheless, it has always been my experience that *no* news
is the only *good* news—so I brace for the worst.) She
continues, "I've brought the last of your clothes along with me
today, and your toys as well, because you won't be coming
back to the children's ward, ever again." "Eber, neber?" "Right,
Teddy! You are going to stay in this house with your new
parents, 'Mr. and Mrs. Thompson'." "And Tipper too?" I
interrupt. "Ha-ha-ha, yes, of course, and the doggie too." she
finishes. "L.L." is obviously pleased with the positive message
she was able to bring to me today.

(I just noticed, not only is she not stuttering today, but also she
actually just *laughed*, a real laugh. I've never even heard her
laugh before today.) "Did you bwing my twike too?" "Yes, your
trike is right out on the porch." she answers. "Oh gweat!"

Oh my. Oh, my goodness, I don't know what to think. Have I
just come through my last revolving door? Can it be possible
these nice folks will really be my forever "parents"? However,
what if they turn mean? What if they stop liking me? What if
they kick me in the ribs? What if they do bad things to me, as
"Rita" did? What if I am bad sometimes—will they send me
back to the orphan asylum? What if they move away and can't
take me with them? What if I cry again and they don't like me
anymore? (What if I never understand who Jesus is—will they
send me packing if I don't get it?)

PART IX: Can My Dreams Really Come True?

Chapter 54: Are My Moving Days Behind Me?

[November 3, 1952, Progress Report to the "C.A.S." Director,

"Soon after Teddy's placement in the "Thompsons'" home, they were thoroughly questioned by his Social Worker and Case Worker to first determine if they were satisfied with Teddy, and secondly to find out if they felt they would be able to cope with his many problems and issues, such as tantrums and seizures. The "Thompsons" expressed how they are 'quite satisfied', *and said,* 'Teddy is a pleasure to have in our lives'. *They find him to be* 'quite bright' *and are* 'happy he has similar interests, such as a love for music—and animals'. *They are,* 'extremely pleased to see how well he gets along with their Collie-dog and how the affection is quite mutual'."

They did express their concern that, 'He eats too little and he seems to be *lonely* at mealtime, welcoming the times when his little friend, John, stays to eat.' *(We suggested they keep the candies out of his reach, except as a* 'reward' *after meals are eaten.) When questioned as to whether they are disappointed in his* 'age', *(as they had originally asked to adopt an infant or toddler, at the very oldest), they stated they were,* 'in no way disappointed and frankly found Teddy to be very cute and endearing'.

They also said how much they 'appreciate his enthusiasm'. *They stated,* 'He is quite excitable and as such can be disobedient, but not really in an angry or belligerent way at all.' *(Our suggestion was to try* 'reasoning' *first, then failing that,* 'isolation in his room' *would be another appropriate type of punishment for a child such as Teddy who has suffered much of his abuse while, being, so-called, punished.)*

Additionally, they both expressed, 'We find it very strange how he hoards worthless items under his bed, such as: pieces of paper, broken toys, and old utensils—useless things. For example, if we are about to dispose of something broken, a pen perhaps, then he always asks if he can have the broken item for himself.' *The 'Thompsons' also asked about,* 'the terribly painful earaches Teddy experiences when it is very windy'. *(We suggested they have his ears checked by their own 'family' physician, as we do not have any documented history of this problem. We did not have a suggestion as to what to do about his* 'hoarding useless items'.*)"*]

Here's the problem. It has *always* been my experience that I *never* know what awaits me around the next corner or through the next invisible *revolving door*. I do know for certain that I always need a hidey-hole ready for me to escape into, whenever the *abuse* starts. But, now that I know how to take care of myself—and a doggie too—I always have to be prepared to run—to escape! This also means I need to collect, (or hoard, as the parents put it), lots of items that may, on the surface, appear to be useless. However, absolutely nothing is useless to me! So whenever I'm in the next new home I will continue to rummage through the daily trash to add useful things to my collection. I think I'll just be more cautious to stash my special items much more secretively! [Naturally, there's no way I could possibly comprehend that this is my permanent adoptive home and parents and that there would be no more moves and no further need to hoard things—ever again. Nevertheless, my hoarding would continue to be a problem, even into my adulthood.]

Revolving Doors

Chapter 55: We are a Real Family! *Now, I Belong!*

Well, true to her word, "Librarian Lady" has not been back to see me in a while. I take this as good news. The "Thompsons" have explained to me how I **belong** with them now, and that I am, "the *part* which makes them a *family*". They have told me repeatedly, "Before you came to us, Teddy, we were just a married couple, but now we are a **family**!" I've noticed they're especially patient while constantly reminding me to call them, "Mum" and "Dad". Whenever I go to say, "Mrs.", or "Mr. Thompson", they will gently say, "No, dear, remember, we are *'mum' and 'dad'* now." They are steadfast in their reassurance that I am their *little boy* and "*nothing in the world could change that*". (I sure hope they're right, because I really like it here.)

Their love is quite palpable and unmistakeable, and my life now is very orderly and happily repetitive. I know what I am supposed to do each day and how I am expected to act. I have my few chores such as making my bed, straightening-up my room and collecting the eggs; however, I don't mind these easy chores. In fact, I think my chores are quite fair, in exchange for my kindly treatment and the level of care I receive in this home. (Actually, my chores are designed to teach me responsibility, accountability and consequences for actions. Nevertheless, I won't understand these concepts for a *very* long time to come.)

"Mrs. Thompson", I mean, "*Mum*" is very affectionate towards me and is always giving me hugs, squeezes and kisses. (Better still, I kiss her back.) She plays lots of great games with me every day, and we sing-along to my records. "Skipper" always turns his head from side-to-side and looks at us as if we are crazy because we are dancing all around the house. Sometimes when mum and I are singing along to the records, "Skipper" actually sings too! He goes, "Ahwhoooo, Ahwhoooo,

Ahwhoooo!" Ha, ha, ha, ha...it's the best fun ever! Mr., I mean, my *"Dad"* is very caring also and is affectionate, in his own ' manly way. I do get hugs from him, but he demonstrates his affection in the loving, patient way he is so adamant about teaching me something *new* at every opportunity. His affection just isn't mushy, like "Mum's" cuddles and kisses are.

"Dad" works at his office a great deal of time during the weekdays; but on the weekends, it's *our* special time and it's then we have a whole lot of fun together. Dad's teaching me to ride our gentle, and beautiful, "Nellie". Horsey riding is more fun than I would have ever imagined experiencing in my whole life! However, he is also teaching me the responsibility of cooling the horsey down after exercise. I am also learning how to groom her with the brushes and how I need to ensure her water basin is always clean and full of fresh water. In addition, I get to give the imposing animal her tiny sugar cube, which, apparently to her, is a great treat.

Dad doesn't expect me to *excel* in every new thing he teaches me, he only expects me to *try*. All my "parents" ask of me is that I am polite, obedient and caring. In exchange for these attributes I am provided a loving, caring home, for the rest of my life, or at least until I turn old enough to make it in the world all by myself. ("Mum" says I can stay here *forever*, but "Dad" says all young boys need to get out on their own by the age of eighteen. It's then "dad" thinks I'll be old enough to make my own living...but "mum" is *winking* again—and her winks always foretell good things.). My life is very easy-going and contented and I have not done any head banging, nor had a temper-tantrum or a seizure since being with these nice folks. In fact, I've even stopped biting my fingernails. Things are really looking up in my life—as long as *I* don't mess-up and do something really awful.

Revolving Doors

Chapter 56: "Moobe Ober, 'Tipper'!"

Of course, out of habit, I've secured a hidey-hole, for myself, just in case I need to escape when the "Thompsons" eventually turn *mean* or *hateful* toward me. Simple enough, it is right under the cellar stairs, in the loose-dirt-floor part of the basement. Certainly, there are spiders and other bugs like rolly-polly bugs and small black beetles, and every so often one of those scary-looking earwigs will raise their ugly heads up and menacingly wave their nasty pincers at me. I am careful to move quickly out of *their* path, because I know, from experience, they can sure give you a nasty pinch if you don't look out! I don't like the bugs very much but, then again, I really don't go down there very much either. Naturally, some of my very deep-rooted habits are impossible to break, and my hoarding of *survival* equipment, and other necessities, is certainly one of them. I have already collected matches, small scissors, a knife and spoon, and some canned foodstuffs—just the basics.

Every now-and-then I forget about "The Golden Rule" [127], which I learned both in Sunday School, and had reinforced repeatedly by "mum" and "dad". That's when I've done some super bad stuff, such as taking other kids' things, (John's slingshot, for example). I feel a little bad about taking that particular item, but I couldn't help myself because I figured, you just never know, it might come in handy for my basic survival someday.

Whenever I've stolen things, it is never, ever play toys—those toys are for babies! I don't need toys for survival! Speaking of toys, whenever I've broken a toy, either out of negligence, or even purposefully, I *lose* the toy. (It's mum's and dad's hard and fast rule, and no second chances, either!) One time, I made my "Hopalong Cassidy's" horse, "Topper", jump down, crashing super hard onto my "Mr. Potato Head", until I broke off one of the horse's legs and irreparably cracked "Potato's" head in the process. Both toys "disappeared" *forever,* as punishment. (Well now, *there is* a lesson you won't have to teach me *more than twice.*)

(Later on, whenever I start doing things bad enough to require more severe discipline than the usual, isolation in my room, I'll need a real "hidey-hole", outside the house. Then I'll take over "Skipper's" doghouse. {I will *go* to the *doghouse* when I am *"in the dog house"*, if that makes any sense. Hee, hee, hee.} The good thing is, my doggy's furry body keeps me warm. However, the bad thing is he wants to play and gives away my clandestine hiding spot every single time I try to sneak out there, even when I'm only playing "Hide and Go Seek" with my friends.)

Most of the time I am obedient to mum and dad, though. I try to be good for these folks because I owe it to them for taking me in and giving me a nice home to stay in, this time around. I do extra things for mum, like helping her water the myriad of her plants around the house. Sometimes I dry the dishes; of course, I have to be very careful with that particular chore. For dad, I help with feeding all the farm animals, (except the pigs). I also help him stack the firewood neatly along the wall at the side of the house, and whenever mum needs it, I even carry it inside too, because I am very strong—they both say so! Of course, every day I clean "Skipper's" bowls and put down his fresh food and water, and I brush him too! He loves his brushing and with his long, beautiful coat, he *really* needs it.

Revolving Doors

Chapter 57: CWISSMAS is Coming!

"Do you know what special time of year it is, Teddy?" mum asks while grinning like the proverbial Cheshire Cat. [111] [111a] "Can you guess who's coming right here to our house?" "Hmmmm…. nope." is my verbal reply. However, "I sure hope it isn't anybody from the 'C.A.S.' to take me away again!" is what I am *really* thinking. "Well, dear, it'll very soon be Christmas and time for Santa to come down our chimney and bring you lots of nice presents!" (Is she serious? Wowee! This is always my very favourite time of the year.) "Do you suppose you've been a very good boy this year, Teddy?" (Oh, um, well, to be honest, it has not exactly been my *best* year, I guess, especially if you consider the sling-shot swiping incident.)

Nonetheless, despite what I'm thinking, "I guess so." is what comes out of my mouth. "Well your dad and I certainly think you *have* and we think Santa will know this also." She tells me this in her usual encouraging tone. You didn't know this, but a couple weeks ago, I wrote Santa Claus a letter to tell him what a wonderful little boy you are and what a special blessing you have been by coming to our family. I am positive he already knows you are a very good little boy, but just in case, I thought he should hear it directly from me. "Tsanks a wot, mum. You're da bestest mum in da world." (Whew! This is very good news because I am certain a "letter from a mother" even a temporary mother, will definitely trump one little swiped sling-shot.)

"What shall we do with ourselves today Teddy?" She asks this in the way she *always does* when she *already knows* the answer. "Should we go for a walk, or go shopping or *put up a Christmas tree*?" There she goes again— "asking and knowing" in the same breath. "Cwissmas twee … can we go get a Cwissmas twee?" I prod. Then I jump up onto mum's lap and hug her neck, pleadingly. "It's a wonderful idea, dear!" she says. "Ra—lph! Ra—lph! Come upstairs when you finish what you're doing. Teddy and I have a *great* idea!" A few minutes later, my *dad* finishes tightening the wringer-rollers on the washing machine and comes up to join us at the kitchen table. "What's up? What's this about a *great idea*?" he asks. "Teddy was asking about a Christmas Tree and I know you have a special surprise for him regarding our tree.", she says coyly and with a *wink of her eye*, which **always** promises something verrrry good is right around the corner.

[What I could not know was, *this was the* **very first moment,** *the* **instant,** a wonderfully special family tradition was born. And this wonderful tradition will recur at this time of year, for many, many wonderful years to come in my life.]

"That's right, Teddy! Let me get my axe and you go get some warm clothes on—and—hurry up, now!" This man, "Mr. Thompson"—my dad, and I walk out, deep into the woods at the back of our property to hunt together, not for an animal, but for the perfect Christmas tree! (I thought you had to buy one from a tree-selling man in the grocery store parking lot or from the Boy Scouts' Santa's Village Tree Farm". Ours isn't going to cost any money at all.) "It has to be 'Pine', and nice and full, and round." my new *dad* informs me. I couldn't agree more. We really don't have to trudge too far when, quite by magic, we simultaneously spot the perfect tree. "Can I chop it down, dad?" I plead. "I'll let you have the first whack at it, but don't let your mum know, O.K? You know, she'd have both our heads!" Then, after a mini lesson in safe axe handling, he did. He let me have the first whack, which was a good one, or so he said. Then a few hard hits by my dad and we had us a tree! By the time we dragged it back to the house mum had already gotten the boxes of decorations down from the attic and *this* tree didn't lose *one* needle all the way home!

Revolving Doors

[My dad and I now had a little secret we would keep to ourselves, for many years to come. I still chuckle when I remember this incident. I was so little, and he was so big; nevertheless, he made me feel very grown-up, just the same.]

Anticipating our chill, mum already has the milk warming-up in the pot, and she makes us hot cocoa with an extra treat of white marshmallows bobbing and swimming around on the surface` of the delectable drink. While dad gets the lights on the tree *first*, mum is popping the corn for a garland, with a little extra for us, of course! This morning, mum prepared a beef pot-roast, and it has been cooking slowly, all day. Naturally, what meal of beef pot-roast would be complete without the suet pudding, (my favourite part)? I love the way she always makes the roast for Sunday dinners with potatoes, carrots and onions cooking in the juices around the meat and Yorkshire pudding too! Yummmm! I also love the way her pot-roast makes our home smell so deee-licious. For dessert, of course, it's mum's homemade Apple Crisp! "Dad and I took a vote: Apple Pie or Apple Crisp? The Crisp won out—*today*!

By the time the decorations box was completely empty and our tummies were completely full, our tree was award-winningly, gorgeous! However, the decorating did not stop at our tree. Oh, no…the tree was only the start of it. Dad and I hung lights in the front bay window, and in the side windows, which you can almost see from the road. He put more lights outside around our front door, on which we hung the wreath, handcrafted by my mum and me. We made it from cut up strips of green plastic trash bags and I helped her tie a million of them on the hanger which my mum had bent into a round circle shape. Then when it needed *more* than the little bells, balls and bows, *I* supplied the tiny—*pinecones!* (It may sound chintzy but it truly turned out great and mum said we can make a new one every year!)

Revolving Doors

Inside the house there wasn't a table or a shelf which didn't have something "Christmas-y" on it and almost every single doodad was made lovingly by my mum's hands. Some knick-knacky things she knitted, some she crocheted, and some she let me help make. For instance, I helped mum fashion the dining room table's centrepiece with pretty, shiny, red, blue and gold tree-ornament-balls, some holly and ivy from the bushes at the side of the house, (which, incidentally, is very prickly), and *my* personal contribution, the little *pine cones*! I collected them and mum dried them in the oven, then we painted the tips of them with silver paint, to resemble snow.

Just now, mum was dozing-off a little in the big old rocker, and dad came to me and whispered, "Teddy, I have an idea! Come in the kitchen with me. Shhhhh!" Then we tiptoed into the kitchen and dad said it might be nice to give mum the night off by doing up the dishes and cleaning the kitchen for her. Great idea! After all, she seems so very tired and we both know she would really appreciate a hand with the cleaning up. Then, ever so quietly, dad washes and, very, very carefully, I dry the dishes with a tea towel. "I hope you two aren't trying to clean up in there." mum, shaking her doziness off, calls out to us. "Just never you mind, dear, this is our little treat tonight!" my dad insists. "Teddy, be careful and please try not to drop any dishes, dear." She just can't help herself. She just *has* to mention this because I dropped a glass, once—once! "I'n O.K., I'n not donna bweak dem, mum, I pwomise."

After a quick kitchen clean-up, (which, my dad says, "everybody knows men are faster at than women"), we all played a game of making finger-shadow puppets on the wall. I don't think I've laughed so much in my whole life, either before the shadow puppets, or maybe even since. Mum made a bunny-rabbit and dad made a dog to chase the bunny. *I made a tree.* Mum made a spider and dad made a hammer to squash the spider. *I made a stick.* Mum made a cat and dad made a house fall down on top of the cat. *I made a ball!* On and on we played. Hee, hee, hee! Next to my already favourite game, "I Spy With My Little Eye", this is definitely the bestest game ever!

After a little while, dad is relaxing with his newspaper. It is the Sunday edition so it's super thick with all the extra sections and the stores' advertisements. It just happens to contain my favourite part, the "funnies"! Mum starts working on dad's surprise, knitted scarf. Then, after chuckling over all the cartoon drawings, I go in my room and drag all my Tinkertoys, [45], out into the living room to start to build a small city underneath our tree. We have a roaring fire going and it keeps the whole upstairs nice and cozy-warm! It is all so perfect, so very, very perfect. Actually, my life here is really too perfect. It certainly is so much more love and fun than this little "guttersnipe" would ever **dream** of deserving. It also feels a little bittersweet to me, because sort of bad thoughts keep crocheting their spider webs in my head. Some thoughts truly torment me—thoughts such as,

"Enjoy this now as it surely won't last much longer!", or,

*"If they only knew the truth of who you really are and what you've done, they wouldn't love you! In fact, they wouldn't even **like** you a little—and you'd be right out of their front door—and kicked all the way to the road!"*, or,

"You'd better get serious about finding the perfect hidey-hole because you'll be out of here and gone from this couple's life, before a flea can sneeze!" (…and "dad" says fleas sneeze incredibly fast!)

Therefore, I smile, laugh, play human wheelbarrow, "Simon Says" and anything else they want to play, for now, because the reality is, it will be over soon enough. "Let's read Teddy's bedtime story in here by the tree tonight, dear." mum suggests, again with a little wink. Her soft words shock me back to the reality of the moment, which is simply, *I am here, I am loved*, and *I am not leaving—ever,* if mum has *her* way. Then, after a little more hot cocoa, dad gets out the pecialist Christmas story of all, and one I've never heard before. It is a poem about Christmas Eve and Santa's ride with his reindeer. It is titled, "*T'was the Night Before Christmas*"! [123] And I love it!

Although we really don't watch a whole lot of television shows in this household, some programs are special enough for the whole family to make a point of enjoying together. Tonight, one of our favourite Christmas stories was made into a movie and is coming on "TV" at seven o'clock. It's called, "A Christmas Carol", [139], and is based on a book of the same title, written a very long time ago by a man named, "Charles Dickens". [140] It *could* be a little bit scary because there are ghosts in it, but with mum, dad and "Skipper" beside me, who could really be frightened? Not me! That's for darn certain!

[There is one other time you will always find us in front of the television. It's every Sunday night, (which isn't offering a special seasonal movie), at seven o'clock, when "The Ed Sullivan Show", [125], comes on. It is a family variety hour and there is always something for every family member to enjoy. I think my favourite are the circus acts! Maybe I could be in a circus someday too! A clown—I could be a *clown*!]

Once we had decorated the tree, I decided I didn't have a whole lot of time before Santa's visit, in which to be a "good little boy". All I could really do was just try to help my folks as much, and as often, as possible. That's why I'm trying to do everything, and be extra good, so I can sort of make up for the "bad" I'd done earlier in the past year, (at least up until the time I arrived at this home). After all, Santa Claus sees you *all* the time, even when you are sleeping, so I had quite a bit of "making up" to do!

I think I must have bugged my mum and dad so much, especially as the remaining days leading up to Christmas became fewer and fewer. The good part was, the more I helped my parents, the faster the days and nights sped by until, finally, it was here! It was Christmas Eve and time for dad to read, "T'was the Night before Christmas" again! Only, by now, he had read it to me so many times to me, he seemed to have it memorized and spoke the words by heart, and my mum recited the poem right along with him!

While "mum" is tucking me into bed, I honestly can't imagine how I can possibly do any sleeping. However, mum and dad reminded me about pretending to sleep. So, remembering how well this has worked in the past, that's exactly what I'm doing, I'm preten……

Suddenly my sleepy ears hear, "Ted-dy! Ted-dy! Santa came last night! Come and see!" It's Christmas morning! Yippee! Santa came! Santa came and left a hundred presents under the tree, and in my stocking too! Oh my gosh! There are a million packages under our tree—and most of them are for me, at least I think so. "Teddy we'll make a nice little pile of yours and you can open them quickly or slowly—any ol' way you'd like!" Mum bubbles with joy as she is almost bursting at the seams watching my reactions. "Oh! It's my "Swinky"!" (I got a new "Slinky" [83], which I wanted very, very much, especially after my first one was lost somewhere in the shuffle of my changing residences).

Oh, boy...I recognize *that* shape. It's a Lifesavers candy book! Santa brought me a Lifesavers Christmas Book with a story about "Lifesavers and Christmas" on the package, and bunches of Lifesaver candy rolls inside. [58] What's this? It is a box with a familiar, funny face on it. It's a new "Mr. Potato Head"! My other one disappeared after I broke it with my "Topper" horsey. (I wonder how Santa knew I needed a new one.) However, before I take all the pieces of the "Mr. Potato Head" out of the box, mum passes another, flat package to me! Oh! It's two more colouring books accompanied by a *new giant* box of crayons!

"Was I *that* good?" I silently ask myself. Perhaps Santa really *cannot* see you every minute. Just then, I remember the letter my mum sent Santa Claus on my behalf. I am thinking she must be some fine letter-writer. Oh boy, some more "Tinkertoys"! [45] Now, I have enough to build some skyscrapers! Oh yes, and in my stocking Santa also left me a large, hollow chocolate "Rudolph", [61], reindeer with a red gum-drop candy for a nose, and a solid chocolate Santa Claus too. I don't even know where to *start* eating Rudolph, or Santa. (Oh, such silly problems for a little guttersnipe.)

Despite all these wonderful gifts from Santa, mum says she think the best present of all is from dad and her, and she walks into the *bathroom* to get it for me. She says she couldn't wrap it and she was so afraid I might pull back the shower curtain and look in the tub, explaining how it would have spoiled their Christmas morning surprise. Of course, I didn't look there...and am I ever surprised! Oh, wow! It's a real, live goldfish in a glass bowl in which are placed a few things to make him a nice little home. There is a tiny bridge, a castle, real seaweed, and some colourful stones in the bottom. Mum hands me the special scooper and a little box of fish food, explaining how much is to be fed daily to the tiny, shiny fishy. ("Goldie" I'll name him, "Goldie".) "What would you like to name you little fish, dear?" mum asks, *reading my mind*. "Gow-die". "Goldie"? It's a perfect name." (How does she always *get* what I am saying?) Seeing the pleased looks on my parents' faces, I suddenly remember my manners and tell them both, while hugging their necks to death, "*Tsank-you mum 'n' dad.*" Then I look up to the sky and say my most sincere "*Tsank You*" to Santa Claus. (I wonder if he's in Heaven.)

Moments later, I witnessed this, (just as someone imagines a love story unfolds). The "Thompsons" lovingly exchanged gifts with each other:

*She gave him a tie. * He gave her perfume. {KISS-KISS}*

*She gave him handsome, pearl cuff links. * He gave her Laura Secord chocolates, [70], (which she immediately shared with me). {KISS-KISS-KISS}*

*She gave him a tie clip to match the cufflinks. * He gave her tickets to a concert they had both expressed a desire to see. {KISS-KISS}*

Everybody was super happy and truly surprised at the wonderful gifts, except for the warm scarf, which she had been knitting him for a couple months. It wasn't exactly a surprise. Nevertheless, it was very handsome with grey and maroon stripes and maroon is my dad's very favourite colour. {KISS-KISS}

(My dad doesn't usually get this mushy, but I guess today is different, isn't it?)

Once all the presents were opened, shared and enjoyed, I had to show my dad how my "Slinky" works. "Dad, come 'ere!" At the back steps, I demonstrate to my dad how I make my Slinky walk down the stairs all by itself. Only now, I must wrestle "Skipper" to keep him from biting the strangely threatening robotic-object. (It's amazing how this metal coil knows how to walk down stairs, one step at a time without missing any.) John asked Santa for a "Slinky" too—Oh-oh! Do you suppose

Revolving Doors

Santa was confused and put it under the tree at my house by mistake?

After we cleaned up all the wrapping paper and ribbons, mum headed to the kitchen to make her very, extra special Christmas morning brekkies! The menu consists of scrambled eggs, farmer's potatoes, kidneys with homemade chilli sauce, fresh-made biscuits and, of course, the raspberry jam made from what would be my, "great-great-great" grandmother's recipe! By the time I am so stuffed, I can't even move, John walks through the front door. "Hey, wanna go tobogganing over on the *big* hill?" He did *not* have to ask *me* twice!

"Guess what! I dot a Swinky pfrom Santa, did you det one too?" I ask him, hopefully. "Yeah! I dot a Swinky too!" he replies, and we both fall down laughing! "Oh, come here 'n' see, Gow-die, my new gold-fiscee!" "Wow, he's weally nice, Teddy. How did Santa bwing him and not spiwl him?" he asks me. "No, he's pfwum mum 'n' dad." "Oh", he remarks, quite satisfied.

Anyway, after a few minutes of watching "Goldie" we head out to spend the day on the big sliding hill nearby, just on the other side of the frozen creek. We slide down, and trudge up, race down, and trudge up, over and over! And the more times we go down, we are actually packing the snow down tighter and tighter, making a super sliding spot with every repetition!

(I really like my friend John. He's a very nice kid, just like me and it's fun how we enjoy the same activities, even though he *is* two years younger. That really doesn't seem to matter to our friendship.)

After a million slides and trudges we go over to his house and have a bite of home-made, just-came-out-of-the-oven, apple pie, with his mum's yummy-in-the-tummy whipped cream! It's a special day at everybody's house and John shows me his presents from Santa too. I brought my "Slinky", [83], in my coat pocket and we race our "Slinkys" down the stairs. What a riot! Later, after a little hot cocoa, we head right back to the sliding hill. Finally, hours later, we are so exhausted, and wet, we can hardly make it back to our homes—just in time for Christmas Dinner!

The "Thompsons'"..., I mean... *"MY"* house is filled with the beautiful smells of a traditional Christmas turkey dinner cooking in my mum's very special way which is, "slow and low", all day long! Mum also made apple pie along with the pumpkin pie, in case I didn't like the taste of pumpkin! "Is it weady, mum? Is the dewicious dinner weady yet?" I frantically try to get an answer out of her. I don't know how she understands me but somehow she always gets my drift. "Not yet, sweetheart, not quite yet. Would you like some soup to tide you over 'till we sit down to supper; because that won't be for about two-and-a-half hours?" I nod affirmatively. Then, in no time at all, I am filling my tummy with a little of mum's homemade chicken noodle soup with the big chunks of carrots floating in it. It's good but it doesn't come close to matching the *deee—licious* scent of the turkey, with all the trimmings, emanating from the kitchen and filling every inch of our home right now.

"Teddy, can you please come down and help me here?" dad calls up from the basement. I scurry right down to find out what I can do for him. He is building a big new workbench for his tools and every-thing, and he needs *my help*, right now. "Hand me the hammer, there, Teddy." "Diss one?" "Yes, son, reach it to me, here, please." "What's dat, dad?" It is called peg-board and it's very handy for hanging my tools and other things. You see?" "What's diss, dad?" It's a pipe wrench for fixing...well...*pipes*. Hahaha! Say, son are you as hungry as I am?" "Yes, sir, I *sur* am!" Dad and I are really just trying to keep ourselves busy right now, and trying NOT to think about dinner; but in actuality, we are really waiting for those *two* magic words.

Suddenly, mum calls down to us, "Dinner's ready! C'mon and eat, boys!" We both race up and bump right into mum's aproned tummy! "Hands washed first!" she reminds.

Oh boy, oh boy, will you look at this turkey! It is utterly perfect—such a nice, rich golden brown, and a fat one too—in fact, it's absolutely oozing its delicious juices everywhere. (For a moment I have a *dark* thought, like an ominous rain cloud, float across my mind, as I wonder if one of our big ol' turkeys is missing from the coop. Then mum, once again reading my mind, says, 'Wasn't this a nice turkey I found at Mr. McCafferty's Market?". Whew! That's good, because I really did *not* want to eat any of my new friends, not unless I absolutely have to, and certainly not yet anyway.)

"Well, would you just look at this spread? It's a meal fit for a royal family!" my dad says, exhibiting more enthusiasm than I've ever before seen from him. "There's turkey, mashed potatoes and gravy, carrots, Brussels sprouts, green beans, turnips and rolls. My dear, you have really outdone yourself this year! Well, let's get started here. I'll do the carving first. Now Teddy, I want to see you really eat well because your mum has worked very hard to put this wonderful meal on the table for us. O.K., son?" "O.K. dad." "What am I forget-ting?" mum muses to herself aloud. "Teddy, would you like some tomato juice?" she asks, while already pouring it. "Oh! The little pickles and vegetable sticks!" she remembers, also aloud.

"What's for dessert honey?" dad pries. "If you both eat you dinner up, I made two nice pies for dessert...and 'Mrs...' sent over some fresh whipping-cream. Lucky for us, she made far too much today." "Yippee!" That's all I have to say! Of course, I

Revolving Doors
have already tasted John's mummy's whipped cream—so,
double yummy!

Chapter 58: "POPS"

"We have a very special place to go today, Teddy", my dad informs me. "We're going down to the train yards to visit my 'Pops', your Grandpa." "Who's dat?" I ask. "He's *my* father, and your mum has prepared a very special Christmas hamper overflowing with yummy foodstuffs for him." "Where's *your* mum" I query. "She's been in Heaven for a long time, Teddy. My "Pops" has lived alone, missing her, for just as long." he explains. (For an instant, I saw a barely noticeable glimpse of sadness in my dad's eyes. I wonder why.)

"My 'Pops' works as a "Watchman" down at the rail-yards, and he lives there too." "Does he lib on a twain?" I wonder aloud, (while secretly thinking how absolutely awesome it would be!). "No, no, Teddy. He lives in a little glass room—a sort-of tower. You'll see when we get there and it'll be *lots* of fun to see the trains coming and going, won't it?" he asks me with another sad look in his eyes. "Yes, yes dad! Wots!" I agree.

Then, off we go in our very nice family car. After a long drive we are at the rail-yards, where there are many railway tracks stretching in every direction as far as your eyes can see. I immediately notice, 'parked' here and there on the rails, there are about fifty train engines and boxcars. All are painted in shades of rust-red, brown, grey or black, with large white numbers and/or letters. I guess they must be resting after returning from their travels to faraway, exotic places unknown. "Phew!" I suddenly complain, while pinching my nose, (because it's very, very stinky around here—sort of like when you're crossing the road and you walk behind a bus—it's the same kind of stench). "Oh, it's the diesel fuel the trains run on, Teddy. It *is* kind of stinky, isn't it?"

To get to the glass room, we must quite deftly step on the

boards, which are laid in ladder-rung-like fashion, in-between, and supporting, all the metal track rails. We step across several rails and head in the direction of a small platform which my dad pointed out to me. It is right smack-dab in the middle, between all of the train tracks. I wonder what *that's* doing there.

I squeeze my dad's hand and tell him, "I'n scared of da twains, dad!" However, my dad reassures me, "Oh, Teddy, you don't need to be scared. Do you know what? I bet I can show you a way to find out if a train is coming, even if it *is* a long way off. I can show you which track it will be riding on, too." "Weally, dad?" Then, he leans down and puts his hand on six or seven different iron track rails as we step between them. Here, touch this rail—this one, right here, Teddy!" Naturally, I do what he says, without the faintest idea why. "Do you feel the vibration?" he asks me. "What's dat?" "The funny buzzy movement in the rail, do you feel it, now?" "Yes, dad." I answer while wondering what it could possibly have to do with the location of *his dad's house.* "It means there is a train coming along this very track!" he explains. Hearing this, I grab his hand with both of mine and try to pull him off the tracks. I urge him to come-on and hurry-up and get to the little platform to be safe. He chuckles and says, "Oh, no—you don't have to worry, son, it's quite a ways off right now, so don't look so distressed." He's smiling but I'm wondering how on earth he could know this and could he possibly be right—and what if he's *wrong and the train is much, much closer—and—and...?*

My mind is focused on the vibration of the oncoming train as I still keep tugging his arm. I'm trying to pull him fast enough to reach the safety of the small, smooth, inlaid-red-brick platform before the great, noisy iron monster arrives angrily growling and spitting at everybody, and everything, in its path! The platform is the anchor for some old, rusty iron stairs going almost straight up. Dad points all the way up saying it's where his dad works, and *lives*. Really? I'm looking at a small, glassed-in, box of a room, which is perched quite high up, at the top of the metal stairs. As we ascend, I immediately discover the ancient stairs wobble and creek badly as we step from one to the next.

At the top, we can see through the tower-room's window, there is an old man, with his back to us. He is sitting in front of a small card table playing a card game of Solitaire. There isn't much of anything inside the room except another wooden, ladder-back chair and a canvas cot. On this bed is a stained, flattened, raggedy old pillow and a grubby-looking, grey-once-blue, frayed blanket.

"Tap, tap, tap…" Dad knocks lightly on the glass pane. The old man reels around and motions with a pointed finger, mouthing the words, "*Just a minute.*" Then he hurries, in his excruciatingly slow, arm pumping, old-man way, to unlock the door for us. (I am wondering why he even has a locked door; after all, exactly how many bad guys would come knocking at *this* door to his little room.)

Inside the glass room, *my* dad, and *his* dad, "Pops", shake hands. "This is your grandpa, Teddy." my dad introduces us, politely, adding, "Say hello, son." "Um, hi-ya.", I say, a little meekly as I am rather overwhelmed by the appearance of this very sickly-looking, old man. He is barely able to stay standing upright as he reaches a bony, arthritic hand towards my small, white, plump, new little one. The veins on his hands are raised up and look blue and purplish. I don't mind admitting, he seems a little scary to me. Nonetheless, I let him shake my little hand, but I keep the rest of myself behind my dad's leg, just in case this is some sort of *trick* to get rid of me by *dumping me* with this old codger, and leaving me *living here* **next.**

Revolving Doors

(Just imagine me, caught up in a revolving door in this train yard. I would be always going in and out, and never stopping long enough to find any sort of a home. Oooh, the thought makes me shudder a little, but when I glance up at my dad, I quickly shake it off.)

"Here, 'Pops', Lillian packed you a little hamper." my dad says while offering the basket we brought. Mum embroidered a small, white linen cloth with geometric patterns in red and green Christmas colours and she draped it over the top, cleverly disguising who-knows-what delicious delights and surprises underneath. "Pops" gratefully acknowledges the gesture of food. From the looks of his pathetic little office-bedroom, I'd say he certainly can use it. When he opens the small refrigerator to put-in the Christmas dinner plate mum fixed him, I can see—well—nothing. There is nothing inside of it, except a small, red, "Coca-Cola" carrying box made to house eight *miniature* bottles of the popular soft drink. [136] I notice four of them are empty bottles and four remain unopened.

Looking around the glass box-house, I notice a coffee percolator sitting on top of one of the crusty, ringed-burners of a two-burner hot plate. On the other burner is a small cast-iron skillet with what appears to be very old bacon grease sliming its surface. Below it, on the shelf is a very, very small, rusted coffee tin, which is obviously only placed there as a receptacle for said bacon grease or, at least, something else, *other than* coffee. Maybe it's used for the over-flow of ciggy butts from the glass insert receptacle of the "Firestone Tire" rubber tire ashtray, on the old man's card table. [138]).

I can immediately see it is very lucky for my grandpa, that my considerate "mum" sent along a new, *large* can of "Maxwell House Coffee". (It must be good stuff, because, according to the TV man, "*It's good to the last drop!*") [129] "Pops" just can't get the coffee percolator going fast enough so he can enjoy a very long-awaited, fresh cup of java, and of course to share a cup of the "good stuff" with company, *my dad*. While he is getting an old, chipped china cup wiped out for dad's coffee, he finds an empty soup-can, for his own, apologizing for not having much to offer *me*. No problem, I don't think I could eat or drink anything in this little glass room anyway, because the diesel-fuel impregnated air is quite overwhelmingly nauseating to me.

Then, quite unexpectedly, grandpa asks, "Would you like a soda-pop, Teddy?" I look up at my dad for a signal and he asks his father, "Are you sure you can spare it, dad?" Grandpa nods affirmatively. A minute later, he inserts the little metal bottle cap into a small hook type of thing, which is screwed onto the wooden wall-slat, beside his table. Then, "wooosssssshhhh" I hear the sound of the fizzy soft drink. What a cute little bottle! It's just my size too. Hmmm, the stuff inside is darn good—almost as good as "Woot Beer".

As my grandpa moves around his small living-working area, I am able to have a little better look at him. I notice he is quite a bit shorter than dad, and is bent over forward, always holding his lower back with one hand, as if he has a boo-boo there. He's wearing a wrinkly, blue work shirt with the sleeves rolled up, and over it are his dirty old overalls which seem to be made of a sturdy-looking material, (which actually looks like bed, or pillow ticking, in a thin black stripe on white, twill-weave pattern). [131] They were obviously new once, but currently are faded and caked in grease. Tucked securely into the roll of his left sleeve are his smokes, ("John Wayne endorsed", non-filtered, "Camels".). [132] What there is of his hair, is very thin and silver-coloured. I suppose he does look a little like my dad, except for his very big ears and extremely wrinkly, colourless, or rather grey complexion. Nonetheless, he *does* have brown eyes like "dad's", and just like my "dad's" today, "Pops'" eyes are full of *sadness*.

When my Grandpa talks, he coughs *a lot*. He isn't smoking right now but the whole room stinks like diesel-exhaust-infused, stale cigarette smoke. In no time, the heavy air is starting to bother my extremely sensitive lungs too, so much so, I'm unable to stifle the little coughs which keep forcing their way up and popping out of my throat. "Are you alright, Teddy?" dad asks me. I just nod, so I don't have to speak. I take little sips of the soda pop and it seems to be helping my coughs go away.

While "Pops" and dad have a little chit-chat about the weather and other unimportant stuff, I peer out through the diesel-grease smeared window for any interesting train movement—especially for the one dad said is going to come down one of the tracks. Just then, my Grandpa stands up and raises his skinny, white arm to point down at one of the tracks. In fact, it is the very one my dad said would soon be occupied. In seconds, a large, noisy monstrosity hurries and hurtles itself toward this sheltered part of the station. "Pops" says, "Look-it, Teddy, *hhhhcllhh*, there's a big one coming in right now—lookee over there, *hhhhcllhh, hhhhcllhh!*" While I await the incoming on track nine, or "niner", as my Grandpa called it, I am more bothered by the appearance of this old man's arms. Their own *tracks* are blue veins, which are raised up, as if something is worming its way, in and out, around his arms. The veins are right below the surface of the loose skin, which is virtually draped down from my grandpa's very old arm bones. Ooooh, very disturbing.

Just as I watch this great machine come squealing in on "niner", I see that, *once again,* **my dad is right!** Then, out of the blue, Grandpa asks, "Teddy, do you, *hhhhcllhh*, know the story of the, *hhhhcllhh,* 'The Murderous, One-eyed, One-armed and One-legged Rail-yard Ghost'? Have you, *hhhhcllhh*, heard that one Teddy?" Then he adds, *"Hhhhcllhh, hhhhcllhh, hhhhcllhh, hhhhcllhh."* coughing-out his question. Then he grins with a broad, knowing expression, very much the same grin as my dad sometimes makes, except my Grandpa's grin exposes the few remaining teeth in his mouth, (which I notice are far out-numbered by the missing ones).

Then, before I can answer, he proceeds to tell me about the scary ghost, and what it looks like, and what it does at night, and such and such. (Wow, he certainly has *my* attention!) However, before "Pops" is very deep into the ghostly tale, my dad, (no doubt having heard the story five-hundred times), makes quite an overt gesture of checking his watch. I am not certain why he did this since there are clocks everywhere you look in these rail yards. Some are even hanging down from the ceiling over the platforms and *two* of them are right in this "Watchman's tower"! Nevertheless, having interrupted the story, dad makes our excuses to leave *his* dad, with apologies, of course. "I'll finish the story, *hhhhcllhh*, the next time you stop by, *Te—hhhhcllhh—ddy—hhhhcllhh.*" he coughs his promise. The two men don't hug or say, "I love you." They just shake hands again, and this time I can't help but notice how young, firm and strong my dad's hands are. All the two men *do say* are their mutual, *"Merry Christmases"*.

We leave my grandpa's house, carefully climbing back down the rickety metal stairs. As we cross back over the tracks, I glance up at my Grandpa's *house*, because I thought he might be waving good-bye to us, but I'm wrong. There's no sign of him. I guess he decided to take a nap.

"How is he doing, Ralph?" mum asks dad when we arrive at home. "Not good, dear—he's not well at all. I'm pretty sure it's emphysema now—he's gone downhill so much since we saw him over at my brother's at Thanksgiving." he replies. "Has he seen a doctor?" mum asks. "I don't know—he steered clear of the topic completely." he answers. "Well, did he enjoy the hamper?" "Yes, oh yes, Lillian, he immediately made us coffee and put the dinner plate into his little fridge, which I couldn't help but notice was not only grimy, but completely devoid of food. Thank-you for thinking about him, dear."

"What do you think of your Grandpa, Teddy?" mum asks me. "He knows a gweat ghost stowy!" I reply, (while forever wondering how the scary ghost story ends).

*[I'll only see this man two more times in my life. The next time, we visit him in the veteran's ward at Sunnybrook Hospital, [137]. My Grandpa is now deathly ill, and bedridden in the Intensive Care Unit where they literally monitor his every breath. He is in-and-out of consciousness, and has his mouth and nose covered with a plastic breathing mask, thus rendering it impossible for him to speak. Just the same, in one of his few lucid moments, I know I saw **something** in his eyes. His eyes were speaking to me, probably finishing his "Ghost Story"! When Grandpa slips out of consciousness, you can see it because his eyes roll up back into his eye-sockets. Those are the times I look up to the corners of the ceiling, just on the off chance he is up there screaming to be set free—just as I was that time I died of pneumonia.*

The time, after the hospital visit, I'll see him in his open-casket, at the funeral. Sadly, my Grandpa had a lung disease called "lung cancer" which is even worse than emphysema, and it was believed at that time to apparently be caused by decades of his being exposed to the airborne particles of diesel-fuel exhaust, which were always so prevalent at the yards. [130] Of course, looking back from an adult's perspective, and knowing what I now know, I am convinced, his decades of chain-smoking those "Camels" served to only doubly exacerbate my Grandpa's degenerating lung issues with the diesel-exhaust.

Revolving Doors

I certainly never got to know "Pops" and never had any other grandparents in my life. Too bad, I think, because I would like to have better understood the stories of his life, which quite obviously left their marks in every deeply etched line on his face. Well, at least I would like to know the ending to the story of the "Murderous Rail-Yard Ghost"...]

Chapter 59: "To School...or *Not* to School?"

Before the Christmas season began, my parents made a promise to the "C.A.S." Workers, after the holidays they would decide if it would be the best thing for me to start kindergarten in January. It would mean my missing the first half-year of school. Since I don't have any friends who already attend school, I don't particularly have any *desire* to attend school yet. (I certainly haven't been *asking* to start school.) Anyway, my days are *filled* with my time spent with mum or dad, chores, meals, playtime by myself, or with "Skipper", or with John, (who, being two years my junior, has not yet started school either). Besides, mum and dad read to me every day and mum is teaching me my alphabet and printing. I already know my colours, I'm good with picture puzzles and I've learned some social skills such as turn-taking, the "Golden Rule", using my manners and so on. I think this just about encompasses what the kids are learning at kindergarten right now, so I believe I am pretty well covered for all those lessons.

It isn't as if I've been totally isolated from other kids. After all, I've already experienced some learning situations and socialization with the other children at the Sunday school. Of course, I do have a problem *trusting* anyone whom I don't know very well. It's the reason I'm not a big socialiser and I tend to stick by my best friend, John. As well, during the first half of each of the adult church services, I learn other things which are related to the church, or what the Bible teaches about Jesus, and God. Also, mum and dad keep insisting I am a "pretty smart cookie", and I learn things the very first time I am ever given an explanation, a demonstration or a lesson about anything. This is especially true when it is my dad who is doing the teaching. He has a wonderful way of explaining things which always makes perfect sense. I love, and cherish, every lesson he ever gives me—especially one of my *first few* lessons, about the, "Flash and the Crash". Everything my folks teach me is something to make my life better and move me forward.

One important factor in aiding my parents' decision is the issue with the location of the nearest school accepting five-year-olds in kindergarten. The rural school, which I should be attending, according to my area of residence, is on North Jane Street in Toronto. Although the school accepts children my age, they are already over-crowded and informed mum they don't have room for me this year. Moreover, it is further than a mile away from our home, which would make it difficult for my mum to get me there and back. Since I am young, new to this area and very insecure, riding a school bus full of strange new children would be out of the question. That is at least until I've lived with my parents long enough to not be frightened about getting on the bus all alone, and travel to and from, my school. That's when I'll be ready, for certain.

My parents also considered the fact, had my birthday been in October instead of August, naturally, I would not be starting kindergarten until the fall of 1953. Therefore, thinking I would not be too far behind others my age, the grown-ups decided I would "be allowed to play now, and begin kindergarten at age six, in the fall of 1953". (*My mum just breathed a huge sigh of relief! She did not want to have to lose her best little play pal— me! Not yet, anyway.* Frankly, I think dad was a little relieved too, but he might not ever admit it.)

Revolving Doors

Chapter 60: My Bestest Pal, "JOHN"

On John's farm, his dad has *milking cows* and I've started to go over there early every morning to help John with his big "milking" chores. It's a good sized job for the two of us, even with his dad helping. Still, it is loads of fun! Whenever we fill up one of the big, metal milk cans, it takes both of us to wrestle it all the way from the barn up into his house. John's mum is just waiting for this can's delivery so she can skim the cream fat off the top and we can help her churn it into butter. There's always lots of milk left for me to take back home to mum and dad. It's a darn good thing we get free milk now, because *I've* started drinking more and more every day. (It is really starting to show on me, because I've obviously grown since I first got here!).

Anyway, we also collect the eggs in John's chicken coop and wash the poop off them for *his mum.* Then we come back over to my place and he helps me get the eggs from our hens and clean them up for *my mum.* ("His mum"…"My mum"…this may sound simple to others, but it "sounds" quite marvellous to me. I wonder how long it will last. I wonder how long I'll get to stay at this house until I am shoved through the next revolving door! Oh, well, right now, just as a dog does when he comes in from the rain, I'll just *shake* that bad thought right out of my head.)

It feels good to work hard at my chores and contribute to the welfare of this family, after all, they certainly don't owe **me** anything. Then, after all of our chores are finished, it's playtime for us boys. Today, just like any other day, John's daddy has to muck-out the barn stalls for the cows and horses to have fresh, clean straw in their beds. John and I help by keeping "Midnight Blue Star" busy, walking him all around, and brushing his coat, or trying to braid his mane, but he keeps flicking it around, and back and forth making our task is an impossible one.

"Hee, hee, hee! It's O.K. boys—you're doing a very good job today. Thank you. My wife is the only one Blue Star will allow to braid his mane." We both love grooming this beautiful colt and our vigorous brushing makes his coat shine like the stars. We would rather just play with "Star", nonetheless, we keep helping with any other things John's daddy needs to be done, in case Santa is watching. But, we can't play until we've gone around filling up the water troughs for all the animals. However, when there are no more jobs to do, playtime definitely begins.

We climb way up on the hay bales then slide all the way again! Then we have to pile them back up so we can slide down back down, of course, knocking them over again, in the process. Sometimes we play hide-and-go-seek and, sometimes, when his dad is not looking, we climb on, *and **ride** the year-old **steers*** all around! Nevertheless, when John's daddy catches us, boy oh boy, do we ever get into trouble. John's daddy chases us all over the place, because when we ride his steers, it makes him as mad as a wet hornet. However, every now and then, John's dad will be extra nice and allow us to climb up onto his big yellow and green "John Deere" [128], tractor. Then he'll give us a nice long ride around the farm! Boy, oh, boy—it's the most fun ever, at least next to steer-riding and shadow puppets!

"Oh-oh!" Here comes my mum—and she isn't looking any too happy. "Ted-dy! Ted-dy! Where on earth have you been? You know you were supposed to be home in *one hour!* That was at *two o'clock,* which was *two hours* ago!" ("In an hour…two o'clock…two hours ago…blah, blah, blah"…it all makes absolutely no sense to me right now.) I attempt to explain, we've been out in the fields riding on the tractor with John's dad, but mum is really steaming because we missed some important new *doctor's* appointment for me. I'm fine! What do I need a doctor for now? I am not sick or banging my head or doing any of those things. I believe I will be the judge of when I'm sick or not and right now, *I am not sick.*

Anyway, how could I know what my parents mean when they say, "One, two or three o'clock". "I'n sorry, mum." Sometimes I make my mum or dad kind of mad because they don't understand I have no grasp of this thing you can't see or touch—this abstract idea of time-telling—something I've never actually been taught. That's why time passes so quickly when I'm having fun with John, and I just don't realize I was supposed to be home much sooner. When my folks say to be home from John's by such-and-such a time, I wander in hours later. I don't do it to anger them, I just can't understand the idea of *passing* time. It's really so much fun playing with John because, he doesn't order me around and I don't need to bully him. We're just having a great time playing, day-in and day-out, and doing anything we can think up, of course, hoping to not be caught at it. Hee, hee, hee!

Chapter 61: My Other Bestest Pal, "MUM"

With a great deal of drama finally behind me and mum and dad right next to me, I am very slowly experiencing life as it begins to get better and better now. At least, it's certainly getting a lot easier. I don't mean my chores aren't hard. I simply mean, my life, as it has become more orderly, controlled and predictable, is better and easier than when it was in chaos. Even when I've completed the tasks assigned to me, I like to help my mum. She and I spend our days together doing whatever is required, either around the house, or on the farm. Every day my mum spends time outside with me having fun playing or sometimes just talking to me. I am learning to accept each day as it unfolds in front of me, (after all, I never know when I'll be *sent back* to the "Big House".)

My mum is such a great sport and she and I do all kinds of fun, but unusual stuff together. Mum just suggested we build a real, wooden wheelbarrow together and it sounded like such an interesting idea, I could do nothing but agree. Therefore, I just decide to follow her lead. We start by drawing a picture of a wheelbarrow on a piece of paper. Then, figuring the measurements, we cut the wood. (Dad has always reminded me when you are making something from wood, always, "measure twice and cut once", because you certainly cannot do it the other way around!) So we do measure twice for all of the woodcutting. Then we screw the sides of the box-part together and we bolt-on the handles and the legs. Then we attach the wheel, which we scavenged from a broken wagon, in order to build it into our fun finished product. [This will not be the only time my mum and I build a wheelbarrow, either.]

The two of us have such great times together. Whenever we finish building one of these, we get to celebrate by me sitting in it and mum running me all around in our yard. One time she also helped me build a real scooter like the one John has! She said it was a whole lot easier structure to make than a wheelbarrow. (The hardest part was finding and sort of borrowing the perfect sized wheels off of something we think dad no longer needed, {and praying dad wouldn't notice them missing!})

Mum is so great to hang out with all day. We have a good system going here. She helps me with the big things, and I help her with the little things. This morning, for instance, she asked me to put the "**BREAD/MILK**" card in the front window. We don't often need the milkman to bring milk or even cream, because we usually get those from John's farm, but we do need cottage cheese or the awesome orange cheddar he often brings. So I put the sign in the window with the word, "MILK" facing out. Then, when he drives by in his van, he is looking for all the little signs in the neighbourhood windows. If he spots ours, he knows to stop at our house. The same technique works for the "BREAD" card, which summons the bread-delivery man when we need something from him. It's a pretty clever system and it is important for me to get the cards the right way around. (I guess it could be said, I can almost read now.) Of course, whenever I see it is one of the deliverymen knocking, mum permits me to answer the door and tell them what she says we need. Once, she even let me *pay money* to the delivery fellow.

My mum is surely the world's best! It's a wonderful thing to finally know what it is like to have such a loving, caring mother. (I suppose she is like the *real* mommy I once knew, but, sadly, it was far too long ago to even try to remember now).

Revolving Doors

Chapter 62: "DAD": My Teacher and My Pfwend

Never one to be outdone by mum, on the weekends, my dad teaches me about all of our farm animals and what is necessary in order to care for each of their needs. He also tells me about the wild animals around here in Ontario, because a kid as adventurous as I am should certainly know his facts when it comes to recognizing animal and bird sounds. If dad didn't tell me about wolves, I would most certainly try to run up and pet, or even *hug*, the first one I see!

Dad is also teaching me about all the "ins and outs" of farming in general, as I help him with increasingly difficult chores, especially those requiring greater skills and expertise. (I really don't like having to catch the chickens for him to wring their necks and chop off their heads. Nevertheless, I have come to accept and understand, that on a farm, the food is grown and cultivated, milk comes from the cows, eggs from the hens, and sometimes our meat comes from the swine, cattle and unproductive birds. It's quite simple, nevertheless *difficult* for a little boy, such as myself, to accept, especially when I've made friends of many of our livestock.)

No matter how exhausted my dad is in the evenings, every night he tirelessly reads me my favourite bedtime stories, even the long ones, if I so choose. Lately, both my dad and my mum are constantly teaching me about "critically important" concepts like "trust" and about their unwavering, "unconditional love" for me, of which, they continually remind me, *I am very deserving*. However, when I purposely don't do as I am told, even my dad can get pretty hot and he usually ends up putting me in "time-out" in the corner—which I hate, or in "isolation" in my room—which I don't mind so much. Dad doesn't discipline me with spankings, at least, not very often. Nonetheless, a black "leather belt" hangs on the wall next to the basement stairs and, every now and then, an oblique reference is made to this object. Actually, because of this belt/strap, I guess I'm a little scared of my dad. I love him and I am scared of him, if I'm making any sense.

However, overall dad is an exceptionally patient man, so I really can't think of a better father for me on this whole planet than the one I have right now. In fact, he'll definitely put up with a lot of stuff I do, or don't do. He even forgives the many times I don't get home when I'm told to, which happens a lot, (for reasons I have already explained). But when I am doing something truly dangerous, such as the "juvenile steer-riding", that's when he lays down the law and quickly dispenses the most appropriate discipline, no doubt to the same degree as John's dad is simultaneously doling out John's punishment. (Whenever dad *has* spanked my bum a little, he always tells me, "It's for your own good, Teddy, and one day you'll under-stand why." Well, that day certainly has *not* come around yet.)

Nevertheless, I've been good today and finished all my chores. I even helped mum hang all the wet laundry up on the line, especially because she wasn't feeling very well today. (She thinks she has a bug in her tummy, or a tummy bug, or some such thing.) However, tonight it's a night for us all to relax after all the hard work we did this whole weekend. Dad and I had to repair the pigpen because "Bobby Boy" decided he wanted to get out and go live somewhere else. Our big, ol', meanie pig just pushed and pushed until he knocked-apart one corner of the split-rail fence! It was a big job getting it fixed fast, but became an even bigger job for us to convince the big ol' boar to get back into his pen, and *stay-put*! He was "SNORTING MAD", to put it mildly!

So, tonight requires a very special reward. We are making it an evening of family television entertainment, by the fireplace. In fact, one of my folks' favourite films, which they saw at the movie theatre, comes on the television tonight. The film is titled, "*It's a Wonderful Life*" [133], and is starring two of his favourite actors, "James Stewart" [134], and "Lionel Barrymore", [135]. Both my folks say it is a great Christmastime movie, which is great for the whole family to see any day of the year. My dad has already cooked-up some maple fudge, and while it is cooling in the fridge, I get to lick the stirringspoon, which is the best part because it is still warm with dripping, oozing fudge.

*(I am beginning to get a little nervous lately because my life seems too good to be true. I keep waiting for the familiar sweep-sweep-sweep of the next "revolving door" to carry me out of this nirvana, [63], to once again struggle in the dark abyss of true homelessness. I am a little like the "daddy" in this movie. He already has the perfect family and the most "wonderful life", but he just doesn't know it, until he loses everyone and everything, including his **faith**. I am always preparing myself to lose again—to lose my family, or my home, or my pet, or at the very least, my belongings—for always that day seems to sweep around, incessantly catching me up in the momentum of its rotation.)*

I suppose the best I can do is enjoy each day with the "Thompsons", and keep preparing my survival necessities, for the day which will inevitably come around. However, I've decided that hiding under the cellar steps, or in the doghouse, won't be good enough for that eventuality. Maybe I could still stow away with "Midnight Blue Star". May—be. After all, I am not adopted yet—am I? (Maybe they can't make up their minds about adopting me because it is so final a step. *Sweep—sweep—sweep.*)

[It will take me a good number of years to completely trust the motives and actions of these "parents"--and everybody else, for that matter.]

Revolving Doors

Chapter 63: Not HER! Not Again!! Not This Time!!!

Wow! Am I ever pooped-out! I've been playing really hard for the better part of the morning and mid-day at John's place, (of course, only after we both completed our daily chores). However, today we played hide-and-go-seek repeatedly, and must have climbed up and down into the hayloft five-thousand times! Anyway, I am famished now, so I tell John I'll be back over after lunch and I take off for home.

As I round the trees and can see my house, I am not particularly happy to see the car belonging to "Librarian Lady's" sister, in our driveway. What the hell is *she* doing here? Today is February 4, 1953, and she was here only two weeks ago, at which time she expressed how *pleased* she was with my progress. I suppose I thought it meant I would never have to see her again—ever! If that were truly the case, what could she want with me, or the "Thompsons", this time?

"Teddy, say hello to 'Mrs...'", mum urges.

"Hi-ya.", I comply, but not with any real enthusiasm.

"Teddy, your mother has just been telling me how well you are doing these days."

"Uh-huh" is my positive response. However, "*O.K., so I guess you can leave now.*" is what I am really thinking.

"Your mum also tells me you are eating better these days."

"Yes." I say while thinking, "*That's right...I'm eating lots of good stuff...so why haven't you left yet?*" Now, I'm beginning to feel a little peeved.

Revolving Doors

"You certainly look like a happy little fellow to me!"

"I guess so." I answer, although my brain is screaming,

"Yepper! That's me! I'm just a happy-go-lucky little feller! So, you can go home now! Yess-sir-ee! I am just as happy as a homeless little guttersnipe deserves to be! So you can go back to your nice office...there is the door...sorry you couldn't stay longer...hope to never see your plain-Jane, librarian face again! O.K., so why aren't you leaving and heading back to the asylum? It's quite fine with me if you give my crib-cage away to the next homeless little bugger!"

"Bye-bye.", I say, while waving frantically and obviously *hinting*!

Without a shred of a clue as to what I might be truly be contemplating in this conversation, the Social Worker I call, "Librarian Lady." said all of the above, ending each sentence on an up note! I am starting to feel more than a little nervous and suspicious now. Nevertheless, when I glance at mum, (who is silently encouraging me with her eyes and her smile), I force the wide grin anticipated by "L.L.", and expected by "Mrs. Thompson".

The phoney grin is also my attempt at disguising my fear, anger and frustration that she is even here in the first place. I must make her think I am perfectly contented with the "Thompsons", so she'll go away, and *stay* away! However, I'm really, really scared because every single time the "mother" in my life has started saying nicey-nice things about me, the next thing I know, I'm stuck right back in the middle of another revolving door! Then I get caught-up in its accelerating swirl, only to either be pushed out once more into the dark oblivion of "foster" life, or else, right back into the steel orphanage cages and the annoying restrictions of asylum life.

"Teddy do you miss having other children around in your family?" she asks me. "Hell No!" is what I am thinking and, "I wanna be da onwy boy here!" are the words which actually spew out of my mouth. Then, knowing me the way she does, mum senses my tension and tells the Social Worker, "Teddy often says he'll never leave, even when he is a grown man!" "Oh, he's so cute! Aren't you cute, Teddy?!" "L.L." exclaims. (I dunno how *cute* I am, but I do know how bloody desperate I am to get this Social Worker back into her borrowed station wagon so I can wave good-bye when I see her tail-lights disappear from the end of the driveway.)

"I'n cute?" I ask, truly wondering, since the term had never before been used to describe me. However, something about my question must be funny since both women start to chuckle. I don't think it's very funny. Oh well, who can understand grown-ups anyway?

The Worker's interrogation of my mum continues with the question, "How are Teddy's coping habits these days? Any temper tantrums, head-banging or the like?" With her notebook and pen in hand, "L.L." awaits my mum's response, ready as usual to make note of whatever any of us say. "No, in that regard he has improved one-hundred percent! In fact, look at his nails—he doesn't even bite them anymore. Uh, no, actually, don't look at them! Teddy, dear, go and scrub those hands!" mum stammers, suddenly a little embarrassed at the sight of my filthy paws. Then mum offers, "Teddy is eating well and drinking a great deal of milk."

Therefore, still trying to get the Social Worker to be satisfied with my progress and leave me here, I try to explain to my Worker, I go over to John's house every morning and milk their cows. However, her response is, "I'm afraid I didn't understand him, 'Mrs. Thompson'." Mum explains I said I "can milk the cows", then she adds how I'm a really good little worker on the *farms*. "*Farms?*" The Worker questions the plural. "Oh yes he goes every morning to help his little friend, John, milk their cows and gather and clean eggs from their hens. Then they both come back over here and gather, and wash, our eggs, and feed our birds as well. These are his chores, but he really enjoys taking care of the animals. Don't you dear?" I nod my "yes", but I don't know if this is a good or bad sign because "Librarian Lady" is madly writing down every single word she hears.

Then mum says, proudly, "He has grown too! Don't you think so, 'Mrs...'?" "Well why don't we just stand him up here and measure how much he has grown since living with you folks." the Worker suggests, while pulling out her trusty little cloth, sewing tape measure. "An inch—Teddy, you've grown a whole inch!" mum bubbles and "L.L." resumes her frantic note-writing. "Wonderful Teddy!" she honestly agrees. Then turning to mum, she adds, "We've always been concerned with his growth and development, especially since he succumbs to so many colds and lung infections. So this is very good news, indeed. Do you know his exact weight now?" "Well, we don't have a bathroom scale but I can certainly tell you from lifting him, he's gotten a whole lot heavier since his first day with us." Mum and I chuckle together.

"Lifting him? Was he hurt? Has he been ill? Why would you be lifting him?" "L.L." changes her tone and digs. "Oh, that's when we play wheelbarrows and such, hee, hee, hee." Then we have a twinkling little moment when mum winks at me and smiles sweetly, and I blink and smile sweetly right back, (because I haven't yet quite mastered the art of the wink). It is in this instant, I realize I love my mum a lot, and I know she loves me a lot too. My Social Worker doesn't really get it, but she writes it all down anyway.

Then moving on with mum's inquisition, "L.L." asks, "Since he didn't start kindergarten yet, we have been a little concerned about the development of his social skills." Mum replies, "Well, of course he has his friend John who lives next door, and those two are inseparable. But he's also in Sunday school and we feel it's a perfect outlet for development of those skills." My Worker pries, "Do you have friends at Sunday School?" "Yes, John is my best pfwend!" "Are you saying, 'John'? Is he the same boy who lives next door?" she asks. "Yes." She writes more stuff, and then aims more questions at mum. "How's his health been, "Mrs. Thompson"? Any colds?" "None, I'm happy to report." Mum slips me off the hook with that one.

Then trying to resume answering the previous question, mum adds, "Teddy's very considerate also. He's always asking me how *I* am feeling and tries to help me with laundry, or whatever I need, especially if I am not feeling up to par." "Are you ill? Is Teddy's care too strenuous for you?" she probes. "I'm sorry? Oh, no, of course not! I only mean, every now and then if I'm a little under the weather, as we all can be sometimes, it's then he's very *attuned* to me and understands how giving me a little help goes a long way.", mum corrects. "Oh, I see." This uninvited guest comments blandly while simultaneously resuming the writing of her full-length novel, in her little note pad.

While the Worker keeps badgering us with her questions, mum has been making me some tomato soup for lunch. "Tea, 'Mrs...'?" She nods, and mum pours.

"Tell me about your trip to the zoo. Weren't you going there soon after my last visit?" the worker questions me.

"Why is she still here?" This is the thought firing my brain cells;

however, this is what comes out of my mouth,

"It was wots of pfun at da zoo! I saw da wions, an' tigers and monkeys! Da monkeys pooped a whole wot!" (What else could she want to know about me? Why doesn't she just go away—forever?)

"Is there anything exciting you are going to be doing soon?" she continues to probe.

"Yes! Saying good-bye to you!" is my pressing thought. However, *"I'n pwanting a darden in da spwing, 'n' I'n donna det a piggy 'n' a duckie too!"* are the actual words jumping from my lips.

Mum, reads the bewilderment which washes across "L.L.'s" pale face. She quickly translates my garble, then nervously adds, "Teddy really loves all the animals." Then I tell the visitor, I know she is the lady who brought me to this house and she acknowledges it's true, then says, "Yes, Teddy, that's right, and I will be coming back to visit you from time to time just to see how big you are growing."

Oh, shit! What a liar! Everybody KNOWS you are coming back sooner or later to take me away from the best house where I've ever stayed. Then I look at mum, who is reading me like a book, and I whisper in her ear, "Is da wady donna tate me away wis her?" "No, dear, no." Mum reassures me quite satisfactorily, without having to explain our whispered secret to the Worker, (whose business it definitely is *not!*).

After countless more questions, finally—her glowing-red taillights announce her departure. Thank God and Santa! I thought she would never go! However, after she leaves this time *I* am starting to feel very nervous myself. As long as she was here, I was so scared my mum might spill-it about my new little problem. I don't understand why, but I've regressed somehow and am wetting my bed almost every night now. I can't explain my nightmares to mum or dad, because I, myself, don't understand them. Nevertheless, in my horrid dreams, somebody is doing something to me which really hurts and feels icky too and I'm crying and trying to run away. Before I know it, I am awakened by the chilly wetness of my peed-in sheets, yet again. Mum doesn't say much even though it has been happening with increased frequency lately. I'm not bad, I'm just scared, and of course ashamed. Somehow, mum seems to understand I can't help myself. She quietly changes my bedding and my jammies, hugs me, and tucks me back in, deftly removing my water glass from the nightstand.

For days after my Social Worker's visit, I find myself quite often hiding in the crawl space under the cellar stairs. I need to think things through. It very much feels as if "L.L." is planning to remove me from this home as well. I don't think I've been a very bad little kid at this "home", certainly not bad enough to be sent back through the invisible revolving doors which open into the "C.A.S." asylum! "Teddy! Teddy!" Oh-oh, mum is calling me. I run up from the basement and she looks puzzled and asks, "Are you alright, Teddy?" I try to explain, I was gonna go back to John's and play, but it's raining now so I decided to play Tinkertoys [45] with "Skipper" in the cellar. "Why don't you play in your room?" "O.K."

A few minutes later mum pokes her head in my door and asks again if I need to talk about anything. However, I don't feel like talking so I barely shake a "no" outta my head and continue our construction of a large, intricate bridge. "Well, I'm grilling some cheese sandwiches for lunch. I hope you're hungry." "Nope." She knows me well and senses something is awry, but leaves me to work out things for myself.

Later on, when dad comes home I'm still feeling very insecure so I confront him immediately with the question firing my neurons and burning my lips. I climb onto his lap and, hugging his neck tightly, I ask him if I am a "bad boy". He looks confused and glances at mum. Then, as usual sensing what is really going on in my head, mum mentions to dad that "Mrs..." had stopped by today and she seemed to make me nervous with all her questions. I just decide to ask them both, flat out,

"Dat wady won't ever take me away will she?" (Of course, it didn't sound exactly like that, but they got the gist of it anyway and they reassured me this would not ever happen. You know, I almost believe them, this time. Anyway, it was a good time for reassuring hugs and kisses all around. There really can never be too many of those.)

[February 4, 1953, the Social Worker's follow-up report to the "C.A.S." read as follows,

"After this visit to the 'Thompsons'' home, I am able to report the child is improving a great deal. 'Mrs. Thompson' says he can sing several tunes very well and has his own record collection. The child has an electric train set and several other mechanical toys, which he operates himself. Both of the adoptive parents are really showing a great deal of understanding and insight into handling Teddy and, in my estimation, I believe this placement could become permanent."]

Considering the next part of my plan, it's unfortunate I don't know it yet, because right now, I'm already one giant-step closer to the finality of adoption.

Revolving Doors

Chapter 64: "BAD Teddy" Almost Ruins Everything!

Although my life here on the "Thompsons'" farm is idyllic most of the time, every now and then I get a wild hair up my bum and absolutely *have to* act-out in one way or another. The first major such incident happened right after this Valentine's Day. I was eating so much of my candy, my dad told me to put it away until after I've had my supper. Now, this seemed like an unreasonable demand since I was certain I could eat my candy *and* my supper without any difficulties. So, I *sorta* said, "No!" and by the shocked look on his face, I could see my response didn't sit too well with him.

"Oh my goodness, don't speak to your dad that way, Teddy!" Mum stepped in, to impress upon me this was not acceptable behaviour in our household. However, once again, I sort of said, "No!" but this time to my "mum". "Tell your mum you're sorry, right now." Uh, well, "No! I won't!" slid sideways out of my pie-hole, slapping my dad right in the face. "Go right to your room and don't come out until you are prepared to apologize to us, and behave properly!" dad insisted. Geeze, again? "*No!*" just flew out of my damn mouth!

I don't know why I had such an attitude, or what I was even thinking. I really didn't intend to be so rude to my folks. I was just feeling really angry inside—really, **really** angry! I simply didn't *want* to "do as I was told" for once. Then dad insisted, "You're going straight to your room, right this minute, young man!", and mum agreed by nodding. Then, damned if, "Who cares!" did not spew forth from my innocent little pink lips. Dad was absolutely aghast! "You get right to your room, Teddy." Ever the pacifist, my mum demanded I go to my favourite place in the world, obviously not wanting to witness the consequence of my instigating such an escalation of wills. "Nope!" Oh, no I did not just say that, did I? Oops!

Revolving Doors

"Lillian, put his candy up where he can't reach it. No more candy until we say so, Teddy!" Oh, no—not that! Then, what do you suppose—right out of the blue there I am down on the floor, kicking and screaming, and totally out of control. The "Thompsons" were completely stunned since they had never yet witnessed one of my tantrums, even though they had a pre-determined plan already in place, should this eventuality arise. The plan was to completely ignore me and leave the room, on the assumption that without an audience, I would simply discontinue my *performance*. This also incorrectly assumed I was somehow *in control* of my behaviour *during* such an episode.

I couldn't consciously quit because I was not consciously in control of my thoughts and actions. In fact, I began acting even worse until my head started banging itself against the hardwood floor. The very next thing I knew, I was across dad's knee and getting a bum spank-in. However, I was not about to let dad know he had won this battle of wills, so I just grinned when he finished three whacks with his hand. He looked fit to be tied and so did mum! (I *really* don't understand why I am suddenly acting like this.)

"Tipper, Tipper…wets go out—si—ide." I casually suggest this, acting as if I did *not just* receive my first real bum spanking. Then, adding insult to injury, dad insisted, "You stay on this property and no playing with John today, either!" "Who cares?!" Like stinking verbal vomit, this actually slewed out of my mouth once more. Dad reached for me, presumably, to finish what the flat of his hand had started, but I scooted past both parents so quickly I was out the door and hiding in "Skipper's" house before they could blink!

Actually, the doggy's house is my second hidey-hole on the

"Thompsons'" farm; in fact, it's a good place to go plunk myself down and just think about stuff. I only needed to move some of his straw into a soft little pile because, of course, my bum was definitely feeling the pain of dad's spanking. However, to a greater degree than my bottom, it was *my feelings,* which were hurting. I really didn't think this would happen here at the "Thompsons'" house. "Time-out" and "isolation" are one level of punishment, but this is a whole *nuther* game. Inside "Skipper's" house, I reformulate my escape plan and decide it must now happen *sooner* rather than *later.*

This sort of acting-out and misbehaving occurred once more, before Easter. This time I blatantly began obeying my dad and *disobeying* my *mum.* I did have the idea, since mum never spanked me, that dad was the only disciplinarian in this family. As such, I believed dad would be the only one I really needed to obey. Just as in the previous incident, this too ended with my lying on the floor, kicking, screaming and bashing the back of my head, almost to the point of haemorrhaging again.

Again, dad resorted to spanking me, because, after all, you do what *you know*, and when *you know better, you do better.* I find it peculiar that both before and after the corporeal punishment, both parents looked quite bewildered by my shocking change of behaviour. However, *after* spanking me, what I saw in my dad's eyes was not anger, or even satisfaction, as you might expect. It was tears—tears in this big, strong, grown-up man's gentle eyes. He had hurt me, but I had hurt him much, much worse.

Therefore, after a quiet discussion between my parents, they confronted me with their version of a solution. Dad said, "Teddy, we know you have been through a great deal of trouble in your life, and we certainly don't want to add to that, or to make you feel unhappy or scared of us. This is your *forever* home now and we think you don't understand that, in our home, your *mum* is just as much the boss as I am, especially when it comes to your behaviour. You must obey her whether or not I am at home to administer immediate physical punishment. If I have somehow led you to believe she is not in charge just as much as I am, I'm sorry. I apparently did not make myself clear. However, now I want you to promise to obey your mum, and not talk back, or be rude, to her. If you *do* behave in a way requiring discipline other than isolation, mum is to give you a spanking, if necessary. I glanced at mum for reassurance only to see her tear-filled eyes turn away from mine. Do you understand what I'm saying?" "Yes." I reply, hugging both their necks and ensuring they know I understand dad's meaning, which, of course, I really did, (and so did my bum), but of far greater importance, so did *my heart*.

Regrettably, what I *said*, and what I really *thought* and *felt*, was incongruous. I had clearly once decided never again to endure any physical abuse, torture or molestation from anyone supposedly in charge of my life. I am not exactly sure where, or even if, a spanking falls into those categories. Nonetheless, I decided to stick to my plan to escape this latest probation adoption home before I could be prevented from getting away—far, far away. I don't care if I'm only five-and-a-half, or if I'll be all alone in the world. I have lived more in these short years than most will experience in a full lifetime! After all, being alone is what I seem to do best. I'll just have to await the proper time and opportunity. I plan to pilfer any necessary canned goods, which might be good for a feller on the move. (Canned foods are better since they don't spoil and are quite compact, compared to the same fruits or vegetables in their raw state.) Certainly, the matches and candle, which I must swipe, are also staple necessities in the business of hidey-holes and escapes.

Following this latest incident, it was of no surprise to me that mum, I mean, *"Mrs. Thompson"*, contacted the "C.A.S." for input on the best way to manage my tantrums and head-banging issues. She explained how she and *"Mr. Thompson"* have handled each individual incident, including disclosure about the spankings, which they've documented on the fridge-calendar. My "Worker" told mum, she and dad were, "already handling [me] better than what [the "C.A.S."] could suggest or advise".

The phone voice explained to mum how they expected I would eventually come around and begin facing my demons. The Social Worker also told mum that whenever I am able to face my own issues, it should give me a sense of mastery over that which is mentally and emotionally tearing me from limb to limb, (metaphorically speaking). (However, nobody knew the true nature of my demons. Nobody knew about "Rita", or the little mausoleum, or the cemetery Angel, or my dead little friends—all **seven** of them! Nobody knew about ALL the revolving doors' swirls I've been caught in…nobody, but me, and now, "Skipper"--but I know *he's* not talking.)

I'm just *so* confused. I really don't want to live on the run again. I really don't want to leave the "Thompsons". Maybe, I can do this! Maybe I can try to be good and not rude or belligerent. I *can* be thankful and appreciative of all the wonderful things given to me by these parents, from a place of love and caring in their hearts. I promise myself, aloud, I will do the most *right* thing I can do in each instance, or in confronting each complication I must face. After all, it's already March of 1953 and I'm doing quite fine! No more tantrums or acting-out. I've been as polite as I know how to be. I haven't even banged my head since the last time I guess I frightened the "Thompsons" half to death. I decide to try not to fight these parents, because, after all, they're the *best* things that have ever, ever happened to me.

Revolving Doors

So, today while I'm playing Jacks out front with John and "Skipper", who should arrive but trusty old "Mrs..." my Social Worker. "Hi Teddy, how are *we* today?" (Irrrrrkkkk! "*We* are fine. Go A-way! Leave! Take-off! Scat! Vamoose!" I mentally make every effort to make her disappear; however, she is still here! I wonder about her purpose for today's visit.)

"Oh gw—e—at!" {spoken in a completely facetious tone!} "I gotta go inside now, John!"

"Dat's O.K...Can I pway wis your jacks?" John pleads.

"O.K." I reply, a little anxious to get this interview over-with and get back on with the business of my life, which is obviously playin!

"Teddy..." she says, repeating her question, "How are..." I halt her words with, "'We' are just pfine, tsanks." (Of course this would sound better with my **front teeth intact**, but what else can you do with so many gaps?")

"Is it my imagination, or are you growing taller, and slimmer?" she pretend-asks.

Therefore, I ask her why she has come to us today, and after mum's translation, she responds, reminding me how she had promised to come and see how I am growing from time to time. This satisfied me for the time being and so I drag her into my room and show her its new decor. Then I drag her to the back door and show her some wooden boxes mum and I had constructed to plant flower seeds in. Outside, I show her the start of my small garden and she makes a comment, and a notation for my file which reads, "*Teddy enjoys outdoor life*".

I don't know what prompted me to do what I did next, except

my urgency for her to leave me here and stay away, once and for all time. I crawled right up onto my Social Worker's lap and start hugging her neck and kissing her. Because I am all dirty and slobbery, I *know* I'm making her quite antsy. She is acting embarrassed, trying to lift me off her. My mum, noticing the Worker's discomfort, feels the need to quickly explain that I am very affectionate and often display this by squeezing my parent's necks.

"Oh! Wook! It's my dad!" I scream and jump down from "L.L.'s" lap. I am so anxious to see dad, I run out after the car before he's even in the garage. "Hi, dad!" I yell and he returns the greeting. "Da wady is here to take me away." "No, Teddy, of course not. She's just making a little check on your progress. I'm sure of it." he reassures. Then the Worker comes outside and tells me that my mum wants me in the kitchen. Of course, it's a ruse to get me to go back into the house where, she obviously supposes, I can't hear the conversation she was about to have with dad. Apparently it will be a conversation about "keeping me", "adopting me", "moving me" to the next foster home, "taking me back" to the asylum, or maybe even about "punishing me" for my *inaction*, because I never did tell any adult how the other children I was living with, or hiding-out with, were DYING...or DEAD!!! (I'm still waiting for the other shoe to drop on that one!)

Anyway, I am far too clever for the likes of this Social Worker. All I need to do is sneak out the back door and around to hide in the doghouse, so I can listen to whatever propaganda she is now feeding my dad. Every now and then, I catch a word or two, "*Socialization ... Christmas ... over-indulge ... candy ... tantrums ... head-banging ... belligerent ... will-full ... pugnacious ... etc.*" Of course I don't understand all the words; however, I get the gist of their conversation well enough to know she is slamming him with all the negativity she can muster to trick him into giving the answers she is hoping to write down.

John has already gone on home, so while "Skipper" and I are snug inside the spacious doggie house, we're in a good spot to find out why this "C.A.S." **spy** is *really* here. I feel sorry for dad as she approaches him, because he is unarmed and unprepared for her onslaught of questions. I don't often I see my dad without a word to say, but in this instance, he is struck dumbfounded! He is even stammering a little. (Relax dad...it's *me* she's after, not you!) Dad glances in the direction of the doghouse, as if he has telepathically received my mental encouragement. I peek out and we connect with a quiet little smile. Still, I wonder exactly what it is she's telling him—and why!

PART X: Is "Fostering" Truly Behind Me?

Chapter 65: I Just Didn't *Get It!*

[*I just didn't understand how this time was different and I was really just awaiting the court's timing to finalize my adoption. How could I fathom what "adoption" would mean? I didn't know I would never, ever again have to scrounge for food, or any other of life's necessities. I couldn't understand that the job of taking care of me, was now a job placed in the "Thompsons'" more than capable hands.*]

[Social Worker's Notes, March 1953,

"*Today, Teddy looked very happy and his eyes danced with excitement when he saw his dad's car heading up the driveway. 'Mrs. Thompson' said Teddy eats very well and drinks a quart of milk each day. He sleeps well and is up early in the morning. I noticed Teddy was very excited when his dad came home for supper and rushed out to squeeze him. I had a chance to discuss Teddy's behaviour with 'Mr. Thompson', while we were outside, alone. 'Mr. Thompson' felt the child had been more difficult in February. He constantly asked 'Mr. Thompson' for presents and would sulk when 'Mr. Thompson' said, 'I only brought myself home for you!' I discussed the upsetting effect of the excitement of Christmas and all the presents, which a child receives; and I suggested the 'Thompsons' minimize gift-giving as much as possible during the next few months.*

(*Oh! No! It's a good thing I don't know she's writing this! I guess this would mean I couldn't eat my leftover Valentine's candies. What about the Easter Bunny's sugary delights, which I will collect over at my Sunday School's Easter Egg*

Hunt? No candy! If that be the case, well life just ain't worth livin', now is it?)

I told 'Mr. Thompson' it was often hard for adoptive parents not to over-indulge in giving a child expensive clothes and presents, (due to the parents' own excitement). 'Mr. Thompson' agreed. He said his wife also takes Teddy out for trike-rides and on little bird-watching expeditions. He enjoys these activities and, as summer progresses, they will be going out more and more. 'Mr. Thompson' expressed feeling worried about Teddy's inability to play well with other children. In describing this, he said Teddy dominates and fights, and he tends to boss a lot of them. I told 'Mr. Thompson' of the competition Teddy had to face in his foster homes and suggested this was one of his ways of reacting to a past unpleasant experience.

I asked 'Mr. Thompson' about their methods of discipline, and he said he and his wife try to first reason with Teddy in every instance. He explained to Teddy how mommy and daddy never quarrelled and they wanted him to get along with everyone too. I suggested that most of our older children go through a period of testing behaviour and then as they begin to feel secure, behaviour problems become less and less difficult to work out. I was impressed with the keen interest 'Mr. Thompson' obviously takes in the little fellow. I gave the added suggestion that what would most likely work the best is firm, but kind, discipline in the manner of depriving him of candy, a favourite toy, or even a television show. I also impressed upon both the parents how consistency in working together would best achieve the desired actions from the child.

*'Mr. Thompson' felt Teddy would benefit from school as he is so bright, and I agreed with this. Teddy does seem to have **high average intelligence,** and combined with his boundless*

energy, he requires infinite patience and understanding in order to function well. 'Mr. Thompson' has a wealth of quiet patience and his wife is also a quiet, relaxed person. I feel that together they should be able to work out Teddy's problems. I praised the 'Thompsons' for their accomplishments with Teddy thus far."]

"What are you doing there, Teddy?", "L.L." inquires. (I hear her talking but I'm busy and not paying any attention to her.) "Teddy, 'Mrs...' asked what you were doing, son." dad presses. "I'n doin' a zigsaw puzzle." "It looks pretty hard to me. Is it a tough one?" she asks me. Since it's the only real puzzle I've ever tried to piece-together, I have no point of reference from which to answer her question. "Guess so. It's a bwack horsey." is all the reply I feel like squeezing out. "*She's* very handsome. Does *she* have a name?" the woman pursues. "**She** is a '**he**', 'n' '**his**' name is 'Midnight Bwue Tsar', just wike John's!" I clarify for her. "What did he say?" she grasps for understanding. Mum replies with, "He's only telling you it's a *male* horse and looks like John's pony, named 'Midnight Blue Star'."

Then, changing direction, she speaks to dad, "Oh...So, 'Mr. Thompson'...of course I understand you have your career and must also tend this farm, but can you tell me how often you and Teddy are able to interact." Dad explains how he and I have our own hour of solid playtime every night, no matter what and dad also tells her he always reads me the bedtime stories as well. "My, how wonderful." she comments while writing. In only a few minutes, I've finished assembling my horsey picture puzzle and the Social Worker seems genuinely impressed. Granted it had large jigsaw pieces, nevertheless it was more of an accomplishment in *her* eyes than I could understand.

"Wanna hear me tsing my new tsongs?" I ask her. (I thought I was clear, nevertheless, she glances back and forth between my parents who simultaneously translate.) "Oh, oh yes, of course, Teddy. What did you want to sing for me?" I start with my "ABC" song and then I sing my all-time favourite, "Old MacDonald's Farm". The best part of the Farm song is when the animals each make their noises and my mum and dad help me make the animal sounds too. We all go, "Oink-oink! Moo-moo! Cwuck-cwuck! Neigh-neigh! Quack-quack!" It's so funny! "L.L." actually seems to enjoy my little performance, but now she is right back at the rapid writing. I glance at mum and plead with my eyes, "Is it time to go back out and play now?" She nods affirmatively. "Tipper! Tipper! Wet's do out 'n' pwa—aaay!" It doesn't matter what I say, or how I say it, "Skipper" always understands and always agrees!

Revolving Doors

Chapter 66: The Great Egg Hut

Today is Easter Sunday. I am all shiny and spiffy today, and dressed in a brand new little grey linen suit, with a white shirt and red bow tie. It is the latest fashion for boys my age, according to the "Wishbook", [32] [32a], and my mum, of course. For the finishing touch, she even bought me another new pair of shiny black patent-leather shoes, because I already out-grew my first pair. Although I remember what black, patent leather shoes *used* to mean to me, it's all behind me now, (I *hope*), and this fashionable footwear will never bother me again, (I *hope*).

Mum and dad are really spruced up too. Dad also has a new spring suit, which is grey like mine and he too is sporting a red bow tie around the collar of his new white shirt. Of course, my mum is the real blossom of our bunch. She is wearing a very beautiful grey, tailored skirt-suit, with a red silk blouse. Fastened to her lapel, is a lovely red tulip right out of our spring garden. As always, mum's hair is so perfectly coiffed with, apparently, very little effort. (However, I finally discovered her secret. She has a collection of wigs which she slips on, so she is always ready to go at the drop of a hat!) My mum is so smart and she certainly knows how to make us a picture-perfect family on such a special church day. In fact, she actually brought her camera along to the church in order to get her best friend, John's mum Florence, to take our little family portrait, which she did. Then mum took a photo of John's family too.

As we are milling around in the church parking lot, I can see that many of the other arriving families, especially those with children in-tow, are *all* dressed to the nines as they head to the front doors. I know Sunday is always the day we have an excuse to be fashionable, but today seems a little excessive to me. Of course, the special significance of Easter Sunday has been lost on most of us little kids who are just waiting for the services to be *over.* That's when we can all get on with the fun business of the promised Egg Hunt, to be held out on the expansive back lawn of the church property! However, the *wait* is trying the patience of each of us kids old enough to walk, or run, and hunt for the Bunny's candy.

All the children in the Sunday School classes are absolutely itching to get outside and hunt for the Easter eggs and other candies. However, the main services are really dragging on and on today, so of course, our Sunday School class is taking an extra-long time to finish as well. Then, finally, the tower bells signal the end of the services. Up the stairs I race, with John right on my heels.

We run straight into the waiting arms of our parents, as usual. "We have to go downstairs to the big meeting hall and get some lunch before it's time for the Egg-Hunt, boys." Oh! Why are we wasting all this time? Can't we just go see where the Bunny left the eggs? What if the other kids go out there first and grab all the eggs and candies while we are all down here eating some boring, potluck lunch? Mum, as usual, reads my mind. "Teddy, all the children will go up at the same time and when the minister blows his whistle you will all start on the egg hunt together. Alright with you?" "O.K." I say, but not meaning it. Nevertheless, mum is always right so I decide to make the best of being stuck here with all the food. I decide to try a little spoonful from each of the four different kinds of macaroni and cheese! Then, before we all are too stuffed on what actually prove to be "yummy" potluck lunch items, it's *time*! Yippeeee!

"Whewwweeeee!" goes the minister's whistle and I am off! Before fifteen minutes are up I'm already dumping my multi-coloured, wicker Easter basket full of loot into mum's lap and I'm running back out to re-load. This is such great fun and

Revolving Doors

John is having a riot too. We are racing each other and so far, we are neck and neck! Then, it seems as if no time has gone by and it's all over. Of course, my basket is full to overflowing again, my dad's pockets are stuffed and mum's purse houses the rest of my great big candy haul! Oh, what fun! "Tsanks a wot mum 'n' dad pfor bwinging me. I wove you." They glance at each other and smile exactly the way they did when they were lovingly exchanging Christmas gifts with each other, only a few months ago.

As we pull into our long driveway, I imagine our car is riding lower with the added weight of all my Easter candies! *I am* crammed full from mac-and-cheese-and-candy when dad asks, "What's for supper, Lillian?" "You can't be serious! You just ate your lunch!" she chuckles, adding, "It's the ham dear. I put it in early this morning so it could cook all day and will be good and juicy by dinnertime." "And all the trimmings?" he pries, while already knowing the answer. "Yes, of course, with all the trimmings!" "Wonderful!" he exclaims with a very broad smile.

"Teddy, here's a cloth dear. Don't forget to wipe the dust off your new shoes off before you put them away in your closet." mum directs. I comply; however, gazing at my sort-of reflection in their sheen sets my mind adrift for a moment, making my rib-lump tingle a little. I subconsciously rub my chest over the spot where my rib was broken and displaced by "Rita's" violent kick. I guess this lump will never go away.

Suddenly...wooosh...back from my *day-mare*, I ask my folks, "Wanna candy?" "Don't you eat too much, now...you'll get a tummy ache." mum warns. Then, with a nod and a gap-tooth grin smeared in chocolate, I agree to follow her directive. What a wonderful Easter I've had this year. I am a *very* lucky little kid, these days. What more could I ask out of my life than loving parents, a great best friend, a wonderful doggie and lots

Revolving Doors
and lots of CANDY!

Chapter 67: Swimmin' Holes and Super Buddies!

Wow, it's a hot day! [*Of course, you don't know hot days if you don't know Southern Ontario summer steaming hot days!*] I'm just lazing around and not feeling like doing much of anything, when I hear the familiar little *tap, tap, tap*. It's John at the front door. "Hey, Teddy, d'ya wanna do swimmin'?" "Yeah! Mu—um...can I go swimmin' with 'John'?" "Alright, dear. Don't you want your bathing suit?" I shake my head to say "No", because when we boys swim in the pond, we skinny-dip—of course! Who needs swim suits? Hahahaha! "Wet's det Mikey too." John suggests and I agree.

In no time we're about to leave Mike's house, when his mum gives the three of us home-made Popsicles she made from freezing grape juice in an ice cube tray with recycled Popsicle sticks. What a great, yummy idea and a good way to get cool before we all get too hot! Then, in no time at all, the three of us are bobbing around in the mirky water of the shallow pond, which is located right at the back of John's property where it just meets up with Mike's farm.

[The overflowing of this pond will later contribute to much of the flooding of ours, and surrounding, farmland when the infamous Hurricane Hazel dumps 300 million tons of water in Southern Ontario on October 15, 1954, when I am just a little over seven years old.] [16] [16a]

"Ow! Ouch!" Mike's hopping around on one foot. "What happened?" I ask. "Sumpin' bit me! It bit me!" We all have a look at the injured patient but can barely see any bite under all the muck on his feet. "You'll live. Stop whining. Ha! At least it didn't bite your wee-wee off!" I tell him. "Shut-up!" Mike screams. Then John and I start laughing and cackling as if we're a couple of hyenas, but Mike is still upset. Oh well, I guess there might be some fish or other things that could bite you, however it's not going to deter me from my main purpose—swimmin' and poking my toes down into the cool mud at the bottom of the pond. That's the best way of cooling down! The pond mud feels all squishy and mushy, and I like it, but Mike hates it, *now*! Therefore, as the day stretches on, John and I swim and sunbathe repeatedly. (Mike is being a big scaredy-cat because he thinks there is a great big crab or some kind of fish with big teeth down in the muck and mire of the little pond.)

Nevertheless, we all soon come to the realization we are absolutely starving. So we head back to Mike's for some grub. "Hi boys!" "Mrs...", (Mike's mum), greets us in her usual cheerful manner. "Momma, I got bit by sumpin' in the pond!" Mike starts explain-whining with what almost looks like tears in his eyes. His mum has a closer look at the injured patient, and tells him it will be fine. Then she turns to us and says, "I betcha I know exactly what you all want right now—some lunch. Am I right?" This diminutive, dark-haired, Italian woman hit a homer with that guess. "Well, you boys go wash up, then sit-down here. I've already made some sandwiches for you." (How did she know? Hmmm, "mums" just never cease to amaze me.)

"D'ya wanna do back swimmin' after wunch?" John asks. "Wet's go pway in your barn." I suggest, since Mike doesn't seem to want to get back into our pond any time soon. Anyway, we all agree on the barn since we've had quite a bit of sun already today and the barn is always cooler, especially the lower, underground part. However, before long, we are all worn out, and it's time for Mike to head on home, anyway. "Can I come to your pwace?" John asks me. "Sure."

As we are walking up my lane, we are trying to beat each other at skipping stones in the creek. Nevertheless, it is a futile effort because the water has all but dried up in most places.

"Whaaaat? Oh no!" I look up to see the station wagon belonging to "Librarian Lady's" sister, parked out front of the house. "Who's dat car?" John innocently asks. He doesn't have a clue about the years of horrible, hidden secrets in my life. "Never mind. It's nobody's." is all I feel like admitting. He takes the hint and doesn't pursue the question.

"Oh, hello, John. John is Teddy's best friend, 'Mrs...'. As always, they're stuck together with glue!" my mum jokes. Then both women break out in laughter. "Oh—dear, say hello to 'Mrs...'" mum says encouragingly. She's probably hoping I won't show my true disappointment and embarrass her. "Oh, hi." I say, with no pleasantness whatsoever, all the time wondering what the hell she is doing here *now—again*. "I wanted to come and visit before June was out, Teddy. How're you doing?" she asks. (Wow, she said "*you*", not "we"!) "I'n pfine—okaaaay." I answer with a measure of disdain. "You boys look wonderful and look at those tans! I can see you've been having a lot of fun at this house." (Oh gosh, I sure hope she doesn't talk about anything like the orphanage, or my foster homes, or moving me again!)

Mum quickly pours some lemonade and puts us in my room with a large plate of cookies on my nightstand. We put my records on and start playing "Tinkertoys" [45], while the women talk in the living room. "I feel like Teddy has steadily improved with every passing day here, 'Mrs...'" mum explains. "How are his skills at interaction with others coming along? And what are you doing in the way of discipline now?" "L.L." pries. "Well, he still tries to be rude and noisy at times but is more easily corrected. In fact, my husband feels much more encouraged particularly in view of the fact that Teddy now shares his toys quite readily. He is also getting along much better with other children now. In fact, we installed the new swing set and teeter-totter out back, on the *condition*, Teddy promises to *share*. These days, we'll hear him say to the other boys, 'Come outside and play on my swing-set!'" Mum continues to explain the changes around here in the manner of discipline they use, including actual physical punishment, and their occasional threats of the *belt*.

"Oh, I almost forgot, our *Director* wanted me to bring you these pamphlets about "Camping", in case you feel Teddy might be interested." "L.L." says while rifling through her rather ample, yet stuffed, hand-bag. "My husband feels summer camp would be good for Teddy so he could mix with many other children, and not only his usual pals, John and Mike. As a matter of fact, in July there's a two-week church camp involving Teddy's Sunday school class." mum discloses. "Actually, 'Mrs. Thompson', I discussed this issue with his Case Worker and we both feel it should be discouraged at this time. We honestly think Teddy might well become upset by leaving a home in which he has lived *less than a year* and we feel next year might be soon enough for this special sort of activity." "Of course, I'll tell my husband how you feel. However, he has actually indicated he wanted Teddy to participate in camp activities so, as he puts it, '*Teddy will grow up into a manly boy and not a sissy.*'" "Certainly, the choice would be left up to you folks, and we can quite understand 'Mr. Thompson's' attitude." my Worker adds, back peddling just a little.

When I see that my Social Worker is about to leave, I decide to show her how well I am able to swim in the little kiddie pool out front of our house. "Good, Teddy, I can see what fun you're having! Well, I'll be off until the next time I come to see you." she says while walking to the car, (not looking at me). "Why does she come here, Teddy?" John asks. "She wants to see how big I'n getting." is my truthful answer, with some obvious omissions in my reply. (I quickly decided it's all the information my younger little friend needs to know about my past.)

Chapter 68: Too Many Doctors, Dammit!

Through the rest of the hot summer months, I am forced to miss many opportunities of playing and having fun. It's because two times a week, and sometimes three, mum drags me to appointments with a team of a new kind of doctors in Toronto. I vehemently hate it! They ask me a million questions. They don't dress in white suits, weigh me, look in my ears or throat or even give me bum-shots. They just sit there and fire questions at me, while writing my answers down word-for-word.

For instance, on Monday, "Dr. Adams" asked me if I knew why I had come to live with the "Thompsons". I looked at mum before I answered his obviously stupid question, but mum was very quiet and evidenced no answers by her facial expressions. I told them, "*I know I have always been a bad boy and have been living with a lot of other people.*" As well, I said, "*I came to my parents when I was five because they wanted a boy of my age.*" After mum's quick, concise translation, the team seemed relatively satisfied, this time anyway.

I really hate going to these doctors because every damn time I am in their office they ask me lots and lots more repetitions of the same questions. Then, without ever looking at me, they frantically write down stuff while I am talking. Today, it was "Dr. Gerhardt" firing the questions at me. (I certainly don't know how he became a doctor. This man talks even *less* understandably than I do and *he* doesn't have anybody, like my mum, to translate for him.)

Sometimes their questions are very difficult to answer. It's not because I'm stupid, but because it *hurts* my head to remember the answers. They often dig to elicit the details behind my broken rib. I tell them "*Her* shoes did it." They ask if I mean my mother's shoes. Dummies—of course not! However, I am still truly terrified to tell them *whose* shoes and exactly what happened, because they might contact "Rita". Then she would come after me and kill me for sure—or worse, she could hurt my parents and *not* kill me.

The doctors actually want me to *remember* the multitude of painful and frightening incidents which occurred while I was stuck at the "hell-house" where "Rita" abused me. I hate her. I don't want to remember. I hate the doctor team and, I am not too very pleased with mum for bringing me here. Then, "Dr. Franklin", a pretty, blonde-haired, lady with deep blue eyes, starts prying about the foster home where I lived with "Big Boy" and the other two kids. I don't *want* to remember that either. It hurts me. At least they don't even know what to *ask* about the last boys' group home because we all ran away! Nobody, absolutely *nobody*, except us boys, "Dog," God and Santa, knew what happened to us kids during our months spent down in the Don Valley.

Another one of the prying team, "Dr. Sanchez", (also speaking in a virtually unintelligible accent), inquires about the toys I like to play with these days. He also questions me about the books I read. Mum answers for me regarding the "books" because, of course, I have not yet learned to read. They even ask silly questions, such as, "What are you afraid of? Is it thunder storms, or spiders, or snakes or what?" Well my truthful and perfect answer is simply, "*Nothing* during the daytime and *everything*, when I'm asleep." Then, pooling their notes, they all give mum suggestions as to how she should be encouraging my reading and writing skills. They keep stacking even more responsibilities on top of mum's already heavily burdened shoulders and, certainly, onto my dad's also. Dad has enough worrisome stuff pushing grey hairs outta his head already. Anyway, mum just nods, agrees and signs all of the papers they push across the desk at her before we are able to make our escape.

["C.A.S." file notation,

"Each time we receive the psychometric, [66], and/or psychological reports from the specialists' office working with this case, we add them to the attached file "B". All entries within this folder are concerned with tracking the child's mental health and his emotional and intellectual growth and development, and also in demonstrating and recording his degree of progress in each of these areas."]

Revolving Doors

Chapter 69: Picnics, Prizes and Playfulness!

Luckily, I quickly realize, the fun picnic activities in the summer months actually far out-weigh the times I've been put through the ringer with all the head-pounding doctors' questions. Happily, the official picnic season began in May when we went to the annual picnic with my *mum's family.* This was my *very first-ever* picnic, though obviously it was not my first time eating out in a nature setting. There was such a varied selection of food brought in by all the women in our extended family. Everyone could find something enjoyable from all the choices and activities. *I* participated in every one of the *picnic-y* games, which were set-up for us little kids! I filled my day with eating, playing, running, swimming, eating, playing, running and swimming.

Then, a month later, in early June, we went to my second picnic with my *dad's family.* It was very much a repeat of my first picnic. I had a little too much food and a little too much sun, though. At this picnic, there was not one game in which I didn't participate. After all, I could never have too much *fun!*

On the weekend of Canada Day's July first celebrations, my *dad's office people* arranged for their *yearly picnic* festivities to be held on Centre Island. They chose this weekend because it was a holiday, and usually the best time of year for good weather as it's almost always dry and warm, but not as sweltering hot as August. Our special picnic day started at the Toronto ferry docks where we met-up with all the other families from dad's workplace who needed to get to the picnic site at the same time. The day's fun activities actually began with our ride on the huge, noisy, slow, stinky ferry-boat across the waterway between downtown Toronto's harbour-front and the recreational areas of Centre and Ward's Islands, and Hanlan's Point. The ferry was far too much fun to ride in, although its diesel-fuel smell, sadly, reminded me of my dead grandpa.

Anyway, once we docked, I couldn't get off fast enough. I pulled and tugged at my parents' hands but they just disembarked in their usual manner—slowly and carefully. Once on the island, the real, actual *picnic* fun started. There was a large area sort of a roped off with some of those colourful plastic flags they hang up to catch your attention at car dealerships. Inside the specified area were picnic tables, prize tables and people doing the last minute buzzing around to make-ready the day's activities. Our roped-off area is decorated everywhere with the company's logo colours of red and white. Even the checkered tablecloths are in the company colours. Attached to the corners of each table, are decorative red and white balloons, drawing attention to the array of food, food, food—no end to the food—on almost every table! When I look around, I under-stand the reason behind our delineated space, because I see many other groups, here and there on the island's picnic area, setting up for their own planned activities. Certainly, none of the kids in each of the groups want to be mixed up in the other's celebrations.

Once our games began, you could choose from several fun activities such as Horse-Shoe Tossing, Three-Legged Race, Sprinting Races, Lawn Bowling, Bean Bag Toss and numerous others. In addition, there were games like Dodge Ball for the bigger kids. For the winners there were prizes of chocolate bars and candy boxes, red, blue and white ribbons, trophies or medallions on long red and white ribbons. Because I am such a fast runner, for a little feller, I easily out-sprint the other kids who aren't trying as hard to win when they think little ol' Teddy is their competition. (Of course, having my mum and dad cheering me on the loudest probably contributed the most to my success!) For reaching the other side first, I received a bright, shiny red ribbon, which a nice woman pinned on my shirt right before handing me a box of candies. Oh boy, what fun!

Some of us kids played on the swings, slides and monkey bars during the in-between times when the organizers were setting up the next activity. Though I had fun doing everything, I think my most favourite game was the Potato-Sack Race. It was a father-son or -daughter race and my dad and I had such a blast! We didn't win, but we laughed and fell down and kept trying until we had tears coming down our faces, we were giggling so hard. The people at dad's company who arranged this event even rented a cotton candy machine, out of which spun my very first taste of the most delectable fuzzy blue treat! It is so yummy and it melts immediately, as soon as it hits on your tongue!

"O—ka-a-ay, da-a-a-ds and ki-i-i-ds, it's ti-i-i-me for the fishing-ing-ing tourne-e-ey." Some man with a reverberating megaphone is announcing this in every direction. I well-remember how to fish for minnows with a stick, string and a safety pin, after all, that experience happened only last summer. Oh, but this is a far more sophisticated little tournament. There are prizes for the "biggest", "tiniest" and "most fish caught". As well, the organizers are supplying the fishing poles and even the bait—real, live, squirmy worms.

[I keep thinking—no, asking myself, "Isn't this just waaaay too much fun for any little, soon-to-be-six-year-old, gutter rat?" I can't help it. I just keep wondering and asking myself, "When is everything gonna change and when am I gonna get kicked out of the 'Thompsons'' home, and lives, forever?"]

Anyway, my thoughts quickly race back into the moment as my dad patiently demonstrates the "basics" any good angler needs to know. In a very short time, dad and I actually come in "second place" for the "biggest" fish caught today! It's a good-sized lake Trout—weighing a whopping eleven-and-a-half pounds. Dad was super excited and, of course, mum was very pleased too. So was I, because it was the very first real fish I ever caught! I think first prize went to the father-*daughter* team for catching a big, ugly thing—a "Carp", I believe they called it. Their nasty looking fish-monster had to be over fifteen pounds. The first prize was a tiny trophy shaped like a fish! Who needs such a silly thing? I got a nice, shiny blue ribbon pinned on my chest for the Second Prize! Huh...at least our Trout was a *pretty* fish.

I can't help thinking this picnic is proving to be equally as much crazy fun as both my families' picnics combined! Only this time I must admit, I've had too much food and sun; however, I'll never admit to having too much *fun*. That would be virtually impossible!

At the end of the fishing competition, you could either throw your catch back into the lake after the judge determined its weight, or you could do what we did and take it on home at the end of the day. I wondered, but didn't ask, why we were transporting the fish wrapped in waxed paper, instead of in a bag, or even a bucket, of lake water. That's because I rather thought, once we got home, we would be putting him in a huge fish bowl and making him my *pet*. However, mum and dad had much different plans for our fishy. They explained they were "going to scale and clean it and cook it for tonight's supper". Really? Seriously? (Well, I for one, just lost my appetite.)

Once at home, I am feeling very sad about the prospect of everybody eating my fish. Certainly, *I* want to keep him and take care of him. However, dad clearly explained how a lake fish needs to live in a great big lake—like Lake Ontario. He said, in order to continue living, the fish must immediately be returned to the lake. (I guess this was an example of the original practice of, "catch and release".) I sort-of understood, but nothing will make me swallow any part of "Mr. Fishy".

Revolving Doors

Regardless of my personal feelings toward our Trout, I watched attentively while my mum and dad toiled hard getting the "fish" part of our dinner prepared. Besides the fish, which proved to be the most work, mum made *my* favourites: corn on the cob, little carrot coins and baked potatoes. I ended up eating all my vegetables, but I just couldn't get one bite of the fish down my throat, because it just closed up. I couldn't help myself...it was "Rita's" stink—right there on my plate. I could *not* tell my parents and they wouldn't possibly know what had happened previously in my life to create in my mind, such an aversion to eating the little pieces of "Mr. Fishy". Mum and dad put it down to my not wanting to eat an animal we just caught—and sort of killed. Therefore, dad tries to impress upon me the fact that, as part of my life on a farm with chickens and turkeys, eventually I will experience a lot more of life's hard lessons. The lessons he is referring to are those having something to do with eating your friends. However, that was not at all my problem with this fish dinner—it was just the smell—***her*** disgusting smell.

Chapter 70: Now We Are "Three" and I Am *Six*!

Today is my sixth birthday and mum has prepared a special party for me—my very first ever, at this house! John, Mike, Travis, Tony and Sonny are all here to help me celebrate. Travis and Sonny are brothers, Travis being the elder at seven years of age. Sonny and I have birthdays one week apart! Both boys have dirty blonde, bowl-cut hair and blue eyes, and both are taller than John and me. Tony, (short for "Anthony"), is a bean-pole of a kid with almost black eyes and no hair at all, because, once his mom shaved it off when he came home from school with the "cooties", (the "head lice" which were, and still are, often treated in boys, by shaving all their hair off). Then their mom decided to keep it that way, at least through the hot summer months. When all the kids first got here, the boys who have not yet gotten to know "Skipper" go crazy petting him and making friends with him, as he jumps all around showing off.

My mum has organized quite an exceptional birthday party for me today. First, she decorated our house all over with streamers and balloons, (and John and I helped her). Then she planned some games for us to play and she even has prizes for the winners. All over the living room are treats of candies, potato chips and pretzels in bowls, so we can all just help ourselves, instead of asking mum every five minutes. Then she made all the little sandwiches for lunch, but they're almost too pretty to eat. Of course, she also baked a wonderful cake for me which is a triple-layer chocolate cake, with chocolate icing in between each layer. She also has chocolate ice cream to go along with the cake and there's even chocolate milk to wash it down, (or you can have white milk if you'd rather). These are all *my* very favourite delights.

There are six lighted candles on my birthday cake and across the cake itself, mum says it actually reads, "Happy Sixth Birthday Teddy", in cursive writing made with blue icing. Also, drawn on it with yellow icing, is an outline of a doggie which looks a lot like "Skipper". When I make my secret wish and blow out my candles, everybody claps, laughs and sings me the "Happy Birthday" song. (I shouldn't tell my wish because everyone reminds me it won't come true then. Nonetheless, I only wished this fun would go on forever and ever—that's all.) Anyway, after we boys have our "gas tanks all sugared-up", as mum puts it, we have to play some "running-around-and-letting-off-steam-games", before we settle down in time for me to open my gifts. So, outside we play Tag, Hopscotch, Leapfrog and Hide-n-Seek! What g-r-e-a-t fun!

O.K., now we are all ready for the big reveal! One at a time, I open the absolute best presents a six-year-old kid could ask for, or ever dream of getting. Travis gave me a "Giant Pan American Clipper Plane", [146], with spinning propellers, landing gear, a luggage wagon and a loading ramp. From Tony I got a "Bomber Exploding Ship" [145]. You fly it over the enemy's target ship and when you drop the bomb onto the exploding ship, it busts into eight parts! Then you make a bombing sound, like, "BOOM-BOOM-*KABOOM*". Sonny got me a "Truck Terminal" [141], with fifty-two pieces. Mike gave me a "Caterpillar Earth-Moving Equipment" set, [142], which has a motor grader, a scraper and a wagon with a tractor and everything has real working action! John got me a "Walkie Talkie Set", [147], which you can talk and listen on at the same time. It even has fifty feet of cord. [147] We are gonna have a blast with it! Then mum and dad gave me a, "Tom Corbett Space Academy" [144], which has space cadets, frogmen, the Space buildings, rocket ships and flying saucers which actually *fly*. The "Gilbert Tool Chest" [143], they gave me has twenty-one real tools just like dad's! Now I can help him build huge things, or mom and I can build a kiddie-car or another wheelbarrow. Then, to top it off, "Skipper" runs outside and fetches me his favourite bone—I'm not kidding!

Thanks everybody! I really *love* everything! Wowee! What a haul! And, what a birthday! As long as I live, I am never gonna forget this first birthday party with ALL my bestest friends, my wonderful mum and dad and my "Skipper". I sure hope I get another party when I turn seven. I hope so, but I guess I will just "have to wait and see", like mum is always reminding me.

Chapter 71: Things Are Just a-Rollin' Right Along...

"Are we ready? Let's go over our list once more." mum worries aloud. She has been running around like one of our chickens that temporarily got loose after my dad chopped his head off. She is trying to get me all ready for my first day of school, called "Kindergarten"! That's tomorrow! I am excited too, but of course, I really have no idea exactly why. Even my dad is all a-buzz too. They will be driving me tomorrow and waiting to bring me home, because it's a shortened day. They really don't want, or expect, me to ride the school bus, (at least not until I've met other children who ride, and we've all met the bus driver, "Mr. St. Pierre", too).

Mum is checking my clothes, my pencil case, and whatever else my teacher told her I might need to bring along on my first day of class. She bought me a special kit to carry my lunch in after my first day. It's a "Hopalong Cassidy" lunch pail! [148] No kidding! Boy oh boy, does my mum ever *know* me. I ask if I can wear my cowboy suit but my parents think it isn't appropriate and instead lay out some regular play clothes for me. They said I *could* wear my "Hopalong Watch", [104], but only on the first day, so it doesn't get broken or lost.

It seems as though no time at all has passed and I have settled into the school routines. Everything is going well, I guess, for the most part, at least. I've gotten the hang of how to behave properly in the classroom, and I try my best to do exactly as my teacher tells me. I have a very nice Kindergarten teacher named, "Miss Barry". Well, at least she went by that name when school first started, but a few weeks after the first day of class, she got married. Because I tend to get my "ts" and my "ss" mixed up, I have trouble pronouncing, her married name, "*Mrs. Waterston*". I think, "Miss Barry" was a whole lot easier to roll off my lips.

Anyway, "Mrs. W" is quite tall and rather lovely with long light brown hair curling all around the bottom. She always wears very pretty dresses—a different one every day, in fact. They are all fashioned in the same style with a fitted blouse type of bodice, which has short, cuffed sleeves and a belted waist, which floats over a very full skirt. Sometimes I find myself daydreaming a little, while mesmerized by the floral prints and the sound of their crinolines beneath, as they swish-swish up, and sash-sashay down the aisles between our row-seats.

Whenever my teacher leans down to help me with something, I notice "Mrs. W" smells very nice, like mum's roses. When she speaks, she has a soft, tender and low, calming tone. Also, I really like her kind and patient manner, which is similar to my mum's and dad's. Overall, my time spent at school is quite delightful and especially enjoyable at snack time, recess and lunchtime. We kids even have our own mats to lie on when it is time to take a nap—which is something we must do every afternoon when "Mrs. W" signals us by turning-out the classroom lights.

Mum doesn't really like me riding on the bus alone, but dad is glad I am "taking a little responsibility". "It's a small step towards your own independence." he says. At least I have Mike to ride with almost every day, unless he is sick or something. I have him and Tony who I hang out the most with at school, but John isn't old enough to go yet. He'll have to wait until next year. Sonny and his brother Travis moved away right before school was to start this year. I guess, other than Mike and Tony, I really don't have any friends at school whom I can truly trust and who don't pick fights with me.

Sadly, some of the boys try to bully me because I am six and just now starting kindergarten. Of course, they also hassle me because I'm just a little feller. However, my dad is teaching me a few 'boxing' moves to handle those kids, (much to my mum's chagrin). That's why I'm feeling like such a big boy these days. I even know how to enter the school from the playground. We have to use the BOYS' side door which opens into the washroom area on the lower level of the school. It is completely blocked off from the GIRLS' lower level side. It's where we have to clean-up our hands and faces or take a pee, but quickly, *before* the second bell rings. This routine is no problem for me because I'm six now and I *get it*.

Unfortunately, however, as big as I am acting at school, there is one little, tiny problem at home, where I realize that I'm not quite as big as I think I am. It's all because a few weeks into the school year, some *bigger girls,* who were in the schoolyard at recess one day, started to pick on me. They made fun of me and even laughed and pointed at me too. I don't know *why* they did this, but I really didn't like it at all and I told them to, "Stop-it!" I really, really wanted to hit them, but my dad has taught me I must always remember the rule, "Never hit a girl." Because I have to stick to this rule, I really don't know what to do when these mean, bully-girls taunt me. So sometimes, out of sheer frustration, I start to cry. Of course, that makes them tease, and laugh at, me even more.

Unfortunately, their relentless mocking seems to have sparked some real whopper nightmares for me lately. In my sleep, I've been re-living the repetitious horrors of torture and sexual abuse I endured at "Rita's" hands. Lately, virtually on a nightly basis, I've been waking up screaming and crying, all over again. My hair and jammies are always as soaking wet as my bed. These dark memories of the ritualistic, horrendous torments, which she inflicted upon me, are giving birth to a new kind of bad dream, and it is one which is far more severe than my regular nightmares. These new kind of dreams are actually termed *night terrors*, and they certainly are! In these unspeakable terrors, I am also re-living the additional abuses, which I've suffered under the so-called *care* of so many of the foster "mothers" in my life.

Then, even worse than recalling those incidents of neglect and/or mistreatment, are my nightmares about illness, dying and death. I don't dream about my own demise, of course, (I don't particularly care about myself), but about mum's and dad's, or "Skipper's", or even John's. Everybody I care about and love is dying or dead, in these dreams. In fact, last night I had another *terror* dream about my own sweet mother who gave birth to me. A very big girl was beating her, causing her bones to crack and making her battered body all bloody! It was unspeakably horrific. However, of course, I can't tell mum the details of my night terrors, or even explain the actual dreams to her. So all I say is "yes" when she asks me, knowingly, if I had another bad dream. She has *ab-so-lute-ly* no earthly idea of the true nature of my night terrors, and she never, ever will. [*In fact, even when mum went to Heaven, I had never disclosed the truth of my former abuses—and she never found out.*]

Oh no, not again! Please, not this again! Not now. I really thought I was doing so well. Oh, damn! My mum just finished cleaning me up and changing my bedding, after another night of accidents. Right now, my head is banging itself against the wall. Here we go again. Bang! Bang! Bang! I am feeling very ashamed of myself right now, and about my *past* also. I truly hope my parents will never know what exactly went on in my life before I came to them. Absolutely nothing beneficial would come of their having such information. So, how do I explain my nightly agony? And, how do I stop it?

"Oh, dear, Teddy. Oh my goodness, son, you've cut your head again. Please stop thrashing about. Please stop, sweetheart." Mum is so worried, and I am feeling no less scared, myself.

Then, having been awakened, dad pokes his head in my door and asks, "What can I do, dear?" Mum tells him to go back to sleep as she has decided if *any* of us are going to get any rest tonight, she'll have to lie down beside me and hold me tightly, all night long. Mum is so very intuitive, reassuring and comforting. With her loving arms around me to keep the night terrors at bay, I believe I am going to be alright now, at least for tonight, anyway.

Chapter 72: We All Give "Thanks"--But *I* Give "Extra"!

Once again, mum, dad and I are sitting at our dining-room table just about to chow down. However, tonight's supper will prove to be quite different from any other night's. That's because today is "Thanksgiving Day" and my mum has done a beautiful job of decorating our table accordingly. First, she put on the very spiffy white linen tablecloth, which boasts lovely, detailed red, orange and yellow leaves, all perfectly embroidered by mum, of course. They form a *running* pattern connected by green stems all around, and just inside, the edges of the cloth. Each side is also finished with scalloped eyelet lace sewn on all around the perimeter. My eyes are fixated on the coloured leaves as my mind drifts to the warm memory of a striking autumn canopy. It is what I viewed so many times as I gazed out across the calico-painted treetops of the Don River valley, (from my safe hiding spot way up in the Necropolis).

However, quite unexpectedly, a chill washes over the back of my neck making the fine little hairs stand at attention. I shiver as I suddenly "*remember everything*". Nevertheless, I am quickly mindful of the fact that "*everything I remember*" is all over now, and I should push it far behind me—forever. It's why I am silently "giving thanks" for the most horrific part of my life being all *over* now. Right now, in this very moment, I am also "giving thanks" for this wonderful mum and dad whom I wish, and hope, will be the very *last* couple to take me into their home and their lives. I sincerely love them and I am sure they genuinely love me too. I really want to grow up with the "Thompsons" as my parents, FOREVER. Could it be possible? I sigh a little, while thinking, "If only wishes could come true." (I could sure use some birthday candles right about now.)"

Revolving Doors

Mum and dad, unaware of my secret thoughts, are smiling as we all gaze at the amazing spread of food before our eyes: turkey, stuffing, mashed potatoes, gravy, carrots, turnips, yellow wax beans and little green Brussels sprouts, always my dad's favourite. Naturally, pumpkin pie with fresh whipped cream is our dessert reward, "if [we] boys eat up good". I am "giving thanks" for my mum, "I think you're the greatest in the whole world, and of course, you too Dad." By the way, both of our turkeys are still running around outside, with their heads on, right? Whew—once again, I am sure glad we aren't eating my friends—very glad. In fact, I'm *truly* "giving thanks".

Over the next several weeks, my life goes on with its regular routines. School is good. My best friends are great. I still *hate* girls. Oh yes, and I'm sick and staying home from school today because mum says I have a cold. I've been coughing and hacking all over the house. She won't let me go outside to play, or not even to walk "Skipper". She's afraid my head cold might turn into "Bronchitis" or "Pneumonia". Well, please don't tell me my old nemeses are about to rear their ugly heads again! I will have none of Thee, Sir "Brown Kites"--nor any of Thee either, Sir "New Onions"! Be gone! Pray, scat! "Swish, swish, swish..." No, it's not a revolving door this time. It's the sound of me jumping around, and "pretend-sword-fighting" in the air, in order to stab those two nasty diseases *to death*.

Today, I'm bored as heck and just sitting with the realistic little porcelain kitty, looking out the bay window. John and Mike are both sick and can't come out to play with me either. That just leaves "Skipper" and me to share our daydreams, while staring out the front window's panes. What the heck?! Ohhhhhhh! Hell nooo! It's "Librarian Lady" driving her sister's station wagon and bumping all along up our long driveway. I take off like a lightning flash and scoot down into the cellar and under the stairs to my nearest hidey-hole. "Skipper" is right beside me wagging his tail wildly and stirring up the dust. "Hey, 'Tipper' get away, shush, go upstairs—wight now!" (I have to really pretend I'm mad at him or else he won't leave my side.) "Go on, now! Go up, I said!" I'm whisper-yelling right now, because I'm desperate to stay quite well hidden and out of my Social Worker's reach. I feel like something **very bad**, regarding my staying here, is about to happen. The proverbial *other shoe* is about to drop and I think it's gonna land right on my head! (Did I just hear a "sweep, sweep, sweep"? On the other hand, am I imagining it?)

The washer has stopped swishing the clothes around, so now I'm easily able to hear the women's conversations from my basement hiding spot. "Ted-dy, Ted-dy! Where are you dear? 'Mrs...' has dropped by to see you. Come to the kitchen please." I really don't want mum to get mad at me, so what can I do but comply? Then mum asks me to say hello and I do so. "Skipper" is jumping all over the place trying to say hello in his own doggie way. (He would not be acting so excited and happy to see this woman if he really knew what she is here for—to take me back to the asylum orphanage.) I flash her a broad smile, and jump right into the conversation in order to *answer* all her questions, before she asks them. I start telling her everything about as rapidly I can fire the words off, with mum scrambling to translate, and catching only about every third word.

I tell "L.L." about the approaching Christmas, and what is going on at my school, also about all our farm animals, including my pet baby duckie, "Missy Quack-Quack" and my baby piggy, "Pinkie Pooper". (I explain why I named her, because, of course, she is pink and she poops a lot). Then, I show my "Worker" several of my books, acquired after my "head doctors" sent her their last report about my mental health status and their suggestions that I need to begin learning how to read. She then asks me to read one of them to her, in a sneaky way of testing me. Fortunately for me, I have them all memorized page by page. Therefore, after I impress her with my reading skills, next, I play a couple of my records and sing-along to] the "Fa wa wa wa wa", Christmas song.

During the whole time she is here, I run around and do everything mum asks of me. Then I jump up on mum's lap and squeeze her neck. "Do you wove me mum? Am I a good wittle boy, mum? Do you need something else I can do?" Then I whisper my **real** question in my mum's ear, "Is she gonna take me away again?" Mum shakes her head to say, "No!" Then I ask her, "Wanna hab a cookie, 'Mrs...'?"

"Is this how he treats every visitor, or is he just so overly attentive because it is me?" she asks mum. (The small quiver in her voice betrays her nervousness, no doubt at the possibility of what either "Skipper", or I, might do next.)

[November 15, 1953, Social Worker's Follow-up Report for Teddy's file,

"*I felt that his relationship with 'Mrs. Thompson' was a happy one. He talked to her, and pointed things out to her. 'Mrs. Thompson' was unexcitable, but remained calm and consistent and obviously enjoyed Teddy. While Teddy was out of the room, 'Mrs. Thompson' explained how she and her husband are very anxious to have the adoption completed. She said, they really think of him as their own son, and all of their family are devoted to him as well. She asked about telling him about his background. Apparently, he tells them they 'couldn't take him until {their} house was finished'. They agreed, they don't deny this story, but also agree to my suggestion they should answer any questions formally and not lead him to believe anything other than the truth.*"]

Revolving Doors

Chapter 73: The "*SIGNING*"

I just asked my parents why we are all being so spruced up today. Is there somewhere special where we are going? I don't think its Sunday, or is it? I am absolutely bursting, I'm so full of questions, but I don't seem to be getting answers. My parents are unusually quiet and just speaking in hushed tones about something that's going to happen today. We are all dressed up in our gray suits, which we wore to Church at Easter. However, today Dad's tie, mum's blouse and my clip-on tie, are all, exactly matching in cornflower blue.

"Hurry up, Teddy! Let's get going!" Moments later, we are already half-way down our long lane when mum asks, "Do you have your glasses, Ralph?" "Oh-No, I don't. It's a good thing you asked me dear, because I'm gonna need them today, aren't I?" We had not even made it to the end of our lane way when dad had to back the car up all the way to the house. "O.K. I know I have everything, now." he assures himself, while handing his eyeglass case to mum. "Did I tell you how lovely you look today dear?" "You uh, probably did, uh, I mean, thank you sweetheart." mum responds, while obviously very distracted by *something*. "I'm pretty hungry. Are you?" dad asks mum. Then, in the next breath, he assures her, "We'll stop at the little family restaurant *after*, if you like." "After? After? After what?" I can only wonder if they're planning to take me back to the "C.A.S." asylum. Maybe they'll just dump me off because I did something wrong. Maybe I cost too much money and they want to dine-out without me. I don't know the reason, but I do know they're getting rid of me and the "hand-off" will happen as soon as we get where we are going, which I'm absolutely certain will be the "C.A.S.".

PART XI: My Last "Revolving Door"

Chapter 74: My Right of Passage

I am still without an answer to my questioning *why* we are all being so spiffed up today. Regardless, we are already on our way to... to... to where? Today is December 13, 1953, and unbeknownst to me, it promises to be a very special day in the lives of all *three* of us. The winter wind is blowing with such a bitter iciness that my woollen coat isn't working at all to keep my body warm. I'm chilled to my very bone marrow. I am quite uncomfortable too. I don't want to be where I am right now. Snow, snow, snow—in every direction you look. I would much rather be *playing,* than driving, in it! Good thing this car has some sort of a heater, although it sure doesn't work the way it needs to! What could I be thinking? I won't be riding in *their* car, or playing on the "Thompsons'" farm, or cuddling "Skipper", or having fun with John, or riding baby steers or brushing "Midnight Blue Star", for very much longer. I won't be doing any of these things after today, now, will I?

I suppose they will keep all my toys and gifts. Who cares! Anyway, I'll need to travel lightly from here on out. I definitely won't be able to tote toys or books or anything, although I certainly could make good use of my "Radio Flyer" wagon, [115], and my trike too for that matter. Unfortunately, they're both back at the "Thompsons'" house, so I just need to concentrate on the necessities. Somehow, I'll have to sneak a few things from the kitchen area in the orphanage. Lemmie see, I'll need a can opener, some canned food, matches—lots of them, and a sharp knife, and food, of course, like apples and potatoes. None of those items should be too hard to round up. Of course, I'll have to steal some of the other kids' blankets to pack for my journey. Nevertheless, right this very minute, I need to find me a hidey-hole and just *think*! My God, how my head hurts! I need to bang the pain and bad thoughts out.

Well, by now I certainly know the route—the way to the "C.A.S.". Of course, that's exactly where we're going. It's the place to drop-off unwanted kids—guttersnipes like me! Just as I suspected, here we are, turning into the familiar parking lot of the "Children's Aid Society". Within minutes of our arrival, we are all standing in the Director's office. Mum and dad are both very nervous. Mum has a little smile on her lips, but not in her eyes. Dad—well my "dad" is strong and firm about what he knows is going to happen next. He is not smiling at all. I am angry with myself right now—angry, I somehow blew this last chance at a normal life, with normal parents. However, even worse, I am also really, really confused and scared. In fact, my brain feels as if it's on fire and my thoughts are *racing along*, virtually spreading the fire as they spark each electrical pathway.

Oh, shit! This is it! They **are** dropping me off—leaving me right here! I just *know* it. "I'n sorry, mum and dad." I try to squeeze in an apology to ward off the inevitable *handing me back* to the "Wart Lady". However, they both just look at me without a response. Oh, hell no! This can't really be happening. I thought everything was going well, or at least better. It's the *night terrors*, isn't it? Or, is it my *fighting* at school? But, my dad taught me to *fight* back. Is it because I've started to *pee in the bed* again? I'm thinking, please don't give me back, please— please!!!! I am told to hush; nevertheless, I continue to plead with my eyes. However, my mum and dad are both quite distracted and not exactly paying attention to me. Certainly, they're aware of the obvious distress I'm experiencing. This is not typical of my parents' behaviour—not like them at all. I guess they don't even want to look at me as they hand me back to the "Wart Lady". Maybe they *should* look into the wards—at the cages—at the sad, unwanted children—at **me**. I am just waiting now for the final, "Good Bye, Teddy." Will I even get a hug, or a kiss? On the other hand, will they just walk away and not even look back like other parents have done?

Shortly all three of my Workers have entered the glass room. I'm waiting to be ushered outside and placed on the hard wooden bench, again. However, this time I am not ordered to sit there. Inside I am actually permitted to sit on my dad's lap. "My dad", "my dad"—those words used to have such a very nice ring. However, now I must stop thinking about the past—which obviously now includes the "Thompsons". I flat out refuse to go to another "foster", or even another "prospective adoptive" home. I will definitely run far away. I don't even care if I die out there in the freezing cold. I just want to get away. I want to bang my head. I need to bash the bad thoughts right out, but I can't do it, not here and not now—not yet. I am squirming so much right now, my dad hands me over to my mum.

At that moment the Director starts speaking to them regarding their urgency in wanting to sign the *final* papers. What? Would those be the final *giving-me-back* papers or are we talking about adoption papers? "Wart" starts the conversation with, "We quite understand your desire to have the documents finally signed and legalized. Of course, in your own minds the love and bonding which you have all experienced is tantamount to the adoption having already taken place." (I am pleading with mum for any hint of hope, but she says nothing. She only winks at me.) "Do you have any final questions?" Mum and dad both shake their heads indicating a negative response.

Wait! Wait! Wait just a minute—my mum *winked* at me—it was always a *good thing* when my mum winked at me! Wasn't it? Oh, my goodness! This formal meeting is *not* about getting rid of me, or giving me back to the orphan asylum. This is about keeping me "forever"! I am dumbstruck by this joyful possibility. I am so happy at the thought of the "Thompsons" becoming my "forever parents" and theirs, becoming my "forever home". Naturally and "Skipper" would be my forever and ever doggie, too! Is it all too much to hope for ... or has it already happened? I wonder and I hope anyway.

After a few minutes of formalities and paper signing by both the "Thompsons", they lean back in the expansive chairs and, while longingly looking at each other, they sigh simultaneously. Then mum kisses me on my head, dad pats me on the back and they grasp each other's hand. "Everything is going to be just fine now, Teddy." mum says, with more reassurance than she has ever expressed. "You won't have anything to worry about ever again, sweetheart." she adds. Then they both tell me how much they love me and commence their explanation of what has just happened in the "Wart's" office. "It's all over now, son..." dad says, adding, "and it's going to be alright from now on, we promise you. You are all ours."

Chapter 75: We Belong to Each Other Now!

[*Only one-step remains to finalize this adoption. What's needed now is a signature by "Judge A. B. Surrey". On May 3, 1954, he will put his hand to these very same documents, the implications of which for three little souls on this earth, are life altering.*]

Therefore, upon *my* promise to **stop worrying** about being good or bad, or being given back, or made to live on the streets, or forced to eat out of garbage cans, (or being abused, or beaten, or molested, or tortured, or **raped**), I get from both of them, the biggest huggy-squeeze ever! (I probably will never get over my concern, my behaviour could still cause me to be returned to the Asylum at *any* time. I couldn't understand the significance of what has just happened in the Director's office. However, I will understand the significance of what happens next.)

Chapter 76: It's Only "Food" ... I Can DO This!

As mum and dad discussed on the way-in to town today, we are celebrating today's *victory for love* by dining out at the little neighbourhood family restaurant called, "***Donna and David's Diner***". We seat ourselves at a good table and are all grinning and laughing at our own little secret when "Sandra" our waitress, approaches the table. "Hi folks! What'll it be today?" she asks in a very happy and friendly, "waitress-y" sort-of manner. "What's the special today, Sandra?" mum asks, (ever mindful of how hard my dad works to earn the money and care for our little *family* of three). The diminutive, pear-shaped, middle-aged woman, wearing a pink uniform and matching little cap, answers, "*Fish 'n' Chips, today, folks.*" "Sounds perfect!" my dad agrees aloud with mum's fervent nod. "I love Fish 'n' Chips, don't you?" mum asks, glancing at dad, then me.

"Mmm, hmmm!" is all dad says.

(I don't answer.)

While we wait for our meal, we all chitchat a little about nothing of any particular importance. We are all very, very happy, now we know we all belong to each other, forever and ever. Boy, my mum sure is doing a lot of winking today. *I* silently vow never to run away, to try to stop peeing in my bed and to quit banging my head. I'm sure I can accomplish these goals, now. I have nothing more on God's green earth to worry about and most certainly no more reasons to escape. These wonderful folks have given me the reassurance I've always needed, wanted and, frankly, *deserved*. They are promising me they will never let me go away from them. I will never, ever, end-up in the asylum again! Certainly, no more crib-cages! No more screaming brats! No more crabby nurses! This is all I need to know. I am content and very much in love with my parents, the "Thompsons". Hee, hee, hee…how funny! Right now, I *am* one of the "Thompsons"--now there are THREE of us "THOMPSONS"—even four if you count "Skipper"!

When our fish dinners arrive, I find myself, for just a moment, somewhat numbly staring at the battered, deep-fried Haddock on the pretty, opaque green, scalloped-edged, glass plate. The fish is a tantalizing, golden-brown colour and is steaming-hot with juices just oozing from it. It does actually *look* tasty. Should I try it? What if it makes me puke? Mum and dad wouldn't understand. "Eat your meal, dear." mum urges. She doesn't have an inkling as to what exactly might be going on in my mind. I observe as mum and dad are already digging into their overloaded plates. "Mmm…Yummm", are the contented sounds coming from both of my parents simultaneously. "Try it, son—you will love it. It's quite delicious!" my dad insists.

Today, I am feeling very happy and contented with my life right now. I know, without a doubt, these kind parents would not make me eat something terrible. For this reason, I force myself to try a couple of fries, which aren't actually touching any part of the fish. "Go on, now, eat up, dear!" mum urges again. I close my eyes to determine if the fish dinner's smell is either inviting, or revolting. After all, what is sitting on my plate is food—just—*food*. It no longer has power over me, nor is it capable of transporting me back to the darkest time in my short life. It's only food, and should no longer stir up those terrible memories, or any awful associations in my mind. (Subconsciously I rub the permanent lump in my chest, but even *it* doesn't bother me anymore. I wonder if maybe my tormentor, "Rita", isn't even able to hurt me anymore, either.)

Next, I consciously decide to try the *fish*—to try and just take a teeny-tiny bite, if only to please my folks. One bite and I swallow. It does actually taste good in my mouth, but the back of my throat rises up a little as I swallow it down. Then, I try again. I take a second, little bite, and swallow. It is starting to taste even better now, and actually sliding down my throat a little easier too. "Why are you picking at your food, Teddy? Don't you like the fish sweetie?" mum asks innocently. "Dunno." "Well, let's see you try a little and if you don't want it, well *I'll* be happy to polish off your plate there, son." my dad says, with a huge grin and a deep chuckle.

O.K., so I *know* I can do this. I take another, then another bite of the fish. It *is* good. In fact, it really is *very* tasty, and flavoured just right too. Suddenly I see how something within *me* has changed. I am in control of eating my own food, even if it *is* fish. "Rita" is no longer in charge of my life. She no longer controls the smells in my nose or the tastes in my mouth. Moreover, I will no longer picture her in my mind. I will no longer smell her stench, in my mind. She is gone now. In this very moment, I have discovered, what has changed for me is not what is actually *on* my plate, but what is *really* at this table. It's "love". The *love* is what has changed me. Because my life is actually *seasoned* with the overflowing *love* given me by these parents, the food on my plate is likewise seasoned. The fish, flavoured with their love, has morphed that which has, for much of my life, frightened and disgusted me, into that, which is now so appetizing and delicious I just can't imagine my life without it.

So I too, dig in, after all, *it's only food—good, wholesome, healthy food.*

Revolving Doors

Chapter 77: My *"Promise"*

In my childhood heart and mind, I inscribed this promise to my mum and dad:

Dear Mum and Dad,

*I promise to always be good and do what you tell me. I promise to not talk back or be rude. I promise not to fight at school anymore. I promise never to wet my bed again. (I can do this. I can stay out of trouble. I absolutely **have** to.) I promise never to do anything bad or wrong. I promise always to live by the "Golden Rule". I promise never to run away. I promise to love you, mom and dad, forever. I promise, even if on one dark day for me, you have to go to Heaven, I promise still to love you ever more, after that, until it's time for me to meet you there.*

Love always and forever,
Your little Teddy.

Epilogue: A Letter to my Reader

Dear friend,

The story you have just read is my true autobiography. I, Richard Ketteringham, was the victim and am the survivor. The events in my early childhood, described in this novel, unknowingly affected every aspect of my life, from the first moment of each of their occurrences, on throughout my life until my treatment for their resulting mental conditions, disorders and illnesses.

*The recollection of absolutely **all** of the events of my first five years of life, whether dramatic or insignificant, up until the time I settled in at the 'Thompsons" farm, would be completely blocked from my memory for the next five decades. I had absolutely **no** conscious recollections of any life event, which occurred prior to the age of six. Of course, I assumed that such a lack of memories was perfectly normal. I simply took it for granted that any other children, or adults, who tried to remember an event occurring in their early years, like myself, could elicit absolutely no recollections whatsoever. This seeming eradication of my memories, sadly, included any remembrance of my birth mother, Berneice Ketteringham Faulconer—what she was like, how she looked, acted, smelled or even how she treated me—and loved me.*

I was shocked into awareness of the fact I did, indeed, have a life, (which included my very first "mother"), and this life existed prior to age of six, when I had first begun accepting the possibility of permanence in the home, and lives, of "Mr. and Mrs. Thompson". Of course, somewhere deep in my brain there indeed existed memories of all the details of such and these memories were closely guarded by some mental gatekeeper.

Revolving Doors

My awakening happened when I was around fifty-four, while participating in one of my many regular group therapy sessions, for my Post-Traumatic Stress Disorder, (P.T.S.D.), [13] [13a], anxiety and depression. It was the moment when the "flood-gates" of my strangely compartmentalized recollections, opened right before my eyes and in front of everyone else's eyes in the group at the same instant! Unbeknownst to me they were all silent witnesses to my twenty-minute blackout and agonizing re-awakening, while actually cowering under my chair, during the session. This incident would be the turning point in both my mental health and my life.

Of course, once opened, despite the degree of pain, which was associated with the vision of my long-withheld memories, there would be no more closing of my brain's protective gates. They had somehow been a creation of my own young mind in order to cocoon me from these deep-seated, horrific secrets, which held the truth of my own repeated incidents of neglect, abuse, molestation, torture and rape. I unknowingly and unwittingly blocked everything from my own conscious self. However, once the gates were flung open, all these dark and degrading incidents, were now suddenly being brought into the light of day, almost as if in a slide show my pre-six-year-old past. At that point, all memories had to be acknowledged, confronted, accepted, locked away and eventually, one at a time, managed. These memories have been my own personal **demons.**

Suddenly, when I had to come eye-to-eye with these so-called, demons in my brain, acceptance of the truths they bore became a very complicated process. This was because the incidents were accompanied by feelings of fear, shame and self-debasement. These blocked-out emotions triggered my repeated episodes of unspeakable depression. I was unable to understand, or control, this depression, which was being sparked and perpetuated, by an incomprehensible level of anxiety, seething just below the surface. (I was always physically trembling and shaking as my unconscious self was trying to rein-in and control my brain's issues within itself.)

Then, at some point in my therapy, something clicked in my brain. Whatever it was, I don't know; however I started suffering distinct episodic cycles of mania, in between my bouts of depression. Eventually, of course, [13] [13a], my newest additional diagnosis was "Bipolar I". [117] The direction of my personal psychotherapy was then altered to add-in the most effective chemotherapies in order to control this incurable mental illness and permit me to lead a relatively normal existence.

*It is my sincere desire, by revealing my own, excruciatingly painful, and shameful memories of the events in my childhood, perhaps other adult survivors of child abuse may be encouraged to take a closer look at their own memories and nightmares. Possibly, also, someone suffering with mental health issues, similar to mine, might be able to accept how such conditions may well be masking demons in their own past, and in their own minds, ("demons", such as mine, which could be holding their own truths captive). I can only hope someone, upon reading **my** autobiography, might move forward in his/her own life, and begin to heal, as I believe I may now finally say, I have **begun** to do.*

If you are that "someone" for whom this book will be a catalyst to facing, accepting and healing, I wish you courage to face, strength to bear and mental and emotional healing to overcome your own darkness. In essence, I wish you love. I believe it's through love and acceptance of my own self, (including my own "loving" the suffering little boy inside me), that I have definitely begun to discover the strength to face and overcome the dark, appalling, atrocious and horrifying

Revolving Doors
secret experiences of my own childhood.

Thanks very much for your interest in, (and forbearance for the length of), this novel—my memoir—my autobiography—my story.

Sincerely,

Richard Ketteringham
Victim and Survivor

Appendix "A"

The Role of the York County Children's Aid Society, and Reason for, the Detestable Overcrowding, in its Orphanages

(a) The "Home Children Movement"
(b) The "Great Depression" [7] [7a]
(c) The "Children's Overseas Reception Board" [1]
(d) The "Children of War Brides" [162], and
(e) The "Baby Boomers"
(f) Halifax's, famed Port of refugee children's entry, *Pier 21,* [6] [6a] [162]

****

(a) The "Home Children Movement" provided Canadian homes for approximately 100,000 homeless and destitute child refugees from England and the, (mostly), western European countries. (As well, there were 13,500 "private evacuations" to Canada). This organization operated from 1680 through the mid-1960s, [2] [4] [4a] [9] [9a], and was named after Dr. Thomas John Barnardo's, [3] [3a], British, *"Children's Homes",* (orphanages).

(b) During the socioeconomic devastations of the Great Depression, [7] [7a], (Oct. 29, 1929-1941), for many families, and especially single parents, there was no longer any way to financially care for their own children, and so many thousands ended up in the orphan-ages, or sent on to foster residences, or the "lucky" ones to adoptive homes. [7] [7a]

(c) The "Children's Overseas Reception Board", or "C.O.R.B.", [1], was an organization which reviewed applications for 211,448 European children, all requesting orphan housing in

Canada. However, after operating for only two months, from July 21, 1940 to Sept. 21, 1940, only a mere 3,127 children safely emigrated before the indiscriminate German bombings of refugee ships, brought an abrupt and untimely end to the program (as well as innocent lives). [1]

(d) There were untold thousands of the "children of war brides" who passed through "Pier 21". [1] [6] [6a] [162]

(e) The Baby Boomers, added another 400,000+ babies born in Canada, between 1943 and 1960. [5] [5a]

(f) Through Halifax's "Pier 21", 22,000 *other* migrant children arrived over the war years. ref. [6] [6a] [162]

All of the immigrant children were not only British, but also from a widespread area across Europe, (the majority coming from the western countries). In most cases, parents, or social and religious agencies, had to petition for the "applicants" who were the children from poverty-stricken families or orphans, to be the ones chosen to have their sailing passage to Canada arranged, and one way or another, paid in full on their behalf. At that time, stringent Canadian immigration policies clearly dictated the preference for "ideal immigrants" who were the children from Great Britain and Western Europe, rather than those from Eastern Europe, the Mediterranean or Asia [10] [10a]

Nevertheless, the reasoning behind this movement may not have been as completely altruistic as it originally appeared to be. The symbiotic design intended for the children to continue working as "child labourers", except, the majority would be working in infinitely better working conditions. That is, they would no longer be forced to toil, in the harsh, unforgiving and unrewarding conditions in the London factories and workhouses of Industrial-era Britain. [11]

*Ideally, these children would be provided a "home" and be in the care of individual fostering families, or in a very limited number of cases, "adopting" families. These living conditions would be exceedingly better than the circumstances experienced by many of the unfortunate children who had been living either in a crowded and cramped **one-or-two-room** dwelling shared with five or six other family members, or otherwise out on the streets. [1]*

*It was the last hope for the great number of pathetic, near-starving, orphans who were barely existing in unthinkably far harsher situations. Due to many circumstances, not the least of which was poverty, some of these "street-children" had been separated or orphaned from, and others even given up by, their parents or guardians. **They** were considered the real "**guttersnipes**". These children were literally "**working in**", (mostly begging, stealing, even **prostituting)** and barely existing in the London gutters which were filthy, disease-ridden and flowing with all manner of garbage, muck, excrement, rodents and deceased animals.*

All of these children had to first be assessed. According to their ages, needs, abilities, talents and strengths, they were placed into "foster care", either in orphan asylums, or on Canadian farms, which badly needed to replace the farming labourers which wartime had claimed. Unfortunately, despite the limited availability of farms requiring workers, the waves of more and more Home Children, [2] [4] [4a] [9] [9a], and other such refugees, kept rolling in.

Whenever there were no immediately available placements, these incoming immigrants had to be situated in "temporary housing" in the orphan asylums. Often the living quarters in these institutions had to be shuffled and rearranged to accommodate more children and beds into the existing space, but without any addition to the care-taking staff. Rarely did the funding dictate, either the expansion of existing asylums, or the construction of new ones, in order to accommodate the deluge of refugee children.

Of course, the "Southwest York County Children's Aid Society", of Toronto, was in no way exempt from this flood of refugee children, which included a great many younger ones, even infants. The consensus was that the younger children were more malleable and therefore could adapt more quickly, and easily accept new cultural idiosyncrasies and adjust to the other major changes in their lives. Certainly, some of the immediate and most difficult adjustments would be felt by the non-English speaking children who were firstly facing the reality of having to learn the language in order to under-stand their change in circumstances, then cope, adapt and fit-in.

During the Great Depression, [7] [7a], there was a slowing of the immigration through this system. In fact, between 1930 and 1939, the children arriving at Halifax, Nova Scotia's bustling and famed "Pier 21", [6] [6a] [162], never exceeded fifteen thousand per year. [7] [7a] But, by the very nature of the economy during the Great Depression, [7] [7a], many Canadian parents no longer had the resources to properly care for their children. In fact, they were either forced to turn them out into the streets, or give them up to institutions such as orphanages.

Naturally, when Canada entered the war on September 10, 1939, child immigration picked up again. Then, by mid-wartime, between 1942 and 1943, there was a continual flood of these Home Children entering the country. [2] [4] [4a] [9] [9a] (Although this contributed to the volume of needy children passing through the system of fostered care-giving, of course this was still prior to Teddy's birthday in 1947.)

Revolving Doors

Immediately before the start of World War II, in order to allow children to, "escape feared German bombings" the philanthropists at the "Children's Overseas Reception Board", (C.O.R.B.), [1], hand-picked 3127 children from 211,448 applications to travel on allied merchant marine ships to Canada. After many horrendous leagues across the Atlantic, the children grew weary of the game of daily practices of abandoning ship. Furthermore, apart from the obviously harrowing fear of German attacks on their poorly defended ships, the most dreadful problem, which plagued virtually all of the children, was seasickness. (It was their most common complaint. In fact, one young evacuee said, "Everything reduced to seasickness...I ate half an apple in eight days!" Another child added, "I've spent most of my four weeks on the [refugee ship] hanging over the rail!") [1]

These "orphan ships" were supposed to be protected by convoys of warships. However, the program, which began on Sunday July 21, 1940, came to a sudden end on September 21 in the same year. The swift end came, because of German attacks upon most of the ships in the emigration convoys, sinking many and killing scores of innocent children, and their well-intentioned chaperones as well. [1]

Sadly, even though most of the children were promised a safe and rapid, post-war return to whatever families were left, for a great number of these children there was nothing whatsoever awaiting them "back home" in 1945. [1] Each and every one of these pathetic young refugees wanted nothing more than dry land, warm clothes, any food and a safe home. Certainly none wanted, nor expected, to end up as just another ward of an orphan institution such as the "Southwest York County Children's Aid Society" in Toronto.

All of the small expatriates who did safely arrive on Canadian shores, disembarked in Halifax. There, with the help of their chaperones, the Canadian Red Cross, and other agents, they were interviewed by the Canadian Immigration officials at Pier 21, [6] [6a]. (The Canadian Red Cross' played a major role in aiding the arriving women and children evacuees, (including the war brides). [162]) Additionally, 22,000 other migrant children were among the millions who passed through this terminal over the years.

The "evacuated" children were all in dire need of food, clothing, safe housing, medical assistance, continuing health care, not to mention social and psychological counselling and guidance. Certainly, their hopes and dreams were of nothing more than individual fostering, or adoption, by a loving, caring family. For the children travelling further west and arriving anywhere in Southern Ontario, it was this region's "Children's Aid Society", which was appointed to manage their immediate and most basic requirements.

Unfortunately, most of these children were unhappy, frightened and confused as to why they had been uprooted and isolated from their own parents and families, only to be forced to accept new guardians and siblings, in a new country, with different customs, and often a language quite unlike their own. But they first had to be evaluated, and documented by the various self-appointed Toronto organizations, [77] [77a], in order to determine each child's individual ethnicity, language, stated religious preference, general health, background, housing needs, personal capabilities and individual fostering requirements. This was done so, ideally, the children would be placed into homes with families offering complementary backgrounds, and thus provide them some semblance of normalcy and also help them achieve an easier assimilation of their newly adopted Canadian culture.

With so many more children than there were adoptive or fostering h homes, or farms, to welcome them, the result was an overwhelming deluge of children who were placed into multi-children group foster homes, or large scale fostering asylums and orphanages. The unfortunate consequence was a great many older, difficult to place, or otherwise not adoptable children living long-term in the orphan asylums. Such extended-term institutional living unfortunately created a number of children suffering with crippling emotional issues, or long-term mental health problems, and some who were simply unable to adapt to the cultural differences. According to the "S.W. York Co. Children's Aid Society's" restrictions on placement, these unfortunate and anomalous children were rendered "unsuitable" to be appropriately placed and assimilated into adoptive Canadian families. (Surely, it would be tantamount to a prison sentence for a child to be held as a captive in such emotional limbo, having to grow-up as a permanent resident of a children's orphanage.)

In 1943, the governments of the Province of Ontario and the Dominion of Canada established the "Dominion-Provincial War-Time Day Nurseries Agreement of 1943", for the children of mothers employed in war industries. It was an insightful, forward-looking, cost-sharing program to provide funding for day nurseries, childcare centres and school feeding programs. By 1946, Toronto alone boasted twenty-two childcare centres for school-age children and thirteen day-nurseries for preschoolers. However, with the war over, by the spring of that year the "temporary war-time program" was scrapped, leaving at least 2500 children who were returned to the full-time care of their mothers, [8] [8a], many of whom were suddenly unemployed and, as such, financially unprepared to properly care for their children. This situation also resulted in many more children over-extending the occupancy of the orphan asylums. [This was immediately prior to Teddy's birth.]

Of course, for the city of Toronto, this entire, well-intentioned evacuation program resulted in the over-abundance of these children occupying the Children's Aid Society and other similar foundling homes. These youngsters needed homes of any sort and not only with the ideal, loving, nuclear families who, with only the best of intentions, were wanting to foster, or eager to adopt a child. Often these displaced children were placed in foster homes with a struggling single mother, and more than a few foster siblings. It seems, due to the lack of space, beds, services and staff to handle these many thousands of children, scores of them ended up being farmed-out to almost anyone willing to take them in or put up with them...[or with me].

About the Author

In Ms. Ketteringham's forty-year career, she began as a Marketing Researcher, Copywriter, and Editorial Assistant. Later she became a Reporter, Journalist, Feature Writer and Assistant Editor for a USA newspaper. She has also been a University Job Analyst, Researcher and Job Description Writer; a University Journalism, Creative Writing and French Tutor; a University Media Coordinator and Language Department six-language Laboratory Tutor and Faculty Liaison. Presently she is sole contributing Author, Editor and CEO of both PARAGON ECLECTIC EDITING and MEMORIES TO MEMOIRS PUBLISHING. She has authored her own personal memoir, *RAPED!!! "PRESUMED INNOCENCE" My Fifty-Yearlong Painful Secret* (Distributed by LULU.com), and edited several newspaper and magazine feature stories and has blogged numerous short stories, essays and poems. At the time of this revised publication she is a candidate for the degree: Doctor of Philosophy in Metaphysical Parapsychology. She holds a Bachelor of Arts with Majors in Philosophy, Psychology and English, Minor: Fine Art; a Master of Arts in Education, Major: The Psychology of Childhood Creative Arts; an Associate Diploma, Majors: Journalism and French; and a Diploma, Major: Early Childhood Special Education. She considers her most meaningful "titles" to be: "Mom", "Gam Gam", "Sis" and "Friend".

References

[1]. Stewart, Patrick. *The Children's Overseas Reception Board.* (n.d.) Halifax, Nova Scotia, Canada. Retrieved from, **http://www.pier21.ca/sites/default/files/uploads/files/First_ 75_Years/research_british_evacuee_children.pdf** (See also, [6] [6a] [162])

[2] *Home Children 1869-1930.* Library and Archives Canada. Govt. of Canada. Ottawa, Ontario. (2014). Retrieved from, **http://www.bac-lac.gc.ca/eng/discover/immigration/immigration-records/home-children-1869-1930/Pages/home-children.aspx**

[3] Barnardo, Thomas John. *Barnardo's Homes.* (2014). Retrieved from, **http://www.barnardos.org.uk/what_we_do/our_history/bar nardos_homes.htm**

[3a] *Thomas John Barnardo.* (2014). Wikipedia. Wikimedia Foundation, Inc. Retrieved from, **http://en.wikipedia.org/wiki/Thomas_John_Barnardo**

[4] New Version of the *Home Children* Database. (1869-1930). Library and Archives, Canada. (2014). Retrieved from, **http://www.collectionscanada.gc.ca/whats-new/013-542-e.html**

[4a] *The British Home Children.* The British Child Emigration Scheme to Canada 1870-1957. Ancestry.com. (2013). Calgary, Alberta. Retrieved from, **http://freepages.genealogy.rootsweb.ancestry.com/~britis hhomechildren/**

[5] Krotki, Karol J. And Henripin, Jaques. *Baby Boom.* (2014). Historica Canada. Retrieved from,

Revolving Doors
http://www.thecanadianencyclopedia.com/articles/baby-boom

[5a] *Baby boomers.* (2014). Wikipedia. Wikimedia Foundation, Inc. Retrieved from,
http://en.wikipedia.org/wiki/Baby_boomer

[6] Yunusov, Elena. (2011). *Pier 21's History.* Canadian Immigrant: Settling in Canada. Metroland Media (2015). Retrieved from, **http://canadianimmigrant.ca/settling-in-canada/pier-21s-history** (See also, [162])

[6a] *Pier 21.* (2014). Wikipedia. Wikimedia Foundation, Inc. Retrieved from, **http://en.wikipedia.org/wiki/Pier_21**

[7] *The Great Depression.* (2010). Making Medicare. The Canadian Museum of History. Gov't. of Canada. Ottawa, Ontario. Retrieved from,
http://www.civilization.ca/cmc/exhibitions/hist/medicare/medic-2c01e.shtml

[7a] *Great Depression.* (2014). Wikipedia. Wikimedia Foundation, Inc. Retrieved from,
http://en.wikipedia.org/wiki/Great_Depression

[8] *On All Fronts: World War Two and the NFB. (2008).* National Film Board of Canada. Ottawa, Ontario. Retrieved from, **http://www3.nfb.ca/ww2/**

[8a] *Canadian Women's Army Corps.* Wikipedia. (2014). Wikimedia Foundation, Inc. Retrieved from,
http://en.wikipedia.org/wiki/Canadian_Women%27s_Army_Corps

[9] Lapointe, E.B. (2003) *Home Children.* Genealogy Today. Retrieved from,
http://www.genealogytoday.com/ca/connect/031202.html

[9a] *Home Children.* Wikipedia. (2014). Wikimedia Foundation, Inc. Retrieved from,
http://en.wikipedia.org/wiki/Home_Children

[10] Displaced persons camp. Wikipedia. (2015). Wikimedia Foundation, Inc. Retrieved from, **http://en.wikipedia.org/wiki/Displaced_persons_camp**

[10a] *Displaced Person Transports: Cargo of Hope.* (2002). U.S. Merchant Marines at War. (1998-2002). Retrieved from, **http://www.usmm.org/dp.html**

[11] Higginbotham, Peter. *The Workhouse: The Story of an Institution. Poplar, Middlesex, London: Up to 1834.* (2015). Retrieved from, **http://www.workhouses.org.uk/Poplar/**

[12] Van Ells, Mark D. (n.d.). *Haunted.* America in World War II. Retrieved from, **http://www.americainwwii.com/articles/haunted/**

[12a] *Combat Stress Reaction.* (2014). Wikipedia. Wikimedia Foundation, Inc. Retrieved from, **http://en.wikipedia.org/wiki/Combat_stress_reaction**

[13] *Post-Traumatic Stress Disorder, (P.T.S.D.).* (2014). Canadian Mental Health Association. Ottawa, Ontario. Retrieved from, **http://www.cmha.ca/mental_health/post-traumatic-stress-disorder/#**

[13a] *Posttraumatic Stress Disorder.* (2014). Wikipedia. Wikimedia Foundation, Inc. Retrieved from, **http://en.wikipedia.org/wiki/Posttraumatic_stress_disorder**

[14] *Adoption.* (2014). Wikipedia. Wikimedia Foundation, Inc. Retrieved from, **http://en.wikipedia.org/wiki/Adoption** (See also, [160])

[15] *Baby Scoop Era.* (2014). Wikipedia. Wikimedia Foundation, Inc. Retrieved from, **http://en.wikipedia.org/wiki/Baby_Scoop_Era** (See also, [161])

[16] *Hurricane Hazel: 60 Years Later.* (n.d.). Toronto and Region Conservation and Thin Data. Retrieved from, **http://www.hurricanehazel.ca/**

Revolving Doors

[16a] *Hurricane Hazel.* (2014). Wikipedia. Wikimedia Foundation, Inc. Retrieved from, **http://en.wikipedia.org/wiki/Hurricane_Hazel**

[17] *Loblaws.* (2014). Wikipedia. Wikimedia Foundation, Inc. Retrieved from, **http://en.wikipedia.org/wiki/Loblaws**

[18] *Pablum Mixed Cereal.* (2014). Wikipedia. Wikimedia Foundation, Inc. Retrieved from, **http://en.wikipedia.org/wiki/Pablum**

[19] *Campbell Soup Company.* (2014). Wikipedia. Wikimedia Foundation, Inc. Retrieved from, **http://en.wikipedia.org/wiki/Campbell_Soup_Company**

[20] *1934 Buick Four-Door Convertible.* (2014). Bing Images. Retrieved from, **http://ts3.mm.bing.net/th?id=HN.607992461277530234&pid =15.1&P=0**

[21] *Convertible.* Wikipedia. (2015). Wikimedia Foundation, Inc. Retrieved from, **http://en.wikipedia.org/wiki/Convertible**

[22] *Chenille fabric.* Wikipedia. (2014). Wikimedia Foundation, Inc. Retrieved from, **http://en.wikipedia.org/wiki/Chenille_fabric**

[23] *Dinky Toys.* Wikipedia. (2014). Wikimedia Foundation, Inc. Retrieved from, **http://en.wikipedia.org/wiki/Dinky_Toys**

[24] *Raggedy Ann.* Wikipedia. (2014). Wikimedia Foundation, Inc. Retrieved from, **http://en.wikipedia.org/wiki/Raggedy_Ann**

[25] *Tiddlywinks.* Wikipedia. (2014). Wikimedia Foundation, Inc. Retrieved from, **http://en.wikipedia.org/wiki/Tiddlywinks**

[26] *The Hospital for Sick Children.* Wikipedia. (2014). Wikimedia Foundation, Inc. Retrieved from, **http://en.wikipedia.org/wiki/Hospital_for_Sick_Children**

[26a] *About Sick Kids.* (1999-2014). Sick Kids. Toronto,

Ontario. **http://www.sickkids.ca/AboutSickKids/index.html**

[27] *Little Golden Books*. Wikipedia. (2014). Wikimedia Foundation, Inc. Retrieved from, **http://en.wikipedia.org/wiki/Little_Golden_Books**

[28] *Playtex.* Wikipedia. (2014). Wikimedia Foundation, Inc. Retrieved from, **http://en.wikipedia.org/wiki/playtex#Products**

[28a] *Playtex Living Bra.* Google Images. **http://www.advertisingarchives.co.uk/preview/20624/1/Magazine-Advert/Playtex/1950s.jpg**

[28b] *Playtex Living Girdle.* Magazine advert 1950s. Google Images. **http://myoldadz.com/images/playtex19400513.jpg**

[29] *Page Boy.* Wikipedia. (2014). Wikimedia Foundation, Inc. Retrieved from, **http://en.wikipedia.org/wiki/Pageboy**

[30] *Penaten Cream.* Dusson. Retrieved from, **http://www.dusson.com/penaten/bc121.html**

[31] *Reye's Syndrome.* Mayo Clinic: Diseases and Conditions. (2014). Retrieved from, **http://www.mayoclinic.com/health/reyes-syndrome/DS00142**

[32] *Sears.* Wikipedia. (2014). Wikimedia Foundation, Inc. Retrieved from, **http://en.wikipedia.org/wiki/Sears_Catalog#Mail_order_catalog**

[32a] *Sears Wishbook Vintage.* (n.d.). Google Images. Retrieved from, **https://www.google.ca/searchq=sears+wishbook+vintage&espv=210&es_sm=93&tbm=isch&tbo=u&source=univ&sa=X&ei=13eCUuisB8KpiQLxwoDAAQ&ved=0CE8QsAQ&biw=1280&bih=667**

[33] *Pig Latin.* Wikipedia. (2015). Wikimedia Foundation, Inc. Retrieved from, **http://en.wikipedia.org/wiki/Pig_Latin**

[34] *Electrocardiography.* Wikipedia. (2015). Wikimedia Foundation, Inc. Retrieved from, **http://en.wikipedia.org/wiki/Electrocardiography**

[35] *Tracheal Intubation.* Wikipedia. (2014). Wikimedia Foundation, Inc. Retrieved from, **http://en.wikipedia.org/wiki/Intubation,_intratracheal**

[36] *House Beautiful.* Wikipedia. (2014). Wikimedia Foundation, Inc. Retrieved from, **http://en.wikipedia.org/wiki/House_Beautiful**

[37] *Better Homes and Gardens (magazine).* Wikipedia. (2014). Wikimedia Foundation, Inc. Retrieved from, **http://en.wikipedia.org/wiki/Better_Homes_and_Gardens_(magazine)**

[38] *Redbook.* Wikipedia. (2014). Wikimedia Foundation, Inc. Retrieved from, **http://en.wikipedia.org/wiki/Redbook_magazine**

[39] *Ladies' Home Journal.* Wikipedia. (2014). Wikimedia Foundation, Inc. Retrieved from, **http://en.wikipedia.org/wiki/Ladies_Home_Journal**

[40] *Trunk (luggage).* Wikipedia. (2014). Wikimedia Foundation, Inc. Retrieved from, **http://en.wikipedia.org/wiki/Trunk_(luggage)**

[41] *Corn flakes.* Wikipedia. (2014). Wikimedia Foundation, Inc. Retrieved from, **http://en.wikipedia.org/wiki/Corn_flakes**

[42] *Christian Child's Prayer.* Wikipedia. (2014). Wikimedia Foundation, Inc. Retrieved from, **http://en.wikipedia.org/wiki/Christian_child%27s_prayer**

[43] Shakespeare, William (1602). *Hamlet.* The Literature Network. Jalic Inc. (2000-2014). Retrieved from, **http://www.onlineliterature.com/shakespeare/hamlet/**

[43a] *"Shuffle off this Mortal Coil".* The Phrase Finder: Phrase Dictionary: Meanings and Origins. Gary Martin (1996-2014).

Revolving Doors
Retrieved from,
http://www.phrases.org.uk/meanings/319800.html

[44] *Simpson's.* Wikipedia. (2014). Wikimedia Foundation, Inc.
Retrieved from,
http://en.wikipedia.org/wiki/Simpsons_(department_store)

[44a] *Simpsons (department store): Wikis.* (n.d.). Wikimedia
Foundation, Inc. Retrieved from,
http://www.thefullwiki.org/Simpsons_(department_store)

[45] *Tinkertoy.* Wikipedia. (2014). Wikimedia Foundation, Inc.
Retrieved from, **http://en.wikipedia.org/wiki/Tinkertoy**

[46] *1940s Vintage Children's Toys With Prices, Descriptions
and Images.* The People History. (2004-2014). Retrieved from,
http://www.thepeoplehistory.com/40stoys.html

[47] *Toronto Streetcar System.* Wikipedia. (2014). Wikimedia
Foundation, Inc. Retrieved from,
http://en.wikipedia.org/wiki/Toronto_streetcar_system

[48] Maitland, Pat. (n.d.). *Toronto's Arcadian Court Restaurant.*
Suite 101. Retrieved from, **https://suite101.com/a/torontos-
arcadian-court-a101596**

[49] *Revolving Doors.* Wikipedia. (2014). Wikimedia
Foundation, Inc. Retrieved from,
http://en.wikipedia.org/wiki/Revolving_door

[50] Unknown author. (late 19C). *Simpson's Department Store
Jingle.* Simpson's. The Department Store Museum. Jingle was
written published and recorded for Robert Simpson's
Department Store. Comment posted by blogger,
"luaprelknie19 January, 2013 11:10". Retrieved Blogspot.ca.,
**http://departmentstoremuseum.blogspot.ca/2010/05/robert
-simpson-company-
ltd.html?showComment=1358611818548#c1702281698520
957512**

[51] *Jack Frost.* (late 19th C.) Wikipedia. (2014). Wikimedia

Revolving Doors
Foundation, Inc. Retrieved from,
http://en.wikipedia.org/wiki/Jack_Frost#History

[52] *Women's Fashion.* 1940s.org. (1940-2013). Retrieved
from, **http://1940s.org/fashion/women/**

[53] *Lipstick.* Wikipedia. (2015). Wikimedia Foundation, Inc.
Retrieved from, **http://en.wikipedia.org/wiki/Lipstick**

[54] *Joan Crawford.* Google Images. (2014). Retrieved from,
**https://www.google.ca/search?q=joan+crawford+hair&biw
=1093&bih=526&tbm=isch&tbo=u&source=univ&sa=X&ei=
AB-nVNyrMY23oQSexYKYCg&ved=0CBwQsAQ**

[55] *Greta Garbo.* Wikipedia. (2015). Wikimedia Foundation,
Inc. Retrieved from,
http://en.wikipedia.org/wiki/Greta_Garbo

[56] *Robert Taylor (actor).* Wikipedia. (2014). Wikimedia
Foundation, Inc. Retrieved from,
http://en.wikipedia.org/wiki/Robert_Taylor_(actor)

[57] Bayer, Friedrich and Co. (1897pat.) *Over 100 Years of
Aspirin: Aspirin History: Who Invented Aspirin?*
DMSORollon.com. Culver City, CA. Web Images. Retrieved
from,
**http://images.search.yahoo.com/yhs/search_adv_prop=im
age&fr=yhs-
visicomlavasoft&va=lifesavers+christmas+book&hspart=v
isicom&hsimp=yhs-lavasoft**

[59] Lee, Thomas. (1903). New York, N.Y. *Adirondack Chair.*
Wikipedia. (2014). Wikimedia Foundation, Inc. Retrieved from,
http://en.wikipedia.org/wiki/Adirondack_chair

[60] Jack and Jill (nursery rhyme). Wikipedia. (2014).
Wikimedia Foundation, Inc. Retrieved from,
**http://en.wikipedia.org/wiki/Jack_and_Jill_(nursery_rhyme
)**

[61] May, Robert. (1939). *Rudolph the Red-Nosed Reindeer.*

Montgomery Ward. MetroLyrics. CBS Interactive Inc., (2013). **http://www.metrolyrics.com/rudolph-the-red-nosed-reindeer-lyrics-christmas-carols.html**

[61a] Chircop, Philip. (2013). *The Story Behind 'Rudolph the Red-Nosed Reindeer'.* A-Mused. Thomas Nelson (2013). Retrieved from, **http://www.philipchircop.com/post/70197960528/the-story-behind-rudolf-the-red-nosed**

[62] Martin, Gary. *Good Night Sleep Tight.* The Phrase Finder: Meanings and Origins. (1996-2014). Retrieved from, **http://www.phrases.org.uk/meanings/sleep%20tight.html**

[63] *Nirvana.* Wikipedia. (2014). Wikimedia Foundation, Inc. Retrieved from, **http://en.wikipedia.org/wiki/Nirvana**

[64] *Canadian Club Whiskey.* (1858). Gooderham and Wortz, Toronto. Wikipedia. (2014). Wikimedia Foundation, Inc. Retrieved from, **http://en.wikipedia.org/wiki/Canadian_Club**

[65] *Health Sciences Centre.* Sunnybrook Hospital. (2015). Univ. Of Toronto Faculty of Medicine. Toronto, Ontario. Retrieved from, **http://sunnybrook.ca/**

[66] *Psychometrics.* Wikipedia. (2014). Wikimedia Foundation, Inc. Retrieved from, **http://en.wikipedia.org/wiki/Psychometrics**

[67] *Intelligence Quotient.* Wikipedia. (2015). Wikimedia Foundation, Inc. Retrieved from, **http://en.wikipedia.org/wiki/IQ**

[68] *IQ Classification.* Wikipedia. (2014). Wikimedia Foundation, Inc. Retrieved from, **http://en.wikipedia.org/wiki/IQ_reference_chart**

[69] Dale, Lucy. *Implications of Intelligence Testing.* eHow Mom. Demand Media. (1999-2015). Retrieved from, **http://www.ehow.com/info_8231933_implications-intelligence-testing.html**

Revolving Doors

[70] O'Connor, Frank P. (mfg. 1913). Laura Secord Chocolates. Ontario. Wikipedia. (2014). Wikimedia Foundation, Inc. Retrieved from,
http://en.wikipedia.org/wiki/Laura_Secord_Chocolates

[71] *Frank Sinatra.* Wikipedia. (2015). Wikimedia Foundation, Inc. Retrieved from,
http://en.wikipedia.org/wiki/Frank_Sinatra

[72] *The Beaches.* Wikipedia. (2014). Wikimedia Foundation, Inc. Retrieved from,
http://en.wikipedia.org/wiki/The_Beaches

[73] *Lego.* (1949). Wikipedia. (2015). Wikimedia Foundation, Inc. Retrieved from, **http://en.wikipedia.org/wiki/Lego**

[74] *Brylcreem.* (1928). County Chemicals (mfg.). Wikipedia.(2014). Wikimedia Foundation, Inc. Retrieved from,
http://en.wikipedia.org/wiki/Brylcreem

[75] *Flight Jacket.* Wikipedia. (Wikimedia Foundation, Inc. Retrieved from, **http://en.wikipedia.org/wiki/Flight_jacket**

[76] *Norman Rockwell.* Wikipedia. Wikimedia Foundation, Inc. Retrieved from,
http://en.wikipedia.org/wiki/Norman_Rockwell

[76a] Rockwell, Norman. *Walking to Church.* Google Images. (2014). Retrieved from,
https://www.google.ca/search?q=walking+to+church+norman+rockwell&espv=210&es_sm=93&tbm=isch&tbo=u&source=univ&sa=X&ei=tlKCUszoN6zWiAKs3lHACA&ved=0CDwQsAQ&biw=1280&bih=667

[77] *The History of the Salvation Army in Canada.* (2015). The Salvation Army in Canada. Retrieved from,
http://www.salvationarmy.ca/history

[77a] *The Salvation Army.* Wikipedia. (2014). Wikimedia Foundation, Inc. Retrieved from,
http://en.wikipedia.org/wiki/The_Salvation_Army#History

[78] Magie, Elizabeth. (inventor, circa, 1902). *History of the Board Game Monopoly.* Wikipedia. (2014). Wikimedia Foundation, Inc. Retrieved from, **http://en.wikipedia.org/wiki/History_of_the_board_game_ Monopoly**

[79] *Medusa.* Wikipedia. (2014). Wikimedia Foundation, Inc. Retrieved from, **http://en.wikipedia.org/wiki/Medusa**

[80] Sun-Maid. Wikipedia. (2014). Wikimedia Foundation, Inc. Retrieved from, **http://en.wikipedia.org/wiki/Sun-Maid**

[81] Plymouth Suburban. Wikipedia. (2014). Wikimedia Foundation, Inc. Retrieved from, **http://en.wikipedia.org/wiki/Plymouth_Suburban**

[82] Board Games. Wikipedia. (2014). Wikimedia Foundation, Inc. Retrieved from, **http://en.wikipedia.org/wiki/Board_games**

[83] James, Richard. (inventor, early 1940s). *Slinky.* Wikipedia. (2014). Wikimedia Foundation, Inc. Retrieved from, **http://en.wikipedia.org/wiki/Slinky**

[84] Binney and Smith. (mfg.). *Silly Putty.* Wikipedia. (2014). Wikimedia Foundation, Inc. Retrieved from, **http://en.wikipedia.org/wiki/Silly_Putty**

[85] *Historical Weather for 1950 in Toronto, Ontario, Canada.* Weatherspark. Cedar Lake Ventures, Inc. Retrieved from, **http://weatherspark.com/history/28448/1950/Toronto-Ontario-Canada**

[86] *SORRY!* (mfg. 1934 Parker Bros.). Wikipedia. (2014). Wikimedia Foundation, Inc. Retrieved from, **http://en.wikipedia.org/wiki/Sorry_(game)**

[87] *Candy Land.* (mfg. 1945 Milton Bradley Co.) Wikipedia. (2014). Wikimedia Foundation, Inc. Retrieved from, **http://en.wikipedia.org/wiki/Candy_land_game**

[88] *Hobby Horse.* Wikipedia. (2014). Wikimedia Foundation,

Revolving Doors
Inc. Retrieved from,
http://en.wikipedia.org/wiki/Hobby_horse_(toy)

[89] *Baby Bathinette 1950s.* LavaSoft Web Images. (2014).
Retrieved from,
**http://images.search.yahoo.com/yhs/search_adv_prop=im
age&fr=yhsvisicomlavasoft&va=baby+bathinette+1950s&h
spart=visicom&hsimp=yhs-lavasoft**

[90] *Chantilly.* (1941). Houbigant. The Perfume Projects,
Lightyears Collection. (2005-2014). Retrieved from,
**http://www.perfumeprojects.com/museum/bottles/Chantill
y.shtml**

[91] Stratemeyer, Edward. (Aka: Laura Lee Hope). (1904). *The
Story of the Bobbsey Twins.* Michael P. Weinstein. (1999).
Retrieved from,
**http://home.netcom.com/~drmike99/aboutbobbsey.html#F
amily**

[92] *Santa Claus is Comin' to Town.* Lonestar Lyrics. AZLyrics.
(2000-2014). Retrieved from,
**http://www.azlyrics.com/lyrics/lonestar/santaclausiscomin
totown.html**

[93] *Tasmanian Devil.* Wikipedia. (2014). Wikimedia
Foundation, Inc. Retrieved from,
http://en.wikipedia.org/wiki/Tasmanian_Devil

[94] *World War I.* Wikipedia. (2015). Wikimedia Foundation,
Inc. Retrieved from,
http://en.wikipedia.org/wiki/World_War_I

[95] *The Bowery Boys* (1946-1958). Monogram Pictures.
Wikipedia. (2014). Wikimedia Foundation, Inc. Retrieved from,
http://en.wikipedia.org/wiki/The_Bowery_Boys

[96] *Rita Hayworth Photos from Cover Girl.* (2011). Internet
Movie Database (IMDb). (1990-2015). Retrieved from,
**http://www.imdb.com/media/rm3968121600/nm0000028?re
f_=nmmi_mi_all_sf_26**

[97] *SPAM (food).* Hormel Foods Corp. (mfg. 1937). Wikipedia. (2014). Wikimedia Foundation, Inc. Retrieved from, **http://en.wikipedia.org/wiki/Spam_(food)**

[98] *Swiss Army knife.* Voctorinox AG (mfg. 1891). Wikipedia. (2014). Wikimedia Foundation, Inc. Retrieved from, **http://en.wikipedia.org/wiki/Swiss_army_knife**

[99] *Equal Partners.* (n.d.). Corporate Communications of the Toronto Police Service. Retrieved from, **http://www.torontopolice.on.ca/publications/files/misc/history/4t.html**

[100] *Buster Brown.* (1902). Wikipedia. (2014). Wikimedia Foundation, Inc. Retrieved from, **http://en.wikipedia.org/wiki/Buster_Brown**

[101] *Jehovah's Witnesses.* Wikipedia. (2015). Wikimedia Foundation, Inc. Retrieved from, **http://en.wikipedia.org/wiki/Jehovah%27s_Witnesses**

[102] *View-Master.* (1939). Wikipedia. (2014). Wikimedia Foundation, Inc. Retrieved from, **http://en.wikipedia.org/wiki/View-Master** (See also, [106])

[103] *Muffin the Mule.* Yahoo Images. (2014). Retrieved from, **http://ca.images.search.yahoo.com/search/images?_adv_prop=image&fr=crmas&va=muffin+the+mule+toy**

[104] *Hopalong Cassidy Watch.* Yahoo Images. (2014). Retrieved from, **http://ca.images.search.yahoo.com/search/images;_ylt=AwrSbjShtqRUeqgA8dDrFAx.;_ylu=X3oDMTB0OW1kMm5qBHNIYwNzYwRjb2xvA2dxMQR2dGlkA0NBQzAwMV8x?_adv_prop=image&fr=crmas&va=hopalong+cassidy+watch**

[105] *Hopalong Cassidy Doll.* Hakes Images. (2014). Retrieved from, **http://ca.images.search.yahoo.com/search/images;_ylt=A0SO8192QKdUHWYAv87rFAx.;_ylu=X3oDMTB0OW1kMm5qBHNIYwNzYwRjb2xvA2dxMQR2dGlkA0NBQzAwMV8x?_**

adv_prop=image&fr=crmas&va=Hopalong+Cassidy+doll

[106] *Hopalong Cassidy and his horse Topper.* View Master Reel. EBay. Retrieved from, http://www.ebay.com/sch/i.html?_from=R40&_trksid=m57 0.l1313&_nkw=ViewMaster+reel+of+hopalong+cassidy+an d+his+horse+topper&_sacat=0 (See also, [102])

[107] *'51 Ford Country Squire Woodie Station Wagon.* Bing Images. (2014). Retrieved from, http://www.bing.com/images/search?q='51+ford+country+ squire+woodie+station+wagon+&qpvt=%2751+ford+count ry+squire+woodie+station+wagon+&FORM=IGRE#view=d etail&id=E08FA7F54F21135D37595AA6EF613FB476408874 &selectedIndex=10

[108] *On Top of Spaghetti.* Bus Songs. (2003-2015). Retrieved from, http://bussongs.com/songs/on-top-of-spaghetti.php

[109] *1940 Ford de Luxe Station Wagon.* Yahoo Images. (2014). Retrieved from, http://ca.images.search.yahoo.com/images/view;_ylt=A2K LdXcsQqdUjgoAWCXtFAx.;_ylu=X3oDMTIyMnIwcWY0BH NIYwNzcgRzbGsDaW1nBG9pZANIY2Y3OWU3YmRINTI0Zj NiNDEzMmJjMmI4MDExYmEzYwRncG9zAzgEaXQDYmIuZ w-- ?.origin=&back=http%3A%2F%2Fca.images.search.yahoo .com%2Fsearch%2Fimages%3F_adv_prop%3Dimage%26 va%3D1940%2BFord%2Bdeluxe%2Bstation%2Bwagon%2 6fr%3Dcrmas%26tab%3Dorganic%26ri%3D8&w=500&h=3 44&imgurl=farm3.staticflickr.com%2F2538%2F3906066858 _0d70cd0184_z.jpg&rurl=http%3A%2F%2Fwww.flickr.com %2Fphotos%2Fargentla%2F3906066858%2F&size=166.2K B&name=%3Cb%3E1940+Ford+Deluxe+station+wagon%3 C%2Fb%3E+side&p=1940+Ford+deluxe+station+wagon&o id=ecf79e7bde524f3b4132bc2b8011ba3c&fr2=&fr=crmas&t t=%3Cb%3E1940+Ford+Deluxe+station+wagon%3C%2Fb %3E+side&b=0&ni=72&no=8&ts=&tab=organic&sigr=11he 7cukb&sigb=13ra8l1eq&sigi=11npq0bf5&sigt=11agjfafm&

sign=11agjfafm&.crumb=WyQ39OjR/06&fr=crmas

[110] *The Three Stooges.* (1925). Wikipedia. (2015).
Wikimedia Foundation, Inc. Retrieved from,
http://en.wikipedia.org/wiki/The_Three_Stooges

[111] Dodgson, Charles Ludwidge. (Aka. Lewis Carroll) *Alice's
Adventures in Wonderland.* (1865). Wikipedia. Wikimedia
Foundation, Inc. Retrieved from,
**http://en.wikipedia.org/wiki/Alice%27s_Adventures_in_Wo
nderland**

[111a] *Cheshire Cat.* Wikipedia. Wikimedia (2014).
Foundation, Inc. Retrieved from,
http://en.wikipedia.org/wiki/Cheshire_Cat

[112] Brownie Hawkeye Flash Model Camera. Yahoo Images.
(2014). Retrieved from,
**http://ca.images.search.yahoo.com/search/images;_ylt=A
0SO81xexKRUJj4AlG7rFAx.;_ylu=X3oDMTB0OW1kMm5q
BHNlYwNzYwRjb2xvA2dxMQR2dGlkA0NBQzAwMV8x_adv
_prop=image&fr=crmas&va=Brownie+Hawkeye+Flash+Mo
del+Camera**

[113] *Tri-colour Film for Black and White TV.* AnswerBag.
(2012). Demand Media. Retrieved from.
http://www.answerbag.com/q_view/2700443

[114] *TV Tray Table.* Wikipedia. (2012). Wikimedia
Foundation, Inc. Retrieved from,
http://en.wikipedia.org/wiki/TV_tray_table

[115] *Radio Flyer.* Wikipedia. (2014). Wikimedia Foundation,
Inc. Retrieved from, **http://en.wikipedia.org/wiki/Radio_Flyer**

[116] *Texaco.* Wikipedia. (2014). Wikimedia Foundation, Inc.
Retrieved from, **http://en.wikipedia.org/wiki/Texaco**

[117] *Bipolar Disorder.* Wikipedia. (2015Wikimedia
Foundation, Inc. Retrieved from,
http://en.wikipedia.org/wiki/Bipolar_disorder

[118] *Hans Christian Andersen.* Wikipedia. Wikimedia Foundation, Inc. Retrieved from, **http://en.wikipedia.org/wiki/Hans_Christian_Andersen**

[119] *Vintage 1950's Children's Fashion Clothes.* The People History. (2004-2014). Retrieved from, **http://www.thepeoplehistory.com/1950skidsfashion.html**

[120] *1952 Chevrolet, Four-Door.* Yahoo Images. Retrieved from, **https://www.google.ca/searchq=1952+chevrolet+4door&bi w=1093&bih=561&tbm=isch&tbo=u&source=univ&sa=X&e i=9kynVKySNsyuogTV6YLwBg&ved=0CBwQsAQ**

[121] *Patent Leather.* Wikipedia. (2014). Wikimedia Foundation, Inc. Retrieved from, **http://en.wikipedia.org/wiki/Patent_leather**

[122] Blue Law. Wikipedia. (2014). Wikimedia Foundation, Inc. Retrieved from, **http://en.wikipedia.org/wiki/Blue_law**

[123] Moore, Clement Clarke. *T'was the Night Before Christmas.* (1822). BlackDog's Christmas Fun and Games. (n.d.). Retrieved from, **http://www.blackdog.net/holiday/christmas/twas.html**

[124] Lerner, George. *Mr. Potato Head* (mfg. Hasbro 1952). Wikipedia. (2014). Wikimedia Foundation, Inc. Retrieved from, **http://en.wikipedia.org/wiki/Mr._Potato_Head**

[125] *The Ed Sullivan Show.* CBS television network. (1948-1971).Wikipedia. (2015). Wikimedia Foundation, Inc. Retrieved from, **http://en.wikipedia.org/wiki/The_Ed_Sullivan_Show**

[126] Bland, Edith Nesbit. (late 19C). *Christmas is Coming.* (2014). Retrieved from, **http://www.carols.org.uk/christmas_is_coming.htm**

[127] *Golden Rule.* Wikipedia. (2015). Wikimedia Foundation, Inc. Retrieved from,

Revolving Doors
http://en.wikipedia.org/wiki/Golden_Rule

[128] *List of John Deere Tractors.* Wikipedia. (2014).
Wikimedia Foundation, Inc. Retrieved from,
http://en.wikipedia.org/wiki/List_of_John_Deere_tractors

[129] Maxwell House. Wikipedia. (2014). Wikimedia
Foundation, Inc. Retrieved from,
http://en.wikipedia.org/wiki/Maxwell)_House

[130] Garshick, Erick et. al. *Lung Cancer in Railroad Workers
Exposed to Diesel Exhaust.* Environmental Health
Perspectives. (2004). and (2005). Retrieved from,
http://www.ncbi.nlm.nih.gov/pmc/articles/PMC1247618/

[131] *Ticking.* Wikipedia. (2013). Wikimedia Foundation, Inc.
Retrieved from, **http://en.wikipedia.org/wiki/Ticking**

[132] *Wayne for Camels: 1950s.* The Pop History Dig. (2015).
Retrieved from,
http://www.pophistorydig.com/?tag=camel-cigarette-ads

[133] *"It's a Wonderful Life" is Released.* (1946). World History
Project. (2015). MCHABU. Retrieved from,
**http://worldhistoryproject.org/1946/12/20/its-a-wonderful-
life-is-released**

[134] *James Stewart.* Wikipedia. (2015). Wikimedia
Foundation, Inc. Retrieved from,
http://en.wikipedia.org/wiki/James_Stewart

[135] *Lionel Barrymore.* Wikipedia. (2014). Wikimedia
Foundation, Inc. Retrieved from,
http://en.wikipedia.org/wiki/Lionel_Barrymore

[136] *Vintage Coca-Cola/Coke Red Plastic 8-Slot Carrier
Caddie for 6.5 oz. Bottles.* EBay. (2014). Retrieved from,

Revolving Doors
http://www.ebay.com/itm/Vintage-Coca-Cola-Coke-Red-Plastic-8-Slot-Carrier-Caddie-for-6-5-oz-Bottles-/281190762558?pt=LH_DefaultDomain_0&hash=item41784 6883e

[137] *Sunnybrook Health Sciences Centre.* Univ. Of Toronto Faculty of Medicine. (2015). Retrieved from, **http://sunnybrook.ca/content/?page=veterans-centre-community**

[138] *Firestone Tire Ash Tray 1950s.* Yahoo Images. Retrieved from, **http://ca.images.search.yahoo.com/search/images_adv_pr op=image&fr=ush-mailn&va=firestone+%27+ashtray+in+1950%27s**

[139] Dickens, Charles. *A Christmas Carol* (1938 film). Charles Dickens, (author, 1843). Wikipedia. (2014). Wikimedia Foundation, Inc. Retrieved from, **http://en.wikipedia.org/wiki/A_Christmas_Carol_(1938)_fil m**

[140] *Charles Dickens.* Wikipedia. (2014). Wikimedia Foundation, Inc. Retrieved from, **http://en.wikipedia.org/wiki/Charles_Dickens**

[141] *Truck Terminal.* 1951 Vintage Toys from the Fifties. The People History. (2004-2014). Retrieved from, **http://www.thepeoplehistory.com/1951toys.html**

[142] *Caterpillar Earth Moving Equipment.*1952 Vintage Toys from the Fifties. The People History. (2004-2014). Retrieved from, **http://www.thepeoplehistory.com/1952toys.html**

[143] *Gilbert Tool Chest.* 1952 Vintage Toys from the Fifties.

The People History. (2004-2014). Retrieved from,
http://www.thepeoplehistory.com/1952toys.html

[144] *Tom Corbett Space Academy.* 1952 Vintage Toys from
the Fifties. The People History. (2004-2014). Retrieved from,
http://www.thepeoplehistory.com/1952toys.html

[145] *Bomber Exploding Ship.* 1953 Vintage Toys from the
Fifties. The People History. (2004-2014). Retrieved from,
http://www.thepeoplehistory.com/1953toys.html

[146] *Giant Pan American Clipper.* 1953 Vintage Toys from the
Fifties. The People History. (2004-2014). Retrieved from,
http://www.thepeoplehistory.com/1953toys.html

[147] *Walkie Talkie.* 1953 Vintage Toys from the Fifties. The
People History. (2004-2014). Retrieved from,
http://www.thepeoplehistory.com/1953toys.html

[148] *Hopalong Cassidy Lunch Pail.* Yahoo Images. (2014).
Retrieved from,
**http://images.search.yahoo.com/yhs/search_adv_prop=im
age&fr=yhsvisicomlavasoft&va=hopalong+cassidy+lunch
+box&hspart=visicom&hsimp=yhs-lavasoft**

[149] KatR. *The Mount Pleasant Necropolis.* Photo Walk
through Toronto's Mount Pleasant Cemetery. Flickr. (2013).
Retrieved from,
http://www.flickr.com/photos/52734530@N06/10343289555

[150] Blake, William. *Auguries of Innocence.* (circa 1803) (pub.
1863). Wikipedia. Wikimedia Foundation, Inc. Retrieved from,
http://en.wikipedia.org/wiki/Auguries_of_Innocence

[151] *Teddy bear.* Wikipedia. (2014). Wikimedia Foundation,
Inc. Retrieved from, **http://en.wikipedia.org/wiki/Teddy_bear**

Revolving Doors

[152] *Tim Horton's.* Wikipedia. (2014). Wikimedia Foundation, Inc. Retrieved from,
http://en.wikipedia.org/wiki/Tim_Hortons

[153] *Humewood House.* Wikipedia. (Toronto, Ontario). (2015). Wikimedia Foundation, Inc. Retrieved from,
http://www.humewoodhouse.com/

[154] *Oxygen Tent.* Wikipedia. (2014). Wikimedia Foundation, Inc. Retrieved from,
http://en.wikipedia.org/wiki/Oxygen_tent

[155] *Old Maytag Ringer-Washing Machine.* YouTube. (2010). Retrieved from,
https://www.youtube.com/watch?v=qHpAm9ui_1Y

[156] *Penicillin.* Wikipedia. (2014). Wikimedia Foundation, Inc. Retrieved from, **http://en.wikipedia.org/wiki/Penicillin**

[157] *Mother Goose.* Wikipedia. (2014). Wikimedia Foundation, Inc. Retrieved from,
http://en.wikipedia.org/wiki/Mother_Goose

[158] *Tinker Bell.* Wikipedia. (2014). Wikimedia Foundation, Inc. Retrieved from, **http://en.wikipedia.org/wiki/Tinker_Bell**

[159] *Shalimar.* Guerlain, Paris France. Fragrantica Perfume Encyclopedia. (2006-2013). Retrieved from,
http://www.fragrantica.com/perfume/Guerlian/Shalimar-53.html

[160] Carlson, Kathryn Blaze. *Curtain Lifts on decades of forced adoptions for unwed mothers in Canada.* (2012) National Post. Retrieved from,
http://news.nationalpost.com/2012/03/09/curtain-lifts-on-decades-of-forced-adoptions-for-unwed-mothers-in-canada (See also, [14])

[161] Grown in My Heart. *The Baby Scoop Era: Women Forced to Give Up Their Babies*, (Daily Telegraph, Toronto, Nov. 1956). Divine Caroline. Meredith Corp. (2015). Retrieved from,
http://www.divinecaroline.com/life-etc/culture-causes/baby-scoop-era-women-forced-give-their-babies
[Quotation Dr. Marion Hilliard of Women's College Hospital, Toronto]

[162] Tinkham, Jennifer. (n.d.) *Lasting Impressions: The Volunteers of Pier 21.* (pdf). Pier 21. Retrieved from,
http://www.pier21.ca/sites/default/files/uploads/files/resear ch_lasting_impressions.pdf

[163] *Florsheim.* Florsheim Shoes. (2014).
http://www.florsheimshoes.ca/shop/index.html

[164] Rey, Hans Augusto and Margret. *Curious George.* Wikipedia. (2014). Wikimedia Foundation, Inc. Retrieved from,
http://en.wikipedia.org/wiki/The_Man_in_the_Yellow_Hat# The_Man_with_the_Yellow_Hat

[165] Caroll, Lewis. (Aka. Charles Lutwidge Dodgson). *Alice's Adventures in Wonderland.* Wikipedia. (2014). Wikimedia Foundation, Inc. Retrieved from,
http://en.wikipedia.org/wiki/Alice%27s_Adventures_in_Wo nderland

[166] *Toronto Transit Commission.* (1997-2014). Retrieved from, **http://www.ttc.ca/Customer_Service/index.jsp**

[167] *Bus Songs: Lyrics to Nursery Rhymes and Kids' Songs.* Bus Songs. (2003-2015). Retrieved from,
http://bussongs.com/songs/

Revolving Doors